Brownlows by Margaret Oliphant

Margaret Oliphant Wilson was born on April 4th, 1828 to Francis W. Wilson, a clerk, and Margaret Oliphant, at Wallyford, near Musselburgh, East Lothian.

Her youth was spent in establishing a writing style and by 1849 she had her first novel published: Passages in the Life of Mrs. Margaret Maitland.

Two years later, in 1851 Caleb Field was published and also an invitation to contribute to Blackwood's Magazine; the beginning of a life time business relationship.

In May 1852, Margaret married her cousin, Frank Wilson Oliphant. Their marriage produced six children but, tragically, three died in infancy. When her husband developed signs of the dreaded consumption (tuberculosis) they moved to Florence, and then to Rome where, sadly, he died.

Margaret was naturally devastated but was also now left without support and only her income from writing to support the family. She returned to England and took up the burden of supporting her three remaining children by her literary activity.

Her incredible and prolific work rate increased both her commercial reputation and the size of her reading audience. Tragedy struck again in January 1864 when her only remaining daughter Maggie died.

In 1866 she settled at Windsor to be closer to her sons, who were being educated at near-by Eton School.

For more than thirty years she pursued a varied literary career but family life continued to bring problems. Cyril Francis, her eldest son, died in 1890. The younger son, Francis, who she nicknamed 'Cecco', died in 1894.

With the last of her children now lost to her, she had little further interest in life. Her health steadily and inexorably declined.

Margaret Oliphant Wilson Oliphant died at the age of 69 in Wimbledon on 20th June 1897. She is buried in Eton beside her sons.

Index of Contents

CHAPTER I

MR. BROWNLOW'S MONEY

Every body in the neighborhood was perfectly aware what was the origin of John Brownlow's fortune. There was no possibility of any mistake about it. When people are very well known and respectable, and inspire their neighbors with a hearty interest, some little penalty must be paid for that pleasant state of affairs. It is only when nobody cares for you, when you are of no importance to the world in general, that you can shroud your concerns in mystery; but the Brownlows were very well known, much respected, and quite unable to hide themselves in a corner. In all Dartfordshire there was no family better known; not that they were county people, or had any pretensions to high connection, but then there was not one family in the county of whom John Brownlow did not know more than they knew themselves, and in his hands, and in the hands of his fathers before him, had reposed the papers and affairs of all the squires about, titled or otherwise, for more years than could be counted. It was clever of the Brownlows to have had so much business in their hands and yet not to be rich; but virtue, when it is exceptional, is perhaps always a little extreme, and so it is probable that an honest lawyer is honester than most honest men who have no particular temptation. They were not rich, and yet, of course, they were far from being poor. They had the kind of substantial old brick house, standing close up to the pavement in the best end of the High Street of Masterton, which would be described as a mansion in an auctioneer's advertisement. It was very red and infinitely clean, and had a multitude of windows all blinking in the sun, and lighting up into impromptu illuminations every winter afternoon, when that blazing red luminary went down, not over the river and the open country, as he ought to have done, but into the rectory garden, which happened to lie in his way as he halted along toward the west. The Brownlows for generations back had lived very comfortably in this red house. It had a great, rich, luxuriant, warm garden behind, with all sorts of comforts attached to it, and the rooms were handsome and old-fashioned, as became a house that had served generations; and once upon a time many good dinners, and much good wine, and the most beautiful stores of fine linen, and crystal, and silver were in the house, for comfort, and not for show. All this was very well, and John Brownlow was born to the possession of it; but there can be no doubt that the house in the High Street was very different from the house he now inhabited and the establishment he kept up in the country. Even the house in the High Street had been more burdened than was usual in the family when it came to his turn to be its master. Arthur, the younger brother, who was never good for much, had just had his debts paid for the second time before his father died. It was not considered by many people as quite fair to John, though some did say that it was he above all who urged the step upon old Mr. Brownlow. Persons who professed to know, even asserted that the elder son, in his generosity, had quite a struggle with his father, and that his argument was always "for my mother's sake." If this, was true, it was all the more generous of him, because his mother was well known to have thought nothing of John in comparison with the handsome Arthur, whom she spoiled as long as she lived. Anyhow, the result was that John inherited the house and the business, the furniture and old crystal and silver, and a very comfortable income, but nothing that could be called a fortune, or that would in any way have justified him in launching out into a more expensive description of life.

At this time he was thirty at least, and not of a speculative turn of mind; and when old Mrs. Thomson's will—a will not even drawn up in his office, which would have been a kind of preparation—was read to him, it is said that he lost his temper on the occasion, and used very unbecoming language to the poor woman in her coffin. What had he to do with the old hag? "What did she mean by bothering him with her filthy money?" he said, and did not show at all the frame of mind that might have been expected under the circumstances. Mrs. Thomson was an old woman, who had lived in a very miserly sort of way, with an old servant, in a little house in the outskirts of the town. Nobody could ever tell what attracted her toward John Brownlow, who never, as he himself said, had any thing to do with her; and she had relations of her own in Masterton—the Fennells—who always knew she had money, and counted upon being her heirs. But they were distant relations, and perhaps they did not know all her story. What petrified the town, however, was, when it was found out that old Mrs. Thomson had left a fortune, not of a few hundreds, as people supposed, but of more than fifty thousand pounds, behind her, and that it was all left in a way to John Brownlow. It was left to him in trust for Mrs. Thomson's daughter Phœbe, a person whose existence no one in Masterton had ever dreamed of, but who, it appeared had married a common soldier, and gone off with him ages before, and had been cursed and cast off by her hard-hearted mother. That was long, long ago, and perhaps the solitary old creature's heart, if she had a heart, had relented to her only child; perhaps, as John Brownlow thought, it was a mere suggestion of Satan to trouble and annoy him, a man who had nothing to do with Phœbe Thomson. Anyhow, this was the substance of the will. The money was all left to John Brownlow in trust for this woman, who had gone nobody knew where, and whose very name by marriage her mother did not state, and nobody could tell. If Phœbe Thomson did not make her appearance within the next twenty-five years, then the money was to pass to John Brownlow and his heirs in perpetuity beyond all power of reclamation. This was the strange event which fell like a shell into the young lawyer's quiet life, and brought revolution and change to every thing around.

He was very much annoyed and put out about it at first; and the Fennells, who had expected to be Mrs. Thomson's heirs, were furious, and not disinclined to turn upon him, blameless as he was. To tell the truth, theirs was a very hard case. They were very poor. Good-for-nothing sons are not exclusively reserved for the well-to-do portion of the community; and poor Mrs. Fennell, as well as the Brownlow family, had a good-for-nothing son, upon whom she had spent all her living. He had disappeared at this time into the darkness, as such people do by times, but of course it was always on the cards that he might come back and be a burden upon his people again. And the father was paralytic and helpless, not only incapable of doing any thing, but requiring to have every thing done for him, that last aggravation of poverty. Mrs. Fennell herself was not a prepossessing woman. She had a high temper and an eloquent tongue, and her disappointment was tragic and desperate. Poor soul! it was not much to be wondered at—she was so poor and so helpless and burdened; and this money would have made them all so comfortable. It was not that she thought of herself, the poor woman said, but there was Fennell, who was cousin to the Thomsons, and there was Tom out in the world toiling for his bread, and killing himself with work. And then there was Bessie and her prospects. When she had talked it all over at the highest pitch of her voice, and stormed at every body, and made poor Fennell shake worse than ever in his paralytic chair, and overwhelmed Bessie with confusion and misery, the poor woman would sit down and cry. Only one thousand pounds of it would have done them such a great deal of good; and there was fifty thousand, and it was all going to be tied up and given to John Brownlow. It was hard upon a woman with a hot head and a warm heart, and no temper or sense to speak of; and to storm at it was the only thing she took any comfort from, or that did her any good.

This money, which Mrs. Fennell regretted so bitterly for a long time, was nothing but a nuisance to John Brownlow. He advertised and employed detectives, and did every thing a man could do to find Phœbe Thomson and relieve himself of the burden. But Phœbe Thomson was not to be found. He sought her far and near, but no such person was to be heard of—for, to be sure, a poor soldier's wife was not very likely to be in the way of seeing the second column of the "Times;" and if she should happen to be Mrs. Smith or Mrs. Doherty by marriage, nobody but herself and her husband might be aware that she had ever been Phœbe Thomson. Anyhow, all the advertisements and all the detectives failed; and after working very hard at it for a year or more, John Brownlow very quietly, and to his own consciousness alone, damned Phœbe Thomson, and gave up the useless investigation.

But he was a man who had eyes, and a strong sense of justice. When he thought of the poor Fennells, his anger rose against the wretched old woman who had laid on him the burden of her money. Poor Mrs. Fennell's son was good for nothing, but she had a daughter who was good for much; and Bessie had a lover who would gladly have married her, had that wicked old miser, as John Brownlow in his indignation said, left only a thousand pounds out of her fifty to help the paralytic father and passionate mother. Bessie's lover was not mercenary—he was not covetous of a fortune with his wife; but he could not marry all the family, or work for the old people, as their daughter had to do. This was what Mrs. Fennell meant when she raved of poor Bessie and her prospects. But Bessie herself said nothing. The lover went very sorrowfully away, and Bessie was silent and went on with her work, and made no show of her trouble. John Brownlow, without knowing it, got to watch her. He was not aware for a long time why it was that, though he always had so much to do, he never missed seeing Bessie when by chance she passed his windows. As luck would have it, it was always at that moment he raised his eyes; and he did his best to get pupils for her, "taking an interest" in her which was quite unusual in so quiet a man. But it was not probable that Bessie could have had much of an education herself, much less was qualified to give it to others. And whether it was want of skill, or the poverty of her surroundings, her poor dress, or her mother's aspect and temper, it is certain that, diligent and patient and "nice" as she was, pupils failed her. She did not get on; yet she kept struggling on, and toiling, keeping a smile in her eyes for every body that looked friendly on her, whatever sinking there might be in her heart. And she was a slight fragile little creature to bear all that weight on her shoulders. John Brownlow, without knowing it, watched her little figure about the streets all the year through, marveling at that "soft invincibility," that steady standing up against defeat and every kind of ill which the gentle soul was capable of. And as he watched her, he had many thoughts in his mind. He was not rich, as we have said; on the contrary, it would have been his bounden duty, had he done his duty, to have married somebody with a modest little fortune, who would have helped him to keep up the house in the High Street, and give the traditionary dinners; and to maintain his wife's family, if he were to marry, was something out of the question. But then that fifty thousand pounds—this money which did not belong to him but to Phœbe Thomson, whosoever she was, and wheresoever she might be. All this produced a confusion of thought which was of very strange occurrence in Mr. Brownlow's office, where his ancestors for generations had pondered over other people's difficulties—a more pleasing operation than attending to one's own. Gradually, as time wore on, Phœbe Thomson grew into a more and more mythical figure to Mr. Brownlow's mind, and Bessie Fennell became more and more real. When he looked up one winter's afternoon and saw her passing the office window in the glow of the frosty sunset, which pointed at her in its clear-sighted way, and made thrice visible the thinness of her cheek and the shabbiness of her dress, Mr. Brownlow's pen fell from his fingers in amaze and self-reproach. She was wearing herself out, and he had permitted her to do so, and had sat at his window thinking about it for two whole years. Two years had passed since Mrs. Thomson's death. All the investigations in the world had not been able to find Phœbe; and John Brownlow was master of the old woman's fifty thousand pounds; and the Fennells might be starving for any thing he could tell. The result was, that he proposed to Bessie, to the unbounded amazement not only of the town of Masterton, but even of the county people, who all knew Mr. Brownlow. Probably Bessie was as much surprised as any body; but she married him after a while, and made him a very good wife. And he pensioned her father and mother in the most liberal way, and saw as little of them as possible. And for a few years, though they did not give many dinners, every thing went on very well in the big brick house.

I tell the story thus briefly, instead of introducing these people to show their existence for themselves, because all this is much prior to the real date of this history. Mrs. Brownlow made a very good and sweet wife; and my own opinion is that she was fond of her husband in a quiet way. But, of course, people said she had married him for his money, and Bessie was one of those veiled souls who go through the world without much faculty of revealing themselves even to their nearest and dearest. When she did, nobody could make quite sure whether she had enjoyed her life or merely supported it. She had fulfilled all her duties, been very kind to every body, very faithful and tender to her husband, very devoted to her family; but she died, and carried away a heart within her of which no man seemed ever to have found the key. Sara and John were very little at the time of her death—so little, that they scarcely remembered their mother. And they were not like her. Little John, for his part, was like big John, as he had a right to be; and Sara was like nobody else that ever had been seen in Masterton. But that is a subject which demands fuller exposition. Mr. Brownlow lived very quietly for some years after he lost his wife; but then, as was natural, the ordinary course of affairs was resumed. And then it was that the change in his fortunes became fully evident. His little daughter was delicate, and he got a carriage for her. He got ponies for her, and costly governesses and masters down from town at the wildest expense; and then he bought that place in the country which had once been Something Hall or Manor, but which Dartfordshire, in its consternation, henceforward called Brownlow's. Brownlow's it was, without a doubt; and Brownlows it became—without the apostrophe—in the most natural way, when things settled down. It was, as old Lady Hetherton said, "quite a place, my dear; not one of your little bits of villas, you know." And though it was so near Masterton that Mr. Brownlow drove or rode in every day to his office, its grounds and gardens and park were equal to those of any nobleman in the county. Old Mrs. Thomson's fifty thousand pounds had doubled themselves, as money skillfully managed has a way of doing. It had got for her executor every thing a man could desire. First, the wife of his choice—though that gift had been taken from him—and every other worldly good which the man wished or could wish for. He was able to surround the daughter, who was every thing to him—who was more to him, perhaps, than even his wife had ever been—with every kind of delightsome thing; and to provide for his son, and establish him in the world according to his inclinations; and to assume, without departing from his own place, such a position as no former Brownlow had ever occupied in the county. All this came to John Brownlow through old Mrs. Thomson; and Phœbe Thomson, to whom the money in reality belonged, had never turned up to claim it, and now there was but one year to run of the five-and-twenty which limited his responsibilities. All this being made apparent, it is the history of this one year that I have now to tell.

CHAPTER II

SARA

Mr. Brownlow had one son and one daughter—the boy, a very good natured, easy-minded, honest sort of young fellow, approaching twenty-one, and not made much account of either at home or abroad. The daughter was Sara. For people who know her, or indeed who are at all acquainted with society in Dartfordshire, it is unnecessary to say more; but perhaps the general public may prefer a clearer description. She was the queen of John Brownlow's house, and the apple of his eye. At the period of which we speak she was between nineteen and twenty, just emerging from what had always been considered a delicate girlhood, into the full early bloom of woman. She had too much character, too much nonsense, too many wiles, and too much simplicity in her, to be, strictly speaking, beautiful; and she was not good enough or gentle enough to be lovely. And neither was she beloved by all, as a heroine ought to be. There were some people who did not like her, as well as some who did, and there were a great many who fluctuated between love and dislike, and were sometimes fond of her, and sometimes affronted with her; which, indeed, was a very common state of mind with herself. Sara was so much a girl of her age that she had even the hair of the period, as the spring flowers have the colors of spring. It was light-brown, with a golden tint, and abundant as locks of that color generally are; but it can not be denied that it was darker than the fashionable shade, and that Sara was not above being annoyed by this fact, nor even above a vague and shadowy idea of doing something to bring it to the correct tint; which may rank as one of the constantly recurring proofs that young women are in fact the least vain portion of the creation, and have less faith in the efficacy of their natural charms than any other section of the race. She had a little rosebud mouth, dewy and pearly, and full eyes, which were blue, or gray, or hazel, according as you looked at them, and according to the sentiment they might happen to express. She was very tall, very slight and flexible, and wavy like a tall lily, with the slightest variable stoop in her pretty shoulders, for which her life had been rendered miserable by many well-meaning persons, but which in reality was one of her charms. To say that she stooped is an ugly expression, and there was nothing ugly about Sara. It was rather that by times her head drooped a little, like the aforesaid lily swayed by the softest of visionary breezes. This, however, was the only thing lily-like or angelic about her. She was not a model of any thing, nor noted for any special virtues. She was Sara. That was about all that could be said for her; and it is to be hoped that she may be able to evidence what little bits of good there were in her during the course of this history, for herself.

"Papa," she said, as they sat together at the breakfast-table, "I will call for you this afternoon, and bring you home. I have something to do in Masterton."

"Something to do in Masterton?" said Mr. Brownlow; "I thought you had got every thing you could possibly want for three months at least when you were in town."

"Yes," said Sara, "every thing one wants for one's bodily necessities—pins and needles and music, and all that sort of thing—but one has a heart, though you might not think it, papa; and I have an idea that one has a soul."

"Do you think so?" said her father, with a smile; "but I can't imagine what your soul can have to do in Masterton. We don't cultivate such superfluities there."

"I am going to see grandmamma," said Sara. "I think it is my duty. I am not fond of her, and I ought to be. I think if I went to see her oftener perhaps it might do me good."

"O! if it's only for grandmamma," said young John, "I go to see her often enough. I don't think you need take any particular trouble to do her good."

Upon which Sara sighed, and drooped a little upon its long stem her lily head. "I hope I am not so stupid and conceited as to think I can do any body good," she said. "I may be silly enough, but I am not like that; but I am going to see grandmamma. It is my duty to be fond of her, and see after her; and I know I never go except when I can't help it. I am going to turn over a new leaf."

Mr. Brownlow's face had been overshadowed at the first mention of the grandmother, as by a faint mist of annoyance. It did not go so far as to be a cloud. It was not positive displeasure or dislike, but only a shade of dissatisfaction, which he expressed by his silence. Sara's resolutions to turn over a new leaf were not rare, and her father was generally much amused and interested by her good intentions; but at present he only went on with his breakfast and said nothing. Like his daughter, he was not fond of the grandmamma, and perhaps her sympathy with his own sentiments in this respect was satisfactory to him at the bottom of his heart; but it was not a thing he could talk about.

"There is a great deal in habit," said Sara, in that experienced way which belongs to the speculatist of nineteen. "I believe you can train yourself to any thing, even to love people whom you don't love by nature. I think one could get to do that if one was to try."

"I should not care much for your love if that was how it came," said young John.

"That would only show you did not understand," said Sara, mildly. "To like people for a good reason, is not that better than liking them merely because you can't help it? If there was any body that it suited papa, for instance, to make me marry, don't you think I would be very foolish if I could not make myself fond of him? and ungrateful too?"

"Would you really do as much for me, my darling?" said Mr. Brownlow, looking up at her with a glimmer of weakness in his eyes; "but I hope I shall never require to put you to the test."

"Why not, papa?" said Sara, cheerfully. "I am sure it would be a much more sensible reason for being fond of any body that you wished it, than just my own fancy. I should do it, and I would never hesitate about it," said the confident young woman; and the father, though he was a man of some experience, felt his heart melt and glow over this rash statement with a fond gratification, and really believed it, foolish as it was.

"And I shall drive down," said Sara, "and look as fine as possible; though, of course, I would far rather have Meg out, and ride home with you in the afternoon. And it would do Meg a world of good," she added, pathetically. "But you know if one goes in for pleasing one's grandmamma, one ought to be content to please her in her own way. She likes to see the carriage and the grays, and a great noise and fuss. If it is worth taking the trouble for at all, it is worth doing it in her own way."

"I walk, and she is always very glad to see me," said John, in what must be allowed was an unpleasant manner.

"Ah! you are different," said Sara, with a momentary bend of her graceful head. And, of course, he was very different. He was a mere man or boy—whichever you prefer—not in the least ornamental, nor of very much use to any body—whereas Sara—But it is not a difference that could be described or argued about; it was a thing which could be perceived with half an eye. When breakfast was over, the two gentlemen went off to Masterton to their business; for young John had gone into his father's office, and was preparing to take up in his turn the hereditary profession. Indeed, it is not clear that Mr. Brownlow ever intended poor Jack to profit at all by his wealth, or the additional state and grandeur the family had taken upon itself. To his eyes, so far as it appeared, Sara alone was the centre of all this magnificence; whereas Jack was simply the heir and successor of the Brownlows, who had been time out of mind the solicitors of Masterton. For Jack, the brick house in the High Street waited with all its old stores; and the fairy accessories of their present existence, all the luxury and grace and beauty—the grays—the conservatories—the park—the place in the country—seemed a kind of natural appanage to the fair creature in whom the race of Brownlow had come to flower, the father could not tell how; for it seemed strange to think that he himself, who was but a homely individual, should have been the means of bringing any thing so fair and fine into the world. Probably Mr. Brownlow, when it came to making his will, would be strictly just to his two children; but in the mean time, in his thoughts, that was, no doubt, how things stood; and Jack accordingly was brought up as he himself had been, rather as the heir of the Brownlows' business, their excellent connection and long-established practice, than as the heir of Brownlows—two very different things, as will be perceived.

When they went away Sara betook herself to her own business. She saw the cook in the most correct and exemplary way. Fortunately the cook was also the housekeeper, and a very good-tempered woman, who received all her young mistress's suggestions with amiability, and only complained sometimes that Miss Brownlow would order every thing that was out of season. "Not for the sake of extravagance," Mrs.

Stock said, in answer to Sara's maid, who had made that impertinent suggestion; "oh, no, nothin' of the sort—only out of always forgettin', poor dear, and always wantin' me to believe as she knows." But as Sara fortunately paid but little attention to the dinner when produced, making no particular criticism—not for want of will, but for want of knowledge—her interview with the cook at least did no harm. And then she went into many small matters which she thought were of importance. She had an hour's talk, for instance, with the gardener, who was, like most gardeners, a little pig-headed, and fond of having his own way; and Sara was rather of opinion that some of her hints had done him good; and she made him, very unwillingly, cut some flowers for her to take to her grandmother. Mrs. Fennell was not a woman to care for flowers if she could have got them for the plucking; but expensive hothouse flowers in the depth of winter were a different matter. Thus Sara reasoned as she carried them in her basket, with a ground-work of moss beneath to keep them fresh, and left them in the hall till the carriage should come round. And she went to the stables, and looked at every thing in a dainty way—not like your true enthusiast in such matters, but with a certain gentle grandeur, as of a creature to whom satin-skinned cattle and busy grooms were vulgar essentials of life, equally necessary, but equally far off from her supreme altitude. She cared no more for the grays in themselves than she did for Dick and Tom, which will be sufficient to prove to any body learned in such matters how imperfect her development was in this respect. All these little occupations were very different from the occupations of her father and brother, who were both of them in the office all day busy with other people's wills and marriage-settlements and conveyances. Thus it would have been as evident to any impartial looker-on as it was to Mr. Brownlow, that the fortune which had so much changed his position in the county, and given him such very different surroundings, all centered in, and was appropriated to, his daughter, while his old life, his hereditary business, the prose and plain part of his existence, was to be carried out in his son.

When all the varieties of occupation in this useful day were about exhausted, Sara prepared for her drive. She wrapped herself up in fur and velvet, and every thing that was warmest and softest and most luxurious; and with her basket of flowers and another little basket of game, which she did not take any personal charge of, rolled away out of the park gates to Masterton. Brownlows had belonged to a very unsuccessful race before it came to be Brownlow's. It had been in the hands of poor, failing, incompetent people, which was, perhaps, the reason why its original name had dropped so completely out of recollection. Now, for the first time in its existence, it looked really like "a gentleman's place." But yet there were eye-sores about. One of these was a block of red brick, which stood exactly opposite the park gates, opposite the lodge which Mr. Brownlow had made so pretty. There were only two cottages in the block, and they were very unpretending and very clean, and made the life of the woman in the lodge twice as lightsome and agreeable; but to Sara's eyes at least, Swayne's Cottages, as they were called, were very objectionable. They were two-storied houses, with windows and doors very flush with the walls; as if, which indeed was the case, the walls themselves were of the slightest construction possible; and Swayne himself, or rather Mrs. Swayne, who was the true head of the house, let a parlor and bedroom to lodgers who wanted country air and quiet at a cheap rate. "Any body might come," Sara was in the habit of saying; "your worst enemy might come and sit down there at your very door, and spy upon every thing you were doing. It makes me shudder when I think of it." Thus she had spoken ever since her father's entrance upon the glories of his "place," egging him up with all her might to attack this little Naboth's vineyard. But there never was a Naboth more obstinate in his rights than Mr. Swayne, who was a carpenter and builder, and had put the two houses together himself, and was proud of them; and Sara was then too young and too much under the sway of her feelings to take upon her in cold blood Jezebel's decisive part.

She could not help looking at them to-day as she swept out, with the two grays spurning the gravel under foot, and the lodge-woman at the gate looking up with awe while she made her courtesy as if to the queen. Mrs. Swayne, too, was standing at her door, but she did not courtesy to Sara. She stood and looked as if she did not care—the splendor and the luxury were nothing to her. She looked out in a calm sort of indifferent way, which was to Sara what, to continue a scriptural symbolism, Mordecai was to another less fortunate personage. And Mrs. Swayne had a ticket of "Lodgings" in her window. It could do her no good, for nobody ever passed along that road who could be desirous of country lodgings at a cheap rate, and this advertisement looked to Sara like an intentional insult. The wretched woman might get about eight shillings a week for her lodgings, and for that paltry sum she could allow herself to post up bills opposite the very gate of Brownlows; but then some people have so little feeling. This trifling incident occupied Sara's mind during at least half her drive. The last lodger had been a consumptive patient, whose pale looks had filled her with compassionate impulses, against which her dislike of Mrs. Swayne contended vainly. Who would it be next? Some other invalid most likely, as pale and as poor, to make one discontented with the world and ashamed of one's self the moment one issued forth from the park gates, and all because of the determination of the Swaynes to annoy their wealthy neighbors. The thought made Sara angry as she drove along; but it was a brisk winter afternoon, with frost in the air, and the hoofs of the grays rang on the road, and even the country waggons seemed to move along at an exhilarated pace. So Sara thought, who was young, and whose blood ran quickly in her veins, and who was wrapped up to the throat in velvet and fur. Now and then another carriage would roll past, when there were people who nodded or kissed their hands to Sara as they passed, with all that clang of hoofs and sweep of motion, merrily on over the hard road beneath the naked trees. And the people who were walking walked briskly, as if the blood was racing in their veins too, and rushing warm and vigorous to healthy cheeks. If any cheeks were blue rather than red, if any hearts were sick with the cold and the weary way, if any body she met chanced to be going heavily home to a hearth where there was no fire, or a house from which love and light had gone, Sara, glowing to the wind, knew nothing of that; and that the thought never entered her mind was no fault of hers.

The winter sky was beginning to dress itself in all the glories of sunset when she got to Masterton. It had come to be the time of the year when the sun set in the rectory garden, and John Brownlow's windows in the High Street got all aglow. Perhaps it brought associations to his mind as the dazzling red radiance flashed in at the office window, and he laid down his pen. But the fact was that this pause was caused by a sound of wheels echoing along the market-place, which was close by. That must be Sara. Such was the thought that passed through Mr. Brownlow's mind. He did not think, as the last gleam came over him, how he used to look up and see Bessie passing—that Bessie who had come to be his wife—nor of any other moving event that had happened to him when the sun was coming in at his windows aslant in that undeniable way. No; all that he thought was, There goes Sara; and his face softened, and he began to put his papers together. The child in her living importance, little lady and sovereign of all that surrounded her, triumphed thus even over the past and the dead.

Mrs. Fennell had lodgings in a street which was very genteel, and opened off the market-place. The houses were not very large, but they had pillars to the doors and balconies to all the first-floor windows; and some very nice people lived there. Mrs. Fennell was very old and not able to manage a house for herself, so she had apartments, she and her maid—one of the first floors with the balconies—a very comfortable little drawing-room, which the care of her friends had filled with every description of comfortable articles. Her paralytic husband was dead ages ago, and her daughter Bessie was dead, and her beloved but good-for-nothing son—and yet the old woman had lived on. Sometimes, when any thing touched her heart, she would mourn over this, and ask why she had been left when every thing was gone that made life sweet to her; but still she lived on; and at other times it must be confessed that she was not an amiable old woman. It is astonishing how often it happens that the sweet domestic qualities do not descend from mother to daughter, but leap a generation as it were, interjecting a passionate, peevish mother to bring out in full relief the devotion of her child—or a selfish exacting child to show the mother's magnanimity. Such contrasts are very usual among women—I don't know if they are visible to the same extent as between father and son. Mrs. Fennell was not amiable. She was proud and quarrelsome and bitter—exacting of every profit and every honor, and never contented. She was proud to think of her son-in-law's fine house and her granddaughter's girlish splendor; and yet it was the temptation of her life to rail at them, to tell how little he had done for her, and to reckon up all he ought to have done, and to declare if it had not been for the Fennells and their friends, it was little any body would ever have heard of John Brownlow. All this gave her a certain pleasure; and at the same time Sara's visit with the grays and the state equipage and the tall footman, and her entrance in her rich dress with her sables, which had cost nobody could tell how much, and her basket of flowers which could not have been bought in Dartfordshire for their weight in gold, was the triumph of her life. As soon as she heard the sound of the wheels in the street—which was not visited by many carriages—she would steal out into her bedroom and change her cap with her trembling hands. She never changed her cap for Jack, who came on foot, and brought every kind of homely present to please her and make her comfortable. But Sara was different—and Sara's presents added not to her comfort, but to her glory, which was quite another affair.

"Well, my dear," she said, with a mixture of peevishness and pleasure, as the girl came in, "so this is you. I thought you were never coming to see me any more."

"I beg your pardon, grandmamma," said Sara. "I know I have been neglecting my duty, but I mean to turn over a new leaf. There are some birds down below that I thought you would like, and I have brought you some flowers. I will put them in your little vases if I may ring for Nancy to bring some water. I made Pitt cut me this daphne, though I think he would rather have cut off my head. It will perfume the whole room."

"My dear, you know I don't like strong smells," said Mrs. Fennell. "I never could bear scents—a little whiff of musk, and that was all I ever cared for—though your poor mamma was such a one for violets and trash. And I haven't got servants to be running up and down stairs as you have at your fine place. One maid for every thing is considered quite enough for me."

"Well, grandmamma," said Sara, "you have not very much to do, you know. If I were you, I would have a nice young maid that would look pleasant and cheerful instead of that cross old Nancy, who never looks pleased at any thing."

"What good do you think I could have of a young maid?" said Mrs. Fennell—"nasty gossiping tittering things, that are twenty times more bother than they're worth. I have Nancy because she suits me, and because she was poor old Mrs. Thomson's maid, as every body has forgotten but her and me. The dead are soon out of mind, especially when they've got a claim on living folks' gratitude. If it wasn't for poor Mrs. Thomson where would your grand carriage have been, and your daphnes, and your tall footmen, and all your papa's grandeur? But there's nobody that thinks on her but me."

"I am sure I have not forgotten her," said Sara. "I wish I could. She must have been a horrible old wretch, and I wish she had left papa alone. I'd rather not have Brownlows if I am always to hear of that wretched old woman. I suppose Nancy is her ghost and haunts you. I hate to hear her horrid old name."

"You are just like all the rest," said the grandmother—"ashamed of your relations because you are so fine; and if it had not been for your relations—she was your poor mamma's cousin, Miss Sairah—if it was only that, and out of respect to me—"

"Don't call me Sairah, please," said the indignant little visitor. "I do hate it so; and I have not done any thing that I know of to be called Miss for. What is the use of quarreling, grandmamma? Do let us be comfortable a little. You can't think how cold it is out of doors. Don't you think it is rather nice to be an old lady and sit by the fire and have every body come to see you, and no need to take any trouble with making calls or any thing? I think it must be one of the nicest things in the world."

"Do you think you would like it?" the old woman said grimly from the other side of the fire.

"It is different, you know," said Sara, drooping her pretty head as she sat before the fire with the red light gleaming in her hair. "You were once as young as me, and you can go back to that in your mind; and then mamma was once as young as me, and you can go back to that. I should think it must feel like walking out in a garden all your own, that nobody else has any right to; while the rest of us, you know—"

"Ah!" said the old woman with a cry; "but a garden that you once tripped about, and once saw your children tripping about, and now you have to hobble through it all alone. Oh child, child! and never a sound in it, but all the voices gone and all the steps that you would give the world to hear!"

Sara roused herself up out of her meditation, and gave a startled astonished look into the corner where the cross old grandmother was sobbing in the darkness. The child stumbled to her feet, startled and frightened and ashamed of what she had done, and went and threw herself upon the old woman's neck. And poor old Mrs. Fennell sobbed and pushed her granddaughter away, and then hugged and kissed her, and stroked her pretty hair and the feather in her hat and her soft velvet and fur. The thoughtless girl had given her a stab, and yet it was such a stab as opens while it wounds. She sobbed, but a touch of sweetness came along with the pain, and for the moment she loved again, and grew human and motherlike, warming out of the chills of her hard old age.

"You need not talk of cold, at least," she said when the little accès was over, and when Sara, having bestowed upon her the first real affectionate kiss she had given her since she came to woman's estate, had dropped again into the low chair before the fire, feeling a little astonished, yet rather pleased with herself for having proved equal to the occasion—"you need not talk of cold with all that beautiful fur. It must have cost a fortune. Mrs. Lyon next door will come to see me to-morrow and she will take you all to pieces, and say it isn't real. And such a pretty feather! I like you in that kind of hat—it is very becoming; and you look like a little princess just now as you sit before the fire."

"Do I?" said Sara. "I am very glad you are pleased, grandmamma. I put on my very best to please you. Do you remember the little cape you made for me, when I was a tiny baby, out of your great old muff? I have got it still. But oh, listen to that daphne how it tells it is here! It is all through the room, as I said it would be. I must ring for some water, and your people, when they come to call, will never say the daphne is not real. It will contradict them to their face. Please, Nancy, some water for the flowers."

"Thomas says it's time for you to be a-going, Miss," said Nancy, grimly.

"Oh, Thomas can say what he pleases; papa will wait for me," cried Sara; "and grandmamma and I are such friends this time. There is some cream in the basket, Nancy, for tea; for you know our country cream is the best; and some of the grapes of my pet vine; don't look sulky, there's an old dear. I am coming every week. And grandmamma and I are such friends—"

"Anyhow, she's my poor Bessie's own child," said Mrs. Fennell, with a little deprecation; for Nancy, who had been old Mrs. Thomson's servant, was stronger even than herself upon the presumption of Brownlows, and how, but for them as was dead and gone and forgotten, such splendor could never have been.

"Sure enough," said Nancy, "and more people's child as well," which was the sole but pregnant comment she permitted herself to make. Sara, however, got her will, as she usually did. She took off her warm cloak, which the two old women examined curiously, and scorned Thomas's recommendations, and made and shared her grandmother's tea, while the grays drove up and down the narrow street, dazzling the entire neighborhood, and driving the coachman desperate. Mr. Brownlow, too, sat waiting and wondering in his office, thinking weakly that every cab that passed must be Sara's carriage. The young lady did not hurry herself. "It was to please grandmamma," as she said; certainly it was not to please herself, for there could not be much pleasure for Sara in the society of those two old women, who were not sweet-tempered, and who were quite as like, according to the mood they might happen to be in, to take the presents for insults as for tokens of love. But, then, there was always a pleasure in having her own way, and one of which Sara was keenly susceptible. When she called for her father eventually, she complained to him that her head ached a little, and that she felt very tired. "The daphne got to be a little overpowering in grandmamma's small room," she said; "I dare say they would put it out of window as soon as I was gone; and, besides, it is a little tiring, to tell the truth. But grandmamma was quite pleased," said the disinterested girl. And John Brownlow took great care of his Sara as they drove out together, and felt his heart grow lighter in his breast when she recovered from her momentary languor, and looked up at the frosty twinkling in the skies above, and chattered and laughed as the carriage rolled along, lighting up the road with its two lamps, and dispersing the silence with a brisk commotion. He was prouder of his child than if she had been his bride—more happy in the possession of her than a young man with his love. And yet John Brownlow was becoming an old man, and had not been without cares and uncomfortable suggestions even on that very day.

CHAPTER III

A SUDDEN ALARM

The unpleasant suggestion which had been brought before Mr. Brownlow's mind that day, while Sara accomplished her visit to her grandmother, came after this wise:

His mind had been going leisurely over his affairs in general, as he went down to his office; for naturally, now that he was so rich, he had many affairs of his own beside that placid attention to other people's affairs which was his actual trade; and it had occurred to him that at one point there was a weakness in his armor. One of his investments had not been so skillful or so prudent as the rest, and it looked as if it might call for farther and farther outlay before it could be made profitable, if indeed it were ever made profitable. When he got to the office, Mr. Brownlow, like a prudent man, looked into the papers connected with this affair, and took pains to understand exactly how he stood, and what farther claims might be made upon him. And while he was doing this, certain questions of date arose which set clearly before him, what he had for the moment forgotten, that the time of his responsibility to Phœbe Thomson was nearly over, and that in a year no claim could be made against him for Mrs. Thomson's fifty thousand pounds. The mere realization of this fact gave him a certain thrill of uncertainty and agitation. He had not troubled himself about it for years, and during that time he had felt perfectly safe and comfortable in his possessions; but to look upon it in actual black and white, and to see how near he was to complete freedom, gave him a sudden sense of his present risk, such as he had never felt before. To repay the fifty thousand pounds would have been no such difficult matter, for Mrs. Thomson's money had been lucky money, and had, as we have said, doubled and trebled itself; but there was interest for five-and-twenty years to be reckoned; and there was no telling what other claims the heir, if an heir should turn up, might bring against the old woman's executor. Mr. Brownlow felt for one sharp moment as if Sara's splendor and her happiness was at the power of some unknown vagabond who might make a sudden claim any moment when he was unprepared upon the inheritance which for all these years had appeared to him as his own. It was a sort of danger which could not be guarded against, but rather, indeed, ought to be invited; though it would be hard—no doubt it would be hard, after all this interval—to give up the fortune which he had accepted with reluctance, and which had cost him, as he felt, a hundred times more trouble than it had ever given him pleasure. Now that he had begun to get a little good out of it, to think of some stealthy vagrant coming in and calling suddenly for his rights, and laying claim perhaps to all the increase which Mr. Brownlow's careful management had made of the original, was an irritating idea. He tried to put it away, and perhaps he might have been successful in banishing it from his mind but for another circumstance that fixed it there, and gave, as it seemed, consistency and force to the thought.

The height of the day was over, and the sun was veering toward that point of the compass from which its rays shone in at John Brownlow's windows, when he was asked if he would see a young man who came about the junior clerk's place. Mr. Brownlow had very nearly made up his mind as to who should fill this junior clerk's place; but he was kind-hearted, and sent no one disconsolate away if it were possible to help it. After a moment's hesitation, he gave orders for the admission of this young man. "If he does not do for that, he may be good for something else," was what John Brownlow said; for it was one of his crotchets, that to help men to work was better than almsgiving. The young man in question had nothing very remarkable in his appearance. He had a frank, straightforward, simple sort of air, which partly, perhaps, arose from the great defect in his face—the projection of the upper jaw, which was well garnished with large white teeth. He had, however, merry eyes, of the kind that smile without knowing it whenever they accost another countenance; but his other features were all homely—expressive, but not remarkable. He came in modestly, but he was not afraid; and he stood respectfully and listened to Mr. Brownlow, but there was no servility in his attitude. He had come about the clerk's place, and he was quite ready to give an account of himself. His father had been a non-commissioned officer, but was dead; and his mother wanted his help badly enough.

"But you are strangers in Masterton," said Mr. Brownlow, attracted by his frank looks. "Had you any special inducement to come here?"

"Nothing of any importance," said the youth, and he colored a little. "The fact is, sir, my mother came of richer people than we are now, and they cast her off; and some of them once lived in Masterton. She came to see if she could hear any thing of her friends."

"And did she?" said John Brownlow, feeling his breath come a little quick.

"They are all dead long ago," said the young man. "We have all been born in Canada, and we never heard what had happened. Her moth—I mean her friends, are all dead, I suppose; and Masterton is just as good as any other place to make a beginning in. I should not be afraid if I could get any thing to do."

"Clerk's salaries are very small," said Mr. Brownlow, without knowing what it was he said.

"Yes, but they improve," said his visitor, cheerfully; "and I don't mind what I do. I could make up books or do any thing at night, or even have pupils—I have done that before. But I beg your pardon for troubling you with all this. If the place is filled up—"

"Nay, stop—sit down—you interest me," said Mr. Brownlow. "I like a young fellow who is not easily cast down. Your mother—belongs—to Masterton, I suppose," he added, with a little hesitation; he, that gave way to no man in Dartfordshire for courage and coolness, he was afraid. He confessed it to himself, and felt all the shame of the new sensation, but it had possession of him all the same.

"She belongs to the Isle of Man," said the young man, with his frank straightforward look and the smile in his eyes. He answered quite simply and point-blank, having no thought that there was any second meaning in his words; but it was otherwise with him who heard. John Brownlow sat silent, utterly confounded. He stared at the young stranger in a blank way, not knowing how to answer or how to conceal or account for the tremendous impression which these simple words made on him. He sat and stared, and his lower lip fell a little, and his eyes grew fixed, so that the youth was terrified, and did not know what to make of it. Of course he seized upon the usual resource of the disconcerted—"I beg your pardon," he said, "but I am afraid you are ill."

"No, no; it is nothing," said Mr. Brownlow. "I knew some people once who came from the Isle of Man. But that is a long time ago. I am sorry she has not found the people she sought for. But, as you say, there is nothing like work. If you can engross well—though how you should know how to engross after taking pupils and keeping books—"

"We have to do a great many things in the colony," said his young visitor. "If a man wants to live, he must not be particular about what he does. I was two years in a lawyer's office in Paris—"

"In Paris?" said Mr. Brownlow, with amazement.

"I mean in Paris, Canada West," said the youth, with a touch of momentary defiance, as who would say, "and a very much better Paris than any you can boast of here."

This little accident did so much good that it enabled Mr. Brownlow to smile, and to shake off the oppression that weighed upon him. It was a relief to be able to question the applicant as to his capabilities, while secretly and rapidly in his own mind he turned over the matter, and asked himself what he should do. Discourage the young man and direct him elsewhere, and gently push him out of Masterton—or take him in and be kind to him, and trust in Providence? The panic of the moment suggested the first course, but a better impulse followed. In the first place, it was not easy to discourage a young fellow with those sanguine brown eyes, and blood that ran so quickly in his veins; and if any danger was at hand, it was best to have it near, and be able to study it, and be warned at once how and when it might approach. All this passed rapidly, like an under-current, through John Brownlow's mind, as he sat and asked innumerable questions about the young applicant's capabilities and antecedents. He did it to gain time, though all young Powys thought was that he had never gone through so severe an examination. The young fellow smiled within himself at the wonderful precision and caution of the old man, with a kind of transatlantic freedom—not that he was republican, but only colonial; not irritated by his employer's superiority, but regarding it as an affair of perhaps only a few days or years.

"I will think it over," said Mr. Brownlow at last. "I can not decide upon any thing all at once. If you settle quietly down and get a situation, I think you may do very well here. It is not a dear place, and if your mother has friends—"

"But she has no friends now that we know of," said the young man, with the unnecessary and persistent explanatoriness of youth.

"If she has friends here," persisted Mr. Brownlow, "you may be sure they will turn up. Come back to me to-morrow. I will think it all over in the mean time, and give you my answer then. Powys—that is a very good name—there was a Lady Powys here some time ago, who was exceedingly good and kind to the poor. Perhaps it was she whom you sought—"

"Oh, no," said the young man, eagerly; "it was my mother's people—a family called—"

"I am afraid I have an engagement now," said Mr. Brownlow; and then young Powys withdrew, with that quiet sense of shame and compunction which belongs only to his years. He, of course, as was natural, could see nothing of the tragic under-current. It appeared to him only that he was intruding his private affairs, in an unjustifiable way, on his probable patron—on the man who had been kind to him, and given him hope. "What an ass I am!" he said to himself as he went away, "as if he could take any interest in my mother's friends." And it troubled the youth all day to think that he had possibly wearied Mr. Brownlow by his explanations and iteration—an idea as mistaken as it was possible to conceive.

When he had left the office, the lawyer fell back in his chair, and for a long time neither moved nor spoke. Probably it was the nature of his previous reflections which gave this strange visit so overwhelming an effect. He sat in a kind of stupor, seeing before him, as it appeared in actual bodily presence, the danger which it had startled him this same morning to realize as merely possible. If it had been any other day, he might have heard, without much remarking, all those singular coincidences which now appeared so startling; but they chimed in so naturally, or rather so unnaturally, with the tenor of his thoughts, that his panic was superstitious and overwhelming. He sat a long time without moving, almost without breathing, feeling as if it was some kind of fate that approached him. After so many years that he had not thought of this danger, it seemed to him at last that the thoughts which had entered his mind in the morning must have been premonitions sent by Providence; and at a glance he went over the whole position—the new claimant, the gradually expanding claim, the conflict over it, the money he had locked up in that one doubtful speculation, the sudden diminution of his resources, perhaps the necessity of selling Brownlows and bringing Sara back to the old house in the High Street where she was born. Such a downfall would have been nothing for himself: for him the old wainscot dining-parlor and all the well-known rooms were agreeable and full of pleasant associations; but Sara—Then John Brownlow gave another wide glance over his social firmament, asking himself if there was any one whom, between this time and that, Sara's heart might perhaps incline to, whom she might marry, and solve the difficulty. A few days before he used to dread and avoid the idea of her marriage. Now all this rushed upon him in a moment, with the violent impulse of his awakened fears. By-and-by, however, he came to himself. A woman might be a soldier's wife, and might come from the Isle of Man, and might have had friends in Masterton who were dead, without being Phœbe Thomson. Perhaps if he had been bold, and listened to the name which was on his young visitor's lips, it might have reassured him, and settled the question; but he had been afraid to do it. At this early stage of his deliberations he had not a moment's doubt as to what he would do—what he must do—at once and without delay, if Phœbe Thomson really presented herself before him. But it was not his business to seek her out. And who could say that this was she? The Isle of Man, after all, was not so small a place, and any one who had come to Masterton to ask after old Mrs. Thomson would have been referred at once to her executor. This conviction came slowly upon Mr. Brownlow's mind as he got over the first wild thrill of fear. He put his terror away from him gradually and slowly. When a thought has burst upon the mind at once, and taken possession of it at a stroke, it is seldom dislodged in the same complete way. It may cease to be a conviction, but it never ceases to be an impression. To this state, by degrees, his panic subsided. He no longer thought it certain that young Powys was Phœbe Thomson's representative; but only that such a thing was possible—that he had something tangible to guard against and watch over. In place of his quiet every-day life, with all its comforts, an exciting future, a sudden whirl of possibilities opened before him. But in one year all this would be over. One year would see him, would see his children, safe in the fortune they had grown used to, and come to feel their own. Only one year! There are moments when men are fain to clog the wheels of time and retard its progress; but there are also moments when, to set the great clock forward arbitrarily and to hasten the measured beating of that ceaseless leisurely pendulum, is the desire that goes nearest the heart. Thus it came to appear to Mr. Brownlow as if it was now a kind of race between time and fate; for as yet it had not occurred to him to think of abstract justice nor of natural rights higher than those of any legal testament. He was thinking only of the letter, of the stipulated year. He was thinking if that time were past that he would feel himself his own master. And this sentiment grew and settled in his mind as he sat alone, and waited for Sara's carriage—for his child, whom in all this matter he thought of the most. He was disturbed in the present, and eager with the eagerness of a boy for the future. It did not even occur to him that ghosts would arise in that future even more difficult to exorcise. All his desire in the mean time was—if only this year were over—if only anyhow a leap could be made through this one interval of danger. And the sharp and sudden pain he had come through gave him at the same time a sense of lassitude and exhaustion. Thus Sara's headache and her fatigue and fanciful little indisposition were very lucky accidents for her father. They gave him an excuse for the deeper compunctious tenderness with which he longed to make up to her for a possible loss, and occupied both of them, and hid his disturbed air, and gave him a little stimulus of pleasure when she mended and resumed her natural chatter. Thus reflection and the fresh evening air, and Sara's headache and company, ended by almost curing Mr. Brownlow before he reached home.

CHAPTER IV

A LITTLE DINNER

There was a very pleasant party that evening at Brownlows—the sort of thing of which people say, that it is not a party at all, you know, only ourselves and the Hardcastles, or whoever else it may happen to be. There was the clergyman of the parish, of course—who is always, if he happens to be at all agreeable, the very man for such little friendly dinners; and there was his daughter; for he was a widower, like Mr. Brownlow—and his Fanny was half as much to him, to say the least, as Sara was to her admiring father. And there was just one guest besides—young Keppel, to wit, the son of old Keppel of Ridley, and brother of the present Mr. Keppel—a young fellow who was not just precisely what is called eligible, so far as the young ladies were concerned, but who did very well for all secondary purposes, and was a barrister with hopes of briefs, and a flying connection with literature, which helped him to keep his affairs in order, and was rather of service to him than otherwise in society, as it sometimes is to a perfectly well-connected young man. Thus there were two girls and two young men, and two seniors to keep each other company; and there was a great deal of talk and very pleasant intercourse, enough to justify the rector in his enthusiastic utterance of his favorite sentiment, that this was true society, and that he did not know what people meant by giving dinners at which there were more than six. Mr. Hardcastle occasionally, it is true, expressed under other circumstances opinions which might be supposed a little at variance with this one; but then a man can not always be in the same mind, and no doubt he was quite sincere in what he said. He was a sort of man that exists, but is not produced now-a-days. He was neither High Church nor Low Church, so to speak. If you had offered to confess your sins to him he would have regarded you with as much terror and alarm as if you had presented a pistol at his head; and if you had attempted to confess your virtues under the form of spiritual experience, he would have turned from you with disgust. Neither was he in the least freethinking, but a most correct orthodox clergyman, a kind of man, as I have said, not much produced in these times. Besides this indefinite clerical character he had a character of his own, which was not at all indefinite. He was a little red-faced, and sometimes almost jovial in his gayety, and at the same time he was in possession of a large stock of personal griefs and losses, which had cost him many true tears and heartaches, poor man, but which were very useful to him in the way of his profession. And he had an easy way of turning from the one phase of life to the other, which had a curious effect sometimes upon impartial spectators. But all the same it was perfectly true and genuine. He made himself very agreeable that night at Brownlows, and was full of jest and frolic; but if he had been called to see somebody in trouble as he went home, he would have gone in and drawn forth from his own private stores of past pain, and manifested plainly to the present sufferer that he himself had suffered more bitterly still. He had "come through" all the pangs that a man can suffer in this world. He had lost his wife and his children, till nothing was left to him but this one little Fanny—and he loved to open his closed-up chambers to your eyes, and to meet your pitiful looks and faltering attempt at consolation; and yet at the same time you would find him very jolly in the evening at Mr. Brownlow's, which hurt the feelings of some sensitive people. His daughter, little Fanny, was pretty and nice, and nothing particular, which suited her position and prospects perfectly well. These were the two principal guests, young Keppel being only a man, as ladies who are in the habit of giving dinners are wont to describe such floating members of the community. And they all talked and made themselves pleasant, and it was as pretty and as lively a little party as you could well have seen. Quantities of flowers and lights, two very pretty girls, and two good-looking young men, were enough to guarantee its being a very pretty scene; and nobody was afraid of any body, and every body could talk, and did so, which answered for the latter part of the description. Such little parties were very frequent at Brownlows.

After dinner the two girls had a little talk by themselves. They came floating into the great drawing-room with those heaps of white drapery about them which make up for any thing that may be intrinsically unamiable[A] in crinoline. Before they went up stairs, making it ready for them, a noble fire, all red, clear, and glowing, was in the room, and made it glorious; and the pretty things which glittered and reddened and softened in the bright warm atmosphere were countless.

[A] If there is anything; most of us think there is not. If the unthinking male creatures who abuse it only knew the comfort of it! and what a weariness it saves us! and as for the people who are burnt, it is not because of their crinolines, but because of losing their heads—a calamity to which in all kinds of dresses we are constantly liable.

There was a bouquet of violets on the table, which was Mr. Pitt the gardener's daily quit-rent to Sara for all the honors and emoluments of his situation, so that every kind of ethereal sense was satisfied. Fanny

Hardcastle dropped into a very low chair at one side of the fire, where she sat like a swan with her head and throat rising out of the white billowy waves which covered yards of space round about her. Sara, who was at home, drew a stool in front of the fire, and sat down there, heaping up in her turn snow-wreaths upon the rosy hearth. A sudden spark might have swallowed them both in fiery destruction. But the spark happily did not come; and they had their talk in great comfort and content. They touched upon a great many topics, skimming over them, and paying very little heed to logical sequences. And at last they stumbled into metaphysics, and had a curious little dive into the subject of love and love-making, as was not unnatural. It is to be regretted, however, that neither of these young women had very exalted ideas on this point. They were both girls of their period, who recognized the necessity of marriage, and that it was something likely to befall both of them, but had no exaggerated notions of its importance; and, indeed, so far from being utterly absorbed in the anticipation of it, were both far from clear whether they believed in such a thing as love.

"I don't think one ever could be so silly as they say in books," said Fanny Hardcastle, "unless one was a great fool—feeling as if every thing was changed, you know, as soon as he was out of the room, and feeling one's heart beat when he was coming, and all that stuff; I don't believe it Sara; do you?"

"I don't know," said Sara, making a screen of her pretty laced handkerchief to protect her face from the firelight; "perhaps it is because one has never seen the right sort of man. The only man I have ever seen whom one could really love is papa."

"Papa!" echoed Fanny, faintly, and with surprise. Perhaps, after all, she had a lingering faith in ordinary delusions; at all events, there was nothing heroic connected in her mind with papas in general; and she could but sit still and gaze and wonder what next the spoiled child would say.

"I wonder if mamma was very fond of him," said Sara, meditatively. "She ought to have been, but I dare say she never knew him half as well as I do. That is the dreadful thing. You have to marry them before you know."

"Oh, Sara, don't you believe in love at first sight?" said Fanny, forgetting her previously expressed sentiments. "I do."

Sara threw up her drooping head into the air with a little impatient motion. "I don't think I believe any thing about it," she said.

"And yet there was once somebody that was fond of you," said little Fanny breathlessly. "Poor Harry Mansfield, who was so nice—every body knows about that—and, I do think, Mr. Keppel, if you would not be so saucy to him—"

"Mr. Keppel!" exclaimed Sara, with some scorn. "But I will tell you plainly what I mean to do. Mind it is in confidence between us two. You must never tell it to any body. I have made up my mind to marry whoever papa wishes me to marry—I don't mind who it is. I shall do whatever he says."

"Oh, Sara!" said her young companion, with open eyes and mouth, "you will never go so far as that."

"Oh yes, I will," said Sara, with calm assurance. "He would not ask me to have any body very old or very hideous; and if he lets it alone I shall never leave him at all, but stay still here."

"That might be all very well for a time," said the prudent Fanny; "but you would get old, and you couldn't stay here forever. That is what I am afraid of. Things get so dull when one is old."

"Do you think so?" said Sara. "I don't think I should be dull—I have so many things to do."

"Oh, you are the luckiest girl in the whole world," said Fanny Hardcastle, with a little sigh. She, for her own part, would not have despised the reversion of Mr. Keppel, and would have been charmed with Jack Brownlow. But such blessings were not for her. She was in no hurry about it; but still, as even now it was dull occasionally at the rectory, she could not but feel that when she was old—say, seven-and-twenty or so—it would be duller still; and if accordingly, in the mean time, somebody "nice" would turn up—Fanny's thoughts went no farther than this. And as for Sara, she has already laid her own views on the subject before her friends.

It was just then that Jack Brownlow, leaving the dining-room, invited young Keppel to the great hall door to see what sort of a night it was. "It looked awfully like frost," Jack said; and they both went with serious countenances to look out, for the hounds were to meet next day.

"Smoke! not when we are going back to the ladies," said Keppel, with a reluctance which went far to prove the inclination which Fanny Hardcastle had read in his eyes.

"Put yourself into this overcoat," said Jack, "and I'll take you to my room, and perfume you after. The girls don't mind."

"Your sister must mind, I am sure," said Keppel. "One can't think of any coarse sort of gratification like this—I suppose it is a gratification—in her presence."

"Hum," said Jack; "I have her presence every day, you know, and it does not fill me with awe."

"It is all very easy for you," said Keppel, as they went down the steps into the cold and darkness. Poor fellow! he had been a little thrown off his balance by the semi-intimacy and close contact of the little dinner. He had sat by Sara's side, and he had lost his head. He went along by Jack's side rather disconsolate, and not even attempting to light his cigar. "You don't know how well off you are," he said, in touching tones, "whereas another fellow would give his head—"

"Most fellows I know want their heads for their own affairs," said the unfeeling Jack. "Don't be an ass; you may talk nonsense as much as you like, but you know you never could be such an idiot as to marry at your age."

"Marry!" said Keppel, a little startled, and then he breathed forth a profound sigh. "If I had the ghost of a chance," he said, and stopped short, as if despair choked farther utterance. As for Jack Brownlow, he was destitute of sensibility, as indeed was suitable to his trade.

"I shouldn't say you had in this case," he said, in his imperturbable way; "and all the better for you. You've got to make your way in the world like the rest of us, and I don't think you're the sort of fellow to hang on to a girl with money. It's all very well after a bit, when you've made your way; but no fellow with the least respect for himself should think of such a thing before, say five-and-thirty; unless, of course, he is a duke, and has a great family to keep up."

"I hope you'll keep to your own standard," said Keppel, with a little bitterness, "unless you think an only son and a duke on equal ground."

"Don't sneer," said Jack; "I'm young Brownlow the attorney; you know that as well as I do. I can't go visiting all over the country at my uncle's place and my cousin's place, like you. Brownlows is a sort of a joke to most people, you know. Not that I haven't as much respect for my father and my family as if we were all princes; and I mean to stand by my order. If I ever marry it will be twenty years hence, when I can afford it; and you can't afford it any more than I can. A fellow might love a woman and give up a great deal for her," Jack added with a little excitement; "but, by Jove! I don't think he would be justified in giving up his life."

"It depends on what you call life," said Keppel. "I suppose you mean society and that sort of thing—a few stupid parties and club gossip, and worse."

"I don't mean any thing of the sort," said Jack, tossing away his cigar; "I mean working out your own career, and making your way. When a fellow goes and marries and settles down, and cuts off all his chances, what use is his youth and his strength to him? It would be hard upon a poor girl to be expected to make up for all that."

"I did not know you were such a philosopher, Jack," said his companion, "nor so ambitious; but I suppose you're right in a cold-blooded sort of way. Anyhow; if I were that duke—"

"You'd make an ass of yourself," said young Brownlow; and then the two congratulated each other that the skies were clouding over, and the dreaded frost dispersing into drizzle, and went in and took off their smoking coats, and wasted a flask of eau-de-cologne, and went up stairs; where there was an end of all philosophy, at least for that night.

And the seniors sat over their wine, drinking little, notwithstanding Mr. Hardcastle's ruddy countenance, which was due rather to fresh air, taken in large and sometimes boisterous drafts, than to any stronger beverage. But they liked their talk, and they were, in a friendly way, opposed to each other on a great many questions; the rector, as in duty bound, being steadily conservative, while the lawyer had crotchets in political matters. They were discussing the representatives of the county, and also those of some of the neighboring boroughs, which was probably the reason why Mr. Hardcastle gave a personal turn to the conversation as he suddenly did.

"If you will not stand for the borough yourself, you ought to put forward Jack," said the rector. "I think he is sounder than you are. The best sign I know of the country is that all the young fellows are tories, Brownlow. Ah! you may shake your head, but I have it on the best authority. Sir Robert would support him, of course; and with your influence at Masterton—"

"Jack must stick to his business," said Mr. Brownlow; "neither he nor I have time for politics. Besides, we are not the sort of people—county families, you know."

"Oh, bother county families!" said Mr. Hardcastle. "You know there is not another place in the county kept up like Brownlows. If you will not stand yourself, you ought to push forward your boy."

"It is out of my way," said Mr. Brownlow, shaking his head, and then a momentary smile passed over his face. It had occurred to him, by means of a trick of thought he had got into unawares—if Sara could but do it! and then he smiled at himself. Even while he did so, the recollection of his disturbed day returned to him; and though he was a lawyer and a self-contained man, and not given to confidences, still something moved in his heart and compelled him, as it were, to speak.

"Besides," he went on, "we are only here on sufferance. You know all about my circumstances—every body in Dartfordshire does, I believe; and Phœbe Thomson may turn up any day and make her claim."

"Nonsense," said the rector; but there was something in John Brownlow's look which made him feel that it was not altogether nonsense. "But even if she were to turn up," he added, after a pause, "I suppose it would not ruin you to pay her her fifty thousand pounds."

"No, that is true enough," said Mr. Brownlow. It was a kind of ease to him to give this hint that he was still human and fallible, and might have losses to undergo; but the same instinct which made him speak closed his lips as to any more disastrous consequences than the loss of the original legacy. "Sara will have some tea for us up stairs," he said, after a pause. And then the two fathers went up to the drawing-room in their turn, and nothing could be more cheerful than the rest of the evening, though there were a good many thoughts and speculations of various kinds going on under this lively flood of talk, as may be perceived.

CHAPTER V

SARA'S SPECULATIONS

The next morning the frost had set in harder than before, contrary to all prognostications, to the great discomfiture of Jack Brownlow and of the Dartfordshire hounds. The world was white, glassy, and sparkling, when they all looked out upon it from the windows of the breakfast-room—another kind of world altogether from that dim and cloudy sphere upon which Jack and his companion had looked with hopes of thaw and an open country. These hopes being all abandoned, the only thing that remained to be thought of was, whether Dewsbury Mere might be "bearing," or when the ice would be thick enough for skaters—which were questions in which Sara, too, took a certain interest. It was the parish of Dewsbury in which Brownlows was situated, and of which Mr. Hardcastle was the parish priest; and young Keppel, along with his brother Mr. Keppel of Ridley, and all the visitors he might happen to have, and Sir Charles Hetherton, from the other side, with any body who might be staying in his house—not to speak of the curate and the doctor, and Captain Stanmore, who lived in the great house in Dewsbury village, and a number of other persons less known in the upper circles of the place, would crowd to the Mere as soon as it was known that it might yield some diversion, which was a scant commodity in the neighborhood. Mr. Brownlow scarcely listened to the talk of the young people as he ate his eggs sedately. He was not thinking of the ice for one. He was thinking of something quite different—of what might be waiting him at his office, and of the changes which any moment, as he said to himself, might produce. He was not afraid, for daylight disperses many ghosts that are terrible by night; but still his fright seemed to have opened his eyes to all the advantages of his present position, and the vast difference there was between John Brownlow the attorney's children, and the two young people from Brownlows. If that change were ever to occur, it would make a mighty alteration. Lady Hetherton would still know Sara, no doubt, but in how different a way! and their presence at Dewsbury then would be of no more importance than that of Fanny Hardcastle or young Stanmore in the village—whereas, now—This was what their father was reflecting, not distinctly, but in a vague sort of way, as he ate his egg. He had once been fond of the ice himself, and was not so old but that he felt the wonted fires burn in his ashes; but the office had an attraction for him which it had never had before, and he drove down by himself in the dog-cart with the vigor and eagerness of a young man, while his son got out his skates and set off to ascertain the prospects of the Mere. In short, at that moment Mr. Brownlow rather preferred to go off to business alone.

As for Sara, she did not allow her head to be turned by the prospect of the new amusement; she went through her duties, as usual, with serene propriety—and then she put all sorts of coverings on her feet and her hands, and her person generally, and set out with a little basket to visit her "poor people." I can not quite tell why she chose the worst weather to visit her poor people—perhaps it was for their sakes, to find out their wants at the worst; perhaps for her own, to feel a little meritorious. I do not pretend to be able to fathom Sara's motives; but this is undeniably what she did. When it rained torrents, she put on a large waterproof, which covered her from head to foot, and went off with drops of rain blown upon her fair cheeks under her hood, on the same charitable mission. This time it was in a fur-trimmed jacket, which was the envy of half the parish. Her father spoiled her, it was easy to see, and gave her every thing she could desire; but her poor people liked to see her in her expensive apparel, and admired and wondered what it might cost, and were all the better pleased with the tea and sugar. They were pleased that she should wear her fine things for them as well as for the fine people she went to visit. I do not attempt to state the reason why.

When she went out at the park gates, Mrs. Swayne was the first person who met Sara's eyes, standing at her door. The lines of the road were so lost in snow that it seemed an expanse of level white from the gate of Brownlows to the door-step, cleared and showing black over the whiteness, upon which Mrs. Swayne stood. She was a stout woman, and the cold did not seem to affect her. She had a black gown on and a little scarlet shawl, as if she meant to make herself unusually apparent; and there she stood defiant as the young lady came out. Sara was courageous, and her spirit was roused by this visible opponent. She gave herself a little shake, and then she went straight over the road and offered battle. "Are you not afraid of freezing up," she said to Mrs. Swayne, with an abruptness which might have taken away any body's breath—"or turning into Lot's wife, standing there at the open door?"

Mrs. Swayne was a woman of strong nerves, and she was not frightened. She gave a little laugh to gain time, and then she retorted briskly, "No, miss, no more nor you in all your wraps; poor folks can stand a deal that rich folks couldn't bear."

"It must be much better to be poor than to be rich, then," said Sara, "but I don't believe that—your husband, for instance, is not half so strong as—but I beg your pardon—I forgot he was ill," she cried, with a compunction which covered her face with crimson, "I did not mean to say that; when one speaks without thinking, one says things one doesn't mean."

"It's a pity to speak without thinking," said Mrs. Swayne; "If I did, I'd say a deal of unpleasant things; but, to be sure, you're but a bit of a girl. My man is independent, and it don't matter to nobody whether he is weakly or whether he is strong."

"I beg your pardon," said Sara, meekly; "I am very sorry he is not strong."

"My man," continued Mrs. Swayne, "is well-to-do and comfortable, and don't want no pity: there's a plenty in the village to be sorry for—not them as the ladies visit and get imposed upon. Poor folks understands poor folks—not as I mean to say we're poor."

"Then, if you are not poor you can't understand them any better than I do," said Sara, with returning courage. "I don't think they like well-to-do people like you; you are always the most hard upon them. If we were never to get any thing we did not deserve, I wonder what would become of us; and besides, I am sure they don't impose upon me."

"They'd impose upon the Apostle Paul," said Mrs. Swayne; "and as for the rector—not as he is much like one of the apostles; he is one as thinks his troubles worse than other folks. It ain't no good complaining to him. You may come through every thing as a woman can come through; but the parson'll find as he's come through more. That's just Mr. Hardcastle. If a poor man is left with a young family, it's the rector as has lost two wives; and as for children and money—though I don't believe for one as he ever had any money—your parsons 'as come through so much never has—"

"You are a Dissenter, Mrs. Swayne," said Sara, with calm superiority.

"Bred and born and brought up in the church, miss," said Mrs. Swayne, indignantly, "but druve to the chapel along of Swayne, and the parson being so aggravatin'. I'm one as likes a bit of sympathy, for my part; but it ain't general in this world," said the large woman, with a sigh.

Sara looked at her curiously, with her head a little on one side. She was old enough to know that one liked a little sympathy, and to feel too that it was not general in this world; but it seemed mighty strange to her that such an ethereal want should exist in the bosom of Mrs. Swayne. "Sympathy?" she said, with a curious tone of wonder and inquiry. She was candid enough, notwithstanding a certain comic aspect which the conversation began to take to her, to want to know what it meant.

"Yes," said Mrs. Swayne, "just sympathy, miss. I'm one as has had my troubles, and as don't like to be told that they ain't troubles at all. The minister at the chapel is 'most as bad, for he says they're blessins in disguise—as if Swayne being weakly and awful worritin' when his rheumatism's bad, could ever be a blessin'. And as for speaking to the rector, you might as well speak to the Mere, and better too, for that's got no answer ready. When a poor body sees a clergyman, it's their comfort to talk a bit and to tell all as they're going through. You can tell Mr. Hardcastle I said it, if you please. Lord bless us! I don't need to go so far if it's only to hear as other folks is worse off. There's old Betty at the lodge, and there's them poor creatures next door, and most all in the village, I'm thankful to say, is worse off nor we are; but I would like to know what's the good of a clergyman if he won't listen to you rational, and show a bit of sympathy for what you've com'd through."

Perhaps Sara's attention had wandered during this speech, or perhaps she was tired of the subject; at all events, looking round her with a little impatience as she listened, her eye was caught by the little card with "Lodgings" printed thereon which hung in Mrs. Swayne's parlor window. It recalled her standing grievance, and she took action accordingly at once, as was her wont.

"What is the good of that?" she said, pointing to it suddenly. "I think you ought to keep your parlor to sit in, you who are so well off; but, at least, it can't do you any good to hang it up there—nobody can see it but people who come to us at Brownlows; and you don't expect them to take lodgings here."

"Begging your pardon, miss," said Mrs. Swayne, solemnly, "It's been that good to me that the lodgings is took."

"Then why do you keep it up to aggravate people?" said Sara; "It makes me wild always when I pass the door. Why do you keep it there?"

"Lodgers is but men," said Mrs. Swayne, "or women, to be more particular. I can't never be sure as I'll like 'em; and they're folks as never sees their own advantages. It might be as we didn't suit, or they wasn't satisfied, or objected to Swayne a-smoking when he's bad with the rheumatism, which is a thing I wouldn't put a stop to not for forty lodgers; for it's the only thing as keeps him from worritin'. So I always keeps it up; it's the safest way in the end."

"I think it is a wretched sort of way," cried Sara, impetuously. "I wonder how you can confess that you have so little faith in people; instead of trying to like them and getting friends, to be always ready to see them go off. I couldn't have servants in the house like that: they might just as well go to lodge in a cotton-mill or the work-house. There can't be any human relations between you."

"Relations!" said Mrs. Swayne, with a rising color. "If you think my relations are folks as go and live in lodgings, you're far mistaken, miss. It's well known as we come of comfortable families, both me and Swayne—folks as keeps a good house over their heads. That's our sort. As for taking 'em in, it's mostly for charity as I lets my lodgings—for the sake of poor folks as wants a little fresh air. You was a different looking-creature when you come out of that stuffy bit of a town. I've a real good memory, and I don't forget. I remember when your papa come and bought the place off the old family; and vexed we all was—but I don't make no doubt as it was all for the best."

"I don't think the old family, as you call them, were much use to anybody in Dewsbury," said Sara, injudiciously, with a thrill of indignation and offended pride.

"Maybe not, miss," said Mrs. Swayne, meekly; "they was the old Squires, and come natural. I don't say no more, not to give offense; but you was a pale little thing then, and not much wonder neither, coming out of a house in a close street as is most fit for a mill, as you was saying. It made a fine difference in you."

"Our house in Masterton is the nicest house I know," said Sara, who was privately furious. "I always want papa to take me back in the winter. Brownlows is very nice, but it is not so much of a house after all."

"It was a different name then," said Mrs. Swayne, significantly; "some on us never can think of the new name; and I don't think as you'd like living in a bit of a poky town after this, if your papa was to let you try."

"On the contrary, I should like it excessively," said Sara, with much haughtiness; and then she gave Mrs. Swayne a condescending little nod, and drew up a corner of her dress, which had drooped upon the snow. "I hope your lodgers will be nice, and that you will take down your ticket," she said; "but I must go now to see my poor people." Mrs. Swayne was so startled by the sudden but affable majesty with which the young lady turned away, that she almost dropped her a courtesy in her surprise. But in fact she only dropped her handkerchief, which was as large as a towel, and which she had a way of holding rolled up like a ball in her hand. It was quite true that the old family had been of little use to any body at Dewsbury; and that they were almost squalid in their poverty and pretensions and unrespected misfortune before they went away; and that all the little jobs in carpentry which kept Mr. Swayne in employment had been wanting during the old régime; in short, it was on Brownlows, so to speak—on the shelfs and stands, and pegs and bits of cupboard, and countless repairs which were always wanting in the now prosperous house—that Swayne's Cottages had been built. This, however, did not make his wife compunctious. She watched Sara's active footsteps over the snow, and saw her pretty figure disappear into the white waste, and was glad she had given her that sting. To keep this old family bottled up, and give the new people a little dose from time to time of the nauseous residue, was one of her pleasures. She went in and arranged the card more prominently in her parlor window, and felt glad that she had put it there; and then she went and sat with her poor neighbor next door, and railed at the impudent little thing in her furs and velvets, whom the foolish father made such an idol of. But she made her poor neighbor's tea all the same, and frightened away the children, and did the woman good, not being bad any more than most people are who cherish a little comfortable animosity against the nearest great folks. Mrs. Swayne, however, not being democratic, was chiefly affected by the fact that the Masterton lawyer's family had no right to be great folks, which was a reasonable grievance in its way.

As for Sara, she went off through the snow, feeling hot at heart with this little encounter, though her feet were cold with standing still. Why had she stood still to be insulted? this was what Sara asked herself; for, after all, Mrs. Swayne was nothing to her, and what could it matter to Brownlows whether or not she had a bill in her window? But yet unconsciously it led her thoughts to a consideration of her present home—to the difference between it and her father's house at Masterton, to all the fairy change which, within the bounds of her own recollection, had passed upon her life. Supposing any thing was to happen, as things continually happened to men in business—supposing some bank was to fail, or some railway to break down—a thing which occurred every day—and her papa should lose all his money? Would she really be quite content to go back to the brick house in which she was born? Sara thought it over with a great deal of gravity. In case of such an event happening (and, to be sure, nothing was more likely), she felt that she would greatly prefer total ruin. Total ruin meant instant retirement to a cottage with or without roses—with only two, or perhaps only one, servants—where she would be obliged, with her own hands to make little dishes for poor papa, and sew the buttons on his shirts, and perhaps milk a very pretty little Alderney cow, and make beautiful little pats of butter for his delectation. This Sara felt that she was equal to. Let the bank or the railway break down to-morrow, and the devoted daughter was ready to go forth with her beloved parent. She smiled to herself at the thought that such a misfortune could alarm her. What was money? she said to herself; and Sara could not but feel that it was quite necessary to take this plan into full consideration in all its details, for nobody could tell at what moment it might be necessary to put it in practice. As for the house at Masterton, that was quite a different matter, which she did not see any occasion for considering. If papa was ruined, of course he would have to give up every thing, and the Masterton house would be as impossible as Brownlows; and so long as he was not ruined, of course every thing would go on as usual. Thus Sara pursued her way cheerfully, feeling that a possible new future had opened upon her, and that she had perceived and accepted her duty in it, and was prepared for whatever might happen. If Mr. Brownlow returned that very night, and said, "I am a ruined man," Sara felt that she was able to go up to him, and say, "Papa, you have still your children;" and the thought was so far from depressing her that she went on very cheerfully, and held her head high, and looked at every body she met with a certain affability, as if she were the queen of that country. And, to tell the truth, such people as she met were not unwilling to acknowledge her claims. There were many who thought her the prettiest girl in Dewsbury parish, and there could be no doubt that she was the richest and most magnificent. If it had been known what heroic sentiments were in her heart, no doubt it would have deepened the general admiration; but at least she knew them herself, and that is always a great matter. To have your mind made up as to what you must and will do in case of a sudden and at present uncertain, but on the whole quite possible, change of fortune, is a thing to be very thankful for. Sara felt that, considering this suddenly revealed prospect of ruin, it perhaps was not quite prudent to promise future bounties to her poor pensioners; but she did it all the same, thinking that surely somehow she could manage to get her promises fulfilled, through the means of admiring friends or such faithful retainers as might be called forth by the occasion—true knights, who would do any thing or every thing for her. Thus her course of visits ended quite pleasantly to every body concerned, and that glow of generosity and magnanimity about her heart made her even more liberal than usual, which was very satisfactory to the poor people. When she had turned back and was on her way home, she encountered the carrier's cart on its way from Masterton. It was a covered waggon, and sometimes, though very rarely, it was used as a means of traveling from one place in the neighborhood to another by people who could not afford more expensive conveyances. There were two such people in it now who attracted Sara's attention—one an elderly woman, tall and dark, and somewhat gaunt in her appearance; the other a girl about Sara's own age, with very dark brown hair cut short and lying in rings upon her forehead like a boy's. She had eyes as dark as her hair, and was closely wrapped in a red cloak, and regarded by her companion with tender and anxious looks, to which her paleness and fragile appearance gave a ready explanation. "It ain't the speediest way of traveling, for I've a long round to make, miss, afore I gets where they're a-going," said the carrier; "they'd a most done better to walk, and so I told 'em. But I reckon the young un ain't fit, and they're tired like, and it's mortal cold." Sara walked on remorseful after this encounter, half ashamed of her furs, which she did not want—she whose blood danced in her veins, and who was warm all over with health and comfort, and happiness and pleasant thoughts. And then it occurred to her to wonder whether, if papa were ruined, he and his devoted child would ever have to travel in a carrier's cart, and go round and round a whole parish in the cold before they came to their destination. "But then we could walk," Sara said to herself as she went briskly up the avenue, and saw the bright fire blinking in her own window, where her maid was laying out her evening dress. This, after all, felt a great deal more natural even than the cottage with the roses, and put out of her mind all thought of a dreary journey in the carrier's cart.

CHAPTER VI

AN ADVENTURE

Jack in the mean time was on the ice.

Dewsbury Mere was bearing, which was a wonder, considering how lately the frost had set in; and a pretty scene it was, though as yet some of the other magnates of the parish, as well as Sara, were absent. It was a round bit of ornamental water, partly natural, partly artificial, touching upon the village green at one side, and on the other side bordered by some fine elm-trees, underneath which in summer much of the love-making of the parish was performed. The church, with its pretty spire, was visible through the bare branches of the plantation, which backed the elm-trees like a little host of retainers; and on the other side—the village side—glittering over the green in the centre of all the lower and humbler dwellings, you could see the Stanmores' house, which was very tall and very red, and glistening all over with reflections from the brass nobs on the door, and the twinkling glass of the windows, and even from the polished holly leaves which all but blocked up the entrance. The village people were in full possession of the Mere without the gêne imposed by the presence of Lady Hetherton or Mrs. Keppel. Fanny Hardcastle, who, if the great people had been there, would have pinned herself on tremblingly to their skirts and lost the fun, was now in the heart of it, not despising young Stanmore's attentions, nor feeling herself painfully above the doctor's wife; and thus rosy and blooming and gay, looked a very different creature from the blue little Fanny whom old Lady Hetherton, had she been there, would have awed into cold and propriety. And the doctor's wife, though she was not exactly in society, was a piquant little woman, and the curate was stalwart, if not interesting, very muscular, and slow to commit himself in the way of speech. Besides, there were many people of whom no account was made in Dewsbury, who enjoyed the ice, and knew how to conduct themselves upon it, and looked just as well as if they had been young squires and squiresses. Jack Brownlow came into the midst of them cordially, and thought there were many more pretty faces visible than were to be seen in more select circles, and was not in the least appalled by the discovery that the prettiest of all was the corn-factor's daughter in the village. When little Polly Huntly from the baker's wavered on her slide, and was near falling, it was Jack who caught her, and his friendliness put some very silly thoughts into the poor little girl's head; but Jack was thinking of no such vanity. He was as pleased to see the pretty faces about as a right-thinking young man ought to be, but he felt that he had a great many other things to think of for his part, and gave very sensible advice, as has been already seen, to other young fellows of less thoroughly established principles. Jack was not only fancy free, but in principle he was opposed to all that sort of thing. His opinion was, that for any body less than a young duke or more than an artisan to marry under thirty, was a kind of social and moral suicide. I do not pretend to justify or defend his opinions, but such were his opinions, and he made no secret of them. He was a young fellow with a great many things to do in this world, or at least so he thought. Though he was only a country solicitor's son, he had notions in his head, and there was no saying what he did not aspire to; and to throw every thing away for the sake of a girl's pretty face, seemed to him a proceeding little short of idiocy. All this he had expounded to many persons of a different way of thinking; and indeed the only moments in which he felt inclined to cast aside his creed were when he found it taken up and advocated by other men of the same opinion, but probably less sense of delicacy than himself.

"Where is your father?" said Mr. Hardcastle; "he used to be as fond as any one of the ice. Gone to business! he'll kill himself if he goes on going to business like this all the year round, every day."

"Oh, no," said Jack, "he'll not kill himself; all the same he might have come, and so would Sara, had we known that the Mere was bearing. I did not think it possible there could have been such good ice to-day."

"Not Sara," said the rector; "this sort of thing is not the thing for her. The village folks are all very well, and in the exercise of my profession I see a great deal of them. But not for Sara, my dear boy—this sort of thing is not in her way."

"Why Fanny is here," said Jack, opening his eyes.

"Fanny is different," said Mr. Hardcastle; "clergywomen have got to be friendly with their poor neighbors—but Sara, who will be an heiress—"

"Is she to be an heiress?" said Jack, with a laugh which could not but sound a little peculiar. "I am sure I don't mind if she is; but I think we may let the future take care of itself. The presence of the cads would not hurt her any more than they hurt me."

"Don't speak of cads," said the rector, "to me; they are all equal—human beings among whom I have lived and labored. Of course it is natural that you should look on them differently. Jack, can you tell me what it is that keeps young Keppel so long about Ridley? What interest has he in remaining here?"

"The hounds, I suppose," said Jack, curtly, not caring to be questioned.

"Oh, the hounds!" repeated Mr. Hardcastle, with a dubious tone. "I suppose it must be that—and nothing particular to do in town. You were quite right, Jack, to stick to your father's business. A briefless barrister is one of the most hopeless wretches in the world."

"I don't think you always thought so, sir," said Jack; "but here is an opening and I'll see you again." He had not come there to talk to the parson. When he had gone flying across the Mere thinking of nothing at all but the pleasure of the motion, and had skirted it round and round and made figures of 8 and all the gambols common to a first outbreak, he stopped himself at a corner where Fanny Hardcastle, whom her father had been leading about, was standing with young Keppel looking very pretty, with her rose cheeks and downcast eyes. Keppel had been mooning about Sara the night before, was the thought that passed through Jack's mind; and what right had he to give Fanny Hardcastle occasion to cast down her eyes? Perhaps it was purely on his friend's account; perhaps because he thought that girls were very hardly dealt with in never being left alone to think of any thing but that confounded love-making; but the fact was that he disturbed them rather ruthlessly, and stood before them, balancing himself on his skates. "Get into this chair, Fanny, and I'll give you a turn of the Mere," he said; and the downcast eyes were immediately raised, and their fullest attention conferred upon him. All the humble maidens of Dewsbury at that moment cast glances of envy and yet awe at Fanny. Alice Stanmore, who was growing up, and thought herself quite old enough to receive attention in her own person, glowered at the rector's daughter with horrible thoughts. The two young gentlemen, the envied of all observers, seemed for the moment, to the female population of the village, to have put themselves at Fanny's feet. Even Mrs. Brightbank, the doctor's little clever wife, was taken in for the moment. For the instant that energetic person balanced in her mind the respective merits of the two candidates, and considered which it would be best for Fanny to marry; never thinking that the whole matter involved was half-a-dozen words of nonsense on Mr. Keppel's part, and on Jack Brownlow's one turn on the ice in the skater's chair.

For it was not until Fanny was seated, and being driven over the Mere, that she looked back with that little smile and saucy glance, and asked demurely, "Are you sure it is quite proper, Mr. John?"

"Not proper at all," said Jack; "for we have nobody to take care of us—neither I nor you. My papa is in Masterton at the office, and yours is busy talking to the old women. But quite as proper as listening to all the nonsense Joe Keppel may please to say."

"I listening to his nonsense!" said Fanny, as a pause occurred in their progress. "I don't know why you should think so. He said nothing that every body might not hear. And besides, I don't listen to any body's nonsense, nor ever did since I was born," added Fanny, with another little soft glance round into her companion's face.

"Never do," said Jack, seizing the chair with renewed vehemence, and rushing all round the Mere with it at a pace which took away Fanny's breath. When they had reached the same spot again, he came to a standstill to recover his own, and stood leaning upon the chair in which the girl sat, smiling and glowing with the unwonted whirl. "Just like a pair of lovers," the people said on the Mere, though they were far enough from being lovers. Just at that moment the carrier's cart came lumbering along noisily upon the hard frosty path. It was on its way then to the place where Sara met it on the road. Inside, under the arched cover, were to be seen the same two faces which Sara afterward saw—the mother's elderly and gaunt, and full of lines and wrinkles; the sweet face of the girl, with its red lips, and pale cheeks, and lovely eyes. The hood of the red cloak had fallen back a little, and showed the short, curling, almost black hair. A little light came into the young face at the sight of all the people on the ice. As was natural, her eyes fixed first on the group so near the edge—pretty Fanny Hardcastle, and Jack, resting from his fatigue, leaning over her chair. The red lips opened with an innocent smile, and the girl pointed out the scene to her mother, whose face relaxed, too, into that momentary look of feigned interest with which an anxious watcher rewards every exertion or stir of reviving life. "What a pretty, pretty creature!" said Fanny Hardcastle, generously, yet with a little passing pang of annoyance at the interruption. Jack did not make any response. He gazed at the little traveler, without knowing it, as if she had been a creature of another sphere. Pretty! he did not know whether she was pretty or not. What he thought was that he had never before seen such a face; and all the while the wagon lumbered on, and kept going off, until the Mere and its group of people were left behind. And Jack Brownlow got to his post again, as if nothing had happened. He drove Fanny round and round until she grew dizzy, and then he rushed back to the field and cut all kinds of figures, and executed every possible gambol that skates will lend themselves to. But, oddly enough, all the while he could not get it out of his head how strange it must look to go through the world like that in a carrier's cart. It seemed a sort of new view of life to Jack altogether, and no doubt that was why it attracted him. People who had so little sense of the importance of time, and so great a sense of the importance of money, as to jog along over the whole breadth of the parish in a frosty winter afternoon, by way of saving a few shillings—and one of them so delicate and fragile, with such a face, such soft little rings of dark hair on the forehead, such sweet eyes, such a soft little smile! Jack did not think he had much imagination, yet he could not help picturing to himself how the country must look as they passed through; all the long bare stretches of wood and the houses here and there, and how the Mere must have flashed upon them to brighten up the tedious panorama; and then the ring of the horses' hoofs on the road, and their breath steaming up into the air, and the crack of the carrier's whip as he walked beside them. Jack, who dashed along in his dog-cart the quickest way, or rode his horse still faster through the well-known lanes, could not but linger on this imagination with the most curious sense of interest and novelty. "It must be poverty," he said to himself; and it was all he could do to keep the words from being spoken out loud.

As for Fanny, I am afraid she never thought again of the poor travelers in the carrier's cart. When the red sunset clouds were gathering in the sky, her father, who was very tender of her, drew her hand within his arm, and took her home. "You have had enough of it," he said, though she did not think so; and when they turned their backs on the village, and took the path toward the rectory under the bare elm-trees, which stood like pillars of ebony in a golden palace against the setting sun, Mr. Hardcastle added a little word of warning. "My love," he said—for he too, like Mr. Brownlow, thought there was nobody like his child—"you must not put nonsense into these young fellows heads."

"I put nonsense into their heads," cried Fanny, feeling, with a slight thrill of self-abasement, that probably it was quite the other way.

"Not a doubt about it," said the rector; "and so far as Jack Brownlow is concerned, I don't know that I should object much; but I don't want to lose my little girl yet awhile; I don't know what I should do all alone in the house."

"Oh papa, I will never leave you," cried Fanny. She meant it, and even, which is more, believed it for the moment. Was he not more to her than all the young men that had ever been dreamed of? But yet it was rather agreeable to Fanny to think that she was suspected of putting nonsense into their heads. She liked the imputation, as indeed most people do, both men and women; and she liked the position—the only lady, with all that was most attractive in the parish at her feet; for Sir Charles Hetherton was considered by most people as very far from bright. And then the recollection of her rapid whirl across the ice came over her like a warm glow of pleasant recollection as she dressed for the evening. It would be nice to have them come in, to talk it all over after dinner—very nice to have little parties, like the last night's party at Brownlows; and notwithstanding her devotion to her father, after they had dined, and she had gone alone into the drawing-room, Fanny could not but find it dull. There was neither girl to gossip with, nor man into whose head it would be any satisfaction to put nonsense, near the rectory, from whom a familiar visit might be expected; and after the day's amusement, the silent evening, with papa down stairs enjoying his after-dinner doze in his chair was far from lively. But it did not occur to Fanny to frame any conjectures upon the two travelers who had looked momentarily out upon her from the carrier's cart.

As for Jack Brownlow, he had a tolerably long walk before him. In summer he would have crossed the park, which much reduced the distance, but, in the dark and through the snow, he thought it expedient to keep the high-road, which was a long way round. He went off very briskly, with the straps of his skates over his shoulders, whistling occasionally, but not from want of thought. Indeed, he had a great many things to think of—the ice itself for one thing, and the pleasant run he had given little Fanny, and the contemptible vacillations of that fellow Keppel from one pretty girl to another, and the office and his work, and a rather curious case which had lately come under his hands. All this occupied him as he went home, while the sunset skies gradually faded. He passed from one thing to another with an unfettered mind, and more than once there just glanced across his thoughts a momentary wonder, where would the carrier's cart be now? Had it got home yet, delivered all its parcels, and deposited its passengers? Had it called at Brownlows to leave his cigars, which ought to have arrived a week ago? That poor little pale face—how tired the little creature must be! and how cold! and then the mother. He would never have thought of them again but for that curious way of moving about, of all ways in the world, among the parcels in the carrier's cart.

This speculation had returned to his mind as he came in sight of the park gates. It was quite dark by this time, but the moon was up overhead, and the road was very visible on either side of that little black block of Swayne's cottages which threw a shadow across almost to the frosted silver gates. Something, however, was going on in this bit of shadow. A large black movable object stood in the midst of it; and from Mrs. Swayne's door a lively ray of red light fell across the snow. Then by degrees Jack identified the horses, with their steaming breath, and the wagon wheel upon which the light fell. He said "by Jove" loud out as he stood at the gate and found out what it was. It was the very carrier's cart of which he had been thinking, and some mysterious transaction was going on in the darkness which he could only guess at vaguely. Something or somebody was being made to descend from the wagon, which some sudden swaying of the horses made difficult. Jack took his cigar from his lips to hear and see the better, and stood and gazed with the vulgarest curiosity. Even the carrier's cart was something to take note of on the road at Brownlows. But when that sudden cry followed, he tossed his cigar away and his skates with it, and crossed the road in two long steps, to the peril of his equilibrium. Somehow he had divined what was happening. He made a stride into the thick of it, and it was he who lifted up the little figure in the red cloak which had slipped and fallen on the snow. It was natural, for he was the only man about. The carrier was at his horses' heads to keep them steady; Mrs. Swayne stood on the door steps, afraid to move lest she too should slip; and as for the girl's mother, she was benumbed and stupefied, and could only raise her child up half-way from the ground, and beg somebody to help. Jack got her up in his arms, pushed Mrs. Swayne out of his way, and carried her in. "Is it here she is to go?" he cried over his shoulder as he took her into the parlor, where the card hung in the window, and the fire was burning. There was nothing in it but firelight, which cast a hue of life upon the poor little traveler's face. And then she had not fainted, but blushed and gasped with pain and confusion. "Oh, thank you, that will do," she cried—"that will do." And then the others fell upon her, who had come in a procession behind, when he set her down. He was so startled himself that he stood still, which was a thing he scarcely would have done had he known what he was about, and looked over their heads and gaped at her. He had put her down in a kind of easy-chair, and there she lay, her face changing from red to pale. Pale enough it was now, while Jack, made by his astonishment into a mere wondering, curious boy, stood with his mouth open and watched. He was not consciously thinking how pretty she was; he was wondering if she had hurt herself, which was a much more sensible thought; but still, of course, he perceived it, though he was not thinking of it. Curls are common enough, you know, but it is not often you see those soft rings, which are so much longer than they look; and the eyes so limpid and liquid all through, yet strained, and pathetic, and weary—a great deal too limpid, as any body who knew any thing about it might have known, at a glance. She made a little movement, and gave a cry, and grew red once more, this time with pain, and then as white as the snow. "Oh, my foot, my foot," she cried, in a piteous voice. The sound of words brought Jack to himself. "I'll wait outside, Mrs. Swayne," he said, "and if the doctor's wanted I'll fetch him; let me know." And then he went out and had a talk with the carrier, and waited. The carrier knew very little about his passenger. He reckoned the young un was delicate—it was along of this here brute swerving when he hadn't ought to—but it couldn't be no more than a sprain. Such was Hobson's opinion. Jack waited, however, a little bewildered in his intellects, till Mrs. Swayne came out to say his services were not needed, and that it was a sprain, and could be mended by ordinary female remedies. Then young Mr. Brownlow got Hobson's lantern, and searched for his skates and flung them over his shoulders. How queer they should have come here—how odd to think of that little face peeping out at Mrs. Swayne's window—how droll that he should have been on the spot just at that moment; and yet it was neither queer nor droll to Jack, but confused his head somehow, and gave him a strange sort of half-commotion in the region of his heart. It is all very well to be sensible, but yet there is certainly something in it when an adventure like this happens, not to Keppel, or that sort of fellow, but actually to yourself.

CHAPTER VII

THE FATHER'S DAY AT THE OFFICE

While Sara and Jack were thus enjoying themselves, Mr. Brownlow went quietly in to his business—very quietly, in the dogcart, with his man driving, who was very steady, and looked as comfortable as his master. Mr. Brownlow was rather pleased not to have his son's company that morning; he had something to do which he could scarcely have done had Jack been there—business which was quite justifiable, and indeed right, but which it would have been a disagreeable matter to have explained to Jack. His mind was much more intent upon his own affairs than were those of either of his children on theirs. They had so much time in life to do all they meant to do, that they could afford to set out leisurely, and go forth upon the world with a sweet vacancy in their minds, ready for any thing that might turn up; but with Mr. Brownlow it was not so; his objects had grown to be very clear before him. He was not so old as to feel the pains or weariness or languor of age. He was almost as able to enjoy, and perhaps better able to do, in the way of his profession at least, than was young Jack. The difference was, that Mr. Brownlow lived only in the present; the future had gradually been cut off, as it were, before him. There was one certainty in his path somewhere a little in advance, but nothing else that could be counted upon, so that whatever he had to do, and anything he might have to enjoy, presented themselves with double clearness in the limited perspective. It was the only time in his life that he had felt the full meaning of the word "Now." The present was his possession, his day in which he lived and worked, with plenty of space behind to go back upon, but nothing reliable before. This gave not only a vividness and distinct character, but also a promptitude, to his actions, scarcely possible to a younger man. To-day was his, but not to-morrow; whereas to Jack and his contemporaries to-morrow was always the real day, never the moment in which they lived.

When Mr. Brownlow reached his office, the first thing he did was to send for a man who was a character in Masterton. He was called by various names, and it was not very certain which belonged to him, or indeed if any belonged to him. He was called Inspector Pollaky by many people who were in the habit of reading the papers; but of course he was not that distinguished man. He was called detective and thief-taker, and many other injurious epithets, and he was a man whom John Brownlow had had occasion to consult before now on matters of business. He was sent for that morning, and he had a long conversation with Mr. Brownlow in his private room. He was that sort of man that understands what people mean even when they do not speak very plainly, and naturally he took up at once the lawyer's object and pledged himself to pursue it. "You shall have some information on the subject probably this afternoon, sir," he said as he went away. After this visit Mr. Brownlow went about his own business with great steadiness and precision, and cast his eyes over his son's work, and was very particular with the clerks—more than ordinarily particular. It was his way, for he was an admirable business man at all times; but still he was unusually energetic that day. And they were all a little excited about Pollaky, as they called him, what commission he might have received, and which case he might be wanted about. At the time when he usually had his glass of sherry, Mr. Brownlow went out; he did not want his midday biscuit. He was a little out of sorts, and he thought a walk would do him good; but instead of going down to Barnes's Pool or across the river to the meadows, which had been lately flooded, and now were one sheet of ice, places which all the clerks supposed to be the most attractive spots for twenty miles round, he took the way of the town and went up into Masterton. He was going to pay a visit, and it was a most unusual one. He was going to see his wife's mother, old Mrs. Fennell, for whom he had no love. It was a thing he did not do for years together, but having been somehow in his own mind thoroughly worked up to it, he took the occasion of Jack's absence and went that day.

Mrs. Fennell was sitting in her drawing-room with only her second-best cap on, and with less than her second-best temper. If she had known he was coming she would have received him with a very different state, and she was mortified by her unpreparedness. Also her dinner was ready. As for Mr. Brownlow, he was not thinking of dinners. He had something on his mind, and it was his object to conceal that he had any thing on his mind—a matter less difficult to a man of his profession than to ordinary mortals. But what he said was that he was anxious chiefly to know if his mother-in-law was comfortable, and if she had every thing according to her desires.

Mrs. Fennell smiled at this inquiry. She smiled, but she rushed into a thousand grievances. Her lodgings were not to her mind, nor her position. Sara, the little puss, had carriages when she pleased, but her grandmamma never had any conveyance at her disposal to take the air in. And the people of the house were very inattentive, and Nancy—but here the old woman, who was clever, put a sudden stop to herself and drew up and said no more. She knew that to complain of Nancy would be of no particular advantage to her, for Mr. Brownlow was not fond of old Mrs. Thomson's maid, and was as likely as not to propose that she should be pensioned and sent away.

"I have told you before," said Mr. Brownlow, "that the brougham should be sent down for you when you want to go out if you will only let me know in time. What Sara has is nothing—or you can have a fly; but it is not fit weather for you to go out at your age."

"You are not so very young yourself, John Brownlow," said the old lady, with a little offense.

"No indeed—far from it—and that is what makes me think," he said abruptly; and then made a pause which she did not understand, referring evidently to something in his own mind. "Did you ever know any body of the name of Powys in the Isle of Man?" he resumed, with a certain nervous haste, and an effort which brought heat and color to his face.

"Powys!" said Mrs. Fennell. "I've heard the name; but I think it was Liverpool-ways and not in the Isle of Man. It's a Welsh name. No; I never knew any Powyses. Do you?"

"It was only some one I met," said Mr. Brownlow, "who had relations in the Isle of Man. Do you know of any body who married there and left? Knowing that you came from that quarter, somebody was asking me."

"I don't know of nobody but one," said the old woman—"one that would make a deal of difference if she were to come back now."

"You mean the woman Phœbe Thomson?" said Mr. Brownlow, sternly. "It is a very strange thing to me that her relatives should know nothing about that woman—not even whom she married or what was her name."

"She married a soldier," said Mrs. Fennell, "as I always heard. She wasn't my relation—it was poor Fennell that was her cousin. As for us, we come of very different folks; and I don't doubt as her name might have been found out," said the old woman, nodding her spiteful old head. Mr. Brownlow kept his temper, but it was by a kind of miracle. This was the sort of thing which he was always subject to on his rare visits to his mother-in-law. "It's for some folks' good that her name couldn't be found out," added the old woman, with another significant nod.

"It would have been for some folks' good if they had never heard of her," said Mr. Brownlow. "I wish a hundred times in a year that I had never administered or taken any notice of the old hag's bequest. Then it would have gone to the crown, I suppose, and all this trouble would have been spared."

"Other things would have had to be spared as well," said Mrs. Fennell, in her taunting voice.

"I should have known what was my own and what was not, and my children would have been in no false position," said Mr. Brownlow, with energy: "but now—" Here he stopped short, and his looks alarmed his companion, unsympathetic as she was. She loved to have this means of taunting and keeping down his pride, as she said; but her grandchildren's advantage was to a certain extent her own, and the thought of injury to them was alarming, and turned her thoughts into another channel. She took fright at the idea of Phœbe Thomson when she saw Mr. Brownlow's face. It was the first time it had ever occurred to her as possible that he, a gentleman, a lawyer, and a clever man, might possibly have after all to give up to Phœbe Thomson should that poor and despised woman ever turn up.

"But she couldn't take the law of you?" Mrs. Fennell said, with a gasp. "She wouldn't know any thing about it. I may talk disagreeable by times, and I own that we never were fond of each other, you and I, John Brownlow; but I'm not the woman that would ever let on to her, to harm my poor Bessie's children—not I—not if she was to come back this very day."

It is useless to deny that Mr. Brownlow's face at that moment looked as if he would have liked to strangle the old woman; but he only made an indignant movement, and looked at her with rage and indignation, which did her no harm. And, poor man, in his excitement perhaps it was not quite true what he himself said—

"If she should come back this very day, it would be your duty to send her to me instantly, that I might give up her mother's trust into her hands," he said. "You may be sure I will never permit poor Bessie's children to enjoy what belongs to another." And then he made a pause and his voice changed. "After all, I suppose you know just as little of her as I do. Did you ever see her?" he said.

"Well, no; I can't say I ever did," said Mrs. Fennell, cowed for the moment.

"Nor Nancy?" said Mr. Brownlow; "you two would be safe guides certainly. And you know of nobody else who left the Isle of Man and married—no relation of Fennell's or of yours?"

"Nobody I know of," said the old woman after a pause. "There might be dozens; but us and the Thomsons and all belonging to us, we've been out of the Isle of Man for nigh upon fifty years."

After that Mr. Brownlow went away. He had got no information, no satisfaction, and yet he had made no discovery, which was a kind of negative comfort in its way; but it was clear that his mother-in-law, though she made so much use of Phœbe Thomson's name, was utterly unable to give him any assistance either in discovering the real Phœbe Thomson or in exposing any false pretender. He went across the market place over the crisp snow in the sunshine with all his faculties, as it were, crisped and sharpened like the air he breathed. This was all the effect as yet which the frosts of age had upon him. He had all his powers unimpaired, and more entirely serviceable and under command than ever they were. He could trust himself not to betray himself, to keep counsel, and act with deliberation, and do nothing hastily. Thus, though his enemies were as yet unknown and unrecognized, and consequently all the more dangerous, he had confidence in his own army of defense, which was a great matter. He returned to his office, and to his business, and was as clearheaded and self-possessed, and capable of paying attention to the affairs of his clients, as if he had nothing particular in his own to occupy him. And the only help he got from circumstances was that which was given him by the frost, which had happily interfered this day of all others to detain Jack. Jack was not his father's favorite child; he was not, as Sara was, the apple of John Brownlow's eye; and yet the lawyer appreciated, and did justice to, as well as loved, his son, in a just and natural way. He felt that Jack's quick eye would have found out that there was something more than usual going on. He knew that his visit to Mrs. Fennell and his unexplained conference with the man of mystery would not have been passed over by Jack without notice; and at the young man's hasty, impetuous time of life, prudence was not to be expected or even desired. If Jack thought it possible that Phœbe Thomson was to be found within a hundred miles, no doubt he would make off without a moment's thought and hunt her up, and put his own fortune, and, what was more, Sara's, eagerly into her hands. This was what Jack would do, and Mr. Brownlow was glad in his heart that Jack would be sure to do it; but yet it might be a very different course which he himself, after much thought and consideration, might think it best to take.

He was long in his office that night, and worked very hard—indeed he would have been almost alone before he left but that one of the clerks had some extra work to do, and another had stayed to keep him company; so that two of them were still there when Inspector Pollaky, as they called him, came back. It was quite late, too late for the ice, or the young men would not have waited—half an hour later at least than the usual time at which Mr. Brownlow left the office. And he closed his door carefully behind his mysterious visitor, and made sure that it was securely shut before he began to talk to him, which naturally was a thing that excited much wondering between the young men.

"Young Jack been a naughty boy?" said one to the other; then they listened, but heard nothing. "More likely some fellow going in for Miss Brownlow, and he wants to pick holes in him," said the second. But when half an hour passed and every thing continued very undisturbed, they betook themselves to their usual talk. "I suppose it's about the Worsley case," they said, and straightway Inspector Pollaky lost interest in their eyes. So long as it was only a client's business it did not matter. Not for such common place concerns would the young heroes of John Brownlow's office interrupt the even tenor of their way.

"I suppose you have brought me some news," said Mr. Brownlow; "come near the fire. Take a chair, it is bitterly cold. I scarcely expected you so soon as to-day."

"Bless you, sir, it's as easy as easy," said the mysterious man—"disgusting easy. If there's any body that I despise in this world, it's folks that have nothing to conceal. They're all on the surface, them folks are. You can take and read them clear off, through and through."

"Well?" said Mr. Brownlow. He turned his face a little away from the light that he might not be spied too closely, though there was not in reality any self-betrayal in his face. His lips were a little white and more compressed than usual, that was all.

"Well, sir, for the first thing, it's all quite true," said the man. "There's seven of a family—the mother comely-like still, but older nor might be expected. Poor, awful poor, but making the best of it—keeping their hearts up as far as I could see. The young fellow helping too, and striving his best. I shouldn't say as they had much of a dinner to-day; but cheerful as cheerful, and as far as I could see—"

"Was this all you discovered?" said Mr. Brownlow, severely.

"I am coming to the rest, sir," said the detective, "and you'll say as I've forgotten nothing. The father, which is dead, was once in the Life Guards. He was one of them sprigs as is to be met with there—run away out of a good family. He came from London first as far as she knows; and then they were ordered to Windsor, and then they went to Canada; but I've got the thread, Mr. Brownlow—I've got the thread. This poor fellow of a soldier got letters regular for a long time from Wales, she says—post-mark was St. Asaphs. Often and often she said as she'd go with him, and see who it was as wrote to him so often. I've been thereabouts myself in the way of my business, and I know there's Powyses as thick as blackberries—that's point number one. Second point was, he always called himself a Welshman and kept St. David's Day. If he'd lived longer he'd have been sent up for promotion, and gone out of the ranks."

"And then?—but go on in your own way, I want to hear it all," said Mr. Brownlow. He was getting more and more excited; and yet somehow it was a kind of pleasure to him to feel that his informant was wasting time upon utterly insignificant details. Surely if the detective suspected nothing, it must be that there was nothing to suspect.

"Yes, sir," he said, "that's about where it is; he was one of the Powyses; naturally the children is Powyses too. But he died afore he went up for promotion; and now they're come a-seeking of their friends. It ain't no credit to me to be employed on such an easy case. The only thing that would put a little credit in it would be, if you'd give me just a bit of a hint what was wanted. If their friends want 'em I'll engage to put 'em on the scent. If their friends don't want 'em—as wouldn't be no wonder; for folks may have a kindness for a brother or a son as is wild, and yet they mightn't be best pleased to hear of a widow a-coming with seven children—if they ain't wanted a word will do it, and no questions asked."

John Brownlow gave the man a sharp glance, and then he fell a-musing, as if he was considering whether to give him this hint or not. In reality, he was contemplating, with a mixture of impatience and vexation and content, the total misconception of his object which his emissary had taken up. He was exasperated by his stupidity, and yet he felt a kind of gratitude to him, and relief, as if a danger had been escaped.

"And what of the woman herself?" he said, in a tone which, in spite of him trembled a little.

"Oh, the woman," said the detective, carelessly; "some bit of a girl as he married, and as was pretty, I don't doubt, in her day. There's nothing particular about her. She's very fond of her children, and very free in her talk, like most women when you take 'em the right way. Bless you, sir, when I started her talking of her husband, it was all that I could do to get her to leave off. She don't think she's got any thing to hide. He was a gentleman, that's clear. He wouldn't have been near so frank about himself, I'll be bound. She ain't a lady exactly, but there's something about her—and awful open in her way, with them front teeth—"

"Has she got front teeth?" said Mr. Brownlow, with some eagerness. He pitched upon it as the first personal attribute he had yet heard of, and then he added, with a little confusion, "like the boy—"

"Yes sir—exactly like the young fellow," said his companion; "but there ain't nothing about her to interest us. She told me as she once had friends as lived in Masterton; but she's the sort of woman as don't mind much about friends as long as her children is well off; and I judge she was of well-to-do folks, that was awful put out about her marriage. A man like that, sir, might be far above her, and have friends that was far above her, and yet it's far from the kind of marriage as would satisfy well-to-do folks."

"I thought she came from the Isle of Man," said Mr. Brownlow, in what he meant for an indifferent way.

"As a child, sir—as a child," said the detective, with easy carelessness. "Her friends left there when she was but a child, and then they went where there was a garrison, where she met with her good gentleman. She was never in Masterton herself. It was after she was married and gone, and, I rather think, cast off by all belonging to her, that they came to live here."

Mr. Brownlow sat leaning over the fire, and a heavy moisture began to rise on his forehead. The speaker was so careless, and yet these calm details seemed to him so terrible. Could it be that he was making terrors for himself—that the man experienced in mystery was right in being so certain that there was no mystery here—or must he accept the awful circumstantial evidence of these simple particulars? Could there be more than one family which had left the Isle of Man so long ago, and gone to live where there was a garrison, and abandoned its silly daughter when she married her soldier? Mr. Brownlow was stupefied, and did not know what to think. He sat and listened while this man whom he had called to his assistance went over again all the facts that seemed to point out that the connection of the family with the Powyses of North Wales was the one thing either to be brought forward or got rid of. This was how he had understood his instructions, and he had carried them out so fully that his employer, fully occupied with the incidental information which seemed to prove all he feared, heard his voice run on without remarking it, and would have told him to stop the babble to which he was giving vent, had his thoughts been sufficiently at leisure to care for what he was saying. When he fully perceived this mistake, Mr. Brownlow looked upon it as "providential," as people say. But, in the mean time, he was not conscious of any thing, except of a possibility still more clear and possible, and of a ridiculous misconception which still it was not his interest to clear up. He let his detective talk, and then he let him go, but half satisfied, and inclined to think that no confidence was reposed in him. And though it was so late, and the brougham was at the door, and the servants very tired of their unusual detention, Mr. Brownlow went back again to the fire, and bent over it, and stretched out his hands to the blaze, and again tried to think. He went over the same ideas a hundred times, and yet they did not seem to grow any clearer to him. He tried to ask himself what was his duty, but duty slunk away, as it were to the very recesses of his soul, and gave no impulse to his mind, nor so much as showed itself in the darkness. If this should turn out to be true, no doubt there were certain things which he ought to do; and yet, if all this could but be banished for awhile, and the year got over which would bring safety—Mr. Brownlow had never in all his life before done what he knew to be a dishonorable action. He was not openly contemplating such a thing now; only somehow his possessions seemed so much more his than any body else's; it seemed as if he had so much better right to the good things he had been enjoying for four-and-twenty years than any woman could have who had never possessed them—who knew nothing about them. And then he did not know that it was this woman. He said to himself that he had really no reason to think so. The young man had said nothing about old Mrs. Thomson. The detective had never even suspected any mystery in that quarter, though he was a man of mystery, and it was his business to suspect every thing. This was what he was thinking when he went back to the fire in his office, and stretched his hands over the blaze. Emotion of any kind somehow chills the physical frame; but when one of the detained clerks came to inform him of the patient brougham which waited outside, and which Sara, by reason of the cold, had sent for him, it was the opinion of the young man that Mr. Brownlow was beginning to age rapidly, and that he looked quite old that evening. But he did not look old; he looked, if any one had been there with eyes to see it, like a man for the first time in his life driven to bay. Some men come to that moment in their lives sooner, some later, some never at all. John Brownlow had been more than five-and-fifty years in the world, and yet he had never been driven to bay before. And he was so now; and except to stand out and resist, and keep his face to his enemies, he did not, in the suddenness of the occurrence, see as yet what he was to do.

In the mean time, however, he had to stoop to ordinary necessities and get into his carriage and be driven home, through the white gleaming country which shone under the moonlight, carrying with him a curious perception of how different it would have been had the house in High Street been home—had he had nothing more to do than to go up to the old drawing-room, his mother's drawing-room, and find Sara there; and eat his dinner where his father had eaten his, instead of this long drive to the great country-house, which was so much more costly and magnificent than any thing his forefathers knew; but then his father, what would he have thought of this complication? What would he have advised, had it been any client of his; nay, what, if it was a client, would Mr. Brownlow himself advise? These thoughts kept turning over in his mind half against his will as he lay back in the corner of the carriage and saw the ghostly trees glimmer past in their coating of snow. He was very late, and Sara was anxious about him; nay, even Jack was anxious, and had come down to the park gates to look out for the carriage, and also to ask how the little invalid was at Mrs. Swayne's. Jack, having this curiosity in his mind, did not pay much attention to his father's looks; but Sara, with a girl's quick perception, saw there was something unusual in his face; and with her usual rapidity she leaped to the conclusion that the bank must have broken or the railway gone wrong of which she had dreamed in the morning. Thus they all met at the table with a great deal on their minds; and this day, which I have recorded with painstaking minuteness, in order that there may be no future doubt as to its importance in the history, came to an end with outward placidity but much internal perturbation—at least came to an end as much as any day can be said to come to an end which rises upon an unsuspecting family big with undeveloped fate.

CHAPTER VIII

YOUNG POWYS

Mr. Brownlow took his new clerk into his employment next morning. It is true that this was done to fill up a legitimate vacancy, but yet it took every body in the office a little by surprise. The junior clerk had generally been a very junior, taken in rather by way of training than for any positive use. The last one, indeed, whom this new-comer had been taken to replace, was an overgrown boy in jackets, very different, indeed, from the tall, well-developed Canadian whose appearance filled all Mr. Brownlow's clerks with amazement. All sorts of conjectures about him filled the minds of these young gentlemen. They all spied some unknown motive underneath, and their guesses at it were ludicrously far from the real case. The conveyancing clerk suggested that the young fellow was somebody's son "that old Brownlow has ruined, you know, in the way of business." Other suppositions fixed on the fact that he was the son of a widow by whom, perhaps, the governor might have been bewitched, an idea which was speedily adopted as the favorite and most probable explanation, and caused unbounded amusement in the office. They made so merry over it that once or twice awkward consequences had nearly ensued; for the new clerk had quick ears, and was by no means destitute of intelligence, and decidedly more than a match, physically, for the most of his fellows. As for the circumstances of his engagement, they were on this wise.

At the hour which Mr. Brownlow had appointed to see him again, young Powys presented himself punctually in the outer office, where he was made to wait a little, and heard some "chaffing" about the governor's singular proceedings on the previous day and his interviews with Inspector Pollaky, which probably conveyed a certain amount of information to the young man. When he was ushered into Mr. Brownlow's room, there was, notwithstanding his frank and open countenance, a certain cloud on his brow. He stood stiffly before his future employer, and heard with only a half-satisfied look that the lawyer, having made inquiries, was disposed to take advantage of his services. To this the young backwoodsman assented in a stilted way, very different from his previous frankness; and when all was concluded, he still stood doubtful, with the look upon his face of having something to say.

"I don't know what more there is to settle, except the time when you enter upon your duties," said Mr. Brownlow, a little surprised. "You need not begin to-day. Mr. Wrinkell, the head-clerk, will give you all the necessary information about hours, and show you all you will have to do—Is there any thing more you would like to say?"

"Why, yes, sir," said the youth abruptly, with a mixture of irritation and compunction. "Perhaps what I say may look very ungrateful; but—why did you send a policeman to my mother? That is not the way to inquire about a man if you mean to trust him. I don't say you have any call to trust me—"

"A policeman!" said Mr. Brownlow, in consternation.

"Well, sir, the fellows there," cried the energetic young savage, pointing behind him, "call him Inspector. I don't mean to say you were to take me on my own word; any inquiries you liked to make we were ready to answer; but a policeman—and to my mother?"

Mr. Brownlow laughed, but yet this explosion gave him a certain uneasiness. "Compose yourself," he said, "the man is not a policeman, but he is a confidential agent, whom when I can't see about any thing myself—but I hope he did not say any thing or ask any thing that annoyed Mrs.—your mother," Mr. Brownlow added, hurriedly; and if the jocular youths in the office had seen something like a shade of additional color rise on his elderly cheek, their amusement and their suspicions would have been equally confirmed.

"Well, no," said young Powys, the compunction gaining ground; "I beg your pardon, sir; you are very kind. I am sure you must think me ungrateful—but—"

"Nonsense!" said Mr. Brownlow; "it is quite right you should stand up for your mother. The man is not a policeman—and I never—intended him—to trouble—your mother," he added, with hesitation. "He went to make inquiry, and these sort of people take their own way; but he did not annoy her, I hope?"

"Oh, no!" said the youth, recovering his temper altogether. "She took it up as being some inquiry about my father, and she was a little excited, thinking perhaps that his friends—but never mind. I told her it was best we should depend only on ourselves, and I am sure I am right. Thank you; I shall have good news to tell her to-day."

"Stop a little," said Mr. Brownlow, feeling a reaction upon himself of the compunction which had passed over his young companion. "She thought it was something about your father? Is there any thing mysterious, then, about your father? I told you there was a Lady Powys who had lived here."

"I don't think there is any thing mysterious about him," said the young man. "I scarcely remember him, though I am the eldest. He died quite young—and my poor mother has always thought that his friends—But I never encouraged her in that idea, for my part."

"That his friends could do something for you?" said Mr. Brownlow.

"Yes, that is what she thought. I don't think myself there is any foundation for it; and seeing they have never found us out all these years—five-and-twenty years—"

"Five-and-twenty years!" Mr. Brownlow repeated, with a start—not that the coincidence was any thing, but only that the mere sound of the word startled him, excited as he was.

"Yes, I am as old as that," said young Powys, with a smile, and then he recollected himself. "I beg your pardon, sir; I am taking up your time, and I hope you don't think I am ungrateful. Getting this situation so soon is every thing in the world to us."

"I am glad to hear it," said Mr. Brownlow: and yet he could not but ask himself whether his young visitor laid an emphasis upon this situation. What was this situation more than another? "But the salary is not very large, you know—do you mean to take your mother and her family on your shoulders with sixty pounds a-year!"

"It is my family," said the young man, growing red. "I have no interest separate from theirs." Then he paused for a moment, feeling affronted; but he could not bear malice. Next minute he relapsed into the frank and confidential tone that was natural to him. "There are only five of us after all," he said—"five altogether, and the little sisters don't cost much; and we have a little money—I think we shall do very well."

"I hope so," said Mr. Brownlow; and somehow, notwithstanding that he intended in his heart to do this young fellow a deadly injury, a certain affectionate interest in the lad sprung up within him. He was so honest and open, and had such an innocent confidence in the interest of others. None of his ordinary clerks were thus garrulous to Mr. Brownlow. It never would have occurred to them to confide in the "guv'nor." He knew them as they came and went, and had a certain knowledge of their belongings—which it was that would have old Robinson's money, and which that had given his father so much uneasiness; but that was very different from a young fellow that would look into your face and make a confidant of you as to his way of spending his sixty pounds a-year. John Brownlow had possessed a heart ever since he was aware of his own individuality. It was that that made him raise his eyes always, years and years ago, when Bessie Fennell went past his windows. Perhaps it would have been just as well had he not been thus moved; and yet sometimes, when he was all by himself and looked up suddenly and saw any passing figure, the remembrance of those moments when Bessie passed would be as clear upon him as if he were young again. Influenced by this same organ, which had no particular business in the breast of a man of his profession at his years, Mr. Brownlow looked up with eyes that were almost tender upon the young man whom he had just taken into his employment—notwithstanding that, to tell the truth, he meant badly by him, and in one particular at least was far from intending to be his friend.

"I hope so," he said; "and if you are steady and suit us, there may be means found of increasing a little. I don't pledge myself to any thing, you know; but we shall see how you get on; and if you have any papers or any thing that may give a clue to your father's family," he continued, as he took up his pen, "bring them to me some day and I'll look over them. That's all in the way of business to us. We might satisfy your mother after all, and perhaps be of some use to you."

This he said with an almost paternal smile, dismissing his new clerk, who went away in an enthusiasm of gratitude and satisfaction. It is so pleasant to be very kindly used, especially to young people who know no better. It throws a glow of comfort through the internal consciousness. It is so very, very good of your patron, and, in a smaller way, it is good of you too, who is patronized. You are understood, you are appreciated, you are liked. This was the feeling young Powys had. To think that Mr. Brownlow would have been as good to any body would not have been half so satisfactory, and he went off with ringing hasty steps, which in themselves were beating a measure of exhilaration, to tell his mother, who, though ready on the spot to worship Mr. Brownlow, would naturally set this wonderful success down to the score of her boy's excellencies. As for the lawyer himself, he took his pen in his hand and wrote a few words of the letter which lay unfinished before him while the young man was going out, as if anxious to make up for the time lost in this interview; but as soon as the door was closed John Brownlow laid down his pen and leaned back in his chair. What was it he had done?—taken in a viper to his bosom that would sting him? or received a generous, open, confiding youth, in order to blind and hoodwink and rob him? These were strong—nay, rude and harsh words, and he did not say them even to himself; but a kind of shadow of them rolled through his mind, and gave him a momentary panic. Was this what he was about to do? With a pretense of kindness, even generosity, to take this open-hearted young fellow into his employment, in order to keep him in the dark, and prevent him from finding out that the fortune was his upon which Brownlows and all its grandeur was founded? Was this what he was doing?

It seemed to John Brownlow for the moment as if the air of the room was suffocating, or rather as if there was no air at all to breathe, and he plucked at his cravat in the horror of the sensation. But then he came to himself. Perhaps, on the other hand, just as likely, he was taking into his house a secret enemy, who, once posted there, would search and find out every thing. Quite likely, very likely; for what did he mean by the emphasis with which he said this situation, and all that about his father, which was throwing dust into Mr. Brownlow's cautious eyes? Perhaps his mind was a little biased by his profession—perhaps he was moved by something of the curious legal uncertainty which teaches a man to plead "never indebted" in the same breath with "already paid;" for amid the hurry and tumult of these thoughts came another which was of a more comforting tendency. After all, he had no evidence that the boy was that woman's son. No evidence whatever—not a shadow. And it was not his duty to go out and hunt for her or her son over all the world. Nobody could expect it of him. He had done it once, but to do it over again would be simply absurd. Let them come and make their claim.

Thus the matter was decided, and there could be no doubt that it was with a thrill of very strange and mingled interest that Mr. Brownlow watched young Powys enter upon his duties. He had thought this would be a trouble to him—a constant shadow upon him—a kind of silent threat of misery to come; but the fact was that it did not turn out so. The young fellow was so frank and honest, so far at least as physiognomy went—his very step was so cheerful and active, and rang so lightly on the stones—he was so ready to do any thing, so quick and cordial and workman-like about his work—came in with such a bright face, spoke with such a pleasant respectful confidence, as knowing that some special link existed between his employer and himself; Mr. Brownlow grew absolutely attached to the new clerk, for whom he had so little use, to whom he was so kind and fatherly, and against whom—good heavens! was it possible? he was harboring such dark designs.

As for young Jack, when he came back to the office after a few days on the ice, there being nothing very important in the way of business going on just then, the sight of this new figure took him very much by surprise. He was not very friendly with his father's clerks on the whole—perhaps because they were too near himself to be looked upon with charitable eyes; too near, and yet as far off, he thought to himself, as if he had been a duke. Not that Jack had those attributes which distinguished the great family of snobs. When he was among educated men he was as unassuming as it is in the nature of a young man to be, and never dreamed of asking what their pedigree was, or what their balance at their banker's. But the clerks were different—they were natural enemies—fellows that might set themselves up for being as good as he, and yet were not as good as he, however you chose to look at the question. In short, they were cads. This was the all-expressive word in which Jack developed his sentiments. Any addition to the cads was irksome to him; and then he, the young prince, knew nothing about it, which was more irksome still.

"Who is that tall fellow?" he said to Mr. Wrinkell, who was his father's vizier. "What is he doing here? You don't mean to say he's en permanence? Who is he, and what is he doing there?"

"That's Mr. Powys, Mr. John," said Mr. Wrinkell, calmly, and with a complacent little nod. The vizier rather liked to snub the heir-apparent when he could, and somehow the Canadian had crept into his good graces too.

"By Jove! and who the deuce is Mr. Powys?" said Jack, with unbecoming impatience, almost loud enough to reach the stranger's ear.

"Hush," said Mr. Wrinkell, "he has come in young Jones's place, who left at Michaelmas, you know. I should say he was a decided addition; steady, very steady—punctual in the morning—clever at his work—always up to his hours—"

"Oh, I see, a piece of perfection," said Jack, with, it must be confessed, a slight sneer. "But I don't see that he was wanted. Brown was quite able for all the work. I should like to know where you picked that fellow up. It's very odd that something always happens when I am absent for a single day."

"The frost has lasted for ten days," said Mr. Wrinkell, with serious but mild reproof—"not that I think there is any thing in that. We are only young once in this life; and there is nothing particular doing. I am very glad you took advantage of it, Mr. John."

Now it was one of Jack's weak points that he hated being called Mr. John, and could not bear to be approved of—two peculiarities of which Mr. Wrinkell was very thoroughly aware. But the vizier had many privileges. He was serious and substantial, and not a man who could be called a cad, as Jack called his own contemporaries in the office. Howsoever tiresome or aggravating he might be, he had to be borne with; and he knew his advantages, and was not always generous in the use he made of them. When the young man went off into his own little private room, Mr. Wrinkell was tempted to give a little inward chuckle. He was a dissenter, and he rather liked to put the young autocrat down. "He has too much of his own way—too much of his own way," he said to himself, and went against Jack on principle, and for his good, which is a kind of conduct not always appreciated by those for whose good it is kept up.

And from that moment a kind of opposition, not to say enmity, crept up between Jack and the new clerk—a sort of feeling that they were rather too like each other, and were not practicable in the same hemisphere. Jack tried, but found it did not answer, to call the new-comer a cad. He did not, like the others, follow Jack's own ways at a woful distance, and copy those things for which Jack rather despised himself, as all cads have a way of doing; but had his own way, and was himself, Powys, not the least like the Browns and Robinsons. The very first evening, as they were driving home together, Jack, having spent the day in a close examination of the new-comer, thought it as well to let his father know his opinion on the subject, which he did as they flew along in their dogcart, with the wicked mare which Jack could scarcely hold in, and the sharp wind whizzing past their ears, that were icy cold with speed.

"I see you have got a new fellow in the office," said Jack. "I hope it's not my idleness that made it necessary. I should have gone back on Monday; but I thought you said—"

"I am glad you didn't come," said Mr. Brownlow, quietly. "I should have told you had there been any occasion. No, it was not for that. You know he came in young Jones's place."

"He's not very much like young Jones," said Jack—"as old as I am, I should think. How she pulls, to be sure! One would think, to see her go, she hadn't been out for a week."

"Older than you are," said Mr. Brownlow—"five-and-twenty;" and he gave an unconscious sigh—for it was dark, and the wind was sharp, and the mare very fresh; and under such circumstances a man may relieve his mind, at least to the extent of a sigh, without being obliged to render a reason. So, at least, Mr. Brownlow thought.

But Jack heard it, somehow, notwithstanding the ring of the mare's hoofs and the rush of the wind, and was confounded—as much confounded as he durst venture on being with such a slippery animal to deal with.

"Beg your pardon, sir," said the groom, "keep her steady, sir; this here is the gate she's always a-shying at."

"Oh, confound her!" said Jack—or perhaps it was "confound you"—which would have been more natural; but the little waltz performed by Mrs. Bess at that moment, and the sharp crack of the whip, and the wind that whistled through all, made his adjuration less distinct than it might have been. When, however, the dangerous gate was past, and they were going on again with great speed and moderate steadiness, he resumed—

"I thought you did not mean to have another in young Jones's place. I should have said Brown could do all the work. When these fellows have too little to do they get into all sorts of mischief."

"Most fellows do," said Mr. Brownlow, calmly. "I may as well tell you, Jack, that I wanted young Powys—I know his people; that is to say," he added hastily, "I don't know his people. Don't take it into your head that I do—but still I've heard something about them—in a kind of a way; and it's my special desire to have him there."

"I said nothing against it, sir," said Jack, displeased. "You are the head, to do whatever you like. I only asked you know."

"Yes, I know you only asked," said Mr. Brownlow, with quiet decision. "That is my business; but I'd rather you were civil to him, if it is the same to you."

"By Jove, I believe she'll break our necks some day," said Jack, in his irritation, though the mare was doing nothing particular. "Going as quiet as a lamb," the groom said afterward in amazement, "when he let out at her enough to make a saint contrairy." And "contrairy" she was up to the very door of the house, which perhaps, under the circumstances, was just as well.

CHAPTER IX

NEW NEIGHBORS

Perhaps one of the reasons why Jack was out of temper at this particular moment was that Mrs. Swayne had been impertinent to him. Not that he cared in the least for Mrs. Swayne; but naturally he took a little interest in the—child—he supposed she was only a child—a little light thing that felt like a feather when he carried her in out of the snow. He had carried her in, and he "took an interest" in her; and why he should be met with impertinence when he asked how the little creature was, was more than Jack could understand. The very morning of the day on which he saw young Powys first, he had been answered by Mrs. Swayne standing in front of her door, and pulling it close behind her, as if she was afraid of thieves or something. "She's a-going on as nicely as could be, and there ain't no cause for anxiety, sir," Mrs. Swayne said, which was not a very impertinent speech after all.

"Oh, I did not suppose there was," said Jack. "It was only a sprain, I suppose; but she looked such a delicate little thing. That old woman with her was her mother, eh? What did she mean traveling with a fragile little creature like that in the carrier's cart?"

"I don't know about no old woman," said Mrs. Swayne; "the good lady as has my front parlor is the only female as is here, and they've come for quiet, Mr. John, not meaning no offense; and when you're a bit nervish, as I knows myself by experience, it goes to your heart every time as there comes a knock at the door."

"You can't have many knocks at the door here," said Jack; "as for me, I only wanted to know how the little thing was."

"Miss is a-doing nicely, sir," Mrs. Swayne answered, with solemnity; and this was what Jack considered a very impertinent reception of his kind inquiries. He was amused by it, and yet it put him a little out of temper too. "As if I could possibly mean the child any harm," he said to himself, with a laugh; rather, indeed, insisting on the point that she was a child in all his thoughts on the subject; and then, as has been seen, the sudden introduction of young Powys and Mr. Brownlow's calm adoption of the sentiment that it was his business to decide who was to be in the office, came a little hard upon Jack, who, after all, notwithstanding his philosophical indifference as to his sister's heiress-ship, liked to be consulted about matters of business, and did not approve of being put back into a secondary place.

Thus it was with a sense of having done her duty by her new lodgers, that Mrs. Swayne paid her periodical visit in the afternoon to the inmates of the parlor, where the object of Jack Brownlow's inquiries lay very much covered up on the little horse-hair sofa. She was still suffering from her sprain, and was lying asleep on the narrow couch, wrapped in all the shawls her mother possessed, and with her own pretty red cloak thrown over the heap. It was rather a grim little apartment, with dark-green painted walls, and coarse white curtains drawn over the single window. But the inmates probably were used to no better, and certainly were quite content with their quarters. The girl lay asleep with a flush upon her cheeks, which the long eyelashes seemed to overshadow, and her soft rings of dark hair pushed back in pretty disorder off her soft, full, childlike forehead. She was sleeping that grateful sleep of convalescence, in which life itself seems to come back—a sleep deep and sound and dreamless, and quite undisturbed by the little murmur of voices which went on over the fire. Her mother was a tall, meagre woman, older than the mother of such a girl ought to have been. Save that subtle, indefinable resemblance which is called family likeness, the two did not resemble each other. The elder woman now sitting in the horsehair easy-chair over the fire, was very tall, with long features, and gray cheeks which had never known any roses. She had keen black passionate eyes, looking as young and full of life as if she had been sixteen instead of nearly sixty; and her hair was still as black as it had been in her youth. But somehow the dead darkness of the hair made the gray face underneath look older than if it had been softened by the silvery tones of white that belong to the aged. She was dressed as poor women, who have ceased to care about their appearance, and have no natural instinct that way, so often dress, in every thing most suited to increase her personal deficiencies. She had a little black lace cap over her black hair, and a black gown with a rim of grayish white round the neck, badly made, and which took away any shape that might ever have been in her tall figure. Her hands were hard, and red, and thin, with no sort of softening between them and the harsh black sleeve which clasped her wrists. She was not a lady, that was evident; and yet you would not have said she was a common woman after you had looked into her eyes.

It was very cold, though the thaw had set in, and the snow was gone—raw and damp with a penetrating chill, which is as bad as frost—or worse, some people think. And the new-comer sat over the fire, leaning forward in the high-backed horse-hair chair, and spreading out her hands to the warmth. She had given Mrs. Swayne a general invitation to come in for a chat in the afternoon, not knowing as yet how serious a business that was; and was now making the best of it, interposing a few words now and then, and yet not altogether without comfort in the companionship, the very hum of human speech having something consolatory in it.

"If it's been a fever, that's a thing as will mend," said Mrs. Swayne, "and well over too; and a thing as you don't have more nor once. When it's here, and there's decline in the family—" she added, putting her hand significantly to her breast.

"There's no decline in my family," said the lodger, quickly. "It was downright sickness always. No, she's quite strong in her chest. I've always said it was a great blessing that they were all strong in their chests."

"And yet you have but this one left," said Mrs. Swayne. "Dear, dear!—when it's decline, it comes kind of natural, and you get used to it like. An aunt o' mine had nine, all took one after the other, and she got that used to it, she'd tell you how it would be as soon as e'er a one o' them began to droop; but when it's them sort of masterful sicknesses as you can't do nothing for—Deary me! all strong in their chests, and yet you have had so many and but this one left."

"Ay," said the mother, wringing her thin hands with a momentary yet habitual action, "it's hard when you've reared them so far, but you said it was good air here?"

"Beautiful air, that's what it is," said Mrs. Swayne, enthusiastically; "and when she gets a bit stronger, and the weather gets milder, and he mends of his rheumatics, Swayne shall drive her out in his spring-cart. It's a fine way of seeing the country—a deal finer, I think, than the gentry in their carriages with a coachman on his box perched up afore them. I ain't one as holds by much doctoring. Doctors and parsons, they're all alike; and I don't care if I never saw one o' them more."

"Isn't there a nice clergyman?" said the lodger—"it's a nice church, for we saw it passing in the cart, and the child took a fancy to it. In the country like this, it's nice to have a nice clergyman—that's to say, if you're church folks."

"There was nothing but church folks heard tell of where I came from," said Mrs. Swayne, with a little heat. "Them as says I wasn't born and bred and confirmed in the church don't know what they're talking of; but since we come here, you know, along of Swayne being a Dissenter, and the rector a man as has no sympathy, I've give up. It's the same with the doctors. There ain't one as I haven't tried, exceptin' the homepathic; and I was turning it over in my mind as soon as Swayne had another bad turn to send for him."

"I hope we shan't want any more doctors," said the mother, once more softly wringing her hands. "But for Pamela's sake—"

"Is that her name?" said Mrs, Swayne; "I never knew one of that name afore; but folks is all for new-fashioned names nowadays. The Pollys and Betsys as used to be in my young days, I never hear tell of them now; but the girls ain't no nicer nor no better behaved as I can see. It's along o' the story-books and things. There's Miss Sairah as is always a-lending books—"

"Is Miss Sairah the young lady in the great house?" asked the stranger, looking up.

Mrs. Swayne assented with a little reluctance. "Oh! yes, sure enough; but they ain't the real old Squires. Not as the old Squires was much to brag of; they was awful poor, and there never was nothing to be made out of them, neither by honest trade-folks nor cottagers, nor nobody; but him as has it now is nothing but a lawyer out of Masterton. He's made it all, I shouldn't wonder, by cheating poor folks out of their own; but there he is as grand as a prince, and Miss Sairah dressed up like a little peacock, and her carriage and her riding-horse, and her school, as if she was real old gentry. It was Mr. John as carried your girl indoors that time when she fell; and a rare troublesome one he can be when he gets it in his head, a-calling at my house, and knocking at the knocker when, for any thing he could tell, Swayne might ha' been in one of his bad turns, or your little maid a-snatching a bit of sleep."

"But why does he come?" said the lodger, once more looking up; "is it to ask after Mr. Swayne?"

Mr. Swayne's spouse gave a great many shakes of her head over this question. "To tell you the truth," she said, "there's a deal of folks thinks if Swayne hadn't a good wife behind him as kept all straight, his bad turns would come very different. That's all as a woman gets for slaving and toiling and understanding the business as well as e'er a man. No; it was not for my husband. I haven't got nothing to say against Mr. John. He's not one of the sort as leads poor girls astray and breaks their hearts; but I wouldn't have him about here, not too often, if I was you. He was a-asking after your girl."

"Pamela?" said the mother, with surprise and almost amusement in her tone, and she looked back to the sofa where her daughter was lying with a flush too pink and roselike for health upon her cheek. "Poor little thing; it is too early for that—she is only a child."

"I don't put no faith in them being only children," said Mrs. Swayne. "It comes terrible soon, does that sort of thing; and a gentleman has nice ways with him. When she's once had one of that sort a-running after her, a girl don't take to an honest man as talks plain and straightforward. That's my opinion; and, thank Providence, I've been in the way of temptation myself, and I know what it all means."

Mrs. Swayne's lodger did not seem at all delighted by these commentaries. A little flush of pride or pain came over her colorless cheek; and she kept glancing back at the sofa on which her daughter lay. "My Pamela is a little lady, if ever there was a lady," she said, in a nervous undertone; but it was evidently a question she did not mean to discuss with her landlady; and thus the conversation came to a pause.

Mrs. Swayne, however, was not easily subdued; and curiosity urged her even beyond her wont. "I think you said as you had friends here?" she said, making a new start.

"No, no friends. We're alone in the world, she and I," said the woman, hastily. "We've been long away, and every body is dead that ever belonged to us. She hasn't a soul but me, poor dear, and I'm old. It's dreadful to be old and have a young child. If I was to die—but we're not badly off," she continued, with a faint smile in answer to an alarmed glance all around the room from Mrs. Swayne, "and I'm saving up every penny for her. If I could only see her as well and rosy as she used to be!"

"That will come in time," said the landlady. "Don't you be afeard. It's beautiful air; and what with fresh milk and new-laid eggs, she'll come round as fast as the grass grows. You'll see she will—they always does here. Miss Sairah herself was as puny a bit of a child as ever you set eyes on, and she's a fine tall lass with a color like a rose—I will say that for her—now."

"And I think you said she was about my child's age," said the mother, with a certain wistful glance out of the window. "Perhaps she and my Pamela—But of course a young lady like that has plenty of friends. Pamela will never be tall—she's done growing. She takes after her father's side, you see," the poor woman added, with a sigh, looking round once more to the sofa where her child lay.

"And it ain't long, perhaps, since you lost your good gentleman?" said Mrs. Swayne, curiosity giving a certain brevity to her speech.

"He was in the army," said the lodger, passing by the direct question, "and it's a wandering sort of life. Now I've come back, all are gone that ever belonged to me, or so much as knew me. It feels dreary like. I don't mind for myself, if I could but find some kind friends for my child."

"Don't you fret," said Mrs. Swayne, rising. "She'll find friends, no fear; and its ridiklus to hear you talk like an old woman, and not a gray hair on your head—But I hear Swayne a-grumbling, Mrs. Preston. He's no better nor an old washerwoman, that man isn't, for his tea."

When the conversation ended thus, the lodger rose, partly in civility, and stood before the fire, looking into the dark little mirror over the mantle-shelf when her visitor was gone. It was not vanity that moved her to look at herself. "Threescore and ten!" she was saying softly—"threescore and ten! She'd be near thirty by then, and able to take care of herself." It was a sombre thought enough, but it was all the comfort she could take. "The child" all this time had to all appearance lain fast asleep under her wraps, with the red cloak laid over her, a childlike, fragile creature. She began to stir at this moment, and her mother's face cleared as if by magic. She went up to the little hard couch, and murmured her inquiries over it with that indescribable voice which belongs only to doves, and mothers croodling over their sick children. Pamela considered it the most ordinary utterance in the world, and never found out that it was totally unlike the usually almost harsh tones of the same voice when addressing other people. The girl threw off her coverings with a little impatience, and came with tottering steps to the big black easy-chair. The limpid eyes which had struck Jack Brownlow when they gazed wistfully out of the carrier's cart, were almost too bright, as her color was almost too warm, for the moment; but it was the flush of weakness and sleep, not of fever. She too, like her mother, wore rusty black; but neither that poor and melancholy garb, nor any other disadvantageous circumstance, could impair the sweetness of the young tender face. It was lovely with the sweetness of spring as are the primroses and anemones; dew, and fragrance, and growth, and all the possibilities of expansion, were in her lovely looks. You could not have told what she might not grow to. Seeing her, it was possible to understand the eagerness with which the poor old mother, verging on threescore, counted her chances of a dozen years longer in this life. These dozen years might make all the difference to Pamela; and Pamela was all that she had in the world.

"You have had a long sleep, my darling. I am sure you feel better," she said.

"I feel quite well, mamma," said the girl; and she sat down and held out her hands to the fire. Then the mother began to talk, and give an account of the conversation she had been holding. She altered it a little, it must be acknowledged. She omitted all Mrs. Swayne's anxieties about Jack Brownlow, and put various orthodox sentiments into her mouth instead. When she had gone on so for some ten minutes,

Pamela, who had been making evident efforts to restrain herself, suddenly opened her red lips with a burst of soft ringing laughter, so that the mother stopped confused.

"I am afraid it was very naughty," said the girl; "but I woke up, and I did not want to disturb you, and I could not help listening. Oh, mamma, how clever you are to make up conversation like that. When you know Mrs. Swayne was talking of Mr. John, and was such fun! Why shouldn't I hear about Mr. John? Because one has been ill, is one never to have any more fun? You don't expect me to die now?"

"God forbid!" said the mother. "But what do you know about Mr. John? Mrs. Swayne said nothing—"

"She said he came a-knocking at the knocker," Pamela said, with a merry little conscious laugh; "and you asked if he came to ask for Mr. Swayne. I thought I should have laughed out and betrayed myself then."

"But, my dear," said Mrs. Preston, steadily, "why shouldn't he have come to ask for Mr. Swayne?"

"Yes, why indeed?" said Pamela, with another merry peal of laughter, which made her mother's face relax, though she was not herself very sensible wherein the joke lay.

"Well," she said, "if he did, or if he didn't, it does not matter very much to us. We know nothing about Mr. John."

"Oh, but I do," said Pamela; "it was he that was standing by that lady's chair on the ice—I saw him as plain as possible. I knew him in a minute when he carried me in. Wasn't it nice and kind of him? and he knew—us;—I am sure he did. Why shouldn't he come and ask for me? I think it is the most natural thing in the world."

"How could he know us?" said Mrs. Preston, wondering. "My darling, now you are growing older you must not think so much about fun. I don't say it is wrong, but—For you see, you have grown quite a woman now. It would be nice if you could know Miss Sara," she added, melting; "but she is a little great lady, and you are but a poor little girl—"

"I must know Miss Sara," cried Pamela. "We shall see her every day. I want to know them both. We shall be always seeing them any time they go out. I wonder if she is pretty. The lady was, that was in the chair."

"How can you see every thing like that, Pamela?" said her mother, with mild reproof. "I don't remember any lady in a chair."

"But I've got a pair of eyes," said Pamela, with a laugh. She was not thinking that they were pretty eyes, but she certainly had a pleasant feeling that they were clear and sharp, and saw every thing and every body within her range of vision. "I like traveling in that cart," she said, after a moment, "if it were not so cold. It would be pleasant in summer to go jogging along and see every thing—but then, to be sure, in summer there's no ice, and no nice bright fires shining through the windows. But mamma, please," the little thing added, with a doubtful look that might be saucy or sad as occasion required, "why are you so dreadfully anxious to find me kind friends?"

This was said with a little laugh, though her eyes were not laughing; but when she saw the serious look her mother cast upon her, she got up hastily and threw herself down, weak as she was, at the old woman's knee.

"Don't you think if we were to live both as long as we could and then to die both together!" cried the changeable girl, with a sudden sob. "Oh, mamma, why didn't you have me when you were young, when you had Florry, that we might have lived ever so long, ever so long together? Would it be wrong for me to die when you die? why should it be wrong? God would know what we meant by it. He would know it wasn't for wickedness. And it would make your mind easy whatever should happen," cried the child, burying her pretty face in her mother's lap. Thus the two desolate creatures clung together, the old woman yearning to live, the young creature quite ready at any word of command that might reach her to give up her short existence. They had nobody in the world belonging to them that they knew of, and in the course of nature their companionship could only be so short, so short! And it was not as if God saw only the outside like men. He would know what they meant by it; that was what poor little Pamela thought.

But she was as lively as a little bird half an hour after, being a creature of a variable mind. Not a magnificent little princess, self-possessed and reflective, like Sara over the way—a little soul full of fancies, and passions, and sudden impulses of every kind—a kitten for fun, a heroine for any thing tragic, such as she, not feared, but hoped, might perhaps fall in her way. And the mother, who understood the passion, did not know very much about either the fun or the fancy, and was puzzled by times, and even vexed when she had no need to be vexed. Mrs. Preston was greatly perplexed even that night after this embrace and the wild suggestion that accompanied it to see how swiftly and fully Pamela's light heart came back to her. She could not comprehend such a proposal of despair; but how the despair should suddenly flit off and leave the sweetest fair skies of delight and hope below was more than the poor woman could understand. However, the fact was that hope and despair were quite capable of living next door in Pamela's fully occupied mind, and that despair itself was but another kind of hope when it got into those soft quarters where the air was full of the chirping of birds and the odors of the spring. She could not sing, to call singing, but yet she went on singing all the evening long over her bits of work, and planned drives in Mr. Swayne's spring-cart, and even in the carrier's wagon, much more joyfully than Sara ever anticipated the use of her grays. Yet she had but one life, one worn existence, old and shattered by much suffering, between her and utter solitude and destitution. No wonder her mother looked at her with silent wonder, she who could never get this woful possibility out of her mind.

CHAPTER X

AT THE GATE

It was not to be expected that Sara could be long unconscious of her humble neighbors. She, too, as well as Jack, had seen them in the carrier's cart; and though Jack had kept his little adventure to himself, Sara had no reason to omit due notice of her encounter. It was quite a new sensation to her when she saw for the first time the little face with its dewy eyes peeping out at Mrs. Swayne's window. And the ticket which offended Sara's sight had been promptly taken down, not by Mrs. Swayne, but by her lodgers themselves. Sara's impulse was to go over immediately and thank them for this good office; but, on second thoughts, she decided to wait another opportunity. They might not be "nice,"—or they might be ladies, and require more ceremonious treatment, notwithstanding the carrier's wagon. The face that peeped from Mrs. Swayne's window might have belonged to a little princess in disguise for any thing that could be said to the contrary. And Sara was still of the age which believes in disguised princesses, at least in theory. She talked about them, however, continually; putting Jack to many hypocritical devices to conceal that he too had seen the little stranger. Though why he should keep that fact secret, nobody, not even himself could tell. And he had confided it to young Keppel, though he did not think of telling the story at home. "I don't know if you would call her pretty, but her eyes are like two stars," was what Jack said; and he was more angry at Keppel's jocular response than was at all needful. But, as for Sara, she was far more eloquent. "She is not pretty," that authority said; "all girls are pretty, I suppose, in a kind of a way—I and Fanny Hardcastle and every body—I despise that. She's lovely; one would like to take and kiss her. I don't in the least care whether I am speaking grammar or not; but I want to know her, and I've made up my mind I'll have her here."

"Softly, Sara," said Mr. Brownlow, with that indulgent look which Sara alone called into his eyes.

"Oh yes, papa, as softly as you please; but I shall never be like her if I were to live a hundred years. I'd like to cut all my hair off, and wear it like that; but what's the use, with this odious light hair?"

"I thought it was golden and Titianesque, and all sorts of fine things," said Jack, "besides being fashionable. I've heard Keppel say—"

"Don't, please; Mr. Keppel is so stupid," and she took in her hand a certain curl she had, which was her favorite curl in a general way, and looked at it with something like disgust.

"It isn't even the right color for the fashion," she said, contemptuously. This was at breakfast, before the gentlemen went to business, which was a favorite hour with all of them, when their minds were free, and the day had not as yet produced its vexations. Mr. Brownlow, for his part, had quite got over any symptoms of discomposure that his children might have perceived on his face. Every thing was going on well again. Young Powys was safely settled in the office, and his employer already had got used to him, and nothing seemed to be coming of it: and every day was helping on the year, the one remaining year of uncertainty. He was very anxious, but still he was not such a novice in life but that he could keep his anxiety to himself.

"Don't forget to make every thing comfortable for your visitors," was what he said, as he drove away; and the fact was, that even Mr. Brownlow cast a glance over Mrs. Swayne's windows; and that Jack brought the mare almost on her haunches, by way of showing his skill, as she dashed out at the gates. And poor little Pamela had limped to the window, for she had not much to amuse her, and the passing of Mr. Brownlow's dog-cart was an event. "Is that the girl?" said Mr. Brownlow; "why she is like your sister, Jack."

"Like Sara!" Jack gasped in dismay. He was so amazed that he could say nothing more for a full minute. "I suppose you think every thing that's pretty is like Sara," he said, when he had recovered his breath.

"Well, perhaps," said the father; "but there's something more there—and yet she's not like Sara either for the matter of that."

"Not the least bit in the world," said Jack, decisively; at which Mr. Brownlow only smiled, making no other reply.

Sara, of course, knew nothing of this; and notwithstanding her admiration for the stranger, it is doubtful whether she would have been flattered by the suggestion. She made great preparations for her visitors. There was to be a dinner-party, and old Lady Motherwell and her son Sir Charles were to stay for a day or two—partly because it was too far for the old lady to drive back that night, and partly, perhaps, for other reasons, which nobody was supposed to know any thing about. In her own mind, however, Sara was not quite unaware of these other reasons. The girl was so unfortunate as to be aware that she was considered a good match in the county, and she knew very well what Sir Charles meant when he came and mounted guard over her at county gatherings. It was commonly reported of Sir Charles Motherwell that he was not bright—but he was utterly opaque to Sara when he came and stood over her and shut out other people who might have been amusing; though, to tell the truth, Miss Brownlow was in a cynical state of mind altogether about amusing people. She thought they were an extinct species, like mastodons, and the other sort of brutes that lived before the creation. Fanny Hardcastle began to unfold her dress as soon as breakfast was over, and to look out her gloves and her shoes and all her little ornaments, and was in a flutter all day about the dinner at Brownlows. But as for Sara, she was not excited. By way of making up to herself for what she might have to suffer in the evening, she went out for a ride, a pleasure of which she had been debarred for some time by the frost; and little Pamela came again to the window and watched—oh, with what delight and envy and admiration!—the slender-limbed chestnut and the pretty creature he carried, as they came down all the length of the avenue.

"Oh, mamma, make haste—make haste! it is a prettier sight than Mr. John," cried the little girl at Mrs. Swayne's window, her cheeks glowing and her eyes shining; "what fun it is to live here and see them all passing!" Probably she enjoyed it quite as much as Sara did. When she had watched the pretty rider as far as that was possible, she sat down by the window to wait till she came back—wondering where she was going—following her as she went cantering along the sunny long stretches of road which Pamela remembered watching from the carrier's cart. What a strange kind of celestial life it must be to be always riding down stately avenues and playing golden-stringed harps, and walking about in glorious silken robes that swept the ground! Pamela laughed to herself at those splendid images—she enjoyed it more than Sara did, though Sara found all these good things wonderfully pleasant too.

"What are you laughing at?" said her mother, who was working at a table at the other end of the room.

"What fun it is to live here!" repeated Pamela. "It is as good as a play; don't you like to see them all riding out and in, and the horses prancing, and the shadows coming down the avenue?—it was the greatest luck in the world to come here."

"Put up your foot, my dear," said her mother, "and don't catch cold at that window. I've seen somebody very like that young lady, but I can't remember where."

"That was Miss Sara, I suppose," said Pamela, with a little awe; and she put up her weak foot, and kept her post till the chestnut and his mistress came back, when the excitement was renewed; and Mrs. Preston herself took another look, and wondered where she had seen some one like that. Thus the life of Brownlows became entangled, as it were, in that of the humble dwellers at their gate, before either were aware.

Lady Motherwell arrived in a very solid family coach, just as the winter twilight set in; and undoubtedly, on this occasion at least, it was Pamela who had the best of it. Sara awaited the old lady in the drawing-room, ready to administer to her the indispensable cup of tea; and Sir Charles followed his mother, a tall fellow with a mustache which looked like a respirator. As for Lady Motherwell, she was not a pleasant visitor to Sara; but that was for reasons which I have already stated. In herself she was not a disagreeable old woman. She had even a certain esprit du corps which made it evident to her that thus to come in force upon a girl who was alone, was a violent proceeding, and apt to drive the quarry prematurely to bay. So she did her best to conciliate the young mistress of the house, even before she had received her cup of tea.

"Charley doesn't take tea," she said. "I think we'll send him off, my dear, to look at the stables, or something. I hate to have a man poking about the room when I want a comfortable chat; and in this nice cozy firelight, too, when they look like tall ghosts about a place. You may go and have your cigar, Charley. Sara and I have a hundred things to say."

Sir Charles was understood to murmur through his respirator that it was awful hard upon a fellow to be banished like this; but nevertheless, being in excellent training, and knowing it to be for his good, he went. Then Lady Motherwell took Sara in her arms for the second time, and gave her a maternal kiss.

"My love, you're looking lovely," she said. "I'm sorry for poor Charley, to tell the truth; but I knew you'd have enough of him to-night. Now tell me how you are, and all about yourself. I have not seen you for an age."

"Oh, thank you, I'm just as well as ever," said Sara. "Sit down in this nice low chair, and let me give you some tea."

"Thank you," said Lady Motherwell. "And how is Jack and the good papa? Jack is a gay deceiver; he is not like my boy. You should have seen him driving the girls about the ice in that chair. I am not sure that I think it very nice, do you know, unless it was a very old friend or—somebody very particular. I was so sorry I could not come for you—"

"Oh, it did not matter," said Sara; "I was there three days. I got on very well; and then I have more things to do than most girls have. I don't care so very much for amusements. I have a great many things to do."

"Quite a little housekeeper," said Lady Motherwell. "You girls don't like to have such things said to you nowadays; but I'm an old-fashioned old woman, and I must say what I think. What a nice little wife you will make one of these days! That used to be the highest compliment that could be paid to us when I was your age."

"Oh, I don't mind it at all," said Sara; "I suppose that is what one must come to. It is no good worrying one's self about it. I am rather fond of housekeeping. Are you going to be one of the patronesses for the Masterton ball, Lady Motherwell? Do you think one should go?"

"No, I don't think one should go," said the old lady, not without a very clear recollection that she was speaking to John Brownlow the solicitor's daughter; "but I think a dozen may go, and you shall come with me. I am going to make up a party—yourself and the two Keppels—"

"No," said Sara, "I am a Masterton girl, and I ought not to go with you grand county folks—oh no, papa must take me; but thank you very much all the same."

"You are an odd girl," said Lady Motherwell. "You forget your papa is one of the very richest of the county folks, as you call us. I think Brownlows is the finest place within twenty miles, and you that have all the charge of it—"

"Don't laugh at me, please—I don't like being laughed at. It makes me feel like a cat," said Sara; and she clasped her soft hands together, and sat back in her soft velvet chair out of the firelight, and sheathed her claws as it were; not feeling sure any moment that she might not be tempted to make a spring upon her flattering foe.

"Well, my dear, if you want to spit and scratch, let Charley be the victim, please," said the old lady. "I think he would rather like it. And I am not laughing in the least, I assure you. I think a great deal of good housekeeping. We used to be brought up to see after every thing when I was young; and really, you know, when you have a large establishment, and feel that your husband looks to you for every thing—"

"We have not all husbands, thank heaven," said Sara, spitefully; "and I am sure I don't want a situation as a man's housekeeper. It is all very well when it's papa."

"You will not always think so," said Lady Motherwell, laughing; "that is a thing a girl always changes her mind about. Of course you will marry some day, as every body does."

"I don't see," said Sara, very decidedly, "why it should be of course. If there was any body that papa had set his heart on, and wanted me to marry—or any good reason—of course I would do what ever was my duty. But I don't think papa is a likely sort of man to stake me at cards, or get into any body's power, or any thing of that sort."

"Sara, you are the most frightful little cynic," cried Lady Motherwell, laughing; "don't you believe that girls sometimes fall in love?"

"Oh yes, all the silly ones," said Sara, calmly, out of her corner. She was not saying any thing that she did not to a certain extent feel; but there is no doubt that she had a special intention at the moment in what she said.

Lady Motherwell had another laugh, for she was amused, and not nearly so much alarmed for the consequences as the young speaker intended she should be. "If all girls had such sentiments, what would become of the world?" she said. "The world would come to an end."

"I wish it would," said Sara. "Why shouldn't it come to an end? It would be easy to make a nicer world. People are very aggravating in this one. I am sure I don't see why we should make ourselves unhappy about its coming to an end. It would always be a change if it did. And some of the poor people might have better luck. Do you think it is such a very nice world?"

"My dear, don't be profane," said Lady Motherwell. "I never did think Mr. Hardcastle was very settled in his principles. I declare you frighten me, Sara, sitting and talking in that sceptical way, in the dark."

"Oh, I can ring for lights," said Sara; "but that isn't sceptical. It's sceptical to go on wishing to live forever, and to make the world last forever, as if we mightn't have something better. At least so I think. And as for Mr. Hardcastle, I don't know what he has to do with it—he never said a word on the subject to me."

"Yes, my dear, but there is a general looseness," said the old lady. "I know the sort of thing. He lets you think whatever you like, and never impresses any doctrines on you as he ought. We are not in Dewsbury parish, you know, and I feel I ought to speak. There are such differences in clergymen. Our vicar is very pointed, and makes you really feel as if you knew what you believed. And that is such a comfort, my dear. Though, to be sure, you are very young, and you don't feel it now."

"No, I don't feel it at all," said Sara; "but, Lady Motherwell, perhaps you would like to go to your room. I think I hear papa's cart coming up the avenue—will you wait and see him before you go?"

Thus the conversation came to an end, though Lady Motherwell elected to wait, and was as gracious to Mr. Brownlow as if he had been twenty county people. Even if Sara did not have Brownlows, as everybody supposed, still she would be rich and bring money enough with her to do a vast deal of good at Motherwell, where the family for a long time had not been rich. Sir Charles's father, old Sir Charles, had not done his duty by the property. Instead of marrying somebody with a fortune, which was clearly the object for which he had been brought into the world, he had married to please a fancy of his own in a very reprehensible way. His wife herself felt that he had failed to do his duty, though it was for her sake; and she was naturally all the more anxious that her son should fulfill this natural responsibility. Sir Charles was not handsome, nor was he bright, nor even so young as he might have been; but all this, if it made the sacrifice less, made the necessity more, and accordingly Lady Motherwell was extremely friendly to Mr. Brownlow. When she came down for dinner she took a sort of natural protecting place, as if she had been Sara's aunt, or bland, flattering, uninterfering mother-in-law. She called the young mistress of the house to her side, and held her hand, and patted it and caressed it. She told Mr. Brownlow how pleased she was to see how the dear child had developed. "You will not be allowed to keep her long," she said, with tender meaning; "I think if she were mine I would go and hide her up so that nobody might see her. But one has to make up one's mind to part with them all the same."

"Not sooner than one can help," said Mr. Brownlow, looking not at Lady Motherwell, but at his child, who was the subject of discourse. He knew what the old lady meant as well as Sara did, and he had been in the way of smiling at it, wondering how any body could imagine he would give his child to a good-tempered idiot; but this night another kind of idea came into his mind. The man was stupid, but he was a gentleman of long-established lineage, and he could secure to Sara all the advantages of which she had so precarious a tenure here. He could give her even a kind of title, so far as that went, though Mr. Brownlow was not much moved by a baronet's title; and if any thing should happen to endanger Brownlows, it would not matter much to Jack or himself. They could return to the house in Masterton, and make themselves as comfortable as life, without Sara, could be anywhere. This was the thought that was passing through Mr. Brownlow's mind when he said, "Not sooner than one can help." He was thinking for the first time that such a bestowal of his child might not be so impossible after all.

Beside her, in the seat she had taken when she escaped from Lady Motherwell, Sir Charles had already taken up his position. He was talking to her through his hard little black mustache—not that he said a great deal. He was a tall man, and she was seated in a low chair, with the usual billows of white on the carpet all round her, so that he could not even approach very near; and she had to look up at him and strain her ear when he spoke, if she wanted to hear—which was a trouble Sara did not choose to take. So she said, "What?" in her indifferent way, playing with her fan, and secretly doing all she could to extend the white billows round her; while he, poor man, bent forward at a right angle till he was extremely uncomfortable, and repeated his very trivial observations with a vain attempt to reach her ear.

"I think I am growing deaf," said Sara; "perhaps it was that dreadful frost—I don't think I have ever got quite thawed yet. When I do, all you have been saying will peal out of the trumpet like Baron Munchausen, you know. So you didn't go to the stables? Wasn't that rather naughty? I am sure it was to the stables your mamma sent you when you went away."

"Tell you what, Miss Brownlow," said Sir Charles, "you are making game of me."

"Oh, no," said Sara; "or did you go to the gate and see such a pretty girl in the cottage opposite? I don't know whether you would fall in love with her, but I have; I never saw any one look so sweet. She has such pretty dark little curls, and yet not curls—something prettier—and such eyes—"

"Little women with black hair are frights," said Sir Charles—"always thought so, and more than ever now."

"Why more than ever now?" said Sara, with the precision of contempt; and then she went on—"If you don't care either for pretty horses or pretty girls, we shan't know how to amuse you. Perhaps you are fond of reading; I think we have a good many nice books."

Sir Charles said something to his mustache, which was evidently an expletive of some kind. He was not the sort of man to swear by Jove, or even by George, much less by any thing more tangible; but still he did utter something in an inarticulate exclamatory way. "A man would be difficult to please if he didn't get plenty to amuse him here," was how it ended. "I'm not afraid—"

"It is very kind of you to say so," said Sara, so very politely that Sir Charles did not venture upon any more efforts, but stood bending down uneasily, looking at her, and pulling at his respirator in an embarrassed way; not that he was remarkable in this, for certainly the moment before dinner is not favorable to animated or genial conversation. And it was not much better at dinner. Sara had Mr. Keppel of Ridley, the eldest brother, at her other side, who talked better than Sir Charles did. His mother kept her eye upon them as well as that was possible from the other end of the table, and she was rather hard upon him afterward for the small share he had taken in the conversation. "You should have amused her and made her talk, and drawn her out," said the old lady. "Oh, she talked plenty," Sir Charles said, in a discomfited tone; and he did not make much more of it in the evening, when young Mrs. Keppel and her sister-in-law, and Fanny Hardcastle, all gathered in a knot round the young mistress of the house. It was a pretty group, and the hum of talk that issued from it attracted even the old people to linger and listen, though doubtless their own conversation would have been much more worth listening to. There was Sara reclining upon the cushions of a great round ottoman, with Fanny Hardcastle by her, making one mass of the white billows; and opposite, Mrs. Keppel, who was a pretty little woman, lay back in a low deep round chair, and Mary Keppel, who was a little fond of attitudes, sat on a stool, leaning her head upon her hands, in the centre. Sometimes they talked all together, so that you could not tell what they said; and they discussed every thing that ought to be discussed in heaven and earth, and occasionally something that ought not; and there was a dark fringe of men round about them, joining in the babble. But as for Sir Charles, he knew his consigne, and stood at his post, and did not attempt to talk. It was an exercise that was seldom delightful to him; and then he was puzzled, and could not make out whether, as he himself said, it was chaff or serious. But he could always stand over the mistress of his affections, and do a sentinel's duty, and keep other people away from her. That was a métier he understood.

"Has it been a pleasant evening, Sara?" said Mr. Brownlow when the guests had all gone, and Sir Charles had disappeared with Jack, and Lady Motherwell had retired to think it all over and invent some way of pushing her son on. The father and daughter were left alone in the room, which was still very bright with lights and fire, and did not suggest any of the tawdry ideas supposed to hang about in the air after an entertainment is over. They were both standing by the fire, lingering before they said good-night.

"Oh, yes," said Sara, "if that odious man would not mount guard over me. What have I done that he should always stand at my elbow like that, with his hideous mustache?"

"You mean Sir Charles?" said Mr. Brownlow. "I thought girls liked that sort of thing. He means it for a great compliment to you."

"Then I wish he would compliment somebody else," said Sara; "I think it is very hard, papa. A girl lives at home with her father, and is very happy and doesn't want any change; but any man that pleases—any tall creature with neither brains nor sense, nor any thing but a mustache—thinks he has a right to come and worry her; and people think she should be pleased. It is awfully hard. No woman ever attempts to treat Jack like that."

Mr. Brownlow smiled, but it was not so frankly as usual. "Are you really quite sure about this matter?" he said. "I wish you would think it over, my darling. He is not bright—but he's a very good fellow in his way—stop a little. And you know I am only Brownlow the solicitor, and if any thing should happen to our money, all this position of ours in the county would be lost. Now Sir Charles could give you a better position—"

"Oh, papa! could you ever bear to hear me called Lady Motherwell?" cried Sara—"young Lady Motherwell! I should hate myself and every body belonging to me. But look here; I have wanted to speak to you for a long time. If you were to lose your money, I don't see why you should mind so very much. I should not mind. We would go away to the country, and get a cottage somewhere, and be very comfortable. After all, money don't matter so much. We could walk instead of driving, which is often far pleasanter, and do things for ourselves."

"What do you know about my money?" said Mr. Brownlow, with a bitter momentary pang. He thought something must have betrayed the true state of affairs to Sara, which would be an almost incredible addition to the calamity.

"Well, not much," said Sara, lightly; "but I know merchants and people are often losing money, and you have an office like a merchant. I should not mind that; but I do mind never being able to turn my head even at home in our very own house, without seeing that man with his horrid mustache."

"Poor Sir Charles!" said Mr. Brownlow, and the anxiety on his face lightened a little. She could not know any thing about it. It must be merely accidental, he thought. Then he lighted her candle for her, and kissed her soft cheek. "You said you would marry any one I asked you to marry," he said, with a smile; but it was not a smile that went deep. Strangely enough he was a little anxious about the answer, as if he had really some plan in his mind.

"And so I should, and never would hesitate," said Sara, promptly, holding his hand, "but not Sir Charles, please, papa."

This was the easy way in which the girl played on what might possibly turn out to be the very verge of the precipice.

CHAPTER XI

THE YOUNG PEOPLE

After all, no doubt it is the young people who are the kings and queens of this world. They don't have it in their own hands, nor their own way in it, which would not be good for them, but all our plots and plans are for their advantage whether they know it or not. For their sakes a great deal of harm is done in this world, which the doers hold excused, sometimes sanctified, by its motive, and the young creatures themselves have a great many things to bear which, no doubt, is for their advantage too. It is the least invidious title of rank which can exist in any community, for we have all been young—all had a great many things done for us which we would much rather had been let alone—and all suffered or profited by the plans of our progenitors. But if they are important in the actual universe, they are still more important in the world of fiction. Here we can not do without these young heroes and heroines. To make a middle-aged man or woman interesting demands genius, the highest concentration of human power and skill; whereas almost any of us can frame our innocent little tale about Edwin and Angelina, and tempt a little circle to listen notwithstanding the familiarity of the subject. Such is the fact, let us account for it as we may. The youths and maidens, and their encounters, and their quarrels, and their makings-up, their walks and talks and simple doings, are the one subject that never fails; so, though it is a wonder how it should be so, let us go back to them and consider their young prospects and their relations to each other before we go farther on in the real progress of our tale.

The way that Sara made acquaintance with the little dweller at her gate was in this wise. It was the day after the dinner-party, when the Motherwells were still at Brownlows. Sara had gone out to convey some consolation to old Betty at the gate, who was a rheumatical old woman. And she thought she had managed to escape very cleverly out of Lady Motherwell's clutches, when, to her horror, Sir Charles overtook her in the avenue. He carried in his manner and appearance all the dignity of a man whose mind is made up. He talked very little, certainly, to begin with—but that was his way; and he caressed his abrupt little black mustache as men do caress any physical adjunct which is a comfort to them in a crisis. Sara could not conceal it from herself that something was coming, and there was no apparent escape for her. The avenue was long; there was nobody visible coming or going. Had the two been on a desert island, Sir Charles could scarcely have had less fear of interruption. I do not pretend to say that Sara was entirely inexperienced in this sort of thing, and did not know how to snub an incipient lover or get out of such a dilemma in ordinary cases; but Sir Charles Motherwell's was not an ordinary case. In the first place, he was staying in the house, and would have to continue there till to-morrow at least, whatever might happen to him now; and in the second, he was obtuse, and might not understand what any thing short of absolute refusal meant. He was not a man to be snubbed graciously or ungraciously, and made to comprehend without words that his suit was not to be offered. Such a point of understanding was too high for him. He was meditating between himself and his mustache what he had to say, and he was impervious to all Sara's delicate indications of an indisposition to listen. How could he tell what people meant unless they said it? Thus he was a man with whom only such solid instruments as Yes and No were of any use; and it would have been very embarrassing if Sara, with at least twenty-four hours of his society to look forward to, had been obliged to say No. She did the very best she could under the emergency. She talked with all her might and tried to amuse him, and if possible lead him off his grand intention. She chatted incessantly with something of the same feelings that inspired Scherazade, speaking against time, though not precisely for her life, and altogether unaware that, in so far as her companion could abstract his thought from the words he was about to say, when he could find them, his complacent consciousness of the trouble she took to please him was rising higher and higher. Poor dear little thing! he was saying to himself, how pleased she will be! But yet, notwithstanding this comfortable thought, it was a difficult matter to Sir Charles in broad daylight, and with the eyes of the world, as it were, upon him, to prevail upon the right words to come.

They were only half way down the avenue when he cleared his throat. Sara was in despair. She knew by that sound and by the last convulsive twitch of his mustache that it was just coming. A pause of awful suspense ensued. She was so frightened that even her own endeavor to ward off extremities failed her. She could not go on talking in the horror of the moment. Should she pretend to have forgotten something in the house and rush back? or should she make believe somebody was calling her and fly forward? She had thrown herself forward on one foot, ready for a run, when that blessed diversion came for which she could never be sufficiently thankful. She gave a start of delightful relief when they came to that break in the trees. "Who can that be?" she said, much as, had she been a man, she would have uttered a cheer. It would not have done for Miss Brownlow to burst forth into an unlooked-for hurrah, so she gave vent to this question instead, and made a little rush on to the grass where that figure was visible. It was a pretty little figure in a red cloak; and it was bending forward, anxiously examining some herbage about the root of a tree. At the sound of Sara's exclamation the stranger raised herself hurriedly, blushed, looked confused, and finally, with a certain shy promptitude, came forward, as if, Sara said afterward, she was a perfect little angel out of heaven.

"I beg your pardon," she said; "perhaps I ought not to be here. I am so sorry; but—it was for old Betty I came."

"You are very welcome to come," said Sara, eagerly—"if you don't mind the damp grass. It is you who live at Mrs. Swayne's? Oh, yes, I know you quite well. Pray, come whenever you please. There are a great many pretty walks in the park."

"Oh, thank you!" said little Pamela. It was the first time she had seen the young great lady so near, and she took a mental inventory of her, all that she was like and all that she had on. Seeing Miss Sara on foot, like any other human creature, was not a thing that occurred every day; and she took to examining her with a double, or rather triple, interest—first, because it was Miss Sara, and something very new; second, to be able to describe minutely the glorious vision to her mother; and thirdly out of genuine admiration. How beautiful she was! and how beautifully dressed! and then the tall gentleman by her side, so unlike any thing Pamela ever saw, who took off his hat to her—actually to her! No doubt, though he was not so handsome as might have been desired, they were going to be married. He must be very good, gallant, and noble, as he was not so very good looking. Pamela's bright eyes danced with eagerness and excitement as she looked at them. It was as good as a play or a story-book. It was a romance being performed for her benefit, actually occurring under her very eyes.

"I know what you were doing," said Sara, "but it is too early yet. 'Round the ashen roots the violets blow'—I know that is what you were thinking of."

Pamela, who knew very little about violets, and nothing about poetry, opened her eyes very wide. "Indeed," she said, anxiously, "I was only looking for some plantain for Betty's bird—that was all. I did not mean to take any—flowers. I would not do any thing so—so—ungrateful."

"But you shall have as many violets as ever you like," said Sara, who was eager to find any pretense for prolonging the conversation. "Do come and walk here by me. I am going to see old Betty. Do you know how she is to-day? Don't you think she is a nice old woman? I am going to tell her she ought to have her grandchild to live with her, and open the gate, now that her rheumatism has come on. It always lasts three months when it comes on. Your Mr. Swayne's, you know, goes on and off. I always hear all about it from my maid."

When she paused for breath, Pamela felt that as the tall gentleman took no part in the conversation, it was incumbent upon her to say something. She was much flattered by the unexpected grandeur of walking by Miss Brownlow's side, and being taken into her confidence; but the emergency drove every idea out of her head, as was natural. She could not think of any thing that it would be nice to say, and in desperation hazarded a question. "Is there much rheumatism about here?" poor Pamela said, looking up as if her life depended on the answer she received; and then she grew burning red, and hot all over, and felt as if life itself was no longer worth having, after thus making a fool of herself. As if Miss Brownlow knew any thing about the rheumatism here! "What an idiot she will think me!" said she to herself, longing that the earth would open and swallow her up. But Miss Brownlow was by no means critical. On the contrary, Sara rushed into the subject with enthusiasm.

"There is always rheumatism where there are so many trees," she said, with decision—"from the damp, you know. Don't you find it so at Motherwell, Sir Charles? You have such heaps of trees in that part of the county. Half my poor people have it here. And the dreadful thing is that one doesn't know any cure for it, except flannel. You never can give them too much flannel," said Sara, raising her eyes gravely to her tall companion. "They think flannel is good for every thing under the skies."

"Don't know, I'm sure," said Sir Charles. "Sure it's very good of you. Don't know much about rheumatism myself. Always see lots about in our place; flannel pettic—hem—oh—beg your pardon. I'm sure—"

When he uttered that unfortunate remark, poor Sir Charles brought himself up with a sudden start, and turned very red. It was his horror and embarrassment, poor man, and fear of having shocked his companion's delicacy. But Sara took the meanest advantage of him. She held out her hand, with a sweet smile. "Are you going?" she said; "it is so kind of you to have come so far with me. I hope you will have a pleasant ride. Please make Jack call at the Rectory, and ask if Fanny's cold is better. Shall you be back to luncheon? But you never are, you gentlemen. Are you never hungry in the middle of the day as we are? Till dinner, then," she said, waving her hand. Perhaps there was something mesmeric in it. The disappointed wooer was so startled that he stood still as under a spell.

"Didn't mean to leave you," he said: "don't care for riding. I'd like to see old Betty too."

"Oh, but that would be much too polite," cried Sara. "Please, never mind me. It is so kind of you to have come so far. Good-bye just now. I hope you will have a pleasant ride." She was gone before he could move or recover from his consternation. He stood in dumb amaze for a full minute looking after her; and then poor Sir Charles turned away with the obedience of despair. He had been too well brought up on the whole. His mother had brought him to such a pitch of discipline that he could not choose but obey the helm, whosesoever hand might touch it. "It was all those confounded petticoats," he said to himself. "How could I be such an ass?" which was the most vigorous speech he had made even to himself for ages. As for Sara, she relaxed from her usual dignity, and went along skipping and tripping in the exhilaration of her heart. "Oh, what a blessing he is gone! oh, what a little angel you were to appear just when you did!" said Sara; and then she gave a glance at her new companion's bewildered face, and composed herself. "But don't let us think of him any more," she continued. "Tell me about yourself—I want to know all about yourself. Wasn't it lucky we met? Please tell me your name, and how old you are, and how you like living here. Of course, you know I am Sara Brownlow. And oh, to be sure, first of all, why did you say ungrateful? Have I ever done any thing to make you grateful to me?"

"Oh, yes, please," said Pamela. "It is so pretty to see you always when you ride, and when you drive out. I am not quite strong yet, and I don't know any body here; but I have only to sit down at the window, and there is always something going on. Last night you can't think how pretty it was. The carriage lamps kept walking up and down like giants with two big eyes. And I can see all up the avenue from my window; and when I looked very close, just as they passed Betty's door, I could see a little glimpse of the ladies inside. I saw one lovely pink dress; and then in the next there was a scarlet cloak all trimmed with swan's down. I could tell it was swan's down, it was so fluffy. Oh, I beg your pardon, I didn't mean to talk so much; but it is such fun living there, just opposite the gate. And that is why I am so grateful to you."

Sara, it was impossible to deny, was much staggered by this speech. Its frankness amazed and yet attracted her. It drove her into deep bewilderment as to the rank of her little companion. Was she a lady? She would scarcely have taken so much pleasure in the sight, had it been within the range of possibility that she could herself join such a party; but then her voice was a refined voice, and her lovely looks might, as Sara had thought before, have belonged to a princess. The young mistress of Brownlows looked very curiously at Pamela, but she could not fathom her. The red cloak was a little the worse for wear, but still it was such a garb as any one might have worn. There was no sort of finery, no sort of pretension, about the little personage. And then Sara had already made up her mind in any case to take her pretty neighbor under her protection. The end of the matter was, that in turning it over in her mind, the amusing side of the question at last caught her eye. How strange it was! While the awful moment before dinner was being got through at the great house, this little creature at the gate was clapping her hands over the sounds and sights out-of-doors. To her it was not heavy people coming to dinner, to be entertained in body and mind for three or four mortal hours; but prancing horses and rolling wheels, and the lamps making their shining progress two and two, and all the cheerful commotion. How odd it was! She must be (whatever her "position") an original little thing, to see so tedious a business in such a novel light.

"It is very odd," said Sara, "that I never thought of that before. I almost think I shouldn't mind having stupid people now and then if I had thought of that. And so you think it fun? You wouldn't think it fun if you had to watch them eating their dinner, and amuse them all the evening. It is such hard work; and then to ask them to sing when you know they can't sing, no more than peacocks, and to stand and say Thank you when it is all over! I wonder what made you think of looking at the lamps. It is very clever of you, you know, to describe them like that. Do you read a great deal? Are you fond of it? Do you play, or do you draw, or what do you like best?"

This question staggered Pamela as much as her description had done Sara. She grew pale and then she grew red. "I am—not in the least clever," she said, "nor—nor accomplished—nor—I am not a great lady like you, Miss Brownlow," the little girl added, with a sudden pang of mortification. She had not been in the least envious of Sara, nor desirous of claiming equality with her. And yet when she thus suddenly perceived the difference, it went to her heart so sharply that she had hard ado not to cry.

As for Sara, she laughed softly, not knowing of any bitterness beneath that reply. She laughed, knowing she was not a great lady, and yet a little disposed to think she was, and pleased to appear so in her companion's eyes. "If you were to speak like that to Lady Motherwell, I wonder what she would say," said Sara; "but I don't want you to be a great lady. I think you are the prettiest little thing I ever saw in my life. There now—I suppose it is wrong to say it, but it is quite true. It is a pleasure just to look at you. If you are not nice and good, it is a great shame, and very ungrateful of you, when God has made you so pretty; but I think you must be nice. Don't blush and tremble like that, as if I were a gentleman. I am just nineteen. How old are you?"

"Seventeen last midsummer," said Pamela, under her breath.

"I knew you were quite a child," said Sara, with dignity. "Don't look so frightened. I mean to come and see you almost every day. And you shall come home with me, and see the flowers, and the pictures, and all my pretty things. I have quantities of pretty things. Papa is so very kind. I have no mother; but that—that—old—lady—is your mother, is she? or your grandmother? Look, there is old Betty at the door. Wicked old woman! what business has she to come out to the door and make her rheumatism worse? Come along a little quicker; but, you poor little dear, what is the matter? Can't you run?"

"I sprained my ankle," said Pamela, blushing more and more, and wondering if Mr. John had perhaps kept that little incident to himself.

"And I trying to make you run!" cried the penitent Sara. "Never mind, take my arm. I am not in the least in a hurry. Lean upon me—there's a good child. They should not let you come so far alone."

Thus it was that the two arrived at Betty's cottage, to the old woman's intense amazement. Pamela herself was flattered by the kind help afforded her, but it is doubtful whether she enjoyed it; and in the exciting novelty of the position, she was glad to sit down in a corner and collect herself while her brilliant young patroness fulfilled her benevolent mission. Betty's lodge was a creation of Miss Brownlow's from beginning to end. It was Sara's design, and Sara had furnished it, up to the pictures on the wall, which were carefully chosen in accordance with what might be supposed to be an old woman's taste, and the little book-shelf, which was filled on the same principles. The fact was, however, that Betty had somewhat mortified Sara by pinning up a glorious colored picture out of the "Illustrated News," and by taking in a tale of love and mystery in penny numbers, showing illegitimate tastes both in literature and art. But she was suffering, and eventually at such a moment her offenses ought to be forgiven.

"You should not stand at the door like that, and go opening the gate in such weather," said Sara. "I came to say you must have one of your son's children to help you,—that one you had last year."

"She's gone to service, Miss," said Betty, with a bob.

"Then one of your daughter's,—the daughter you have at Masterton—she has dozens and dozens of children. Why can not one of them come out and take care of you?"

"Please, Miss," said Betty, "a poor man's childer is his fortune—leastways in a place where there's mills and things. They're all a-doing of something, them little things. I'm awful comfortable, Miss, thanks to you and your good papa"—at this and all other intervals of her speech, Betty made a courtesy—"but I ain't got money like to pay 'em wages, and saving when one's a bit delicate, or that—"

"Betty, sit down, please, and don't make so many courtesies. I don't understand that. If I had a nice old grandmother like you"—said Sara; and then she paused and blushed, and bethought herself—perhaps it might be as well not to enter upon that question.

"Anyhow it is very easy to pay them something," she said. "I will pay it for you till your rheumatism is better. And then there is your other son, who was a tailor or something—where is he?"

"Oh, if I could but tell!" said Betty. "Oh, Miss, he's one o' them as brings down gray hairs wi' sorrow—not as I have a many to lose, though when I was a young lass, the likes o' me for a 'ead of 'air wasn't in all Dewsbury. But Tom, I'm afeard, I'm afeard, has tooken to terrible bad ways."

"Drinking or something?" asked Sara, in the tone of a woman experienced in such inevitable miseries.

"Worse than that, Miss. I don't say as it ain't bad enough when a man takes to drinking. Many a sore heart it's giv' me, but it always comes kind o' natural like," said Betty, with her apron at her eyes. "But poor Tom, he's gone and come out for a Radical, Miss, and sets hisself up a-making speeches and things. It's that as brought it on me so bad. I've not been so bad before, not sin' his poor father died."

"Then don't stand and courtesy like that, please," said Sara. "A Radical—is that all? I am a little of a Radical myself, and so is papa."

"Ah, the like of you don't know," said Betty. "Mr. John wouldn't say nothing for him. He said, 'That's very bad, very bad, Betty,' when I went and told him; and a young gentleman like that is the one to know."

"He knows nothing about it," said Sara; "he's a University man, and Eton, you know; he is all in the old world way; but papa and I are Radicals, like Tom. Are you?—but I suppose you are too young to know. And oh, here it is just time for luncheon, and you have never told me your name. Betty, make haste and send for Tom or somebody to help you. And there's something coming in a basket; and if you want any thing you must send up to the house."

"You're very kind, Miss," said Betty, "and the neighbors is real kind, and Mrs. Swayne, though she has queer ways—And as for Miss Pammly here—"

"Pamela," said the little girl, softly, from her chair.

"Is that your name?" said Sara. "Pamela—I never knew any one called Pamela before. What a pretty name! Sara is horrible. Every soul calls me Sairah. Look here, you are a little darling; and you don't know what you saved me from this morning; and I'll come to see you the moment Lady Motherwell goes away."

Upon which Sara dropped a rapid kiss upon her new friend's cheek and rushed forth, passing the window like an arrow, rushing up the long avenue like a winged creature, with the wind in her hair and in her dress. The little lodge grew darker to Pamela's dazzled eyes when she was gone.

"Is that really Miss Brownlow, Betty?" she said, after the first pause.

"Who could it be else, I would like to know?" said Betty; "a-leaving her orders like that, and never giving no time to answer or nothing. I wonder what's coming in the basket. Not as I'm one o' the greedy ones as is always looking for something; but what's the good o' serving them rich common folks if you don't get no good out of them? Oh for certain sure it's Miss Sara; and she taken a fancy to you."

"What do you mean by common folks?" asked Pamela, already disposed, as was natural, to take up the cudgels for her new friend. "She is a lady, oh, all down to the very tips of her shoes."

"May be as far as you knows," said Betty, "but I've been here off and on for forty years, and I mind the old Squires; not saying no harm of Miss Sara, as is very open-handed; but you mind my words, you'll see plenty of her for a bit—she's took a fancy to you."

"Do you think so, really, Betty?" said Pamela, with brightening eyes.

"What I says is for a bit," said Betty; "don't you take up as I'm meaning more—for a bit, Miss Pammly; that's how them sort does. She's one as 'ill come every day, and then, when she's other things in hand, like, or other folks, or feels a bit tired—"

"Yes, perhaps," said Pamela, who had grown very red; "but that need not have any effect on me. If I was fond of any one, I would never, never change, whatever they might do—not if they were to be cruel and unkind—not if they were to forget me—"

Here the little girl started, and became very silent all in a moment. And the blush of indignation on her cheek passed and was followed by a softer sweeter color, and her words died away on her lips. And her eyes, which had been shining on old Betty with all the magnanimity of youth, went down, and were covered up under the blue-veined, long-fringed eyelids. The fact was, some one else had come into the lodge—had come without knocking, in a very noiseless, stealthy sort of way—"as if he meant it." And this new-comer was no less a person than Mr. John.

"My sister says you are ill, Betty," said Jack; "what do you mean by being ill? I am to send in one of your grandchildren from Masterton. What do you say? Shall I? or should you rather be alone?"

"It's allays you for the thoughtful one, Mr. John," said Betty, gratefully; "though you're a gentleman, and it don't stand to reason. But Miss Sara's a-going to pay; and if there's a little as is to be arned honest, I'm not one as would send it past my own. There's little Betsy, as is a tidy bit of a thing. But I ain't ill, not to say ill, no more nor Miss Pammly here is ill—her as had her ankle sprained in that awful snow."

Mr. John made what Pamela thought a very grand bow at this point of Betty's speech. He had taken his hat off when he came in. Betty's doctor, when he came to see her, did not take off his hat, not even when Pamela was present. The little girl had very quick eyes, and she did not fail to mark the difference. After he had made his bow, Mr. John somehow seemed to forget Betty. It was to the little stranger his words, his eyes, his looks, were addressed. "I hope you are better?" he said. "I took the liberty of going to your house to ask, but Mrs. Swayne used to turn me away."

"Oh, thank you; you are very kind," said Pamela; and then she added, "Mrs. Swayne is very funny. Mamma would have liked to have thanked you, I am sure."

"And I am sure I did not want any thanks," said Jack; "only to know. You are sure you are better now?"

"Oh, much better," said Pamela; and then there came a pause. It was more than a pause. It was a dead stop, with no apparent possibility of revival. Pamela, for her part, like an inexperienced little girl, fidgeted on her chair, and wrapped herself close in her cloak. Was that all? His sister had a great deal more to say. Jack, though he was not inexperienced, was almost for the moment as awkward as Pamela. He went across the room to look at the picture out of the "Illustrated News;" and he spoke to Betty's bird, which had just been regaled with the bit of plantain Pamela had brought; and, at last, when all those little exercises had been gone through, he came back.

"I hope you like living here," he said. "It is cold and bleak now, but in summer it is very pretty. You came at the worst time of the year; but I hope you mean to stay?"

"Oh yes, we like it," said Pamela; and then there came another pause.

"My sister is quite pleased to think of having you for a neighbor," said Jack. It was quite extraordinary how stupid he was. He could talk well enough sometimes; but at this present moment he had not a syllable to say. "Except Miss Hardcastle at the Rectory, she has nobody near, and my father and I are so much away."

Pamela looked up at him with a certain sweet surprise in her eyes. Could he too really think her a fit friend for his sister? "It is very kind of Miss Brownlow," she said, "but I am only—I mean I don't think I am—I—I am always with my mother."

"But your mother would not like you to be shut up," said Jack, coming a little nearer. "I always look over the way now when I pass. To see bright faces instead of blank windows is quite pleasant. I dare say you never notice us."

"Oh yes," cried Pamela. "And that pretty horse! It is such fun to live there and see you all passing." She said this forgetting herself, and then she met old Betty's gaze and grew conscious again. "I mean we are always so quiet," she said, and began once more to examine the binding of her cloak.

At this moment the bell from the great house began to tinkle pleasantly in the wintry air: it was another of Pamela's amusements. And it marked the dinner hour at which her mother would look for her; but how was she to move with this young man behind her chair? Betty, however, was not so delicate. "I always set my clock by the luncheon-bell," said old Betty. "There it's a-going, bless it! I has my dinner by it regular, and I sets my clock. Don't you go for to stir, Miss Pammly. Bless you, I don't mind you! And Mr. John, he's a-going to his lunch. Don't you mind. I'll set my little bit of a table ready; but I has it afore the fire in this cold weather, and it don't come a-nigh of you."

"Oh, mamma will want me," said Pamela. "I shall come back another time and see you." She made Jack a little curtsy as she got up, but to her confusion he came out with her and opened the gate for her, and sauntered across the road by her side.

"I am not going to lunch—I am going to ride. So you have noticed the mare?" said Jack. "I am rather proud of her. She is a beauty. You should see how she goes when the road is clear. I suppose I shall have to go now, for here come the horses and Motherwell. He is one of those men who always turn up just when they're not wanted," Jack continued, opening the gate of Mrs. Swayne's little garden for Pamela. Mrs. Swayne herself was at the window up stairs, and Mrs. Preston was at the parlor window looking out for her child. They both saw that wonderful sight. Young Mr. Brownlow with his hat off holding open the little gate, and looking down into the little face, which was so flushed with pleasure and pride, and embarrassment and innocent shame. As for Pamela herself, she did not know if she were walking on solid ground or on air. When the door closed behind her, and she found herself in the dingy little passage with nothing but her dinner before her, and the dusky afternoon, and her work, her heart gave a little cry of impatience. But she was in the parlor time enough to see Jack spring on his horse and trot off into the sunshine with his tall companion. They went off into the sunshine, but in the parlor it was deepest shade, for Mr. Swayne had so cleverly contrived his house that the sunshine never entered. Its shadow hung across the road, stretching to the gate of Brownlows, almost the whole day, which made every thing dingier than it was naturally. This was what Pamela experienced when she came in out of the bright air, out of sight of those young faces and young voices. Could she ever have any thing to do with them? Or was it only a kind of dream, too pleasant, too sweet to come to any thing? It was her very first outset in life, and she was aware that she was not much of a heroine. Perhaps it was only the accident of an hour; but even that was pleasant if it should be no more. This, when she had told all about it, and filled the afternoon with the reflected glory, was the philosophical conclusion to which Pamela came at last.

CHAPTER XII

NEWS OF FRIENDS

"But you must not set your heart upon it, my darling," said Mrs. Preston. "It may be or it mayn't be—nobody can say. And you must not get to blame the young lady if she thinks better of it. They are very rich, and they have all the best people in the county coming and going. And you are but my poor little girl, with no grand friends; and you mustn't take it to heart and be disappointed. If you were doing that, though it's such good air and so quiet, I'd have to take my darling away."

"I won't, mamma," said Pamela; "I'll be good. But you say yourself that it may be—"

"Yes," said the mother; "young creatures like that are not so worldly-minded—at least, sometimes they're not. She might take a fancy to you; but you mustn't build on it, Pamela. That's all, my dear. We're humble folks, and the like of us don't go visiting at great houses. And even you've not got the education, my darling: and nothing but your black frocks—"

"Oh, mamma, do you think I want to visit at great houses?" cried Pamela. "I should not know what to say nor how to behave. What I should like would be to go and see her in the mornings when nobody was there, and be her little companion, and listen to her talking, and to see her dressed when she was going out. I know we are poor; but she might get fond of me for all that—"

"Yes, dear," said Mrs. Preston, "I think she is a very nice young lady. I wish her mamma had been living, Pamela. If there had been a good woman that had children of her own, living at that great house, I think it would have been a comfort to me."

"Mamma, I can't think why you should always be speaking like that," said Pamela, with a cloud on her brow.

"You would soon know why if you were as old as me," said the mother. "I can't forget I'm old, and how little strength I've got left. And I shouldn't like my pet to get disappointed," she said, rising and drawing Pamela's pretty head to her, as she stood behind her chair; "don't you build upon it, dear. And now I'm going into the kitchen for five minutes to ask for poor Mr. Swayne."

It was a thing she did almost every night, and Pamela was not surprised; perhaps it was even a relief to her to have a few minutes all to herself to think over the wonderful events of the day. To be sure, it had been about Sara alone, and her overtures of friendship, that the mother and daughter had been talking. But when Pamela was by herself, she recollected, naturally, that there had been another actor on the scene. She did not think of asking her mother, or even herself, if Mr. John was to be depended on, or if there was any danger of disappointment in respect to him. Indeed, Pamela was so wise that she did not, as she said to herself, think at all about this branch of the subject; for, of course, it was not likely she would ever make great friends with a young gentleman. The peculiarity of the matter was that, though she was not thinking of Mr. John, she seemed to see him standing before her, holding the gate open, looking into her face, and saying that Motherwell was one of the men that always turned up when they were least wanted. She was not thinking of Jack; and was it her fault if this picture had fixed itself on her retina, if that is the name of it? She went and sat down on the rug before the fire, and gazed into the glow, and thought it all over. After a while she even put her hands over her eyes, that she might think over it the more perfectly. And it is astonishing how often this picture came between her and her thoughts; but, thank heaven, it was only a picture! Whatever Pamela might be thinking of, it was certainly not of Mr. John.

Mrs. Swayne's kitchen was by far the most cheerful place in the house. It had a brick floor, which was as red as the hearth was white, and a great array of shining things about the walls. There was a comfortable cat dozing and blinking before the fire, which was reflected out of so many glowing surfaces, copper, pewter, and tin, that the walls were hung with a perfect gallery of cats. Mrs. Swayne herself had a wickerwork chair at one side, which she very seldom occupied; for there was a great multiplicity of meals in the house, and there was always something just coming to perfection in the oven or on the fire. But opposite, in a high-backed chair covered with blue and white checked linen, was Mr. Swayne, who was the object of so much care, and was subject to the rheumatics, like Betty. The difference of his rheumatics was, that they went off and on. One day he would be well—so well as to go out and see after his business; and the next day he would be fixed in his easy-chair. Perhaps, on the whole, it was more aggravating than if he had gone in steadily for a good long bout when he was at it, and saved his wife's time. But then that was the nature of the man. There was a visitor in the kitchen when Mrs. Preston went in—no less a personage than old Betty, who, with a daring disregard for her rheumatics, had come across the road, wrapped in an old cloak, to talk over the news of the day. It was a rash proceeding, no doubt; but yet rheumatics were very ordinary affairs, and it was seldom—very seldom—that any thing so exciting came in Betty's way. Mrs. Swayne, for her part, had been very eloquent about it before her lodger appeared.

"I'd make short work with him," she said, "if it was me. I'd send him about his business, you take my word. It ain't me as would trust one of 'em a step farther than I could see 'em. Coming a-raging and a-roaring round of a house, as soon as they found out as there was a poor little tender bit of a lamb to devour."

"What is that you say about a bit o' lamb, Nancy?" cried Mr. Swayne; "that's an awful treat, that is, at this time of the year. I reckon it's for the new lodgers and not for us. I'll devour it, and welcome, my lass, if you'll set it afore me."

Mrs. Swayne gave no direct answer to this question. She cast a glance of mild despair at Betty, who answered by lifting up her hands in sympathy and commiseration. "That's just like the men," said Mrs. Swayne. "Talk o' something to put into them, and that's all as they care for. It's what a poor woman has to put up with late and early. Always a-craving and a-craving, and you ne'er out of a mess, dinner and supper—dinner and supper. But as I was a-saying, if it was me, he should never have the chance of a word in her ear again."

"It's my opinion, Mrs. Swayne," said Betty, unwinding her shawl a little, "as in those sort of cases it's mostly the mother's fault."

"I don't know what you mean by the mother's fault," said Mrs. Swayne, who was contradictory, and liked to take the initiative. "She never set eyes on him, as I can tell, poor soul. And how was she to know as they were all about in the avenue? It's none o' the mother's fault; but if it was me, now as they've took the first step—"

"That was all as I meant," said Betty humbly; "now as it's come to that, I would take her off, as it were, this very day."

"And a deal of good you'd do with that," said Mrs. Swayne, with natural indignation; "take her off! and leave my parlor empty, and have him a-running after her from one place to another. I thought you was one as knew better; I'd brave it out if it was me—he shouldn't get no advantages in my way o' working. Husht both of you, and hold your tongues; I never see the like of you for talk, Swayne—when here's the poor lady out o' the parlor as can't abide a noise. Better? ay, a deal better, Mrs. Preston: if he wasn't one as adored a good easy-chair afore the fire—"

"And a very good place, too, this cold weather," said Mr. Swayne with a feeble chuckle. "Nancy, you tell the lady about the lamb."

Mrs. Swayne and Betty once more exchanged looks of plaintive comment. "That's him all over," she said; "but you're one as understands what men is, Mrs. Preston, and I've no mind to explain. I hear as Miss Sara took awful to our young Miss, meeting of her promiscuous in the avenue. Betty here, she says as it was wonderful; but I always thought myself as that was how it would be."

"Yes," said the gratified mother; "not that I would have my Pamela build upon it. A young lady like that might change her mind; but I don't deny that it would be very nice. Whatever is a pleasure to Pamela is twice a pleasure to me."

"And a sweet young lady as ever I set eyes on," said Betty, seizing the opportunity, and making Mrs. Preston one of her usual bobs.

Pamela's mother was not a lady born; the two women, who were in their way respectful to her, saw this with lynx eyes. She was not even rich enough, poor soul, to have the appearance of a lady; and it would have been a little difficult for them to have explained why they were so civil. No doubt principally it was because they knew so little of her, and her appearance had the semi-dignity of preoccupation—a thing very difficult to be comprehended in that region of society which is wont to express all its sentiments freely. She had something on her mind, and she did not relieve herself by talking, and she lived in the parlor, while Mrs. Swayne contented herself with the kitchen. That was about the extent of her claim on their respect.

"I suppose you are all very fond of Miss Sara, knowing her all her life," Mrs. Preston said, after she had received very graciously Betty's tribute to her own child. Though she warned Pamela against building on it, it would be hard to describe the fairy structures which had already sprung in her own mind on these slight foundations; and though she would not have breathed his name for worlds, it is possible that Pamela's mother, in her visions, found a place for Mr. John too.

"Fond! I don't know as we're so fond of her neither," said Mrs. Swayne. "She's well, and well enough, but I can't say as she's my sort. She's too kind of familiar like—and it ain't like a real county lady neither. But it's Betty as sees her most. And awful good they are, I will say that for them, to every creature about the place."

"Ah, mum, they ain't the real old gentry," said Betty, with a touch of pathos. "If I was one as had come with 'em, or that—but I'm real old Dewsbury, me, and was at the Hall, coming and going, for twenty years afore their time. I ain't got nothing to say again' Miss Sara. She comed there, that's all—she wasn't born. It makes a difference when folks have been forty years and more about a place. To see them pass away as has the right," said Betty growing sentimental, "and them come in as has only a bag o' money!"

"Little enough money the old Squire had," said Mrs. Swayne, turning her head, "nor manners neither. Don't you be ungrateful, Betty Caley. You was as poor as a church-mouse all along o' your old Squires, and got as fat as fat when the new folks come and put you all comfortable. Deny it, if you can. I would worship the very ground Miss Sara sets foot on, if I was you."

"Ah, she ain't the real old gentry," said Betty, with a sigh.

Perhaps Mrs. Preston had a weakness for real old gentry too, and she had a dull life, poor woman, and was glad of a little gossip. She had heard the story before, but she asked to hear it again, hoping for a little amusement; for a woman, however bowed down to the level of her fortune, gets tired sometimes, even of such a resource as needlework. She would not sit down, for she felt that might be considered lowering herself to their level. But she stood with her hand upon the back of an old high wooden chair, and asked questions. If they were not the real old gentry, and were such upstarts, why was it that the place was called by their name, and how did they come there?

"Some say as it was a poor old creature in Masterton as give him the money," said Mrs. Swayne, "away from her own child as was gone off a-soldiering. I wouldn't say it was money that would thrive. He was called to make the will for her, or something; an old miser, that was what she was; and with that he bought the place. And the folks laughed and said it was Brownlow's. But he ain't a man to laugh at, ain't Mr. Brownlow hisself. A body may have their opinion about the young folks. Young folks ain't nothing much to build upon, as you was a-saying, Mrs. Preston, at their best; but I wouldn't be the one as would cross him hisself. He's terrible deep, and terrible close, like all them lawyers. And he has a way of talking as is dreadful deceiving. Them as tries to fight honest and open with the likes of him hasn't no chance. He ain't a hard neighbor, like, nor unkind to poor folk; but I wouldn't go again' him, not for all the world, if it was me."

"That's all you know, you women," said Mr. Swayne; "he's the easiest-minded gentleman going, is Mr. Brownlow. He's one as pays your little bits o' bills like a prince, and don't ask no bothering questions—what's this for, and what's that for, and all them niggle-naggles. He's as free with his money—What are you two women a-shaking of your heads off for, as if I was a-saying what isn't true?"

"It's true, and it ain't true," said Mrs. Swayne; "and if you ever was any way in trouble along of the young folks, Mrs. Preston, or had him to do with, I give you my warning you'll have to mind."

"I shall never have any thing to do with Mr. Brownlow," said the lodger, with a half-frightened smile. "I'm independent. He can't have any thing to say to me."

Mrs. Swayne shook her head, and so did Betty, following her lead. The landlady did not very well know why, and neither did the old woman. It was always a practicable way of holding up the beacon before the eyes of Pamela's mother. And that poor soul, who was not very courageous, grew frightened, she could not tell why.

"But there was something to-day as made me laugh," said old Betty—"not as I was in spirits for laughing—what with my back, as was like to split, and my bad knee, and them noises in my ears. But just to see how folks forget! Miss Sara she came in. She was along of your young miss, mum, and a-making a fuss over her; and she says, 'Betty,' says she, 'we ain't a-going to let you open the gate, and your rheumatics so bad; send for one of them grandchildren o' yours.' Atween oursels, I was just a-thinking o' that; for what's enough for one is enough for two, and it's allays a saving for Polly. My Polly has seven on 'em, mum, and hard work a-keeping all straight. So I up and says, 'A poor man's childer is his fortin', Miss,' says I; 'they're all on 'em a-working at summat, and I can't have 'em without paying.' And no more I oughtn't to, serving rich folks. 'What! not for their grandmother?' says she. 'If I had a nice old grandmother like you—'"

"Law!" said Mrs. Swayne, "and her own grandmother living in a poky bit of a place in Masterton, as every body knows—never brought out here for a breath of fresh air, nor none of them going a-nigh of her! To think how little folks is sensible when it's themselves as is to blame!"

"That's what it is," said the triumphant Betty. "When she said that, it was her conscience as spoke. She went as red as red, and stopped there and then. It was along of old Mrs. Fennell, poor old soul! Why ain't she a-living out here, and her own flesh and blood to make her comfortable? It was on my lips to say, Law! Miss, there's old Mrs. Fennell is older nor me."

"Fennell?" said Mrs. Preston; "I ought to know that name."

"It was her own mamma's name," said Betty, "and I've met wi' them as seen the old lady with their own eyes. Hobson, the carrier, he goes and sees her regularly with game and things; but what's game in comparison with your own flesh and blood?"

"Perhaps the mother died young," said Mrs. Preston with some anxiety—"that breaks the link, like. Fennell? I wonder what Fennells she belongs to. I once knew that name well. I wish the old lady was living here."

"You take my word, she'll never live here," said Mrs. Swayne. "She ain't grand enough. Old grandmothers is in the way when young folks sets up for lords and ladies. And it ain't that far to Masterton but you could go and see her. There's Hobson, he knows; he'd take you safe, never fear."

Mrs. Preston shrunk back a little from the suggestion. "I'm not one to pay visits," she said. "But I'll say good-night to you all, now. I hope you'll soon be better, Mr. Swayne. And, Betty, you should not be out-of-doors on such a cold night. My child will be dull, all by herself." So saying, she left them; but she did not that moment return to Pamela. She went up stairs by herself in the dark, with her heart beating quick in her ears. "Fennell!" she was saying to herself—"I ought to know that name." It was very dark on the road, and there was nothing visible from the window but the red glow from Betty's lodge, where the door stood innocently open; but notwithstanding, Mrs. Preston went and looked out, as if the scene could have thrown any enlightenment upon her thoughts. She was excited about it, unimportant though the matter seemed. What if perhaps she might be on the trace of friends—people who would be good to Pamela? There was once a Fennell—Tom Fennell—who ages ago—No doubt he was dead and gone, with every body who had belonged to her far-off early life. But standing there in the darkness, pressing her withered cheek close to the window, as if there was something to be seen outside, it went through the old woman's mind how, perhaps, if she had chosen Tom Fennell instead of the other one, things might have been different. If any life could ever have been real to the liver of it, surely her hard life, her many toils and sufferings, must have been such sure fact as to leave no room for fancy. Yet so truly, even to an unimaginative woman, was this fantastic existence such stuff as dreams are made of, that she stopped to think what the difference might have been if—She was nearly sixty, worn even beyond her years, incapable of very much thinking; and yet she took a moment to herself ere she could join her child, and permitted herself this strange indulgence. When she descended the stairs again, still in the dark, going softly, and with a certain thrill of excitement, Mrs. Preston's mind was full of dreams more unreal than those which Pamela pondered before the fire. She was forming visions of a sweet, kind, fair old lady who would be good to Pamela. Already her heart was lighter for the thought. If she should be ill or feel any signs of breaking up, what a comfort to mount into the carrier's cart and go and commend her child to such a protector! If she had conceived at once the plan of marrying Pamela to Mr. John, and making her at one sweep mistress of Brownlows, the idea would have been wisdom itself in comparison; but she did not know that, poor soul! She came down with a visionary glow about her heart, the secret of which she told to no one, and roused up Pamela, who looked half dazed and dazzled as she drew her hands from before her face and rose from the rug she had been seated on. Pamela had been dreaming, but not more than her mother. She almost looked as if she had been sleeping as she opened her dazzled eyes. There are times when one sees clearer with one's eyes closed. The child had been looking at that picture of hers so long that she felt guilty when her mother woke her up. She had a kind of shamefaced consciousness, Mr. John having been so long about, that her mother must find his presence out—not knowing that her mother was preoccupied and full of her own imaginations too. But they did not say any thing to each other about their dreams. They dropped into silence, each over her work, as people are so ready to do who have something to think of. Pamela's little field of imagination was limited, and did not carry her much beyond the encounters of to-day; but Mrs. Preston bent her head over her sewing with many an old scene coming up in her mind. She remembered the day when Tom Fennell "spoke" to her first, as vividly in all its particulars as Pamela recollected Jack Brownlow's looks as he stood at the door. How strange if it should be the same Fennells! if Pamela's new friends should be related to her old one—if this lady at Masterton should be the woman in all the world pointed out by Providence to succor her darling. Poor Mrs. Preston uttered praises to Providence unawares—she seemed to see the blessed yet crooked ways by which she had been drawn to such a discovery. Her heart accepted it as a plan long ago concerted in heaven for her help when she was most helpless, to surprise her, as it were, with the infinite thought taken for her, and tender kindness. These were the feelings that rose and swelled in her mind and went on from step to step of farther certainty. One thing was very confusing, it is true; but still when a woman is in such a state of mind, she can swallow a good many confusing particulars. It was to make out what could be the special relationship (taking it for granted that there was a relationship) between Tom Fennell and this old lady. She could not well have been his mother; perhaps his wife—his widow! This was scarcely a palatable thought, but still she swallowed it—swallowed it, and preferred to think of something else, and permitted the matter to fall back into its former uncertainty. What did it matter about particulars when Providence had been so good to her? Dying itself would be little if she could but make sure of friends for Pamela. She sang, as it were, a "Nunc dimittis" in her soul.

Thus the acquaintance began between the young people at the great house and little Pamela in Mrs. Swayne's cottage. It was not an acquaintance which was likely to arise in the ordinary course of affairs, and naturally it called forth a little comment. Probably, had the mother been living, as Mrs. Preston wished, Sara would never have formed so unequal a friendship; but it was immaterial to Mr. Brownlow, who heard his child talk of her companion, and was pleased to think she was pleased: prepossessed as he was by the pretty face at the window which so often gleamed out upon him, he himself, though he scarcely saw any more of her than that passing glimpse in the morning, was taken with a certain fondness for the lovely little girl. He no longer said she was like Sara; she was like a face he had seen somewhere, he said, and he never failed to look out for her, and after a while gave her a friendly nod as he passed. It was more difficult to find out what were Jack's sentiments. He too saw a great deal of the little stranger, but it was in, of course, an accidental way. He used to happen to be in the avenue when she was coming or going. He happened to be in the park now and then when the spring brightened, and Pamela was able to take long walks. These things of course were pure accident, and he made no particular mention of them. As for Pamela herself, she would say, "I met Mr. John," in her innocent way, but that was about all. It is true that Mrs. Swayne in the cottage and Betty at the lodge both kept very close watch on the young people's proceedings. If these two had met at the other end of the parish, Betty, notwithstanding her rheumatics, would have managed to know it. But the only one who was aware of this scrutiny was Jack. Thus the spring came on, and the days grew pleasant. It was pleasant for them all, as the buds opened and the great chestnut-blossoms began to rise in milky spires among the big half folded leaves. Even Mrs. Preston opened and smoothed out, and took to white caps and collars, and felt as if she might live till Pamela was five-and-twenty. Five-and-twenty is not a great age, but it is less helpless than seventeen, and in a last extremity there was always Mrs. Fennell in Masterton who could be appealed to. Sometimes even the two homely sentinels who watched over Pamela would relax in those lingering spring nights. Old Betty, though she was worldly-minded, was yet a motherly kind of old woman; her heart smote her when she looked in Pamela's face. "And why shouldn't he be honest and true, and marry a pretty lass if it was his fancy?" Betty would say. But as for Mrs. Swayne, she thanked Providence she had been in temptation herself, and knew what that sort meant; which was much more than any of the others did, up to this moment—Jack, probably, least of all.

CHAPTER XIII

A CRISIS

All this time affairs had been going on very quietly in the office. Mr. Brownlow came and went every day, and Jack when it suited him, and business went on as usual. As for young Powys, he had turned out an admirable clerk. Nothing could be more punctual, more painstaking than he was. Mr. Wrinkell, the head-clerk, was so pleased, that he invited him to tea and chapel on Sunday, which was an offer the stranger had not despised. And it was known that he had taken a little tiny house in the outskirts, not the Dewsbury way, but at the other side of the town—a little house with a garden, where he had been seen planting primroses, to the great amusement of the other clerks. They had tried jeers, but the jeers were not witty, and Powys's patience was found to have limits. And he was so big and strong, and looked so completely as if he meant it, that the merriment soon came to an end and he was allowed to take his own way. They said he was currying favor with old Wrinkell; they said he was trying to humbug the governor; they said he had his pleasures his own way, and kept close about them. But all these arrows did not touch the junior clerk. Mr. Brownlow watched the young man out of his private office with the most anxious mixture of feelings. Wrinkell himself, though he was of thirty years' standing in the office, and his employer and he had been youths together, did not occupy nearly so much room in Mr. Brownlow's favor as this "new fellow." He took a livelier interest even in the papers that had come through his protégé's hands. "This is Powys's work, is it?" he would say, as he looked at the fair sheets which cost other people so much trouble. Powys did his work very well for one thing, but that did not explain it. Mr. Brownlow got into a way of drawing back the curtain which covered the glass partition between his own room and the outer office. He would draw back this curtain, accidentally as it were, the least in the world, and cast his eyes now and then on the desk at which the young man sat. He thought sometimes it was a pity to keep him there, a broad-shouldered, deep-chested fellow like that, at a desk, and consulted with himself whether he could not make some partial explanation to him, and advance him some money and send him off to a farm in his native Canada. It would be better for Powys, and it would be better for Brownlows. But he had not the courage to take such a direct step. Many a thought was in his mind as he sat glancing by turns from the side of the curtain—compunctions and self-reproaches now and then, but chiefly, it must be confessed, more selfish thoughts. Business went on just the same, but yet it cannot be denied that an occasional terror seized Mr. Wrinkell's spirit that his principal's mind was "beginning to go." "And young John never was fit to hold the candle to him," Mr. Wrinkell said, in those moments of privacy when he confided his cares to the wife of his bosom. "When our Mr. Brownlow goes, the business will go, you'll see that. His opinion on that Waterworks case was not so clear as it used to be—not near so clear as it used to be; he'll sit for an hour at a time and never put pen to paper. He is but a young man yet, for his time of life, but I'm afraid he's beginning to go; and when he goes, the business will go. You'll see young John, with his fine notions, will never keep it up for a year."

"Well, Thomas, never mind," said Mrs. Wrinkell; "It's sure to last out our time."

"Ah! that's just like women," said her husband—"after me the deluge; but I can tell you I do mind." He had the same opinion of women as Mrs. Swayne had of men, and it sprung from personal superiority in both cases, which is stronger than theory. But still he did let himself be comforted by the feminine suggestion. "There will be peace in my time;" this was the judgment formed by his head clerk, who knew so well of Mr. Brownlow's altered ways.

All this went on for some months after the admission of young Powys, and then all at once there was a change. The change made itself apparent in the Canadian, to begin with. At first it was only like a shadow creeping over the young man; then by degrees the difference grew more and more marked. He ceased to be held up as a model by the sorrowing Wrinkell; he ceased to be an example of the punctual and accurate. His eyes began to be red and bloodshot in the mornings; he looked weary, heavy, languid—sick of work, and sick of every thing. Evidently he had taken to bad ways. So all his companions in the office concluded, not without satisfaction. Mr. Wrinkell made up his mind to it sorrowing. "I've seen many go, but I thought the root of the matter was in him," he said to his domestic counselor. "Well, Thomas, we did our best for him," that sympathetic woman replied. It was not every body that Mr. Wrinkell would have asked to chapel and tea. And this was how his kindness was to be rewarded. As for Mr. Brownlow, when he awoke to a sense of the change, it had a very strange effect upon him. He had a distinct impression of pain, for he liked the lad, about whom he knew so much more than any body else knew. And in the midst of his pain there came a guilty throb of satisfaction, which woke him thoroughly up, and made him ask himself sternly what this all meant. Was he glad to see the young man go wrong because he stood in his own miserable selfish way? This was what a few months of such a secret had brought him to. It was now April, and in November the year would be out, and all the danger over. Once more, and always with a deeper impatience, he longed for this moment. It seemed to him, notwithstanding his matured and steady intellect, that if that day had but come, if that hour were but attained, his natural freedom would come back to him. If he had been consulted about his own case, he would have seen through this vain supposition; but it was his own case, and he did not see through it. Meanwhile, in the interval, what was he to do? He drew his curtain aside, and sat and watched the changed looks of this unfortunate boy. He had begun so innocently and well, was he to be allowed to end badly, like so many? Had not he himself, in receiving the lad, and trading as it were on his ignorance, taken on himself something of the responsibility? He sat thinking of this when he ought to have been thinking of other people's business. There was not one of all his clients whose affairs were so complicated and engrossing as his own. He was more perplexed and beaten about in his own mind than any of the people who came to ask him for his advice. Oh, the sounding nothings they would bring before him; he who was engaged in personal conflict with the very first principles of honor and rectitude. Was he to let the lad perish? was he to interfere? What was he to do?

At the very height of his perplexity, one of those April days, Mr. Brownlow was very late at the office. Not exactly on account of the confusion of mind he was in, and yet because the intrusion of this personal subject had retarded him in his business. He was there after all the clerks were gone—even Mr. Wrinkell. He had watched young Powys go away from that very window where he had once watched Bessie Fennell passing in her thin cloak. The young man went off by himself, taking the contrary road, as Mr. Brownlow knew, from that which led to his home. He looked ill—he looked unhappy; and his employer watched him with a sickening at his heart. Was it his fault? and could he mend it or stop the evil, even were he to make up his mind to try? After that he had more than an hour's work, and sent off the dogcart to wait for him at the Green Man in the market-place. It was very quiet in the office when all his people were gone. As he sat working, there came over him memories of other times when he had worked like this, when his mother would come stealing down to him from the rooms above; when Bessie would come with her work to sit by him as he finished his. Strange to think that neither Bessie nor his mother were up stairs now; strange to believe, when you came to think of it, that there was nobody there—that the house was vacant and his home elsewhere, and all his own generation, his own contemporaries, cut off from his side. These ideas floated through his mind as he worked, but they did not impair the soundness of the work, as some other thoughts did. His mind was not beginning to go, though Mr. Wrinkell thought so. It was even a wonder to himself how quickly, how clearly he got through it; how fit he was for work yet, though the world was so changed. He had finished while it was still good daylight, and put away his papers and buttoned his coat, and set out in an easy way. There was nothing particular to hurry him. There was Jack's mare, which flew rather than trotted, to take him home. Thus thinking, he went out, drawing on his gloves. Opposite him, as he opened the door, the sky was glowing in the west after the sunset, and he could see a woman's figure against it passing slowly, as if waiting for some one. Before he could shut the door, it became evident that it was for himself that she was waiting. Somehow he divined who she was before she said a word. A comely, elderly, motherly woman, dressed like a farmer's or a shopkeeper's wife, in the days when people dressed like their condition. She had a large figured shawl on, and a bonnet with black ribbons. And he knew she was Powys's mother—the woman on earth he most dreaded, come to speak to him about her son.

"Mr. Brownlow," she said, coming up to him with a nervous movement of her hands, "I've been waiting about this hour not to be troublesome. Oh! could you let me speak to you ten minutes? I won't keep you. Oh, please, if I might speak to you five minutes now."

"Surely," he said; he was not quite sure if it was audible, but he said it with his lips. And he went in and held the door open for her. Then, though he never could tell why, he took her up stairs—not to the office which he had just closed, but up to the long silent drawing-room which he had not entered for years. There came upon his mind an impression that Bessie was surely about somewhere, to come and stand by him, if he could only call her. But in the first place he had to do with his guest. He gave her a chair and made her sit down, and stood before her. "Tell me how I can serve you," he said. It seemed to him like a dream, and he could not understand it. Would she tell her fatal name and make her claim, and end it all at once? That was folly. But still it seemed somehow natural to think that this was why she had come. The woman he had hunted for far and wide—whom he had then neglected and thought no more of—whom lately he had woke up to such horror and fear of, his greatest danger, his worst enemy—was it she who was sitting so humbly before him now?

"I have no right to trouble you, Mr. Brownlow," she said; "it's because you were so kind to my boy. Many a time I wanted to come and thank you; and now—oh, it's a different thing now!"

"Your son is young Powys," said Mr. Brownlow—"yes; I knew by—by the face. He has gone home some time ago. I wonder you did not meet him in the street."

"Gone away from the office—not gone home," said Mrs. Powys. "Oh, Mr. Brownlow, I want to speak to you about him. He is as good as gold. He never had another thought in his mind but his sisters and me. He'd come and spend all his time with us when other young men were going about their pleasure. There never was such a son as he was, nor a brother. And oh, Mr. Brownlow, now it's come to this! I feel as if it would break my heart."

"What has it come to?" said Mr. Brownlow. He drew forward a chair and sat down facing her, and the noise he made in doing so seemed to wake thunders in the empty house. He had got over his agitation by this time, and was as calm as he always was. And his profession came to his help and opened his eyes and ears to every thing that might be of use to him, notwithstanding the effect the house had upon him in its stillness, and this meeting which he had so much reason to fear.

"Oh, sir, it's come to grief and trouble," said the poor woman. "Something has come between my boy and me. We are parted as far as if the Atlantic was between us. I don't know what is in his heart. Oh, sir, it's for your influence I've come. He'll do any thing for you. It's hard to ask a stranger to help me with my own son, and him so good and so kind; but if it goes on like this, it will break my heart."

"I feared there was something wrong," said Mr. Brownlow; "I feared it, though I never thought it could have gone so far. I'll do what I can, but I fear it is little I can do. If he has taken to bad ways—"

But here the stranger gave a cry of denial which rung through the room. "Bad ways! my boy!" said the mother. "Mr. Brownlow, you know a great deal more than I do, but you don't know my son. He taken to bad ways! I would sooner believe I was wicked myself. I am wicked, to come and complain of him to them that don't know."

"Then what in the name of goodness is it?" said the lawyer, startled out of his seriousness. He began to lose the tragic sense of a dangerous presence. It might be the woman he feared; but it was a homely, incoherent, inconsequent personage all the same.

Mrs. Powys drew herself up solemnly. She too was less respectful of the man who did not understand. "What it is, sir," she said slowly, and with a certain pomp, "is, that my boy has something on his mind."

Something on his mind! John Brownlow sunk again into a strange fever of suspense and curiosity and unreasonable panic. Could it be so? Could the youth have found out something, and be sifting it to get at the truth? The room seemed to take life and become a conscious spectator, looking at him, to see how he would act in this emergency. But yet he persevered in the course he had decided on, not giving in to his own feelings. "What can he have on his mind?" he asked. His pretended ignorance sounded in his own ears like a lie; but nevertheless he went on all the same.

"That's what I don't know, sir," said Mrs. Powys, putting her handkerchief to her eyes. "He's been rummaging among my papers, and he's may be found something, or he's heard some talk that has put things in his head. I know he has heard things in this very house—people talking about families, and wills, and all that. His father was of a very good family, Mr. Brownlow. I don't know them, but I know they're rich people. May be it's that, or perhaps—but I don't know how to account for it. It's something that is eating into his heart. And he has such a confidence in you! It was you that took him up when we were strangers, and had nobody to look to us. I have a little that my poor husband left me; but it's very little to keep four upon; and I may say it's you that gave us bread, for that matter. There's nothing in this world my boy wouldn't do for you."

Then there was a pause. The poor woman had exhausted her words and her self-command and her breath, and stopped perforce, and Mr. Brownlow did not know how to reply. What could he say to her? It was a matter of death and life between him and her boy, instead of the indifferent question she thought. "Would you like me to speak to him?" he said at last, with a little difficulty of utterance; "should I ask him what is occupying his mind? But he might not choose to tell me. What would you wish me to do?"

"Oh, sir, you're very good," said Mrs. Powys, melting into gratitude. "I never can thank God enough that my poor boy has met with such a kind friend."

"Hush!" said Mr. Brownlow, rising from his chair. He could not bear this; thanking God, as if God did not know well enough, too well, how the real state of the matter was! He was not a man used to deception, or who could adapt himself to it readily. He had all the habits of an honest life against him, and that impulse to speak truth and do right which he struggled with as if it were a temptation. Thus his position was awfully the reverse of that of a man tempting and falling. He was doing wrong with all the force of his will, and striving against his own inclination and instinct of uprightness; but here was one thing beyond his strength. To bring God in, and render him, as it were, a party, was more than he could bear. "I am not so kind as you think," he said hoarsely. "I am not—I mean your son deserves all that I can do."

"Oh, sir, that's kind—that's kindness itself to say so," cried the poor mother. "Nothing that could be said is so kind as that—and me, that was beginning to lose faith in him! It was to ask you to speak to him, Mr. Brownlow. If you were to ask him, he might open his heart to you. A gentleman is different from a poor woman. Not that any body could feel for him like me, but he would think such a deal of your advice. If you would speak and get him to open his heart. That's what I wanted to ask you, if it's not too much. If you would be so kind—and God knows, if ever it was in my power or my children's, though I'm but a poor creature, to do any thing in this world that would be a service to you—"

God again. What did the woman mean? And she was a widow, one of those that God was said to take special charge of. It was bad enough before without that. John Brownlow had gone to the fireless hearth, and was standing by it leaning his head against the high carved wooden mantel-piece, and looking down upon the cold vacancy where for so many years the fire that warmed his inmost life had blazed and sparkled. He stood thus and listened, and within him the void seemed as cold, and the emptiness as profound. It was his moment of fate. He was going to cast himself off from the life he had lived at that hearth—to make a separation forever and ever between the John Brownlow, honest and generous, who had been trained to manhood within these walls, and had loved and married, and brought his bride to this fireside—and the country gentleman who, in all his great house, would never more find the easy heart and clear conscience which were natural to this atmosphere. He stood there and looked down on the old domestic centre, and asked himself if it was worth the terrible sacrifice; honor and honesty and truth—and all to keep Brownlows for Sara, to preserve the grays, and the flowers, and the park, and Jack's wonderful mare, and all the superfluities that these young creatures treated so lightly? Was it worth the price? This was the wide fundamental question he was asking himself, while his visitor, in her chair between him and the window, spoke of her gratitude. But there was no trace in his face, even if she could have seen it, that he had descended into the very depths, and was debating with himself a matter of life and death. When her voice ceased, Mr. Brownlow's self-debate ceased too, coming to a sharp and sudden end, as if it was only under cover of her words that it could pass unnoted. Then he came toward her slowly, and took the chair opposite to her, and met her eye. The color had gone out of his face, but he was too self-possessed and experienced a man to show what the struggle was through which he had just come. And the poor woman thought it so natural that he should be full of thought. Was he not considering, in his wonderful kindness, what he could do for her boy?

"I will do what you ask me," he said. "It may be difficult, but I will try. Don't thank me, for you don't know whether I shall succeed. I will do—what I can. I will speak to your son, perhaps to-morrow—the earliest opportunity I have. You were quite right to come. And—you may—trust him—to me," said Mr. Brownlow. He did not mean to say these last words. What was it that drew them—dragged them from his lips? "You may trust him to me." He even repeated it twice, wondering at himself all the while, and not knowing what he meant. As for poor Mrs. Powys, she was overwhelmed by her gratitude.

"Oh, sir, with all my heart," she cried, "him, and all my hopes in this world!" And then she bade God bless him, who was so good to her and her boy. Yes, that was the worst of it. John Brownlow felt that but too clearly all through. It was hard enough to struggle with himself, with his own conscience and instincts; but behind all that there was another struggle which would be harder still—the struggle with God, to whom this woman would appeal, and who, he was but too clearly aware, knew all about it. But sufficient unto the moment was its own conflict. He took his hat after that, and took his visitor down stairs, and answered the amazed looks of the housekeeper, who came to see what this unusual disturbance meant, with a few words of explanation, and shook hands with Mrs. Powys at the door. The sunset glow had only just gone, so short a time had this conversation really occupied, though it involved so much, and the first magical tone of twilight had fallen into the evening air. When Mr. Brownlow left the office door he went straight on, and did not remember the carriage that was waiting for him. He was so much absorbed by his own affairs, and had so many things to think of, that even the strength of habit failed him. Without knowing, he set out walking upon the well-known way. Probably the mere fact of movement was a solace to him. He went along steadily by the budding hedgerows and the little gardens and the cottage doors, and did not know it. What he was really doing was holding conversations with young Powys, conversations with his children, all mingled and penetrated with one long never-ending conflict with himself. He had been passive hitherto, now he would have to be active. He had contented himself simply with keeping back the knowledge which, after all, it was not his business to give. Now, if he was to gain his object, he must do positively what he had hitherto done negatively. He must mislead—he must contradict—he must lie. The young man's knowledge of his rights, if they were his rights, must be very imperfect. To confuse him, to deceive him, to destroy all possible evidence, to use every device to lose his time and blind his eyes, was what Mr. Brownlow had now to do.

And there can be no doubt that, but for the intervention of personal feelings, it would have been an easy thing enough to do. If there had been no right and wrong involved, no personal advantage or loss, how very simple a matter to make this youth, who had such perfect confidence in him, believe as he pleased; and how easy after to make much of young Powys, to advance him, to provide for him—to do a great deal better for him, in short, than he could do for himself with old Mrs. Thomson's fifty thousand pounds! If there was no right and wrong involved! Mr. Brownlow walked on and on as he thought, and never once observed the length of the way. One thing in the world he could not do—that was, to take away all the sweet indulgences with which he had surrounded her, the delights, the luxuries, the position, from his child. He could not reduce Sara to be Brownlow the solicitor's daughter in the dark old-fashioned house at Masterton. He went over all her pretty ways to himself as he went on. He saw her gliding about the great house which seemed her natural sphere. He saw her receiving his guests, people who would not have known her, or would at least have patronized her from a very lofty distance, had she been in that house at Masterton; he saw her rolling forth in her pretty carriage with the grays, which were the envy of the county. All these matters were things for which, in his own person, John Brownlow cared not a straw. He did not care even to secure them for his son, who was a man and had his profession, and was no better than himself; but Sara—and then the superb little princess she was to the rest of the world! the devoted little daughter she was to him! Words of hers came somehow dropping into his ears as the twilight breathed around him. How she had once said—Good heavens! what was that she had said?

All at once Mr. Brownlow awoke. He found himself walking on the Dewsbury road, instead of driving, as he ought to have been. He remembered that the dog-cart was waiting for him in the market-place. He became aware that he had forgotten himself, forgotten every thing, in the stress and urgency of his thoughts. What was the galvanic touch that brought him back to consciousness? The recollection of half a dozen words once spoken by his child—girlish words, perhaps forgotten as soon as uttered; yet when he stopped, and turned round to see how far he had come, though he had been walking very moderately and the evening was not warm, a sudden rush of color, like a girl's blush, had come to his face. If the mare had been in sight, in her wildest mood, it would have been a relief to him to seize the reins, and fight it out with her, and fly on, at any risk, away from that spot, away from that thought, away from the suggestion so humbling, so saving, so merciful and cruel, which had suddenly entered his mind. But the mare was making every body very uncomfortable in the market-place at Masterton, and could not aid her master to escape from himself. Then he turned again, and went on. It was a seven miles walk, and he had come three parts of the way; but even the distance that remained was long to a man who had suddenly fallen into company with a new idea which he would rather not entertain. He felt the jar in all his limbs from this sudden electric shock. Sara had said it, it was true—she had meant it. He had her young life in his hands, and he could save Brownlows to her, and yet save his soul. Which was the most to be thought of, his soul or her happiness? that was the question. Such was the sudden tumult that ran through John Brownlow's veins. He seemed to be left there alone in the country quiet, in the soft twilight, under the dropping dew, to consider it, shut out from all counsel or succor of God or man. Man he himself shut out, locking his secret in his own breast—God! whom he knew his last struggle was to be with, whom that woman had insisted on bringing in, a party to the whole matter—was not He standing aside, in a terrible stillness, a spectator, waiting to see what would come of it, refusing all participation? Would God any more than man approve of this way of saving John Brownlow's soul? But the more he tried to escape from it the more it came back. She had said it, and she had meant it, with a certain sweet scorn of life's darker chances, and faith unbounded in her father, of all men, who was God's deputy to the child. Mr. Brownlow quickened his pace, walked faster and faster, till his heart thumped against his breast, and his breath came in gasps; but he could not go so fast as his thoughts, which were always in advance of him. Thus he came to the gate of Brownlows before he knew. It was the prettiest evening scene. Twilight had settled down to the softest night; big stars, lambent and dilating, were coming softly out, as if to look at something out of the sweet blue. And it was no more dark than it was light. Old Betty, on her step, was sitting crooning, with many quavers, one of her old songs. And Pamela, who had just watered her flowers, leaned over the gate, smiling, and listening with eyes that were very like the stars. Somehow this picture went to Mr. Brownlow's heart. He went up to the child as he passed, and laid a kind hand upon her pretty head, on the soft rings of her dark hair. "Good-night, little one," he said, quite softly, with that half shame which a man feels when he betrays that he has a heart in him. He had never taken so much notice of her before. It was partly because any thing associated with Sara touched him to the quick at this moment; partly for her own sake, and for the sake of the dews and stars; and partly that his mind was overstrained and tottering. "Poor little thing," he said to himself, as he went up the avenue, "she is nobody, and she is happy." With this passing thought, Mr. Brownlow fell once more into the hands of his demon, and, thus agitated and struggling, reached his home.

CHAPTER XIV

Next morning Mr. Brownlow was not well enough to go to business. He was not ill. He repeated the assurance a score of times to himself and to his children. He had not slept well, that was all—and perhaps a day's rest, a little quiet and tranquillity, would do him good. He had got up at his usual hour, and was down to breakfast, and read his paper, and every thing went on in its ordinary way; but yet he was indisposed—and a day's rest would do him good. Young John assented heartily, and was very willing to take his father's place for the day and manage all his business. It was a bright morning, and the room was full of flowers and the young leaves fluttered at the windows in the earliest green of spring. It was exhilarating to stand in the great recesses of the windows and look out upon the park, all green and budding, and think it was all yours and your children's—a sort of feeling which had little effect upon the young people, but was sweet yet overwhelming to their father as he stood and looked out in the quiet of the morning. All his—all theirs; yet perhaps—

"I don't think I shall go down to-day," he said. "You can tell Wrinkell to send me up the papers in the Wardell case. He knows what I want. He can send the—the new clerk up with them—Powys I mean."

"Powys?" said Jack.

"Well, yes, Powys. Is there any reason why he should not send Powys?" said Mr. Brownlow peremptorily, feeling hot and conscious, and ready to take offense.

"No, certainly," said Jack, with some surprise. He did not take to Powys, that was unquestionable; yet the chances are he would never have remarked upon Mr. Brownlow's choice of him but for the curious impatience and peremptoriness in his father's tone.

"I like him," said Mr. Brownlow—"he knows what he has to do and—he does it. I like a man who does that—it gives one confidence for the time to come."

"Yes," said Jack. "I never cared for him, sir, as you know. He is not my ideal of a clerk—but that is nothing; only I rather think Wrinkell has changed his opinion lately. The young fellow gets on well enough—but there is a difference. I suppose that sort of extra punctuality and virtue can only last a certain time."

"I dare say these are very fine notions, Jack," said his father; "but I am not quite such an accomplished man of the world, I suppose, as if I had been brought up at Eton. I believe in virtue lasting a long time. You must bear with my old-fashioned prejudices." This Mr. Brownlow said in a way which puzzled Jack, for he was not a man given to sneers.

"Of course, if you take it like that, sir, I have not another word to say," said the young man, and he went away feeling bitterly hostile to Powys, who seemed to be the cause of it all. He said to himself that to be snubbed on account of a clerk was a new experience, and lost himself in conjectures as to the cause of this unexplained partiality—"a fellow who is going to the bad and all," Jack said to himself; and his feeling was somewhat vindictive, and he did not feel so sorry as he ought to have done that Powys was going to the bad. It seemed on the whole a kind of retribution. Mr. Wrinkell himself had been sent for to Brownlows on various occasions, but it was not an honor that had been accorded to any of the clerks; and now this young fellow, whose appearance and conduct had both begun to be doubtful, was to have the privilege. Jack did not comprehend it; uneasy unexpressed suspicions came into his mind, all utterly wide of the mark, yet not the less uncomfortable. The mare was a comfort to him as she went off in one of her long dashes, without ever taking breath, like an arrow down the avenue; and so was the momentary glimpse of a little face at the window, to which he took off his hat; but notwithstanding these consolations, he was irritated and somewhat disturbed. On account of a cad! He had no right to give such a title to his father's favorite; but still it must be allowed that it was a little hard.

"Who is Powys?" said Sara, when her brother was gone. "And why are you angry, papa? You are cross, you know, and that is not like you. I am afraid you must be ill."

"Cross, am I?" said Mr. Brownlow. "I suppose I am not quite well—I told you I had a bad night."

"Yes—but what has Powys to do with it? and who is he?" said Sara looking into his face.

Then various possibilities rushed into her father's mind; should he tell her what he was going to ask of her? Should he claim her promise and hold her to her word? Should he make an attempt, the only one possible, to secure for himself a confidante and counselor? Ah, no! that was out of the question. He might sully his own honor, but never, never his child's. And he felt, even with a certain exultation, that his child would not have yielded to the temptation—that she would balk him instead of obeying him, did she know why. He felt this in his inmost mind, and he was glad. She would do what he asked her, trusting in him, and in her it would be a virtue—only his should be the sin.

"Who is he?" he said, with a doubtful smile which resulted from his own thoughts, and not from her question. "You will know who he is before long. I want to be civil to him, Sara. He is not just like any other clerk. I would bring him, if you would not be shocked—to lunch—"

"Shocked!" said Sara, with one of her princess airs—"I am not a great lady. You are Mr. Brownlow the solicitor, papa—I hope I know my proper place."

"Yes," said John Brownlow; but the words brought an uneasy color to his face, and confounded him in the midst of his projects. To keep her from being merely Mr. Brownlow the solicitor's daughter, he was going to soil his own honor and risk her happiness; and yet it was thus that she asserted her condition whenever she had a chance. He left her as soon as he could, taking no such advantage of his unusual holiday as Sara supposed he would. He left the breakfast-room which was so bright, and wandered away into the library, a room which, busy man as he was, he occupied very seldom. It was of all the rooms in Brownlows the one which had most appearance of having been made by a new proprietor. There were books in it, to be sure, which had belonged to the Brownlows, the solicitors, for generations, but these were not half or quarter part enough to fill the room, which was larger than any two rooms in the High Street—and consequently it had been necessary to fill the vacant space with ranges upon ranges of literature out of the bookseller's, which had not mellowed on the shelves, nor come to belong to them by nature. Mr. Brownlow did not think of this, but yet he was somehow conscious of it when, with the prospect of a long unoccupied day before him, he went into this room. It was on the other side of the house, turned away from the sunshine, and looking out upon nothing but evergreens, sombre corners of shrubberies, and the paths which led to the kitchen and stables. He went in and sat down by the table, and looked round at all the shelves, and drew a blotting-book toward him mechanically. What did he want with it? he had no letters to write there—nothing to do that belonged to that luxurious leisurely place. If there was work to be done, it was at the office that he ought to do it. He had not the habit of writing here—nor even of reading. The handsome library had nothing to do with his life. This, perhaps, was why he established himself in it on the special day of which we speak. It seemed to him as if any moment his fine house might topple down about his ears like a house of cards. He had thought over it in the High Street till he was sick and his head swam; perhaps some new light might fall on the subject if he were to think of it here. This was why he established himself at the table, making in his leisure a pretense to himself of having something to do. If he had been used to any sort of guile or dishonorable dealing, the chances are it would have been easier for him; but it is hard upon a man to change the habits of his life. John Brownlow had to maintain with himself a fight harder than that which a man ordinarily has to fight against temptation; for the fact was that this was far, very far from being his case. He was not tempted to do wrong. It was the good impulse which in his mind had come to be the thing to be struggled against. What he wanted was to do what was right; but with all the steadiness of a virtuous resolution he had set himself to struggle against his impulse and to do wrong.

Here was the state of the case: He had found, as he undoubtedly believed, the woman whom more than twenty years ago he had given himself so much trouble to find. She was here, a poor woman—to whom old Mrs. Thomson's fifty thousand pounds would be equal to as many millions—with a son, whose every prospect would be changed, whose life would begin on a totally different level, if his legitimate inheritance came to him as it ought: this was all very distinct and clear. But, on the other hand, to withdraw that fifty thousand pounds from his own affairs at this moment, would be next to ruin to John Brownlow. It would be a loss to him of almost as much more. It would reduce him again hopelessly to the character of the country solicitor—a character which he had not abandoned, which he had, in short, rather prided himself in keeping up, but which was very different, in conjunction with his present standing in the county, from what it would be were he Brownlow the solicitor alone. And then there was the awful question of interest, which ought to have been accumulating all these five-and-twenty years. He thought to himself as he reflected, that his best course would have been to reject young Powys's application and throw him off, and leave him to find occupation where he could. Then, if the young man had discovered any thing, it would at least have been a fair fight. But he had of his own will entered into relations with him; he had him under his eyes day by day, a standing temptation, a standing reproach; he had kept him close by him to make discoveries that otherwise he probably never would have made; and he had made discoveries. At any moment the demand might come which should change the character of the position altogether. All this was old ground over which he had gone time after time. There was nothing new in it but the sudden remedy which had occurred to him on the previous night as he walked home. He had not as yet confessed to himself that he had accepted that suggestion, and yet only half voluntarily he had taken the first steps to bring it about. It was a remedy almost as bad as the original danger—very unpalatable, very mortifying—but it was better than utter downfall. By moments Mr. Brownlow's heart revolted altogether against it. It was selling his child, even though it was for her own sake—it was taking advantage of her best instincts, of her rash girlish readiness to put her future in his hands. And there were also other questions involved. When it came to the point, would Sara hold by her promise—had she meant it, in earnest, as a real promise when she made it? And then she was a girl who would do any thing, every thing for her father's sake, in the way of self-sacrifice, but would she understand sacrificing herself to save, not her father, but Brownlows? All these were very doubtful questions. Mr. Brownlow, who had never before been in any body's power, who knew nothing about mysteries, found himself now, as it were, in every body's power, threading a darkling way, from which his own efforts could never deliver him. He was in the power of young Powys, who any day could come to his door and demand—how much? any sum almost—his whole fortune—with no alternative but that of a lawsuit, which would take his good name as well. He was in the power of his son, who, if he heard of it, might simplify matters very summarily, and the chances were would do so; and he was in the power of Sara, who could save him if she would—save him not only from the consequences but from the sin—save his conscience and his credit, and her own position. Why should not she do it? Young Powys was poor, and perhaps not highly educated; but he was pleasanter to look at, more worth talking to, than Sir Charles Motherwell. If he gave his daughter to this youth, John Brownlow felt that he would do more than merely make him amends for having taken his inheritance. It would be restoring the inheritance to him, and giving him over and above it something that was worth more than compound interest. When he had come to this point, however, a revulsion occurred in his thoughts. How could he think of marrying his child, his Sara, she of whom he had made a kind of princess, who might marry any body, as people say—how could he give her to a nameless young man in his office? What would the world say? What inquiries, what suspicions would arise, if he gave up his house and all its advantages to a young fellow without a penny? And then Sara herself, so delicate in all her tastes, so daintily brought up, so difficult to please! If she were so little fastidious at the end, what would be thought of it? She had refused Sir Charles Motherwell, if not actually yet tacitly—and Sir Charles had many advantages, and was very nearly the greatest man in the county—refused him and was going to take her father's uncultivated clerk. Would she, could she do it? was it a thing he ought to ask of her? or was it not better that he should take it upon his conscience boldly to deceive and wrong the stranger than to put such a burden on the delicate shoulders of his child?

Thus he passed the morning, driven about from one idea to another and feeling little comfort in any, longing for Powys's arrival, that he might read in his eyes how much he knew, and yet fearing it, lest he might know too much. If any of his clients had come to him in such a state of mind, John Brownlow would have looked upon that man with a certain pity mingled with contempt, and while advising him to his best, would have said to himself, How weak all this shilly-shally is! one way or other let something be decided. But it is a very different matter deciding on one's own affairs and on the affairs of other people. Even at that moment, notwithstanding his own agitation and mental distress, had he been suddenly called upon for counsel, he could have given it clearly and fully—the thing was, that he could not advise himself.

And to aggravate matters, while he sat thus thinking it all over and waiting for Powys, and working himself up almost to the point of preparing for a personal contest with him, the Rector chanced to call, and was brought triumphantly into the library. "Papa is so seldom at home," Sara had said, with a certain exultation; "come and see him." And Mr. Hardcastle was exultant too. "How lucky that I should have come to-day of all others," he said. "One never sees you by day-light."

"Well, yes," said Mr. Brownlow, who was cross and out of temper in spite of himself; "I am visible by day-light to every body on the road between this and Masterton. I don't think I shut myself up."

"That's exactly what I mean," said the Rector; "but you have been overdoing it, Brownlow. You're ill. I always told you you ought to give yourself more leisure. A man at your time of life is not like a young fellow. We can't do it, my dear sir—we can't do it. I am up to as much as most men of my age; but it won't do morning and night—I have found that out."

"It suits me very well," said Mr. Brownlow. "I am not ill, thank you. I had a restless night—rather—"

"Ah, that's just it," said Mr. Hardcastle. "The brain is fatigued—that is what it is. And you ought to take warning. It is the beginning of so many things. For instance, last year when my head was so bad—"

"Don't speak of it," said Mr. Brownlow. "My head is not bad; I am all right. I have a—a clerk coming with some papers; that is what I am waiting for. Is Fanny with you to-day?"

"No," said Mr. Hardcastle. "They have begun to have her up at Ridley more than I care to see her. And there is that young Keppel, you know. Not that he means any thing, I suppose. Indeed, I thought he was devoted to Sara a short time ago. Ah, my dear Brownlow, it is a difficult matter for us, left as we both are with young girls who have never known maternal care—"

It was not a moment when Mr. Brownlow could enter upon such a subject. But he instinctively changed his expression, and looked solemn and serious, as the occasion demanded. Poor Bessie!—he had probably been a truer lover to her than the Rector had been to the two Mrs. Hardcastles, though she had not been in his mind just then; but he felt bound to put on the necessary melancholy look.

"Yes," he said; "no doubt it is difficult. My clerk is very late. He ought to have been here at twelve. I have a good many pressing matters of business just now—"

"I see, I see; you have no time for private considerations," said the Rector. "Don't overdo it, don't overdo it,—that is all I have got to say. Remember what a condition I was in only two years since—took no pleasure in any thing. Man delighted me not, nor woman either—not even my little Fanny. If ever there was a miserable state on earth, it is that. I see a fine tall young fellow straying about there among the shrubberies. Is that your clerk?"

Mr. Brownlow got up hastily and came to the window, and there beyond all question was Powys, who had lost his way, and had got involved in the maze of paths which divided the evergreens. It was a curious way for him to approach the house, and he was not the man to seek a back entrance, however humble his circumstances had been. But anyhow it was he, and he had got confused, and stood under one of the great laurels, looking at the way to the stables, and the way to the kitchen, feeling that neither way was his way, and not knowing where to turn. Mr. Brownlow opened the window and called to him. Many a day after he thought of it, with that vague wonder which such symbolical circumstances naturally excite. It did not seem important enough to be part of the symbolism of Providence at the moment. Yet it was strange to remember that it was thus the young man was brought into the house. Mr. Brownlow set the window open, and watched him as he came forward, undeniably a fine tall young fellow, as Mr. Hardcastle said. Somehow a kind of pride in his good looks, such as a father might have felt, came into John Brownlow's mind. Sir Charles, with his black respirator, was not to be named in the same day with young Powys, so far as appearance went. He was looking as he did when he first came to the office, fresh, and frank, and open-hearted. Those appearances which had so troubled the mind of Mr. Wrinkell and alarmed Mr. Brownlow himself, were not visible in his open countenance. He came forward with his firm and rapid step, not the step of a dweller in streets. And Mr. Hardcastle, who had a slight infusion of muscular Christianity in his creed, could not refrain from admiration.

"That is not much like what one looks for in a lawyer's clerk," said the Rector. "What a chest that young fellow has got! Who is he, Brownlow?—not a Masterton man, I should think."

"He is a Canadian," said Mr. Brownlow, "not very long in the office, but very promising. He has brought me some papers that I must attend to—"

"Yes, yes, I understand," said Mr. Hardcastle—"always business; but I shall stay to luncheon as you are at home. I suppose you mean to allow yourself some lunch?"

"Surely," said Mr. Brownlow; but it was impossible to reply otherwise than coldly. He had wanted no spy upon his actions, nobody to speculate on what he meant in the strange step he was about to take. He could not send his neighbor away; but at the same time he could not be cordial to him as if he desired his company. And then he turned to speak to his clerk, leaving the Rector, who went away in a puzzled state of mind, wondering whether Mr. Brownlow meant to be rude to him. As for young Powys, he came in by the window, taking off his hat, and looking at his employer with an honest mixture of amusement and embarrassment. "I beg your pardon, sir," he said; "I had lost my way; I don't know where I was going—"

"You were going to the stables," said Mr. Brownlow, "where I dare say you would have found something much more amusing than with me. Come in. You are later than I expected. How is it you did not come up in the dogcart? My son should have thought of that."

"He did not say any thing about it," said Powys, "but I liked the walk. Mr. Wrinkell told me to bring you these, sir. They are the papers in the Wardell case; and he gave me some explanations which I was to repeat to you—some new facts that have just come out—"

"Sit down," said Mr. Brownlow. He gave the young man a seat at his table, and resumed his own, and drew the papers to him. But he was not thinking of the papers or of the Wardell case. His attention was fixed upon his young companion. Perhaps it was the walk, perhaps some new discovery, perhaps because he began to see his way to the recovery of that which John Brownlow was determined not to give up, but certainly his eye was as bright and his color as fresh as when he had first come to the office innocent and unsuspecting. He sat down with none of the affectation either of humility or of equality which a Masterton youth of his position would have shown. He was not afraid of his employer, who had been kind to him, and his transatlantic ideas made him feel the difference between them, though great in the mean time, to be rather a difference of time than of class. Such at least was the unconscious feeling in his mind. It is true that he had begun to learn that more things than time, or even industry and brains, are necessary in an old and long-constituted social system, but his new and hardly purchased knowledge had not affected his instincts. He was respectful, but he did not feel himself out of place in Mr. Brownlow's library. He took his seat, and looked round him with the interest of a man free to observe or even to comment, which, considering that even Mr. Wrinkell was rather disposed at Brownlows to sit on the edge of his chair, was a pleasant variety. Mr. Brownlow drew the papers to him, and bent over them, leaning his head on both his hands; but the fact was, he was looking at Powys from under that cover, fixing his anxious gaze upon him, reading what was in the unsuspicious face—what was in it, and most likely a great deal which was not in it. When he had done this for some minutes he suddenly raised his head, removed his hands from his forehead to his chin, and looked steadily at his young companion.

"I will attend to these by-and-by," he said, abruptly; "in the mean time, my young friend, I have something to say to you."

Then Powys, whose eyes had been fixed upon a dark picture over and beyond, at some distance, Mr. Brownlow's head, came to himself suddenly, and met the look fixed upon him. The elder man thought there was a little defiance in the glance which the younger cast upon him; but this is one of the things in which one sees always what one is prepared to see. Powys, for his part, was not in the least defiant; he was a little surprised, a little curious, eager to hear and reply, but he was utterly unconscious of the sentiments which the other read in his eyes.

"I thought a little while ago," said Mr. Brownlow, in his excitement going farther than he meant to go, "that I had found in you one of the best clerks that ever I had."

Here he stopped for a moment, and Powys regarded him open-mouthed, waiting for more. His frank face clouded over a little when he saw that Mr. Brownlow made a pause. "I was going to say Thank you, sir," said the young man; "and indeed I do say Thank you; but am I to understand that you don't think so now?"

"I don't know what to think," said Mr. Brownlow. "I take more interest in you than—than I am in the habit of taking in a—in a stranger; but they tell me at the office there is a change, and I see there is a change. It has been suggested to me that you were going to the bad, which I don't believe; and it has been suggested to me that you had something on your mind—"

The young man had changed color, as indeed he could scarcely help doing; his amour propre was still as lively and as easily excited as is natural to his age. "If you are speaking of my duties in the office, sir," he said, "you have a perfect right to speak; but I don't suppose they could be influenced one way or another by the fact that I had something on my mind—"

"I am not speaking to you so much as your employer as—as your friend," said Mr. Brownlow. "You know the change has been visible. People have spoken about it to me—not perhaps the people you would imagine to have interfered. And I want to speak to you as an old man may speak to a young man—as I should wish, if the circumstances make it needful, any one would speak to my son. Why do you smile?"

"I beg your pardon, sir; but I could not but smile at the thought of Mr. John—"

"Never mind Mr. John," said Mr. Brownlow, discomfited. "He has his way, and we have ours. I don't set up my son as an example. The thing is, that I should be glad if you would take me into your confidence. If any thing is wrong I might be able to help you; and if you have something on your mind—"

"Mr. Brownlow," said young Powys, with a deep blush, "I am very sorry to seem ungrateful, but a man, if he is good for any thing, must have something he keeps to himself. If it is about my work, I will hear whatever you please to say to me, and make whatever explanations you require. I am not going to the bad; but for any thing else I think I have a right to my own mind."

"I don't deny it—I don't deny it," said Mr. Brownlow, anxiously. "Don't think I want to thrust myself into your affairs; but if either advice or help—"

"Thank you," said the young man. He smiled, and once more Mr. Brownlow, though not imaginative, put a thousand meanings into the smile. "I will be more attentive to my work," he said; "perhaps I have suffered my own thoughts to interfere with me. Thank you, sir, for your kindness. I am very glad that you have given me this warning."

"But it does not tempt you to open your heart," said Mr. Brownlow, smiling too, though not with very pleasurable feelings.

"There is nothing in my heart that is worth opening," said Powys; "nothing but my own small affairs—thank you heartily all the same."

This is how Mr. Brownlow was baffled, notwithstanding his superior age and prudence and skill. He sat silent for a time with that curious feeling of humiliation and displeasure which attends a defeat even when nobody is to be blamed for it. Then by way of saving his dignity, he drew once more toward him the Wardell papers, and studied them in silence. As for the young man, he resumed, but with a troubled mind, his examination of the dark old picture. Perhaps his refusal to open his heart arose as much from the fact that he had next to nothing to tell as from any other reason, and the moment the conversation ceased his heart misgave him. Young Powys was not one of the people possessed by a blessed certainty that the course they themselves take is the best. As soon as he had closed his mouth a revulsion of feeling came upon him. He seemed to himself hard-hearted, ungrateful, odious, and sat thinking over all Mr. Brownlow's kindness to him, and his detestable requital of that kindness, and asking himself how he could recommence the interrupted talk. What could he say to show that he was very grateful, and a devoted servant, notwithstanding that there was a corner of his heart which he could not open up? or must he continue to lie under this sense of having disappointed and refused to confide in so kind a friend? A spectator would have supposed the circumstances unchanged had he seen the lawyer seated calmly at the table looking over his papers, and his clerk at a little distance respectfully waiting his employer's pleasure; but in the breast of the young man, who was much too young to be sure of himself, there was a wonderful change. He seemed to himself to have made a friend into an enemy; to have lost his vantage ground in Mr. Brownlow's good opinion, and above all to have been ungrateful and unkind. Thus they sat in dead silence till the bell for luncheon—the great bell which amused Pamela, bringing a lively picture before her of all that was going on at the great house—began to sound into the stillness. Then Mr. Brownlow stirred, gathered his papers together, and rose from his chair. Powys sat still, not knowing what to do; and it may be imagined what his feelings were when his employer spoke.

"Come along, Powys," said Mr. Brownlow,—"you have had a long walk, and you must be hungry—come and have some lunch."

CHAPTER XV

LUNCHEON

It was like a dream to the young Canadian when he followed the master of the house into the dining-room;—not that that, or any other social privilege, would have struck the youth with astonishment or exultation as it would have done a young man from Masterton: but because he had just behaved so ungratefully and ungraciously, and had no right to any such recompense. He had heard enough in the office about Brownlows to know that it was an unprecedented honor that was being paid him; but it was the coals of fire thus heaped upon his head which he principally felt. Sara was already at the head of the table in all that perfection of dainty apparel which dazzles the eyes of people unused to it. Naturally the stranger knew nothing about any one particular of her dress, but he felt without knowing how, the difference between that costly simplicity and all the finery of the women he was accustomed to see. It was a different sphere and atmosphere altogether from any he had ever entered; and the only advantage he had over any of his fellow-clerks who might have been introduced in the same way was, that he had mastered the first grand rule of good-breeding, and had forgotten himself. He had no time to think how he ought to behave in his own person. His mind was too much occupied by the novelty of the sphere into which he was thus suddenly brought. Sara inclined her head graciously as he was brought in, and was not surprised; but as for Mr. Hardcastle, whose seat was just opposite that of young Powys, words could not express his consternation. One of the clerks! Mr. Brownlow the solicitor was not such a great man himself that he should feel justified in introducing his clerks at his table; and after that, what next? A rapid calculation passed through Mr. Hardcastle's mind as he stared at the new-comer. If this sort of thing was to go on, it would have to be looked to. If Mr. Brownlow thought it right for Sara, he certainly should not think it right for his Fanny. Jack Brownlow himself, with Brownlows perhaps, and at least a large share of his father's fortune, was not to be despised; but the clerks! The Rector even felt himself injured—though to be sure, young Powys or any other clerk could not have dreamed of paying addresses to him. And it must be admitted that the conversation was not lively at table. Mr. Brownlow was embarrassed as knowing his own intentions, which, of course, nobody else did. Mr. Hardcastle was astonished and partially affronted. And Powys kept silence. Thus there was only Sara to keep up a little appearance of animation at the table. It is at such moments that the true superiority of womankind really shows itself. She was not embarrassed—the social difference which, as she thought, existed between her and her father's clerk was so great and complete that Sara felt herself as fully at liberty to be gracious to him, as if he had been his own mother or sister. "If Mr. Powys walked all the way he must want his luncheon, papa," she said. "Don't you think it is a pretty road? Of course it is not grand like your scenery in Canada. We don't have any Niagaras in England; but it is pleasant, don't you think?"

"It is very pleasant," said young Powys; "but there are more things in Canada than Niagara."

"I suppose so," said Sara, who was rather of opinion that he ought to have been much flattered by her allusion to Canada; "and there are prettier places in England than Dewsbury—but still people who belong to it are fond of it all the same. Mr. Hardcastle, this is the dish you are so fond of—are you ill, like papa, that you don't eat to-day?"

"Not ill, my dear," said the Rector, with meaning—"only like your papa, a little out of sorts."

"I don't know why people should be out of sorts who have every thing they can possibly want," said Sara. "I think it is wicked both of papa and you. If you were poor men in the village, with not enough for your children to eat, you would know better than to be out of sorts. I am sure it would do us all a great deal of good if we were suddenly ruined," the young woman continued, looking her father, as it happened, full in the face. Of course she did not mean any thing. It came into her head all at once to say this, and she said it; but equally of course it fell with a very different significance on her father's ears. He changed color in spite of himself—he dropped on his plate a morsel he was carrying to his mouth. A sick sensation came over him. Sara did not know very much about the foundation of his fortune, but still she knew something; and she was just as likely as not to let fall some word which would throw final illumination upon the mind of the young stranger. Mr. Brownlow smiled a sickly sort of smile at her from the other end of the table.

"Don't use such strong language," he said. "Being ruined means with Sara going to live in a cottage covered with roses, and taking care of one's aged father; but, my darling, your father is not yet old enough to give in to being ruined, even should such a chance happen to us. So you must make up your mind to do without the cottage. The roses you can have, as many as you like."

"Sara means by ruin, that is to say," said the Rector, "something rather better than the best that I have been able to struggle into, and nothing to do for it. I should accept her ruin with all my heart."

"You are laughing at me," said Sara, "both of you. Fanny would know if she were here. You understand, don't you, Mr. Powys? What do I care for cottages or roses? but if one were suddenly brought face to face with the realities of life—"

"You have got that out of a book, Sara," said the Rector.

"And if I have, Mr. Hardcastle?" said Sara. "I hope some books are true. I know what I mean, whether you know it or not. And so does Mr. Powys," she added, suddenly meeting the stranger's eye.

This appeal was unlucky, for it neutralized the amusement of the two elder gentlemen, and brought them back to their starting-point. It was a mistake in every way, for Powys, though he was looking on with interest and wonder, did not understand what Sara meant. He looked at her when she spoke, and reddened, and faltered something, and then betook himself to his plate with great assiduity, to hide his perplexity. He had never known any thing but the realities of life. He had known them in their most primitive shape, and he was beginning to become acquainted with them still more bitterly in the shape they take in the midst of civilization, when poverty has to contend with more than the primitive necessities. And to think of this dainty creature, whose very air that she breathed seemed different from that of his world, desiring to be brought face to face with such realities! He had been looking at her with great reverence, but now there mingled with his reverence just that shade of conscious superiority which a man likes to feel. He was not good, sweet, delightsome, celestial, as she was, but he knew better—precious distinction between the woman and the man.

But Sara, always thinking of him as so different from herself that she could use freedom with him, was not satisfied. "You understand me?" she said, repeating her appeal.

"No," said young Powys; "at least if it is real poverty she speaks of, I don't think Miss Brownlow can know what it means." He turned to her father as he spoke with the instinct of natural good-breeding. And thereupon there occurred a curious change. The two gentlemen began to approve of the stranger. Sara, who up to this moment had been so gracious, approved of him no more.

"You are quite right," said the Rector; "what Miss Brownlow is thinking of is an imaginary poverty which exists no longer—if it ever existed. If your father had ever been a poor curate, my dear Sara, like myself, for instance—"

"Oh, if you are all going to turn against me—" said Sara, with a little shrug of her shoulders. And she turned away as much as she could do it without rudeness from the side of the table at which young Powys sat, and began in revenge to talk society. "So Fanny is at Ridley," she said; "what does she mean by always being at Ridley? The Keppels are very well, but they are not so charming as that comes to. Is there any one nice staying there just now?"

"Perhaps you and I should not agree about niceness," said the Rector. "There are several people down for Easter. There is Sir Joseph Scrape, for instance, who was Chancellor of the Exchequer once, before you were born. I am very fond of him, but you would prefer his grandson, Sara, if he happened to have a grandson."

"On the contrary, I like old gentlemen," said Sara. "I never see any thing else, for one thing. There is yourself, Mr. Hardcastle, and papa—"

"Well, I suppose I am an old gentleman," said the Rector, ruefully; "at least to babies like you. That is how things go in this world—one shifts the burden on to one's neighbor. Probably Sir Joseph is of my mind, and thinks somebody else old. And then, in revenge, we have nothing to do but to call you young creatures babies, though you have the world in your hands," Mr. Hardcastle added, with a sigh; for he was a vigorous man, and a widower, and had been already twice married, and saw no reason why he should not take that step again. And it was hard upon him to be called an old gentleman in this unabashed and open way.

"Well, they have the world before them," said Mr. Brownlow; "but I am not so sure that they have it in their hands."

"We have nothing in our hands," said Sara, indignantly—"even I, though papa is awfully good to me. I don't mean to speak slang, but he is awfully good, you know; and what does it matter? I daren't go anywhere by myself, or do any thing that every body else doesn't do. And as for Fanny, she would not so much as take a walk if she thought you did not like it."

"Fanny is a very good girl," said Mr. Hardcastle, with a certain melting in his voice.

"We are all very good girls," said Sara; "but what is the use of it? We have to do every thing we are told just the same; and have old Lady Motherwell, for example, sitting upon one, whenever she has a chance. And then you say we have the world in our hands! If you were to let us do a little as we pleased, and be happy our own way—"

"Then you have changed your mind," said Mr. Brownlow. He was smiling, but yet underneath that he was very serious, not able to refrain from giving in his mind a thousand times more weight than they deserved to his daughter's light and random words, though he knew well enough they were random and light. "I thought you were a dutiful child, who would do what I asked you, even in the most important transaction of your life—so you said once, at least."

"Any thing you asked me, papa?" cried Sara, with a sudden change of countenance. "Yes, to be sure! any thing! Not because I am dutiful, but because—you are surely all very stupid to-day—because—Don't you know what I mean?"

"Yes," said young Powys, who all this time had not spoken a word. Perhaps in her impatience her eye had fallen upon him; perhaps it was because he could not help it; but however that might be, the monosyllable sent a little electric shock round the table. As for the speaker himself, he had no sooner uttered it than he reddened like a girl up to his very hair. Sara started a little, and became suddenly silent, looking at the unexpected interpreter she had got; and as for the Rector, he stared with the air of a man who asks himself, What next?

The sudden pause thus made in the conversation by his inadvertent reply, confused the young man most of all. He felt it down to the very tips of his fingers. It went tingling through him, as if he were the centre of the electricity—as indeed he was. His first impulse, to get up and run away, of course could not be yielded to; and as luncheon was over by this time, and the servants gone, and the business of the meal over, it was harder than ever to find any shelter to retire behind. Despair at last, however, gave him a little courage. "I think, sir," he said, turning to Mr. Brownlow, "if you have no commands for me, that I had better go. Mr. Wrinkell will want to know your opinion; unless, indeed—"

"I am not well enough for work," said Mr. Brownlow, "and you may as well take a holiday as you are here. It will do you good. Go and look at the horses, and take a stroll in the park. Of course you are fond of the country. I don't think there is much to see in the house—"

"If Mr. Powys would like to see the Claude, I will take him into the drawing-room," said Sara, with all her original benignity. Powys, to tell the truth, did not very well know whether he was standing on his head, or on the other and more ordinary extremity. He was confounded by the grace showed to him. And being a backwoodsman by nature, and knowing not much more than Masterton in the civilized world, the fact is that at first, before he considered the matter, he had not an idea what a Claude was. But that made no difference; he was ready to have gone to Pandemonium if the same offer had been made to show the way. Not that he had fallen in love at first sight with the young mistress of Brownlows. He was too much dazzled, too much surprised for that; but he had understood what she meant, and the finest little delicate thread of rapport had come into existence between them. As for Sara's condescension and benignity, he liked it. Her brother would have driven him frantic with a tithe of the affability which Sara thought her duty under the circumstances; but from her it was what it ought to be. The young man did not think it was possible that such a privilege was to be accorded to him, but he looked at her gratefully, thanking her with his eyes. And Sara looked at him, and for an instant saw into those eyes, and became suddenly sensible that it was not her father's clerk, but a man, a young man, to whom she had made this obliging offer. It was not an idea that had entered her head before; he was a clerk whom Mr. Brownlow chose to bring in to luncheon. He might have been a hundred for any thing Sara cared. Now, all at once it dawned upon her that the clerk was a man, and young, and also well-looking, a discovery which filled her with a certain mixture of horror and amusement. "Well, how was I to know?" she said to herself, although, to be sure, she had been sitting at the same table with him for about an hour.

"Certainly, if Powys likes, let him see the Claude; but I should think he would prefer the horses," said Mr. Brownlow; and then Sara rose and shook out her long skirt, and made a little sign to the stranger to follow her. When the two young creatures disappeared, Mr. Hardcastle, who had been staring at them, open-mouthed, turned round aghast and pale with consternation upon his friend.

"Brownlow, are you mad?" he said; "good heavens! if it was any body but you I should think it was softening of the brain."

"It may be softening of the brain," said Mr. Brownlow, cheerfully; "I don't know what the symptoms are. What's wrong?"

"What's wrong?" said the Rector—he had to stop and pour himself out a glass of wine to collect his faculties—"why, it looks as if you meant it. Send your clerk off with your child, a young fellow like that, as if they were equals! Your clerk! I should not permit it with my Fanny, I can tell you that."

"Do you think Sara will run away with him?" said Mr. Brownlow, smiling. "I feel sure I can trust him not to do it. Why, what nonsense you are speaking! If you have no more confidence in my little friend Fanny, I have. She would be in no danger from my clerk if she were to see him every day, and show him all the pictures in the world."

"Oh, Fanny,—that is not the question," said the Rector, half suspicious of the praise, and half pleased. "It was Sara we were talking of. I don't believe she would care if a man was a chimney-sweep. You have inoculated her with your dreadful Radical ideas—"

"I? I am not a Radical," said Mr. Brownlow; and he still smiled, though he entered into no farther explanation. As for the Rector, he gulped down his wine, and subsided into his neck-cloth, as he did when he was disturbed in his mind. He had no parallel in his experience to this amazing indiscretion. Fanny?—no; to be sure Fanny was a very good girl, and knew her place better—she would not have offered to show the Claude, though it had been the finest Claude in the world, even to a curate, much less to a clerk. And then it seemed to Mr. Hardcastle that Mr. Brownlow's eyes looked very heavy, and that there were many tokens half visible about him of softening of the brain.

Meanwhile Sara went sweeping along the great wide fresh airy passages, and through the hall, and up the grand stair-case. Her dress was of silk, and rustled—not a vulgar rustle, like that which announces some women offensively wherever they go, but a soft satiny silvery ripple of sound, which harmonized her going like a low accompaniment. Young Powys had only seen her for the first time that day, and he was a reasonable young fellow, and had not a thought of love or love-making in his mind. Love! as if any thing so preposterous could ever arise between this young princess and a poor lawyer's clerk, maintaining his mother and his little sisters on sixty pounds a year. But yet, he was a young man, and she was a girl; and following after her as he did, it was not in human nature not to behold and note the fair creature, with her glistening robes and her shining hair. Now and then, when she passed through a patch of sunshine from one of the windows, she seemed to light up all over, and reflect it back again, and send forth soft rays of responsive light. Though she was so slender and slight, her step was as steady and free as his own, Canadian and backwoodsman as he was; and yet, as she moved, her pretty head swayed by times like the head of a tall lily upon the breeze, not with weakness, but with the flexile grace that belonged to her nature. Powys saw all this, and it bewitched him, though she was altogether out of his sphere. Something in the atmosphere about her went to his head. It was the most delicate intoxication that ever man felt, and yet it was intoxication in a way. He went up stairs after her, feeling like a man in a dream, not knowing what fairy palace, what new event she might be leading him to; but quite willing and ready, under her guidance, to meet any destiny that might await him. The Claude was so placed in the great drawing-room, that the actual landscape, so far as the mild greenness of the park could be called landscape, met your eye as you turned from the immortal landscape of the picture. Sara went straight up to it without a pause, and showed her companion where he was to stand. "This is the

Claude," she said, with a majestic little wave of her hand by way of introduction. And the young man stood and looked at the picture, with her dress almost touching him. If he did not know much about the Claude at the commencement, he knew still less now. But he looked into the clear depths of the picture with the most devout attention. There was a ripple of water, and a straight line of light gleaming down into it, penetrating the stream, and casting up all the crisp cool glistening wavelets against its own glow. But as for the young spectator, who was not a connoisseur, his head got confused somehow between the sun on Claude's ripples of water, and the sun as it had fallen in the hall upon Sara's hair and her dress.

"It is very lovely," he said, rather more because he thought it was the thing he ought to say than from any other cause.

"Yes," said Sara; "we are very proud of our Claude; but I should like to know why active men like papa should like those sort of pictures; he prefers landscapes to every thing else—whereas they make me impatient. I want something that lives and breathes. I like pictures of life—not that one everlasting line of light fixed down upon the canvas with no possibility of change."

"I don't know much about pictures," said Powys—"but yet—don't you think it is less natural still to see one everlasting attitude—like that, for instance, on the other wall? people don't keep doing one particular thing all their lives."

"I should like to be a policeman and tell them to move on," said Sara. "That woman there, who is giving the bread to the beggar—she has been the vexation of my life; why can't she give it and have done with it? I think I hate pictures—I don't see what we want with them. I always want to know what happened next."

"But nothing need happen at all here," said Powys, with unconscious comprehension, turning to the Claude again. He was a little out of his depth, and not used to this kind of talk, but more and more it was going to his head, and that intoxication carried him on.

"That is the worst of all," said Sara. "Why doesn't there come a storm?—what is the good of every thing always being the same? That was what I meant down stairs when you pretended you did not understand."

What was the poor young fellow to say? He was penetrated to his very heart by the sweet poison of this unprecedented flattery—for it was flattery, though Sara meant nothing more than the freemasonry of youth. She had forgotten he was a clerk, standing there before the Claude; she had even forgotten her own horror at the discovery that he was a man. He was young, like herself, willing to follow her lead, and he "understood;" which after all, though Sara was not particularly wise, is the true test of social capabilities. He did know what she meant, though in that one case he had not responded; and Sara, like every body else of quick intelligence and rapid mind, met with a great many people who stared and did not know what she meant. This was why she did the stranger the honor of a half reproach;—it brought the poor youth's intoxication to its height.

"But I don't think you understand," he said, ruefully, apologetically, pathetically, laying himself down at her feet as it were, to be trod upon if she pleased. "You don't know how hard it is to be poor; so long as it was only one's self, perhaps, or so long as it was mere hardship; but there is worse than that; you have to feel yourself mean and sordid—you have to do shabby things. You have to put yourself under galling obligations; but I ought not to speak to you like this—that is what it really is to be poor."

Sara stood and looked at him, opening her eyes wider and wider. This was not in the least like the cottage with the roses, but she had forgotten all about that; what she was thinking of now was whether he was referring to his own case—whether his life was like that—whether her father could not do something for him; but for the natural grace of sympathy which restrained her, she would have said so right out; but in her simplicity she said something very near as bad. "Mr. Powys," she said, quite earnestly, "do you live in Masterton all alone?"

Then he woke up and came to himself. It was like falling from a great height, and finding one's feet, in a very confused, sheepish sort of way, on the common ground. And the thought crossed his mind, also, that she might think he was referring to himself, and made him still more sheepish and confused. But yet, now that he was roused, he was able to answer for himself. "No, Miss Brownlow," he said; "my mother and my little sisters are with me. I don't live alone."

"Oh, I beg your pardon," said Sara, whose turn it now was to blush. "I hope you like Masterton?" This very faltering and uncomfortable question was the end of the interview; for it was very clear no answer was required. And then she showed him the way down stairs, and he went his way by himself, retracing the very steps which he had taken when he was following her. He felt, poor fellow, as if he had made a mistake somehow, and done something wrong, and went out very rueful into the park, as he would have gone to his desk, in strict obedience to his employer's commands.

CHAPTER XVI

Late in the afternoon Mr. Brownlow did really look as if he were taking a holiday. He came forth into the avenue as Sara was going out, and joined her, and she seized her opportunity, and took his arm, and led him up and down in the afternoon sunshine. It is a pretty sight to see a girl clinging to her father, pouring all her guesses and philosophies into his ears, and claiming his confidence. It is a different kind of intercourse, more picturesque, more amusing, in some ways even more touching, than the intercourse of a mother and daughter, especially when there is, as with these two, no mother in the case, and the one sole parent has both offices to fulfill. Sara clung to her father's arm, and congratulated herself upon having got him out, and promised herself a good long talk. "For I never see you, papa," she said; "you know I never see you. You are at that horrid office the whole long day."

"Only all the mornings and all the evenings," said Mr. Brownlow, "which is a pretty good proportion, I think, of life."

"Oh, but there is always Jack or somebody," said Sara, tightening her clasp on his arm; "and sometimes one wants only you."

"Have you something to say to me then," said her father, with a little curiosity, even anxiety,—for of course his own disturbed thoughts accompanied him everywhere, and put meanings into every word that was said.

"Something!" said Sara, with indignation; "heaps of things. I want to tell you and I want to ask you;—but, by-the-by, answer me first, before I forget, is this Mr. Powys very poor?"

"Powys!" said Mr. Brownlow, with a suppressed thrill of excitement. "What of Powys? It seems to me I hear of nothing else. Where has the young fellow gone?"

"I did not do any thing to him," said Sara, turning her large eyes full of mock reproach upon her father's face. "You need not ask him from me in that way. I suppose he has gone home—to his mother and his little sisters," she added, dropping her voice.

"And what do you know about his mother and his little sisters?" said Mr. Brownlow, startled yet amused by her tone.

"Well, he told me he had such people belonging to him, papa," said Sara; "and he gave me a very grand description before that of what it is to be poor. I want to know if he is very poor? and could I send any thing to them, or do any thing? or are they too grand for that? or couldn't you raise his salary or something? You ought to do something, since he is a favorite of your own."

"Did he complain to you?" said Mr. Brownlow, in consternation; "and I trust in goodness, Sara, you did not propose to do any thing for them as you say?"

"No indeed; I had not the courage," said Sara. "I never have sense enough to do such things. Complain! oh, dear no; he did not complain. But he was so much in earnest about it, you know, apropos of that silly speech I made at luncheon, that he made me quite uncomfortable. Is he a—a gentleman, papa?"

"He is my clerk," said Mr. Brownlow, shortly; and then the conversation dropped. Sara was not a young woman to be stopped in this way in ordinary cases, though she did stop this time, seeing her father fully meant it; but all the same she did not stop thinking, which indeed, in her case, was a thing very difficult to do.

Then Mr. Brownlow began to nerve himself for a great effort. It excited him as nothing had excited him for many a long year. He drew his child's arm more closely through his own, and drew her nearer to him. They were going slowly down the avenue, upon which the afternoon sunshine lay warm, all marked and lined across by columns of trees, and the light shadows of the half-developed foliage. "Do you know," he said, "I have been thinking a great deal lately about a thing you once said to me. I don't know whether you meant it—"

"I never say any thing I don't mean," said Sara, interrupting him; but she too felt that something more than usual was coming, and did not enlarge upon the subject. "What was it, papa?" she said, clinging still closer to his arm.

"You refused Motherwell," said Mr. Brownlow, "though he could have given you an excellent position, and is, they tell me, a very honest fellow. I told you to consider it, but you refused him, Sara."

"Well, no," said Sara, candidly; "refusing people is very clumsy sort of work, unless you want to tell of it after, and that is mean. I did not refuse him. I only contrived, you know, that he should not speak."

"Well, I suppose that it comes to about the same thing," said Mr. Brownlow. "What I am going to say now is very serious. You once told me you would marry the man I asked you to marry. Hush, my darling, don't speak yet. I dare say you never thought I would ask such a proof of confidence from you; but there are strange turns in circumstances. I am not going to be cruel, like a tyrannical father in a book; but if I were to ask you to do such a great thing for me—to do it blindly without asking questions, to try to love and to marry a man, not of your own choice, but mine—Sara, would you do it? Don't speak yet. I would not bind you. At the last moment you should be free to withdraw from the bargain—"

"Let me speak, papa!" cried Sara. "Do you mean to say that you need this—that you really want it? Is it something that can't be done any other way? first tell me that."

"I don't think it can be done any other way," said Mr. Brownlow sadly, with a sigh.

"Then of course I will do it," said Sara. She turned to him as she spoke, and fixed her eyes intently on his face. Her levity, her lightness, her careless freedom were all gone. No doubt she had meant the original promise, as she said, but she had made it with a certain gay bravado, little dreaming of any thing to follow. Now she was suddenly sobered and silenced. There was no mistaking the reality in Mr. Brownlow's face. Sara was not a careful, thoughtful woman; she was a creature who leaped at conclusions, and would not linger over the most solemn decision. And then she was not old enough to see both sides of a question. She jumped at it, and gave her pledge, and fixed her fate more quickly than another temperament would have chosen a pair of gloves. But for all that she was very grave. She looked up in her father's face, questioning him with her eyes. She was ready to put her life in his hands, to give him her future, her happiness, as if it had been a flower for his coat. But yet she was sufficiently roused to see that this was no laughing matter. "Of course I will do it," she repeated without any grandeur of expression; but she never looked so grave, or had been so serious all her life.

As for her father, he looked at her with a gaze that seemed to devour her. He wanted to see into her heart. He wanted to look through and through those two blue spheres into the soul which was below, and he could not do it. He was so intent upon this that he did not even perceive at the first minute that she had consented. Then the words caught his ear and went to his heart—"Of course I will do it." When he caught the meaning, strangely enough his object went altogether out of his mind, and he thought of nothing but of the half pathetic, unhesitating, magnificent generosity of his child. She had not asked a question, why or wherefore, but had given herself up at once with a kind of prodigal readiness. A sudden gush of tears, such as had not refreshed them for years, came into Mr. Brownlow's eyes. Not that they ran over, or fell, or displayed themselves in any way, but they came up under the bushy eyebrows like water under reeds, making a certain glimmer in the shade. "My dear child!" he said, with a voice that had a jar in it such as profound emotion gives; and he gathered up her two little hands into his, and pressed them together, holding her fast to him. He was so touched that his impulse was to give her back her word, not to take advantage of it; to let every thing go to ruin if it would, and keep his child safe. But was it not for herself? It was in the moment when this painful sweetness was going to his very heart that he bent over her and kissed her on the forehead. He could not say any thing, but there are many occasions, besides those proper to lovers, when that which is inexpressible may be put into a kiss. The touch of her father's lips on Sara's forehead told her a hundred things; love, sorrow, pain, and a certain poignant mixture of joy and humiliation. He could not have uttered a word to save his life. She was willing to do it, with a lavish youthful promptitude; and he, was he to accept the sacrifice? This was what John Brownlow was thinking when he stooped over her and pressed his lips on his child's brow. She had taken from him the power of speech.

Such a supreme moment can not last. Sara, too, not knowing why, had felt that serrement du cœur, and had been pierced by the same poignant sweetness. But she knew little reason for it, and none in particular why her father should be so moved, and her spirits came back to her long before his did. She walked along by his side in silence, feeling by the close pressure of her hands that he had not quite come to himself for some time after she had come back to herself. With every step she took the impression glided off Sara's mind; her natural light-heartedness returned to her. Moreover, she was not to be compelled to marry that very day, so there was no need for being miserable about it just yet at least. She was about to speak half a dozen times before she really ventured on utterance; and when at last she took her step out of the solemnity and sublimity of the situation, this was how Sara plunged into it, without any interval of repose.

"I beg your pardon, papa; I would not trouble you if I could help it. But please, now it is all decided, will you just tell me—am I to marry any body that turns up? or is there any one in particular? I beg your pardon, but one likes to know."

Mr. Brownlow was struck by this demand, as was to be expected. It affected his nerves, though nobody had been aware that he had any nerves. He gave an abrupt, short laugh, which was not very merry, and clasped her hands tighter than ever in his.

"Sara," he said, "this is not a joke. Do you know there is scarcely any thing I would not have done rather than ask this of you? It is a very serious matter to me."

"I am sure I am treating it very seriously," said Sara. "I don't take it for a joke; but you see, papa, there is a difference. What you care for is that it should be settled. It is not you that have the marrying to do; but for my part it is that that is of the most importance. I should rather like to know who it was, if it would be the same to you."

Once more Mr. Brownlow pressed in his own the soft, slender hands he held. "You shall know in time—you shall know in good time," he said, "if it is inevitable;" and he gave a sort of moan over her as a woman might have done. His beautiful[B] child! who was fit for a prince's bride, if any prince were good enough. Perhaps even yet the necessity might be escaped.

[B] The fact was, Sara was not beautiful. There was not the least trace of perfection about her; but her father had prepossessions and prejudices, such as parents are apt to have, unphilosophical as it may be.

"But I should like to know now," said Sara; and then she gave a little start, and colored suddenly, and looked him quickly, keenly in the face. "Papa!" she said;—"you don't mean—do you mean—this Mr. Powys, perhaps?"

Mr. Brownlow actually shrank from her eye. He grew pale, almost green; faltered, dropped her hands—"My darling!" he said feebly. He had not once dreamt of making any revelation on this subject. He had not even intended to put it to her at all, had it not come to him, as it were, by necessity; and consequently he was quite unprepared to defend himself. As for Sara, she clung to him closer, and looked him still more keenly in the eyes.

"Tell me," she said; "I will keep my word all the same. It will make no difference to me. Papa, tell me! it is better I should know at once."

"You ought not to have asked me that question, Sara," said Mr. Brownlow, recovering himself; "if I ask such a sacrifice of you, you shall know all about it in good time. I can't tell; my own scheme does not look so reasonable to me as it did—I may give it up altogether. But in the mean time don't ask me any more questions. And if you should repent, even at the last moment—"

"But if it is necessary to you, papa?" said Sara, opening her eyes—"if it has to be done, what does it matter whether I repent or not?"

"Nothing is necessary to me that would cost your happiness," said Mr. Brownlow. And then they went on again for some time in silence. As for Sara, she had no inclination to have the magnificence of her sacrifice thus interfered with. For the moment her feeling was that, on the whole, it would even be better that the marriage to which she devoted herself should be an unhappy and unfit one. If it were happy it would not be a sacrifice; and to be able to repent at the last, like any commonplace young woman following her own inclinations, was not at all according to Sara's estimation of the contract. She went on by her father's side, thinking of that and of some other things in silence. Her thoughts were of a very different tenor from his. She was not taking the matter tragically as he supposed—no blank veil had been thrown over Sara's future by this intimation, though Mr. Brownlow, walking absorbed by her side, was inclined to think so. On the contrary, her imagination had begun to play with the idea lightly, as with a far-off possibility in which there was some excitement, and even some amusement possible. While her father relapsed into painful consideration of the whole subject, Sara went on demurely by his side, not without the dawnings of a smile about the corners of her mouth. There was nothing said between them for a long time. It seemed to Mr. Brownlow as if the conversation had broken off at such a point that it would be hard to recommence it. He seemed to have committed and betrayed himself without doing any good whatever by it; and he was wroth at his own weakness. Softening of the brain! there might be something in what the Rector said. Perhaps it was disease, and not the pressure of circumstances, which had made him take so seriously the first note of alarm. Perhaps his whole scheme to secure Brownlows and his fortune to Sara was premature, if not unnecessary. It was while he was thus opening up anew the whole matter, that Sara at last ventured to betray the tenor of her thoughts.

"Papa," she said, "I asked you a question just now, and you did not answer me; but answer me now, for I want to know. This—this—gentleman—Mr. Powys. Is he—a gentleman, papa?"

"I told you he was my clerk, Sara," said Mr. Brownlow, much annoyed by the question.

"I know you did, but that is not quite enough. A man may be a gentleman though he is a clerk. I want a plain answer," said Sara, looking up again into her father's face.

And he was not without the common weakness of Englishmen for good connections—very far from that. He would not have minded, to tell the truth, giving a thousand pounds or so on the spot to any known family of Powys which would have adopted the young Canadian into its bosom. "I don't know what Powys has to do with the matter," he said; and then unconsciously his tone changed. "It is a good name; and I think—I imagine—he must belong somehow to the Lady Powys who once lived near Masterton. His father was well born, but, I believe," added Mr. Brownlow, with a slight shiver, "that he married—beneath him. I think so. I can't say I am quite sure."

"I should have thought you would have known every thing," said Sara. "Of course, papa, you know I am dying to ask you a hundred questions, but I won't, if you will only just tell me one thing. A girl may promise to accept any one—whom—whom her people wish her to have; but is it as certain," said Sara, solemnly, "that he—will have me?"

Then Mr. Brownlow stood still for a moment, looking with wonder, incomprehension, and a certain mixture of awe and dismay upon his child. Sara, obeying his movement, stood still also with her eyes cast down, and just showing a glimmer of malice under their lids, with the color glowing softly in her cheeks, with the ghost of a smile coming and going round her pretty mouth. "Oh child, child!" was all Mr. Brownlow said. He was moved to smile in spite of himself, but he was more moved to wonder. After all, she was making a joke of it—or was it really possible that, in this careless smiling way, the young creature, who had thrust her life into his hands like a flower, to be disposed of as he would, was going forward to meet all unknown evils and dangers? The sober, steady, calculating man could understand a great many things more abstruse, but he could not understand this.

This, however, was about the end of their conference, for they had reached old Betty's cottage by this time, who came out, ungrateful old woman as she was, to courtesy as humbly to Mr. Brownlow as if he had been twenty old squires, and to ask after his health. And Sara had occasion to speak to her friend Pamela on the other side of the way. It was not consistent with the father's dignity, of course, to go with her to visit those humble neighbors, but he stood at the gate with old Betty behind in a whirl of courtesies, watching while Sara's tall, straight, graceful figure went across the road, and Pamela with her little, fresh, bright, dewy face, like an April morning, came running out to meet her. "Poor little thing!" Mr. Brownlow said to himself—though he could not have explained why he was sorry for Pamela; and then he turned back slowly and went home, crossing the long shadows of the trees. He was not satisfied with himself or with his day's work. He was like a doctor accustomed to regard with a cool and impartial eye the diseases of others, but much at a loss when he had his own personal pains in hand. He was uneasy and ashamed when he was alone, and reminded himself that he had managed very badly. What was he to do? Was he to act as a doctor would, and put his domestic malady into the hands of a brother practitioner? But this was a suggestion at which he shuddered. Was he to take Jack into his counsel and get the aid of his judgment?—but Jack was worse, a thousand times worse, than a stranger. He had all his life been considered a very clever lawyer, and he knew it; he had got scores of people out of scrapes, and, one way or other, half the county was beholden to him; and he could do nothing but get himself deeper and deeper into his own miserable scrape. Faint thoughts of making it into "a case" and taking opinions on it—taking Wrinkell's opinion, for instance, quietly, his old friend who had a clear head and a great deal of experience—came into his mind. He had made a muddle of it himself. And then the Rector's question recurred to him with still greater force—could it be softening of the brain? Perhaps it would be best to speak to the doctor first of all.

Meanwhile Sara had gone into Mrs. Swayne's little dark parlor, out of the sunshine, and had seated herself at Pamela's post in the window, very dreamy and full of thought. She did not even speak for a long time, but let her little friend prattle to her. "I saw you and Mr. Brownlow coming down the avenue," said Pamela; "what a long time you were, and how strange it looked! Sometimes you had a great deal to say, and then for a long time you would walk on and on, and never look at each other. Was he scolding you? Sometimes I thought he was."

Sara made no answer to this question; she only uttered a long, somewhat demonstrative sigh, and then went off upon a way of her own. "I wonder how it would have felt to have had a mother?" she said, and sighed again, to her companion's great dismay.

"How it would have felt!" said Pamela; "that is just the one thing that makes me feel I don't envy you. You have quantities and quantities of fine things, but I have mamma."

"And I have papa," said Sara, quickly, not disposed to be set at a disadvantage; "that was not what I meant. Sometimes, though you may think it very wicked, I feel as if I was rather glad; for, of course, if mamma had been living it would have been very different for me; and then sometimes I think I would give a great deal—Look here. I don't like talking of such things; but did you ever think what you would do if you were married? Fanny Hardcastle likes talking of it. How do you think you should feel? to the gentleman, you know?"

"Think," said Pamela; "does one need to think about it? love him, to be sure." And this she said with a rising color, and with two rays of new light waking up in her eyes.

"Ah, love him," said Sara; "it is very easy to talk; but how are you to love him? that does not come of itself just when it is told, you know; at least I suppose it doesn't—I am sure I never tried."

"But if you did not love him, of course you would not marry him," said Pamela, getting confused.

"Yes—that is just one of the things it is so easy to say," said Sara; "and I suppose at your age you don't know any better. Don't you know that people have to marry, whether they like it or not? and when they never, never would have thought of it themselves? I suppose," said Sara, in the strength of her superior knowledge, "that most of us are married like that. Because it suits our people, or because—I don't know what—any thing but one's own will." And this little speech the young martyr again rounded with a sigh.

"Are you going to be married?" said Pamela, drawing a footstool close to her friend's feet, and looking up with awe into her face. "I wish you would tell me. Mamma has gone to Dewsbury, and she will not be back for an hour. Oh, do tell me—I will never repeat it to any body. And, dear Miss Brownlow, if you don't love him—"

"Hush," said Sara; "I never said any thing about a him. It is you who are such a romantic little girl. What I was speaking of was one's duty; one has to do one's duty, whether one likes it or not."

This oracular speech was very disappointing to Pamela. She looked up eagerly with her bright eyes, trying to make out the romance which she had no doubt existed. "I can fancy," she said, softly, "why you wanted your mother;" and her little hand stole into Sara's, which lay on her knee. Sara did not resist the soft caress. She took the hand, and pressed it close between her own, which were longer, and not so rounded and childlike; and then, being a girl of uncertain disposition, she laughed, to Pamela's great surprise and dismay.

"I think, perhaps, I like to be my own mistress best," she said; "if mamma had lived she never would have let me do any thing I wanted to do—and then most likely she would not have known what I meant. It is Jack, you know, who is most like mamma."

"But he is very nice," said Pamela, quickly; and then she bent down her head as quickly, feeling the hot crimson rushing to her face, though she did not well know why. Sara took no notice of it—never observed it, indeed—and kept smoothing down in her own her little neighbor's soft small hand.

"Oh yes," she said, "and I am very fond of my brother; only he and I are not alike, you know. I wonder who Jack will marry, if he ever marries; but it is very fine to hear him talk of that—perhaps he never did to you. He is so scornful of every body who falls in love, and calls them asses, and all sorts of things. I should just like to see him fall in love himself. If he were to make a very foolish marriage it would be fun. They say those dreadfully wise people always do."

"Do they?" said Pamela; and she bent down to look at the border of her little black silk apron, and to set it to rights, very energetically, with her unoccupied hand. But she did not ask any farther question; and so the two girls sat together for a few minutes, hand clasped in hand, the head of the one almost touching the other, yet each far afield in her own thoughts; of which, to tell the truth, though she was so much the elder and the wiser, Sara's thoughts were the least painful, the least heavy, of the two.

"You don't give me any advice, Pamela," she said at last. "Come up the avenue with me at least. Papa has gone home, and it is quite dark here out of the sun. Put on your hat and come with me. I like the light when it slants so, and falls in long lines. I think you have a headache to-day, and a walk will do you good."

"Yes, I think I have a little headache," said Pamela, softly; and she put on her hat and followed her companion out. The sunshine had passed beyond Betty's cottage, and cut the avenue obliquely in two—the one end all light, the other all gloom. The two young creatures ran lightly across the shady end, Sara, as always, leading the way. Her mind, it is true, was as full as it could be of her father's communication, but the burden sat lightly on her. Now and then a word or two would tingle, as it were, in her ears; now and then it would occur to her that her fate was sealed, as she said, and a sigh, half false half true, would come to her lips, but in the mean time she was more amused by the novelty of the position than discouraged by the approach of fate.

"What are you thinking of?" she said, when they came into the tender light in the farther part of the avenue; for the two, by this time, had slackened their pace, and drawn close together, as is the wont of girls, though they did not speak.

"I was only looking at our shadows going before us," said Pamela, and this time the little girl echoed very softly Sara's sigh.

"They are not at all beautiful to look at; they are shadows on stilts," said Sara; "you might think of something more interesting than that."

"But I wish something did go before us like that to show the way," said Pamela. "I wish it was true about guardian angels—if we could only see them, that is to say; and then it is so difficult to know—"

"What?" said Sara; "you are too young to want a guardian angel; you are not much more than a little angel yourself. When one has begun to go daily farther from the cast, one knows the good of being quite a child."

"But I am not quite a child," said Pamela, under her breath.

"Oh yes, you are. But look, here Jack must be coming; don't you hear the wheels? I did not know it was so late. Shall you mind going back alone, for I must run and dress? And please come to me in the morning as soon as ever they are gone, I have such heaps of things to say."

Saying this, Sara ran off, flying along under the trees, she and her shadow; and poor little Pamela, not so much distressed as perhaps she ought to have been to be left alone, turned back toward the house. The dog-cart was audible before it dashed through the gate, and Pamela's heart beat, keeping time with the ringing of the mare's feet and the sound of the wheels. But it stopped before Betty's door, and some one jumped down, and the mare and the dog-cart and the groom dashed past Pamela in a kind of whirlwind. Mr. John had keen eyes, and saw something before him in the avenue; and he was quick-witted, and timed his inquiries after Betty in the most prudent way. Before Pamela, whose heart beat louder than ever, was half way down the avenue, he had joined her, evidently, whatever Betty or Mrs. Swayne might say to the contrary, in the most purely accidental way.

"This is luck," said Jack; "I have not seen you for two whole days, except at the window, which doesn't count. I don't know how we managed to endure the dullness before that window came to be inhabited. Come this way a little, under the chestnuts—you have the sun in your eyes."

"Oh, I don't mind," said Pamela, "and I must not wait; I am going home."

"I suppose you have been walking with Sara, and she has left you to go home alone," said Jack; "it is like her. She never thinks of any thing. But tell me what you have been doing these two frightfully long days?"

From which it will be seen that Mr. John, as well as his sister, had made a little progress toward intimacy since he became first acquainted with the lodgers at Mrs. Swayne's.

"I don't think they have been frightfully long days," said Pamela, making the least little timid response to his emphasis and to his eyes—wrong, no doubt, but almost inevitable. "I have been doing nothing more than usual; mamma has wanted me, that's all."

"Then it is too bad of mamma," said Jack; "you know you ought to be out every day. I must come and talk to her about it—air and exercise, you know."

"But you are not a doctor," said Pamela, with a soft ring of laughter—not that he was witty, but that the poor child was happy, and showed it in spite of herself; for Mr. John had turned, and was walking down the avenue, very slowly, pausing almost every minute, and not at all like a man who was going home to dinner. He was still young. I suppose that was why he preferred Pamela to the more momentous fact which was in course of preparation at the great house.

"I am a little of every thing," he said; "I should like to go out to Australia, and get a farm, and keep sheep. Don't you like the old stories and the old pictures with the shepherdesses? If you had a little hut all covered with flowers, and a crook with ribbons—"

"Oh, but I should not like to be a shepherdess," cried Pamela, in haste.

"Shouldn't you? Well, I did not mean that; but to go out into the bush, or the backwoods, or whatever they call it, and do every thing and get every thing for one's self. Shouldn't you like that? Better than all the nonsense and all the ceremony here," said Jack, bending down to see under the shade of her hat, which as it happened was difficult enough.

"We don't have much ceremony," said Pamela, "but if I was a lady like your sister—"

"Like Sara!" said Jack, and he nodded his head with a little brotherly contempt. "Don't be any thing different from what you are, please. I should like people to wear always the same dress, and keep exactly as they were when—the first time, you know. I like you, for instance, in your red cloak. I never see a red cloak without thinking of you. I hope you will keep that one forever and ever," said the philosophical youth. As for Pamela, she could not but feel a little confused, wondering whether this, or Sara's description of her brother, was the reality. And she should not have known what to answer but that the bell at the house interfered in her behalf, and began to send forth its touching call—a sound which could not be gainsayed.

"There is the bell," she cried; "you will be too late for dinner. Oh, please don't come any farther. There is old Betty looking out."

"Bother dinner," said Mr. John, "and old Betty too," he added, under his breath. He had taken her hand, the same hand which Sara had been holding, to bid her good-bye, no doubt in the ordinary way. At all events, old Betty's vicinity made the farewell all that politeness required. But he did not leave her until he had opened the gate for her, and watched her enter at her own door. "When my sister leaves Miss Preston in the avenue," he said, turning gravely to Betty, with that severe propriety for which he was distinguished, "be sure you always see her safely home; she is too young to walk about alone." And with these dignified words Mr. John walked on, having seen the last of her, leaving Betty speechless with amazement. "As if I done it!" Betty said. And then he went home to dinner. Thus both Mr. Brownlow's children, though he did not know it, had begun to make little speculations for themselves in undiscovered ways.

CHAPTER XVII

A CATASTROPHE

After that day of curious abandonment and imprudence, Mr. Brownlow returned to his natural use and wont. He could not account to himself next day even for his want of control, for his injudiciousness. What end could it serve to lay open his plans to Sara? He had supposed she would take it seriously, as he had done, and, lo! she had taken it very lightly, as something at the first glance rather amusing than otherwise. Nothing could have so entirely disconcerted her father. His position, his good name, his very life, seemed to hang upon it, and Sara had taken it as a singularly piquant novelty, and nothing more. Then it was that it had occurred to him about that softening of the brain, and the thought had braced him up, had reawakened all his energies, and sealed his lips, and made him himself again. He went to the office next day, and all the following days, and took no more notice of young Powys than if he had never tried to win his confidence, and never introduced him to his daughter. No doubt it was a disappointment to the young man. No doubt a good deal of the intoxication of the moment had remained in Powys's brain. He had remembered and dwelt upon the effect of that passing sunbeam on Miss Brownlow's hair and her dress, much more than he need have done. And though he did not look at it much, the young Canadian had hung up the Claude in his memory—the Claude with a certain setting round it more important than its actual frame. This he had done naturally, as a kind of inevitable consequence. And it was not to be denied that he watched for Mr. Brownlow's coming next morning, and waited for some little sign of special friendship, something that should show, on his employer's part as well, a consciousness of special favor extended. But no such sign came. He might have been a cabbage for all the notice Mr. Brownlow took of him as he passed to his own office. Not a glance, not a word, betrayed any thing different from the ordinary not unkind but quite indifferent demeanor of the lawyer to his clerks. Then, as was to be expected, a certain surprise and painful enlightenment—such as every body has to encounter, more or less, who are noticed by their social superiors—came upon the young man. It was all a caprice, then, only momentary and entirely without consequences, which had introduced him to Mr. Brownlow's table and his daughter. He belonged to a different world, and it was vain to think that the other world would ever open to him. He was too unimportant even to be kept at a distance. He was her father's clerk. In Canada that would not have mattered so much, but in this old hard long-established England—Poor young fellow! he knew so little. The thought brought with it a gush of indignation. He set his teeth, and it seemed to him that he was able to face that horrible conventional system, and break a lance upon it, and make good his entrance. He forgot his work even, and laid down his pen and stared at Mr. John, who was younger than himself. How was he better than himself? that was the question. Then an incipient sneer awoke in the soul of the young backwoodsman. If there was such a difference between the son of a country solicitor and his clerk, what must there be between the son and the clients, all the county people who came to have their difficulties solved? But then Mr. Brownlow was something more than a solicitor. If these two men—the one old and full of experience, the other young and ignorant, with only a screen of glass and a curtain between them—could have seen into each other's thoughts, how strange would have been the revelation. But happily that is one refuge secured for humanity. They were each safe, beyond even their own powers of self-interpretation, in the recesses of their hearts.

Mr. Brownlow, by a superhuman effort not only took no notice of young Powys, but, so far as that was possible, dismissed all thought of him from his mind. It was a difficult thing to do, but yet he all but did it, plunging into the Wardell case, and other cases, and feeling with a certain relief that, after all, he had not any particular symptoms of softening of the brain. The only thing he could not do was to banish from his own mind the consciousness of the young man's presence. Busy as he was, occupied to the full extent of his powers, considering intently and with devotion fine points of law and difficult social problems, he never for one minute actually forgot that young Powys was sitting on the other side of the screen. He could forget any thing else without much difficulty. Neither Sara nor Brownlows were in his mind as he labored at his work. He thought no more of Jack's presence in the office, though he knew very well he was there, than of the furniture; but he could have made a picture of the habitual attitude in which his clerk sat, of the way he bent over his work, and the quick upward glance of his eyes. He could not forget him. He could put out of his mind all his own uncomfortable speculations, and even the sense that he had conducted matters unwisely, which is a painful thought to such a man. All this he could do, but he could not get rid of Powys's presence. He was there a standing menace, a standing reminder. He did not even always recall to himself, in the midst of his labors, why it was that this young man's presence disturbed him, but he never could for a moment get free of the consciousness that he was there.

At the same time he regarded him with no unfriendly feelings. It was not hatred any more than it was love that moved him. He carried the thought with him, as we carry about with us, as soon as they are gone, that endless continual thought of the dead which makes our friends in the unseen world so much closer to us than any body still living to be loved and cherished. Mr. Brownlow carried his young enemy, who at the same time was not his enemy, about with him, as he would have carried the thought of a son who had died. It came to his mind when he got up in the morning. It went side by side with him wherever he went—not a ghost, but yet something ghostly in its perseverance and steady persistency. When he laid down his pen, or paused to collect his thoughts for a moment, the spectre of this youth would cross him, whatever he might be doing. While Mr. Wrinkell was talking to him, there would suddenly glide across Mr. Wrinkell's substantial person the apparition of a desk and a stool and the junior clerk. All this was very trying; but still Mr. Brownlow wisely confined himself to this one manifestation of Powys's presence, and sternly silenced in his own mind all thought on the subject. On that one unlucky day of leisure he had gone too far; in the rebound he determined to do nothing, to say nothing—to wait.

This was perhaps as little satisfactory to Sara as it was to young Powys. She had, there can not be a doubt, been much amused and a little excited by her father's extraordinary proposal. She had not taken it solemnly indeed, but it had interested her all the same. It was true he was only her father's clerk, but he was young, well-looking, and he had amused her. She felt in her soul that she could (or at least so she thought) make an utter slave of him. All the absurdities that ever were perpetrated by a young man in love would be possible to that young man, or else Sara's penetration failed her, whereas the ordinary young men of society were incapable of absurdities. They were too much absorbed in themselves, too conscious of the possibility of ridicule, to throw themselves at a girl's feet heart and soul; and the girl who was still in the first fantastic freshness of youth despised a sensible and self-respecting lover. She would have been pleased to have had the mysterious Canadian produced again and again to be operated upon. He was not blasé and instructed in every thing like Jack. And as for having to marry him, if he was the man, that was still a distant evil, and something quite unexpected no doubt would come of it; he would turn out a prince in disguise, or some perfectly good reason which her father was now concealing from her, would make every thing suitable. For Sara knew too well the important place she held in her father's opinion to imagine for a moment that he meant to mate her unworthily. This was how the tenor of her thoughts was turned, and Mr. Brownlow was not insensible to the tacit assaults that were made upon him about his protégé. She gave up her judgment to him as she never had done before, with a filial self-abandonment that would have been beautiful had there been no arrière pensée in it. "I will do as papa thinks proper. You know best, papa," she said, in her new-born meekness, and Mr. Brownlow understood perfectly what she meant.

"You have turned dreadfully good all of a sudden," said Jack. "I never knew you so dutiful before."

"The longer one lives, one understands one's duties the better," said Sara, sententiously; and she looked at her father with a mingled submission and malice which called forth a smile about the corners of his mouth.

"I hope so," said Mr. Brownlow; "though you have not made the experiment long enough to know much about it yet."

"There are moments which give one experience as much as years," said Sara, in the same lofty way, which was a speech that tempted the profane Jack to laughter, and made Mr. Brownlow smile once more. But though he smiled, the suggestion did not please him much. He laid his hand caressingly on her head, and smoothed back her pretty hair as he passed her; but he said nothing, and showed no sign of consciousness in respect to those moments which give experience. And the smile died off his lip almost before his hand was withdrawn from her hair. His thought as he went away was that he had been very weak; he had betrayed himself to the child who was still but a child, and knew no better than to play with such rude edge-tools. And the only remedy now was to close his lips and his heart, to tell nobody any thing, never to betray himself, whatever might happen. It was this thought that made him look so stern as he left Brownlows that morning—at least that made Pamela think he looked stern, as the dog-cart came out at the gate. Pamela had come to be very learned in their looks as they flashed past in that rapid moment in the early sunshine. She knew, or she thought she knew, whether Mr. John and his father were quite "friends," or if there had been a little inevitable family difference between them, as sometimes happened; and it came into her little head that day that Mr. Brownlow was angry with his son, perhaps because—She would not put the reason into words, but it filled her mind with many reflections. Was it wrong for Mr. John to come home early so often?—to stay at home so often the whole day?—to time his expeditions so fortunately that they should end in stray meetings, quite accidental, almost every day? Perhaps he ought to be in the office helping his father instead of loitering about the avenue and elsewhere, and finding himself continually in Pamela's way. This she breathed to herself inarticulately with that anxious aim at his improvement which is generally the first sign of awakening tenderness in a girl's heart. It occurred to her that she would speak to him about it when she saw him next; and then it occurred to her with a flash of half guilty joy that he had not been in the dog cart as it dashed past, and that, accordingly, some chance meeting was very sure to take place that day. She meant to remonstrate with him, and put it boldly before him whether it was his duty to stay from the office; but still she could not but feel rather glad that he had stayed from the office that day.

As for Mr. John, he had, or supposed he had—or at least attempted to make himself suppose that he had—something to do at home on that particular day. His fishing-tackle had got out of order, and he had to see to that, or there was something else of equal importance which called his attention, and he had been in Masterton for two days in succession. Thus his conscience was very clear. It is true that he dawdled the morning away looking for Pamela, who was not to be found, and was late in consequence—so late that young Keppel, whom he had meant to join, had gone off with his rod on his shoulder to the Rectory to lunch, and was on his way back again before Jack found his way to the water-side. There are certain states of mind in which even dinner is an indifferent matter to a young man; and as for luncheon, it was not likely he would take the trouble to think of that.

"You are a nice fellow," said Keppel, "to keep a man lounging here by himself all the time that's any good; and here you are now when the sun is at its height. I don't understand that sort of work. What have you been about all day?"

"I have not been lunching at the Rectory," said Jack. "Have a cigar, old fellow? Now we are here, let's make the best of it. I've been waiting about, kicking my heels, while you've been having lunch with Fanny Hardcastle. But I'll tell you what, Keppel; I'd drop that if I were you!"

"Drop what?" cried Mr. Keppel, guiltily.

"Dancing about after every girl who comes in your way," said Jack. "Why, you were making an ass of yourself only the other day at Brownlows."

"Ah, that was out of my reach," said Keppel, shaking his head solemnly, and he sighed. The sigh was such that Jack (who, as is well known, was totally impervious to sentimental weaknesses) burst into a fit of laughter.

"I suppose you think little Fanny is not out of your reach," he said; "but Fanny is very wide awake, I can tell you. You haven't got any money; you're neglecting your profession."

"It is my profession that is neglecting me," said Keppel, meekly. "Don't be hard upon a fellow, Jack. They say here that is you who are making an ass of yourself. They say you are to be seen about all the lanes—"

"Who says?" said Jack; and he could not prevent a certain flush from rising to his face. "Let every man mind his own business, and woman too. As for you, Keppel, you would be inexcusable if you were to do any thing ridiculous in that way. A young fellow with a good profession that may carry him as high as he likes—as high as he cares to work for, I mean; of course nothing was ever done without work—and you waste your time going after every girl in the place—Fanny Hardcastle one day, somebody else the next. You'll come to a bad end, if you don't mind."

"What is a fellow to do?" said Keppel. "When I see a nice girl—I am not a block of wood, like you—I can't help seeing it. When a man has got eyes in his head, what is the use of his being reasoned with by a man who has none?"

"As good as yours any day," said Jack, with natural indignation. "What use do you make of your eyes? I have always said marrying early was a mistake; but, by Jove, marrying early is better than following every girl about like a dog. Fanny Hardcastle would no more have you than Lady Godiva—"

"How do you know that?" said Keppel, quickly. "Besides—I—don't—want her to have me," he added, with deliberation; and thereupon he occupied himself for a long time very elaborately in lighting his cigar.

"It is all very well to tell me that," said Jack. "You want every one of them, till you have seen the next. But look here, Keppel; take my advice: never look at a woman again for ten years, and then get married off-hand, and you'll bless me and my good counsel for all the rest of your life."

"Thank you," said Keppel. "You don't say what I'm to do with myself during the ten years; but, Jack, good advice is admirable, only one would like to know that one's physician healed himself."

"Physicians never heal themselves; it is an impossibility upon the face of it," said Jack, calmly. "A doctor is never such an idiot as to treat his own case. Don't you know that? When I want ghostly counsel, I'll go to—Mr. Hardcastle. I never attempt to advise myself—"

"You think he'd give Fanny to you," said Keppel, ruefully, "all for the sake of a little money. I hate moneyed people,—give us another cigar;—but she wouldn't have you, Jack. I hope I know a little better than that."

"So much the better," said Jack; "nor you either, my boy, unless you come into a fortune. Mr. Hardcastle knows better than that. Are we going to stay here all day? I've got something to do up at the house."

"What have you got to do? I'll walk up that way with you," said Keppel, lifting his basket from the grass.

"Well, it is not exactly at the house," said Jack. "The fact is, I am in no particular hurry; I have somebody to see in the village—that is, on the road to Ridley; let's walk that way, if you like."

"Inhospitable, by Jove!" said Keppel. "I believe, after all, what they say must be true."

"What do they say?" said Jack, coldly. "You may be sure, to start with, that it is not true; what they say never is. Come along, there's some shade to be had along the river-side."

And thus the two young men terminated the day's fishing for which Jack had abandoned the office. They strayed along by the river-side until he suddenly bethought himself of business which led him in quite an opposite direction. When this recollection occurred to his mind, Jack took leave of his friend with the air of a man very full of occupation, and marched away as seriously and slowly as if he had really been going to work. He was not treating his own case. He had not even as yet begun to take his own case into consideration. He was simply intent upon his own way for the moment, and not disposed to brook any contradiction, or even inquiry. No particular intention, either prudent or imprudent, made his thoughts definite as he went on; no aims were in his mind. A certain soft intoxication only possessed him. Somehow to Jack, as to every body else, his own case was entirely exceptional, and not to be judged by ordinary rules. And he neither criticised nor even inquired into his personal symptoms. With Keppel the disease was plain, and the remedy quite apparent; but as for himself, was he ill at all, that he should want any physician's care?

This question, which Jack did not consider for himself, was resolved for him in the most unexpected way. Mr. Brownlow had gone thoughtful and almost stern to the office, reflecting upon his unfortunate self-betrayal—vexed and almost irritated by the way in which Sara essayed to keep up the private understanding between them. He came back, no doubt, relieved of the cloud on his face; but still very grave, and considering within himself whether he could not tell his daughter that the events of that unlucky day were to count for nothing, and that the project he had proposed to her was given over forever. His thoughts were still so far incomplete, that he got down at the gate in order to walk up the avenue and carry them on at leisure. As he did so he looked across, as he too had got a habit of doing, at Mrs. Swayne's window—the bright little face was not there. It was not there; but, in place of it, the mother was standing at the door, shading her eyes from the rare gleam of evening sun which reached the house, and looking out. Mr. Brownlow did not know any thing about this mother, and she was not so pleasant to look at as Pamela; yet, unawares, there passed through his mind a speculation, what she was looking for? Was she too, perhaps, in anxiety about her child? He felt half disposed to turn back and ask her, but did not do it; and by the time he had found old Betty's cottage the incident had passed entirely from his mind. Once more the sunshine was slanting through the avenue, throwing the long tree-shadows and the long softly-moving figure of the wayfarer before him as he went on. He was not thinking of Jack, or any thing connected with him, when that startling apparition met his eyes, and brought him to a stand-still. The sight which made him suddenly stop short was a pretty one, had it been regarded with indifferent eyes; and, indeed, it was the merest chance, some passing movement of a bird or flicker of a branch, that roused Mr. Brownlow from his own thoughts and revealed that pretty picture to him. When the little flutter, whatever it was, roused him and he raised his eyes, he saw among the trees, at no great distance from him, a pair such as was wont to wander over soft sod, under blue sky, and amid all the sweet interlacements of sunshine and shade—two creatures—young, hopeful, and happy—the little one half-timid, half-trustful, looking up into her companion's face; he so much taller, so much stronger, so much bolder, looking down upon her—taking the shy hand which she still withdrew, and yet still left to be retaken;—two creatures, unaware as yet why they were so happy—glad to be together, to look at each other, to touch each other—thinking no evil. Mr. Brownlow stood on the path and looked, and his senses seemed to fail him. It was a bit out of Arcadia, out of fairy-land, out of Paradise; and he himself once in his life had been in Arcadia too. But in the midst of this exquisite little poem one shrill discord of fact was what most struck the father's ear—was it Jack? Jack!—he who was prudence itself—too prudent, even so far as words went, for Mr. Brownlow's simple education and habits. And, good heavens! the little neighbor, the little bright face at the window which had won upon them all with its sweet friendly looks! Mr. Brownlow was a man, and not sentimental, but yet the sight after the first surprise gave him a pang at his heart. What did it mean? or could it mean any thing but harm and evil? He waited, standing on the path, clearly visible while they came softly forward absorbed in each other. He was fixed, as it were, in a kind of silent trance of pain and amazement. She was Sara's little humble friend—she was the little neighbor, whose smiles had won even his own interest—she was the child of the worn woman at the cottage door, who stood shading her eyes and looking out for her with that anxious look in her face. All these thoughts filled Mr. Brownlow's eyes with pity and even incipient indignation. And Jack! was this the result of his premature prudence, his character as a man of the world? His father's heart ached as they came on so unconsciously. At last there came a moment when that curious perception of another eye regarding them, which awakens even sleepers, came over the young pair. Poor little Pamela gave a start and cry, and fell back from her companion's side. Jack, for perhaps the first time in his life thoroughly confounded and overwhelmed, stood stock-still, gazing in consternation at the unthought-of spectator. Mr. Brownlow's conduct at this difficult conjuncture was such as some people might blame. When he saw their consternation he did not at that very moment step in to improve the occasion. He paused that they might recognize him; and then he took off his hat very gravely, with a certain compassionate respect for the woman—the little weak fool-hardy creature who was thus playing with fate; and then he turned slowly and went on. It was as if a thunderbolt had fallen at the feet of the foolish young pair. Hitherto, no doubt, these meetings had been clandestine, though they did not know it; but now all at once illumination flashed upon both. They were ashamed to be found together, and in a moment, in the twinkling of an eye, both of them became conscious of the shame. They gave one glance at each other, and then looked no more. What had they been doing all those stolen hours?—all those foolish words, all those soft touches of the warm rosy young fingers—what did they all mean? The shock was so great that they scarcely moved or spoke for a minute, which felt like an age. Perhaps it was greatest to Jack, who saw evidently before him a paternal remonstrance, against which his spirit rose, and a gulf of wild possibilities which made him giddy. But still Pamela was the one whom it overwhelmed the most. She grew very pale, poor child! the tears came to her eyes. "Oh, what will he think of me?" she said, wringing her poor little hands. "Never mind what he thinks," said Jack; but he could not keep out of his voice a certain tone which told the effect which this scene had had upon him also. He walked with her to the gate, but it was in a dutiful sort of way. And then their shame flashed upon them doubly when Pamela saw her mother in the distance waiting for her at the door. "Don't come any farther," she said, under her breath, not daring to look at him; and thus they parted ashamed. They had not only been seen by others; they had found themselves out.

CHAPTER XVIII

TREATING HIS OWN CASE

It may be imagined after this with what sort of feelings the unhappy Jack turned up the avenue in cold blood, and walked home to dinner. He thought he knew what awaited him, and yet he did not know, for up to this moment he had never come seriously in collision with his father. He did not know what was going to be said to him, what line of reproach Mr. Brownlow would take, what he could reply; for in reality he himself had made as great or a greater discovery than his father had done. He was as totally unaware what he meant as Mr. Brownlow was. What did he mean? Nothing—to be happy—to see the other fair little creature happy, to praise her, to admire her, to watch her pretty ways—to see her look up with her dewy eyes, tender and sweet, into his face. That was all he had meant; but now that would answer no longer. If he had been a little less brave and straightforward, Jack would have quailed at the prospect before him. He would have turned his back upon the awful dinner-table, the awful hour after dinner, which he felt awaited him. But at the same time his spirit was up, and he could not run away. He went on doggedly, seeing before him in the distance his father still walking slowly, very slowly he thought, up to the house. Jack had a great respect for his father, but he had been so differently educated, his habits and ways of thinking were so different, that perhaps in ordinary cases the young man was a little impatient of paternal direction; and he did not know now how he could bear it, if Mr. Brownlow took matters with a high hand. Besides, even that was not the most urgent question. How could he answer any one? what could he say for himself? He did not know what he meant. He could not acknowledge himself a fool, and admit that he meant nothing. His thoughts were not pleasant as he went slowly after his father up the avenue. Perhaps it would convey but an uncomfortable impression of Jack were I to say that he had been quite sincere, and was quite sincere even now in what he had said about marriage. He had no particular desire to change his own condition in any way. The idea of taking new responsibilities upon him had not entered into his mind. He had simply yielded to a very pleasurable impulse, meaning no harm; and all at once, without any warning, his pleasure had turned into something terrible, and stood staring at him with his father's eyes—with eyes still more severe and awful than his father's. In an hour or two, perhaps even in a minute or two, he would be called to account; and he could not tell what to answer. He was utterly confounded and stupefied by the suddenness of the event, and by the startling revelation thus made to him; and now he was to be called up to the bar, and examined as to what he meant. These thoughts were but necessary companions as he went home, where all this awaited him; and he did not know whether to be relieved or to feel more disconcerted still, when he met a messenger at the door, who had just been sent in hot haste to the Rectory to ask Mr. Hardcastle to join the Brownlows party—a kind of thing which the Rector, in a general way, had no great objection to do. Was Mr. Hardcastle to be called in to help to lecture him? This was the thought that crossed Jack's mind as he went—it must be acknowledged, very softly and quietly—up stairs to his own room. He met nobody on the way, and he was glad. He let the bell ring out, and made sure that every body was ready, before he went down stairs. And he could not but feel that he looked like a culprit when finally he stole into the drawing-room, where Mr. Hardcastle was waiting along with his father and sister. Mr. Brownlow said, "You are late, Jack," and Jack's guilty imagination read volumes in the words; but nothing else was said to him. The dinner passed on as all dinners do; the conversation was just as usual. Jack himself was very silent, though generally he had his own opinion to give on most subjects. As he sat and listened, and allowed the talk to float over his head, as it were, a strong conviction of the nothingness of general conversation came over him. He was full to brimming with his own subject, and his father at least might be also supposed to be thinking more of that than of any thing else. Yet here they were talking of the most trifling matters, feeling bound to talk of any thing but the one thing. He had known this before, no doubt, in theory, but for the first time it now appeared to him in reality. When Sara left the room, it is not to be denied that his heart gave a jump, thinking now perhaps they would both open upon him. But still not a word was said. Mr. Hardcastle talked in his usual easy way, and with an evident unconsciousness of any particular crisis. Mr. Brownlow was perhaps more silent than usual, and left the conversation more in the hands of his guest. But he did not speak at his son, or show him any displeasure. He was grave, but otherwise there was no difference in him. Thus the evening passed on, and not a word was said. When Mr. Hardcastle went away Jack went out with him to walk part of the way across the park, and then only a certain consciousness showed itself in his father's face. Mr. Brownlow gave his son a quick warning look—one glance, and no more. And when Jack returned from his walk, which was a long and not a comfortable one, his father had gone to his room, and all chances of collision were over for that evening at least. He had escaped, but he had not escaped from himself. On the contrary, he sat half the night through thinking over the matter. What was he to do?—to go away would be the easiest, perhaps in every way the best. But yet, as he sat in the silence of the night, a little fairy figure came and stood beside him. Could he leave her, give her up, let her remain to wake out of the dream, and learn bitterly by herself that it was all over? He had never seen any one like her. Keppel might rave about his beauties, but not one of them was fit to be named beside Pamela.

So sweet too, and fresh and innocent, with her dear little face like a spring morning. Thinking of that, Jack somehow glided away from his perplexities. He made a leap back in his mind to that frosty, icy day on which he had seen her in the carrier's cart—to the moment when she sprained her ankle—to all the trifling pleasant events by which they had come to this present point. And then all at once, with a start, he came back to their last meeting, which had been the sweetest of all, and upon which hard fate, in the shape of Mr. Brownlow, had so solemnly looked in. Poor Jack! it was the first time any thing of the kind had ever happened to him. He had gone through a little flirtation now and then before, no doubt, as is the common fate of man; but as for any serious crisis, any terrible complication like this, such a thing had never occurred in his life; and the fact was, after all, that the experienced-man-of-the-world character he was in the habit of putting on did him no service in the emergency. It enabled him to clear his brow, and dismiss his uncomfortable feelings from his face during the evening, but it did him no good now that he was by himself; and it threw no light upon his future path. He could talk a little polite cynicism now and then, but in his heart he was young, and fresh, and honest, and not cynical. And then Pamela. It was not her fault. She had suffered him to lead her along those primrose paths, but it was always he who had led the way, and now was he to leave her alone to bear the disappointment and solitude, and possibly the reproach? She had gone home confused, and near crying, and probably she had been scolded when she got home, and had been suffering for him. No doubt he too was suffering for her; but still the sternest of fathers can not afflict a young man as a well-meaning mother can afflict a girl. Poor little Pamela! perhaps at this moment her pretty eyes were dim with tears. And then Jack melted altogether and broke down. There was not one of them all that was fit to hold a candle to her—Sara! Sara was handsome, to be sure, but no more to be compared to that sweet little soul—So he went on, the foolish young fellow. And if he did not know what he meant at night, he knew still less in the morning, after troublous hours of thought, and a great deal of discomfort and pain.

In the morning, however, what he had been dreading came. As bad luck would have it he met his father on the stairs going down to breakfast; and Mr. Brownlow beckoned his son to follow him into the library, which Jack did with the feelings of a victim. "I want to speak to you, Jack," Mr. Brownlow said; and then it came.

"When I met you yesterday you were walking with the—with Mrs. Swayne's young lodger," said Mr. Brownlow, "and it was evidently not for the first time. You must know, Jack, that—that—this sort of thing will not do. It puts me out as much—perhaps more than it can put you out—to have to speak to you on such a subject. I believe the girl is an innocent girl—"

"There can be no doubt about that, sir," cried Jack, firing up suddenly and growing very red.

"I hope not," said Mr. Brownlow, "and I hope—and I may say I believe—that you don't mean any harm. But it's dangerous playing with edge-tools; harm might come of it before you knew what you were doing. Now look here, Jack; I know the time for sermons is passed, and that you are rather disposed to think you know the world better than I do, but I can't leave you without warning. I believe the girl is an innocent girl, as I have said; but there are different kinds of innocence—there is that which is utterly beyond temptation, and there is that which has simply never been tempted."

"It is not a question I can discuss, sir," cried Jack. "I beg your pardon. I know you don't mean to be hard upon me, but as for calling in question—her—innocence, I can't have it. She is as innocent as the angels; she doesn't understand what evil means."

"I am glad you think so," said Mr. Brownlow; "but let me have out my say. I don't believe in seduction in the ordinary sense of the word—"

"Sir!" cried Jack, starting to his feet with a countenance flaming like that of an angry angel. Mr. Brownlow only waved his hand and went on.

"Let me have out my say. I tell you I don't believe in seduction; but there are people in the world—and the most part of the people in the world—who are neither good nor bad, and to such a sudden impulse one way or other may be every thing. I would not call down upon a young man's foolish head all the responsibility of such a woman's misery," said Mr. Brownlow, thoughtfully, "but still it would be an awful thought that somebody else might have turned the unsteady balance the right way, and that your folly had turned it the wrong. See, I am not going into it as a question of personal vice. That your own heart would tell you of; but I don't believe, my boy—I don't believe you mean any harm. I say this to you once for all. You could not, if you were a hundred times the man you are, turn one true, good, pure-hearted girl wrong. I don't believe any man could; but you might develop evil that but for you would only have smouldered and never come to positive harm. Who can tell whether this poor child is of the one character or the other? Don't interrupt me. You think you know, but you can't know. Mind what you are about. This is all I am going to say to you, Jack."

"It is too much," cried Jack, bursting with impatience, "or it is not half, not a hundredth part enough. I, sir—do you think I would harm her? Not for any thing that could be offered me—not for all the world!"

"I have just said as much," said Mr. Brownlow, calmly. "If I had thought you capable of a base intention, I should have spoken very differently; but intention is one thing and result another. Take care. You can't but harm her. To a girl in her position every word, every look of that kind from a young man like you is a kind of injury. You must know that. Think if it had been Keppel—ah, you start—and how is it different, being you?"

"It may not be different, sir," exclaimed Jack, "but this I know, I can't carry on this conversation. Keppel! any man in short—that is what you mean. Good heavens, how little you know the creature you are talking of! She talk to Keppel or to any one! If it was not you who said it—"

Mr. Brownlow's grave face relaxed for one half moment. It did not come the length of a smile, but it had unawares the same effect upon his son which a momentary lightening of the clouds has, even though no break is visible. The atmosphere, as it were, grew lighter. The young man stopped almost without knowing it, and his indignation subsided. His father understood better than he thought.

"If all you say is true," said Mr. Brownlow, "and I am glad to see that you believe it at least, how can you reconcile yourself to doing such a girl such an injury? You and she belong to different spheres. You can do her nothing but harm, she can do you no good. What result can you look for? What do you mean? You must see the truth of what I say."

Upon which Jack fell silent, chilled in the midst of his heat, struck dumb. For he knew very well that he had not meant any thing; he had no result to propose. He had not gone so far as to contemplate actual practical consequences, and he was ashamed and had nothing to say.

"This is the real state of the case," said Mr. Brownlow, seeing his advantage. "You have both been fools, both you and she, but you the worst, as being a man and knowing better; and now you see how matters stand. It may give you a little pang, and I fear it will give her a pang too; but when I say you ought to make an immediate end of it, I know I advise what is best for both. I am not speaking to you as your judge, Jack. I am speaking to you as your friend."

"Thanks," said Jack, briefly; his heart was full, poor fellow, and to tell the truth, he said even that much reluctantly, but honesty drew it out of him. He felt that his father was his friend, and had not been dealing hardly with him. And then he got up and went to the window, and looked out upon the unsuspicious shrubberies full of better thoughts. Make an end of it! make an end of the best part of his life—make an end of her probably. Yes, it was a very easy thing to say.

"I will not ask any answer or any promise," said Mr. Brownlow. "I leave it to your own good sense and good feeling, Jack. There, that is enough; and if I were you I would go to the office to-day."

This was all he said. He went out of the library leaving his son there, leaving him at liberty to follow out his own reflections. And poor Jack's thoughts were not pleasant. When his father was gone he came from the window, and threw himself into the nearest chair. Make an end of it! Yes, that was it. Easy to say, very easy to advise, but how to do it? Was he simply to skulk away like a villain, and leave her to pine and wonder—for she would wonder and pine, bless her! She believed in him, whatever other people might do. Keppel, indeed! as if she would look at Keppel, much less talk to him, walk with him, lift her sweet eyes to him as she had begun to do. And good heavens, this was to end! Would it not be better that life itself should end? That, perhaps, would please every body just as well. Poor Jack! this was the wild way he got on thinking, until the solemn butler opened the door and begged his pardon, and told him breakfast was ready. He could have pitched something at poor Willis's head with pleasure, but he did not do it. He even got up and thrust back his thoughts into the recesses of his brain, as it were, and after a while settled his resolution and went to breakfast. That was one good of his higher breeding. It did not give him much enlightenment as to what he should do, but it taught him to look as if nothing was the matter with him and to put his trouble in his pocket, and face the ordinary events of life without making a show of himself or his emotions, which is always a triumph for any man. He could not manage to eat much, but he managed to bear himself much as usual, though not entirely to conceal from Sara that something had happened; but then she was a woman, and knew every change of his face. As for Mr. Brownlow, he was pleased by his son's steadiness. He was pleased to see that he bore it like a man, and bore no malice; and he was still more pleased when Jack jumped into the dogcart and took the reins without saying any thing about his intention. It is true the mare had her way that morning, and carried them into Masterton at the speed of an express train, scattering every body on her route as if by magic. Their course was as good as a charge of cavalry through the streets of the suburb they had to go through. But notwithstanding his recklessness, Jack drove well, and nobody came to any harm. When he threw the reins to the groom the mare was straining and quivering in every muscle, half to the admiration, half to the alarm of her faithful attendant, whose life was devoted to her. "But, bless you, she likes it," he said in confidence to his friends, when he took the palpitating animal to her stable at the Green Man. "Nothing she likes better, though he's took it out of her this morning, he have. I reckon the governor have been a-taking it out of 'im."

The governor, however, was a man of honor, and did not once again recur to the subject-matter on the way, which would have been difficult, nor during the long day which Jack spent in the office within his father's reach. In the afternoon some one came in and asked him suddenly to dinner, somewhere on the other side of Masterton, and the poor young fellow consented in a half despair which he tried to think was prudence. He had been turning it over and over in his mind all day. Make an end of it! These words seemed to be written all over the office walls, as if it was so easy to make an end of it! And poor Jack jumped at the invitation in despairing recklessness, glad to escape from himself anyhow for the moment. Mr. Brownlow thus went home alone. He was earlier than usual, and he found Sara at Mrs. Swayne's door, praying, coaxing and teasing Pamela to go up the avenue with her. "Oh, please, I would rather not," Mr. Brownlow heard her say, and then he caught the quiet upward glance, full of a certain wistful disappointment, as she looked up and saw that Jack was not there. Poor Pamela did not know what to say or what to think, or how to look him in the face for confusion and shame, when he alighted at the gate and came toward the two girls. And then for the first time he began to talk to her, though her mind was in such a strange confusion that she could not tell what he said. He talked and Sara talked, drawing her along with them, she scarcely could tell how, to the other side of the road, to the great open gates. Then Mr. Brownlow gave his daughter suddenly some orders for old Betty; and Pamela, in utter consternation and alarm, found herself standing alone by his side, with nobody to protect her. But he did not look unkind. He looked down upon her, on the contrary, pitifully, almost tenderly, with a kind of fatherly kindness. "My poor child," he said, "you live with your mother, don't you? I dare say you must think it dull sometimes. But life is dull to a great many of us. You must not think of pleasure or amusement that is bought at the expense of better things."

"I?" said Pamela, in surprise; "indeed I never have any amusement;" and the color came up hotly in her cheeks, for she saw that something was in the words more than met the ear.

"There are different kinds of amusement," said Mr. Brownlow. "Does not your mother come out with you when you come to walk? You are too young to be left by yourself. Don't be vexed with me for saying so. You are but a child;—and I once knew some one who was like you," he said, looking at her again with friendly compassionate eyes. He was thinking as he looked at her that Jack had been right. He was even sorry in an inexorable way for her disappointment, her inevitable heart-break, which he hoped, at her age, would be got over lightly. Yes; no doubt she was innocent, foolish, poor little thing, and it was she who would have to pay for that—but spotless and guileless all through, down to the very depths of her dewy eyes.

Pamela stood before her mentor with her cheeks blazing and burning and her eyes cast down. Then she saw but too well what he had meant. He had seen her yesterday with his son, and he had sent Mr. John away, and it was all ended forever. This was what it meant, as Pamela thought. And it was natural that she should feel her heart rise against him. He was very kind, but he was inexorable. She stood by him with her heart swelling so against her bosom that she thought it would burst, but too proud to make any sign. This was why he had addressed her, brought her away from her mother's door, contrived to speak to her alone. Pamela's heart swelled, and a wild anger took possession of her; but she stood silent before him, and answered not a single word. He had no claim upon her that she should take his advice or obey him. To him at least she had nothing to say.

"It is true, my poor child," he said again, "there are some pleasures that are very costly, and are not worth the cost. You are angry, but I can not help it. Tell your mother, and she will say the same thing as I do—and go with her when you go out. You are very young, and you will find this always best."

"I don't know why you should speak to me so," said Pamela, with her heart beating, as it were, in her very ears. "Miss Brownlow goes out by herself—I—I—am a poor girl—I can not be watched always—and, oh, why should I, why should I?" cried the girl, with a little burst of passion. Her cheeks were crimson, and her eyes were full, but she would not have dropped the tears that were brimming over her eyelids, or let him see her crying—not for the world.

"Poor child!" said Mr. Brownlow. It was all he said; and it gave the last touch to her suppressed rage and passion—how did he dare call her poor child? But Sara came out just then from old Betty's, and stood stock-still, confounded by her friend's looks. Sara could see that something had happened, but she could not tell what it was. She looked from Pamela to her father, and from her father to Pamela, and could make nothing of it. "What is the matter?" she asked, in surprise; and then it was Pamela's turn to bethink herself, and defend her own cause.

"There is nothing the matter," she said, "except that you have left me standing here, Miss Brownlow, and I must go home. I have my own business to think of, but I can't expect you to think of that. There is nothing wrong."

"You are angry because I left you," said Sara in dismay. "Don't be so foolish, Pamela. I had something to say to old Betty—and then papa was here."

"And mamma is waiting for me," said Pamela in her passion. "Good-bye. She wants me, and you don't. And I dare say we shall not be very long here. Good-night, good-night." Thus she left them, running, so that she could not hear any call, though indeed her heart was beating too loud to let any thing else be audible, jarring against her ears like an instrument out of tune. "She has got her father—she doesn't want me. Nobody wants me but mamma. We will go away—we will go away!" Pamela said to herself; and she ran passionately across the road, and disappeared before any thing could be done to detain her. The father and daughter looked after her from the gate with different thoughts: Sara amazed and a little indignant—Mr. Brownlow very grave and compassionate, knowing how it was.

"What ails her?" said Sara—"papa, what is the matter? Is she frightened for you? or what have I done? I never saw her like this before."

"You should not have left her so long by herself," said Mr. Brownlow, seizing upon Pamela's own pretext.

"You told me to go," cried Sara, injured. "I never thought little Pamela was so quick-tempered. Let me go and tell her I did not mean it. I will not stay a moment—wait for me, papa."

"Not now," said Mr. Brownlow, and he took his daughter's arm and drew it within his own with quiet decision. "Perhaps you have taken too much notice of little Pamela. It is not always kind, though you mean it to be kind. Leave her to herself now. I have something to say to you," and he led her away up the avenue. It was nothing but the promise of this something to say which induced Sara, much against her will, to leave her little friend unconsoled; but she yielded, and she was not rewarded for yielding. Mr. Brownlow had nothing to say that either explained Pamela's sudden passion or threw any light upon other matters which might have been still more interesting. However, she had been taken home, and dinner was impending before Sara was quite aware of this, and Pamela, poor child, remained unconsoled.

She was not just then thinking of consolation. On the contrary, she would have refused any consolation Sara could have offered her with a kind of youthful fury. She rushed home, poor child, thinking of nothing but of taking refuge in her mother's bosom, and communicating her griefs and injuries. She was still but a child, and the child's impulse was strong upon her; notwithstanding that all the former innocent mystery of Mr. John's attentions had been locked in her own bosom, not so much for secrecy's sake as by reason of that "sweet shamefacedness" which made her reluctant, even to herself, to say his name, or connect it anyhow with her own. Now, as was natural, the lesser pressure yielded to the greater. She had been insulted, as she thought, her feelings outraged in cold blood, reproach cast upon her which she did not deserve, and all by the secret inexorable spectator whose look had destroyed her young happiness, and dispelled all her pleasant dreams. She rushed in just in time to hide from the world—which was represented by old Betty at her lodge window, and Mrs. Swayne at her kitchen door—the great hot scalding tears, big and sudden, and violent as a thunder-storm, which were coming in a flood. She threw the door of the little parlor open, and rushed in and flung herself down at her mother's feet. And then the passion of sobs that had been coming burst forth. Poor Mrs. Preston in great alarm gathered up the little figure that lay at her feet into her arms, and asked, "What was it?—what was the matter?" making a hundred confused inquiries; until at last, seeing all reply was impossible, the mother only soothed her child on her bosom, and held her close, and called her all the tender names that ever a mother's fancy could invent. "My love, my darling, my own child," the poor woman said, holding her closer and closer, trembling with Pamela's sobs, beginning to feel her own heart beat loud in her bosom, and imagining a thousand calamities. Then by degrees the short broken story came. Mr. John had been very kind. He used to pass sometimes, and to say a word or two, and Mr. Brownlow had seen them together. No, Mr. John had never said any thing—never, oh, never any thing that he should not have said—always had been like—like—Rude! Mamma! No, never, never, never! And Mr. Brownlow had come and spoken to her. He had said—but Pamela did not know what he had said. He had been very cruel, and she knew that for her sake he had sent Mr. John away. The dog-cart had come up without him. The cruel, cruel father had come alone, and Mr. John was banished—"And it is all for my sake!" This was Pamela's story. She thought in her heart that the last was the worst of all, but in fact it was the thing which gave zest and piquancy to all. If she had known that Mr. John was merely out to dinner, the chances are that she would never have found courage to tell her pitiful tale to her mother. But when the circumstances are so tragical the poor little heroine-victim becomes strong. Pamela's disappointment, her anger, and the budding sentiment with which she regarded Mr. John, all found expression in this outburst. She was not to see him to-night, nor perhaps ever again. And she had been seeing him most days and most evenings, always by chance, with a sweet unexpectedness which made the expectation always the dearer. When that was taken out of her life, how grey it became all in a moment. And then Mr. Brownlow had presumed to scold her, to blame her for what she had been doing, she whom nobody ever blamed, and to talk as if she sought amusement at the cost of better things. And Pamela was virtuously confident of never seeking amusement. "He spoke as if I were one to go to balls and things," she said through her tears, not remembering at the moment that she did sometimes think longingly of the youthful indulgences common enough to other young people from which she was shut out. All this confused and incoherent story Mrs. Preston picked up in snatches, and had to piece them together as best she could. And as she was not a wise woman, likely to take the highest ground, she took up what was perhaps the best in the point of view of consolation at least. She took her child's part with all the unhesitating devotion of a partisan. True, she might be uneasy about it in the bottom of her heart, and startled to see how much farther than she thought things had gone; but still in the first place and above all, she was Pamela's partisan, which was of all devices that could have been contrived the one most comforting. As soon as she had got over her first surprise, it came to her naturally to pity her child, and pet and caress her, and agree with her that the father was very cruel and unsympathetic, and that poor Mr. John had been carried off to some unspeakable banishment. Had she heard the story in a different way, no doubt she would have taken up Mr. Brownlow's rôle, and prescribed prudence to the unwary little girl; but as soon as she understood that Pamela had been blamed, Mrs. Preston naturally took up arms in her child's defense. She laid her daughter down to rest upon the horse-hair sofa, and got her a cup of tea, and tended her as if she had been ill; and as she did so all her faculties woke up, and she called all her reason together to find some way of mending matters. Mr. John! might he perhaps be the protector—the best of all protectors—with whom she could leave her child in full security? Why should it not be so? When this wonderful new idea occurred to her, it made a great commotion in her mind, and called to life a project which she had put aside some time before. It moved her so much, and took such decided and immediate form, that Mrs. Preston even let fall hints incomprehensible to Pamela, and to which, indeed, absorbed as she was, she gave but little attention. "Wait a little," Mrs. Preston said, "wait a little; we may do better than you think for. Your poor mother can do but little for you, my pet, but yet we may find friends—" "I don't know who can do any thing for us," Pamela answered, disconsolately. And then her mother nodded her head as if to herself, and went with the gleam of a superior constantly in her eye. The plan was one that could not be revealed to the child, and about which, indeed, the child, wrapped up in her own thoughts, was not curious. It was not a new intention. It was a plan she had been hoarding up to be made use of should she be ill—should there be any danger of leaving her young daughter alone in the world. Now, thank heaven, the catastrophe was not so appalling as that, and yet it was appalling, for Pamela's happiness was concerned. She watched over her child through all that evening, soothed, took her part, adopted her point of view with a readiness that even startled Pamela; and all the time she was nursing her project in her own heart. Under other circumstances, no doubt, Mrs. Preston would have been grieved, if not angry, to hear of the sudden rapid development of interest in Mr. John and all their talks and accidental meetings of which she now heard for the first time. But Pamela's outburst of grief and rage had taken her mother by storm; and then, if some one else had assailed the child, whom had she but her mother to take her part? This was Mrs. Preston's reasoning. And it was quite as satisfactory to her as if it had been a great deal more convincing. She laid all her plans as she soothed her little daughter, shaking as it were little gleams of comfort from the lappets of her cap, as she nodded reasoningly at her child. "We may find friends yet, Pamela," she would say; "we are not so badly off as to be without friends." Thus she concealed her weakness with a mild hopefulness, knowing no more what results they were to bring about, what unknown wonders would come out of them, than did the little creature by her side, whose narrow thoughts were bounded by the narrow circle which centred in Mr. John. Pamela was thinking, where was he now? was he thinking of her? was he angry because it was through her he was suffering? and then with bitter youthful disdain of the cruel father who had banished him and reproved her, and who had no right—no right! Then the little girl, when her passion was spent, took up another kind of thought—the light of anger and resistance began to fade out of her eyes. After all, she was a poor girl—they were all poor, every body belonging to her. And Mr. John was a rich man's son. Would it, perhaps, be right for the two poor women to steal away, softly, sadly, as they came; and go out into the world again, and leave the man who was rich and strong and had a right to be happy to come back and enjoy his good things? Pamela's tears and her looks both changed with her thoughts—her wavering pretty color, the flush of agitation and emotion went off her cheeks, and left her pale as the sky is when the last sunset tinge has disappeared out of it. Her tears became cold tears, wrung out as from a rock, instead of the hot, passionate, abundant rain. She did not say any thing, but shivered and cried piteously on her mother's shoulders, and complained of cold. Mrs. Preston took her to bed, as if she had been still a child, and covered her up, and dried her eyes, and sat by the pale little creature till sleep stepped in to her help. But the mother had not changed this time in sympathy with her child. She was supported by something Pamela heard not of. "We may find friends—we are not so helpless as that," she said to herself; and even Pamela's sad looks did not change her. She knew what she was going to do. And it seemed to her, as to most inexperienced plotters, that her plan was elaborate and wise in the extreme, and that it must be crowned with success.

CHAPTER XIX

It was only two days after this when Mr. Brownlow received that message from old Mrs. Fennell which disturbed him so much. The message was brought by Nancy, who was in the office waiting for him when he made his appearance in the morning. Nancy, who had been old Mrs. Thomson's maid, was not a favorite with Mr. Brownlow, and both she and her present mistress were aware of that; but Mrs. Fennell's message was urgent, and no other messenger was to be had. "You was to come directly, that was what she said." Such was Nancy's commission. She was a very tall gaunt old woman, and she stood very upright and defiant, as in an enemy's country, and no questions could draw any more from her. "She didn't tell me what she was a-wanting of. I'm not one as can be trusted," said Nancy. "You was to go directly, that was what she said."

"Is she ill?" said Mr. Brownlow.

"No, she ain't ill. She's crooked; but she's always crooked since ever I knew her. You was to come directly; that's all as I know."

"Is it about something she wants?" said Mr. Brownlow again; he was keeping himself down, and trying not to allow his anxiety to be reawakened. "I am very busy. My son shall go over. Or if she will let me know what it is she wants."

"She wants you," said Nancy. "That's what she wants. I can't say no more, for, I scorn to deny it, I don't know no more; but it ain't Mr. John she wants, it's you."

"Then tell her I will come about one o'clock," said Mr. Brownlow; and he returned to his papers. But this was only a pretense. He would not let even such a despicable adversary as old Nancy see that the news disturbed him. He went on with his papers, pretending to read them, but he did not know what he was reading. Till one o'clock! It was but ten o'clock then. No doubt it might be some of her foolish complaints, some of the grievances she was constantly accumulating; or, on the other hand, it might be—Mr. Brownlow drew his curtain aside for a minute, and he saw that young Powys was sitting at his usual desk. The young man had fallen back again into the cloud from which he had seemed to be delivered at the time of his visit to Brownlows. He was not working at that moment; he was leaning his head on his hand, and gazing with a very downcast look at some minute characters on a bit of paper before him—calculations of some kind it seemed. Looking at him, Mr. Brownlow saw that he began to look shabby—white at the elbows, as well as clouded and heavy over the eyes. He drew back the curtain again and returned to his place, but with his mind too much agitated even for a pretense at work. Had the old woman's message any thing to do with this youth? Had his calculations which he was attending to when he ought to have been doing his work any connection with Mrs. Fennell's sudden summons? Mr. Brownlow was like a man surrounded by ghosts, and he did not know from what quarter or in what shape they might next assail him. But he had so far lost his self-command that he could not wait and fight with his assailants till the hour he mentioned. He took up his hat at last, hurriedly, and called to Mr. Wrinkell to say that he was going out. "I shall be back in half an hour," Mr. Brownlow said. The head-clerk stood by and watched his employer go out, and shook his head. "He'll retire before long," Mr. Wrinkell said to himself. "You'll see he will; and I would not give a sixpence for the business after he is gone." But Mr. Brownlow was not aware of this thought. He was thinking nothing about the business. He was asking himself whether it was the compound interest that young Powys was calculating, and what Mrs. Fennell knew about it. All his spectres, after a moment of ineffectual repression, were bursting forth again.

Mrs. Fennell had put on her best cap. She had put it on in the morning before even she had sent Nancy with her message. It was a token to herself of a great emergency, even if her son-in-law did not recognize it as such. And she sat in state in her little drawing-room, which was not adorned by any flowers from Brownlows at that moment, for Sara had once more forgotten her duties, and had not for a long time gone to see her grandmother. But there was more than the best cap to signalize the emergency. The fact was, that its wearer was in a very real and genuine state of excitement. It was not pretense but reality which freshened her forehead under her grim bands of false hair, and made her eyes shine from amid their wrinkles. She had seated herself in state on a high arm-chair, with a high foot-stool: but it was because, really and without pretense, she had something to say which warranted all her preparations. A gleam of pleasure flashed across her face when she heard Mr. Brownlow knock at the door. "I thought he'd come sooner than one," she said, with irrepressible satisfaction, even though Nancy was present. She would not betray the secret to the maid whom she did not trust, but she could not but make a little display to her of the power she still retained. "I knew he'd come," she went on, with exultation; to which Nancy, on her part, could not but give a provoking reply.

"Them as plots against the innocent always comes early," said Nancy. "I've took notice of that afore now."

"And who is it in this house that plots against the innocent?" said Mrs. Fennell, with trembling rage. "Take you care what you say to them that's your mistress, and more than your mistress. You're old, and you'd find it harder than you think to get another home like this. Go and bring me the things I told you of. You've got the money. If it wasn't for curiosity and the key-hole, you'd been gone before now."

"And if it wasn't as there's something to be cur'us about it you wouldn't have sent me, not you," said Nancy, which was so near the truth that Mrs. Fennell trembled in her chair. But Nancy did not feel disposed to go to extremities, and as Mr. Brownlow entered she disappeared. He had grown pale on his way up the stairs. The moment had come when, perhaps, he must hear his own secret discovery proclaimed as it were on the housetop, and it can not be denied that he had grown pale.

"Well?" he said, sitting down opposite to his mother-in-law on the nearest chair. His breath and his courage were both gone, and he could not find another word to say.

"Well, John Brownlow," she said, not without a certain triumph mingled with her agitation. "But before I say a word let us make sure that Nancy and her long ears is out of the way."

Mr. Brownlow rose with a certain reluctance, opened the door, and looked up and down the stair. When he came in again a flush had taken the place of his paleness, and he came and drew his chair close to Mrs. Fennell, bending forward toward her. "What is the matter?" he said; "is it any thing you want, or any thing I can do for you? Tell me what it is!"

"If it was any thing as I wanted it might pass," said Mrs. Fennell, with a little bitterness; "you know well it wasn't that you were thinking of. But I don't want to lose time. There's no time to be lost, John Brownlow. What I've got to say to you is that she's been to see me. I've seen her with my own eyes."

"Who?" said Mr. Brownlow.

Then the two looked at each other. She, keen, eager, and old, with the cunning of age in her face, a heartless creature beyond all impressions of honesty or pity—he, a man, very open to such influences, with a heart both true and tender, and yet as eager, more anxious than she. They faced each other, he with eyes which, notwithstanding their present purpose, "shone clear with honor," looking into her bleared and twinkling orbs. What horrible impulse was it that, for the first time, united two such different beings thus?

"I've seen her," said Mrs. Fennell. "There's no good in naming names. She's turned up at last. I might have played you false, John Brownlow, and made better friends for myself, but I thought of my Bessie's bairns, and I played you true. She came to see me yesterday. My heart's beating yet, and I can't get it stopped. I've seen her—seen her with my own eyes."

"That woman? Phœbe—?" Mr. Brownlow's voice died away in his throat; he could not pronounce the last word. Cold drops of perspiration rose to his forehead. He sank back in his chair, never taking his eyes from the weird old woman who kept nodding her head at him, and gave no other reply. Thus it had come upon him at last without any disguise. His face was as white as if he had fainted; his strong limbs shook; his eyes were glassy and without expression. Had he been any thing but a strong man, healthy in brain and in frame, he would have had a fit. But he was healthy and strong; so strong that the horrible crisis passed over him, and he came to himself by degrees, and was not harmed.

"But you did not know her," he said, with a gasp. "You never saw her; you told me so. How could you tell it was she?"

"Tell, indeed!" said Mrs. Fennell, with scorn; "me that knew her mother so well, and Fennell that was her blood relation! But she did not make any difficulty about it. She told me her name, and asked all about her old mother, and if she ever forgave her, and would have cried about it, the fool, though she's near as old as me."

"Then she did not know?" said Mr. Brownlow, with a great jump of his laboring breast.

"Know! I never gave her time to say what she knew or what she did not know," cried Mrs. Fennell; "do you think I was going to have her there, hanging on, a-asking questions, and may be Nancy coming in that knew her once? I hope I know better than that, for my Bessie's children's sake. I packed her off, that was what I did. I asked her how she could dare to come nigh me as was an honest woman, and had nothing to do with fools that run away. I told her she broke her mother's heart, and so she would, if she had had a heart to break. I sent her off quicker than she came. You have no call to be dissatisfied with me."

Here John Brownlow's heart, which was in his breast all this time, gave a great throb of indignation and protest. But he stifled it, and said nothing. He had to bring himself down to the level of his fellow-conspirator. He had no leisure to be pitiful: a little more courtesy or a little less, what did it matter? He gave a sigh, which was almost like a groan, to relieve himself a little, but he could not speak.

"Oh yes, she came to me to be her friend," said the old woman, with triumph: "talking of her mother, indeed! If her mother had had the heart of a Christian she would have provided for my poor Fennell and me. And to ask me to wrong my Bessie's children for a woman I never saw—"

"What did she ask you?" said Mr. Brownlow, sternly; "better not to talk about hearts. What did she know? what did she say?"

"John Brownlow," said Mrs. Fennell, "you've not to speak like that to me, when I've just been doing you a service against myself, as it were. But it was not for you. Don't you think it was for you. It was for my Bessie's bairns. What do you think she would know? She's been away for years and years. She's been a-soldiering at the other side of the world. But I could have made her my friend forever, and got a good provision, and no need to ask for any thing I want. Don't you think I can't see that. It was for their sake."

Mr. Brownlow waved his hand impatiently; but still it was true that he had brought himself to her level, and was in her power. After this there was a silence, broken only by the old woman's exclamations of triumph. "Oh yes; I sent her away. I am not one that thinks of myself, though I might have made a kind friend," said Mrs. Fennell; and her son intently sat and listened to her, gradually growing insensible to the honor, thinking of the emergency alone.

"Did she say any thing about her son?" he asked at last; he glanced round the room as he did so with a little alarm. He would scarcely have been surprised had he seen young Powys standing behind him with that calculation of compound interest in his hand.

"I don't know about no son," said Mrs. Fennell. "Do you think I gave her time to talk? I tell you I packed her off faster, a deal faster, than she came. The impudence to come to me! But she knows you, John Brownlow, and if she goes to you, you had best mind what you say. Folk think you're a good lawyer, but I never had any opinion of your law. You're a man that would blurt a thing out, and never think if it was prudent or not. If she goes to you, she'll get it all out of you, unless you send her to me—ay, send her to me. To come and cry about her mother, the old fool, and not far short of my age!"

"What was she like?" said Mr. Brownlow again. He did not notice the superfluous remarks she made. He took her answer into his mind, and that was all; and as for her opinion of himself, what did that matter to him? At any other time he would have smiled.

"Like? I don't know what she was like," said Mrs. Fennell; "always a plain thing all her life, though she would have made me think that Fennell once—stuff and nonsense, and a pack of lies—like? She was like—Nancy, that kind of tall creature. Nancy was a kind of a relation, too. But as for what she was like in particular, I didn't pay no attention. She was dressed in things I wouldn't have given sixpence for, and she was in a way—"

"What sort of a way? what brought her here? How did she find you out?" said Mr. Brownlow. "Afterward I will listen to your own opinions. I beg of you to be a little more exact. Tell me simply the facts now. Remember of how much importance it is."

"If I had not known it was of importance I should not have sent for you," said Mrs. Fennell; "and as for my opinions, I'll give them when I think proper. You are not the man to dictate to me. She was in a way, and she came to me to stand her friend. She thought I had influence, like. I didn't tell her, John Brownlow, as she was all wrong, and I hadn't no influence. It's what I ought to have, me that brought the mother of these children into the world; but folks forget that, and also that it was of us the money came. I told her nothing, not a word. It's least said that's soonest mended. I sent her away, that's all that you want to know."

Mr. Brownlow shook his head. It was not all he wanted to know. He knew it was not over, and ended with this one appearance, though his dreadful auxiliary thought so in her ignorance. For him it was but the beginning, the first step in her work. There were still five months in which she could make good her claims, and find them out first if she did not know them, prove any thing, every thing, as people did in such cases. But he did not enter into vain explanations.

"It is not all over," he said. "Do not think so. She will find something out, and she will turn up again. I want to know where she lives, and how she found you out. We are not done with her yet," said Mr. Brownlow, again wiping the heavy moisture from his brow.

"You are done with her if you are not a fool to go and seek her," said Mrs. Fennell. "I can't tell you what she is, nor where she is. She's Phœbe Thomson. Oh, yes, you're frightened when I say her name—frightened that Nancy should hear; but I sent Nancy out on purpose. I am not one to forget. Do you think I got talking with her to find out every thing? I sent her away. That's what I did for the children, not asking and asking, and making a talk, and putting things into her head as if she was of consequence. I turned her to the door, that's what I did; and if you're not a fool, John Brownlow, or if you have any natural love for your children, you'll do the same."

Again Mr. Brownlow groaned within himself, but he could not free himself from this associate. It was one of the consequences of evil-doing, the first obvious one which had come in his way. He had to bear her insults, to put himself on her level, even to be, as she was, without compunction. Their positions were changed, and it was he now who was in the old woman's power; she had a hundred supposed injuries hoarded up in her mind to avenge upon him, even while she did him substantial service. And she was cruel with the remorseless cold-blooded cruelty of a creature whose powers of thought and sympathy were worn out. He wondered at her as he sat and saw her old eyes glisten with pleasure at the thought of having sent this poor injured robbed woman away. And he was her accomplice, her instigator, and it was for Bessie's children. The thought made him sick and giddy. It was only with an effort that he recovered himself.

"When a woman comes back after twenty-five years, she does not disappear again," he said. "I am not blaming you. You did as was natural to you. But tell me everything. It might have been an impostor—you never saw her. How can you be sure it was Phœbe Thomson? If Nancy even had been here—"

"I tell you it was Phœbe Thomson," said Mrs. Fennell, raising her voice. And then all of a sudden she became silent. Nancy had come quietly up stairs, and had opened the door, and was looking in upon her mistress. She might have heard more, she might not even have heard that. She came in and put down some small purchases on the table. She was quite self-possessed and observant, looking as she always did, showing no signs of excitement. And Mr. Brownlow looked at her steadily. Like Nancy! but Mrs. Powys was not like Nancy. He concluded as this passed through his mind that Mrs. Fennell had named Nancy only as the first person that occurred to her. There was no likeness—not the slightest. It went for nothing, and yet it was a kind of relief to him all the same.

"Why do you come in like that, without knocking, when I've got some one with me?" said Mrs. Fennell, with tremulous wrath. "It's like a common maid-of-all-work, that knows no better. I have told you that before."

"It's seldom as one of the family is here," said Nancy, "or I'd think on't. When things happen so rare, folks forgets. Often and often I say as you're left too much alone; but what with the lady yesterday and Mr. Brownlow to-day—"

"What lady yesterday?" cried Mrs. Fennell. "What do you know about a lady yesterday? Who ever said there was a lady yesterday? If you speak up to me bold like that, I'll send you away."

"Oh, it's nothing to me," said Nancy. "You know as I was out. They most always comes when I'm out. Fine folks is not partial to me; but if you're a-going to be better looked to, and your own flesh and blood to come and see you, at your age, it will be good news to me."

"My own flesh and blood don't think a great deal about an old woman," said Mrs. Fennell, swallowing the bait. "I'm little good to any body now. I've seen the day when it was different. And I can still be of use to them that's kind to me," she said, with significance. Mr. Brownlow sat and listened to all this, and it smote him with disgust. He got up, and though it cost him an effort to do so, held out his hand to the old woman in her chair.

"Tell me, or tell Jack, if you want anything," he said. "I can't stay now; and if any thing occurs let me know," he added. He took no notice of the vehement shaking of her hand as she turned toward Nancy. He looked at Nancy again, though he did not like her. She at least was not to be in the conspiracy, and he had a satisfaction in showing that at least he was not afraid of her. "If there is any thing that can make your mistress more comfortable," he said, sternly, "I have already desired you to let me know; and you understand that she is not to be bullied either by you or any one else—good-day."

"Bullied!" said Nancy, in consternation; but he did not condescend to look at her again. He went away silently, like a man in a dream. Up to this moment he had been able to doubt. It was poor comfort, yet there was some comfort in it. When the evidence looked the most clear and overwhelming, he had still been able to say to himself that he had no direct proof, that it was not his business, that still it might all be a mistake. Now that last standing-ground was taken from under his feet. Mrs. Thomson's heir had made herself known, she had told her name and her parentage, and claimed kindred with his mother-in-law, who, if she had been an impostor, could have convicted her; and the old woman, on the contrary, had been convinced. It was a warm summer day, but Mr. Brownlow shivered with cold as he walked along the familiar streets. If she had but come twenty years, five-and-twenty years ago! If he had but followed his own instincts of right and wrong, and left this odious money untouched! It was for Bessie's sake he had used it, to make his marriage practicable, and now the whirligig of time had brought about its revenges. Bessie's daughter would have to pay for her mother's good fortune. He felt himself swing from side to side as he went along, so confused was he with the multitude of his thoughts, and recovered himself only with a violent effort. The decisive moment had come. It had come too soon—before the time was out at which Phœbe Thomson would be harmless. He could not put himself off any longer with the pretext that he was not sure. And young Powys in the office, whom he had taken in, partly in kindness and partly with evil intent, sat under his eyes calculating the amount of that frightful interest which would ruin him. Mr. Brownlow passed several of his acquaintances in the street without noticing them, but not without attracting notice. He was so pale that the strangers who passed turned round to look at him. No farther delay—no putting off—no foolish excuses to himself. Whatever had to be done must be done quickly. Unconsciously he had quickened his pace, and went on at a speed which few men could have kept up with. He was strong, and his excitement gave him new strength. It must be done, one thing or another; there was no way of escaping the alternative now.

There are natures which are driven wild and frantic by a great excitement, and there are others which are calmed and steadied in face of an emergency. Mr. Brownlow entered his private office with the feeling of a man who was about to die there, and might never come out alive. He did not answer any one—even waved Wrinkell away, who was coming to him with a bag of papers. "I have some urgent private business," he said; "take every thing to my son, and don't let me be disturbed." He said this in the office, so that every one heard him; and though he looked at nobody, he could see Powys look up from his calculations, and Jack come in some surprise to the open door of his room. They both heard him, both the young men, and wondered. Jack, too, was dark and self-absorbed, engaged in a struggle with himself. And they looked at the master, the father, and said to themselves, in their youthful folly, that it was easy for him to talk of not being disturbed. What could he have to trouble him—he who could do as he liked, and whom nobody interfered with? Mr. Brownlow, for his part, saw them both without looking at them, and a certain bitter smile at his son's reserve and silence came to him inwardly. Jack thought it a great matter to be checked in his boyish love-making; while, good heavens! how different were the burdens, how much harder the struggles of which the boy was ignorant! Mr. Brownlow went in and shut the door. He was alone then—shut out from every body. No one could tell or even guess, the conflict in his mind—not even his young adversary outside, who was reckoning up the compound interest. He paused a little, and sat down, and bent his head on his hands. Was he praying? He could not have told what it was. It was not prayer in words. If it had been, it would have been a prayer for strength to do wrong. That was what he was struggling after—strength to shut out all compunctions—to be steadily cruel, steadily false. Could God have granted him that? but his habits were those of a good man all the same. He paused when he was in perplexity, and was silent, and collected his thoughts, not without a kind of mute customary appeal; and then flung his hands away from his face, and started to his feet with a thrill of horror. "Help me to sin!" was that what it had been in his heart to say?

He spent the whole day in the office, busy with very hard and heavy work. He went minutely into all those calculations which he supposed young Powys to be making. And when he had put down the last cipher, he opened all his secret places, took out all his memorandums, every security he possessed, all his notes of investments, the numberless items which composed his fortune. He worked at his task like a clerk making up ordinary accounts, yet there was something in his silent speed, his wrapt attention, the intense exactness of every note, which was very different from the steady indifference of daily work. When he had put every thing down, and made his last calculation, he laid the two papers together on his desk. A little glimmering of hope had, perhaps, awakened in him, from the very fact of doing something. He laid them down side by side, and the little color that had come into his face vanished out of it in an instant. If there had been but a little over! If he could have felt that he had something left, he might still, at the eleventh hour, have had strength to make the sacrifice; but the figures which stared him in the face meant ruin. Restitution would cost him every thing—more than every thing. It would leave him in debt; it would mortgage even that business which the Brownlows of Masterton had maintained so long. It would plunge his children down, down in an instant out of the place they had been educated to fill. It would take from himself the means of being as he was—one of the benefactors of the county, foremost in all good works. Good works! when it was with the inheritance of the widow and the orphans that he did them. All this came before him as clearly as if it had been written in lines of light—an uneducated, imprudent woman—a creature who had run away from her friends, abandoned her mother—a boy who was going to the bad—a family unaccustomed to wealth, who would squander and who would not enjoy it. And, on the other hand, himself who had increased it, used it well, served both God and man with it. The struggle was long, and it was hard, but in the end the natural result came. His half-conscious appeal was answered somehow, though not from on high. The strength came to him which he had asked for—strength to do wrong. But all the clerks started, and Mr. Wrinkell himself took off his spectacles, and seriously considered whether he should send for a doctor, when in the evening, just before the hour for leaving the office, Mr. Brownlow suddenly opened the door and called young Powys into his private room.

CHAPTER XX

POWYS'S BITS OF PAPER

Mr. Brownlow, perhaps, did not know very well what he meant when he called young Powys into his room. He was in one of those strange states of mental excitement in which a man is at once confused and clear; incapable of seeing before him what he is about to do, yet as prompt and distinct in the doing of it as if it had been premeditated to the last detail. He could not have explained why nor told what it was he proposed to himself; in short, he had in his own mind proposed nothing to himself. He was swayed only by a vague, intense, and overwhelming necessity to have the matter before him set straight somehow, and, confused as his own mind was, and little as he knew of his own intentions, he yet went on, as by the directest inspiration, marching boldly, calmly, yet wildly, in a kind of serious madness, into the darkness of this unknown way. He called the young man to him in sharp, decided tones, as if he knew exactly what he wanted, and was ready to enter fully into it at once; and yet he did not in the least know what he wanted, nor what question he was to ask, nor what he was to say the next moment; the only thing that helped him was, that as he looked out of his office to call Powys, he could see him pick up hastily and put in his pocket the bits of paper all dotted over with calculations, which he had already remarked on the young man's desk.

"Sit down," said Mr. Brownlow; "I have something to say to you;" and he resumed his own seat at his writing-table as if there had been nothing particular in the conference, and began mechanically to arrange the papers before him: as for Powys, he put his hand upon the back of the chair which stood on the other side of the table, and waited, but did not sit down, being bewildered a little, though not half so much as his employer was, by this sudden summons.

"Sit down," said Mr. Brownlow—"sit down; I want to speak to you: I hope you know that I have always intended to be your friend—"

"Intended! sir," said Powys; "I know that you have been my friend, and a far better friend than I deserved—" Here he made one of those pauses of embarrassment which sometimes mean so much, and often mean so little. Mr. Brownlow, who knew more than Powys did, took it to signify a great deal, and the idea gave him strength to proceed; and the fact is that for once the two, unknown to each other, were thinking of the same thing—of the bits of paper covered with figures that were in Powys's pocket—only their thoughts ran in a very different strain.

"That must be decided rather by the future than by the past," said Mr. Brownlow. "I can say for myself without any doubt thus far, that I have meant to be your friend—but I must have your confidence in return; I do not think you can have any more trustworthy counselor." As Mr. Brownlow said this, it seemed to him that some one else, some unseen third party, was putting the words into his mouth; and his heart gave a flutter as he said them, though it was little in accordance either with his age or character that the heart should take any such prominent part in his concerns.

As for the young man, there came over his face a quick flush, as of shame. He touched with his hand instinctively, and without knowing it, the breast-pocket in which these papers were—all of which actions were distinct and full of meaning to the anxious eyes that were watching him—and he faltered as he spoke. "I know that you would be my most trustworthy counselor—and I don't know how to thank you," he said; but he had lowered his voice and cast down his eyes. He stood holding the back of the chair, and it trembled in his grasp. He could not meet the gaze that was fixed upon him. He stood shuffling his feet, looking down, red with embarrassment, confusion, and shame. Was it that he felt himself a traitor? eating the Brownlow's bread, receiving their kindness, and plotting against them? It seemed to his companion as clear as day.

"Sit down," said Mr. Brownlow, feeling his advantage; "let us talk of it as friends—" and then he himself made a pause, and clenched his hand unawares, and felt his heart contract as he put the last decisive question. "What are those calculations you have been making all day?"

Young Powys started, and became violently red, and looked up suddenly into his employer's face. No doubt this was what he had been thinking of; but the question was so sudden, so point-blank, that it dispersed all the involuntary softenings of which he had been conscious, and brought back to him all his youthful pride and amour propre and reserve about his own affairs. He looked Mr. Brownlow full in the face, and his agitation took a different form. "Calculations, sir!" he said, with even a touch of indignation in his voice; and then he too stopped, lest he should be uncourteous to his employer, who he was confident wished him well, though he was so strangely curious. "The only calculations I have made are about my own affairs," he went on. "They are of no interest to any one. I am sorry you should have thought I was taking up my time—"

"I did not think of your time," said Mr. Brownlow, with an impatient sigh. "I have seen many young men like you who have—who have—gone wrong—from lack of experience and knowledge of the world. I wish to serve you. Perhaps—it is possible—I may have partly divined what is on your mind. Can't you see that it would be best in every way to make a confidant of me?"

All this the lawyer said involuntarily, as it were, the words being put into his mouth. They were false words, and yet they were true. He wanted to cheat and ruin the young man before him, and yet he wanted to serve him. He desired his confidence that he might betray it, and yet he felt disposed to guide and counsel him as if he had been his son. The confusion of his mind was such that it became a kind of exaltation. After all he meant him well—what he would do for him would be the best. It might not be justice—justice was one thing; kindness, friendship, bounty, another—and these last he was ready to give. Thus, in the bewilderment of motives and sentiments that existed in his mind, he came to find himself again, as it were, and to feel that he did really mean well to the boy. "I wish to serve you," he repeated, with a kind of eagerness. Would not this be to serve him better than by giving to his inexperienced hands a fairy fortune of which he would not know how to make use? These thoughts went vaguely but powerfully through Mr. Brownlow's mind as he spoke. And the result was that he looked up in the young man's face with a sense of uprightness which had for some time deserted him. It would be best in every way that there should be confidence between them—best for the youth, who, after all, had he ever so good a case, would probably be quite unaware how to manage it—and best, unquestionably best, for himself, as showing at once what he had to hope or fear. Of this there could be no doubt.

As for Powys, he was touched, and at the same time alarmed. It was the same subject which occupied them both, but yet they looked upon it with very different eyes. The Canadian knew what was in those scraps of paper with their lines of figures and awful totals, and it seemed to him that sooner than show them to any one, sooner than make a clean breast of what was in them, he would rather die. Yet the kindness went to his heart, and made him in his own eyes a monster. "Divined!" he said half to himself, with a look of horror. If Mr. Brownlow had divined it, it seemed to Powys that he never could hold up his head before him again. Shame would stand between them, or something he thought shame. He had not done much that was wrong, but he could have shrunk into the very ground at the idea that his thoughts and calculations were known. In spite of himself he cast a piteous glance at the whiteness of his elbows—was that how it came about that Mr. Brownlow divined? Pride, shame, gratitude, compunction, surged up in his mind, into his very eyes and throat, so that he could not speak or look at the patron who was so good to him, yet whom he could not yield to. "Sir," he stammered, when he had got a little command of himself—"you are mistaken. I—I have nothing on my mind—nothing more than every man has who has a—a—life of his own. Indeed, sir," the poor youth continued with eagerness, "don't think I am ungrateful—but I—I—can't tell you. I can't tell my own mother. It is my own fault. It is nothing to any other creature. In short," he added, breaking off with an effort, and forcing a smile, "it is nothing—nothing!—only I suppose that I am unaccustomed to the world—"

"Sit down," said Mr. Brownlow; "come nearer to me, and sit down upon this chair. You are very young—"

"I am five-and-twenty," said Powys. He said it hastily, answering what he thought was a kind of accusation; and the words struck the lawyer like a blow. It was not new to him, and yet the very statement of that momentous number seemed to carry a certain significance. The ill-omened fortune which made these two adversaries had come to the one just when the other was born.

"Well," said Mr. Brownlow, who felt his utterance stopped by these innocent words, "it does not matter. Sit down; I have still a great deal to say—"

And then he stopped with a gasp, and there was a pause like a pause in the midst of a battle. If Powys had not been preoccupied by the subject which to him was so absorbing, though he denied its interest to any other, he could not have failed to be struck by the earnestness, and suppressed excitement, and eager baffled looks of his employer. But he was blinded by his own anxieties, and by that unconscious self-importance of youth which sees nothing wonderful in the fact of other people's interest in its own fortunes. He thought Mr. Brownlow was kind; it did not occur to him that a stronger motive was necessary for these persistent questions and for this intense interest. He was not vain—but yet it came natural to receive such attention, and his mind was not sufficiently disengaged to be surprised.

As for the lawyer, he paused and took breath, and looked into the frank yet clouded face which was so open and communicative, and yet would not, could not, reveal to him the secret he wanted to seize. It was not skill, it was not cunning, that preserved the young man's secret—was it innocence? Had he been mistaken? was there really in Powys's consciousness at least no such secret, but only some youthful trouble, some boyish indiscretion, that was "on his mind." As Mr. Brownlow paused, and looked at his young companion, this thought gradually shaped itself within him, and for the moment it gave him a strange relief. He too was absorbed and preoccupied, and thrust out of the region of such light as might have been thrown on the subject by the whiteness of the seams of the young fellow's coat; and then he had come to be in such deadly earnest that any lighter commonplace explanation would have seemed an insult to him. Yet he paused, and after a few moments felt as if a truce had been proclaimed. It had not come yet to the last struggle for death or life. There was still time to carry on negotiations, to make terms, to convert the enemy into a firm friend and supporter. This conviction brought comfort to his mind, notwithstanding that half an hour before he had started up in the temerity of despair, and vowed to himself that, for good or evil, the decisive step must be taken at once. Now the clouds of battle rolled back, and a soft sensation of peace fell upon Mr. Brownlow's soul—peace at least for a time. It melted his heart in spite of himself. It made him think of his home, and his child, and the gentle evening that awaited him after the excitement of the day; and then his eye fell upon Powys again.

"I have still a great deal to say," he went on—and his voice had changed and softened beyond all doubt, and Powys, himself surprised, had perceived the change, though he had not an idea what it meant—"I have been pleased with you, Powys. I am not sure that you have quite kept up during the last few weeks; but you began very well, and if you choose to steady yourself, and put away any delusion that may haunt you"—here Mr. Brownlow made a little pause to give force to his words—"you may be of great service to me. I took you only on trial, you know, and you had the junior clerk's place; but now I think I am justified in treating you better—after this your salary shall be double—"

Powys gave a great start in his seat, and looked at Mr. Brownlow with a look of stupefaction. "Double!" he cried, with an almost hysterical gasp. He thought his ears or his imagination were deceiving him. His wonder took all the expression, almost all the intelligence, out of his face. He sat gazing with his mouth open, waiting to hear what it could mean.

"I will double your salary from the present time," said Mr. Brownlow, smiling in spite of himself.

Then the young man rose up. His face became the color of fire. The tears sprang into his eyes. "This was why you said you divined!" he said, with a voice that was full of tears and an ineffable softness. His gratitude was beyond words. His eyes seemed to shoot arrows into Mr. Brownlow's very soul—arrows of sharp thanks, and praise, and grateful applause, which the lawyer could not bear. The words made him start, too, and threw a sudden flood of light upon the whole subject; but Mr. Brownlow could not get the good of this, for he was abashed and shame-struck by the tender, undoubting, half-filial gratitude in the young man's eyes.

"But I don't deserve it," cried Powys, in his eagerness—"I don't deserve it, though you are so good. I have not been doing my work as I ought—I know I have not. These bills have been going between me and my wits. I have not known what I was doing sometimes. Oh! sir, forgive me; I don't know what to say to you, but I don't deserve it—the other fellows deserve it better than I."

"Never mind the other fellows," said Mr. Brownlow, collecting himself; "I mean to make a different use of you. You may be sure that it is not out of goodness I am doing this," he added, with a strange smile that Powys could not understand—"you may be sure it is because I see in you certain—certain—capabilities—"

Mr. Brownlow paused, for his lips were dry; he was telling the truth, but he did not mean it to be received as truth. This was how he went on from one step to another. To tell a lie, or to tell a truth as if it were a pleasant fiction, which was worst? The lie seemed the most straightforward, the most innocent of the two; and this was why his lips were dry, and he had to make a pause in his speech.

Powys sat down again, and leaned on the table, and looked across at his master, his benefactor. That was how the young man was calling him in his heart. His eyes were shining as eyes only do after they have been moistened by tears. They were soft, tender, eager, moved by those last words into a deeper gratitude still, an emotion which awoke all his faculties. "If I have any capabilities," he said, "I wish they were a hundred and a hundred times more. I can't tell you, sir—you can't imagine—how much you have done for me in a moment. And I was ashamed when you said you had divined! I have been very miserable. I have not known what to do."

"So that was all," said Mr. Brownlow, drawing a long breath. "My young friend, I told you you should confide in me. I know sixty pounds a year is very little, and so you must remember is twice sixty pounds a year—"

"Ah, but it is double," said young Powys, with a tremulous smile. "But I have not worked for it," he went on, clouding over—"I have not won it, I know I don't deserve it; only, sir, if you have something special—any thing in this world, I don't care how hard—that you mean to give me to do—"

"Yes," said Mr. Brownlow, "I have something very special; I can't enter upon the details just now. The others in the office are very well; but I want some one I can depend upon, who will be devoted to me."

Upon this the young man smiled; smiled so that his face lighted up all over—every line in it answering as by an individual ray. "Devoted!" he said, "I should think so indeed—not to the last drop of blood, for that would do you no good—but to the last moment of work, whatever, however, you please—"

"Take care," said Mr. Brownlow, "you may be too grateful; when a man promises too much he is apt to break down."

"But I shall not break down," said the Canadian. "You took me in first when I had nobody to speak for me, and now you save from what is worse than starving—from debt and hopeless struggles. And I was beginning to lose heart; I felt as if we could not live on it, and nobody knew but me. I beg your pardon sir, for speaking so much about myself—"

"No, no; go on about yourself," said Mr. Brownlow. He was leaning back on his chair like a man who had had a fit and was recovering from it. His whole countenance had relaxed in a manner wonderful to behold. He listened to the young fellow's open-hearted babble as if it had been celestial music. It was music to his ears. It distilled upon him like the dew, as the Bible says, penetrating through and through, pervading his whole being with a sense of blessed ease, and relief and repose. He lay back in his chair and was content to listen. He did not care to move or think, but only to realize that the crisis had passed over; that for the moment all was still rest and security and peace. It was the best proof how much his nerves had been tried in the former part of the day.

"But you must recollect," he said at last, "that this great fortune you have come into is, after all, only a hundred and twenty pounds a year; it is a very small income. You will have to be careful; but if you get into any difficulties again, the thing you ought to do is to come to me. I will always be ready to give you my advice, and perhaps help, if you want it. Don't thank me again; I shall have a great many things for you to do, which will make up."

"Nothing will ever make up for the kindness," said young Powys; and then he perceived that his audience was over. Already even the lines were beginning to tighten in Mr. Brownlow's face. The young man withdrew and went back to his desk, walking on air as he thought. It was a very small matter to be so glad about, but yet there are circumstances in which ten pounds to pay and only five pounds to pay it with will make as much anguish as the loss of a battle or a kingdom—especially to the inexperienced, the sensitive, and proud. This awful position he was suddenly relieved from when he saw no hope. And no wonder that he was elated. It was not a chronic malady to which he had grown accustomed. The truth was he had never been in debt before all his life. This may be accounted for by the fact that he had never had any money to speak of, and that he had been brought up in the backwoods.

Mr. Brownlow did not change his position for some time after his clerk had left him. Passion was new to him, though he was on the declining side of life. The sharp tension, the sudden relief, the leap from anxiety, suspicion, and present danger into calm and tranquillity, was new to him. His mind had never been disturbed by such conflicts while he was young, and accordingly they came now in all their freshness, with a power beyond any thing in his experience, to his soul. Thus he continued motionless, leaning back in his chair, taking the good of his respite. He knew it was only a temporary respite; he knew the danger was not past; but withal it was a comfort to him. And then, as he had this time disquieted himself in vain, who could tell if perhaps his other fears might vanish in the same way? God might be favorable to him, even though perhaps his cause was not just such a cause as could with confidence be put into God's hands. It was not always justice that prevailed in this world; and perhaps—So strangely does personal interest pervert the mind, that this was how John Brownlow, an upright man by nature and by long habit, calculated with himself. It seemed to him natural somehow that God should enter into the conspiracy with him—for he meant no harm even to the people who were to be his victims. Far from that; he meant, on the contrary, bit by bit, to provide for them, to surround them with comforts, to advance and promote in every way the young man whose inheritance he had so long enjoyed. He meant to be as good to him as any father, if only he could be successful in alienating forever and ever his just right from him. Possibly he might still even carry out the plan he had conceived and abandoned, and give the crown of all his possessions, his beautiful child, to the lucky youth. Any thing but justice. As he sat and rested, a certain sense of that satisfaction which arises from happiness conferred came into Mr. Brownlow's mind. In the mean time, he had been very good to Powys. Poor young fellow! how grateful, how elated, how joyous he was—and all about a hundred and twenty pounds a year! His trouble had involved only a little money, and how easy it was to make an end of that! It was not by a long way the first time in Mr. Brownlow's life at which this opportunity of bringing light out of darkness had occurred to him. There were other clerks, and other men not clerks, who could, if they would, tell a similar tale. He had never been a hard man; he had been considerate, merciful, lending like the righteous man, and little exacting as to his recompense. He had served many in his day, and though he never boasted of it, he knew it. Was it in reason to give up without a struggle his power of serving his neighbors, all the admirable use he had made of his fortune, when he might keep his fortune, and yet withal do better for the real heir than if he gave it up to him? The sense of coming ruin, and the awful excitement of that conflict for life and death which he had anticipated when he called Powys into his office, had exhausted him so entirely that he allowed himself to be soothed by all those softer thoughts. The danger was not over—he knew that as well as any one; but he had a reprieve. He had time to make of his adversary a devoted friend and vassal, and it was even for his adversary's good.

Such were the thoughts that went softly, as in a veiled and twilight procession, through his mind. After a while he raised himself up, and gathered together all the calculations at which he had been working so hard, and locked all his private drawers, and put all his memorandums by. As he did so, his halcyon state by degrees began to be invaded by gleams of the every-day day-light. He had doubled Powys's salary, and he had a right to do so if he pleased; but yet he knew that when he told it to Mr. Wrinkell, that functionary would be much surprised, and that a sense of injury would be visible upon the countenances of the other clerks. Certainly a man has a right to do what he likes with his own, but then every man who does so must make up his mind to certain little penalties. He will always be able to read the grudge of those who have borne the burden and heat of the day in their faces, however silent they may be; and even an emperor, much less a country lawyer, can not fail to be conscious when he is tacitly disapproved of. How was he to tell Wrinkell of it even? how to explain to him why he had taken so unusual a step? The very fact was a kind of confession that something more was in it than met the eye. And Jack—; but Jack and Wrinkell too would have greater cause of astonishment still, which would throw even this into the shade. Mr. Wrinkell knocked at Mr. Brownlow's door when he had come this length in his thoughts. The manager had not troubled him so long as he had been alone and apparently busy; but after the long audience accorded to young Powys, Mr. Wrinkell did not see how he could be shut out. He came in accordingly, and already Mr. Brownlow saw the disapproval in his eye. He was stately, which was no doubt a deportment becoming a head clerk, but not precisely in the private office of his principal; and he did not waste a single word in what he had to say. He was concise almost to the point of abruptness; all of which particulars of disapprobation Mr. Brownlow perceived at once.

"Wrinkell," he said, when they had dismissed in this succinct way the immediate business in hand, "I want to speak to you about young Powys. I am interested in that young fellow. I want to raise his salary. But I should like to know first what you have got to say."

It was a hypocritical speech, but Mr. Wrinkell happily was not aware of that; he pursed up his lips and screwed them tight together, as if, in the first place, he did not mean to say any thing, but relented after a moment's pause.

"At the present moment, sir," said Mr. Wrinkell, "I am doubtful what to say. Had you asked me three months since, I should have answered, 'By all means.' If you had asked me one month since, I should have said, 'Certainly not.' Now, I avow my penetration is baffled, and I don't know what to say."

"You mean he is not doing so well as he did at first?" said Mr. Brownlow. "Nobody ever does that I know of. And better than he did later? Is that what you mean to say?"

"Being very concise," said Mr. Wrinkell, slowly, "I should say that was a sort of a summary. When he came first he was the best beginner I ever had in hand; and I did not leave him without signs of my approval. I had him to my 'umble 'ome, Mr. Brownlow, as perhaps you are aware, and gave him the opportunity of going to chapel with us. I don't hesitate to avow," said Mr. Wrinkell, with a little solemnity, "that I had begun to regard him as a kind of son of my own."

"And then there was a change?" said the lawyer, with a smile.

"There was a great change," said Mr. Wrinkell. "It was no more the same young man—a cheerful bright young fellow that could laugh over his tea of a Sunday, and walk steadily to chapel after with Mrs. Wrinkell and myself. We are not of those Christians who think a little cheerfulness out of season of a Sunday. But he changed of that. He would have no tea, which is a bad sign in a young man. He yawned in my very pew by Mrs. Wrinkell's side. It grieved me, sir, as if he had been my own flesh and blood; but of course we had to give up. The last few weeks he has been steadier," Mr. Wrinkell added, quickly; "there can't be any doubt about that."

"But he might decline tea and yawn over a sermon without going to the bad," said Mr. Brownlow. "I hope so at least, for they are two things I often do myself."

"Excuse me," said Mr. Wrinkell, who liked now and then to take high ground. "There is all the difference. I fully admit the right of private judgment. You judge for yourself; but a young man who has kind friends anxious to serve him—there is all the difference. But he has been steady of late," the head clerk added, with candor; "I gladly acknowledge that."

"Perhaps he had something on his mind," said Mr. Brownlow. "At all events, I don't think much harm has come of it. I take an interest in that young fellow. You will double his salary, Mr. Wrinkell, next quarter-day."

"Double it!" said Mr. Wrinkell, with a gasp. He fell back from his position by the side of the table, and grew pale with horror. "Double it?" he added, after a pause, inquiringly. "Did I understand, sir? was that what you said?"

"That was what I said," said Mr. Brownlow; and, after the habit of guilty men, he began immediately to defend himself. "I trust," he said, unconsciously following the old precedent, "that I have a right to do what I like with my own."

"Certainly—certainly," said Mr. Wrinkell; and then there was a pause. "I shall put these settlements in hand at once," he resumed, with what the lawyer felt was something like eagerness to escape the subject. "Mr. Robinson is waiting for the instructions you have just given me. And the Wardell case is nearly ready for your revision—and—May I ask if the—the—increase you mention in Mr. Powys's salary is to begin from next quarter-day, or from the last?"

"From the last," said Mr. Brownlow, with stern brevity.

"Very well, sir," said Mr. Wrinkell. "I can not conceal from you that it may have a bad effect—a painful effect."

"Upon whom?" said Mr, Brownlow.

"Upon the other clerks. They are pretty steady—neither very good nor very bad; and he has been both good and bad," said Mr. Wrinkell, stoutly. "It will have an unpleasant effect. They will say we make favorites, Mr. Brownlow. They have already said as much in respect to myself."

"They had better mind their own affairs," was all Mr. Brownlow said; but, nevertheless, when he went out into the office afterward, he imagined (prematurely, for it had not yet been communicated to them) that he read disgust in the eyes of his clerks; and he was not unmoved by it, any more than General Haman was by the contempt of the old man who sat in the gate.

CHAPTER XXI

HOW A MAN CAN DO WHAT HE LIKES WITH HIS OWN

It was not for some days that the clerks in Mr. Brownlow's office found out the enormity of which their employer had been guilty—which was almost unfortunate, for he gave them full credit for their disapproval all the time. As it was, Mr. Wrinkell embodied within his own person all the disapprobation on a grand scale. It was not that he disapproved of Powys's advancement. Without being overwhelmingly clever or fascinating, the young Canadian was one of those open-hearted open-eyed souls who find favor with most good people. There was no malice nor envy nor uncharitableness about him; he was ready to acknowledge every body's good qualities, ready to appreciate whatever kindness might be offered to him, open to see all that was noble or pleasant or of good report—which is the quality of all others most generally wanting in a limited community, from an office up to—even a University. Mr. Wrinkell was a head clerk and a Dissenter, and not a tolerant man to speak of, but he liked the more generous breadth of nature without very well knowing why; and he was glad in his heart that the young fellow had "got on." But still, for all that, he disapproved—not of Powys, but of Mr. Brownlow. It was caprice, and caprice was not to be supported—or it was from consideration of capability, apart from all question of standing in the office, which was, it must be allowed, more insupportable still. Mr. Wrinkell reflected that he had himself been nearly forty years in the employment of the Brownlows of Masterton without once having his salary doubled. And he felt that if such a dangerous precedent were once established, the consequences might be tremendous. Such a boy, for example, if he but happened to be clever and useful, might be put over every body's head, before any body was aware. Mr. Wrinkell, who was grand vizier, was not afraid for his own place, but he felt that it was an example to be summarily discouraged. After all, when a man is not clever it is not his fault; whereas, when he is respectable and steady, the virtue and praise is purely his own. "It's revolutionary," he said to his wife. "There is Brown, who has been years and years in the office—there never was a steadier fellow. I don't remember that he ever lost a day—except when he had that fever, you know; but twenty pound a year increase was as much as ever was given to him."

"When he had the fever they were very kind to him," said Mrs. Wrinkell; "and, after all, Mr. Brownlow has a right to do what he likes with his own."

"He may have a right," said Mr. Wrinkell, doubtfully, "but it's a thing that always makes a heart-burning, and always will."

"Well, William, we may be thankful it can't make any difference to us," said his wife. This was the sum of the good woman's philosophy, but it answered very well. It was always her conviction that there will be peace in our day.

As for Brown, when he first heard the news, he went home to the bosom of his family with bitterness in his heart. "I can't call to mind a single day I ever missed, except that fever, and the day Billy was born," he said to Mrs. Brown, despondingly; "and here's this young fellow that's been six months in the office—"

"It's a shame," said that injured woman; "it's a black burning shame. A bit of a lad picked up in the streets that don't know what money is; and you a married man with six—not to say the faithful servant you have been. I wonder for my part how Mr. Brownlow dares to look you in the face."

"He don't mind much about that. What he thinks is, that the money's his own," said poor Brown, with a sigh.

"But it ain't his own," said the higher spirited wife. "I would just like to know who works hardest for it, him or you. If I saw him every day as you do, I would soon give him a piece of my mind."

"And lose my place altogether," said the husband. But, notwithstanding, though he did not give Mr. Brownlow a piece of his mind, Brown did not hesitate to express his feelings a little in the tone of his voice, and the disapproval in his eye.

All this, however, was as nothing to the judgment which Mr. Brownlow brought upon himself on the following Sunday. The fact that his father had doubled any clerk's salary was a matter of great indifference to Jack. He smiled in an uncomfortable sort of way when he heard it was young Powys on whom this benefit had fallen; but otherwise it did not affect him. On Sunday, however, as it happened, something occurred that brought Mr. Brownlow's favoritism—his extraordinary forgetfulness of his position and of what was due to his children—home in the most striking way to his son. It was a thing that required all Mr. Brownlow's courage; and it can not be said that he was quite comfortable about it. He had done what never had been done before to any clerk since the days of Brownlows began. He had invited young Powys to dinner. He had even done more than that—he had invited him to come early, to ramble about the park, as if he had been an intimate. It was not unpleasant to him to give the invitation, but there is no doubt that the thought of how he was to communicate the fact to his children, and prepare them for their visitor, did give him a little trouble. Of course it was his own house. He was free to ask any one he liked to it. The choice lay entirely with himself; but yet—He said nothing about it until the very day for which his invitation had been given—not that he had forgotten the fact, but somehow a certain constraint came over him whenever he so much as approached the subject. It was only Thursday when he asked young Powys to come, and he had it on his mind all that evening, all Friday and Saturday, and did not venture to make a clean breast of it. Even when Jack was out of the way, it seemed to the father impossible to look into Sara's face, and tell her of the coming guest. Sunday was very bright—a midsummer day in all its green and flowery glory. Jack had come to the age when a young man is often a little uncertain about his religious duties. He did not care to go and hear Mr. Hardcastle preach. So he said; though the Rector, good man, was very merciful, and inflicted only fifteen minutes of sermon; and then he was very unhappy, and restless, and uneasy about his own concerns; and he was misanthropical for the moment, and disliked the sight and presence of his fellow-creatures. So Jack did not go to church. And Sara and her father did, walking across the beautiful summer park, under the shady trees, through the paths all flecked with sunshine. Sara's white figure gave a centre to the landscape. She was not angelic, notwithstanding her white robes, but she was royal in her way—a young princess moving through a realm that belonged to her, used to homage, used to admiration, used to know herself the first. Though she was as sweet and as gracious as the morning, all this was written in her face; for she was still very young, and had not reached the maturer dignity of unconsciousness. Mr. Brownlow, as he went with her, was but the first subject in her kingdom. Nobody admired her as he did. Nobody set her up above every competitor with the perfect faith of her father; and to see her clinging to his arm, lifting up her fresh face to him, displaying all her philosophies and caprices for his benefit, was a pretty sight. But yet, all through that long walk to Dewsbury and back, he never ventured to disclose his secret to her. All the time it lay on his heart, but he could not bring himself to say it. It was only when they were all leaving the table, after luncheon, that Mr. Brownlow unburdened himself. "By the way," he said suddenly, as he rose from his chair, "there is some one coming out to dinner from Masterton. Oh, not any body that makes much difference—a young fellow—"

"Some young fellows make a great deal of difference," said Sara. "Who is it, papa?"

"Well—at present he is—only one of my clerks," said Mr. Brownlow, with an uneasy and, to tell the truth, rather humble and deprecating smile—"one you have seen before—he was out here that day I was ill."

"Oh, Mr. Powys," said Sara; and in a moment, before another word was spoken, her sublime indifference changed into the brightest gleam of malice, of mischief, of curiosity, that ever shone out of two blue eyes. "I remember him perfectly well—all about him," she said, with a touch of emphasis that was not lost on her father. "Is there any body else, papa?"

"Powys!" said Jack, turning back in amaze. He had been going out not thinking of any thing; but this intimation, coming just after the news of the office about Powys's increase of salary, roused his curiosity, and called him back to hear.

"Yes, Powys," said Mr. Brownlow, standing on his defense like a guilty man. "I hope you have not any objection."

"Objection, sir?" said Jack; "I don't know what you mean. It is your house, to ask any body you like. I never should have thought of making any objection."

"Yes, it is my own house," said Mr. Brownlow. It made him feel a little sore to have the plea about doing what he liked with his own thus taken, as it were, out of his very mouth.

"But I don't remember that you ever asked any of the clerks before," said Jack. It was not that he cared much about the invitation to the clerk; it was rather because he was disagreeable himself, and could not resist the chance of being disagreeable to others, being in a highly uncomfortable state of mind.

"I don't regard Powys as a mere clerk—there are circumstances," said Mr. Brownlow. "It is useless to explain at this moment; but I don't put him on the same level with Brown and Robinson. I should be glad if you could manage to be civil to him, Jack."

"Of course I shall be civil," said Jack. But he said, "That beggar again!" through his clenched teeth. Between himself and Powys there was a natural antagonism, and just now he was out of sorts and out of temper. Of course it was his father's house, not his, that he should make any pretension to control it, and of course he would be civil to his father's guests; but he could not help repeating, "That beggar!" to himself as he went out. Was his father bewitched? He had not the slightest idea what there could be to recommend this clerk, or to distinguish him from other clerks; and as for the circumstances of difference of which Mr. Brownlow spoke, Jack did not believe in them. He would be civil, of course; but he certainly did not undertake to himself to be any thing more cordial. And he went away with the determination not to be visible again till dinner. Powys!—a pretty thing to have to sit at table and make conversation for the junior clerk.

"Never mind, papa," said Sara. "Jack is dreadfully disagreeable just now; but you and I will entertain Mr. Powys. He is very nice. I don't see that it matters about his being one of the clerks."

"I was once a clerk myself," said Mr. Brownlow. "I don't know what difference it should make. But never mind; I have not come to that pitch that I require to consult Jack."

"No," said Sara, a little doubtfully. Even she, though she was a dutiful child, was not quite so clear on this subject. Mr. Brownlow had a right to do what he would with his own—but yet—Thus Sara remonstrated too. She did not give in her whole adhesion, right or wrong. She was curious and mischievous, and had no objection to see Powys again; but she was not quite clear in her mind, any more than the other people, about a man's utter mastery over his own. Mr. Brownlow saw it, and left her with something of the same feeling of discomfort which he had in the presence of Mr. Wrinkell and Mr. Brown. Was there any thing in this world which a man could really call his own, and of which he was absolutely free to dispose? It seemed to the lawyer, thinking it over, that there was no such absolute personal possession. After all, he of the vineyard settled the matter in a quite arbitrary way; and nowadays, amid all the intricacies of extreme civilization, such a simple way of cutting the knot was impracticable. Nobody knew that Mr. Brownlow's house, and money, and goods were not entirely and honestly his own property; and yet nobody would consent that he should administer them absolutely in his own way. He could not but smile at the thought as he went into the library, where he always felt himself so little at home. His position and relationship to every thing around him seemed to have changed in these days. He had been a just man all his life; but now it seemed to him that justice stood continually in his way. It was a rigid, unmanageable, troublesome principle, which did harm by way of doing right, and forbade the compromises which were essential in this world. Justice to Brown denied him the liberty to advance his clever junior. Justice to Jack forbade him his natural right to entertain whomsoever he pleased at his table. In fact, it was vain to use the possessive pronoun at all; nothing was his—neither his office, nor his money, nor his house—unless under the restriction of every body else's rights, and of public opinion beyond all. So Mr. Brownlow mused as he left Sara and retired to his solitude. "Is thine eye evil because I am good?" But then in the days of the parable there were fewer complications, and a man was more confident in his own power.

As for Sara, in her reflections on the subject, it occurred to her as very probable that Mr. Powys was coming early, and she stayed in-doors accordingly. She put herself into her favorite corner, by the window—that window which was close to the Claude—and took a little pile of books with her. Sunday afternoon, especially when one is very young, is a difficult moment. One never knows exactly what one ought to read. Such at least was Sara's experience. Novels, except under very rare and pressing circumstances, were clearly inadmissible—such circumstances, for instance, as having left your heroine in such a harrowing position that common charity required you to see her through it without delay. And real good books—those books which it is a merit to read—were out of Sara's way. I should be afraid to tell which were the special volumes she carried with her to the window, in case it might convey to some one, differently brought up perhaps, a false impression of the soundness of her views. She had Eugenie de Guerin's Letters in her hand, which ought to cover a multitude of sins; but she was not reading them. There was the ghost of a smile, a very ghost, appearing and disappearing, and never taking bodily shape, about her pretty mouth. What she was thinking was, who, for instance, this Mr. Powys could be? She did not believe he was a mere clerk. If he were a mere clerk, was it possible that he would be brought here and presented to her like this? That was not to be thought of for a moment. No doubt it was a prince in disguise. He might be an enchanted prince, bewitched out of his proper shape by some malignant fairy; but Sara knew better than to believe for a moment that he could be only a clerk. And he was very nice—he had nice eyes, and a nice smile. He was not exactly what you would call handsome, but he had those special gifts which are indispensable. And then poor papa was in a way about him, afraid to tell his secret, compelled to treat him as if he were only a clerk, afraid Jack should be uncivil. Jack was a bear, Sara concluded to herself, and at this moment more a bear than ever; but she should take care that the enchanted prince should not be rendered uncomfortable by his incivility. Sara's musings were to this effect, as she sat in her corner by the window, with Eugenie de Guerin in her hand. A soft, warm, balmy, sunny afternoon, one of those days in which the very air is happiness, and into which no trouble seems capable of entering—nineteen years old—a fairy prince in disguise, coming to test her disposition under his humble incognito. Do you think the young creature could forget all that, and enter even into Mademoiselle de Guerin's pure virginal world of pensive thoughts and world-renunciation, because it was Sunday? But Sara did all she could toward this end. She held that tender talisman in her hand; and, no doubt, if there were any ill spirits about, it kept them out of the way.

Powys for his part was walking up the avenue with a maze of very pleasant thoughts in his mind. He was not thinking particularly of Miss Brownlow. He was too sensible not to know that for him, a junior clerk just promoted to the glory of a hundred and twenty pounds a year, such an idea would have been pure madness. He was thinking, let us say, of the Claude, of how it hung, and all the little accessories round it, and of the sunshine that fell on Sara's dress, and on her hair, and how it resembled the light upon the rippled water in the picture, and that he was about to witness all that again. This is what he was thinking of. He was country bred, and to breathe the fresh air, and see the trees waving over his head, was new life to him; and warm gratitude, and a kind of affection to the man who generously gave him this pleasure, were in his mind. And notwithstanding the horrible effect that the burden of debt had so recently had upon him, and the fact that a hundred and twenty pounds a year are far, very far, from being a fortune, there was no whiteness now visible at his seams. He was as well dressed as he could be made in Masterton, which was a commencement at which Mr. Wrinkell, or any other good economist, would have frowned. Mr. Brownlow went to join his daughter in the drawing-room as soon as he heard that his visitor had come to the door, and met him in the hall, to Powys's great comfort and satisfaction. And they went up stairs together. The sunshine crossed Mr. Brownlow's grizzled locks, just as it had crossed the ripply shining hair, which glistened like the water in Claude's picture. But this time Powys did not take any notice of the effect. Sara was reading when they went in, and she rose, and half closed her book, and gave the guest a very gracious majestic welcome. It was best to be in-doors just then, while it was so hot, Sara thought. Yes, that was the Claude—did he recollect it? Most likely it was simply because he was a backwoodsman, and entirely uncivilized, that Powys conducted himself so well. He did not sit on the edge of his chair, as even Mr. Wrinkell did. He did not wipe his forehead, nor apologize for the dust, as Mr. Brown would have done. And he was grateful to Mr. Brownlow, and not in the least anxious to show that he was his equal. After a while, in short, it was the master of the house who felt that he was set at ease, as it was he who had been the most embarrassed and uncomfortable, and whose mind was much more occupied than that of his visitor was by thinking of the effect that Powys might produce.

At dinner, however, it was more difficult. Jack was present, and Jack was civil. It is at such a moment that breeding shows; any body, even the merest pretender, can be rude to an intruder, but it requires careful cultivation to be civil to him. Jack was so civil that he all but extinguished the rest of the party. He treated Mr. Powys with the most distinguished politeness. He did not unbend even to his father and sister. As for Willis, the butler, Jack behaved to him as if he had been an archbishop; and such very fine manners are troublesome when the party is a small one and disposed to be friendly and agreeable. Under any circumstances it would have been difficult to have kept up the conversation. They could not talk of their friends and ordinary doings, for Powys knew nothing about these; and though this piece of courtesy is by no means considered needful in all circles, still Mr. Brownlow was old-fashioned, and it was part of his code of manners. So they had to talk upon general subjects, which is always difficult; about books, the universal resource; and about the park, and the beauties of nature, and the difference of things in Canada; and about the music in Masterton church, and whether the new vicar was High or Low, which was a very difficult question for Powys, and one to which he did not know how to reply.

"I am sure he is High," said Sara. "The church was all decorated with flowers on Ascension Day. I know, for two of the maids were there and saw them; and what does it matter about a sermon in comparison with that?"

"Perhaps it was his wife's doing," said Mr. Brownlow, "for I think the sermon the best evidence. He is Low—as Low as you could desire."

"As I desire!" cried Sara. "Papa, you are surely forgetting yourself. As if I could be supposed to like a Low Churchman! And Mr. Powys says they have good music. That is proof positive. Don't you think so, Jack?"

This was one of many little attempts to bring back Jack to common humanity; for Sara, womanlike, could not be contented to leave him disagreeable and alone.

"I think Mr. Powys is extremely good to furnish you with information; but I can't say I am much interested in the question," said Jack, which brought the talk to a sudden pause.

"Mr. Powys has not seen our church, papa," Sara resumed. "It is such a dear old place. The chancel every body says is pure Norman, and there are some bits of real old glass in the west window. You should have gone to see it before dinner. Are you very fond of old glass?"

"I am afraid I don't know," said Powys, who was bright enough to see the manufactory of conversation which was being carried on, and was half amused by it and half distressed. "We have no old churches in Canada. I suppose they could scarcely be looked for in such a new world."

"Tell me what sort of churches you have," said Sara. "I am very fond of architecture. We can't do any thing original nowadays, you know. It is only copying and copying. But there ought to be a new field in a new world. Do tell me what style the people there like best."

"You strain Mr. Powys's powers too far," said Jack. "You can not expect him to explain every thing to you from the vicar's principles upward—or downward. Mr. Powys is only mortal, I presume, like the rest of us. He can't know every thing in heaven or earth."

"I know a little of that," said Powys. "Out there we are Jacks-of-all-trades. I once made the designs for a church myself. Miss Brownlow might think it original, but I don't think she would admire it. We have to think less of beauty than of use."

"As if use and beauty could not go together," said Sara, with a little indignation. "Please don't say those things that every body says. Then you can draw if you have made designs? and I want some cottages so much. Papa, you promised me these cottages; and now Mr. Powys will come and help me with the plans."

"There is a certain difference between a cottage and a church," said Mr. Brownlow; but he made no opposition to the suggestion, to the intense amazement and indignation of Jack.

"You forget that Mr. Powys's time is otherwise engaged," he said; "people can't be Jacks-of-all-trades here."

Mr. Brownlow gave his son a warning glance, and Sara, who had been very patient, could bear it no longer.

"Why are you so disagreeable, Jack?" she said; "nobody was speaking to you. It was to Mr. Powys I was speaking. He knows best whether he will help me or not."

"Oh, it was to Mr. Powys you were speaking!" said Jack. "I am a very unimportant person, and I am sorry to have interposed."

Then there came a very blank disagreeable pause. Powys felt that offense was meant, and his spirit rose. But at the same time it was utterly impossible to take offense; and he sat still and tried to appear unconscious, as people do before whom the veil of family courtesy is for a moment blown aside. There are few things which are more exquisitely uncomfortable. He had to look as if he did not observe any thing; and he had to volunteer to say something to cover the silence, and found it very hard to make up his mind as to what he ought to say.

Perhaps Jack was a little annoyed at himself for his freedom of speech, for he said nothing farther that was disagreeable, until he found that his father had ordered the dog-cart to take the visitor back to Masterton. When he came out in the summer twilight, and found the mare harnessed for such an ignoble purpose, his soul was hot within him. If it had been any other horse in the stable—but that his favorite mare should carry the junior clerk down to his humble dwelling-place, was bitterness to Jack. He stood and watched in a very uncomfortable sort of way, with his hands in his pockets, while Powys took his leave. The evening was as lovely as the day had been, and Sara too had come out, and stood on the steps, leaning on her father's arm. "Shall you drive, sir?" the groom had asked, with a respect which sprang entirely from his master's cordiality. It was merely a question of form, for the man expected nothing but a negative; but Powys's countenance brightened up. He held out his hands for the reins with a readiness which perhaps savored more of transatlantic freedom than ought to have been the case; but then he had been deprived of all such pleasures for so long. "Good heavens!" cried Jack, "Tomkins, what do you mean? It's the bay mare you have in harness. He can't drive her. If she's lamed, or if she lames you—"

And he went up to the side of the dog-cart, almost as if he would have taken the reins out of Powys's hand. The Canadian grew very red, and grasped the whip. They were very ready for a quarrel—Jack standing pale with anger, talking with the groom; Powys red with indignation, holding his place. But it was the latter who had the most command of himself.

"I shall not lame her," he said quietly, "nor let any one be lamed; jump up." He was thus master of the situation. The groom took his place; the mare went off straight and swift as an arrow down the avenue. But Jack knew by the look, as he said, of the fellow's wrist, by the glance in his eye, that he knew what he was about, though he did not at this moment confess the results of his observation. They stood all three on the steps when that fiery chariot wheeled away; and Jack, to tell the truth, did not feel very much satisfied with himself.

"Jack," said Mr. Brownlow, calmly, "when I have any one here again, I must require of you to keep from insulting them. If you do not care for the feelings of the stranger, you may at least have some regard for yourself."

"I had no intention of insulting any one, sir," said Jack, with a little defiance; "if you like him to break his neck or the horse's knees it is not my affair; but for a fellow who probably never had the reins in his hand before, to attempt with that mare—"

"He has had the reins in his hand oftener than either I or you," said Mr. Brownlow. The fact was he said it at hazard, thinking it most likely that Powys could drive, but knowing nothing more about it, while Jack knew by sight and vision, and felt himself in his heart a snob as he strolled away from the door. He was uncomfortable, but he succeeded in making his father more uncomfortable still. The mare, too, was his own, though it was Jack's favorite, and if he liked to have it he might. Such was the Parthian arrow which

Mr. Brownlow received at the end of the day. Clearly that was a distant land—a land far removed from the present burden of civilization—a primitive and blessed state of existence, in which a man could be permitted to do what he liked with his own.

CHAPTER XXII

THE DOWNFALL OF PHILOSOPHY

Jack Brownlow was having a very hard time of it just at that moment. There had been a lapse of more than a week, and he had not once seen the fair little creature of whom every day he had thought more and more. It was in vain that he looked up at the window—Pamela now was never there. He never saw her even at a distance—never heard so much as her name. Sara, who had been ready enough to speak of her friend—even Sara, indiscreet, and hasty, and imprudent—was silent. Poor Jack knew it was quite right—he recognized, even though he hated it, the force that was in his father's arguments. He knew he had much better never see her—never even speak of her again. He understood with his intelligence that utter separation between them was the only prudent and sensible step to be taken; but his heart objected to understand with a curious persistency which Jack could scarcely believe of a heart of his. He had found his intellect quite sufficient to guide him up to this period; and when that other part of him, with which he was so much less acquainted, fought and struggled to get the reins in hand, it would be difficult to express the astonishment he felt. And then he was a young man of the present day, and he was not anxiously desirous to marry. A house of his own, with all its responsibilities, did not appear to him the crown of delight which perhaps it ought to have done. He was content to go on with his life as it had been, without any immediate change. It still appeared to him, I am sorry to admit, that for a young man, who had a way to make in the world, a very early marriage was a sort of suicidal step to take. This was all very well for his mind, which wanted no convincing. But for his heart it was very different. That newly discovered organ behaved in the most incomprehensible sort of way. Even though it possibly gave a grunt of consent to the theory about marriage, it kept on longing and yearning, driving itself frantic with eagerness just to see her, just to hear her, just to touch her little hand, just to feel the soft passing rustle of her dress. That was all. And as for talking reason to it, or representing how profitless such a gratification would be, he might as well have preached to the stones. He went back and forward to the office for a whole week with this conflict going on within him, keeping dutifully to his work, doing more than he had done for years at Masterton, trying to occupy himself with former thoughts, and with anticipations of the career he had once shaped out for himself. He wanted to get away from the office, to get into public life somehow, to be returned for the borough, and have a seat in Parliament. Such had been his ambition before this episode in his life. Such surely ought to be his ambition now; but it was amazing, incredible, how this new force within him would break through all his more elevated thoughts with a kind of inarticulate cry for Pamela. She was what he wanted most. He could put the other things aside, but he could not put her aside. His heart kept crying out for her, whatever his mind might be trying to think. It was extraordinary and despicable, and he could not believe it of himself; but this was how it was. He knew it was best that he should not see her; yet it was no virtue nor self-denial of his that kept them apart. It was she who would not be visible. Along the roads, under the trees, at the window, morning or evening, there was no appearance of her. He thought sometimes she must have gone away. And his eager inquiries with himself whether this separation would make her unhappy gradually gave way to irritation and passionate displeasure. She had gone away, and left no sign; or she was shutting herself up, and sacrificing all that was pleasant in his existence. She was leaving him alone to bear the brunt; and he would gladly have taken it all to spare her—but if he bore it, and was the victim, something at least he ought to have had for his recompense. A last meeting, a last look, an explanation, a farewell—at least he had a right to that. And notwithstanding his anger he wanted her all the same—wanted to see her, to speak to her, to have her near him, though he was not ready to carry her off or marry her on the spot, or defy his father and all the world on her account. This was the painful struggle that poor Jack had to bear as he went back and forward all those days to Masterton. He held very little communication with his father, who was the cause of it all. He chose to ride or to walk rather than have those tête-à-tête drives. He kept his eyes on every turn of the way, on every tree and hedge which might possibly conceal her; and yet he knew he must part from her, and in his heart was aware that it was a right judgment which condemned him to this sacrifice. And it was not in him, poor fellow, to take it cheerfully or suffer with a good grace. He kept it to himself, and scorned to betray to his father or sister what he was going through. But he was not an agreeable companion during this interval, though the fact was that he gave them very little of his society, and struggled, mostly by himself, against his hard fate.

And probably he might have been victorious in the struggle. He might have fought his way back to the high philosophical ground from which he was wont to preach to his friend Keppel. At the cost of all the first freshness of his heart, at the cost of many buds of grace that never would have bloomed again, he might have come out victor, and demonstrated to himself beyond all dispute that in such matters a strong will is every thing, and that there is no love or longing that may not be crushed on the threshold of the mind. All this Jack might have done, and lived to profit by it and smart for it, but for a chance meeting by which fate, in spite of a thousand precautions, managed to balk his philosophy. He had gone home early in the afternoon, and he had been seen by anxious eyes behind the curtains of Mrs. Swayne's window—not Pamela's eyes, but those of her mother—to go out again dressed, about the time when a man who is going to dinner sets out to fulfill his engagement. And Jack was going out to dinner; he was going to Ridley, where the family had just come down from town. But there had come that day a kind of crisis in his complaint, and when he was half way to his friend's house a sudden disgust seized him. Instead of going on he jumped down from the dog-cart, and tore a leaf out of his pocket-book, on which he scribbled a hasty word of apology to Keppel. Then, while the groom went on with his note, he turned and went sauntering home along the dusty road in his evening coat. Why should he go and eat the fellow's dinner? What did he care about it? Go and make an ass of himself, and laugh and talk when he would much rather run a tilt against all the world! And what could she mean by shutting herself up like this, and never so much as saying good-bye? It could harm nobody to say good-bye. Thus Jack mused in pure despite and contrariety, without any intention of laying a snare for the object of his thoughts. He had gone a long way on the road to Ridley before he changed his mind, and consequently it was getting late when he drew near Brownlows coming back. It was a very quiet country road, a continuation of that which led to Masterton. Here and there, was a clump of great trees making it sombre, and then a long stretch of hedgerow with the fragrant meadow on the other side of it, and the cows lowing to go home. There was nobody to be seen up or down the road except a late carter with his horse's harness on his shoulder, and a boy and a girl driving home some cows. In the distance stood Swayne's Cottages, half lost in the twilight, with two faint curls of smoke going up into the sky. All was full of that dead calm which chafes the spirit of youth when it is in the midst of its troubles—that calm which is so soothing and so sweet when life and we have surmounted the first battles, and come to a moment of truce. But there was no truce as yet in Jack Brownlow's thoughts. He wanted to have his own way and he could not have it; and he knew he ought not to have it, and he would not give it up. If he could have kicked at the world, and strangled Nature and made an end of Reason, always without making a fool of himself, that would have been the course of action most in consonance with his thoughts.

And it was just then that a certain flutter round the corner of the lane which led to Dewsbury caught his eye—the flutter of the soft evening air in a black dress. It was not the "creatura bella vestita in bianca" which comes up to the ideal of a lover's fancy. It was a little figure in a black dress, with a cloak wrapped round her, and a broad hat shading her face, all dark among the twilight shadows. Jack saw, and his heart sprang up within him with a violence which took away his breath. He made but one spring across the road. When they had parted they had not known that they were lovers; but now they had been a week apart and there was no doubt on the subject. He made but one spring, and caught her and held her fast. "Pamela!" he cried out; and though there had been neither asking nor consent, and not one word of positive love-making between them, and though no disrespectful or irreverent thought of her had ever entered his mind, poor Jack, in his ardor and joy and surprise and rage, kissed her suddenly with a kind of transport. "Now I have you at last!" he cried. And this was in the open road, where all the world might have seen them; though happily, so far as was apparent, there was nobody to see.

Pamela, too, gave a cry of surprise and fright and dismay. But she was not angry, poor child. She did not feel that it was unnatural. Her poor little heart had not been standing still all this time any more than Jack's. They had gone over all those tender, childish, celestial preliminaries while they were apart; and now there could not be any doubt about the bond that united them. Neither the one nor the other affected to believe that farther preface was necessary—circumstances were too pressing for that. He said, "I have you at last," with eyes that gleamed with triumph; and she said, "Oh, I thought I should never, never see you again!" in a voice which left nothing to be confessed. And for the moment they both forgot every thing—fathers, mothers, promises, wise intentions, all the secondary lumber that makes up the world.

When this instant of utter forgetfulness was over, Pamela began to cry, and Jack's arm dropped from her waist. It was the next inevitable stage. They made two or three steps by each other's side, separate, despairing, miserable. Then it was the woman's turn to take the initiative. She was crying, but she could still speak—indeed, it is possible that her speech would have been less natural had it been without those breaks in the soft voice. "I am not angry," she said, "because it is the last time. I shall never, never forget you; but oh, it was all a mistake, all from the beginning. We never—meant—to grow fond of each other," said Pamela through her sobs; "it was all—all a mistake."

"I was fond of you the very first minute I saw you," said Jack; "I did not know then, but I know it now. It was no mistake;—that time when I carried you in out of the snow. I was fond of you then, just as I am now—as I shall be all my life."

"No," said Pamela, "oh no. It is different—every day in your life you see better people than I am. Don't say any thing else. It is far better for me to know. I have been a—a little—contented ever since I thought of that."

These words once more put Jack's self-denial all to flight. "Better people than you are?" he cried. "Oh, Pamela! I never saw any body half as sweet, half as lovely, all my life."

"Hush! hush! hush!" said Pamela; they were not so separate now, and she put her soft little hand up, as if to lay it on his lips. "You think so, but it is all—all a mistake!"

Then Jack looked into her sweet tearful eyes, nearer, far nearer than he had ever looked before—and they were eyes that could bear looking into, and the sweetness and the bitterness filled the young man's heart. "My little love!" he cried, "it is not you who are a mistake." And he clasped her, almost crushed her waist with his arm in his vehemence. Every thing else was a mistake—himself, his position, her position, all the circumstances; but not Pamela. This time she disengaged herself, but very softly, from his arm.

"I do not mind," she said, looking at him with an innocent, wistful tenderness, "because it is the last time. If you had not cared, I should have been vexed. One can't help being a little selfish. Last time, if you had said you were fond of me, I should have been frightened; but now I am glad, very glad you are fond of me. It will always be something to look back to. I shall remember every word you said, and how you looked. Mamma says life is so hard," said Pamela, faltering a little, and looking far away beyond her lover, as if she could see into a long stretch of life. So she did; and it looked a desert, for he was not to be there.

"Don't speak like that," cried Jack; "life shall not be hard to you—not while I live to take care of you—not while I can work—"

"Hush, hush!" said the girl, softly. "I like you to say it, you know. One feels glad; but I know there must be nothing about that. I never thought of it when—when we used to see each other so often. I never thought of any thing. I was only pleased to see you; but mamma has been telling me a great deal—every thing, indeed: I know better now—"

"What has she been telling you?" said Jack. "She has been telling you that I would deceive you; that I was not to be trusted. It is because she does not know me, Pamela. You know me better. I never thought of any thing either," he added, driven to simplicity by the force of his emotions, "except that I could not do without you, and that I was very happy. And Pamela, whatever it may cost, I can't live without you now."

"But you must," said Pamela: "if you could but hear what mamma says! She never said you would deceive me. What she said was, that we must not have our own way. It may break our hearts, but we must give up. It appears life is like that," said Pamela, with a deep sigh. "If you like any thing very much, you must give it up."

"I am ready to give up every thing else," said Jack, carried on by the tide, and forgetting all his reason; "but I will not give you up. My little darling, you are not to cry—I did not know I was so fond of you till that day. I didn't even know it till now," cried the young man. "You mustn't turn away from me, Pamela—give me your hand; and whatever happens to us, we two will stand by each other all our lives."

"Ah, no," said Pamela, drawing away her hand; and then she laid the same hand which she had refused to give him on his shoulder and looked up into his face. "I like you to say it all," she went on—"I do—it is no use making believe when we are just going to part. I shall remember every word you say. I shall always be able to think that when I was young I had some one to say these things to me. If your father were to come now, I should not be afraid of him; I should just tell him how it was. I am glad of every word that I can treasure up. Mamma said I was not to see you again; but I said if we were to meet we had a right to speak to each other. I never thought I should have seen you to-night. I shouldn't mind saying to your father himself that we had a right to speak. If we should both live long and grow old, and never meet for years and years, don't you think we shall still know each other in heaven?"

As for poor Jack, he was driven wild by this, by the sadness of her sweet eyes, by the soft tenderness of her voice, by the virginal simplicity and sincerity which breathed out of her. Pamela stood by him with the consciousness that it was the supreme moment of her existence. She might have been going to die; such was the feeling in her heart. She was going to die out of all the sweet hopes, all the dawning joys of her youth; she was going out into that black desert of life where the law was that if you liked any thing very much you must give it up. But before she went she had a right to open her heart, to hear him disclose his. Had it been possible that their love should have come to any thing, Pamela would have been shy and shamefaced; but that was not possible. But a minute was theirs, and the dark world gaped around to swallow them up from each other. Therefore the words flowed in a flood to Pamela's lips. She had so many things to say to him—she wanted to tell him so much; and there was but this minute to include all. But her very composure—her tender solemnity—the pure little white martyr that she was, giving up what she most loved, gave to Jack a wilder thrill, a more headlong impulse. He grasped her two hands, he put his arm round her in a sudden passion. It seemed to him that he had no patience with her or any thing—that he must seize upon her and carry her away.

"Pamela," he cried, hoarsely, "it is of no use talking—you and I are not going to part like this. I don't know any thing about heaven, and I don't want to know—not just now. We are not going to part, I tell you. Your mother may say what she likes, but she can't be so cruel as to take you from a man who loves you and can take care of you—and I will take care of you, by heaven! Nobody shall ever come between us. A fellow may think and think when he doesn't know his own mind: and it's easy for a girl like you to talk of the last time. I tell you it is not the last time—it is the first time. I don't care a straw for any thing else in the world—not in comparison with you. Pamela, don't cry; we are going to be together all our life."

"You say so because you have not thought about it," said Pamela, with an ineffable smile; "and I have been thinking of it ever so long—ever so much. No; but I don't say you are to go away, not yet. I want to have you as long as I can; I want to tell you so many things—every thing I have in my heart."

"And I will hear nothing," said Jack—"nothing except that you and I belong to each other. That's what you have got to say. Hush, child! do you think I am a child like you? Pamela, look here—I don't know when it is to be, nor how it is to be, but you are going to be my wife."

"Oh, no, no," said Pamela, shrinking from him, growing red and growing pale in the shock of this new suggestion. If this was how it was to be, her frankness, her sad openness, became a kind of crime. She had suffered his embrace before, prayed him to speak to her, thought it right to take full advantage of the last indulgence accorded to them; and now the tables were turned upon her. She shrank away from him, and stood apart in the obscure twilight. There had not been a blush on her cheek while she opened her innocent young heart to him in the solemnity of the supposed farewell, but now she was overwhelmed with sudden shame.

"I say yes, yes, yes," said Jack vehemently, and he seized upon the hands that she had clasped together by way of safeguard. He seized upon them with a kind of violence appropriating what was his own. His mind had been made up and his fate decided in that half hour. He had been full of doubts up to this moment; but now he had found out that without Pamela it was not worth while to live—that Pamela was slipping through his fingers, ready to escape out of his reach; and after that there was no longer any possibility of a compromise. He had become utterly indifferent to what was going on around as he came to this point. He had turned his back on the road, and could not tell who was coming or going. And thus it was that the sudden intrusion which occurred to them was entirely unexpected, and took them both by surprise. All of a sudden, while neither was looking, a substantial figure was suddenly thrust in between them. It was Mrs. Swayne, who had been at Dewsbury and was going home. She did not put them aside with her hands, but she pushed her large person completely between the lovers, thrusting one to one side and the other to the other. With one of her arms she caught Pamela's dress, holding her fast, and with the other she pushed Jack away. She was flushed with walking and haste, for she had seen the two figures a long way off, and had divined what sort of meeting it was; and the sight of her fiery countenance between them startled the two so completely that they fell back on either side and gazed at her aghast, without saying a word. Pamela, startled and overcome, hid her face in her hands, while Jack made a sudden step back, and got very hot and furious, but for the moment found himself incapable of speech.

"For shame of yourself!" said Mrs. Swayne, panting for breath; "I've a'most killed myself running, but I've come in time. What are you a persuadin' of her to do, Mr. John? Oh for shame of yourself! Don't tell me! I know what young gentlemen like you is. A-enticin' her and persuadin' her and leading her away, to bring her poor mother's gray hairs with sorrow to the grave. Oh for shame of yourself! And her mother just as simple and innocent, as would believe any thing you liked to tell her; and nobody as can keep this poor thing straight and keep her out o' trouble but me!"

While she panted out this address, and thrust him away with her extended hand, Jack stood by in consternation, furious but speechless. What could he do? He might order her away, but she would not obey him. He might make his declaration over again in her presence, but she would not believe him, and he did not much relish the idea; he could not struggle with this woman for the possession of his love, and at the same time his blood boiled at her suggestions. If she had been a man he might have knocked her down quietly, and been free of the obstruction, but women take a shabby advantage of the fact that they can not be knocked down. As he stood thus with all his eloquence stopped on his lips, Pamela, from across the bulky person of her champion, stretched out her little hand to him and interposed.

"Hush," she said; "we were saying good-bye to each other, Mrs. Swayne. I told mamma we should say good-bye. Hush, oh hush, she doesn't understand; but what does that matter? we must say good-bye all the same."

"I shall never say good-bye," said Jack; "you ought to know me better than that. If you must go home with this woman, go—I am not going to fight with her. It matters nothing about her understanding; but, Pamela, remember it is not good-bye. It shall never be good-bye—"

"Understand!" said Mrs. Swayne, whose indignation was furious, "and why shouldn't I understand? Thank Providence I'm one as knows what temptation is. Go along with you home, Mr. John; and she'll just go with this woman, she shall. Woman, indeed! And I don't deny as I'm a woman—and so was your own mother for all so fine as you are. Don't you think as you'll lay your clutches on this poor lamb, as long as Swayne and me's to the fore. I mayn't understand, and I may be a woman, but—Miss Pamela, you'll just come along home."

"Yes, yes," said Pamela; and then she held up her hand to him entreatingly. "Don't mind what she says—don't be angry with me; and I will never, never forget what you have said—and—good-bye," said the girl, steadily, holding out her hand to him with a wonderful glistening smile that shone through two big tears.

As for Jack, he took her hand and gave it an angry loving grasp which hurt it, and then threw it away. "I am going to see your mother," he said, deigning no reply. And then he turned his back on her without another word, and left her standing in the twilight in the middle of the dusty road, and went away. He left the two women standing amazed, and went off with quick determined steps that far outstripped their capabilities. It was the road to the cottage—the road to Brownlows—the road anywhere or everywhere. "He's a-going home, and a blessed riddance," said Mrs. Swayne, though her spirit quaked within her. But Pamela said nothing; he was not going home. The girl stood and watched his quick firm steps and worshiped him in her heart. To her mother! And was there any thing but one thing that her mother could say?

CHAPTER XXIII

ALL FOR LOVE

It was almost dark when Jack reached Swayne's Cottages, and there was no light in Mrs. Preston's window to indicate her presence. The only bit of illumination there was in the dim dewy twilight road, was a gleam from old Betty's perennial fire, which shone out as she opened the door to watch the passage of the dog-cart just then returning from Ridley, where it ought to have carried Mr. John to dinner. The dog-cart was just returning home, in an innocent, unconscious way; but how much had happened in the interval! the thought made Jack's head whirl a little, and made him half smile; only half smile—for such a momentous crisis is not amusing. He had not had time to think whether or not he was rapturously happy, as a young lover ought to be: on the whole, it was a very serious business. There were a thousand things to think of, such as take the laughter out of a man; yet he did smile as it occurred to him in what an ordinary commonplace sort of way the dog-cart and the mare and the groom had been jogging back along the dusty roads, while he had been so weightily engaged; and how all those people had been calmly dining at Ridley—were dining now, no doubt—and mentally criticising the dishes, and making feeble dinner table-talk, while he had been settling his fate; in less time than they could have got half through their dinner—in less time than even the bay mare could devour the way between the two houses! Jack felt slightly giddy as he thought of it, and his face grew serious again under his smile. The cottage door stood innocently open; there was nobody and nothing between him and his business; he had not even to knock, to be opened to by a curious indifferent servant, as would have been the case in another kind of house. The little passage was quite dark, but there was another gleam of fire-light from the kitchen, where Mr. Swayne sat patient with his rheumatism, and even Mrs. Preston's door was ajar. Out of the soft darkness without, into the closer darkness within, Jack stepped with a beating heart. This was not the pleasant part of it; this was not like the sudden delight of meeting Pamela—the sudden passion of laying hold on her and claiming her as his own. He stopped in the dark passage, where he had scarcely room to turn, and drew breath a little. He felt within himself that if Mrs. Preston in her black cap and her black gown fell into his arms and saluted him as her son, that he would not be so deeply gratified as perhaps he ought to have been. Pamela was one thing, but her mother was quite another. If mothers, and fathers too for that matter, could but be done away with when their daughters are old enough to marry, what a great deal of trouble it would spare in this world! But that was not to be thought of. He had come to do it, and it had to be done. While he stood taking breath and collecting himself, Mr. Swayne feeling that the step which had crossed his threshold was not his wife's step, called out to the intruder. "Who are you?" cried the master of the house; "you wait till my missis comes and finds you there; she don't hold with no tramp; and I see her a-coming round the corner," he continued, in tones in which exultation had triumphed over fright. No tramp could have been more moved by the words than was Jack. He resisted the passing impulse he had to stride into the kitchen and strangle Mr. Swayne in passing; and then, with one knock by way of preface, he went in without further introduction into the parlor where Mrs. Preston was alone.

It was almost quite dark—dark with that bewildering summer darkness which is more confusing than positive night. Something got up hastily from the sofa at the sight of him, and gave a little suppressed shriek of alarm. "Don't be alarmed—it is only I, Mrs. Preston," said Jack. He made a step forward and looked at her, as probably she too was looking at him; but they could not see each other, and it was no comfort to Pamela's mother to be told by Jack Brownlow, that it was only I.

"Has any thing happened?" she cried; "what is it? what is it? oh my child!—for God's sake, whoever you are, tell me what it is."

"There is nothing the matter with her," said Jack, steadily. "I am John Brownlow, and I have come to speak to you; that is what it is."

"John Brownlow," said Mrs. Preston, in consternation—and then her tone changed. "I am sorry I did not know you," she said; "but if you have any business with me, sir, I can soon get a light."

"Indeed I have the most serious business," said Jack—it was in his mind to say that he would prefer being without a light; but there would have been something too familiar and undignified for the occasion in such a speech as that.

"Wait a moment," said Mrs. Preston, and she hastened out, leaving him in the dark parlor by himself. Of course he knew it was only a pretext—he knew as well as if she had told him that she had gone to establish a watch for Pamela to prevent her from coming in while he was there; and this time he laughed outright. She might have done it an hour ago, fast enough; but now to keep Pamela from him was more than all the fathers and mothers in the world could do. He laughed at the vain precaution. It was not that he had lost all sense of prudence, or that he was not aware how foolish a thing in many respects he was doing; but notwithstanding, he laughed at the idea that any thing, stone walls and iron bars, or admonitions, or parental orders, could keep her from him. It might be very idiotic—and no doubt it was; but if any body dreamed for a moment that he could be made to give her up! or that she could be wrested out of his grasp now that he had possession of her—any deluded individual who might entertain such a notion could certainly know nothing of Jack.

Mrs. Preston was absent for some minutes, and before she came back there had been a soft rustle in the passage, a subdued sound of voices, in one of which, rapidly suppressed and put a stop to, Jack could discern Mrs. Swayne's voluble tones. He smiled to himself in the darkness as he stood and waited; he knew what was going on as well as if he had been outside and had seen it all. Pamela was being smuggled into the house, being put somewhere out of his way. Probably her mother was making an attempt to conceal from her even the fact that he was there, and at this purely futile attempt Jack again laughed in his heart; then in his impatience he strode to the window, and looked out at the gates which were indistinctly visible opposite, and the gleam of Betty's fire, which was now apparent only through her window. That was the way it would have been natural for him to go, not this—there lay his home, wealthy, luxurious, pleasant, with freedom in it, and every thing that ministered most at once to his comfort and his ambition: and yet it was not there he had gone, but into this shabby little dingy parlor, to put his life and all his pleasure in life, and his prospects and every thing for which he most cared, at the disposal, not of Pamela, but of her mother. He felt that it was hard. As for her, the little darling! to have taken her in his arms and carried her off and built a nest for her would not have been hard—but that it should all rest upon the decision of her mother! Jack felt at the moment that it was a hard thing that there should be mothers standing thus in the young people's way. It might be very unamiable on his part, but that was unquestionably his feeling: and indeed, for one second, so terrible did the prospect appear to him, that the idea of taking offense and running away did once cross his mind. If they chose to leave him alone like this, waiting, what could they expect? He put his hand upon the handle of the door, and then withdrew it as if it had burned him. A minute after Mrs. Preston came back. She carried in her hand a candle, which threw a bright light upon her worn face, with the black eyes, black hair, black cap and black dress close round her throat which so much increased the gauntness of her general appearance. This time her eyes, though they were old, were very bright—bright with anxiety and alarm—so bright that for the moment they were like Pamela's. She came in and set down her candle on the table, where it shed a strange little pale inquisitive light, as if, like Jack, it was looking round, half dazzled by the change out of complete darkness, at the unfamiliar place; and then she drew down the blind. When she had done this she came to the table near which Jack was standing. "Mr. Brownlow, you want to speak to me?" she said.

"Yes," said Jack. Though his forefathers had been Brownlows of Masterton for generations, which ought to have given him self-possession if any thing could, and though he had been brought up at a public-school, which was still more to the purpose, this simple question took away the power of speech from him as completely as if he had been the merest clown. He had not felt the least difficulty about what he was going to say, but all at once to say any thing at all seemed impossible.

"Then tell me what it is," said Mrs. Preston, sitting down in the black old-fashioned high-backed easy-chair. Her heart was melting to him more and more every moment, the sight of his confusion being sweet to her eyes, but of course he did not know this—neither, it is to be feared, would Jack have very much cared.

"Yes," he said again; "the fact was—I—wanted to speak to you—about your daughter. I suppose this sort of thing is always an awkward business. I have seen her with—with my sister, you know—we couldn't help seeing each other; and the fact is, we've—we've grown fond of each other without knowing it: that is about the state of the case."

"Fond of each other?" said Mrs. Preston, faltering. "Mr. Brownlow, I don't think that is how you ought to speak. You mean you have grown fond of Pamela. I am very, very sorry; but Heaven forbid that my poor girl—"

"I mean what I say," said Jack, sturdily—"we've grown fond of each other. If you ask her she will tell you the same. We were not thinking of any thing of the kind—it came upon us unawares. I tell you the whole truth, that you may not wonder at me coming so unprepared. I don't come to you as a fellow might that had planned it all out and turned it over in his mind, and could tell you how much he had a year, and what he could settle on his wife, and all that. I tell you frankly the truth, Mrs. Preston. We were not thinking of any thing of the kind; but now, you see, we have both of us found it out."

"I don't understand you," said the astonished mother; "what have you found out?"

"We've found out just what I've been telling you," said Jack—"that we're fond of each other. You may say I should have told you first; but the truth was, I never had the opportunity—not that I would have been sure to have taken advantage of it if I had. We went on without knowing what we were doing, and then it came upon us all at once."

He sat down abruptly as he said this, in an abstracted way; and he sighed. He had found it out, there could be no doubt of that; and he did not hide from himself that this discovery was a very serious one. It filled his mind with a great many thoughts. He was no longer in a position to go on amusing himself without any thought of the future. Jack was but mortal, and it is quite possible he might have done so had it been in his power. But it was not in his power, and his aspect, when he dropped into the chair, and looked into the vacant air before him and sighed, was rather that of a man looking anxiously into the future—a future that was certain—than of a lover waiting for the sentence which (metaphorically) is one of life or death; and Mrs. Preston, little experienced in such matters, and much agitated by the information so suddenly conveyed to her, did not know what to think. She bent forward and looked at him with an eagerness which he never perceived. She clasped her hands tightly together, and gazed as if she would read his heart; and then what could she say? He was not asking any thing from her—he was only intimating to her an unquestionable fact.

"But, Mr. Brownlow," she said at last, tremulously, "I think—I hope you may be mistaken. My Pamela is very young—and so are you—very young for a man. I hope you have made a mistake. At your age it doesn't matter so much."

"Don't it, though?" said Jack, with a flash in his eyes. "I can't, say to you that's our business, for I know, of course, that a girl ought to consult her mother. But don't let us discuss that, please. A fact can't be discussed, you know. It's either true or it's false—and we certainly are the only ones who can know."

Then there was another pause, during which Jack strayed off again into calculations about the future—that unforeseen future which had leaped into existence for him only about an hour ago. He had sat down on the other side of the table, and was gazing into the blank hearth as if some enlightenment might have been found there. As for Mrs. Preston, her amazement and agitation were such that it cost her a great effort to compose herself and not to give way.

"Is this all you have to say to me?" she said at last, with trembling lips.

Then Jack roused himself up. Suddenly it occurred to him that the poor woman whom he had been so far from admiring was behaving to him with a generosity and delicacy very different from his conduct to her; and the blood rushed to his face at the thought.

"I beg your pardon," he said. "I have already explained to you why it is that I come in such an unprepared way. I met her to-night. Upon my life I did not lay any trap for her. I was awfully cut up about not seeing her; but we met by accident. And the fact was, when we met we couldn't help showing that we understood each other. After that it was my first duty," said Jack, with a thrill of conscious grandeur, "to come to you."

"But do you mean to say," said Mrs. Preston, wringing her hands, "that my Pamela—? Sir, she is only a child. She could not have understood you. She may like you in a way—"

"She likes me as I like her," said Jack, stoutly. "It's no use struggling against it. It is no use arguing about it. You may think her a child, but she is not a child; and I can't do without her, Mrs. Preston. I hope you haven't any dislike to me. If you have," said Jack, warming up, "I will do any thing a man can do to please you; but you couldn't have the heart to make her unhappy, and come between her and me."

"I make her unhappy?" said Mrs. Preston, with a gasp. She who had no hope or desire in the world but Pamela's happiness! "But I don't even see how it came about. I—I don't understand you. I don't even know what you want of me."

"What I want?" said Jack, turning round upon her with wondering eyes—"What could I want but one thing? I want Pamela—that's very clear. Good heavens, you are not going to be ill, are you? Shall I call somebody? I know it's awfully sudden," said the young fellow ruefully. Nobody could be more sensible of that than he was. He got up in his dismay and went to a side-table where there stood a carafe of water and brought her some. It was the first act of human fellowship, as it were, that had passed between the two, and somehow it brought them together. Mrs. Preston took the water with that strange half-sacramental feeling with which a soul in extremity receives the refreshment which brings it back to life. Was it her friend, her son, or her enemy that thus ministered to her? Oh, if she could only have seen into his heart! She had no interest in the world but Pamela, and now the matter in hand was the decision for good or for evil of Pamela's fate.

"I am better, thank you," she said faintly. "I am not very strong, and it startled me. Sit down, Mr. Brownlow, and let us talk it over. I knew this was what it would have come to if it had gone on; but I have been talking a great deal to my child, and keeping her under my eye—"

"Yes," said Jack, with some indignation, "keeping her out of my way. I knew you were doing that."

"It was the only thing I could do," said Mrs. Preston. "I did try to find another means, but it did not succeed. When I asked you what you wanted of me, I was not doubting your honor. But things are not so easy as you young people think. Your father never will consent."

"I don't think things are easy," said Jack. "I see they are as crooked and hard as possible. I don't pretend to think it's all plain sailing. I believe he won't consent. It might have been all very well to consider that three months ago, but you see we never thought of it then. We must just do without his consent now."

"And there is more than that," said Mrs. Preston. "It would not be right for him to consent, nor for me either. If you only found it out so suddenly, how can you be sure of your own mind, Mr. John—and you so young? I don't say any thing of my own child. I don't mean to say in my heart that I think you too grand for her. I know if ever there was a lady born it's—; but that's not the question," she continued, nervously wringing her hands again. "If she was a princess, she's been brought up different from you. I did think once there might have been a way of getting over that; but I know better now; and you're very young; and from what you say," said Pamela's mother, who, after all, was a woman, a little romantic and very proud, "I don't think you're one that would be content to give up every thing for love."

Jack had been listening calmly enough, not making much in his own mind of her objections; but the last words did strike home. He started, and he felt in his heart a certain puncture, as if the needle in Mrs. Preston's work, which lay on the table, had gone into him. This at least was true. He looked at her with a certain defiance, and yet with respect. "For love—no," said Jack half fiercely, stirred, like a mere male creature as he was, by the prick of opposition; and then a softening came over his eyes, and a gleam came into them which, even by the light of the one pale candle, made itself apparent; "but for Pamela—yes. I'll tell you one thing, Mrs. Preston," he added, quickly, "I should not call it giving up. I don't mean to give up. As for my father, I don't see what he has to do with it. I can work for my wife as well as any other fellow could. If I were to say it didn't matter, you might mistrust me; but when a man knows it does matter," said Jack, again warming with his subject, "when a man sees it's serious, and not a thing to be done without thinking, you can surely rely upon him more than if he went at it blindly? I think so at least."

So saying, Jack stopped, feeling a little sore and incompris. If he had made a fool of himself, no doubt the woman would have believed in him; but because he saw the gravity of what he was about to do, and felt its importance, a kind of doubt was in his hearer's heart. "They not only expect a man to be foolish, but they expect him to forget his own nature," Jack said to himself, which certainly was hard.

"I don't mistrust you," said Mrs. Preston, but her voice faltered, and did not quite carry out her words; "only, you know, Mr. John, you are very young. Pamela is very young, but you are even younger than she is—I mean, you know, because you are a man; and how can you tell that you know your own mind? It was only to-day that you found it out, and to-morrow you might find something else out—"

Here she stopped half frightened, for Jack had risen up, and was looking at her over the light of the candle, looking pale and somewhat threatening. He was not in a sentimental attitude, neither was there any thing about him that breathed the tender romance for which in her heart Mrs. Preston sighed, and without which it cost her an effort to believe in his sincerity. He was standing with his hands thrust down to the bottom of his pockets, his brow a little knitted, his face pale, his expression worried and impatient. "What is the use of beginning over and over again?" said Jack. "Do you think I could have found out like this a thing that hadn't been in existence for months and months? Why, the first time I saw you in Hobson's cart—the time I carried her in out of the snow—" When he had got this length, he walked away to the window and stood looking out, though the blind was down, with his back turned upon her—"with her little red cloak, and her pretty hair," said Jack, with a curious sound which would not bear classification. It might have been a laugh, or a sob, or a snort—and it was neither; anyhow, it expressed the emotion within him better than half a hundred fine speeches. "And you don't believe in me after all that!" he said, coming back again and looking at her once more over the light of the candle. Perhaps it was something in Jack's eyes, either light or moisture, it would be difficult to tell which, that overpowered Mrs. Preston, for the poor woman faltered and began to cry.

"I do believe in you," she said. "I do—and I love you for saying it; but oh, Mr. John, what am I to do? I can't let you ruin yourself with your father. I can't encourage you when I know what it will cost you; and then, my own child—"

"That's it," said Jack, drawing his chair over to her side of the table, with his first attempt at diplomacy—"that's what we've got to think of. It doesn't matter for a fellow like me. If I got disappointed and cut up I should have to bear it; but as for Pamela, you know—dear little soul! You may think it strange, but," said Jack, with a little affected laugh, full of that supreme vanity and self-satisfaction with which a man recognizes such a fact, "she is fond of me; and if she were disappointed and put out, you know—why, it might make her ill—it might do her no end of harm—it might—Seriously, you know," said Jack, looking in Mrs. Preston's face, and giving another and another hitch to his chair. Though her sense of humor was not lively, she dried her eyes and looked at him with a little bewilderment, wondering was he really in earnest? did he mean it? or what did he mean?

"She is very young," said Mrs. Preston; "no doubt it would do her harm; but I should be there to nurse her—and—and—she is so young."

"It might kill her," said Jack, impressively; "and then whom would you have to blame? Not my father, for he has nothing to do with it; but yourself, Mrs. Preston—that's how it would be. Just look at what a little delicate darling she is—a little bit of a thing that one could carry away in one's arms," he went on, growing more and more animated—"a little face like a flower; and after the bad illness she had. I would not take such a responsibility for any thing in the world," he added, with severe and indignant virtue. As for poor Mrs. Preston, she did not know what to do. She wrung her hands; she looked at him beseechingly, begging him with her eyes to cease. Every feature of the picture came home to her with a much deeper force than it did to her mentor. Jack no more believed in any danger to Pamela than he did in his own ultimate rejection; but the poor mother beheld her daughter pining, dying, breaking her heart, and trembled to her very soul.

"Oh, Mr. John," she cried, with tears, "don't break my heart! What am I to do? If I must either ruin you with your father—"

"Or kill your child," said Jack, looking at her solemnly till his victim shuddered. "Your child is more to you than my father: besides," said the young man, unbending a little, "it would not ruin me with my father. He might be angry. He might make himself disagreeable; but he's not a muff to bear malice. My father," continued Jack, with emphasis, feeling that he owed his parent some reparation, and doing it magnificently when he was about it, "is as true a gentleman as I know. He's not the man to ruin a fellow. You think of Pamela, and never mind me."

But it took a long time and much reiteration to convince Mrs. Preston. "If I could but see Mr. Brownlow, I could tell him something that would perhaps soften his heart," she said; but this was far from being a pleasant suggestion to Jack. He put it down summarily, not even asking in his youthful impatience what the something was. He had no desire to know. He did not want his father's heart to be softened. In short, being as yet unaccustomed to the idea, he did not feel any particular delight in the thought of presenting Pamela's mother to the world as belonging to himself. And yet this same talk had made a wonderful difference in his feeling toward Pamela's mother. The thought of the explanation he had to make to her was repugnant to him when he came in. He had all but run away from it when he was left to wait alone. And now, in less than an hour, it seemed so natural to enter into every thing. Even if she had bestowed a maternal embrace upon him, Jack did not feel as if he would have resisted; but she gave him no motherly kiss. She was still half frightened at him, half disposed to believe that to get rid of him would be the best thing; and Jack had no mind to be got rid of. Neither of them could have told very exactly what was the understanding upon which they parted. There was an understanding, that was certain—an arrangement, tacit, inexpressible, which, however, was not hostile. He was not permitted in so many words to come again; but neither was he sent away. When he had the assurance to ask to see Pamela before he left, Mrs. Preston went nervously through the passage before him and opened the door, opening up the house and their discussion as she did so, to the big outside world and wakeful sky, with all its stars, which seemed to stoop and look in. Poor little Pamela was in the room up stairs, speechless, motionless, holding her breath, fixed as it were to the window from which she must see him go out; hearing the indistinct hum of voices underneath, and wondering what her mother was saying to him. When the parlor door opened, her heart leaped up in her breast. She could hear his voice, and distinguish, as she thought, every tone of it, but she could not hear what he said. For an instant it occurred to her too that she might be called down stairs. But then the next moment the outer door opened, a breath of fresh air stole into the house, and she knew he was dismissed. How had he been dismissed? For the moment? for the night? or forever? The window was open to which Pamela clung in the darkness, and she could hear his step going out. And as he went he spoke out loud enough to be heard up stairs, to be heard by any body on the road, and almost for that matter to be heard at Betty's cottage. "If I must not see her," he said, "give her my dear love." What did it mean. Was his dear love his last message of farewell? or was it only the first public indication that she belonged to him? Pamela sank down on her knees by the window, noiseless, with her heart beating so in her ears that she felt as if he must hear it outside. The whole room, the whole house, the whole air, seemed to her full of that throbbing. His dear love! It seemed to come in to her with the fresh air—to drop down upon her from the big stars as they leaned out of heaven and looked down; and yet she could not tell if it meant death or life. And Mrs. Preston was not young, and could not fly, but came so slowly, so slowly, up the creaking wooden stair!

Poor Mrs. Preston went slowly, not only because of her age, but because of her burden of thoughts. She could not have told any one whether she was very happy or deadly sad. Her heart was not fluttering in her ears like Pamela, but beating out hard throbs of excitement. He was good, he was true; her heart accepted him. Perhaps he was the friend she had so much longed for, who would guard Pamela when she was gone. At present, however, she was not gone; and yet her sceptre was passing away out of her hands, and her crown from her head. Anyhow, for good or for evil, this meant change; the sweet sceptre of love, the crown of natural authority and duty, such as are the glory of a woman who is a mother, were passing away from her. She did not grudge it. She would not have grudged life, nor any thing dearer than life, for Pamela; but she felt that there was change coming: and it made her sick—sick and cold and shivering, as if she was going to have a fever. She would have been glad to have had wings and flown to carry joy to her child; but she could not go fast for the burden and heaviness of her thoughts.

Meanwhile Jack crossed the road briskly, and went up the avenue under the big soft lambent stars. If it was at him in his character of lover that they were looking, they might have saved themselves the trouble, for he took no notice whatever of these sentimental spectators. He went home, not in a lingering meditative way, but like a man who has made up his mind. He had no sort of doubt or disquietude for his part about the acceptance of his love. He knew that Pamela was his, though her mother would not let him see her. He knew he should see her, and that she belonged to him, and nobody on earth could come between them. He had known all this from the first moment when the simple little girl had told him that life was hard; and as for her mother or his father, Jack did not in his mind make much account of the opposition of these venerable personages—such being his nature. What remained now was to clear a way into the future, to dig out a passage, and make it as smooth as possible for these tremulous little feet. Such were the thoughts he was busy with as he went home—not even musing about his little love. He had mused about her often enough before. Now his practical nature resumed the sway. How a household could be kept up, when it should be established, by what means it was to be provided, was the subject of Jack's thoughts. He went straight to the point without any circumlocution. As it was to be done, it would be best to be done quickly. And he did not disguise from himself the change it would make. He knew well enough that he could not live as he had lived in his father's house. He would have to go into lodgings, or to a little house; to have one or two indifferent servants—perhaps a "child-wife"—perhaps a resident mother-in-law. All this Jack calmly faced and foresaw. It could not come on him unawares, for he considered the chances, and saw that all these things were possible. There are people who will think the worse of him for this; but it was not Jack's fault—it was his constitution. He might be foolish like his neighbors on one point, but on all other points he was sane. He did not expect that Pamela, if he translated her at once into a house of her own, should be able to govern him and it on the spot by natural intuition. He knew there would be, as he himself expressed it, many "hitches" in the establishment, and he knew that he would have to give up a great many indulgences. This was why he took no notice of the stars, and even knitted his brows as he walked on. The romantic part of the matter was over. It was now pure reality, and that of the most serious kind, that he had in hand.

CHAPTER XXIV

A NEW CONSPIRATOR

"I don't say as you're to take my advice," said Mrs. Swayne. "I'm not one as puts myself forward to give advice where it ain't wanted. Ask any one as knows. You as is church folks, if I was you, I'd send for the rector; or speak to your friends. There ain't one living creature with a morsel of sense as won't say to you just what I'm saying now."

"Oh please go away—please go away," said Pamela, who was standing with crimson cheeks between Mrs. Preston and her would-be counselor; "don't you see mamma is ill?"

"She'll be a deal worse afore all's done, if she don't listen in time; and you too, Miss Pamela, for all so angry as you are," said Mrs. Swayne. "It ain't nothing to me. If you like it, it don't do me no harm; contrairaways, it's my interest to keep you quiet here, for you're good lodgers—I don't deny it—and ain't folks as give trouble. But I was once a pretty lass myself," she added, with a sigh; "and I knows what it is."

Pamela turned with unfeigned amazement and gazed upon the big figure that stood in the door-way. Once a pretty lass herself! Was this what pretty lasses came to? Mrs. Swayne, however, did not pause to inquire what were the thoughts that were passing through the girl's mind; she took a step or two farther into the room, nearer the sofa on which Mrs. Preston lay. She was possessed with that missionary zeal for other people's service, that determination to do as much as lay in her power to keep her neighbors from having their own way, or to make them very uncomfortable in the enjoyment of the luxury, which is so common a development of virtue. Her conscience was weighted with her responsibility: when she had warned them what they were coming to, then at least she would have delivered her own soul.

"I don't want to make myself disagreeable," said Mrs. Swayne; "it ain't my way; but, Mrs. Preston, if you go on having folks about, it's right you should hear what them as knows thinks of it. I ain't a-blaming you. You've lived in foreign parts, and you're that silly about your child that you can't a-bear to cross her. I'm one as can make allowance for that. But I just ask you what can the likes of that young fellow want here? He don't come for no good. Poor folks has a deal of things to put up with in this world, and women folks most of all. I don't make no doubt Miss Pamela is pleased to have a gentleman a-dancing after her. I don't know one on us as wouldn't be pleased; but them as has respect for their character and for their peace o' mind—"

"Mrs. Swayne, you must not speak like this to me," said Mrs. Preston, feebly, from the sofa. "I have a bad headache, and I can't argue with you; but you may be sure, though I don't say much, I know how to take care of my own child. No, Pamela dear, don't cry; and you'll please not to say another word to me on this subject—not another word, or I shall have to go away."

"To go away!" said Mrs. Swayne, crimson with indignation. But this sudden impulse of self-defense in so mild a creature struck her dumb. "Go away!—and welcome to!" she added; but her consternation was such that she could say no more. She stood in the middle of the little dark parlor, in a partial trance of astonishment. Public opinion itself had been defied in her person. "When it comes to what it's sure to come to, then you'll remember as I warned you," she said, and rushed forth from the room, closing the door with a clang which made poor Mrs. Preston jump on her sofa. Her visit left a sense of trouble and dismay on both their minds, for they were not superior women, nor sufficiently strong-minded to laugh at such a monitor. Pamela threw herself down on her knees by her mother's side and cried—not because of Mrs. Swayne, but because the fright and the novelty overwhelmed her, not to speak of the lively anger and disgust and impatience of her youth.

"Oh, mamma, if we had only some friends!" said Pamela; "everybody except us seems to have friends. Had I never any uncles nor any thing? It is hard to be left just you and me in the world."

"You had brothers once," said Mrs. Preston, with a sigh. Then there was a pause, for poor Pamela knew and could not help knowing that her brothers, had they been living, would not have improved her position now. She kept kneeling by her mother's side, but though there was no change in her position, her heart went away from her involuntarily—went away to think that the time perhaps had come when she would never more want a friend—when somebody would always be at hand to advise her what to do, and when no such complications could arise. She kept the gravity, even sadness of her aspect, with the innocent hypocrisy which is possible at her age; but her little heart went out like a bird into the sunny world outside. A passing tremor might cross her, ghosts might glide for a moment across the way, but it was only for a moment, and she knew they were only ghosts. Her mother was in a very different case. Mrs. Preston had a headache, partly because of the shock of last night, partly because a headache was to her, as to so many women, a kind of little feminine chapel, into which she could retire to gain time when she had any thing on her mind. The course of individual history stops when those headaches come on, and the subject of them has a blessed moment to think. Nothing could be done, nothing could be said, till Mrs. Preston's head was better. It was but a small matter had it been searched to its depths, but it was enough to arrest the wheels of fate.

"Pamela," she said, after a while, "we must be doubly wise because we have no friends. I can't ask any body's advice, as Mrs. Swayne told me to do. I am not going to open up our private affairs to strangers: but we must be wise. I think we must go away."

"Go away!" said Pamela, looking up with a face of despair—"away! Mamma, you don't think of—of—him as she does? You know what he is. Go away! and perhaps never, never see him again. Oh, mamma!"

"I did not mean that," said Mrs. Preston; "but we can't stop here, and live at his father's very door, and have him coming under their eyes to vex them. No, my darling; that would be cruel, and it would not be wise."

"Do you think they will mind so very much?" said Pamela, looking wistfully in her mother's face. "What should I do if they hated me? Miss Brownlow, you know—Sara—she always wanted me to call her Sara—she would never turn against me. I know her too well for that."

"She has not been here for a long time," said Mrs. Preston; "you have not noticed it, but I have, Pamela. She has never come since that day her father spoke to you. There is a great difference, my darling, between the sister's little friend and the brother's betrothed."

"Mamma, you seem to know all about those wretched things," cried Pamela, impulsively. "Why did you never tell me before? I never, never would have spoken to him—if I had known."

"How was I to know, Pamela?" said Mrs. Preston. "It appears you did not know yourselves. And then, when you told me what Mr. Brownlow said, I thought I might find you a friend. I think yet, if I could but see him; but when I spoke last night of seeing Mr. Brownlow, he would not hear of it. It is very hard to know what to do."

Then there ensued another pause—a long pause, during which the mother, engaged with many thoughts, did not look at her child. Pamela, too, was thinking; she had taken her mother's long thin hand into her own, and was smoothing it softly with her soft fingers; her head was bent over it, her eyes cast down; now and then a sudden heaving, as of a sob about to come, moved her pretty shoulders. And her voice was very tuneless and rigid when she spoke. "Mamma," she said, "speak to me honestly, once for all. Ought I to give it all up? I don't mean to say it would be easy. I never knew a—a—any one before—never any body was like that to me. You don't know—oh, you don't know how he can talk, mamma. And then it was not like any thing new—it felt natural, as if we had always belonged to each other. I know it's no use talking. Tell me, mamma, once for all, would it really be better for him and—every body, if I were to give him quite up?"

Pamela held herself upright and rigid as she asked the question. She held her mother's hand fast, and kept stroking it in an intermittent way. When she had finished she gave her an appealing look—a look which did not ask advice. It was not advice she wanted, poor child: she wanted to be told to do what she longed to do—to be assured that that was the best; therefore she looked not like a creature wavering between two opinions, but like a culprit at the bar, awaiting her sentence. As for Mrs. Preston, she only shook her head.

"It would not do any good," she said. "You might give him up over and over, but you would never get him to give you up, Pamela. He is that sort of a young man; he would not have taken a refusal from me. It would be of no use, my dear."

"Are you sure?—are you quite sure?" cried Pamela, throwing her arms round her mother's neck, and giving her a shower of kisses. "Oh you dear, dear mamma. Are you sure, you are quite sure?"

"You are kissing me for his sake," said Mrs. Preston, with a little pang; and then she smiled at herself. "I never was jealous before," she said. "I don't mean to be jealous. No, he will never give in, Pamela; we shall have to make the best of it; and perhaps," she continued, after a pause, "perhaps this was the friend I was always praying for to take care of my child before I die."

"Oh, mamma," said Pamela, "how can you talk of dying at such a time as this? when, perhaps, we're going to have—every thing we want in the world; when, perhaps, we are going to be—as happy as the day is long!" she said, once more kissing the worn old face which lay turned toward her, in a kind of sweet enthusiasm. The one looked so young and the other so old; the one so sure of life and happiness, the other so nearly done with both. Mrs. Preston took the kiss and the clasp, and smiled at her radiant child; and then she closed her eyes, and retreated into her headache. She was not going to have every thing she wanted in the world, or to be as happy as the day was long; so she retreated and took to her handy domestic little malady. The child could not conceive that there were still a thousand things to be thought over, and difficulties without number to be overcome.

As for Pamela, she sprang to her feet lightly, and went off to make the precious cup of tea which is good for every feminine trouble. As she went she fell into song, not knowing it. She was as near dancing as decorum would permit. She went into the kitchen where Mr. Swayne was, and cheered him up more effectually than if he had been well for a week. She made him laugh, though he was in low spirits. She promised him that he should be quite well in three months. "Ready to dance if there was any thing to dance at," was what Pamela said.

"At your wedding, Miss Pamela," said poor Swayne, with his shrill little chuckle. And Pamela too laughed with a laugh that was like a song. She stood by the fire while the kettle boiled, with the fire-light glimmering in her pretty eyes, and reddening her white forehead under the rings of her hair. Should she have to boil the kettle, to spread the homely table for him? or would he take her to Brownlows, or some other such house, and make her a great little lady like Sara? On the whole Pamela thought she would like the first best. She made the tea before the bright fire in such perfection as it never was made at Brownlows, and poured it out hot and fragrant, like one who knew what she was about. But the tea was not so great a cordial as the sight of her own face. She had come clear out of all her perplexities. There was no longer even a call upon that anxious faculty for self-sacrifice which belongs to youth. In short, self-sacrifice would do no good—the idol would simply decline to receive the costly offering. It was in his hands, and nothing that she could do would make any difference. Perhaps, if Pamela had been a self-asserting young woman, her pride would have suffered from this thought; but she was only a little girl of seventeen, and it made her as light as a bird. No dreadful responsibility rested on her soft shoulders—no awful question of what was best remained for her to consider. What use could there be in giving up when he would not be given up? What end would it serve to refuse a man who would not take a refusal? She had made her tragic little effort in all sincerity, and it had come to the sweetest and most complete failure. And now her part had been done, and no farther perplexity could overwhelm her. So she thought, flitting out and in upon a hundred errands, and thinking tenderly in her heart that her mother's headache and serious looks and grave way of looking at every thing was not so much because there was any thing serious in the emergency, as because the dear mother was old—a fault of nature, not of circumstances, to be mended by love and smiles, and all manner of tender services on the part of the happy creature who was young.

When Mrs. Swayne left the parlor in the manner which we have already related, she rushed out, partly to be relieved of her wrath, partly to pour her prophecies of evil into the ears of the other Cassandra on the other side of the road, old Betty of the Gates. The old woman was sitting before her fire when her neighbor went in upon her. To be sure it was summer, but Betty's fire was eternal, and burned without intermission on the sacred hearth. She was mending one of her gowns, and had a whole bundle of bits of colored print—"patches," for which some of the little girls in Miss Brownlow's school would have given their ears—spread out upon the table before her. Bits of all Betty's old gowns were there. It was a parti-colored historical record of her life, from the gay calicoes of her youth down to the sober browns and olives of declining years. With such a gay centre the little room looked very bright. There was a geranium in the window, ruby and emerald. There were all manner of pretty confused cross-lights from the open door and the latticed window in the other corner and the bright fire; and the little old face in its white cap was as brown and as red as a winter apple. Mrs. Swayne was a different sort of person. She came in, filling the room with shadows, and put herself away in a big elbow-chair, with blue and white cushions, which was Betty's winter throne, but now stood pushed into a corner out of reach of the fire. She uttered a sigh which blew away some of the patches on the table, and swayed the ruby blossoms of the big geranium. "Well," she said, "I've done my best—I can say I've done my best. If the worst comes to the worst, there's none as can blame me."

"What is it?—what is it, Mrs. Swayne?" said Betty, eagerly, dropping her work, "though I've something as tells me it's about that poor child and our Mr. John."

"I wash my hands of them," said the visitor, doing so in a moist and demonstrative way. "I've done all as an honest woman can do. Speak o' mothers!—mothers is a pack o' fools. I'd think o' that child's interest if it was me. I'd think what was best for her character, and for keeping her out o' mischief. As for cryin', and that sort, they all cry—it don't do them no harm. If you or me had set our hearts on marryin' the first gentleman as ever was civil, what would ha' become of us? Oh the fools as some folks is! It's enough to send a woman with a bit of sense out o' her mind."

"Marryin'?" said Betty, with a little shriek; "you don't mean to say as they've gone as far as that."

"If they don't go farther afore all's done, it'll be a wonder to me," said Mrs. Swayne; "things is always like that. I don't mean to take no particular credit to myself; but if she had been mine, I'd have done my best for her—that's one thing as I can say. She'd not have got into no trouble if she had been mine. I'd have watched her night and day. I know what the gentlemen is. But that's allays the way with Providence. A woman like me as has a bit of experience has none to be the better of it; and the likes of an old stupid as don't know her right hand from her left, it's her as has the children. I'd have settled all that different if it had been me. Last night as ever was, I found the two in the open road—in the road, I give you my word. It's over all the parish by this, as sure as sure; and after that what does my gentleman do but come to the house as bold as brass. It turns a body sick—that's what it does; but you might as well preach to a stone wall as make 'em hear reason; and that's what you call a mother! much a poor girl's the better of a mother like that."

"All mothers is not the same," said Betty, who held that rank herself. "For one as don't know her duty, there's dozens and dozens—"

"Don't speak to me," said Mrs. Swayne, "I know 'em—as stuck up as if it was any virtue in them, and a shuttin' their ears to every one as gives them good advice. Oh, if that girl was but mine! I'd keep her as snug as if she was in a box, I would. Ne'er a gentleman should get a chance of so much as a look at her. It's ten times worse when a girl is pretty; but, thank heaven, I know what the gentlemen is."

"But if he comed to the house, he must have made some excuse," said Betty. "I see him. He come by himself, as if it was to see your good gentleman, Mrs. Swayne. Knowing as Miss Pamela was out, I don't deny as that was my thought. And he must have made some excuse."

"Oh, they find excuses ready enough—don't you be afeard," said Mrs. Swayne; "they're plenty ready with their tongues, and don't stick at what they promise neither. It's all as innocent as innocent if you was to believe them; and them as believes comes to their ruin. I tell you it's their ruin—that and no less; but I may speak till I'm hoarse," said Cassandra, with melancholy emphasis—"nobody pays no attention to me."

"You must have knowed a deal of them to be so earnest," said old Betty, with the deepest interest in her eyes.

"I was a pretty lass mysel'," said Mrs. Swayne; and then she paused; "but you're not to think as I ever give in to them. I wasn't that sort; and I had folks as looked after me. I don't say as Swayne is much to look at, after all as was in my power; but if Miss Pamela don't mind, she'll be real thankful afore she's half my age to take up with a deal worse than Swayne; and that's my last word, if I was never to draw a breath more."

"Husht!" said Betty. "Don't take on like that. There's somebody a-coming. Husht! It's just like as if it was a child of your own."

"And so I feel," said Mrs. Swayne; "worse luck for her, poor lass. If she was mine—"

"Husht!" said Betty again; and then the approaching steps which they had heard for the last minute reached the threshold, and a woman presented herself at the door. She was not a woman that either of them knew. She was old, very tall, very thin, and very dusty with walking. "I'm most dead with tiredness. May I come in and rest a bit?" she said. She had a pair of keen black eyes, which gleamed out below her poke bonnet, and took in every thing, and did not look excessively tired; but her scanty black gown was white with dust. Old Betty, for her own part, did not admire the stranger's looks, but she consented to let her come in, "manners" forbidding any inhospitality, and placed her a chair as near as possible to the door.

"I come like a stranger," said the woman, "but I'm not to call a stranger neither. I'm Nancy as lives with old Mrs. Fennell, them young folks' grandmamma. I had summat to do nigh here, and I thought as I'd like to see the place. It's a fine place for one as was nothing but an attorney once. I allays wonder if they're good folks to live under, such folks as these."

"So you're Nancy!" said the old woman of the lodge. "I've heard tell of you. I heard of you along of Stevens as you recommended here. I haven't got nothing to say against the masters; they're well and well enough; Miss Sara, she's hasty, but she's a good heart."

"She don't show it to her own flesh and blood," said Nancy, significantly. "Is this lady one as lives about here?"

Then it was explained to the stranger who Mrs. Swayne was. "Mr. Swayne built them cottages," said Betty; "they're his own, and as nice a well-furnished house and as comfortable; and his good lady ain't one of them that wastes or wants. She has a lodger in the front parlor, and keeps 'em as nice as it's a picture to see, and as respected in the whole parish—"

"Don't you go on a-praising me before my face," said Mrs. Swayne, modestly; "we're folks as are neither rich nor poor, and can give our neighbors a hand by times and times. You're a stranger, as is well seen, or you wouldn't be cur'ous about Swayne and me."

"I'm a stranger sure enough," said Nancy. "We're poor relations, that's what we are; and the likes of us is not wanted here. If I was them I'd take more notice o' my own flesh and blood, and one as can serve them yet, like she can. It ain't what you call a desirable place," said Nancy; "she's awful aggravating sometimes, like the most of old women; but all the same they're her children's children, and I'd allays let that count if it was me."

"That's old Mrs. Fennell?" said Betty; "she never was here as I can think on but once. Miss Sara isn't one that can stand being interfered with; but they sends her an immensity of game, and vegetables, and flowers, and such things, and I've always heard as the master gives her an allowance. I don't see as she's any reason to complain."

"A woman as knows as much as she does," said Nancy, solemnly, "she ought to be better looked to;" and then she changed her tone. "I've walked all this long way, and I have got to get back again, and she'll be as cross as cross if I'm long. And I don't suppose there's no omnibus or nothing going my way. If it was but a cart—"

"There's a carrier's cart," said Betty; "but Mrs. Swayne could tell you most about that. Her two lodgers come in it, and Mrs. Preston, that time she had something to do in Masterton—"

"Who is Mrs. Preston?" said Nancy quickly. "I've heard o' that name. And I've heard in Masterton of some one as came in the carrier's cart. If I might make so bold, who is she? Is she your lodger? I once knew some folks of that name in my young days, and I'd like to hear."

"Oh yes, she's my lodger," said Mrs. Swayne, "and a terrible trouble to me. I'd just been a-grumbling to Betty when you came in. She and that poor thing Pamela, they lay on my mind so heavy, I don't know what to do. You might give old Mrs. Fennell a hint to speak to Mr. John. He's a-running after that girl, he is, till it turns one sick; and a poor silly woman of a mother as won't see no harm in it. If the old lady was to hear in a sort of a side way like, she might give Mr. John a talking to. Not as I have much confidence in his mending. Gentlemen never does."

"Oh," said Nancy, with a strange gleam of her dark eyes, "so she's got a daughter! and it was her as came into Masterton in the carrier's cart? I just wanted to know. May be you could tell me what kind of a looking woman she was. There was one as I knew once in my young days—"

"She ain't unlike yourself," said Mrs. Swayne, with greater brevity than usual; and she turned and began to investigate Nancy with a closeness for which she was not prepared. Another gleam shot from the stranger's black eyes as she listened. It even brought a tinge of color to her gray cheek, and though she restrained herself with the utmost care, there was unquestionably a certain excitement in her. Mrs. Swayne's eyes were keen, but they were not used to read mysteries. A certain sense of something to find out oppressed her senses; but, notwithstanding her curiosity, she had not an idea what secret there could be.

"If it's the same person, it's years and years since I saw her last," said Nancy; "and so she's got a daughter! I shouldn't think it could be a very young daughter if it's hers; she should be as old as me. And it was her as came in to Masterton in the carrier's cart! Well, well! what droll things does happen to be sure."

"I don't know what's droll about that," said Mrs. Swayne; "but I don't know nought about her. She's always been quiet and genteel as a lodger—always till this business came on about Mr. John. But I'd be glad to know where her friends was, if she's got any friends. She's as old as you, or older, and not to say any thing as is unpleasant—it's an awful thing to think of—what if folks should go and die in your house, and you not know their friends?"

"If it's that you're thinking of, she's got no friends," said Nancy, with a vehemence that seemed unnatural and uncalled-for to her companions—"none as I know of nowheres—but may be me. And it isn't much as I could do. She's a woman as has been awful plundered and wronged in her time. Mr. John! oh, I'd just like to hear what it is about Mr. John. If that was to come after all, I tell you it would call down fire from heaven."

"Goodness gracious me!" said Mrs. Swayne, "what does the woman mean?" And Betty too uttered a quavering exclamation, and they both drew their chairs closer to the separated seat, quite apart from the daïs of intimacy and friendship, upon which the dusty stranger had been permitted to rest.

Nancy, however, had recollected herself. "Mean?" she said, with a look of innocence; "oh, I didn't mean nothing; but that I've a kind of spite—I don't deny it—at them grand Brownlows, that don't take no notice to speak of their own flesh and blood. That's all as I mean. I ain't got no time to-day, but if you'll say as Nancy Christian sends her compliments and wants badly to see Mrs. Preston, and is coming soon again, I'll be as obliged as ever I can be. If it's her, she'll think on who Nancy Christian was; and if it ain't her, it don't make much matter," she continued, with a sigh. She said these last words very slowly, looking at neither of her companions, fixing her eyes upon the door of Swayne's cottage, at which Pamela had appeared. The sun came in at Betty's door and dazzled the stranger's eyes, and it was not easy for her at first to see Pamela, who stood in the shade. The girl had looked out for no particular reason, only because she was passing that way; and as she stood giving a glance up and a glance down the road—a glance which was not wistful, but full of a sweet confidence—Nancy kept staring at her, blinking her eyes to escape the sunshine. "Is that the girl?" she said, a little hoarsely. And then all the three looked out and gazed at Pamela in her tender beauty. Pamela saw them also. It did not occur to her whose the third head might be, nor did she care very much. She felt sure they were discussing her, shaking their heads over her imprudence; but Pamela at the moment was too happy to be angry. She said, "Poor old things," to herself. They were poor old things; they had not the blood dancing in their veins as she had; they had not light little feet that flew over the paths, nor light hearts that leaped in their breasts, poor old souls. She waved her hand to them half kindly, half saucily, and disappeared again like a living bit of sunshine into the house which lay so obstinately in the shade. As for Nancy, she was moved in some wonderful way by this sight. She trembled when the girl made that half-mocking, half-sweet salutation; the tears came to her eyes. "She could never have a child so young," she muttered half to herself, and then gazed and gazed as if she had seen a ghost. When Pamela disappeared she rose up and shook the dust, not from her feet, but from her skirts, outside old Betty's door. "I've only a minute," said Nancy, "but if I could set eyes on the mother I could tell if it was her I used to know."

"I left her lyin' down wi' a bad headache," said Mrs. Swayne. "If you like you can go and take a look through the parlor window; or I'll ask if she's better. Them sort of folks that have little to do gets headaches terrible easy. Of an afternoon when their dinner's over, what has the likes of them to take up their time? They takes a sleep on my sofa, or they takes a walk, and a headache comes natural-like when folks has all that time on their hands. Come across and look in at the window. It's low, and if your eyes are good you can just see her where she lays."

Nancy followed her new companion across the road. As she went out of the gates she gave a glance up through the avenue, and made as though she would have shaken her fist at the great house. "If you but knew!" Nancy said to herself. But they did not know, and the sunshine lay as peacefully across the pretty stretch of road as if there had been no dangers there. The old woman crossed over to Mrs. Swayne's cottage, and went into the little square of garden where Pamela sometimes watered the flowers. Nancy stooped over the one monthly rose and plucked a bit of the homely lads'-love in the corner which flourished best of all, and then she drew very close to the window and looked in. It was an alarming sight to the people within. Mrs. Preston had got a second cup of tea, and raised herself up on her pillow to swallow it, when all at once this gray visage, not unlike her own, surrounded with black much like her own dress, looked in upon her, a stranger, and yet somehow wearing a half-familiar aspect. As for Pamela, there was something awful to her in the vision. She turned round to her mother in a fright to compare the two faces. She was not consciously superstitious, but yet dim thoughts of a wraith, a double, a solemn messenger of doom, were in her mind. She had heard of such things. "Go and see who it is," said Mrs. Preston; and Pamela rushed out, not feeling sure that the strange apparition might not have vanished. But it had not vanished. Nancy stood at the door, and when she was looked into in the open day-light she was not so dreadfully like Mrs. Preston's wraith.

"Good-day, miss," said Nancy; "I thought as may be I might have had a few words with your mother. If she's the person I take her for, I used to know her long, long ago; and I've a deal that's very serious to say."

"You frightened us dreadfully looking in at the window," said Pamela. "And mamma has such a bad headache; she has been a good deal—worried. Would you mind coming back another time?—or is it any thing I can say?"

"There's something coming down the road," said Nancy; "and I am tired and I can't walk back. If it's the carrier I'll have to go, miss. And I can't say the half nor the quarter to you. Is it the carrier? Then I'll have to go. Tell her it was one as knew her when we was both young—knew her right well, and all her ways—knew her mother. And I've a deal to say; and my name's Nancy Christian, if she should ask. If she's the woman I take her for, she'll know my name."

"And you'll come back?—will you be sure to come back?" asked Pamela, carelessly, yet with a girl's eagerness for every thing like change and news. The cart had stopped by this time, and Mrs. Swayne had brought forth a chair to aid the stranger in her ascent. The place was roused by the event. Old Betty stood at her cottage, and Swayne had hobbled out from the kitchen, and even Mrs. Preston, forgetting the headache, had stolen to the window, and peeped out through the small Venetian blind which covered the lower part of it to look at and wonder who the figure belonged to which had so strange a likeness to herself. Amid all these spectators Nancy mounted, slowly shaking out once more the dust from her skirts.

"I'll be late, and she'll give me an awful talking to," she said. "No; I can't stop to-day. But I'll come again—oh yes, I'll come again." She kept looking back as long as she was in sight, peeping round the hood of the wagon, searching them through and through with her anxious gaze; while all the bystanders looked on surprised. What had she to do with them? And then her looks, and her dress, and her black eager eyes, were so like Mrs. Preston's. Her face bore a very doubtful, uncertain look as she was thus borne solemnly away. "I couldn't know her after such a long time; and I don't see as she could have had a child so young," was what Nancy was saying to herself, shaking her head, and then reassuring herself. This visit made a sensation which almost diverted public attention from Mr. John; and when Nancy's message was repeated to Mrs. Preston, it was received with an immediate recognition which increased the excitement. "Nancy Christian!" Mrs. Preston repeated all the evening long. She could think of nothing else. It made her head so much worse that she had to go to bed, where Pamela watched her to the exclusion of every other interest. This was Nancy's first visit. She did not mean, even had she had time, to proceed to any thing more important that day.

CHAPTER XXV

HOW SARA REGARDED THE MOTE IN HER BROTHER'S EYE

A few days after these events, caprice or curiosity led Sara to Swayne's cottage. She had very much given up going there—why, she could scarcely have explained. In reality she knew nothing about the relationship between her brother and her friend; but either that, unknown to herself, had exercised some kind of magnetic repulsion upon her, or her own preoccupation had withdrawn Sara from any special approach to her little favorite. She would have said she was as fond of her as ever; but in fact she did not want Pamela as she had wanted her. And the consequence was that they had been much longer apart than either of them, occupied with their own concerns, had been aware. The motive which drew Sara thither after so long an interval was about as mysterious as that which kept her away. She went, but did not know why; perhaps from some impulse of those secret threads of fate which are ever being drawn unconsciously to us into another and another combination; perhaps simply from a girlish yearning toward the pleasant companion of whom for a time she had made so much. Mrs. Preston had not recovered when Sara went to see her daughter—she was still lying on the sofa with one of her nervous attacks, Pamela said—though the fact was that neither mother nor daughter understood what kind of attack it was. Anxiety and excitement and uncertainty had worn poor Mrs. Preston out; and then her headache was so handy—it saved her from making any decision—it excused her to herself for not settling immediately what she ought to do. She was not able to move, and she was thankful for it. She could not undergo the fatigue of finding some other place to live in, of giving Mr. John his final answer. To be sure he knew and she knew that his final answer had been given—that there could be no doubt about it; but still every practical conclusion was postponed by the attack, and in this point of view it was the most fortunate thing which could have occurred.

Things were thus with them when Sara, after a long absence, one day suddenly lighted down upon the shady house in the glory of her summer attire, like a white dove lying into the bosom of the clouds. Perhaps it would be wrong to say that Pamela in her black frock stood no chance in the presence of her visitor; but it is certain that when Miss Brownlow came floating in with her light dress, and her bright ribbons and her shining hair, every thing about her gleaming with a certain reflection from the sunshine, Pamela and her mother could neither of them look at any thing else. She dazzled them, and yet drew their eyes to her, as light itself draws every body's eyes. Pamela shrank a little from her friend's side with a painful humility, asking herself whether it was possible that this bright creature should ever be her sister; while even Mrs. Preston, though she had all a mother's admiration for her own child, could not but feel her heart sink as she thought how this splendid princess would ever tolerate so inferior an alliance. This consciousness in their minds made an immediate estrangement between them. Sara was condescending, and she felt she was condescending, and hated herself; and as for the mother and daughter, they were constrained and stricken dumb by the secret in their hearts. And thus there rose a silent offense on both sides. On hers because they were so cold and distant; on theirs because it seemed to them that she had come with the intention of being affable and kind to them, they who could no longer accept patronage. The mother lay on the sofa in the dark corner, and Sara sat on the chair in the window, and between the two points Pamela went straying, ashamed of herself, trying to smooth over her own secret irritation and discontent, trying to keep the peace between the others, and yet at the same time wishing and longing that her once welcome friend would leave them to themselves. The circumstances of their intercourse were changed, and the intercourse itself had to be organized anew. Thus the visit might have passed over, leaving only an impression of pain on their minds, but for an accident which set the matter in a clearer light. Pamela had been seated at the window with her work before Sara entered, and underneath the linen she had been stitching lay an envelope directed to her by Jack Brownlow. Jack had not seen his little love for one entire day, and naturally he had written her a little letter, which was as foolish as if he had not been so sensible a young man. It was only the envelope which lay thus on the table under Pamela's work. Its enclosure was laid up in quite another sanctuary, but the address was there, unquestionably in Jack's hand. It lay the other way from Sara's eyes, tantalizing her with the well-known writing. She tried hard—without betraying herself, in the intervals of the conversation—to read the name on it upside down, and her suspicion had not, as may be supposed, an enlivening effect upon the conversation. Then she stooped and pretended to look at Pamela's work; then she gave the provoking envelope a little stealthy touch with the end of her parasol. Perhaps scrupulous honor would have forbidden these little attempts to discover the secret; but when a sister perceives her brother's handwriting on the work-table of her friend, it is hard to resist the inclination to make sure in the first place that it is his, in the second place to whom it is addressed. This was all that Sara was guilty of. She would not have peeped into the note for a kingdom, but she did want to know whom it was written to. Perhaps it was only some old scrap of paper, some passing word about mendings or fittings to Mr. Swayne. Perhaps—and then Sara gave the envelope stealthily that little poke with her parasol.

A few minutes after she got up to go: her complexion had heightened suddenly in the strangest way, her eyes had taken a certain rigid look, which meant excitement and wrath. "Will you come out with me a little way? I want to speak to you," she said, as Pamela went with her to the door. It was very different from those old beseeching, tender, undeniable invitations which the one had been in the habit of giving to the other; but there was something in it which constrained Pamela, though she trembled to her very heart, to obey. She did not know any thing about the envelope; she had forgotten it—forgotten that she had left it there, and had not perceived Sara's stealthy exertions to secure a sight of it. But nevertheless she knew there was something coming. She took down her little black hat, trembling, and stole out, a dark little figure, beside Sara, stately in her light flowing draperies. They did not say a word to each other as they crossed the road and entered at the gates and passed Betty's cottage. Betty came to the door and looked after them with a curiosity so great that she was tempted to follow and creep under the bushes, and listen; but Sara said nothing to betray herself as long as they were within the range of old Betty's eye. When they had got to the chestnut-trees, to that spot where Mr. Brownlow had come upon his son and his son's love, and where there was a possibility of escaping from the observation of spectators at the gate, Sara's composure gave way. All at once she seized Pamela's arm, who turned round to her with her lips apart and her heart struggling up into her mouth with terror. "Jack has been writing to you," said Sara; "tell me what it has been about."

"What it has been about!" said Pamela, with a cry. The poor little girl was so taken by surprise that all her self-possession forsook her. Her knees trembled, her heart beat, fluttering wildly in her ears; she sank down on the grass in her confusion, and covered her face with her hands. "Oh, Miss Brownlow!" was all that she was able to say.

"That is no answer," said Sara, with all her natural vehemence. "Pamela, get up, and answer me like a sensible creature. I don't mean to say it is your fault. A man might write to you and you might not be to blame. Tell me only what it means. What did he write to you about?"

Then Pamela bethought herself that she too had a certain dignity to preserve; not her own so much as that which belonged to her in right of her betrothed. She got up hastily, blushing scarlet, and though she did not meet Sara's angry questioning eyes, she turned her downcast face toward her with a certain steadfastness. "It is not any harm," she said, softly, "and, Miss Brownlow, you are no—no—older than me."

"I am two years older than you," said Sara, "and I know the world, and you don't; and I am his sister. Oh, you foolish little thing! don't you know it is wicked? If you had told me, I never, never would have let him trouble you. I never thought Jack would have done any thing so dreadful. It's because you don't know."

"Mamma knows," said Pamela, with a certain self-assertion; and then her courage once more failed her. "I tried to stop him," she said with the tears coming to her eyes, "and so did mamma. But I could not force him; not when he—he—would not. What I think of," cried Pamela, "is him, not myself; but if he won't, what can I do?"

"If he won't what?" said Sara, in her amazement and wrath.

But Pamela could make no answer; half with the bitterness of it, half with the sweetness of it, her heart was full. It was hard to be questioned and taken to task thus by her own friend; but it was sweet to know that what she could do was nothing, that her efforts had been vain, that he would not give up. All this produced such a confusion in her that she could not say another word. She turned away, and once more covered her face with her hand; not that she was at all miserable—or if indeed it was a kind of misery, misery itself is sometimes sweet.

As for Sara, she blazed upon her little companion with an indignation which was splendid to behold. "Your mamma knows," she said, "and permits it! Oh, Pamela! that I should have been so fond of you, and that you should treat me like this!"

"I am not treating you badly—it is you," said Pamela, with a sob which she could not restrain, "who are cruel to me."

"If you think so, we had better part," said Sara, with tragic grandeur. "We had better part, and forget that we ever knew each other. I could have borne any thing from you but being false. Oh, Pamela! how could you do it? To be treacherous to me who have always loved you, and to correspond with Jack!"

"I—don't—correspond—with Jack," cried Pamela, the words being wrung out of her; and then she stopped short, and dried her eyes, and grew red, and looked Sara in the face. It was true, and yet it was false; and the consciousness of this falsehood in the spirit made her cheeks burn, and yet startled her into composure. She stood upright for the first time, and eyed her questioner, but it was with the self-possession not of innocence but of guilt.

"I am very glad to hear it," said Sara—"very glad; but you let him write to you. And when I see his handwriting on your table, what am I to think? I will speak to him about it to-night; I will not have him tease you. Pamela, if you will trust in me, I will bring you through it safe. Surely it would be better for you to have me for a friend than Jack?"

Poor Pamela's eyes sank to the ground as this question was addressed to her. Her blush, which had begun to fade, returned with double violence. Such a torrent of crimson rushed to her face and throat that even Sara took note of it. Pamela could not tell a lie—not another lie, as she said to herself in her heart; for the fact was she did prefer Jack—preferred him infinitely and beyond all question; and such being the case, could not so much as look at her questioner, much less breathe a word of assent. Sara marked the silence, the overwhelming blush, the look which suddenly fell beneath her own, with the consternation of utter astonishment. In that moment a renewed storm of indignation swept over her. She stamped her foot upon the grass in the impatience of her thoughts.

"You prefer Jack," she cried, in horror—"you prefer Jack! Oh, heaven! but in that case," she added, gathering up her long dress in her arms, and turning away with a grandeur of disdain which made an end of Pamela, "it is evident that we had better part. I do not know that there is any thing more I can say. I have thought more of you than I ought to have done," said Sara, making a few steps forward and then turning half round with the air of an injured princess, "but now it is better that we should part."

With this she waved her hand and turned away. It was in her heart to have turned and gone back five-and-twenty times before she reached the straight line of the avenue from which they had strayed. Before she got to the first laurel in the shrubberies her heart had given her fifty pricks on the subject of her cruelty; but Sara was not actually so moved by these admonitions as to go back. As for Pamela, she stood for a long time where her friend had left her, motionless under the chestnut-trees, with tears dropping slowly from her downcast eyes, and a speechless yet sweet anguish in her heart. Her mother had been right. The sister's little friend and the brother's betrothed were two different things. This was how she was to be received by those who were nearest in the world to him; and yet he was a man, and his own master; all she could do was in vain, and he could not be forced to give up. Pamela stood still until his sister's light steps began to sound on the gravel; and when it was evident the parting had been final, and that Sara did not mean to come back, the poor child relieved her bosom by a long sob, and then went home very humbly by the broad sunny avenue. She went and poured her troubles into her mother's bosom, which naturally was so much the worse for Mrs. Preston's headache. It was very hard to bear, and yet there was one thing which gave a little comfort; Jack was his own master, and giving him up, as every body else adjured her to do, would be a thing entirely without effect.

The dinner-table at Brownlows was very grave that night. Mr. Brownlow, it is true, was much as usual, and so was Jack; they were very much as they always were, notwithstanding that very grave complications surrounded the footsteps of both. But as for Sara, her aspect was solemnity itself; she spoke in monosyllables only; she ate little, and that little in a pathetic way; when her father or her brother addressed her she took out her finest manners and extinguished them. Altogether she was a very imposing and majestic sight; and after a few attempts at ordinary conversation, the two gentlemen, feeling themselves very trifling and insignificant personages indeed, gave in, and struggled no longer against an influence which was too much for them. There was something, too, in her manner—something imperceptible to Mr. Brownlow, perceptible only to Jack—which made it clear to the latter that it was on his account his sister was so profoundly disturbed. He said "Pshaw!" to himself at first, and tried to think himself quite indifferent; but the fact was he was not indifferent. When she left the room at last, Jack had no heart for a chat with his father over the claret. He too felt his secret on his mind, and became uncomfortable when he was drawn at all into a confidential attitude; and to-day, in addition to this, there was in his heart a prick of alarm. Did Sara know? was that what she meant? Jack knew very well that sooner or later every body must know; but at the present moment a mingled sense of shame and pride and independence kept him silent. Even supposing it was the most prudent marriage he could make, why should a fellow go and tell every body like a girl? It might be well enough for a girl to do it—a girl had to get every body's consent, and ask every body's advice, whereas he required neither advice nor consent. And so he had not felt himself called upon to say any thing about it; but it is nervous work, when you have a secret on your mind, to be left alone with your nearest relative, the person who has the best right to know, and who in a way possesses your natural confidence and has done nothing to forfeit it. So Jack escaped five minutes after Sara, and hastened to the drawing-room looking for her. Perhaps she had expected it—at all events she was there waiting for him, still as solemn, pathetic and important as it is possible to conceive. She had some work in her hands which of itself was highly significant. Jack went up to her, and she looked at him, but took no farther notice. After that one glance she looked down again, and went on with her work—things were too serious for speech.

"What's the matter?" said Jack. "Why are you making such a tragedy-queen of yourself? What has every body done? My opinion is you have frightened my father to death."

"I should be very sorry if I had frightened papa," said Sara, meekly; and then she broke forth with vehemence, "Oh, how can you, Jack? Don't you feel ashamed to look me in the face?"

"I ashamed to look you in the face?" cried Jack, in utter bewilderment; and he retired a step, but yet stared at her with the most straightforward stare. His eyes did not fall under the scrutiny of hers, but gradually as he looked there began to steal up among his whiskers an increasing heat. He grew red, though there was no visible cause for it. "I should like to know what I have done," he said, with an affected laugh. "Anyhow, you take high ground."

"I couldn't take too high ground," said Sara solemnly. "Oh, Jack! how could you think of meddling with that innocent little thing? To see her about so pretty and sweet as she was, and then to go and worry her and tease her to death!"

"Worry and tease—whom?" cried Jack in amaze. This was certainly not the accusation he expected to hear.

"As if you did not know whom I mean!" said his sister. "Wasn't it throwing themselves on our kindness when they came here? And to make her that she dares not walk about or come out anywhere—to tease her with letters even! I think you are the last man in the world from whom I should have expected that."

Jack had taken to bite his nails, not well knowing what else to do. But he made no direct reply even to the solemnity of this appeal. A flush of anger sprang up over his face, and yet he was amused. "Has she been complaining to you?" he said.

"Complaining," said Sara. "Poor little thing! No, indeed. She never said a word. I found it out all by myself."

"Then I advise you to keep it all to yourself," said her brother. "She don't want you to interfere, nor I either. We can manage our own affairs; and I think, Sara," he added, with an almost equal grandeur, "if I were you I would not notice the mote in my brother's eye till I had looked after the beam in my own."

The beam in her own! what did he mean? But Jack went off in a lofty way, contenting himself with this Parthian arrow, and declining to explain. The insinuation, however, disturbed Sara. What was the beam in her own? Somehow, while she was puzzling about it, a vision of young Powys crossed her mind, papa's friend, who began to come so often. When she thought of that, she smiled at her brother's delusion. Poor Jack! he did not know that it was in discharge of her most sacred duty that she was civil to Powys. She had been very civil to him. She had taken his part against Jack's own refined rudeness, and delivered him even from the perplexed affabilities of her father, though he was her father's friend. Both Mr. Brownlow and Jack were preoccupied, and Sara had been the only one to entertain the stranger. And she had done it so as to make the entertainment very amusing and pleasant to herself. But what had that to do with a beam in her eye? She had made a vow, and she was performing her vow. And he was her father's friend; and if all other arguments should be exhausted, still the case was no parallel to that of Pamela. He was not a poor man dwelling at the gate. He was a fairy prince, whom some enchantment had transformed into his present shape. The case was utterly different. Thus it was with a certain magnificent superiority over her brother's weakness that Sara smiled to herself at his delusion. And yet she was grieved to think that he should take refuge in such a delusion, and did not show any symptom of real sorrow for his own sin.

Jack had hardly gone when Mr. Brownlow came up stairs. And he too asked Sara why it was that she sat apart in such melancholy majesty. When he had heard the cause, he was more disturbed than either of his children had been. Sara had supposed that Jack might be trifling with her poor little friend—she thought that he might carry the flirtation so far as to break poor Pamela's heart, perhaps. But Mr. Brownlow knew that there were sometimes consequences more serious than even the breaking of hearts. To be sure he judged, not with the awful severity of a woman, but with the leniency of a man of the world; but yet it seemed to him that worse things might happen to poor Pamela than an innocent heart-break, and his soul was disturbed within him by the thought. He had warned his son, with all the gravity which the occasion required; but Jack was young, and no doubt the warning had been ineffectual. Mr. Brownlow was grieved to his soul; and, what was strange enough, it never occurred to him that his son could have behaved as he had done, like a Paladin. Jack's philosophy, which had so little effect upon himself, had deceived his father. Mr. Brownlow felt that Jack was not the man to sacrifice his position and prospects and ambitions to an early marriage, and the only alternative was one at which he shuddered. For the truth was, his eye had been much attracted by the bright little face at the gate. It recalled some other face to him—he could not recall whose face. He had thought she was like Sara at first, but it was not Sara. And to think of that fresh sweet blossoming creature all trodden down into dust and ruin! The thought made Mr. Brownlow's heart contract with positive pain. He went down into the avenue, and walked about there for hours waiting for his son. It must not be, he said to himself—it must not be! And all this time Jack, not knowing what was in store for him, was hearing over and over again, with much repetition, the story of the envelope and Sara's visit, and was drying Pamela's tears, and laughing at her fright, and asking her gloriously what any body could do to separate them?—what could any body do? A girl might be subject to her parents; but who was there who could take away his free will from a Man? This was the scope of Jack's conversation, and it was very charming to his hearer. What could any one do against that magnificent force of resolution? Of course his allowance might be taken from him; but he could work. They had it all their own way in Mrs. Swayne's parlor, though Mrs. Swayne herself did not hesitate to express her disapproval; but as yet Mr. John knew nothing about the anxious parent who walked up and down waiting for him on the other side of the gate.

CHAPTER XXVI

A DOUBLE HUMILIATION

Jack entered the avenue that evening in a frame of mind very different from his feelings on his last recorded visit to Swayne's cottage. He had been sitting with Pamela all the evening. Mrs. Preston had retired up stairs with her headache, and, with an amount of good sense for which Jack respected her, did not come down again; and the young fellow sat with Pamela, and the minutes flew on angels' wings. When he came away his feelings were as different as can be conceived from those with which he marched home, resolute but rueful, after his first interview with Mrs. Preston. Pamela and her mother were two very different things—the one was duty, and had to be got through with; but the other—Jack went slowly, and took a little notice of the stars, and felt that the evening air was very sweet. He had put his hands lightly in his pockets, not thrust down with savage force to the depths of those receptacles; and there was a kind of half smile, the reflection of a smile, about his mouth. Fumes were hanging about the youth of that intoxication which is of all kinds of intoxication the most ethereal. He was softly dazzled and bewildered by a subdued sweetness in the air, and in the trees, and in the sky—something that was nothing perceptible, and yet that kept breathing round him a new influence in the air. This was the sort of way in which his evenings, perhaps, were always to be spent. It gave a different view altogether of the subject from that which was in Jack's mind on the first dawning of the new life before him. Then he had been able to realize that it would make a wonderful difference in all his plans and prospects, and even in his comforts. Now, the difference looked all the other way. Yes, it would indeed be a difference! To go in every night, not to Brownlows with his father's intermitting talk and Sara's "tantrums" (this was his brotherly way of putting it), and the monotony of a grave long established wealthy existence, but into a poor little house full of novelty and freshness, and quaint poverty, and amusing straits, and—Pamela. To be sure that last was the great point. They had been speculating about this wonderful new little house, as was natural, and she had laughed till the tears glistened in her pretty eyes at thought of all the mistakes she would make—celestial blunders, which even to Jack, sensible as he was, looked (to-night) as if they must be pleasanter and better and every way more fitting than the wisest actions of the other people. In this kind of sweet insanity the young fellow had left his little love. Life somehow seemed to have taken a different aspect to him since that other evening. No doubt it was a serious business; but then when there are two young creatures, you understand, setting out together, and a hundred chances before them, such as nobody could divine—one to help the other if either should stumble, and two to laugh over every thing, and a hundred devices to be contrived, and Crusoe-like experiments in the art of living, and droll little mishaps, and a perpetual sweet variety—the prospect changes. This is why there had come, in the starlight, a sort of reflection of a smile upon Jack's mouth. It was, on the whole, so very considerate and sensible of Mrs. Preston to have that headache and stay up stairs. And Pamela, altogether apart from the fact that she was Pamela, was such charming company—so fresh, so quick, so ready to take up any thing that looked like fun, so full of pleasant changes, catching the light upon her at so many points. This bright, rippling, sparkling, limpid stream was to go singing through all his life. He was thinking of this when he suddenly saw the shadow under the chestnuts, and found that his father had come out to meet him. It was rather a startling interruption to so pleasant a dream.

Jack was very much taken aback, but he did not lose his self-possession; he made a brave attempt to stave off all discussion, and make the encounter appear the most natural thing in the world, as was the instinct of a man up to the requirements of his century. "It's a lovely night," said Jack; "I don't wonder you came out. I've been myself—for a walk. It does a fellow more good than sitting shut up in these stuffy rooms all night."

Now the fact was Jack had been shut up in a very stuffy room, a room smaller than the smallest chamber into which he had ever entered at Brownlows; but there are matters, it is well known, in which young men do not feel themselves bound by the strict limits of fact.

"I was not thinking about the night," said Mr. Brownlow; "there are times when a man is glad to move about to keep troublesome things out of his mind; but luckily you don't know much about that."

"I know as much about it as most people, I suppose, sir," said Jack, with a little natural indignation; "but I hope there is nothing particular to put you out—that Wardell case—"

"I was not thinking of the Wardell case either," said Mr. Brownlow, with an impatient momentary smile. "I fear my clients' miseries don't impress me so much as they ought to do. I was thinking of things nearer home—"

Upon which there was a moment's pause. If Jack had followed his first impulse, he would have asked, with a little defiance, if it was any thing in his conduct to which his father particularly objected. But he was prudent, and refrained; and they took a few steps on together in silence toward the house, which shone in front of them with all its friendly lights.

"No," said Mr. Brownlow, in that reflective way that men think it competent and proper to use when their interlocutor is young, and can not by any means deny the fact. "You don't know much about it; the hardest thing that ever came in your way was to persuade yourself to give up a personal indulgence: and even that you have not always done. You don't understand what care means. How should you? Youth is never really occupied with any thing but itself."

"You speak very positively, sir," said Jack, affronted. "I suppose it's no use for a man in that selfish condition to say a word in his own defense."

"I don't know that it's selfish—it's natural," said Mr. Brownlow: and then he sighed. "Jack, I have something to say to you. We had a talk on a serious subject some time ago—"

"Yes," said Jack. He saw now what was coming, and set himself to face it. He thrust his hands deep down into his pockets and set up his shoulders to his ears, which was a good warning, had Mr. Brownlow perceived it, that, come right or wrong, come rhyme or reason, this rock should fly from its firm base as soon as Jack would—and that any remonstrance on the subject was purely futile. But Mr. Brownlow did not perceive.

"I thought you had been convinced," his father continued. "It might be folly on my part to think any sort of reason would induce a young fellow, brought up as you have been, to forego his pleasure; but I suppose I had a prejudice in favor of my own son, and I thought you saw it in the right point of view. I hear from Sara to-night—"

"I should like to know what Sara has to do with it," said Jack, with an explosion of indignation. "Of course, sir, all you may have to say on this or any other subject I am bound to listen to with respect; but as for Sara and her interference—"

"Don't be a fool, Jack," said Mr. Brownlow, sharply. "Sara has told me nothing that I could not have found out for myself. I warned you, but it does not appear to have been of any use; and now I have a word more to say. Look here. I take an interest in this little girl at the gate. There is something in her face that reminds me—but never mind that. I feel sure she's a good girl, and I won't have her harmed. Understand me once for all. You may think it a small matter enough, but it's not a small matter. I won't have that child harmed. If she should come to evil through you, you shall have me to answer to. It is not only her poor mother to any poor friend she may have—"

"Sir," cried Jack, boiling over, "do you know you are insulting me?"

"Listen to what I am saying," said his father. "Don't answer. I am in earnest. She is an innocent child, and I won't have her harmed. If you can't keep away from her, have the honesty to tell me so, and I'll find means to get you away. Good Lord, sir! is every instinct of manhood so dead in you that you can not overcome a vicious inclination, though it should ruin that poor innocent child?"

A perfect flood of fury and resentment swept through Jack's mind; but he was not going to be angry and lose his advantage. He was white with suppressed passion, but his voice did not swell with anger, as his father's had done. It was thus his self-possession that carried the day.

"When you have done, sir," he said, taking off his hat with a quietness which cost him an immense effort, "perhaps you will hear what I have got to say."

Mr. Brownlow for the moment had lost his temper, which was very foolish. Probably it was because other things too were going wrong, and his sense of justice did not permit him to avenge their contrariety upon the purely innocent. Now Jack was not purely innocent, and here was an outlet. And then he had been walking about in the avenue for more than an hour waiting, and was naturally sick of it. And, finally, having lost his own temper, he was furious with Jack for not losing his.

"Speak out, sir," he cried; "I have done. Not that your speaking can make much difference. I repeat, if you hurt a hair of that child's head—"

"I will thank you to speak of her in a different way," said Jack, losing patience also. "You may think me a villain if you please; but how dare you venture to suppose that I could bring her to harm? Is she nobody? is that all you think of her? By Jove! the young lady you are speaking of, without knowing her," said Jack, suddenly stopping himself, staring at his father with calm fury, and speaking with deadly emphasis, "is going to be—my wife."

Mr. Brownlow was so utterly confounded that he stood still and stared in his turn at his audacious son. He gave a start as if some one had shot him; and then he stood speechless and stared, wondering blankly if some transformation had occurred, or if this was actually Jack that stood before him. It ought to have been a relief to his mind—no doubt if he had been as good a man as he ought to have been, he would have gone down on his knees and given thanks that his son's intentions were so virtuous; but in the mean time amaze swallowed up every other sentiment. "Your wife!" he said, with the utmost wonder which the human voice is capable of expressing in his voice. The wildest effort of imagination could never have brought him to such an idea—Jack's wife! His consternation was such that it took the strength out of him. He could not have said a word more had it been to save his life. If any one had pushed rudely against him he might have dropped on the ground in the weakness of his amaze. "You might have knocked him down with a feather," was the description old Betty would have given; and she would have been right.

"Yes," said Jack, with a certain magnificence; "and as for my power, or any man's power, of harming—her. By Jove!—though of course you didn't know—"

This he said magnanimously, being not without pity for the utter downfall which had overtaken his father. Their positions, in fact, had totally changed. It was Mr. Brownlow who was struck dumb. Instead of carrying things with a high hand as he had begun to do, it was he who was reduced into the false position. And Jack was on the whole sorry for his father. He took his hands out of the depths of his pockets, and put down his shoulders into their natural position. And he was willing "to let down easy," as he himself expressed it, the unlucky father who had made such an astounding mistake.

As for Mr. Brownlow, it took him some time to recover himself. It was not quite easy to realize the position, especially after the warm, not to say violent, way in which he had been beguiled into taking Pamela's part. He had meant every word of what he said. Her sweet little face had attracted him more than he knew how to explain; it had reminded him, he could not exactly tell of what, of something that belonged to his youth and made his heart soft. And the thought of pain or shame coming to her through his son had been very bitter to him. But he was not quite ready all the same to say, Bless you, my children. Such a notion, indeed, had never occurred to him. Mr. Brownlow had never for a moment supposed that his son Jack, the wise and prudent, could have been led to entertain such an idea; and he was so much startled that he did not know what to think. After the first pause of amazement he had gone on again slowly, feeling as if by walking on some kind of mental progress might also be practicable; and Jack had accompanied him in a slightly jaunty, magnanimous, and forgiving way. Indeed, circumstances altogether had conspired, as it were, in Jack's favor. He could not have hoped for so good an opportunity of telling his story—an opportunity which not only took all that was formidable from the disclosure, but actually presented it in the character of a relief and standing evidence of unthought-of virtue. And Jack was so simple-minded in the midst of his wisdom that it seemed to him as if his father's anticipated opposition were summarily disposed of, to be heard of no more—a thing which he did not quite know whether to be sorry for or glad.

Perhaps it staggered him a little in this idea when Mr. Brownlow, after going on, very slowly and thoughtfully, almost to the very door of the house, turned back again, and began to retrace his steps, still as gravely and quietly as ever. Then a certain thrill of anticipation came over Jack. One fytte was ended, but another was for to say. Feeling had been running very high between them when they last spoke; now there was a certain hushed tone about the talk, as if a cloud had suddenly rolled over them. Mr. Brownlow spoke, but he did not look at Jack, nor even look up, but went on moodily, with his eyes fixed on the ground, now and then stopping to kick away a little stone among the gravel, a pause which became almost tragic by repetition. "Is it long since this happened?" he said, speaking in a very subdued tone of voice.

"No," said Jack, feeling once more the high color rushing up into his face, though in the darkness there was nobody who could see—"no, only a few days."

"And you said your wife," Mr. Brownlow added—"your wife. Whom does she belong to? People don't go so far without knowing a few preliminaries, I suppose?"

"I don't know who she belongs to, except her mother," said Jack, growing very hot; and then he added, on the spur of the moment, "I dare say you think it's not very wise—I don't pretend it's wise—I never supposed it was; but as for the difficulties, I am ready to face them. I don't see that I can say any more."

"I did not express any opinion," said Mr. Brownlow, coldly; "no—I don't suppose wisdom has very much to do with it. But I should like to understand. Do you mean to say that every thing is settled? or do you only speak in hope?"

"Yes, it is quite settled," said Jack: in spite of himself this cold questioning had made a difference even in the sound of his voice. It all came before him again in its darker colors. The light seemed to steal out of the prospect before him moment by moment. His face burned in the dark; he was disgusted with himself for not having something to say; and gradually he grew into a state of feverish irritation at the stones which his father took the trouble to kick away, and the crunching of the gravel under his feet.

"And you have not a penny in the world," said Mr. Brownlow, in his dispassionate voice.

"No," said Jack, "I have not a penny in the world."

And then there was another pause. The very stars seemed to have gone in, not to look at his discomfiture, poor fellow! A cold little wind had sprung up, and went moaning out and in eerily among the trees; even old Betty at the lodge had gone to bed, and there was no light to be seen from her windows. The prospect was black, dreary, very chilling—nothing to be seen but the sky, over which clouds were stealing, and the tree-tops swaying wildly against them; and the sound of the steps on the gravel. Jack had uttered his last words with great firmness and even a touch of indignation; but there can be no doubt that heaviness was stealing over his heart.

"If it had been any one but yourself who told me, Jack," said his father, "I should not have believed it. You of all men in the world—I ought to beg your pardon for misjudging you. I thought you would think of your own pleasure rather than of any body's comfort, and I was mistaken. I beg your pardon. I am glad to have to make you an apology like this."

"Thanks," said Jack, curtly. It was complimentary, no doubt; but the compliment itself was not complimentary. I beg your pardon for thinking you a villain—that was how it sounded to his ears; and he was not flattered even by his escape.

"But I can't rejoice over the rest," said Mr. Brownlow—"it is going against all your own principles, for one thing. You are very young—you have no call to marry for ten years at least—and of course if you wait ten years you will change your mind."

"I have not the least intention of waiting ten years," said Jack.

"Then perhaps you will be so good as to inform me what your intentions are," said his father, with a little irony; "if you have thought at all on the subject it may be the easier way."

"Of course I have thought on the subject," said Jack; "I hope I am not a fellow to do things without thinking. I don't pretend it is prudent. Prudence is very good, but there are some things that are better. I mean to get married with the least possible delay."

"And then?" said Mr. Brownlow.

"Then, sir, I suppose," said Jack, not without a touch of bitterness, "you will let me remain in the office, and keep my clerkship; seeing that, as you say, I have not a penny in the world."

Then they walked on together again for several minutes in the darkness. It was not wonderful that Jack's heart should be swelling with a sense of injury. Here was he, a rich man's son, with the great park breathing round him in the darkness, and the great house shining behind, with its many lights, and many servants, and much luxury. All was his father's—all, and a great deal more than that: and yet he, his father's only son, had "not a penny in the world." No wonder Jack's heart was very bitter within him; but he was too proud to make a word of complaint.

"You think it cruel of me to say so," Mr. Brownlow said, after that long pause; "and so it looks, I don't doubt. But if you knew as much as I do, it would not appear to you so wonderful. I am neither so rich nor so assured in my wealth as people think."

"Do you mean that you have been losing money?" said Jack, who was half touched, in the midst of his discontent, by his father's tone.

"I have been losing—not exactly money," said Mr. Brownlow, with a sigh; "but never mind: I can't hide from you, Jack, that you have disappointed me. I feel humbled about it altogether. Not that I am a man to care for worldly advantages that are won by marriage; but yet—and you did not seem the sort of boy to throw yourself away."

"Look here, father," said Jack; "you may be angry, but I must say one word. I think a man, when he can work for his wife, has a right to marry as he likes—at least if he likes," added the young philosopher, hastily, with a desperate thought of his consistency; "but I do think a girl's friends have something to do with it. Yet you set your face against me, and let that fellow see Sara constantly—see her alone—talk with her—I found them in the flower-garden the other day—and then, by Jove! you pitch into me."

"You are speaking of young Powys," said Mr. Brownlow, with sudden dignity; "Powys is a totally different thing—I have told you so before."

"And I have told you, sir, that you are mistaken," said Jack. "How is Powys different? except that he's a young—cad—and never had any breeding. As for any idea you may have in your head about his family—have you ever seen his mother?"

"Have you?" said Mr. Brownlow; and his heart, too, began to beat heavily, as if there could be any sentimental power in that good woman's name.

"Yes," said Jack, in his ignorance, "she is a homely sort of sensible woman, that never could have been any thing beyond what she is; and one look at her would prove that to you. I don't mean to say I like people that have seen better days; but you would never suppose she had been any thing more than what she is now; she might have been a Masterton shopkeeper's daughter from Chestergate or Dove Street," Jack continued, "and she would have looked just as she looks now."

Mr. Brownlow, in spite of himself, gave a long shuddering sigh. He drew a step apart from his son, and stumbled over a stone in the gravel, not having the heart even to kick it away. Jack's words, though they were so careless and so ignorant, went to his father's heart. As it happened, by some curious coincidence, he had chosen the very locality from which Phœbe Thomson would have come. And it rang into the very centre of that unsuspected target which Mr. Brownlow had set up to receive chance shots, in his heart.

"I don't know where she has come from," he said; "but yet I tell you Powys is different; and some day you will know better. But whatever may be done about that has nothing to do with your own case. I repeat to you, Jack, it is very humbling to me."

Here he stopped short, and Jack was doggedly silent, and had not a word of sympathy to give him. It was true, this second mésalliance was a great blow to Mr. Brownlow—a greater blow to his pride and sense of family importance than any body would have supposed. He had made up his mind to it that Sara must marry Powys; that her grandeur and her pretty state could only be secured to her by these means, and that she must pay the price for them—a price which, fortunately, she did not seem to have any great difficulty about. But that Jack should make an ignoble marriage too, that people could be able to say that the attorney's children had gone back to their natural grade, and that all his wealth, and their admittance into higher circles, and Jack's education, and Sara's sovereignty, should end in their marrying, the one her father's clerk, the other the little girl in the cottage at the gate, was a very bitter pill to their father. He had never schemed for great marriages for them, never attempted to bring heirs and heiresses under their notice; but still it was a downfall. Even the Brownlows of Masterton had made very different alliances. It was perhaps a curious sort of thing to strike a man, and a man of business, but nevertheless it was very hard upon him. In Sara's case—if it did come to any thing in Sara's case—there was an evident necessity, and there was an equivalent; yet even there Mr. Brownlow knew that when the time came to avow the arrangement, it would not be a pleasant office. He knew how people would open their eyes, how the thing would be spoken of, how his motives and her motives would be questioned. And to think of Jack adding another story to the wonder of the county! Mr. Brownlow did not care much for old Lady Motherwell, but he knew what she would say. She would clasp her old hands together in their brown gloves (if it was morning), and she would say, "They were always very good sort of people, but they were never much in our way—and it is far better they should settle in their own condition of life. I am glad to hear the young people have had so much sense." So the county people would be sure to say, and the thought of it galled Mr. Brownlow. He would not have felt it so much had Jack alone been the culprit, and Sara free to marry Sir Charles Motherwell, or any other county potentate; but think of both!—and of all the spectators that were looking on, and all their comments! It was mere pride and personal feeling, he knew—even feeling that was a little paltry and scarcely worthy of him—but he could not help feeling the sting and humiliation; and this perhaps, though it was merely fanciful, was the one thing which galled him most about Jack.

Jack for his part had nothing to say in opposition. He opened his eyes a little in the dark to think of this unsuspected susceptibility on his father's part, but he did not think it unjust. It seemed to him on the whole natural enough. It was hard upon him, after he had worked and struggled to bring his children into this position. Jack did not understand his father's infatuation in respect to Powys. It was infatuation. But he could well enough understand how it might be very painful to him to see his only son make an obscure marriage. He was not offended at this. He felt for his father, and even he felt for himself, who had the thing to do. It was not a thing he would have approved of for any of his friends, and he did not approve of it in his own case. He knew it was the only thing he could do; and after an evening such as that he had passed with little Pamela, he forgot that there was any thing in it but delight and sweetness. That, however, was a forgetfulness which could not last long. He had felt it could not last long even while he was taking his brief enjoyment of it, and he began again fully to realize the other side of the question as he walked slowly along in the dark by his father's side. The silence lasted a long time, for Mr. Brownlow had a great deal to think about. He walked on mechanically almost as far as Betty's cottage, forgetting almost his son's presence, at least forgetting that there was any necessity for keeping up a conversation. At last, however, it was he who spoke.

"Jack," he said, "I wish you would reconsider all this. Don't interrupt me, please. I wish you'd think it all over again. I don't say that I think you very much to blame. She has a sweet face," said Mr. Brownlow, with a certain melting of tone, "and I don't say that she may not be as sweet as her face; but still, Jack, you are very young, and it's a very unsuitable match. You are too sensible not to acknowledge that; and it may injure your prospects and cramp you for all your life. In justice both to yourself and your family, you ought to consider all that."

"As it happens, sir, it is too late to consider all that," said Jack, "even if I ever could have balanced secondary motives against—"

"Bah!" said Mr. Brownlow; and then he added, with a certain impatience, "don't tell me that you have not balanced—I know you too well for that. I know you have too much sense for that. Of course you have balanced all the motives. And do you tell me that you are ready to resign all your advantages, your pleasant life here, your position, your prospects, and go and live on a clerk's income in Masterton—all for love?" said Mr. Brownlow. He did not mean to sneer, but his voice, as he spoke, took a certain inflection of sarcasm, as perhaps comes natural to a man beyond middle age, when he has such suggestions to make.

Jack once more thrust his hands into the depths of his pockets, and gloom and darkness came into his heart. Was it the voice of the tempter that was addressing him? But then, had he not already gone over all that ground?—the loss of all comforts and advantages, the clerk's income, the little house in Masterton. "I have already thought of all that," he said, "as you suggest; but it does not make any difference to me." Then he stopped and made a long pause. "If this is all you have to say to me, sir, perhaps it will be best to stop here," said Jack; and he made a pause and turned back again with a certain determination toward the house.

"It is all I have to say," said Mr. Brownlow, gravely; and he too turned round, and the two made a solemn march homeward, with scarcely any talk. This is how Jack's story was told. He had not thought of doing it, and he had found little comfort and encouragement in the disclosure; but still it was made, and that was so much gained. The lights were beginning to be extinguished in the windows, so late and long had been their discussion. But as they came up, Sara became visible at the window of her own room, which opened upon a balcony. She had come to look for them in her pretty white dressing-gown, with all her wealth of hair streaming over her shoulders. It was a very familiar sort of apparel, but still, to be sure, it was only her father and her brother who were witnesses of her little exhibition. "Papa, I could not wait for you," she cried, leaning over the balcony, "I couldn't keep Angelique sitting up. Come and say good-night." When Mr. Brownlow went in to obey her, Jack stood still and pondered. There was a difference. Sara would be permitted to make any marriage she pleased—even with a clerk in his father's office; whereas her brother, who ought to have been the principal—However, to do him justice, there was no grudge in Jack's heart. He scorned to be envious of his sister. "Sara will have it all her own way," he said to himself a little ruefully, as he lighted his candle and went up the great staircase; and then it occurred to him to wonder what she would do about Pamela. Already he felt himself superseded. It was his to take the clerk's income and subside into inferiority, and Sara was to be the queen of Brownlows—as indeed she had always been.

CHAPTER XXVII

SARA'S OWN AFFAIRS

Sara's affairs were perhaps not so interesting, as indeed they were far from being so advanced, as those of Jack; but still all this time they were making progress. It was not without cause that the image of Powys stole across her mental vision when Jack warned her to look at the beam in her own eye. There could be little doubt that Mr. Brownlow had encouraged Powys. He had asked him to come generally, and he had added to this many special invitations, and sometimes, indeed, when Jack was not there, had given the young man a seat in the dog-cart, and brought him out. All this was very confusing, not to Sara, who, as she thought, saw into the motives of her father's conduct, and knew how it was; but to the clerk in Mr. Brownlow's office, who felt himself thus singled out, and could not but perceive that no one else had the same privilege. It filled him with many wondering and even bewildered thoughts. Perhaps at the beginning it did not strike him so much, semi-republican as he was; but he was quick-witted, and when he looked about him, and saw that his neighbors did not get the same advantages, the young Canadian felt that there must be something in it. He was taken in, as it were, to Mr. Brownlow's heart and home, and that not without a purpose, as was told him by the angry lines in Jack's forehead. He was taken in and admitted into the habits of intimacy, and had Sara, as it were, given over to him; and what did it mean? for that it must mean something he could not fail to see.

Thus young Powys's position was very different from that of Jack. Jack had been led into his scrape unwittingly, having meant nothing. But it would have been impossible for Powys to act in the same way. To him unconsciousness was out of the question. He might make it clear to himself, in a dazzled self-conscious way, that his own excellence could have nothing to do with it; that it must be accident, or good fortune, or something perfectly fortuitous; but yet withal the sense remained that he and no other had been chosen for this privilege, and that it could not be for nothing. He was modest and he had good sense, more than could have been expected from his age and circumstances; but yet every thing conspired to make him forget these sober qualities. He had not permitted himself so much as to think at his first appearance that Miss Brownlow, too, was a young human creature like himself. He had said to himself, on the contrary, that she was of a different species, that she was as much out of his reach as the moon or the stars, and that if he suffered any folly to get into his head, of course he would have to suffer for it. But the folly had got into his head, and he had not suffered. He had been left with her, and she had talked to him, and made every thing very sweet to his soul. She had dropped the magic drop into his cup, which makes the mildest draught intoxicating, and the poor young fellow had felt the subtle charm stealing over him, and had gone on bewildered, justifying himself by the tacit encouragement given him, and not knowing what to think or what to do. He knew that between her and him there was a gulf fixed. He knew that of all men in the world he was the last to conceive any hopes in which such a brilliant little princess as Sara could be involved. It was doubly and trebly out of the question. He was not only a poor clerk, but he was a poor clerk with a family to support. It was all mere madness and irredeemable folly; but still Mr. Brownlow took him out to his house, and still he saw, and was led into intimate companionship with his master's daughter. And what could it mean, or how could it end? Powys fell into such a maze at last, that he went and came unconsciously in a kind of insanity. Something must come of it one of these days. Something;—a volcanic eruption and wild blazing up of earth and heaven—a sudden plunge into madness or into darkness. It was strange, very strange to him, to think what Mr. Brownlow could mean by it; he was very kind to him—almost paternal—and yet he was exposing him to this trial, which he could neither fly from nor resist. Thus poor Powys pondered to himself many a time, while, with a beating heart, he went along the road to Brownlows. He could have delivered himself, no doubt, if he would, but he did not want to deliver himself. He had let all go in a kind of desperation. It must end, no doubt, in some dreadful sudden downfall of all his hopes. But indeed he had no hopes; he knew it was madness; yet it was a madness he was permitted, even encouraged in; and he gave himself up to it, and let himself float down the stream, and said to himself that he would shut his eyes, and take what happiness he could get in the present moment, and shut out all thoughts of the future. This he was doing with a kind of thrill of prodigal delight, selling his birthright for a mess of pottage, giving up all the freshness of his heart, and all its force of early passion, for what?—for nothing. To throw another flower in the path of a girl who trod upon nothing but flowers; this was what he felt it to be in his saner moments. But the influence of that sanity never stopped him in what he was doing. He had never in his life met with any thing like her, and if she chose to have this supreme luxury of a man's heart and life offered up to her all for nothing—what then? He was not the man to grudge her that richest and most useless gift. It was not often he went so deep as this, or realized what a wild cause he was embarked on: but when he did, he saw the matter clearly enough, and knew how it must be.

As for Sara, she was very innocent of any such thoughts. She was not the girl to accept such a holocaust. If she had known what was in his heart, possibly she might have scorned him for it; but she never suspected what was passing in his heart. She did not know of that gulf fixed. His real position, that position which was so very true and unquestionable to him, was not real at all to Sara. He was a fairy prince, masquerading under that form for some reason known to himself and Mr. Brownlow; or if not that, then he was the man to whom, according to her father's will, she was to give herself blindly out of pure filial devotion. Anyhow something secret, mysterious, beyond ordinary ken, was in it; something that gave piquancy to the whole transaction. She was not receiving a lover in a commonplace sort of way when she entertained young Powys, but was instead a party to an important transaction, fulfilling a grand duty, either to her father menaced by some danger, or to a hero transformed whom only the touch of a true maiden could win back to his rightful shape. As it happened, this fine devotion was not disagreeable to her; but Sara felt, no doubt, that she would have done her duty quite as unswervingly had the fairy prince been bewitched into the person of the true Beast of the story instead of that of her father's clerk.

It was a curious sort of process to note, had there been any spectator by sufficiently at ease to note it; but there was not, unless indeed Mr. Hardcastle and Fanny might have stood in that capacity. As for the rector, he washed his hands of it. He had delivered his own soul just as Mrs. Swayne had delivered hers in respect to the other parties. He had told Mr. Brownlow very plainly what his opinion was. "My dear fellow," he had said, "you don't know what you are doing. Be warned in time. You don't think what kind of creatures girls and boys are at that age. And then you are compromising Sara with the world. Who do you think would care to be the rival of your clerk? It is very unfair to your child. And then Sara is just one of the girls that are most likely to suffer. She is a girl that has fancies of her own. You know I am as fond of her almost as I am of my Fanny, but there could not be a greater difference than between the two. Fanny might come safely through such an ordeal, but Sara is of a different disposition; she is capable of thinking that it doesn't matter, she is capable, though one does not like even to mention such an idea, of falling in love—"

Mr. Brownlow winced a little at this suggestion. I suppose men don't like to think of their womenkind falling in love. There is a certain desecration in the idea. "No," he said, with something in his voice that was half approval and half contempt, "you need not be afraid of Fanny; and as for Sara, I trust Providence will take care of her—as you seem to think she has so poor a guardian in me."

"Ah, Brownlow, we must both feel what a disadvantage we are at," said Mr. Hardcastle, with a sigh, "with our motherless girls; and theirs is just the age at which it tells."

"Yes," said Mr. Brownlow, shaping his face a little, unawares, into the right look. The rector had had two mothers for Fanny, and was used to this kind of thing; indeed it was never off the cards, as Fanny herself was profoundly aware, that there might be a third; and accordingly he had a right to be effusive about it: whereas Mr. Brownlow had had but one love in his life, and could not talk on the subject. But he knew his duty sufficiently to look solemn, and assent to his pastor's proposition about the motherless girls.

"On that account, if on no other, we ought to give them our double attention," the rector continued. "You know I can have but one motive. Take my word for it, it is not fit that your clerk should be brought into your daughter's society. If any foolish complication should come of it, you would never forgive yourself; and only think of the harm it would do Sara in the world."

"Softly, Hardcastle," said Mr. Brownlow, "don't go too far. Sara and the world have nothing to do with each other. That sort of thing may answer well enough for your hackneyed girls who have gone through a few seasons and are up to every thing; but to the innocent—"

"My dear Brownlow," said the rector, with a certain tone of patronage and compassion, "I know how much I am inferior to you in true knowledge of the world; but perhaps—let us say—the world of fashion—may be a little better known to me than to you."

Mr. Brownlow was roused by this. "I don't know how it should be so," he said, looking very steadily at the rector. Mr. Hardcastle had a second cousin who was an Irish peer. That was the chief ground of his social pretensions, and the world of fashion, to tell the truth, had never fallen much in his way; but still a man who has a cousin a lord, when he claims superior knowledge of society to that possessed by another man who has no such distinction, generally, in the country at least, has his claim allowed.

"You think not?" he said, stammering and growing red. "Oh, ah—well—of course—in that case I can't be of any use. I am sorry to have thrust my opinion on you. If you feel yourself so thoroughly qualified—"

"Don't take offense," said Mr. Brownlow. "I have no such high opinion of my qualifications. I don't think we are, either of us, men of fashion to speak of, but, as it happens, I know my own business. It suits me to have my clerk at hand—and he is not just an ordinary clerk; and I hope Sara is not the sort of girl to lose her head and go off into silly romances. I have confidence in her, you see, as you have in Fanny—though perhaps it may not be so perfectly justified," Mr. Brownlow added, with a smile. Fanny was known within her own circle to be a very prudent little woman, almost too prudent, and this was a point which the rector always felt.

"Well, I hope you will find it has been for the best," Mr. Hardcastle answered, and he sighed in reply to his friend's smile: evidently he did not expect it would turn out for the best—but at all events he had delivered his soul.

And Fanny, in the mean time, was delivering her little lecture to Sara. They had been dining at Brownlows, and there were no other guests, and the two girls were alone in the drawing-room, in that little half-hour which the gentlemen spent over their temperate glass of claret. It is an hour much bemoaned by fast young women, but, as the silent majority are aware, it is not an unpleasant hour. Fanny Hardcastle and Sara Brownlow were great friends in their way. They were in the habit of seeing each other continually, of going to the same places, of meeting the same people. It was not exactly a friendship of natural affinity, but rather of proximity, which answers very well in many cases. Probably Fanny, for her part, was not capable of any thing more enthusiastic. They told each other every thing—that is, they each told the other as much as that other could understand. Fanny, by instinct, refrained from putting before Sara all the prudences and sensible restrictions that existed in her own thoughts; and Sara, equally by instinct, was dumb about her own personal feelings and fancies, except now and then when carried away by their vehemence. "She would not understand me, you know," both of them would have said. But to-night Fanny had taken upon herself the prophetic office. She, too, had her burden of warning to deliver, and to free her own soul from all responsibility in her neighbor's fate.

"Sara," she said, "I saw you the other day when you did not see me. You were in the park—down there, look, under that tree; and that Mr. Powys was with you. You know I once saw him here."

"I do not call that the park—I call that the avenue," said Sara; but she saw that her companion spoke with intention, and a certain quickening of color came to her face.

"You may call it any thing you please, but I am sure it is the park," said Fanny, "and I want to speak to you about it. I am sure I don't know who Mr. Powys is—I dare say he is very nice—but do you think it is quite right walking about with him like that? You told me yourself he was in your papa's office. You know Sara, dear, I wouldn't say a word to you if it wasn't for your good."

"What is for my good?" said Sara—"walking in the park? or having you to speak to me? As for Mr. Powys, I don't suppose you know any thing about him, so of course you can't have any thing to say."

"I wish you would not gallop on like that and take away one's breath," said Fanny. "Of course I don't know any thing about him. He may be very nice—I am sure I can't say; or he may be very amusing—they often are," Fanny added, with a sigh, "when they are no good. But don't go walking and talking with him, Sara; don't, there's a dear; people will talk; you know how they talk. And if he is only in your papa's office—"

"I don't see what difference that can possibly make," said Sara with a little vehemence.

"But it does make a difference," said Fanny, once more with a sigh. "If he were ever so nice, it could be no good. Mr. Brownlow may be very kind to him, but he would never let you marry him, Sara. Yes, of course, that is what it must come to. A girl should not stray about in the park with a man unless he was a man that she could marry if he asked her. I don't mean to say that she would marry, but at least that she could. And, besides, a girl owes a duty to herself even if her father would consent. You, in your position, ought to make a very different match."

"You little worldly-minded wretch," cried Sara, "have you nearly done?"

"Any body would tell you so as well as me," said Fanny. "You might have had that big Sir Charles if you had liked. Papa is only a poor clergyman, and we have not the place in society we might have; but you can go everywhere, you who are so rich. And then the gentlemen always like you. If you were to make a poor marriage it would be a shame."

"When did you learn all that?" said Fanny's hearer, aghast. "I never thought you were half so wise."

"I always knew it, dear," said little Fanny, with complacency. "I used to be too frightened to speak, and then you always talked so much quicker and went on so. But when I was at my aunt's in spring—"

"I shall always hate your aunt;" cried Sara—"I did before by instinct: did she put it all into your head about matches and things? You were ten thousand times better when you had only me. As if I would marry a man because he would be a good marriage! I wonder what you take me for, that you speak so to me!"

"Then what should you marry him for!" said little Fanny, with a toss of her pretty head.

"For!" cried Sara, "not for any thing! for nothing at all! I hate marrying. To think a girl can not live in this world without having that thrust into her face! What should I marry any body for? But I shall do what I like, and walk when I like, and talk to any body that pleases me," cried the impetuous young woman. Her vehemence brought a flush to her face and something like tears into her eyes; and Fanny, for her part, looked on very gravely at an appearance of feeling of which she entirely disapproved.

"I dare say you will take your own way," she said—"you always did take your own way; but at least you can't say I did not warn you; and I hope you will never be sorry for not having listened to me, Sara. I love you all the same," said Fanny, giving her friend a soft little kiss. Sara did not return this salutation with the warmth it deserved. She was flushed and angry and impatient, and yet disposed to laugh.

"You don't hope any thing of the sort," she said; "you hope I shall live to be very sorry—and I hate your aunt." This was how the warning ended in the drawing-room. It was more elegantly expressed than it had been by Mrs. Swayne and old Betty; but yet the burden of the prophecy was in some respects the same.

When Sara thought over it at a later period of the night, she laughed a little in her own mind at poor Fanny's ignorance. Could she but know that the poor clerk was an enchanted prince! Could she but guess that it was in pure obedience to her father's wishes that she had given him such a reception! When he appeared in his true shape, whatever that might be, how uncomfortable little Fanny would feel at the recollection of what she had said! And then Sara took to guessing and wondering what his true shape might be. She was not romantic to speak of in general. She was only romantic in her own special case; and when she came to think of it seriously, her good sense came to her aid—or rather not to her aid—to her hindrance and confusion and bewilderment. Sara knew very well that in those days people were not often found out to be princes in disguise. She knew even that for a clerk in her father's office to turn out the heir to a peerage or even somebody's son would be so unusual as to be almost incredible. And what, then, could her father mean? Neither was Mr. Brownlow the sort of man to pledge his soul on his daughter in any personal emergency. Yet some cause there must be. When she had come this length, a new sense seemed suddenly to wake up in Sara's bosom, perhaps only the result of her own thoughts, perhaps suggested, though she would not have allowed that, by Fanny Hardcastle's advice—a sudden sense that she had been coming down from her natural sphere, and that her father's clerk was not a fit mate for her. She was very generous, and hasty, and high-flown, and fond of her father, and fond of amusement—and moved by all these qualities and affections together she had jumped at the suggestion of Mr. Brownlow's plan; but perhaps she had never thought seriously of it as it affected herself that night. Now it suddenly occurred to her how people might talk. Strangely enough, the same thought which had been bitterness to her father, stung her also, as soon as her eyes were opened. Miss Brownlow of Brownlows, who had refused, or the same thing as refused, Sir Charles Motherwell—whom young Keppel had regarded afar off as utterly beyond his reach—the daughter of the richest man, and herself one of the most popular (Sara did not even to herself say the prettiest; she might have had an inkling of that too, but certainly she did not put it into articulate thought) girls in the county—she bending from her high estate to the level of a lawyer's clerk; she going back to the hereditary position, reminding every body that she was the daughter of the Masterton attorney, showing the low tastes which one generation of higher culture could not be supposed to have effaced! How could she do it? If she had been a duke's daughter it would not have mattered. In such a case nobody could have thought of hereditary low tastes; but now—As Sara mused, the color grew hotter and hotter in her cheeks. To think that it was only now, so late in the day, that this occurred to her, after she had gone so far in the way of carrying out her father's wishes! To think that he could have imposed such a sacrifice upon her! Sara's heart smarted and stung her in her breast as she thought of that. And then there suddenly came up a big indignant blob of warm dew in either eye, which was not for her father nor for her own dignity, but for something else about which she could not parley with herself. And then she rushed at her candles and put them out, and threw herself down on her bed. The fact was that she did sleep in half an hour at the farthest, though she did not mean to, and thus escaped from her thoughts; but that was not what she calculated upon. She calculated on lying awake all night and saying many very pointed and grievous things to her father when in the morning he should ask her the meaning of her pale face and heavy eyes; but unfortunately her cheeks were as fresh as the morning when the morning duly came, and her eyes as bright, and Mr. Brownlow, seeing no occasion for it, asked no questions, but had himself to submit to inquiries and condolences touching a bad night and a pale face. He too had been moved by Mr. Hardcastle's warning—moved, not of course to any sort of acceptance of the rector's advice, but only to the length of being uncomfortable, while he took his own way, which is at all times the only one certain result of good advice. And he was depressed too about Jack's communication which had been made to him only two nights before, and of which he had spoken to nobody. The thought of it was a humiliation to him. His two children whom he had brought up so carefully, his only ones, in whom he had expected his family to make a new beginning—and yet they both meant to descend far below the ancestral level which he had hoped to see them leave utterly behind! He was not what is called a proud man, and he had never been ashamed of his origin or of his business. But yet, two such marriages in one family, and one generation—! It was a bitter thought.

As for Sara, she would have said, had she been questioned, that she thought of nothing else all day; and in fact it was her prevailing pre-occupation. All the humiliations involved in it came gleaming across her mind by intervals. Her pride rose up in arms. She did not know as yet about the repetition or rather anticipation of her case which her brother had been guilty of. But she did ponder over the probable consequences. The hardest thing of all was that they would say it was the fault of her race, that she was only returning to her natural level, and that it was not wealth nor even admiration which could make true gentlefolks; all which were sentiments to which Sara would have subscribed willingly in any but her own case. When Powys arrived with Mr. Brownlow in the evening, she received him with a stateliness that chilled the poor young fellow to his heart. And he too had so many thoughts, and just at that moment was wondering with an intensity which put all the others to shame how it could possibly end, and what his honor required of him, and what sort of a grey and weary desert life would be after this dream was over. It seemed to him absolutely as if the dream was coming to an end that night. Jack, who was never very courteous to the visitor, left them immediately after dinner, and Mr. Brownlow retired to the library for some time, and Powys had no choice but to go where his heart had gone before him, up to the drawing-room where Sara sat alone. Of course she ought to have had a chaperone; but then this young man, being only a clerk from the office, did not count.

She was seated in the window, close to the Claude, which had been the first thing that brought these two together; but to-night she was in no meditative mood. She had provided herself with work, and was laboring at it fiercely in a way which Powys had never seen before. And he did not know that her heart too was beating very fast, and that she had been wondering and wondering whether he would have the courage to come up stairs. He had really had that courage, but now that he was there, he did not know what to do. He came up to her at first, but she kept on working and did not take any notice of him, she who up to this moment had always been so sweet. The poor young fellow was cast down to the very depths; he thought they had but taken him up and played upon him for their amusement, and that now the end had come. And he tried, but ineffectually, to comfort himself with the thought that he had always known it must come to an end. Almost, when he saw her silence, her absorbed looks, the constrained little glance she gave him as he came into the room, it came into his mind that Sara herself would say something to bring the dream to a distinct conclusion. If she had told him that she divined his presumption, and that he was never more to enter that room again, he would not have been surprised. It had been a false position throughout—he knew that, and he knew that it must come to an end.

But, in the mean time, a fair face must be put upon it. Powys, though he was a backwoodsman, knew enough of life, or had sufficient instinct of its requirements, to know that. So he went up to the Claude, and looked at it sadly, with a melancholy he could not restrain.

"It is as you once said, Miss Brownlow," said Powys—"always the same gleam and the same ripples. I can understand your objections to it now."

"The Claude?" said Sara, with unnecessary vehemence, "I hate it. I think I hate all pictures; they are so everlastingly the same thing. Did Jack go out, Mr. Powys, as you came up stairs?"

"Yes; he went out just after you had left us," said Powys, glad to find something less suggestive on which to speak.

"Again?" said Sara, plunging at the new subject with an energy which proved it to be a relief to her also. "He is so strange. I don't know if papa told you; he is giving us a great deal of trouble just now. I am afraid he has got fond of somebody very, very much below him. It will be a dreadful thing for us if it turns out to be true."

Poor Powys's tongue clove to the roof of his mouth. He gave a wistful look at his tormentor, full of a kind of dumb entreaty. What did she say it for? was it for him, without even the satisfaction of plain-speaking, to send him away for ever?

"Of course you don't know the circumstances," said Sara, "but you can fancy when he is the only son. I don't think you ever took to Jack; but of course he is a great deal to papa and me."

"I think it was your brother who never took to me," said Powys; "he thought I had no business here."

"He had no right to think so, when papa thought differently," said Sara; "he was always very disagreeable; and now to think he should be as foolish as any of us." When she had said this, Sara suddenly recollected herself, and gave a glance up at her companion to see if he had observed her indiscretion. Then she went on hastily with a rising color—"I wish you would tell me, Mr. Powys, how it was that you first came to know papa."

"It is very easy," said Powys; but there he too paused, and grew red, and stopped short in his story with a reluctance that had nothing to do with pride. "I went to him seeking employment," he continued, making an effort, and smiling a sickly smile. He knew she must know that, but yet it cost him a struggle; and somehow every thing seemed to have changed so entirely since those long-distant days.

"And you never knew him before?" said Sara—"nor your father?—nor any body belonging to you?—I do so want to know."

"You are surprised that he has been so kind to me," said Powys, with a pang; "and it is natural you should. No, there is no reason for it that I know of, except his own goodness. He meant to be very, very kind to me," the young fellow added, with a certain pathos. It seemed to him as he spoke that Mr. Brownlow had in reality been very cruel to him, but he did not say it in words. Sara, for her part, gave him a little quick fugitive glance; and it is possible, though no explanation was given, that she understood what he did not speak.

"That was not what I meant," she said, quickly; "only I thought there was something—and then about your family, Mr. Powys?" she said, looking up into his face with a curiosity she could not restrain. Certainly the more she thought it over the more it amazed her. What could her father mean?

"I have no family that I know of," said Powys, with a momentary smile, "except my mother and my little sisters. I am poor, Miss Brownlow, and of no account whatever. I never saved Mr. Brownlow's life, nor did any thing he could be grateful to me for. And I did not know you nor this house," he went on, "when your father brought me here. I did not know, and I could live without—Don't ask me any more questions, please; for I fear I don't know what I am saying to-day."

Here there was a pause, for Sara, though fearless enough in most cases, was a little alarmed by his suppressed vehemence. She was alarmed, and at the same time she was softened, and her inquisitiveness was stronger than her prudence. His very prayer that she would ask him no more questions quickened her curiosity; and it was not in her to refrain for fear of the danger—in that, as in most other amusements, "the danger's self was lure alone."

"But I hope you don't regret having been brought here," she said softly, looking up at him. It was a cruel speech, and the look and the tone were more cruel still. If she had meant to bring him to her feet, she could not have done any thing better adapted to her purpose, and she did not mean to bring him to her feet. She did it only out of a little personal feeling and a little sympathy, and the perversity of her heart.

Powys started violently, and gave her a look under which Sara, courageous as she was, actually trembled; and the next thing he did was to turn his back upon her, and look long and intently at the nearest picture. It was not the Claude this time. It was a picture of a woman holding out a piece of bread to a beggar at her door. The wretch, in his misery, was crouching by the wall and holding out his hand for it, and within were the rosy children, well-fed and comfortable, looking large-eyed upon the want without. The young man thought it was symbolical, as he stood looking at it, quivering all over with emotion which he was laboring to shut up in his own breast. She was holding out the bread of life to him, but it would never reach his lips. He stood struggling to command himself, forgetting every thing but the desperation of that struggle, betraying himself more than any words could have done—fighting his fight of honor and truth against temptation. Sara saw all this, and the little temptress was not satisfied. It would be difficult to tell what impulse possessed her. She had driven him very far, but not yet to the farthest point; and she could not give up her experiment at its very height.

"But you do not answer my question," she said, very softly. The words were scarcely out of her lips, the tingle of compunction had not begun in her heart, when her victim's strength gave way. He turned round upon her with a wild breathlessness that struck Sara dumb. She had seen more than one man who supposed he was "in love" with her; but she had never seen passion before.

"I would regret it," he said, "if I had any sense or spirit left; but I have not, and I don't regret. Take it all—take it!—and then scorn it. I know you will. What could you do but scorn it? It is only my heart and my life; and I am young and shall have to live on hundreds of years, and never see your sweetest face again."

"Mr. Powys!" said Sara in consternation, turning very pale.

"Yes," he said, melting out of the momentary swell of excitement, "I think I am mad to say so. I don't grudge it. It is no better than a flower that you will put your foot on; and now that I have told you, I know it is all over. But I don't grudge it. It was not your doing; and I would rather give it to you to be flung away than to any other woman. Don't be angry with me—I shall never see you again."

"Why?" said Sara, not knowing what she said—"what is it?—what have I done? Mr. Powys, I don't think you—either of us—know what you mean. Let us forget all about it. You said you did not know what you were saying to-day."

"But I have said it," said the young man in his excitement. "I did not mean to betray myself, but now it is all over. I can never come here again. I can never dare look at you again. And it is best so; every day was making it worse. God bless you, though you have made me miserable. I shall never see your face again."

"Mr. Powys!" cried Sara, faintly. But he was gone beyond hearing of her voice. He had not sought even to kiss her hand, as a despairing lover has a prescriptive right to do, much less the hem of her robe, as they do in romances. He was gone in a whirlwind of wild haste, and misery, and passion. She sat still, with her lips apart, her eyes very wide open, her face very white, and listened to his hasty steps going away into the outside world. He was gone—quite gone, and Sara sat aghast. She could not cry; she could not speak; she could but listen to his departing steps, which echoed upon her heart as it seemed. Was it all over? Would he never see her face again, as he said? Had she made him miserable? Sara's face grew whiter and whiter as she asked herself these questions. Of one thing there could be no doubt, that it was she who had drawn this explanation from him. He had not wished to speak, and she had made him speak. And this was the end. If a sudden thunder-bolt had fallen before her, she could not have been more startled and dismayed. She never stirred for an hour or more after he had left her. She let the evening darken round her, and never asked for lights. Every thing was perfectly still, yet she was deafened by the noises in her ears, her heart beating, and voices rising and contending in it which she had never heard before. And was this the end? She was sitting still in the window like a thing in white marble when the servant came in with the lamp, and he had almost stumbled against her as he went to shut the window, and yelled with terror, thinking it was a ghost. It was only then that Sara regained command of herself. Was it all over from to-night?

CHAPTER XXVIII

DESPAIR

It was nearly two hours after this when Jack Brownlow met Powys at the gate. It was a moonlight night, and the white illumination which fell upon the departing visitor perhaps increased the look of excitement and desperation which might have been apparent even to the most indifferent passer-by. He had been walking very quickly down the avenue; his boots and his dress gleamed in the moonlight as if he had been burying himself among the wet grass and bushes in the park. His hat was over his brows, his face haggard and ghastly. No doubt it was partly the effect of the wan and ghostly moonlight, but still there must have been something more in it, or Jack, who loved him little, would not have stopped as he did to see what was the matter. Jack was all the more bent upon stopping that he could see Powys did not wish it, and all sorts of hopes and suspicions sprang up in his mind. His father had dismissed the intruder, or he had so far forgotten himself as to betray his feelings to Sara, and she had dismissed him.

Once more curiosity came in Powys's way. Jack was so resolute to find out what it was, that, for the first time in his life, he was friendly to his father's clerk. "Are you walking?" he said; "I'll go with you a little way. It is a lovely night."

"Yes," said Powys; and he restrained his headlong course a little. It was all he could do—that, and to resist the impulse to knock Jack down and be rid of him. It might not have been so very easy, for the two were tolerably well matched; but poor Powys was trembling with the force of passion, and would have been glad of any opportunity to relieve himself either in the way of love or hatred. Nothing of this description, however, seemed practicable to him. The two young men walked down the road together, keeping a little apart, young, strong, tall, full of vigor, and with a certain likeness in right of their youth and strength. There should even have been the sympathy between them which draws like to like. And yet how unlike they were! Jack had taken his fate in his hand, and was contemplating with a cheerful daring, which was half ignorance, a descent to the position in which his companion stood. It would be sweetened in his case by all the ameliorations possible, or so at least he thought; and, after all, what did it matter? Whereas Powys was smarting under the miserable sense of having been placed in a false position in addition to all the pangs of unhappy love, and of having betrayed himself and the confidence put in him, and sacrificed his honor, and cut himself off forever from the delight which still might have been his. All these pains and troubles were struggling together within him. He would have felt more keenly still the betrayal of the trust his employer had placed in him, had he not felt bitterly that Mr. Brownlow had subjected him to temptations which it was not in flesh and blood to bear. Thus every kind of smart was accumulated within the poor young fellow's spirit—the sense of guilt, the sense of being hardly used, the consciousness of having shut himself out from paradise, the knowledge, beyond all, that his love was hopeless and all the light gone out of his life. It may be supposed how little inclination he had to enter into light conversation, or to satisfy the curiosity of Jack.

They walked on together in complete silence for some minutes, their footsteps ringing in harmony along the level road, but their minds and feelings as much out of harmony as could be conceived. Jack was the first to speak. "It's pleasant walking to-night," he said, feeling more conciliatory than he could have thought possible; "how long do you allow yourself from here to Masterton? It is a good even road."

"Half an hour," said Powys, carelessly.

"Half an hour! that's quick work," said Jack. "I don't think you'll manage that to night. I have known that mare of mine do it in twenty minutes; but I don't think you could match her pace."

"She goes very well," said the Canadian, with a moderation which nettled Jack.

"Very well! I never saw any thing go like her," he said—"that is, with a cart behind her. What kind of cattle have you in Canada? I suppose there's good sport there of one kind or another. Shouldn't you like to go back?"

"I am going back," said Powys. He said it in the depth of his despair, and it startled himself as soon as it was said. Go back? yes! that was the only thing to do—but how?

"Really?" said Jack with surprise and no small relief, and then a certain human sentiment awoke within him. "I hope you haven't had a row with the governor?" he said; "it always seemed to me he had too great a fancy for you. I beg your pardon for saying so just now, especially if you're vexed; but look here—I'm not much of a one for a peace-maker; but if you don't mind telling me what it's about—"

"I have had no row with Mr. Brownlow; it is worse than that," said Powys; "it is past talking of; I have been both an ass and a knave, and there's nothing for me but to take myself out of every body's way."

Once more Jack looked at him in the moonlight, and saw that quick heave of his breast which betrayed the effort he was making to keep himself down, and a certain spasmodic quiver in his lip.

"I wouldn't be too hasty if I were you," he said. "I don't think you can have been a knave. We're all of us ready enough to make fools of ourselves," the young philosopher added, with a touch of fellow-feeling. "You and I haven't been over-good friends, you know, but you might as well tell me what it's all about."

"You were quite right," said Powys, hastily. "I ought never to have come up here. And it was not my doing. It was a false position all along. A man oughtn't to be tempted beyond his strength. Of course I have nobody to blame but myself. I don't suppose I would be a knave about money or any thing of that sort. But it's past talking of; and besides I could not, even if it were any good, make a confidant of you."

It was not difficult for Jack to divine what this despair meant, and he was touched by the delicacy which would not name his sister's name. "I lay a hundred pounds it's Sara's fault," he said to himself. But he gave no expression to the sentiment. And of course it was utterly beyond hope, and the young fellow in Powys's position who should yield to such a temptation must indeed have made an ass of himself. But in the circumstances Jack was not affronted at the want of confidence in himself.

"I don't want to pry into your affairs," he said. "I don't like it myself; but I would not do any thing hastily if I were you. A man mayn't be happy, but, so far as I can see, he must live all the same."

"Yes, that's the worst," said Powys; "a fellow can't give in and get done with it. Talk is no good; but I shall have to go. I shall speak to your father to-morrow, and then—Good-night. Don't come any farther. I've been all about the place to say good-bye. I am glad to have had this talk with you first. Good-night."

"Good-night," said Jack, grasping the hand of his fellow. Their hands had never met in the way of friendship before. Now they clasped each other warmly, closely, with an instinctive sympathy. Powys's mind was so excited with other things, so full of supreme emotion, that this occurrence, though startling enough, did not have much effect upon him. But it made a very different impression upon Jack, who was full of surprise and compunction, and turned, after he had made a few steps in the direction of Brownlows, with a reluctant idea of "doing something" for the young fellow who was so much less lucky than himself. It was a reluctant idea, for he was prejudiced, and did not like to give up his prejudices, and at the same time he was generous, and could not but feel for a brother in misfortune. But Powys was already far on his way, out of hearing, and almost out of sight. "He will do it in the half-hour," Jack said to himself, with admiration. "By Jove! how the fellow goes! and I'll lay you any thing it's all Sara's fault." He was very hard upon Sara in the revulsion of his feelings. Of course she could have done nothing but send her presumptuous admirer away. But, then, had she not led him on and encouraged him? "The little flirt!" Jack said to himself; and just then he was passing Swayne's cottage, which lay in the deep blackness of the shadow made by the moonlight. He looked up tenderly at the light that burned in the upper window. He had grown foolish about that faint little light, as was only natural. There was one who was no flirt, who never would have tempted any man and drawn him on to the breaking of his heart. From the height of his own good fortune Jack looked down upon poor Powys speeding along with despair in his soul along the Masterton road. Something of that soft remorse which is the purest bloom of personal happiness softened his thoughts. Poor Powys! And there was nothing that could be done for him. He could not compel his fate as Jack himself could do. For him there was nothing in store but the relinquishment of all hope, the giving up of all dreams. The thought made Jack feel almost guilty in his own independence and well-being. Perhaps he could yet do or say something that would smooth the other's downfall—persuade him to remain at least at Masterton, where he need never come in the way of the little witch who had beguiled him, and afford him his own protection and friendship instead. As Jack thought of the little house that he himself, separated from Brownlows and its comforts, was about to set up at Masterton, his benevolence toward Powys grew still stronger. He was a fellow with whom a man could associate on emergency; and no doubt this was all Sara's fault. He went home to Brownlows disposed to stand Powys's friend if there was any question of him. But when Jack reached home there was no question of Powys. On the whole it was not a cheerful house into which he entered. Lights were burning vacantly in the drawing-room, but there was nobody there. Lights were burning dimly down stairs. It looked like a deserted place as he went up and down the great staircase, and through the silent rooms, and found nobody. Mr. Brownlow himself was in the library with the door shut, where, in the present complexion of affairs, Jack did not care to disturb him; and Miss Sara had gone to bed with a headache, he was told, when, after searching for her everywhere, he condescended to inquire. Sara was not given to headaches, and the intimation startled her brother. And he went and sat in the drawing-room alone, and stared at the lights, and contrasted this solitary grandeur with the small house whose image was in his mind. The little cozy, tiny, sunshiny place, where one little bright face would always smile; where there would always be some one ready to listen, ready to be interested, ready to take a share in every thing. The picture looked very charming to him after the dreariness of this great room, and Sara gone to bed, and poor Powys banished and broken-hearted. That was not to be his own fate, and Jack grew pious and tender in his self-gratulations. After all, poor Powys was a very good sort of fellow; but as it happened, it was Jack who had drawn all the prizes of life. He did think at one time of going down stairs notwithstanding the delicate state of his own relations with his father, and making such excuses as were practicable for the unfortunate clerk, who had permitted himself to be led astray in this foolish manner. "Of course it was a great risk bringing him here at all," Jack thought of saying, that Mr. Brownlow might be brought to a due sense of his own responsibility in the matter; but after long consideration, he wisely reflected that it would be best to wait until the first parties to the transaction had pronounced themselves. If Sara did not mean to say any thing about it, nor Powys, why should he interfere? upon which conclusion, instead of going down stairs, he went to bed, thinking again how cheerless it was for each member of the household to start off like this without a single good-night, and how different it would be in the new household that was to come.

Sara came to breakfast next morning looking very pale. The color had quite gone out of her cheeks, and she had done herself up in a warm velvet jacket, and had the windows closed as soon as she came into the room. "They never will remember that the summer's over," she said, with a shiver, as she took her place; but she made no farther sign of any kind. Clearly she had no intention of complaining of her rash lover;—so little, indeed, that when Mr. Brownlow was about to go away, she held out a book to him timidly, with a sudden blush. "Mr. Powys forgot to take this with him last night; would you mind taking it to him, papa?" she said, very meekly; and as Jack looked at her, Sara blushed redder and redder. Not that she had any occasion to blush. It might be meant as an olive-branch or even a pledge of hope; but still it was only a book that Powys had left behind him. Mr. Brownlow accepted the charge with a little surprise, and he, too, looked at her so closely that it was all she could do to restrain a burst of tears.

"Is it such a wonder that I should send back a book when it is left?" she cried, petulantly. "You need not take it unless you like, papa; it can always go by the post."

"I will take it," said Mr. Brownlow; and Jack sat by rather grimly, and said nothing. Jack was very variable and uncertain just at that moment in his own feelings. He had not forgotten the melting of his heart on the previous night; but if he had seen any tokens of relenting on the part of his sister toward the presumptuous stranger, Jack would have again hated Powys. He even observed with suspicion that his father took little notice of Sara's agitation; that he shut his eyes to it, as it were, and took her book, and evaded all farther discussion. Jack himself was not going to Masterton that day. He had to see that every thing was in order for the next day, which was the 1st of September. So far had the season wheeled round imperceptibly while all the variations of this little domestic drama were ripening to their appointed end.

Jack, however, did not go to inspect his gun, and consult with the gamekeeper, immediately on his father's departure. He waited for a few minutes, while Sara, who had been so cold, rushed to the window, and threw it open. "There must be thunder in the air—one can scarcely breathe," she said. And Jack watched her jealously, and did not lose a single look.

"You were complaining of cold just now," he said. "Sara, mind what you are about. If you think you can play that young Powys at the end of your line, you're making a great mistake."

"Play whom?" cried Sara, blazing up. "You are a nice person to preach to me! I am playing nobody at the end of my line. I have no line to play with; and you that are making a fool of that poor little simple Pamela—"

"Be quiet, will you?" said Jack, furious. "That poor little simple Pamela, as you call her, is going to be my wife."

Sara gazed at him for a moment thunderstruck, standing like something made into stone, with her velvet jacket, which she had just taken off, in her hands. Then the color fled from her cheeks as quickly as it had come to them, and her great eyes filled suddenly, like crystal cups, with big tears. She threw the jacket down out of her hands, and rushed to her brother's side, and clasped his arm. "You don't mean it, Jack?—do you mean it?" she cried, piteously, gazing up into his face; and a crowd of different emotions, more than Jack could discriminate or divine, was in her voice. There was pleasure and there was sorrow, and sharp envy and pride and regret. She clasped his arm, and looked at him with a look which said—"How could you?—how dare you?—and, oh, how lucky you are to be able to do it!"—all in a breath.

"Of course I mean it," said Jack, a little roughly; but he did not mean to be rough. "And that is why I tell you it is odious of you, Sara, to tempt a man to his destruction, when you know you can do nothing for him but break his heart."

"Can't I?" said Sara, dropping away from his arm, with a faint little moan; and then she turned quickly away, and hid her face in her hands. Jack, for his part, felt he was bound to improve the occasion, though his heart smote him. He stood secure on his own pedestal of virtue, though he did not want her to copy him. Indeed, such virtue in Sara would have been little short of vice.

"Nothing else," said Jack, "and yet you creatures do it without ever thinking of the sufferings you cause. I saw the state that poor fellow was in when he left you last night; and now you begin again sending him books! What pleasure can you have in it! It is something inconceivable to me."

This Jack uttered with a superiority and sense of goodness so lofty that Sara's tears dried up. She turned round in a blaze of indignation, too much offended to trust herself to answer. "You may be an authority to Pamela, but you are not an authority to me," she cried, drawing herself up to her fullest state. But she did not trust herself to continue the warfare. The tears were lying too near the surface, and Sara had been too much shaken by the incident of the previous night. "I am not going to discuss my own conduct; you can go and talk to Pamela about it," she added, pausing an instant at the door of the room before she went out. It was spiteful, and Jack felt that it was spiteful; but he did not guess how quickly Sara rushed up stairs after her dignified progress to the door, nor how she locked herself in, nor what a cry she had in her own room when she was safe from all profane eyes. She was not thinking of Pamela, and yet she could have beaten Pamela. She was to be happy, and have her own way; but as for Sara, it was an understood duty that the only thing she could do for a man was to break his heart! Her tears fell down like rain at this thought. Why should Jack be so free and she so fettered? Why should Pamela be so well off? Thus a sudden and wild little hail-storm of rage and mortification went over Sara's head, or rather heart.

Meanwhile Mr. Brownlow went very steadily to business with the book in his pocket. He had been a little startled by Sara's look, but by this time it was going out of his mind. He was thinking that it was a lovely morning, and still very warm, though the child was so chilly; and then he remembered, with a start, that next day was the 1st of September. Another six weeks, and the time of his probation was over. The thought sent the blood coursing through his veins, as if he had been a young man. Every thing had gone on so quietly up to that moment—no farther alarms—nothing to revive his fears—young Powys lulled to indifference, if indeed he knew any thing; and the time of liberation so near. But with that thrill of satisfaction came a corresponding excitement. Now that the days were numbered, every day was a year in itself. It occurred to him suddenly to go away somewhere, to take Sara with him and bury himself in some remote corner of the earth, where nobody could find him for those fated six weeks; and so make it quite impossible that any application could reach him. But he dismissed the idea. In his absence might she not appear, and disclose herself? His own presence somehow seemed to keep her off, and at arm's length; but he could not trust events for a single day if he were gone. And it was only six weeks. After that, yes, he would go away, he would go to Rome or somewhere, and take Sara, and recover his calm after that terrible tension. He would need it, no doubt;—so long as his brain did not give way.

Mr. Brownlow, however, was much startled by the looks of Powys when he went into the office. He was more haggard than he had ever been in the days when Mr. Wrinkell was suspicious of him. His hair hung on his forehead in a limp and drooping fashion—he was pale, and there were circles round his eyes. Mr. Brownlow had scarcely taken his place in his own room when the impatient young man came and asked to speak to him. The request made the lawyer's hair stand up on his head, but he could not refuse the petition. "Come in," he said, faintly. The blood seemed to go back on his heart in a kind of despair. After all his anticipations of approaching freedom, was he to be arrested after all, before the period of emancipation came?

As for Powys, he was too much excited himself to see any thing but the calmest composure in Mr. Brownlow, who indeed, throughout all his trials, though they were sharp enough, always looked composed. The young man even thought his employer methodical and matter of fact to the last degree. He had put out upon the table before him the book Sara had intrusted him with. It was a small edition of one of the poets which poor Powys had taken with him on his last unhappy expedition to Brownlows; and Mr. Brownlow put his hand on the book, with a constrained smile, as a school-master might have put his hand on a prize.

"My daughter sent you this, Powys," he said, "a book which it appears you left last night; and why did you go away in such a hurry without letting me know?"

"Miss Brownlow sent it?" said Powys, growing crimson; and for a minute the poor young fellow was so startled and taken aback that he could not add another word. He clutched at the book, and gazed at it hungrily, as if it could tell him something, and then he saw Mr. Brownlow looking at him with surprise, and his color grew deeper and deeper. "That was what I came to speak to you about, sir," he said, hot with excitement and wretchedness. "You have trusted me, and I am unworthy of your trust. I don't mean to excuse myself; but I could not let another day go over without telling you. I have behaved like an idiot—and a villain—"

"Stop, stop!" said Mr. Brownlow. "What is all this about? Don't be excited. I don't believe you have behaved like a villain. Take time and compose yourself, and tell me what it is."

"It is that you took me into your house, sir, and trusted me," said Powys, "and I have betrayed your trust. I must mention her name. I saw your daughter too often—too much. I should have had the honor and honesty to tell you before I betrayed myself. But I did not mean to betray myself. I miscalculated my strength; and in a moment, when I was not thinking, it gave way. Don't think I have gone on with it," he added, looking beseechingly at his employer, who sat silent, not so much as lifting his eyes. "It was only last night—and I am ready at the moment, if you wish it, to go away."

Mr. Brownlow sat at his table and made no reply. Oh, those hasty young creatures, who precipitated every thing! It was, in a kind of way, the result of his own scheming, and yet his heart revolted at it, and in six weeks' time he would be free from all such necessity. What was he to do? He sat silent, utterly confounded and struck dumb—not with surprise and horror, as his young companion in the fullness of his compunction believed, but with confusion and uncertainty as to what he ought to say and do. He could not offend and affront the young man on whose quietness and unawakened thoughts so much depended. He could not send Powys away, to fall probably into the hands of other advisers, and rise up against himself. Yet could he pledge himself, and risk Sara's life, when so short a time might set him free? All this rushed through his mind while he sat still in the same attitude in which he had listened to the young fellow's story. All this pondering had to be done in a moment, for Powys was standing beside him in all the vehemence of passion, thinking every minute an hour, and waiting for his answer. Indeed he expected no answer. Yet something there was that must be said, and which Mr. Brownlow did not know how to say.

"You betrayed yourself?" he said, at last; "that means, you spoke. And what did Sara say?"

The color on Powys's face flushed deeper and deeper. He gave one wild, half-frantic look of inquiry at his questioner. There was nothing in the words, but in the calm of the tone, in the naming of his daughter's name, there was something that looked like a desperate glimmer of hope; and this unexpected light flashed upon the young man all of a sudden, and made him nearly mad. "She said nothing," he answered, breathlessly. "I was not so dishonorable as to ask for any answer. What answer was possible? It was forced out of me, and I rushed away."

Mr. Brownlow pushed his chair away from the table. He got up and went to the window, and stood and looked out, he could not have told why. There was nothing there that could help him in what he had to say. There was nothing but two children standing in the dusty road, and a pale, swarthy organ-grinder, with two big eyes, playing "Ah, che la morte" outside. Mr. Brownlow always remembered the air, and so did Powys, standing behind, with his heart beating loud, and feeling that the next words he should listen to might convey life or death.

"If she has said nothing," said Mr. Brownlow at last from the window, speaking with his back turned, "perhaps it will be as well for me to follow her example." When he said this he returned slowly to his seat, and took his chair without ever looking at the culprit before him. "Of course you were wrong," he added; "but you are young. You ought not to have been placed in such temptation. Go back to your work, Mr. Powys. It was a youthful indiscretion; and I am not one of those who reject an honorable apology. We will forget it for ever—we, and every body concerned—"

"But, sir—" cried Powys.

"No more," said Mr. Brownlow. "Let by-gones be by-gones. You need not go up to Brownlows again till this occurrence has been forgotten. I told you Sara had sent you the book you left. It has been an unfortunate accident, but no more than an accident, I hope. Go back to your work, and forget it. Don't do any thing rash. I accept your apology. Such a thing might have happened to the best of us. But you will be warned by it, and do not err again. Go back to your work."

"Then I am not to leave you?" said Powys, sorely tossed between hope and despair, thinking one moment that he was cruelly treated, and the next overwhelmed by the favor shown him. He looked so wistfully at his employer, that Mr. Brownlow, who saw him though he was not looking at him, had hard ado not to give him a little encouragement with his eyes.

"If you can assure me this will not be repeated, I see no need for your leaving," said Mr. Brownlow. "You know I wish you well, Powys. I am content that it should be as if it had never been."

The young man did not know what to say. The tumult in his mind had not subsided. He was in the kind of condition to which every thing which is not despair is hope. He was wild with wonder, bewilderment, confusion. He made some incoherent answer, and the next moment he found himself again at his desk, dizzy like a man who has fallen from some great height, yet feels himself unhurt upon solid ground after all. What was to come of it all? And Sara had sent him his book. Sara? Never in his wildest thoughts had he ventured to call her Sara before. He did not do it wittingly now. He was in a kind of trance of giddiness and bewilderment. Was it all real, or had it happened in a dream?

Meanwhile Mr. Brownlow too sat and pondered this new development. What was it all to come to? He seemed to other people to be the arbiter of events; but that was what he himself asked, in a kind of consternation, of time and fate.

CHAPTER XXIX

NEWS

It was the beginning of September, as we have said, and the course of individual history slid aside as it were for the moment, and lost itself in the general web. Brownlows became full of people—friends of Jack's, friends of Mr. Brownlow, even friends of Sara—for ladies came of course to break the monotony of the shooting-party—and in the press of occupation personal matters had to be put aside. Mr. Brownlow himself almost forgot, except by moments when the thought came upon him with a certain thrill of excitement, that the six weeks were gliding noiselessly on, and that soon his deliverance would come. As for Sara, she did not forget the agitating little scene in which she had been only a passive actor, but which had woven a kind of subtle link between her and the man who had spoken to her in the voice of real passion. The sound of it had scared and perplexed her at first, and it had roused her to a sense of the real difference, as well as the real affinities, between them; but whatever she might feel, the fact remained that there was a link between them—a link which she could no more break than the Queen could—a something that defied all denial or contradiction. She might never see him again, but—he loved her. When a girl is fancy-free, there is no greater charm; and Sara was, or had been, entirely fancy-free, and was more liable than most girls to this attraction. When the people around her were stupid or tiresome, as to be sure the best of people are sometimes, her thoughts would make a sudden gleam like lightning upon the man who had said he would never see her face again. Perhaps he might have proved tiresome too, had he gone out in the morning with his gun, and come home tired to dinner; but he was absent; and there are times when the absent have the best of it, notwithstanding all proverbs. She was much occupied, and by times sufficiently well amused at home, and did not feel it in the least necessary to summon Powys to her side; but still the thought of him came in now and then, and gave an additional zest to her other luxuries. It was a supreme odor and incense offered up to her, as he had thought it would be—a flower which she set her pretty foot upon, and the fragrance of which came up poignant and sweet to her delicate nostril. If any body had said as much to Sara it would have roused her almost to fury; but still such were the facts of the case.

Jack, for his part, was less excusable if he was negligent, and he was rather negligent just then, in the first fervor of the partridges, it must be allowed—not that he cared a straw for the ladies of the party, and their accomplishments, and their pretty dresses, and their wiles, poor Pamela believed in her heart. Apart from Pamela, Jack was a stoic, and wasted not a thought on womankind; but when a man is shooting all day, and is surrounded by a party of fellows who have to be dined and entertained in the evening, and is, besides, quite confident in his mind that the little maiden who awaits him has no other seductive voice to whisper in her ear, he may be pardoned for a little carelessness or unpunctuality—at least Jack thought he ought to be pardoned, which comes very much to the same thing. Thus the partridges, if they did not affect the affairs of state, as do their Highland brethren the grouse, at least had an influence upon the affairs of Brownlows, and put a stop, as it were, to the undivided action of its private history for the time.

It was during this interval that the carrier's cart once more deposited a passenger on the Brownlows road. She did not get down at the gate, which, she already knew, was a step calculated to bring upon her the eyes of the population, but was set down at a little distance, and came in noiselessly, as became her mission. It was a September afternoon, close and sultry. The sky was a whitish blue, pale with the blaze that penetrated and filled it. The trees looked parched and dusty where they overhung the road. The whole landscape round Brownlows beyond the line of these dusty trees was yellow with stubble, for the land was rich, and there had been a heavy crop. The fields were reaped, and the kindly fruits of earth gathered in, and there seemed no particular need for all that blaze of sunshine. But the sun blazed all the same, and the pedestrian stole slowly on, casting a long oblique shadow across the road. Every thing was sleepy and still. Old Betty's door and windows were open, but the heat was so great as to quench even curiosity; or perhaps it was only that the stranger's step was very stealthy, and until it suddenly fell upon a treacherous knot of gravel, which dispersed under her weight and made a noise, had given no sign of its approach. Betty came languidly to her door when she heard this sound, but she went in again and dropped back into her doze upon her big chair when she saw it was but the slow and toiling figure of a poor woman, no way attractive to curiosity. "Some poor body a-going to Dewsbury," she said to herself; and thus Nancy stole on unnoticed. The blind was down in the parlor window of Mrs. Swayne's neighbor, and her door closed, and Mrs. Swayne herself was out of the way for the moment, seeing to the boiling of the afternoon kettle. Nancy crept in, passing like a vision across Mrs. Preston's open window. Her step made no appreciable sound even in the sleepy stillness of the house, and the sole preface they had to her appearance in the parlor was a shadow of something black which crossed the light, and the softest visionary tap at the door. Then the old woman stood suddenly before the mother and the daughter, who were sitting together dull enough. Mrs. Preston was still poorly, and disturbed in her mind. And as for Pamela, poor child, it was a trying moment for her. As from a watch-tower, she could see what was going on at Brownlows, and knew that they were amusing themselves, and had all kinds of pleasant parties, in which Jack, who was hers and no other woman's, took the chief part; and that amid all these diversions he had no time to come to see her though she had the only right to him, and that other girls were by, better born, better mannered, better dressed, and more charming than her simple self. Would it be his fault if he were fickle? How could he help being fickle with attractions so much greater around him? This was how Pamela was thinking as she sat by the sofa on which her mother lay. It was not weather for much exertion, and in the peculiar position of affairs, it was painful for these two to run the risk of meeting anybody from Brownlows; therefore they did not go out except furtively now and then at night, and sat all day in the house, and brooded, and were not very cheerful. Every laugh she heard sounding down the avenue, every carriage that drove out of or into the gates, every stray bit of gossip about the doings at the great house, and the luncheon parties at the cover-side, and the new arrivals, sounded to poor little Pamela like an injury. She had meant to be so happy and she was not happy. Only the sound of the guns was a little comfort to her. To be sure when he was shooting he was still amusing himself away from her; but at the same time he was not near the fatal beauties whom every evening Pamela felt in her heart he must be talking to, and smiling upon, and growing bewitched by. Such was the tenor of her thoughts as she sat by the sofa working, when old Nancy came in so suddenly at the door.

Pamela sprang up from her seat. Her nerves were out of order, and even her temper, poor child! and all her delicate organization set on edge "It is her again! and oh, what do you want?" said Pamela, with a little shriek. As for Mrs. Preston, she too sat bolt upright on the sofa and started not without a certain fright, at the sudden apparition. "Nancy Christian!" she said, clasping her hands together; "Nancy Christian! Is this you?"

"Yes, it's me," said Nancy; "I said I would come, and here I am, and I've a deal to say. If you don't mind, I'll take a chair, for it's a long way walking in this heat, all the way from Masterton." This she said without a blush, though she had been set down not fifty yards off from the carrier's cart.

"Sit down," said Mrs. Preston, anxiously, herself rising from the sofa. "It is not often I lie down," (though this was almost as much a fiction as Nancy's), "but the heat gets the better of one. I remember your name as long as I remember any thing; I always hoped you would come back. Pamela, if there is any thing that Nancy would like after her long walk—"

"A cup of tea is all as I care for," said Nancy. "It's a many years since we've met, and you've changed, ma'am," she added, with a cordiality that was warmer than her sincerity; "but I could allays see as it was you."

"I have reason to be changed," said Mrs. Preston. "I was young when you saw me last, and now I'm an old woman. I've had many troubles. I've had a hard fight with the world, and I've lost all my children but this one. She's a good child, but she can't stand in the place of all that I've lost—And oh, Nancy Christian, you're a woman that can tell me about my poor old mother. Many a thought I have had of her, and often, often it seemed a judgment that my children should be taken from me. If you could but tell me she forgave me before she died!"

Nancy made no direct answer to this appeal, but she looked at Pamela, and then at her mother, with a significant gesture. The two old women had their world to go back into of which the young creature knew nothing, and where there were many things which might not bear her inspection; while she, on the other hand, was absorbed in her own new world, and scarcely heard or noticed what they were saying. She stood between them in her youth, unaware of the look they exchanged, unaware that she was in the way of their confidences—thinking, in fact, nothing of much importance in the world except what might be going on in the great house over the way.

"Pamela," said Mrs. Preston, "go and see about the tea, and run out to the garden, dear, and get a breath of air; for I have a deal to ask, and Nancy has a deal to tell me; and there will be no one passing at this time of the day."

"If they were all passing it would not matter to me," said Pamela, and she sighed, and put down her languid work, and went away to make the tea. But she did not go out to the garden; though she said it did not matter, it did matter mightily. She went up stairs to the window and sat down behind the curtain, and fixed her hungry eyes upon the gate and the avenue beyond; and then she made little pictures to herself of the ladies at Brownlows, and how Jack must be enjoying himself, and gathered some big bitter tears in her eyes, and felt herself forsaken. It was worse than the Peri at the gate of Eden. So long as Jack had come to the cottage, it mattered little to Pamela who was at the great house. In those days she could think, "They are finer than I am, and better off, and even prettier, but he likes me best;" but now this was all changed—the poor little Peri saw the blessed walking in pairs and pleasant companies, and her own young archangel, who was the centre of the Paradise, surrounded and taken possession of by celestial sirens—if such things can be. To be sure Jack Brownlow was not much like an archangel, but that mattered little. What a change it was! and all to come about in a week or two. She, too, was like the flower upon which the conqueror set his foot; and Pamela was not passive, but resisted and struggled. Thus she was not curious about what old Nancy could be saying to her mother. What could it be? some old gossip or other, recollections of a previous state of existence before any body was born—talk about dead things and dead people that never could affect the present state of being. If Pamela thought of it at all, she was half glad that poor mamma should have some thing to amuse her, and half jealous that her mother could think of any thing except the overwhelming interest of her own affairs. And she lingered at the window unawares, until the tea was spoiled oblivious of Nancy's fatigue; and saw the gentlemen come in from their shooting, with their dogs and guns and keepers, and the result of their day's work, and was aware that Jack lingered, and looked across the road, and waited till everybody was gone; then her heart jumped up and throbbed loudly as he came toward the house. She was about to rush down to him, to forget her griefs, and understand how it was and that he could not help it. But Pamela was a minute too late. She was on her way to the door, when suddenly her heart stood still and the color went out of her face, and she stopped short like one thunderstruck. He was going away again, astonished, like a man in a dream, with the birds in his hand which he had been bringing as a peace-offering. And Pamela heard her mother's voice, sharp and harsh, speaking from the door. "I am much obliged to you, Mr. Brownlow, but I never eat game, and we are both very much engaged, and unable to see any one to-day;" these were the words the poor girl heard; and then the door, which always stood open—the fearless hospitable cottage door, was closed sharply, and with a meaning. Pamela stood aghast, and saw him go away with his rejected offering; and then the disappointment and wonder and quick change of feeling came raining down from her eyes in big tears. Poor Jack! It was not his fault—he was not unfaithful nor careless—but her own; and her mother to send him away! It all passed, in a moment, and she had not time or self-possession to throw open the window and hold out her hands to him and call him back, but only stood speechless and watched him disappearing, himself speechless with amazement, crossing the road backward with his birds in his hand. Then Pamela's dreams came suddenly to an end. She dried her eyes indignantly—or rather the sudden hot flush on her cheeks dried them without any aid—and smoothed back her hair, and went down flaming in youthful wrath to call her mother to account. But Mrs. Preston too was a changed creature. Pamela did not know what to make of it when she went into the little parlor. Old Nancy was sitting on a chair by the wall, just as she had done when she came in, and looking the same; but as for Mrs. Preston, she was a different woman. If wings had suddenly budded at her shoulders the revolution could scarcely have been greater. She stood upright near the window, with no stoop, no headache, no weariness—ten years younger at least—her eyes as bright as two fires, and even her black dress hanging about her in different folds. Pamela's resentment and indignation and rebellious feelings came to an end at this unwonted spectacle. She could only stand before her mother and stare at her, and wonder what it could mean.

"It is nothing," said Mrs. Preston. "Mr. Brownlow, who brought us some game—you know I don't care for game; and then people change their minds about things. Sit down, Pamela, and don't stare at me. I have been getting too languid about every thing, and when one rouses up every body wonders what one means."

"Mamma," said Pamela, too much astonished to know what to answer, "you sent him away!"

"Yes, I sent him away; and I will send any one away that I think mercenary and selfish," said Mrs. Preston. Was it she who spoke? Could it be her mild uncertain lips from which such words came; and then what could it mean? How could he be mercenary—he who was going to give up every thing for his love's sake? No words could express Pamela's consternation. She sat down weak with wonder, and gazed at her mother. The change was one which she could not in any way explain to herself.

"Old Mrs. Fennell was very rude to me," said Mrs. Preston. "I fear you have not a very comfortable place, Nancy Christian; but we can soon change that. You that were so faithful to my poor mother, you may be sure you'll not be forgotten. You are not to think of walking back to Masterton. If I had known you were coming I would have spoken to Hobson the carrier. I never was fond of the Fennells from the earliest I remember; though Tom, you know, poor fellow—but he was a great deal older than me."

"He was nigh as old as your mother," said Nancy; "many's the time I've heard her say it. 'He wanted my daughter,' she would say; 'her a slip of a girl, and him none so much younger than I am myself; but now he's catched a tartar;' and she would laugh, poor old dear; but when she knew as they were after what she had—that's what drove her wild you may say—"

"Yes, yes," said Mrs. Preston; "yes, yes; you need say no more Nancy; I see it all—I see it all. Wherever there's money it's a snare, and no mortal that I can see escapes. If I had but known a month ago! but after this they shall see they can't do what they please with me. No; though it may be hard upon us—hard upon us. Oh, Nancy Christian," she said, flinging up her arms into the air, "if you had but come to tell me a month ago!"

Pamela listened to this conversation with gradually increasing dismay. She did not know what it meant; but yet by some instinctive sense, she knew that it concerned herself—and Jack. She rose up and went to her mother with vague terrors in her heart. "Mamma, what is it? tell me what it is," she said, putting two clinging hands around her arm.

At these words Mrs. Preston suddenly came to herself. "What is what?" she said. "Sit down, Pamela, and don't ask foolish questions; or rather go and see after the tea. It has never come, though I told you Nancy was tired. If you left it by Mrs. Swayne's fire it will be boiled by this time; and you know when it stands too long I can't bear it. Go, dear, and get the tea."

"But, mamma," said Pamela, still clinging to her, and speaking in her ear, "mamma! I know there must be something. Why did you send him away?"

Mrs. Preston gave her child a look which Pamela, driven to her wits' end, could not interpret. There was pity in it and there was defiance, and a certain fierce gleam as of indignation. "Child, you know nothing about it," she said, with suppressed passion; "nothing; and I can't tell you now. Go and get us the tea."

Pamela gazed again, but she could make nothing of it. It was, and yet it was not her mother—not the old, faded, timid, hesitating woman who had nothing in the world but herself; but somebody so much younger, so much stronger—with those two shining, burning eyes, and this sudden self-consciousness and command. She gave a long look, and then she sighed and dropped her mother's arm, and went away to do her bidding. It was the first appeal she had ever made in vain, and naturally it filled her with a painful amaze. It was such a combination of events as she could not understand. Nancy's arrival, and Jack's dismissal and this curious change in Mrs. Preston's appearance. Her little heart had been full of pain when she left the room before, but it was pain of a very different kind. Now the laggard had come who was all the cause of the trouble then, and he had been sent away without reason or explanation, and what could it mean? "If I had but known a month ago!" What could it be that she had heard? The girl's heart took to beating again very loud and fast, and her imagination began to work, and it is not difficult to divine what sort of theories of explanation rose in her thoughts. The only thing that Pamela could think of as raising any fatal barrier between herself and Jack was unfaithfulness or a previous love on his part. This, without doubt, was Nancy's mission. She had come to tell of his untruthfulness; that he loved somebody else; perhaps had pledged himself to somebody else; and that between him and his new love, instant separation, heartbreak, and despair must ensue. "He need not have been afraid to tell me," Pamela said to herself, with her heart swelling till it almost burst from her breast. All her little frame, all her sensitive nerves, thrilled with pain and pride. This was what it was. She was not so much stunned by the blow as roused up to the fullest consciousness. Her lip would have quivered sadly had she been compelled to speak; her voice might have broken for any thing she could tell, and risen into hard tones and shrieks of pain. But she was not obliged to speak to any one, and so could shut herself in and keep it down. She went about mechanically, but with nervous haste and swiftness, and covered the little table with its white cloth, and put bread on it, and the tea for which Nancy and her mother sighed; and she thought they looked at her with cruel coldness, as if it was they who were concerned and not she. As if it could be any thing to any body in comparison to what it was to her! As if she must not be at all times the principal in such a matter! Thus they sat down at the little round table. Nancy, who was much in her ordinary, ate, drank and was very comfortable, and pleased with the country cream in her tea; but the mother and the daughter neither ate nor drank. Mrs. Preston sat, saying now and then a word or two to Nancy which Pamela could not understand, but mostly was silent, pondering and full of thoughts, while Pamela, with her eyes cast down, and a burning, crimson color on her cheeks, sat still and brooded over the cruelty she thought they were showing her. Nancy was the only one who "enjoyed," as she said, "her tea."

"You may get a drop of what's called cream in a town, but it ain't cream," said Nancy. "It's but skim-milk frothed up, and you never get the taste of the tea. It's a thing as I always buys good. It's me as lays in all the things, and when there ain't a good cup o' tea at my age there ain't nothing as is worth in life. But the fault's not in the tea. It's the want of a drop of good cream as does it. It's that as brings out the flavor, and gives it a taste. A cup o' good tea's a cheering thing; but I wouldn't say as you was enjoying it, Mrs. Preston, like me."

"I have other things in my mind," said Mrs. Preston; "you've had a long walk, and you must want it. As for me, my mind's all in a ferment. I don't seem to know if it's me, or what has happened. You would not have come and told me all this if you had not been as sure as sure of what you had to say!"

"Sure and sure enough," said Nancy. "I've knowed it from first to last, and how could I go wrong! If you go to London, as you say, you can judge for yourself, and there won't be nothing for me to tell; but you'll think on as I was the first—for your old mother's sake—"

"You'll not be forgot," said Mrs. Preston; "you need not fear. I am not the one to neglect a friend—and one that was good to my poor mother; you may reckon on me." She sat upright in her chair, and every line in her face had changed. Power, patronage, and protection were in her tone—she who had been herself so poor and timid and anxious. Her very words were uttered more clearly, and with a distincter intonation. And Pamela listened with all her might, and grew more and more bewildered, and tried vainly to make out some connection between this talk and the discovery which she supposed must have been made. But what could Jack's failure in good faith have to do with any body's old mother! It was only Nancy who was quite at her ease. "I will take another cup, if you please, Miss Pamela," said Nancy, "and I hope as I'll live to see you in your grandeur, feasting with lords and ladies, instead of pouring out an old woman's tea—for them as is good children is rewarded. Many's the day I've wished to see you, and wondered how many of you there was. It's sad for your mother as there's only you; but it's a fine thing for yourself, Miss Pamela—and you must always give your mind to do what your mamma says."

"How should it be a fine thing for me!" said Pamela; "or how should I ever feast with lords and ladies? I suppose you mean to make fun of us. As for doing what mamma says, of course I always do—and she never tells me to do any thing unreasonable," the girl added, after a momentary pause, looking doubtfully at her mother. If she were told to give up Jack, Pamela felt that it would be something unreasonable, and she had no inclination to pledge herself. Mrs. Preston was changed from all her daughter's previous knowledge of her; and it might be that her demands upon Pamela's obedience would change too.

"It's nigh my time to go," said Nancy. "I said to the carrier as he was to wait for me down the road. I wouldn't be seen a-getting into the wagon here. Folks talks awful when they're so few; and thank you kindly, Mrs. Preston, for the best cup of tea as I've tasted for ten years. Them as can get cream like that, has what I calls some comfort in this life."

"Pamela," said Mrs. Preston, "you can walk along with Nancy as far as Merryfield Farm, and give my compliments; and if they'd put a drop of their best cream in a bottle—It's all I can do just now, Nancy Christian; but I am not one that forgets my friends, and the time may come—"

"The time will come, ma'am," said Nancy, getting up and making her patroness a courtesy, "and I'm none afraid as you'll forget; and thank you kindly for thinking o' the cream—if it ain't too much trouble to Miss Pamela. If you go up there, as you think to do, and find all as I say, you'll be so kind as to let me know?"

"I'll let you know, you may be sure," said Mrs. Preston, in her short decisive tones of patronage. And then the girl, much against her will, had to put on her hat and go with Nancy. She did it, but it was with an ill grace; for she was longing to throw herself upon her mother and have an explanation of all this—what had happened, and what it meant. The air had grown cool, and old Betty had come out to her door, and Mrs. Swayne was in the little garden watering the mignonnette. And it was not easy to pass those two pairs of eyes and preserve a discreet incognito. To do her justice, Nancy tried her best; but it was a difficult matter to blind Mrs. Swayne.

"I thought as it was you," said that keen observer. "I said as much to Swayne when he told me there was a lady to tea in the parlor. I said, 'You take my word it's her as come from Masterton asking after them.' And I hope, mum, as I see you well. Mrs. Preston has been but poorly; and you as knows her constitootion and her friends—"

"She knows nothing about us," said Pamela, with indignation; "not now; I never saw her in my life before. And how can she know about mamma's constitution, or her friends either? Nancy, come along; you will be too late for Hobson if you stand talking here."

"It's never no loss of time to say a civil word, Miss Pamela," said Nancy. "It's years and years since I saw her, and she's come through a deal since then. And having a family changes folks' constitootions. If it wasn't asking too much, I'd ask for a bit o' mignonnette. Town folks is terrible greedy when they comes to the country—and it's that sweet as does one's heart good. Nice cream and butter and new-laid eggs, and a bit o' lad's love, or something as smells sweet—give me that, and I don't ask for none o' your grandeurs. That's the good o' the country to me."

"They sends all that country stuff to old Mrs. Fennell, don't they?" said Betty, who in the leisure of the evening had crossed the road. "I should have thought you'd been sick of all them things—and the fruit and the partridges as I see packed no later then this very afternoon. I should have said you had enough for six, if any one had asked me."

"When the partridges is stale and the fruit rotten," said Nancy, shrugging her shoulders; "and them as has such plenty, where's the merit of it? I suppose there's fine doings at the house, with all their shootings and all the strangers as is about—"

"They was at a picnic to-day," said Betty. "Mr. John, he's the one! He makes all them ladies leave their comfortable lunch, as is better than many a dinner, and down to the heath with their cold pies and their jellies and such like. Give me a bit of something 'ot. But they think he's a catch, being the only son; and there ain't one but does what he says."

Pamela had been standing plucking a bit of mignonnette to pieces, listening with tingling ears. It was not in human nature not to listen; but she roused herself when Betty's voice ceased, and went softly on, withdrawing herself from the midst of them. Her poor little heart was swelling and throbbing, and every new touch seemed to add to its excitement; but pride, and a sense of delicacy and dignity, came to her aid. Jack's betrothed, even if neglected or forsaken, was not in her fit place amid this gossip. She went on quietly, saying nothing about it, leaving her companion behind. And the three women gave each other significant glances as soon as she had turned her back on them. "I told 'em how it would be," said Mrs. Swayne, under her breath, "it's allays the way when a girl is that mad to go and listen to a gentleman." And Betty, though she sneered at her employers with goodwill, had an idea of keeping up their importance so far as other people were concerned. "Poor lass!" said Betty, "she's been took in. She thought Mr. John was one as would give up every thing for the like of her; but he has her betters to choose from. He's affable like, but he's a deal too much pride for that."

"Pride goes afore a fall," said Nancy, with meaning; "and the Brownlows ain't such grand folks after all. Nothing but attorneys, and an old woman's money to set them up as wasn't a drop's blood to them. I don't see no call for pride."

"The old squires was different, I don't deny," said Betty, with candor; "but when folks is bred gentlefolks, and has all as heart can desire—"

"There's gentlefolks as might do worse," said Nancy, fiercely; "but it ain't nothing to you nor me—"

"It ought to be a deal to both of you," said Mrs. Swayne, coming in as moderator, "eating their bread as it were, and going on like that. And both of you with black silks to put on of a Sunday, and sure of your doctor and your burial if you was to fall ill. I wouldn't be that ungrateful if it was me."

"It's no use quarreling," said Nancy; "and I'll say good-night, for I've a long way to go. If ever you should want any thing in Masterton, I'd do my best to serve you. Miss Pamela's a long way on, and walking fast ain't for this weather; so I'll bid you both good-night. We'll have time for more talk," she added significantly, "next time I come back; and I'd like a good look at that nice lodge you've got." Old Betty did not know what the woman meant, but those black eyes "went through and through her," she said; and so Nancy's visit came to an end.

CHAPTER XXX

WHAT FOLLOWED

Pamela could make nothing of her companion. Nancy was very willing to talk, and indeed ran on in an unceasing strain; but what she said only confused the more the girl's bewildered faculties; and she saw her mount at last into the carrier's cart, and left her with less perception than ever of what had happened. Then she went straying home in the early dusk, for already the days had begun to grow short, and that night in especial a thunder-storm was brewing, and the clouds were rolling down darkly after the sultry day. Pamela crossed over to the shade of the thick hedge and fence which shut in the park, that nobody might see her, and her thoughts as she went along were not sweet. She thought of Jack and the ladies at Brownlows, and then she thought of the wish her mother had uttered—Had she but known this a month ago! and between the terrible suspicion of a previous love, and the gnawing possibility of present temptation, made herself very miserable, poor child. Either he had deceived her, and was no true man; or if he had not yet deceived her, he was in hourly peril of doing so, and at any moment the blow might come. While she was thus lingering along in the twilight, something happened which gave Pamela a terrible fright. She was passing a little stile when suddenly a man sprang out upon her and caught hold of her hands. She was so sure that Jack was dining at Brownlows, and yielding to temptation then, that she did not recognize him, and screamed when he sprang out; and it was dark, so dark that she could scarcely see his face. Jack, for his part, had been so conscience-stricken when Mrs. Preston refused him entrance that he had done what few men of this century would be likely to do. He had gone in with the other men, and gulped down some sherry at the sideboard, and instead of proceeding to his dressing-room as they all did after, had told a very shocking fib to Willis the butler, for the benefit of his father and friends, and rushed out again. He might have been proof against upbraiding, but compunction seized him when Mrs. Preston closed the door. He had deserved it, but he had not expected such summary measures; and "that woman," as he called her in his dismay, was capable of taking his little love away and leaving him no sign. He saw it in her eye; for he, too, saw the change in her. Thus Jack was alarmed, and in his fright his conscience spoke. And he had seen Pamela go out, and waylaid her; and was very angry and startled to see she did not recognize him. "Good heavens, do you mean to say you don't know me?" he cried, almost shaking her as he held her by the hands. To scream and start as if the sight of him was not the most natural thing in the world, and the most to be looked for! Jack felt it necessary to begin the warfare, to combat his own sense of guilt.

"I thought you were at dinner," said Pamela, faintly. "I never thought it could be you."

"And you don't look a bit glad to see me. What do you mean by it?" said Jack. "It is very hard, when a fellow gives up every thing to come and see you. And your mother to shut the door upon me! She never did it before. A man has his duties to do, whatever happens. I can't go and leave these fellows loafing about by themselves. I must go out with them. I thought you were going to take me for better for worse, Pamela, not for a month or a week."

"Oh, don't speak so," said Pamela. "It was never me. It must have been something mamma had heard. She does not look a bit like herself; and it is all since that old woman came."

"What old woman?" said Jack, calming down. "Look here, come into the park. They are all at dinner, and no one will see; and tell me all about it. So long as you are not changed, nothing else is of any consequence. Only for half an hour—"

"I don't think I ought," said Pamela; but she was on the other side of the stile when she said these words; and her hand was drawn deeply through Jack's arm, and held fast, so that it was clearly a matter of discreet submission, and she could not have got away had she wished it. "I don't think I ought to come," said Pamela, "you never come to us now; and it must have been something that mamma had heard. I think she is going away somewhere; and I am sure, with all these people at Brownlows, and all that old Nancy says, and you never coming near us, I do not mind where we go, for my part."

"As if I cared for the people at Brownlows!" said Jack, holding her hand still more tightly. "Don't be cruel to a fellow, Pamela. I'll take you away whenever you please, but without me you shan't move a step. Who is old Nancy, I should like to know? and as for any thing you could have heard—Who suffers the most, do you suppose, from the people at Brownlows? To know you are there, and that one can't have even a look at you—"

"But then you can have a great many looks at other people," said Pamela, "and perhaps there was somebody else before me—don't hold my hand so tight. We are poor, and you are rich—and it makes a great difference. And I can't do just what I like. You say you can't, and you are a man, and older than I am. I must do what mamma says."

"But you know you can make her do what you like; whereas, with a lot of fellows—" said Jack. "Pamela, don't—there's a darling! You have me in your power, and you can put your foot upon me if you like. But you have not the heart to do it. Not that I should mind your little foot. Be as cruel as you please; but don't talk of running away. You know you can make your mother do whatever you like."

"Not now," said Pamela, "not now—there is such a change in her; and oh, Jack, I do believe she is angry, and she will make me go away."

"Tell me about it," said Jack, tenderly; for Pamela had fallen into sudden tears, without any regard for her consistency. And then the dialogue became a little inarticulate. It lasted a deal longer on the whole than half an hour, and the charitable clouds drooped lower, and gave them shade and shelter as they emerged at last from the park, and stole across the deserted road to Swayne's cottage. They were just in time; the first drops of the thunder-shower fell heavy and big upon Pamela before they gained shelter. But she did not mind them much. She had unburdened her heart, and her sorrows had flown away; and the ladies at Brownlows were no longer of any account in her eyes. She drew her lover in with her at the door, which so short a time before had been closed on him. "Mamma, I made him come in with me, not to get wet," said Pamela; and both the young people looked with a little anxiety upon Mrs. Preston, deprecating her wrath. She was seated by the window, though it had grown dark, perhaps looking for Pamela; but her aspect was rather that of one who had forgotten every thing external for the moment, than of an anxious mother watching for her child. They could not see the change in her face, as they gazed at her so eagerly in the darkness; but they both started and looked at each other when she spoke.

"I would not refuse any one shelter from a storm," she said, "but if Mr. Brownlow thinks a little, he will see that this is no place for him." She did not even turn round as she spoke, but kept at the window, looking out, or appearing to look out, upon the gathering clouds.

Jack was thunderstruck. There was something in her voice which chilled him to his very bones. It was not natural offense for his recent short-comings, or doubt of his sincerity. He felt himself getting red in the darkness. "It was as if she had found me out to be a scoundrel, by Jove," he said to himself afterward, which was a very different sort of thing from mere displeasure or jealousy. And in the silence that ensued, Mrs. Preston took no notice of anybody. She kept her place at the window, without looking round or saying another word; and in the darkness behind stood the two bewildered, trying to read in each other's faces what it could mean.

"Speak to her," said Pamela, eagerly whispering close to his ear; but Jack, for his part, could not tell what to say. He was offended, and he did not want to speak to her; but, on the contrary, held Pamela fast, with almost a perverse desire to show her mother that the girl was his, and that he did not care. "It is you I want, and not your mother," he said. They could hear each other speak, and could even differ and argue and be impassioned without anybody else being much the wiser. The only sound Mrs. Preston heard was a faint rustle of whispers in the darkness behind her. "No," said Jack, "if she will be ill-tempered, I can't help it. It is you I want," and he stood by and held his ground. When the first lightning flashed into the room, this was how it found them. There was a dark figure seated at the window, relieved against the gleam, and two faces which looked at each other, and shone for a second in the wild illumination. Then Pamela gave a little shriek and covered her face. She was not much more than a child, and she was afraid. "Come in from the window, mamma! do come, or it will strike you; and let us close the shutters," cried Pamela. There was a moment during which Mrs. Preston sat still, as if she did not hear. The room fell into blackness, and then blazed forth again, the window suddenly becoming "a glimmering square," with the one dark outline against it. Jack held his little love with his arm, but his eyes were fascinated by that strange sight. What could it mean? Was she mad? Had something happened in his absence to bring about this wonderful change? The mother, however, could not resist the cry that Pamela uttered the second time. She rose up, and closed the shutters with her own hands, refusing Jack's aid. But when the three looked at each other, by the light of the candles, they all looked excited and disturbed. Mrs. Preston sat down by the table, with an air so different from her ordinary looks, that she seemed another woman. And Jack, when her eyes fell upon him, could not help feeling something like a prisoner at the bar.

"Mr. Brownlow," she said, "I dare say you think women are very ignorant, especially about business—and so they are; but you and your father should remember—you should remember that weak folks, when they are put to it—Pamela! sit down, child, and don't interfere; or, if you like, you can go away."

"What have I done, Mrs. Preston!" said Jack. "I don't know what you mean. If it is because I have been some days without coming, the reason is—But I told Pamela all about it. If that is the reason—"

"That!" cried Mrs. Preston, and then her voice began to tremble; "if you think your coming or—or going is—any—any thing—" she said, and then her lips quivered so that she could articulate no more. Pamela, with a great cry, rushed to her and seized her hands, which were trembling too, and Jack, who thought it was a sudden "stroke," seized his hat and rushed to the door to go for a doctor; but Mrs. Preston held out her shaking hands to him so peremptorily that he stopped in spite of himself. She was trembling all over—her head, her lips, her whole frame, yet keeping entire command of herself all the time.

"I am not ill," she said; "there is no need for a doctor." And then she sat resolutely looking at him, holding her feet fast on the floor and her hand flat on the table to stop the movement of her nerves. It was a strange sight. But when the two who had been looking at her with alarmed eyes, suddenly, in the height of their wonder, turned to each other with a glance of mutual inquiry and sympathy, appealing to each other what it could mean, Mrs. Preston could not bear it. Her intense self-command gave way. All at once she fell into an outbreak of wailing and tears. "You are two of you against me," she said. "You are saying to each other, What does she mean! and there is nobody on earth—nobody to take my part." The outcry went to Jack Brownlow's heart. Somehow he seemed to understand better than even Pamela did, who clung to her mother and cried, and asked what was it—what had she done! Jack was touched more than he could explain. The thunder was rolling about the house, and the rain falling in torrents; but he had not the heart to stay any longer and thrust his happiness into her face, and wound her with it. Somehow he felt ashamed; and yet he had nothing to be ashamed about, unless, in presence of this agitation and pain and weakness, it was his own strength and happiness and youth.

"I don't mind the storm," he said. "I am sure you don't want any one here just now. Don't let your mother think badly of me, Pamela. You know I would do any thing—and I can't tell what's wrong; and I am going away. Good-night."

"Not till the storm is over," cried Pamela. "Mamma, he will get killed—you know he will, among those trees."

"Not a bit," said Jack, and he waved his hand to them and went away, feeling, it must be confessed, a good deal frightened—not for the thunder, however, or the storm, but for Mrs. Preston's weird look and trembling nerves, and his poor little Pamela left alone to nurse her. That was the great point. The poor woman was right. For herself there was nobody to care much. Jack was frightened because of Pamela.

His little love, his soft little darling, whom he would like to take in his arms and carry away from every trouble—that she should be left alone with sickness in its most terrible shape, perhaps with delirium, possibly with death! Jack stepped softly into Mrs. Swayne's kitchen, and told her his fears. He told her he would go over to Betty's lodge and wait there, in case the doctor should be wanted, and that she was not to let Miss Pamela wear herself out. As for Mrs. Swayne, though she made an effort to be civil, she scoffed at his fears. When she had heard what he had to say she showed him out grimly, and turned with enjoyment the key in the door. "The doctor!" she said to herself in disdain; "a fine excuse! But I don't hold with none o' your doctors, nor with gentlemen a-coming like roaring lions. I ain't one to be caught like that, at my time of life; and you don't come in here no more this night, with your doctors and your Miss Pamelas." In this spirit Mrs. Swayne fastened the house up carefully, and shut all the shutters, before she knocked at the parlor door to see what was the matter. But when she did take that precaution she was not quite so sure of her own wisdom. Mrs. Preston was lying on the sofa, shivering and trembling, with Pamela standing frightened by her. She had forbidden the girl to call any one, and was making painful efforts by mere resolution to stave it off. She said nothing, paid no attention to any body, but with her whole force was struggling to put down the incipient illness, and keep disease at bay. And Pamela, held by her glittering eye, too frightened to cry, too ignorant to know what to do, stood by, a white image of terror and misery, wringing her hands. Mrs. Swayne was frightened too; but there was some truth in her boast of experience. And, besides, her character was at stake. She had sent Jack away, and disdained his offer of the doctor, and it was time to bestir herself. So they got the stricken woman up stairs and laid her in her bed, and chafed her limbs, and comforted her with warmth. Jack, waiting in old Betty's, saw the light mount to the higher window and shine through the chinks of the shutters, until the storm was over, and he had no excuse for staying longer. It was still burning when he went away, and it burned all night through, and lighted Pamela's watch as she sat pale at her mother's bedside. She sat all through the night and watched her patient—sat while the lightning still flashed and the thunder roared, and her young soul quaked within her; and then through the hush that succeeded, and through the black hours of night and the dawning of the day. It was the first vigil she had ever kept, and her mind was bewildered with fear and anxiety, and the confusion of ignorance. She sat alone, wistful and frightened, afraid to move lest she should disturb her mother's restless sleep, falling into dreary little dozes, waking up cold and terrified, hearing the furniture, and the floor, and the walls and windows—every thing about her, in short—giving out ghostly sounds in the stillness. She had never heard those creaks and jars before with which our inanimate surroundings give token of the depth of silence and night. And Mrs. Preston's face looked grey in the faint light, and her breathing was disturbed; and by times she tossed her arms about, and murmured in her sleep. Poor Pamela had a weary night; and when the morning came with its welcome light, and she opened her eyes after a snatch of unwitting sleep, and found her mother awake and looking at her, the poor child started up with a sharp cry, in which there was as much terror as relief.

"Mamma!" she cried. "I did not mean to go to sleep. Are you better? Shall I run and get you a cup of tea?"

"Come and speak to me, Pamela," said Mrs. Preston. "I am quite well—at least I think I am well. My poor darling, have you been sitting up all night?"

"It does not matter," said Pamela; "it will not hurt me; but I was frightened. Are you sure you are better? Poor mamma, how ill you have been! You looked—I can not tell you how you looked. But you have your own eyes again this morning. Let me go and get you some tea."

"I don't want any tea," said Mrs. Preston. "I want to speak to you. I am not so strong as I used to be, and you must not cross me, Pamela. I have something to do before I die. It upset me to hear of it, and to think of all that might happen. But I must get well and do it. It is all for your sake; and you must not cross me, Pamela. You must think well of what I say."

"No," said Pamela, though her heart sank a little. "I never did any thing to cross you, mamma; but Mrs. Swayne said you were not to talk; and she left the kettle by the fire that you might have some tea."

"I do not care for tea; I care for nothing but to get up and do what has to be done," said her mother. "It is all for your sake. Things will be very different, Pamela, from what you think: but you must not cross me. It is all for you—all for you."

"Oh, mamma, don't mind me," said Pamela, kissing her grey cheek. "I am all right, if you will only be well; and I don't know any thing you can have to do. You are not fit for any thing but to lie still. It is very early yet. I will draw the curtains if you will try to go to sleep."

"I must get up and go," said Mrs. Preston. "This is no time to go to sleep; but you must not cross me—that is the chief thing of all; for Pamela, every thing will be yours—every thing; and you are not to be deceived and taken in, and throw it all away."

"Oh, mamma dear, lie still and have a little more rest," cried Pamela, ready to cry with terror and distress. She thought it was delirium, and was frightened and overwhelmed by the unexpected calamity. Mrs. Preston, however, did not look like a woman who was raving; she looked at the old silver watch under her pillow, drawing it out with a feeble hand, which still trembled, and when she saw how early it still was, she composed herself again as with an effort. "Come and lie down, my poor darling," she said. "We must not spend our strength; and my Pamela will be my own good child and do what I say."

"Yes, mamma," said the poor child, answering her mother's kiss; but all the while her heart sank in her breast. What did it mean? What form was her submission to take? What was she pledging herself to? She lay down in reluctant obedience, trembling and agitated; but she was young and weary, and fell fast asleep in spite of herself and all her fears. And the morning light, as it brightened and filled the little room, fell upon the two together, who were so strange a contrast—the young round sweet face, to which the color returned as the soft sleep smoothed and soothed it, with eyes so fast closed, and the red lips a little apart, and the sweet breath rising and falling: and the dark, weary countenance, worn out of all freshness, now stilled in temporary slumber, now lighting up with two big dark eyes, which would wake suddenly, and fix upon the window, eager with thought, and then veil over again in the doze of weakness. They lay thus till the morning had advanced, and the sound of Mrs. Swayne's entrance made Pamela wake, and spring ashamed from her dead sleep. And finally, the cup of tea, the universal cordial, was brought. But when Mrs. Preston woke fully, and attempted to get up, with the eager look and changed manner which appalled her daughter, it was found to be impossible. The shock, whatever it was, had been too much for her strength. She fell back again upon her bed with a look of anguish which went to Pamela's heart. "I can't do it—I can't do it," she said to herself, in a voice of despair. The convulsive trembling of the previous night was gone; but she could not stand, could not walk, and still shook with nervous weakness. "I can't do it—I can't do it," she said over and over, and in her despair wept; which was a sight overwhelming even to Mrs. Swayne, who was standing looking on.

"Hush, hush," said that surprised spectator. "Bless your poor soul, don't take on. If you can't do it to-day, you'll do it to-morrow; though I don't know, no more than Adam, what she's got to do, Miss

Pamela, as is so pressing. Don't take on. Keep still, and you'll be better to-morrow. Don't go and take no liberties with yourself. You ain't fit to stand, much less to do any thing. Bless you, you'll be as lively as lively to-morrow, if you lie still and take a drop of beef-tea now and again, and don't take on."

"Yes, I'll do it to-morrow. It'll do to-morrow; a day don't signify," said Mrs. Preston; and she recovered herself, and was very quiet, while Pamela took her place by the bedside. Either she was going to be ill, perhaps to die, or something had happened to change her very nature, and turn the current of her life into another channel. Which of these things it was, was beyond the discrimination of the poor girl who watched by her bedside.

CHAPTER XXXI

SUSPICION

Neither the next day, however, nor the next again, was Mrs. Preston able to move. The doctor had to be brought at last, and he enjoined perfect quiet and freedom from care. If she had any thing on her mind, it was to be exorcised and put away, he ordered, speaking to Mrs. Swayne and Pamela, who had not a notion what she had on her mind. As for the patient, she made her effort to rise every morning, and failed, and turned upon her watchers such looks of despair as bewildered them. Every morning Jack Brownlow would come to ask for her, which was the only moment of the day in which Pamela found a little comfort; but her mother found it out instinctively, and grew so restless, and moaned so pitifully when her child left her, that even that sorrowful pleasure had to be given up. The young people did not know what to think. They persuaded themselves sometimes that it was only the effect of illness, and that a fancy so sudden and unexplainable would, when she was better, vanish as unreasonably as it came; but then, what was it she had to do? When she had lain for several days in this state of feebleness, always making vain efforts after strength, another change came over Mrs. Preston. The wild look went out of her eyes. One morning she called Pamela to her with more than her usual energy. "I am going to be very quiet and still for a week," she said; "if I am not better then, I will tell you what you must do, Pamela. You must send for the rector and for Nancy Christian from old Mrs. Fennell's in Masterton. This is Tuesday, and it is the 30th; and I will try for a week. If I am not better next Tuesday, you must send for the rector. Promise me to do exactly what I say."

"Yes, mamma," said Pamela; "but oh! what for?—if you would only tell me what it is for! You never kept any thing secret from me."

Mrs. Preston turned a wistful look upon her child. "I must not tell you," she said; "I can not tell you. If I did you would not thank me. You will know it soon enough. Don't ask me any questions for a week. I mean to try and get well to do it myself; but if I don't get well, no more time must be lost. You must not cross me, Pamela. What do you think I should care if it was not for you?"

"And perhaps if I knew I should not care," cried the poor little girl, wringing her hands. She did not know what it was; but still it became as clear as daylight to her that it was something against Jack.

"You would tell it to him," Mrs. Preston said, with a deep sigh. Perhaps Pamela did not hear her, for the words were spoken almost under her breath; but the girl heard the sigh, and divined what it meant. It was bitter to her, poor child, and hard to think that she could not be true to both—that her mother was afraid of trusting her—and that Jack and Mrs. Preston were ranged on different sides, with her love and faith, as a bone of contention, between them. Perhaps it was all the harder that she could not cry over it, or get any relief to her soul. Things by this time had become too serious for crying. The little soft creature grew without knowing into a serious woman. She had to give up such vain pleasures as that of tears over her trouble. No indulgence of the kind was possible to her. She sat by her mother's bedside all day long, and with her mother's eye upon her, had to feign composure when she little possessed it. Mrs. Preston was unreasonable for the first time in her life as regarded Pamela. She forgot what was needful for the child's health, which was a thing she had never done in her life before. She could not bear her daughter out of her sight. If she went down stairs for half an hour, to breathe the fresh air, her mother's eyes would follow her to the door with keen suspicion and fear. Pamela was glad to think that it must be her illness, and that only, which had this effect. Even Mrs. Swayne was more considerate. She was ready to come as often as it was possible to watch by the sick-bed and let the poor little nurse free; but Mrs. Preston was not willing to let her free. As it happened, however, Mrs. Swayne was in the room when her lodger gave Pamela instructions about calling the rector if she were not better in a week, and it startled the curious woman. She told it to her neighbor and tenant in the next house, and she told it to old Betty; and the thing by degrees grew so patent to the parish that at last, and that no later than the Friday, it came to Mr. Hardcastle's ears. Naturally it had changed in the telling. Whereas Mrs. Preston had directed him to be sent for in a certain desperate case, and as a last resource, the rector heard that Mrs. Swayne's inmate was troubled in her mind, and was anxious to confide some secret to him. What the secret was was doubtful, or else it would not have been a secret; but all Dewsbury believed that the woman was dying, and that she had done something very bad indeed, and desired the absolution of a priest before she could die in peace. When he heard this, it was equally natural that Mr. Hardcastle should feel a little excited. He was disposed toward High Church views, though he was not a man to commit himself, and approved of people who wanted absolution from a priest. Sometimes he had even a nibble at a confession, though unfortunately the people who confessed to him had little on their minds, and not much to tell. And the idea of a penitent with a real burden on her conscience was pleasant. Accordingly he got himself up very carefully on the Saturday, and set out for Mrs. Swayne's. He went with the wisdom of a serpent and the meekness of a dove, not professedly to receive a confession, but to call, as he said, on his suffering parishioner; and he looked very important and full of his mission when he went up stairs. Mrs. Swayne had gone astray after the new lights of Dissent, and up to this moment the dwellers under her roof had received no particular notice from Mr. Hardcastle, so that it was a little difficult to account for his solicitude now.

"I heard you were ill," said the rector; "indeed I missed you from church. As you are a stranger, and suffering, I thought there might be something that we could do—"

"You are very kind," said Mrs. Preston; and then she looked askance both at Mrs. Swayne and Pamela, keenly searching in their eyes to see if they had sent for him. And as Pamela, who knew nothing about it, naturally looked the guiltiest, her mother's heart was smitten with a sharp pang at the thought that she had been betrayed.

"Not kind at all," said Mr. Hardcastle, with animation. "It is my duty, and I am never tired of doing my duty. If you have any thing to say to me now—"

Once more Mrs. Preston cast a keen glance at her daughter. And she asked slowly, "What should I have to say?" looking not at the rector, but suspiciously into Pamela's face.

"My dear friend, how can I tell?" said Mr. Hardcastle. "I have seen a great deal of the world in my time, and come through a great deal. I know how suffering tries and tests the spirit. Don't be shy of speaking to me. If," the rector added, drawing a little nearer her pillow, "you would like me to send your attendants away—"

"Am I dying?" said Mrs. Preston, struggling up upon her bed, and looking so pale that Pamela ran to her, thinking it was so. "Am I so ill as that? Do they think I can not last out the time I said?"

"Mamma, mamma, you are a great deal better—you know you are a great deal better. How can you say such dreadful things?" said Pamela, kneeling by the bedside.

"If I am not dying, why do you forestall my own time?" said Mrs. Preston. "Why did you trouble Mr. Hardcastle? It was soon enough on the day I said."

"My dear friend," said the rector, "I hope you don't think it is only when you are dying that you have need of good advice and the counsel of your clergyman. I wish it was more general to seek it always. What am I here for but to be at the service of my parishioners night and day? And every one who is in mental difficulty or distress has a double claim upon me. You may speak with perfect freedom—whatever is said to me is sacred."

"Then you knew I wanted to speak to you?" said Mrs. Preston. "Thank you, you are very kind. I am not ungrateful. But you knew I wanted to ask your assistance? Somebody sent for you, perhaps?"

"I can not say I was sent for," said Mr. Hardcastle—with a little confusion, "but I heard—you know, in a country place the faintest wish you can express takes wings to itself, and becomes known everywhere. I understood—I heard—from various quarters—that if I came here—I might be of use to you."

All the answer Mrs. Preston made to this was to turn round to the head of the bed where Pamela stood, half hidden, in the corner. "That you might have something to tell him a little sooner!" she said. Her voice, though it was very low, so low as to be inaudible to the visitor, was bitter and sharp with pain, and she cast a glance full of reproach and anguish at her only child. She thought she had been betrayed. She thought that, for the lover's sake, who was dearer than father or mother, her own nursling had forfeited her trust. It was a bitter thought, and she was ill, and weak, and excited, and her mind distorted, so that she could not see things in their proper light. The bitterness was such that Pamela, utterly innocent as she was, sank before it. She did not know what she had done. She did not understand what her mother's look meant; but she shrank back among the curtains as if she had been really guilty, and it brought to a climax her sense of utter confusion and dismay.

"I will tell you what the case is," Mrs. Preston added quickly, the color coming back to her cheek. "I am not in very good health, as you see, but I have something very important to do before I die. It concerns the comfort of my child. So far as I am involved, it would not matter—it would not matter—for I shall not live long," she added with a certain plaintive tremor of self-pity in her voice. "It is all for Pamela, sir—though Pamela—but lately I grew frightened, and thought myself worse; and I told them—I told her—that if I was no better next Tuesday, they were to send for you. I would not trouble you if I were well enough myself. It was in case I should not be able, and I thought of asking your help; that is how it was. I suppose it was their curiosity. Curiosity is not a sin: but—they say I am not worse—they say I am even a little better. So I will not trouble you, Mr. Hardcastle. By that time I shall be able for what I have to do."

"You must not be too sure of that," said the rector; and he meant it kindly, though the words had but a doubtful sound; "and you must not think I am prying or intrusive. I was not sent for: but I understood—that—I might be of use. It is not giving me trouble. If there is any thing I can do for you if you have no friends—"

"We shall soon have plenty of friends," said Mrs. Preston quickly, with a certain mocking tone in her voice; "plenty of friends. We have not had many hitherto; but all that will soon change. Yes, I shall be able for what I have to do. I feel quite sure of it. You have done me a great deal of good. After it is done," she said, with that desolate look which Pamela felt to the bottom of her heart, but could not understand, "there will be time enough to be ill, and to die too, if God pleases. I will not mind it much when I leave her with many friends."

"Mamma!" cried Pamela, with a mingled appeal and reproach; but though she bent over her she could not catch her mother's eyes.

"It is true," said Mrs. Preston. "I was like to break my heart when I thought how old I was, and that I might die and leave you without any body to care for you; but now you will have many friends—plenty of friends. And it don't so much matter." She ended with such a sigh as moved even the heart of the rector, and touched Mrs. Swayne, who was not of a very sympathetic disposition, to tears.

"You must not talk of leaving your child without a protector," said Mr. Hardcastle; "if you knew what it was to have a motherless girl to bring up, you would not speak of it lightly. That is my case. My poor little Fanny was left motherless when she was only ten. There is no misfortune like it to a girl. Nobody knows how to manage a young creature but a mother. I feel it every day of my life," said the rector, with a sigh. It was very, very different from Mrs. Preston's sigh. There was neither depth in it nor despair like that which breathed in hers. Still, its superficial sadness was pathetic to the women who listened. They believed in him in consequence, more perhaps than he believed in himself, and even Mrs. Swayne was affected against her will.

"Miss Fanny has got them as is father and mother both in one," she said; "but bless you, sir, she ain't always like this. It's sickness as does it. One as is more fond of her child, nor prouder of her child, nor more content to live and see her 'appy, don't exist, when she's in her ordinary. And now, as the rector has come hisself, and 'as comforts at hand, you'll pluck up a spirit, that's what you'll do. Miss Pamela, who's as good as gold, don't think of nothing but a-nursing and a-looking after her poor dear mamma; and if so be as you'd make good use o' your time, and take the rector's advice—"

Mrs. Preston closed her lips tight as if she was afraid that some words would come through against her will, and faced them all with an obstinate resolution, shaking her head as her only answer. She faced them half seated on her bed, rising from among her pillows as if they were all arrayed against her, and she alone to keep her own part. Her secret was hers, and she would confide it to nobody; and already, in the shock of this intrusion, it seemed to her as if the languid life had been stirred in her veins, and her forces were mustering to her heart to meet the emergency. When she had made this demonstration, she came down from those heights of determination and responded to the rector's claim for sympathy as he knew well every woman would respond. "A girl is the better of a mother," she said, "even when she don't think it. Many a one is ungrateful, but we are not to look for gratitude. Yes, I know a mother is still something in this world. Pamela, you'll remember some day what Mr. Hardcastle said; and if Miss

Fanny should ever want a friend—But I am getting a little tired. Good-by, Mr. Hardcastle; perhaps you will come and see me again. And after a while, when I have done what I have to do—"

"Good-by," said the rector, after waiting vainly for the close of the sentence; and he rose up and took his leave, feeling that he had been dismissed, and had no right to stay longer. "If you should still want assistance—though I hope you will be better, as you expect—"

Mrs. Preston waved her hand in reply, and he went down stairs much confused, not knowing what to make of it. The talk he had with Mrs. Swayne in the passage threw but little light on the matter. Mrs. Swayne explained that they were poor; that she thought there was "something between" Miss Pamela and Mr. John; that she herself had essayed strenuously to keep the young people apart, knowing that nothing but harm would come of it; but that it was only lately, very lately, that Mrs. Preston had seemed to be of her opinion. A week ago she had received a visit, and had shut the door upon the young man, and fallen ill immediately after. "And all this talk o' something to do has begun since that," she added; "she's never had nothing to do as long as she's been here. There's a bit of a pension as is paid regular, and there never was no friends as I know of as could die and leave her money. It's some next-of-kin business, that's my idea, Mr. Hardcastle—some o' that rubbish as is in the papers—folks of the name of Smith or such like as is advertised for, and something to come to their advantage. But she's awful close and locked up, as you may say, in her own bosom, and never said a rational word to me."

"You don't think it's this?" said Mr. Hardcastle, putting his hand significantly to his forehead.

"Oh, bless you, it ain't that," said Mrs. Swayne. "She's as clear as clear—a deal clearer, for the matter of that, than she was afore; the first time as she had the sense to turn Mr. John from the door was the night as she was took. It ain't that. She's heard o' something, you take my word, and it's put fancies in her head; and as for that poor Pamela, she's as jealous of every look that poor child gives; and I don't call it no wonder myself, if you let a girl see a deal of a gentleman, that she should think more of him than's good for her. It should have been stopped when it began; but nobody will ever listen to me."

Mr. Hardcastle left the house with altogether a new idea in his mind. He had lectured his neighbor about young Powys and Sara, but he had not known any thing of this still more serious scandal about Jack. He murmured to himself over it as he went away with a great internal chuchotement. Poor Mr. Brownlow! both his son and his daughter thus showing low tastes. And he could not refrain from saying a few words about it to Jack, whom he met returning with his shooting-party—words which moved the young man to profound indignation. He was very angry, and yet it was not in nature that he should remain unmoved by the suggestion that Pamela's mother was either mad or had something on her mind. He had himself seen enough to give it probability. And to call Mr. Hardcastle a meddling parson, or even by some of those stronger and still less graceful epithets which sometimes follow the course of a clergyman's beneficent career, did but little good. Jack was furious that any body should have dared to say such words, but the words themselves rankled in his heart. As soon as he could steal out after dinner he did so, and went to the gate and saw the glimmering light in Mrs. Preston's window, and received Mrs. Swayne's ungracious report. But Pamela was not to be seen. She was never to be seen.

"They will kill her with this watching," he said to himself, as he stood and watched the light, and ground his teeth with indignation. But he could do nothing, although she was his own and pledged to him. He was very near cursing all mothers and fathers, as well as interfering priests and ungracious women, as he lingered up the avenue going home, and sucked with indignation and disgust at his extinguished cigar.

Poor little Pamela was no better off up stairs. She was doubted, suspected, feared—she who had been nothing but loved all her life. The child did not understand it, but she felt the bitterness of the cloud into which she had entered. It made her pale, and weighed upon her with a mysterious depth of distress which would not have been half so heavy had she been guilty. If she had been guilty she would have known exactly the magnitude of the offense, and how much she was suspected of; but being utterly innocent she did not know. Her sweet eyes turned deprecating, beseeching, to her mother's but they won no answer. The thought that her child had conspired against her, that she had planned to entrap her secret from her and betray it to her lover, that she was a traitor to the first and tenderest of affections, and that the new love had engrossed and swallowed up every thing—was the bitter thought that filled Mrs. Preston's mind, and hid from her the wistful innocence in Pamela's eyes. When the girl arranged her pillows or gave her medicine, her mother thanked her with formality, and answered her sharply when she spoke. "Dear mamma, are you not tired?" the poor child would say; and Mrs. Preston answered, "No, you need not think it, Pamela; people sometimes balk their own purpose. I shall be able after all. Your rector has done me good."

"He is not my rector, mamma," said Pamela. "I never spoke to him before. Oh! if you would only tell me why you are angry with me."

"I am not angry. I suppose it is human nature," said Mrs. Preston, and this was all the answer she would give. So that Pamela, poor child, had nothing for it but to retire behind the curtains and cry. This time the tears would well forth. She had been used to so much love, and it was hard to do without it; and when her mother repulsed her, in her heart she cried out for Jack. She cried out for him in her heart, but he could not hear her, though at that very moment he was no farther off than in the avenue, where he was lingering along very indignant and heavy-hearted, with his cigar out, though he did not know. It might not be a very deadly trouble to either of the young sufferers, but it was sharp enough in its way.

CHAPTER XXXII

THE REAL TRAITOR

While these things were going on at the gate of Brownlows, a totally different scene was being enacted in Masterton. Mr. Brownlow was at his office, occupied with his business and the people in his house, and the hundred affairs which make up a man's life. And as he had little time to brood over it, it had very much gone out of his mind how near he was to the crisis of his fate. An unexperienced sailor when he sees the port near is apt to be lulled into a dream of safety, though the warier seaman knows that it is the most dangerous moment. Mr. Brownlow was not inexperienced, but yet he allowed himself to be deluded into this sense of security after all his terrors. Young Powys came to business every day, and was very steady and regular, and a little disconsolate, evidently having nothing in his mind which could alarm his employer. When Mr. Brownlow looked up and saw the young fellow going steadily and sadly about his business, it sometimes gave him a sense of compunction, but it no longer filled him with fear. He had come to think the youth was harmless, and with the base instinct of human nature no longer cared for him. At least he cared for him in a different way; he promised to himself to make it all up to him afterward—to be his providence, and looked after him and establish him in the world—to give him no reason to repent having entrusted his fortunes to his hands. This was how Mr. Brownlow was thinking; and he had succeeded in making himself believe that this course was far the best for Powys. As for justice, it was rarely to be had under any circumstances. This young fellow had no more right to it than another; probably if mere justice had been dealt to him it would have been the ruin of him, as well as the ruin of other people. His real advantage after all was what Mr. Brownlow studied. Such thoughts by dint of practice became easier and more natural. The lawyer actually began to feel and believe that for every body concerned he was taking the best course; and the September days wore on, blazing, sultry, splendid, with crack of guns over the stubble, and sound of mirth in-doors, where every room was full and every association cheerful. It would only have been making Powys uncomfortable (Mr. Brownlow reflected) to have invited him at that moment among so many people, even if the accident with Sara had not prevented it. By and by, when all was safe, Sara should go away in her turn to visit her friends, and Powys should be had out to Brownlows, and have the remains of the sport, and be received with paternal kindness. This was the plan Mr. Brownlow had formed, and in the mean time he was cheerful and merry, and no way afraid of his fate.

Things were so when one morning he received a sudden message from old Mrs. Fennell. He had not been to see her for a long time. He had preferred, as far as possible, to ignore her very existence. His own conduct appeared to him in a different light when he saw her. It was blacker, more heinous, altogether vile, when he caught the reflection of it as in a distorted mirror in the old woman's suggestions. And it made Mr. Brownlow very uncomfortable. But this morning the summons was urgent. It was conveyed in a note from his mother-in-law herself. The billet was written on a scrap of paper, in a hand which had never been good, and was now shaky and irregular with old age. "I want to speak to you particular." Mrs. Fennell wrote. "It's about old Nancy and her goings on. There's something astir that is against your advantage and the children. Don't waste any time, but come to me;" and across the envelope she had written Immediate in letters half an inch long. Mr. Brownlow had a momentary thrill, and then he smiled to himself in the imbecility of self-delusion. "Some fancy she has taken into her head," he said. Last time she had sent for him her fears had come to nothing, and his fears, which were exaggerated, as he now thought, had worn out all his capabilities of feeling. He took it quite calmly now. When he had freed himself of his more pressing duties, he took his hat, and went leisurely across the market-place, to his mother-in-law's lodgings. The door was opened to him by Nancy, in whose looks he discovered nothing particular; and it did not even strike him as singular that she followed him up stairs, and went in after him to Mrs. Fennell's sitting-room. The old lady herself was sitting in a great chair, with her foot upon a high footstool, and all her best clothes on, as for an occasion of great solemnity. Her head was in continued palsied motion, and her whole figure trembling with excitement. She did not even wait until Mr. Brownlow had taken the chair which Nancy offered him with unusual politeness. "Shut the door," she cried. "Nancy, don't you go near Mr. Brownlow with your wiles, but shut the door and keep in your own place. Keep in your own place—do; and don't fuss about a gentleman as if that was to change his opinion, you old fool, at your age."

"I'm but doing my duty," said Nancy; "it's little change my wiles could make on a gentleman—never at no age as I know on—and never with Mr. Brownlow—"

"Hold your peace," cried Mrs. Fennell. "I know your tricks. You're old, and you should know better; but a woman never thinks as it's all over with her. John Brownlow, you look in that woman's face and listen to me. You've given her food and clothes and a roof over her head for years and years, and a wage that I never could see the reason for; and here she's been a-conspiring and a-treating with your enemies. I've found her out, though I am old and feeble. Ne'er a one of them can escape me. I tell you she's been conspiring with your enemies. I don't say that you've been overkind to me; but I can't sit by and see my Bessie's children wronged; and I've brought you here to set you face to face and hear what she's got to say."

Mr. Brownlow listened to her without changing countenance; he held his breath hard, and when she ceased speaking he let it go with a long respiration, such as a man draws after a great shock. But that was the only sign of emotion he showed; partly because he was stunned by the unexpected blow; partly because he felt that her every word betrayed him, and that nothing but utter self-command could do him any good.

"What does this mean?" he said, turning from Mrs. Fennell to Nancy. "Who are my enemies? If you have any thing to say against Nancy, or if Nancy has any thing to say—"

"She's a traitor," cried Mrs. Fennell, with a voice which rose almost to a scream. "She's a real traitor;—she eats your bread, and she's betrayed you. That's what I mean and it's as clear as day."

All this time Nancy stood steadily, stolidly by, with her hand on the back of the chair, not defiant but watchful. She had no wish to lose her place, and her wages, and her comforts; but yet, if she were sent away, she had a claim upon the other side. She had made herself a friend like the unjust steward. And she stood and watched and saw all that passed, and formed her conclusions.

Therefore she was in no way disturbed when Mr. Brownlow turned round and looked her in the face. He was very steady and self-possessed, yet she saw by the way that he turned round on his chair, by the grasp he took of the back of it, by the movement of his eyelids, that every word had told upon him. "You must speak a little more plainly," he said, with an attempt at a smile. "Perhaps you will give me your own account of it, Nancy. Whom have you been conspiring with? Who are my enemies? I think I am tolerably at peace with all the world, and I don't know."

Nancy paused with momentary hesitation, whether to speak the simple truth, and see the earthquake which would ensue, which was a suggestion made by the dramatic instinct within her—or whether to keep on the safe side and deny all knowledge of it. If she had been younger, probably she would have preferred the former for the sake of excitement; but being old she chose the latter. She grew meek under Mr. Brownlow's eyes, so meek that he felt it an outrage on his good sense, and answered softly as became a woman anxious to turn away wrath.

"Nor me, sir," said Nancy, "I don't know. If I heard of one as was your enemy, it would be reason enough to me for never looking nigh, him. I've served you and yours for long, and it's my place to be faithful. I've been a-seeing of some old friends as lives a little bit out o' Masterton. I'm but a servant, Mr. Brownlow, but I've some friends; and I never heard as you was one to think as poor folks had no heart. It was a widow woman, as has seen better days; it ain't much I can do for her, but she's old, and she's poor, and I go to see her a bit times and times. I hope there ain't nothing in that that displeases you. If I stayed longer than I ought last time—"

"What is all this to me?" said Mr. Brownlow. "Who is your widow woman? Do you want me to do any thing for her? has she a family? There are plenty of charities in Masterton if she belongs to the place. But it does not seem worth while to have brought me here for this."

"You know better than that, John Brownlow," said Mrs. Fennel, in a kind of frenzy. "If it was any poor woman, what would I have cared? Let 'em starve, the hussies, as brings it all on themselves. There's but one woman as would trouble me, and you know who it is, John Brownlow; and that old witch there, she knows, and it's time to put a stop to it all. It's time to put a stop to it all, I say. She's a-carrying on with that woman; and my Bessie's children will be robbed before my very eyes; and I'm a poor old creature, and their own father as ought to take their part! I tell you, it's that woman as she's a-carrying on with; and they'll be robbed and ruined, my pretty dears, my Bessie's children! and she'll have it all, that wretch! I'd kill her, I'd strangle her, I'd murder her, if it was me!"

Mrs. Fennell's eyes were blood-shot, and rolled in their sockets wildly—her head shook with palsied rage—her voice stammered and staggered—and she lifted her poor old lean hands with wild, incoherent gestures. She was half-mad with passion and excitement. She, who was so terribly in earnest, so eager in her insane desire to save him, was in reality the traitor whom he had most to fear; and Mr. Brownlow had his senses sufficiently about him to perceive this. He exerted himself to calm her down and soothe her. "I will see after it—I will see after it," he said. "I will speak to Nancy—don't excite yourself." As for Mrs. Fennell, not his persuasion, but her own passion wore her out presently, and reduced her to comparative calm; after awhile she sank into silence, and the half doze, half stupor of extreme age. When this re-action had come on, Mr. Brownlow left the room, making a sign to Nancy to follow him, which the old woman did with gradually-rising excitement, feeling that now indeed her turn had come. But he did not take her apart, as she had hoped and supposed, to have a desperate passage of arms. He turned round on the stair, though the landlady stood below within hearing ready to open the door, and spoke to her calmly and coldly. "Has she been long like this?" he said, and looked Nancy so steadily in the face that, for the first time, she was discomfited, and lost all clue to his meaning. She stood and stared at him for a minute, not knowing what to say.

"Has she been long like this?" Mr. Brownlow repeated a little sharply. "I must see after a doctor at once. How long has it lasted? I suppose no one can tell but you?"

"It's lasted—but I don't know, sir," said Nancy, "I don't know; I couldn't say, as it was nothing the matter with her head. She thinks as there's a foundation. It's her notion as I've found out—"

"That will do," said Mr. Brownlow; "I have no curiosity about your friends. It is your mistress's health I am thinking of. I will call on Dr. Bayley as I go back; and you will see that she is kept quiet, and has every attention. I am grieved to see her in such an excited state. And, by the way, you will have the goodness not to leave her again. If your friends require your visits, let me know, and I will send a nurse. If it has been neglect that has brought this on, you may be sure it will tell on yourself afterward," Mr. Brownlow added, as he went out. All this was said in the presence of the mistress of the house, who heard and enjoyed it. And he went away without another look at her, without another word, without praying for her silence, or pleading with her for her secret, as she had expected. Nancy was confounded, notwithstanding all her knowledge. She stood and stared after him with a sinking heart, wondering if there were circumstances she did not know, which held him harmless, and whether after all it had been wise of her to attach herself to the cause of his adversaries. She was disappointed with the effect she had produced—disappointed of the passage of arms she had expected, and the keen cross-examination which she had been prepared to baffle. She looked so blank that the landlady, looking on, felt that she too could venture on a passing arrow.

"You'll take my word another time, Nancy," she said. "I told you as it was shameful neglect to go and leave her all by herself, and her so old and weakly, poor soul! You don't mind the likes of us, but you'll have to mind what your master says."

"He ain't no master of mine," said Nancy, fiercely, "nor you ain't my mistress, Lord be praised. You mind your own business, and I'll mind mine. It's fine to be John Brownlow, with all his grandeur; but pride goes before a fall, is what I says," the old woman muttered, as she went back to Mrs. Fennell's room. She had said so at Brownlows, looking at the avenue which led to the great house, and at the cozy little lodge out of which she had already planned to turn old Betty. That vision rose before her at this trying moment, and comforted her a little. On the one side the comfortable lodge, and an easy life, and the prospect of unbounded tyranny over a new possessor, who should owe every thing to her; but, on the other side, dismissal from her present post, which was not unprofitable, an end of her good wages and all her consolations. Nancy drew her breath hard at the contrast; the risk seemed to her as great almost as the hope.

Mr. Brownlow left the door composed and serious, as a man does who has just been in the presence of severe perhaps fatal illness, and he went to Dr. Bayley, and told that gentleman that his mother-in-law's brain was, he feared, giving way, and begged him to see her immediately; and then he went to the office, grave and silent, without a touch of apparent excitement. When he got there, he stopped in the outer office, and called Powys into his own room. "We have not seen you at Brownlows for a long time," he said. "Jack has some young fellows with him shooting. You had better take a week's holiday, and come up with me to-night. I shall make it all right with Wrinkell. You can go home and get your bag before the dog-cart comes."

He said this quickly, without any pause for consideration, as if he had been giving instructions about some deed drawing out; and it was some time before Powys realized the prospect of paradise thus opening before him. "I, sir—do you mean me?" he cried, in his amazement. "To-night?" And Mr. Brownlow appeared to his clerk as if he had been an angel from heaven.

"Yes," he said, with a smile, "to-night. I suppose you can do it? You do not want much preparation for pleasure at your age."

Then poor Powys suddenly turned very pale. Out of the first glow of delight he sank into despondency. "I don't know, sir—if you may have forgotten—what I once said to you—about—about my folly," faltered the young man, not daring to look into his employer's face.

"About—?" said Mr. Brownlow; and then he made as though he suddenly recollected, and laughed. "Oh, yes, I remember," he said. "I suppose all young men are fools sometimes in that respect. But I don't see it is any business of mine. You can settle it between you. Be ready for me at six o'clock."

And thus it was all arranged. Powys went out to get his things, not knowing whether he walked or flew, in such a sudden amaze of delight as few men ever experience; and when he was gone Mr. Brownlow put down his ashy face into his clasped hands. Heaven! had it come to this? At the last moment, when the shore was so near, the tempest well-nigh spent, deliverance at hand, was there no resource but this, no escape? All his precautions vain, his wiles, his struggle of conscience! His face was like that of a dead man as he sat by himself and realized what had happened. Why could not he fly to the end of earth, and escape the Nemesis? Was there nothing for it but, like that other wretched father, to sacrifice his spotless child?

CHAPTER XXXIII

ONLY MR. BROWNLOW'S CLERK

There was a pleasant bustle about the house that evening when the dog-cart drove up. The sportsmen had been late of getting in, and nobody as yet had gone to dress; the door was open, and in the hall and about the broad door-steps pretty groups were lingering. Sara and her friends on their way up stairs had encountered the gentlemen, fresh from their sport, some of whom had no doubt strayed to the sideboard, which was visible through the open door of the dining-room; but the younger ones were about the hall in their shooting-dresses talking to the girls and giving an account of themselves. There was about them all that sense of being too late, and having no right to be there, which gives a zest to such stolen moments. The men were tired with their day's work, and, for that matter, the ladies too, who, after the monotony of the afternoon and their cup of tea, wanted a little amusement; and there was a sound of talk and of laughter and pleasant voices, which could be heard half-way down the avenue. They had all been living under the same roof for some days at least, and people get to know each other intimately under such circumstances. This was the scene upon which young Powys, still bewildered with delight, alighted suddenly, feeling as if he had fallen from the clouds. He jumped down with a light heart into the bright reflection of the lamp which fell over the steps, but somehow his heart turned like a piece of lead within his heart the moment his foot touched the flags. It grew like a stone within him without any reason, and he did not know why. Nobody knew him, it is true; but he was not a shy boy to be distressed by that. He jumped down, and his position was changed. Between him and Mr. Brownlow, who was so kind to him, and Jack, who was so hostile yet sympathetic, and Sara, whom he loved, there were unquestionable relations. But when he heard the momentary pause that marked his appearance, the quick resuming of the talk with a certain interrogative tone, "Who is he?" the glance at him askance, the sudden conviction rushed into his mind that all the better-informed were saying, "It is only his clerk"—and it suddenly occurred to Powys that there existed no link of possible connection between himself and all those people. He knew nobody—he had no right to know any body among them. He was there only by Mr. Brownlow's indiscreet favoritism, taken out of his own sphere. And thus he fell flat out of his foolish elysium. Mr. Brownlow, too, felt it as he stepped out into the midst of them all; but his mind was preoccupied, and though it irritated, it did not move him. He looked round upon his guests, and he said, with a smile which was not of the most agreeable kind, "You will be late for dinner, young people, and I am as hungry as an ogre. I shan't give you any grace. Sara, don't you see Powys? Willis, send Mr. Powys's things up to the green room beside mine. Come along, and I'll show you the way."

To say Sara was not much startled would be untrue; but she too had been aware of the uncomfortable moment of surprise and dismay among the assembled guests, and a certain fine instinct of natural courtesy which she possessed came to her aid. She made a step forward, though her cheeks were scarlet, and her heart beating loud, and held out her hand to the new visitor: "I am very glad to see you," she said. Not because she was really glad, so much as because these were the first words that occurred to her. It was but a moment, and then Powys followed Mr. Brownlow up stairs. But when Sara turned round to her friends again she was unquestionably agitated, and it appeared to her that every body perceived she was so. "How cross your papa looks," said one of them; "is he angry?—what have we done?" And then the clock struck seven. "Oh, what a shame to be so late! we ought all to have been ready. No wonder Mr. Brownlow is cross," said another; and they all fluttered away like a flock of doves, flying up the staircase. Then the young men marched off too, and the pretty scene was suddenly obliterated, and nothing left but the bare walls, and Willis the butler gravely superintending his subordinates as they gave the finishing touches to the dinner-table. The greater part of the company forgot all about this little scene before five minutes had elapsed, but there were two or three who did not forget. These were Powys, first of all, who was tingling to the ends of his fingers with Sara's words and the momentary touch of her little hand. It was but natural, remembering how they parted, that he should find a special meaning in what she said, and he had no way of knowing that his arrival was totally unexpected, and that she was taken by surprise. And as for Sara herself, her heart fluttered strangely under the pretty white dress which was being put on. Madlle. Angelique could not make out what it was that made her mistress so hard to manage. She would not keep still as a lady ought when she is getting dressed. She made such abrupt movements as to snatch her long bright locks out of Angelique's hands, and quite interfere with the management of her ribbons. She too had begun to recollect what were the last words Powys had addressed to her. And she to say she was glad to see him! Mr. Brownlow had himself inducted his clerk into the green room, next door to his own, which was one of the best rooms in the house; and his thoughts would not bear talking of. They were inarticulate, though their name was legion; they seemed to buzz about him as he made his rapid toilette, so that he almost thought they must make themselves heard through the wall. Things had come to a desperate pass, and there was no time to be biased by thoughts. He had dressed in a few minutes, and then he went to his daughter. Sara at the best of times was not so rapid. She was still in her dressing-gown at that moment with her hair in Angelique's hands, and it was too late to send the maid away.

"Sara," said Mr. Brownlow, very tersely, "you will take care that young Powys is not neglected at dinner. Mind that you arrange it so—"

"Shall he take me in?" said Sara, with a sudden little outbreak of indignation which did her good. "I suppose you do not mean that?"

"I am speaking in earnest," said Mr. Brownlow, with some offense. "I have put him in the green room. Recollect that I think nothing in the house too good for this young man—nothing. I hope you will recollect what I say."

"Nothing?" said Sara, with a little surprise; and then the instinct of mischief returned to her, and she added, demurely, "that is going a long way."

"It is going a very long way—as far as a man can go," said Mr. Brownlow, with a sigh—"farther than most men would go." And then he went away. As for Sara, her very ears thrilled with the significance of his tone. It frightened her into her senses when perhaps she might have been excused for being partly out of them. If she was kind to Powys—as kind as her father's orders required—what could he think? Would he remember what he had ventured to say? Would he think she was giving him "encouragement?" Notwithstanding this perplexity she allowed Angelique to dress her very nicely with her favorite blue ribbons and ornaments; and when she set out to go down stairs, perhaps there was a little touch of Iphigenia in her air; but the martyrdom was not to call disagreeable. He was in the drawing-room when she went in. He was in a corner looking at photographs, which is the general fate of a poor man in a large party who knows nobody. Sara had a little discussion with herself whether it was her duty to go at once to Powys and take him under her protection. But when she looked at him—as she managed to do, so to speak, without looking—it became apparent to her that the young Canadian was too much a man to be treated with any such condescension; he was very humble, very much aware that his presumption in lifting his eyes to the height on which she sat was unpardonable; but still, if she had gone to him and devoted herself to his amusement, there is no telling what the results might have been. He was not one to take it meekly. The room gradually filled and grew a pretty sight as Sara made these reflections. The ladies came down like butterflies, translated out of their warm close morning-dresses into clouds of vapory white and rosy color and sparkles of ornament like evening dew; and the sportsmen in their knickerbockers had melted into spotless black figures, relieved with patches of spotless white, as is the use of gentlemen. The talk scarcely began again with its former freedom, for the moment before dinner is a grim moment, especially when men have been out all day and are hungry. Accordingly, the black figures massed themselves well up about the fire-place, and murmured through their beards such scraps of intelligence as suit the masculine capacity; while the ladies settled all round like flower borders, more patient and more smiling. Nobody took any particular notice of Powys in his corner, except, indeed, Mr. Brownlow who stood very upright by the mantle-piece and did not speak, but looked at Sara, sternly as she thought, and then at the stranger. It was a difficult position for the young mistress of the house. When her father's glance became urgent she called a friend to her aid—a young woman of a serviceable age, not young and not old—who happened to be good-natured as well. "He is a friend of papa's," she said—"a great friend, but he knows nobody." And, strengthened by this companionship, she ventured to draw near the man who, in that very room, not far from that very spot, had told her he loved her. He was looking at a picture—the same picture of the woman holding out bread to the beggar—and he was thinking, Should he ever have that bread?—was it possible? or only a mockery of imagination? As Sara approached him the memory of that other scene came over her so strongly, and her heart began to beat so loudly, that she could scarcely hear herself speaking. "I want to introduce you to my friend Miss Ellerslie," she said. "Mr. Powys, Mary—you will take her in to dinner." And then she came to a dead stop, breathless with confusion. As for poor Powys, he made his new acquaintance a bow, and very nearly turned his back upon her, not seeing her for the dazzle in his eyes. This was about all the intercourse that passed between them, until, for one minute, and one only, after dinner, when he found himself by accident close to Sara's chair. He stood behind her, lingering, scarcely seeing her, for she was almost hidden by the high back of the chair, yet feeling her all round him in the very air, and melted, poor fellow, into the languor of a sweet despair. It was despair, but yet it was sweet, for was he not there beside her? and though his love was impossible, as he said to himself, still there are impossibilities, which are more dear than any thing that can be compassed by man. As he stood, not venturing to say any thing—not knowing, indeed, what to say—Sara suddenly turned round and discovered him. She looked up, and neither did she say any thing; but when their eyes met, a sudden violent scorching blush flashed over her face. Was it anger, indignation, displeasure? He could not tell—but one thing was very clear, that it was recollection. She had not forgotten his wild words any more than he had. They were tingling in her ears as in his, and she did not look at him with the steady look of indignation putting him down. On the contrary, it was her eyes which sank before his, though she did not immediately turn away her face. That was all—and no rational human creature could have said it meant any thing; but yet when it came to be Powys's fate to address himself once more to the photographs, he did so with the blood coursing through all his veins, and his life as it were quickened within him. The other people with whom she was intimate, who were free to crowd around her, to talk to her, to occupy her attention, were yet nothing to her in comparison with what he was. Between these two there was a consciousness that existed between no other two in the party, friendly and well-acquainted as they all were. The Canadian was in such a state of mind that this one point in the evening made every thing else comparatively unimportant. His companion at dinner had been kind and had talked to him; but after dinner, when the ladies left, the men had snubbed the intruder. Those who were near him had rushed into talk about people and places of whom he had no knowledge, as ill-bred persons are apt to do—and he had not found it pleasant. They had made him feel that his position was an anomalous one, and the backwoodsman had longed in his heart to show his sense of their rudeness and get up and go away. But after he had seen Sara's blush, he forgot all about the young fellows and their impertinence. He was at the time of life when such a thing can happen. He was for the moment quite content with the photographs, though he had not an idea what they were like. He was not hoping any thing, nor planning any thing, nor believing that any thing could come of it. He was slightly delirious, and did not know what he was about—that was all.

"Are you fond of this sort of thing?" Mr. Brownlow said, coming up. Mr. Brownlow paid him an uneasy sort of attention, which made Powys more uncomfortable than the neglect of the others, for it implied that his host knew he was being neglected and wanted to make it up to him; "but then you should have seen all these places before you can care for them. And you have never been abroad."

"No, except on the other side of the Atlantic," said Powys, with colonial pride; "and you don't seem to think any thing of that."

"Ah, yes, Canada," said Mr. Brownlow; and then he was so anxious to keep his young visitor in good-humor that he began to talk solidly and heavily of Canada and its resources and future prospects. Mr. Brownlow was distrait, and not very well informed, and Powys had not the heart to laugh at Sara's father even when he made mistakes, so that the conversation was not very lively between them. This, however, was all the amusement the stranger got on his first evening at Brownlows. The proposal to go there had thrown him into a kind of ecstasy, but this was all the result. When he got into his own room at night and thought it all over, an impulse of good sense came to his aid. It was folly. In the office at Masterton he was in his fit place, and nobody could object to him; but this was not his fit place. It might be uncivil and bad manners on their part to make him feel it, but yet the party at Brownlows was right. He had nothing to do there. If he could think that Miss Brownlow's heart had softened a little toward him, it was his duty all the more to deny himself and take himself out of her way. What had love to do between her and him? It was monstrous—not to be thought of. He had been insane when he came, but to-morrow he would go back, and make a stern end of all those dreams. These were Powys's thoughts within himself. But there was a conversation going on about him down stairs of a very different kind.

When the company had all retired, Jack detained his father and his sister to speak to them. Jack was highly uncomfortable in his mind himself, and naturally he was in a very rampant state of virtue. He could not endure that other people should have their cakes and ale; and he did not like his father's looks nor Sara's, and felt as if the honor of his house was menaced somehow. He took Sara's candle from her after his father had lighted it, and set it down on the table. "The nuisance of having all these people," said Jack, "is, that one never has a moment to one's self, and I want to speak to you. I don't mean to say any thing against Powys, sir—nobody knows any thing about him. Has he told you what he said to Sara when he was last here?"

"Jack! how dare you?" said Sara, turning on her brother; but Jack took no notice of her beautiful blazing eyes.

"Did he tell you, that you are so well informed?" said Mr. Brownlow. If either of his children had been cool enough to observe it, they would have perceived that he was too quiet, and that his calm was unnatural; but they suspected nothing, and consequently they did not observe.

"He told me enough to make me understand," said Jack; "and I dare say you've forgotten how young men think, and don't suppose it's of any consequence. Sara knows. If it was a mere nothing, I should not take the trouble," added the exemplary brother; "but, in the circumstances, it's my duty to interfere. After what he said, when you bring him here again it is giving him license to speak; it is giving him a kind of tacit consent. She knows," said Jack, pointing to his sister, who confronted him, growing pale and growing scarlet. "It's as good as saying you will back him out; and, good heavens, when you consider who he is—"

"Do you know who he is?" said Mr. Brownlow. He was very hard put to it for that moment, and it actually occurred to him to deliver himself of his secret, and throw his burden on their shoulders—the two who, in their ignorance, were thus putting the last touch of exasperation to his ordeal. He realized the blank amazement with which they would turn to him, the indignation, the—Ah, but he could not go any farther. What would have succeeded to the first shock of the news he dared not anticipate—beggary probably, and utter surrender of every thing; therefore Mr. Brownlow held his peace.

"I know he is in the office at Masterton," said Jack—"I know he is your clerk, and I don't suppose he is a prince in disguise. If he is honest, and is who he professes to be—I beg your pardon, sir, for saying so—but he ought not to be brought into my sister's society, and he has no business to be here."

"Papa!" cried Sara, breathless, "order him to be quiet! Is it supposed that I can't see any one without being in danger of—of—that any man whom papa chooses to bring is to be kept away for me? I wonder what you think of me? We girls are not such wretched creatures, I can tell you; nor so easily led; nor so wicked and proud—nor—Papa! stop this immediately, and let Jack mind his own affairs."

"I have just one word to say, Jack," said Mr. Brownlow,—"my darling, be quiet—never mind;—Powys is more important to me than if he were a prince in disguise. I know who he is. I have told your sister that I think nothing in this house too good for him. He is my clerk, and you think he is not as good as you are; but he is very important to me. I give you this explanation, not because I think you have any right to it, after your own proceedings. And as for you, my dear child," he added, putting his arm round her, with an involuntary melting of his heart, "my pretty Sara! you are only to do what your heart suggests, my darling. I once asked a sacrifice of you, but I have not the heart now. If your heart goes this way, it will be justice. Yes, justice. I know you don't understand me; but if not, Sara, I will not interfere with you. You are to do according to your own heart."

"Papa!" said Sara, clinging to him, awed and melted and astonished by the emotion in his eyes.

"Yes," Mr. Brownlow repeated, taking her face in his hands, and kissing it. If he had been a soft-hearted man he would have been weeping, but there was something in his look beyond tears. "It will be just, and the best way—but only if it's after your own heart. And I know you don't understand me. You'll never understand me, if all goes well; but all the same, remember what I say."

And then he took up the candle which Jack had taken out of Sara's hand. "Never understand me—never, if all goes well," he muttered to himself. He was strained to the last point, and he could not bear any more. Before his children had recovered from their amaze he had gone away, not so much as looking at them again. They might talk or speculate as they would; he could bear no more.

Jack and Sara looked in each other's faces as he disappeared. They were both startled, but in a different way. Was he mad? his son thought; and Jack grew pale over the possibility: but as for Sara, her life was bound up in it. It was not the blank of dismay and wonder that moved her. She did not speculate on what her father meant by justice. Something else stirred in her heart and veins. As for Jack, he was thunderstruck. "He must be going mad!" he said. "For heaven's sake, Sara, don't give any weight to these delusions; he can't be in his right mind."

"Do you mean papa?" said Sara, stamping her foot in indignation; "he is a great deal wiser than you will ever be. Jack, I don't know what you mean; it must be because you are wicked yourself that you think every body else is going wrong; but you shall not speak so to me."

"Yes; I see you are going to make a fool of yourself," said Jack, in his superiority. "You are shutting your eyes and taking your own way. When you come to a downfall you will remember what I say. You are trying to make a fool of him, but you won't succeed—mind I tell you, you won't succeed. He knows what he is about too well for that."

"If it is Mr. Powys you are speaking of—" said Sara; but she paused, for the name betrayed her somehow—betrayed her even to herself, bringing the color to her cheeks and a gleam to her eyes. Then she made believe as if she scorned to say more, and held her little head high with lofty contempt, and lighted her candle. "I am sure we should not agree on that subject, and it is better we should not try," said Sara, and followed her father loftily up stairs, leaving Jack discomfited, with the feeling of a prophet to whom nobody would listen. He said to himself he knew how it would be—his father had got some wild idea in his head! and Sara was as headstrong and fanciful as ever girl was, and would rush to her own destruction. Jack went out with this sense of approaching calamity in his mind, and lighted his cigar, and took a turn down the avenue as far as the gate, where he could see the light in Mrs. Preston's window. It seemed to him that the world was losing its balance—that only he saw how badly things were turning, and nobody would listen to him. And, strangely enough, his father's conduct seemed so mad to him altogether that his mind did not fix on the maddest word of it—the word which by this time had got into Sara's head, and was driving her half wild with wonder. Justice! What did it mean? Sara was thinking in her agitation: but Jack, taking things in general as at their worst, passed over that particular. And thus they all separated and went to bed, as was to be supposed, in the most natural and seemly way. People slept well at Brownlows in general, the air being so good, and all the influences so healthful, after these long days out-of-doors; and nobody was the wiser for it if "the family" were any way disturbed among themselves.

As for Mr. Brownlow, he threw himself down on his bed in a certain lull of despair. He was dead tired. It was pitiful to see him thus worn out, with too little hope to make any exertion, driven to his last resource, thinking of nothing but of how to forget it all for a little and get it out of his mind. He tried to sleep and to be still, and when he found he could not sleep, got up again and took some brandy—a large fiery dose—to keep his thoughts away. He had thought so much that now he loathed thinking. If he could but go on and let fortune bring him what it might; if he could but fall asleep—asleep, and not wake again till all was over—not awake again at all for that matter. There was nothing so delightful in the world that he should wish very much to wake again. Not that the faintest idea of putting an end to himself ever crossed his mind. He was only sick of it all, tired to death, disgusted with every thing—his own actions, and the frivolity and folly of others who interfered with his schemes, and the right that stood in his way, and the wrong that he was trying to do. At that moment he had not heart enough to go on with any thing. Such moments of disgust come even to those who are the most energetic and ready. He seemed to have thrown the guidance of affairs out of his hands, and be trusting to mere blind chance—if any thing is ruled by chance. If this boy and girl should meet, if they should say to each other certain foolish words, if they should be idiots enough, the one and the other, as to commit themselves, and pledge their lives to an act of the maddest absurdity, not unmixed with wickedness—for it would be wicked of Powys, poor as he was, and burdened as he was, to ask Sara to marry him, and it would be insanity on her part to consent—if this mad climax should arrive, then a kind of salvation in ruin, a kind of justice in wrong, would be wrought. And to this chance Mr. Brownlow, after all his plans and schemes, after all his thought and the time he had spent in considering every thing, had come as the sole solution of his difficulties. He had abdicated, as it were, the throne of reason, and left himself to chance and the decision of two ignorant children. What wind might veer their uncertain intentions, or sudden impulse change them, he could not tell. He could not influence them more, could not guide them, any farther. What could he do but sleep? Oh, that he could have but slept, and let the crisis accomplish itself and all be over! Then he put out his light and threw himself upon his bed, and courted slumber like a lover. It was the only one thing in the world Mr. Brownlow could now do, having transferred, as it were, the responsibility and the power of action into other hands.

CHAPTER XXXIV

AN IMPOSTOR

Next morning Powys was up early, with his wise resolution very strong in his mind. He seemed to see the folly of it all more clearly in the morning light. Such a thing might be possible in Canada; but in this conventional artificial existence there were a hundred things more important than love or happiness. Even that, too, he felt was an artificial way of looking at it; for, after all, let the laws of existence be ever so simple, a man who has already a family to support, and very little to do it on, is mad, and worse than mad, if he tries to drag a girl down into the gulf of poverty with him. And as for Sara having enough for both, Powys himself was not sufficiently unconventional and simple-minded to take up that idea. Accordingly he felt that the only thing to do was to go away; he had been crazy to think of any thing else, but now his sanity had returned to him. He was one of the earliest of the party down stairs, and he did not feel himself so much out of place at the breakfast-table; and when the young men went out, Jack, by way of keeping the dangerous visitor out of his sister's way, condescended to be civil, and invited him to join the shooting-party. Powys declined the invitation. "I am going to the office with Mr. Brownlow," he said, a decision which was much more satisfactory to Jack.

"Oh, I thought you had come for a few days," said Jack. "I beg your pardon; not that the sport is much to offer any one—the birds are getting scarce; but I thought you had come for some days."

"No, I am going back to-day," said Powys, not without a strangled inaudible sigh; for the sight of the dogs and the guns went to his heart a little, notwithstanding his love and despair. And Jack's conscience pricked him that he did not put in a word of remonstrance. He knew well enough that Powys had not meant to go away, and he felt a certain compunction and even sympathy. But he reflected that, after all, it was far best for himself that every pretension should be checked in the bud. Powys stood on the steps looking after them as they went away; and it can not be denied that his feelings were dreary. It seemed hard to be obliged to deny himself every thing, not happiness alone, but even a little innocent amusement, such as reminded him of the freedom of his youth. He was too manly to grumble, but yet he felt it, and could not deny himself the pleasure of wondering how "these fellows" would like the prairies, and whether they would disperse in double-quick time if a bear or a pack of wolves came down upon them in place of their innocent partridges. No doubt "these fellows" would have stood the trial extremely well, and at another moment Powys would not have doubted that; but in the mean time a little sneer was a comfort to him. The dog-cart came up as he waited, and Mr. Brownlow made his appearance in his careful morning-dress, perfectly calm, composed, and steady as usual—a man whose very looks gave consolation to a client in trouble. But yet the lines of his face were a little haggard, if there had been any body there with eyes to see. "What, Powys!" he said, "not gone with the others?"

He said it with a smile, and yet it raised a commotion in his mind. If he had not gone with the others, Mr. Brownlow naturally concluded it must be for Sara's sake, and that the crisis was very near at hand.

"No, sir," said Powys; "in fact I thought of going in with you to the office, if you will take me. It is the fittest place for me."

Then it occurred to Mr. Brownlow that the young man had spoken and had been rejected, and the thought thrilled him through and through, but still he tried to make light of it. "Nonsense," he said; "I did not bring you up last night to take you down this morning. You want a holiday. Don't set up having an old head on young shoulders, but stay and enjoy yourself. I don't want you at the office to-day."

"If an old head means a wise one, I can't much boast of that," said Powys; and then he saw Sara standing in the door-way of the dining-room looking at him, and his heart melted within him. One more day! he would not say a word, not a word, however he might be tempted; and what harm could it do any one? "I think I ought to go," he added, faintly; but the resolution had melted out of his words.

"Nonsense!" said Mr. Brownlow, from the dog-cart, and he waved his hand, and the mare set off at her usual pace down the avenue, waiting for no one. And Powys was left alone standing on the steps. The young men had gone who might have been in the way, and the ladies had already dispersed from the breakfast-table, some to the morning-room on the other side of the hall, some up stairs for their hats and cloaks, before straying out on their morning perambulations. And Sara, who had her housekeeping to do, save the mark! was the only creature visible to whom he turned as her father drove away. Courtesy required (so she said to herself) that she should go forward into the hall a step or two, and say something good-natured to him. "If you are not of Jack's party," she said, "you must go and help to amuse the people who are staying at home; unless you want to write or do any thing, Mr. Powys. The library is on that side; shall I show you the way?"

And a minute after he found himself following her into the room, which was the first room he had ever been in at Brownlows. It was foolish of Sara—it was a little like the way in which she had treated him before. Her own heart was beating more quickly than usual, and yet she was chiefly curious to know what he would do, what he would say. There was something of the eagerness of an experiment in her mind, although she had found it very serious after he left her the last time, and any thing but amusing on the previous night.

"Thanks," said poor Powys, whose head was turning round and round; "I ought to have gone to the office. I am better there than here."

"That is not very complimentary to us," said Sara, with a little nervous laugh.

And then he turned and looked at her. She was making a fool of him, as Jack would have said. She was torturing him, playing with him, making her half-cruel, half-rash experiment. "You should not say so," he said, with vehemence—"you know better. You should not tempt me to behave like an idiot. You know I am ready enough to do it. If I were not an idiot I should never have come here again."

"Not when my father brought you?" said Sara—"not when I—but I think you are rude, Mr. Powys; I will leave you to write your letters, and when you have finished you will find us all up stairs."

With that she vanished, leaving the young man in such a confusion of mind as words would ill describe. He was angry, humiliated, vexed with himself, rapt into a kind of ecstasy. He did not know if he was most wretched or happy. Every thing forbade him saying another word to her; and yet had not her father brought him, as she said? was not she herself surrounding him with subtle sweet temptation? He threw himself down in a chair and tried to think. When that would not do, he got up and began to pace about the room. Then he rushed suddenly to the door, not to fly away from the place, or to throw himself at Sara's feet, as might have been supposed. What he did was to make a wild dash at his traveling-bag, which had been packed and brought into the hall. It was still standing there, a monument of his irresolution. He plunged at it, seized it, carried it into the library, and there unpacked it again with nervous vehemence. Any one who should have come in and seen his collars and handkerchiefs scattered about on the floor would have thought Powys mad. But at length, when he had got to the bottom of the receptacle, his object became apparent. From thence he produced a bundle of papers, yellow and worn, and tied up with a ribbon. When he had disinterred them, it was not without a blush, though there was nobody to see, that he packed up every thing again in the capacious traveling-bag. He had gone into Mr. Brownlow's library because Sara took him there, without a thought of any thing to do, but suddenly here was his work ready for him. He sat down in Mr. Brownlow's chair, and opened out the papers before him, and read and arranged and laid them out in order. When he had settled them according to his satisfaction, he made another pause to think, and then began to write. It was a letter which demanded thought; or at least it appeared so, for he wrote it hotly three times over, and tore it up each time; and on the fourth occasion, which was the last, wrote slowly, pausing over his sentences and biting his nails. The letter which cost all this trouble was not very long. Judging by the size of it, any body might have written it in five minutes; but Powys felt his hand trembling and his brain throbbing with the exertion when he had done. Then he folded it up carefully and put it into an envelope, and addressed it to Mr. Brownlow, leaving it with the bundle of papers on his employer's writing-table. When he had accomplished this he sat for some time irresolute, contemplating his packet on the table, and pondering what should follow. He had put it to the touch to win or lose, but in the mean time what was he to do? She had said he would find them up stairs. She had implied that he would be expected there; and to spend the day beside her would have been a kind of heaven to him; but that was a paradise which he had himself forfeited. He could not be in her company now as any other man might. He had said too much, had committed himself too deeply. He had betrayed the secret which another man more reticent might have kept, undisclosed in words, and it was impossible for him to be with her as another might. Even she, though she had never said a word to him that could be construed into encouragement, except those half dozen words at the library door, was different toward him and other men. She was conscious too; she remembered what he had said. He and she could not be together without remembering it, without carrying on, articulately or inarticulately, that broken interview. Powys did the only thing that remained to him to do. He did not bound forth in the track of the dog-cart, and follow it to Masterton, though that would not have been difficult to him; but he went out into the park, and roamed all about the house in widening circles, hearing sometimes the crack of the guns in the distance, sometimes in alleys close at hand the sound of voices, sometimes catching, as he thought, the very rustle of Sara's dress. He avoided them with much care and pains, and yet he would have been glad to meet them; glad to come upon the shooting-party, though he kept far from the spot where he had heard they were to meet some of the ladies and lunch. It was not for him to seek a place among them. Thus he wandered about, not feeling forlorn or disconsolate, as a man might be supposed to do under such circumstances, but, on the contrary, excited and hopeful. He had set forth what he felt was his best claim to consideration before her father. If Mr. Brownlow had not treated him with such inconceivable favor and indulgence, he never would have ventured upon this. But he had been favored,—he had been encouraged. Grace had been shown to him enough to turn any young man's head, and he knew no reason for it. And at last he had ventured to lay before Mr. Brownlow those distant problematical claims to gentility which were all the inheritance he had, and to tell him what was in his mind. He was not a victim kept out of Paradise. He was a pilgrim of hope, keeping the gates in sight, and feeling, permitting himself to feel, as if they might open any moment and he might be called in.

While this was going on it happened to him, as it happens so often, to come direct in the way of the very meeting which he had so carefully avoided. Turning round the corner of a great old yew, hanging rich with scarlet berries, he came all of a sudden, and without any warning, upon Sara herself, walking quickly from the village with a little basket in her hand. If it was difficult to meet her with a body-guard of ladies in the shelter of her father's house, it may be supposed what it was to meet her in the silence, without another soul in sight, her face flaming with sudden recognition and confusion. Powys stood still, and for a moment speculated whether he should not fly; but it was only that moment of consideration that fled, and he found himself turning by her side, and taking her basket from her hand. She was no more mistress of the situation than he was: she was taken by surprise. The calm with which she had led the way into the library that morning, secure in her office of mistress of the house, had vanished away. She began hurriedly, eagerly, to say where she had been, and how it happened that she was returning alone. "The rest went off to the rectory," she said. "Have you seen it? I think it is such a pretty house. They went to see Fanny Hardcastle. You have met her—I know you have, or I would not have mentioned her," said Sara, with a breathless desire to hear her own voice, which was unlike her. The sound of it gave her a little courage, and perhaps if she spoke a little loud and fast, it might attract some stray member of the party who might be wandering near. But no one came; and there were the two together, alone, in the position of all others most difficult in the circumstances—the green, silent park around them, not an eye to see nor an ear to hear; the red October sunshine slanting across their young figures, catching the ripple in Sara's hair as it had done that day, never to be forgotten, on which he first saw her. This was how fate or fortune, or some good angel or some wicked fairy, defeated Powys's prudent intention of keeping out of harm's way.

"But I wonder you did not go with Jack," Sara resumed. "I should, if I had been you. Not that I should care to kill the poor birds—but it seems to come natural at this time of the year. Did you have much sport in Canada? or do you think it stupid when people talk to you of Canada? Every body does, I know, as soon as they hear you have been there."

"You never could say any thing that was stupid," said Powys, and then he paused, for he did not mean to get upon dangerous ground—honestly, he did not mean it, if circumstances had not been too strong for him. "Canada is a kind of common ground," he said. "It is a good thing to begin conversation on. It is not easy to exhaust it; but people are sadly ignorant," he added, with lively colonial feeling. He was scornful, in short, of the ignorance he met with. Even Mr. Brownlow talked, he could not but recollect, like a charity-school boy on this subject, and he took refuge in his nationality as a kind of safeguard.

"Yes, I know I am very ignorant," said Sara, with humility. "Tell me about Canada. I should like to learn."

These words shook Powys sadly. It did not occur to him that she was as glad as he was to plunge into a foreign subject. There sounded something soft and confiding in the tone, and his heart gave a leap, as it were, toward her. "And I should like to teach you," he said, a little too warmly, and then stopped short, and then began hastily again. "Miss Brownlow, I think I will carry your basket home and leave you by yourself. I can not be near without remembering things, and saying things. Don't despise me—I could nor bear to think you despised me." He said this with growing agitation, but he did not quicken his steps or make any attempt to leave her; he only looked at her piteously, clasping the slender handle of her little basket in both his hands.

"Why should I despise you, Mr. Powys? I don't like Americans," said Sara, demurely; "but you are not American—you are English, like all the rest of us. Tell me about Niagara and the Indians, and the backwoods and the skating and the snow. You see I am not quite so ignorant. And then your little sisters and your mother, do they like being at home? Tell me their names and how old they are," said Sara, herself becoming a little tremulous. "I am fond of little girls."

And then there ensued a breathless, tremendous pause. He would have fled if he could, but there was no possibility of flight; and in a moment there flashed before him all the evidences of Mr. Brownlow's favor. Would he refuse him this supreme gift and blessing? Why had he brought him here if he would refuse him? Thus Powys broke down again, and finally. He poured out his heart, giving up all attempt at self-control when the tide had set in. He told how he had been keeping out of the way—the way of temptation. He described to her how he had been trying to command himself. He told her the ground she trod on was fairy-land: the air she breathed musical and celestial; the place she lived in, paradise; that he hoped nothing, asked for nothing, but only to be allowed to tell her that she was—not an angel—for he was too much in earnest to think of hackneyed expressions—but the only creature in the world for whom he had either eyes or thoughts. All this poured upon Sara as she walked softly, with downcast eyes, along the grassy path. It poured upon her, a perfect flood of adulation, sweet flattery, folly, and delirium—insane and yet quite true. And she listened, and had not a word to say. Indeed he did not ask for a word; he made her no petition; he emptied out his heart before her like a libation poured to the gods; and then suddenly became silent, tremulous, and hoarse as his passion worked itself out.

It was all so sudden, and the passion was so real, that they were both rapt by it, and went on in the silence after he had ceased, without knowing, until the impetus and rush of the outburst had in a measure worn out. Then Sara woke up. She had been quite quiet, pale, half frightened, wholly entranced. When she woke up she grew scarlet with sudden blushes; and they both raised their eyes at the same moment and found that, unawares, they had come in sight of the house. Powys fell back at the sight with a pang of dismay and consternation; but it gave Sara courage. They were no longer entirely alone, and she regained her self-command.

"Mr. Powys," she said, tremulously, "I don't know what to say to you. I am not so good as that. I—I don't know what to say. You have not asked me any thing. I—I have no answer to give."

"It is because I want to ask every thing," said poor Powys; "but I know—I know you can have nothing to say."

"Not now," said Sara, under her breath; and then she held out her hand suddenly, perhaps only for her basket. There was nobody at the windows, heaven be praised, as she afterward said to herself, but not until she had rushed up to her own room and pulled off that glove, and looked at it with scarlet cheeks, and put it stealthily away. No, thank heaven! even Angelique was at the other side of the house at a window which looked out upon the innocent shrubberies. Only the placid, silent house, blank and vacant, had been the witness. Was it a seal of any thing, a pledge of any thing, or only a vague touch, for which she was not responsible, that had fallen upon Sara's glove?

Mr. Brownlow had gone away, his heart positively aching with expectation and anxiety. He did not know what might happen while he was gone. It might be more than life or death to him, as much more as honor or dishonor go beyond mere life and death; and yet he could not stay and watch. He had to nerve himself to that last heroism of letting every thing take its chance, and going on with his work whatever happened. He went to the office with his mind racked by this anxiety, and got through his work all the same, nobody being the wiser. As he returned, a little incident for the moment diverted him from his own thoughts. This was the sight of the carrier's cart standing at Mrs. Swayne's door, and Mrs. Swayne's lodger in the act of mounting into it with the assistance of a chair. Mr. Brownlow, as he passed in the dog-cart, could not but notice this. He could not but observe how pale and ill she looked. He was interested in them partly with that displeased and repellent interest excited by Jack's "entanglement," partly because of Pamela's face, which reminded him of something, and partly—he could not tell why. Mrs. Preston stumbled a little as she mounted up, and Mr. Brownlow, who was waiting for old Betty to open the gate, sprang down from the dog-cart, being still almost as active as ever, and went across the road to assist. He took off his hat to her with the courtesy which all his family possessed, and asked if she was going away. "You do not look well enough to be setting out on a journey," he said, a little moved by the sight of the pale old woman mounting into that uneasy conveyance. "I hope you are not going alone." This he said, although he could see she was going alone, and that poor little Pamela's eyes were big with complaint and reproach and trouble. Somehow he felt as if he should like to take the little creature home with him, and pet and cherish her, though, of course, as the cause of Jack's entanglement, nothing should have made him notice her at all.

But Mrs. Preston looked at him fiercely with her kindled eyes, and rejected his aid. "Thank you," she said abruptly, "I don't want any help—thank you. I am quite able to travel, and I prefer to be alone."

"In that case, there is nothing farther to say," said Mr. Brownlow, politely; and then his heart melted because of little Pamela, and he added, almost in spite of himself, "I hope you are not going away."

"Only to come back," said Mrs. Preston, significantly—"only to come back; and, Mr. Brownlow, I am glad to have a chance of telling you that we shall meet again."

"It will give me much pleasure, I am sure," he said, taking off his hat, but he stared, as Pamela perceived. Meet again! what had he to do with the woman? He was surprised, and yet he could have laughed. As if he should care for meeting her! And then he went away, followed by her fierce look, and walked up the avenue, dismissing the dog-cart. The act might make him a little late for dinner, but on the whole he was glad to be late. At least there could be no confidences made to him before he had been refreshed with food and wine, and he wanted all the strength that could be procured in that or any other way. Thus it was that he had not time to go into the library before dinner, but went up stairs at once and dressed, and down stairs at once into the drawing-room, looking at Sara and at his young guest with an eye whose keenness baffled itself. There was something new in their faces, but he could not tell what it was; he saw a certain gleam of something that had passed, but it was not distinct enough to explain itself, not having been, as will be perceived, distinct at all, at least on the more important side. He kept looking at them, but their faces conveyed no real information, and he could not take his child aside and ask her what it was, as her mother might have done. Accordingly after dinner, instead of going up to the drawing-room and perplexing himself still farther with anxious looks, he went into the library. The suspense had to be borne whether he liked it or not, and he was not a man to make any grievance about it. The smile which he had been wearing in deference to the usages of society faded from his face when he entered that sheltering place. His countenance fell into the haggard lines which Powys had not observed in the morning. A superficial spectator would have supposed that now he was alone his distresses had come back to him; but on the contrary his worn and weary look was not an evidence of increased pain—it was a sign of ease and rest. There he did not need to conceal the anxiety which was racking him. In this state of mind, letting himself go, as it were, taking off the restraints which had been binding him, he went into the library, and found Powys's letter, and the bundle of papers that were put up with it, placed carefully on his table before his chair.

The sight gave him a shock which, being all alone and at his ease, he did not attempt to conceal. The light seemed to go out of his eyes, his lip drooped a little, a horrible gleam of suffering went over his face: now no doubt the moment had come. He even hesitated and went away to the other extremity of the room, and turned his back upon the evidence which was to seal his fate. Then it occurred to him how simple-minded the young fellow was—to thrust his evidences thus, as it were, into the hands of the man whose interest it was to destroy them!—and a certain softening came over him, a thrill of kindness, almost of positive affection for the youth who was going to ruin him. Poor fellow!—he would be sorry—and then Sara would still have it, and he would be good to her. Mr. Brownlow's mind was in this incoherent state when he came back to the table, and, steeling himself for the effort, sat down before the fated papers. He undid the ribbon with trembling hands. Powys's letter was written on his own paper, with "Brownlows" on it in fantastic Gothic letters, according to Sara's will and pleasure; and a thrill of anger shot over him as he perceived this. Strange that as he approached the very climax of his fate he should be able to be moved by such troubles! Then Mr. Brownlow opened the letter. It was very short, as has been said, and this was the communication which had cost the young man so much toil:

"DEAR SIR—It seems strange to write to you thus calmly, at your own table, on your own paper ["Ah! then he felt that!" Mr. Brownlow said to himself], and to say what I am going to say. You have brought me here notwithstanding what I told you, but the time is past when I could come and be like any common acquaintance. I wanted to leave to-day to save my honesty while I could, but you would not let me. I can not be under the same roof with Miss Brownlow, and see her daily, and behave like a stock or stone. I have no right to address her, but she knows, and I can not help myself. I want to lay before you the only claim I have to be looked upon as any thing more than your clerk. It was my hope to work into a higher position by my own exertions, and then to find it out. But in case it should count for any thing with you, I put it before you now. It could not make me her equal; but if by any wonderful chance that should seem possible in your eyes, which to mine seems but the wildest yet dearest dream, I want you to know that perhaps if it could be traced out we are a little less lowly than we seem.

"I enclose my father's papers, which we have always kept with great care. He took care of them himself, and told me before he died that I ought to find my fortune in them. I never had much hope of that, but I send them to you, for they are all I have. I do not ask you to accept of me, to give me your daughter. I know it looks like insanity. I feel it is insane. But you have been either very, very kind or very cruel to me. You have brought me here—you have made it life or death to me. She has every thing that heart of man can desire. I have—what poor hope there may be in these papers. For God's sake look at them, and look at me, and tell me if I am mad to hope. Tell me to go or stay, and I will obey you—but let it be clear and definitive, for mercy's sake.

"C. I. POWYS."

Mr. Brownlow was touched by the letter. He was touched by its earnestness, and he was also touched by its simplicity. He was in so strange a mood that it brought even the moisture to his eye. "To have every thing I possess in the world in his power, and yet to write like this," he said to himself, and drew a long sigh, which was as much relief as apprehension. "She will still have it all, and he deserves to have her," Mr. Brownlow thought to himself; and opened up the yellow papers with a strange mixture of pain and satisfaction which even he could not understand.

He was a long time over them. They were letters chiefly, and they took a great many things for granted of which Mr. Brownlow was completely ignorant, and referred to many events altogether unknown to him. He was first puzzled, then almost disappointed, then angry. It seemed like trifling with him. These could not be the papers Powys meant to enclose. There were letters from some distressed mother to a son who had made a foolish marriage, and there were letters from the son, pleading that love might still be left to him, if not any thing else, and that no evil impression might be formed of his Mary. Who was his Mary? Who was the writer? What had he to do with Brownlows and Sara and Phœbe Thomson's fortune? For a long time Mr. Brownlow toiled on, hoping to come to something which bore upon his own case. The foregone conclusion was so strong in his mind, that he grew angry as he proceeded, and found his search in vain. Powys was trifling with him, putting him off—thrusting this utterly unimportant correspondence into his hands, instead of confiding, as he had thought, his true proofs to him. This distrust, as Mr. Brownlow imagined it, irritated him in the most curious way. Ask his advice, and not intrust him with the true documents that proved the case! Play with his good sense, and doubt his integrity! It wounded him with a certain keen professional sting. He had worked himself up to the point of defrauding the just heir; but to suspect that the papers would not be safe in his hands was a suggestion that cut him to the heart. He was very angry, and he had so far forgotten the progress of time that, when he rang sharply to summon some one, the bell rang through all the hushed echoes of the house, and a servant—half asleep, and considerably frightened—came gaping, after a long interval, to the library door.

"Where is Mr. Powys?" said Mr. Brownlow. "If he is in the drawing-room give him my compliments, and ask him to be so good as to step down here for a few minutes to me."

"Mr. Powys, sir?" said the man—"the gentleman as came yesterday, sir? The drawing-room is all shut up, sir, long ago. The ladies is gone to bed, but some of the gentlemen is in the smoking-room, and I can see if he's there."

"Gone to bed!" said Mr. Brownlow; "why were they in such a hurry?" and then he looked at his watch and found, to his great surprise, that it was past midnight. A vague wonder struck him once again whether his mind could be getting impaired. The suggestion was like a passing stab in the dark dealt him by an unseen enemy. He kept staring at the astonished servant, and then he continued sharply, "Go and see if he is in the smoking-room, or if not, in his own room. Ask him to come to me."

Powys had gone up stairs late, and was sitting thinking, unable to rest. He had been near her the whole evening, and though they had not exchanged many words, there had been a certain sense between them that they were not as the others were. Once or twice their eyes had met, and fallen beneath each other's glance. It was nothing, and yet it was sweeter than any thing certain and definite. And now he sat and thought. The night had crept on, and had become chilly and ghostly, and his mind was in a state of strange excitement. What was to come of it all? What could come of it? When the servant came to his door at that late hour, the young man started with a thrill of apprehension, and followed him down stairs almost trembling, feeling his heart sink within him; for so late and so peremptory a summons seemed an omen of evil. Mr. Brownlow had collected himself before Powys came into the room, and received him with an apology. "I am sorry to disturb you so late. I was not aware it was so late; but I want to understand this—" he said; and then he waited till the servant had left the room, and pointed to a chair on the other side of the table. "Sit down," he said, "and tell me what this means."

"What it means?" said Powys taken by surprise.

"Yes, sir, what it means," said Mr. Brownlow, hoarsely. "I may guess what your case is; but you must know that these are not the papers to support it. Who is the writer of these letters? who is the Mary he talks of? and what has it all to do with you?"

"It has every thing to do with me," said Powys. "The letters were written by my father—the Mary he speaks of is my mother—"

"Your mother?" said Mr. Brownlow, with a sharp exclamation, which sounded like an oath to the young man's astonished ears; and then he thrust the papers away with trembling hands, and folded his arms on the table, and looked intently into Powys's face. "What was your mother's name?"

"My mother's name was Mary Christian," said Powys, wondering; "but the point is—Good heavens! what is the matter? what do you mean?"

His surprise was reasonable enough. Mr. Brownlow had sprung to his feet; he had dashed his two clenched hands through the air, and said, "Impostor!" through his teeth. That was the word—there could be no mistake about it—"Impostor!" upon which Powys too jumped up, and faced him with an expression wavering between resentment and surprise, repeating more loudly in his consternation, "What do you mean?"

But the young man could only stand and look on with increasing wonder when he saw Mr. Brownlow sink into his chair, and bury his face in his hands, and tremble like a palsied old man. Something like a sob even came from his breast. The relief was so amazing, so unlooked for, that at the first touch it was pain. But Powys, standing by, knew nothing of all this. He stood, not knowing whether to be offended, hesitating, looking for some explanation; and no doubt the time seemed longer to him than it really was. When Mr. Brownlow raised his head his face was perfectly colorless, like the face of a man who had passed through some dreadful experiment. He waved his hand to his young companion, and it was a minute before he could speak.

"I beg your pardon," he said. "It is all a mistake—an entire mistake, on my part. I did not know what I was saying. It was a sudden pain. But never mind, I am better. What did you mean me to learn from these papers?" he added, after a pause, with a forced smile.

Then Powys knew his fate. There was a change which could not be described. In an instant, tone, look, manner, every thing was altered. It was his master who said these last words to him; his employer, very kind and just, but unapproachable as a king. One moment before, and Mr. Brownlow had been in his power, he did not know how or why; and in an instant, still without his knowing wherefore, his power had totally departed. Powys saw this in all the darkness of utter ignorance. His consternation was profound and his confusion. In a moment his own presumption, his own hopelessness, the misery of loss and disappointment, overwhelmed him, and yet not a word bearing upon the real matter at issue had been said.

"They are my father's papers," said poor Powys. "I thought—that is, I supposed—I hoped there might be some indication in them—I am sorry if I have troubled you unnecessarily. He belonged to a good family, and I imagined I might perhaps have reclaimed—but it doesn't matter. If that is what you think—"

"Oh yes, I see," said Mr. Brownlow; "you can leave them, and perhaps another time—But in the mean time, if you feel inclined, my groom can drive you down to-morrow morning. I am not sure that I shall be going myself; and I will not detain you any longer to-night."

"Very well, sir," said Powys. He stood for a moment looking for something more—for some possible softening; but not one word of kindness came except an abrupt good-night. Good-night—yes, good-night to every thing—hope, love, happiness, fortune. Farewell to them all; and Sara, she who had almost seemed to belong to him. It seemed to Powys as if he was walking on his own heart as he left the room, trampling on it, stamping it down, crying fool, fool! Poor fellow, no doubt he had been a fool; but it was a hard awakening, and the fault, after all, was not his own.

Mr. Brownlow, however, was too much occupied with his own deliverance to think of Powys. He said that new name over to himself again and again, to realize what had happened. Mary Christian—Mary Christian—surely he had heard it before; but so long as it was not Phœbe Thomson, what did it matter who was his mother? Not Phœbe Thomson. She was dead perhaps—dead, and in a day or two more it would not matter. Two days, that was all—for it was now October. She might turn up a week hence if she would; but now he was free—free, quite free; without any wrong-doing or harm to any body; Brownlows and every thing else his own. Could it be true? Mary Christian—that was the name. And she came from the Isle of Man. But there was plenty of time to inquire into all that. The thing in the mean time was that he was released. When he got up and roused himself he found he could scarcely stand. He had been steady enough during all the time of his trial; but the sudden relief took all his forces from him. He shook from head to foot, and had to hold by the tables and chairs as he went out. And he left the lamp burning in forlorn dreariness on the library-table. The exertion of walking up stairs was almost too much for him. He had no attention to give to the common things surrounding him. All his powers, all his senses were absorbed in the one sensation of being free. Only once as he went up stairs did his ordinary faculties return to him, as it were, for a moment. It was when he was passing the great window in the staircase, and glancing out saw the white moonlight glimmering over all the park, and felt the cold of the night. Then it occurred to him to wonder if the pale old woman whom he had seen getting into the carrier's cart could be traveling through this cold night. Poor old soul! He could not but think for the moment how chilly and frozen it would be. And then he bethought himself that he was safe, might go where he liked, do what he liked, had nobody menacing him, no enemy looking on to watch an opportunity—and no harm done! Thus Mr. Brownlow paused in the weakness of deliverance, and his heart melted within him. He made not vows to the saints of new churches or big tapers, but secret, tender resolutions in his heart. For this awful danger escaped, how should he show his gratitude to God? He was himself delivered, and goodness seemed to come back to him, his natural impulse. He had been saved from doing wrong, and without doing wrong all he wanted had been secured to him. What reason had not he to be good to every body; to praise God by serving his neighbor? This was the offering of thanksgiving he proposed to render. He did not at the moment think of young Powys sitting at his window looking out on the same moonlight, very dumb and motionless and heart-stricken, thinking life henceforward a dreary desert. No harm was done, and Mr. Brownlow was glad. But it did not occur to him to offer any healing in Powys's case. If there was to be a victim at all, it was best that he should be the victim. Had he not brought it on himself?

CHAPTER XXXV

AN UNLOOKED-FOR VISITOR

Powys was proud, and his pride was up in arms. He slept little that night, and while he sat and brooded over it all, the hopelessness and folly of his hope struck him with tenfold distinctness. Early next morning, before any one was up, he came down the great silent staircase, and left the house in the morning sunshine. The distance to Masterton was nothing to him. It was the second time he had left the house with despair in his heart. It would be the last time, he said to himself as he paused to look up at the closed windows; he would never suffer himself to be deluded—never be led away by deceptive hopes again; and he went away, not without bitterness, yet with a certain stern sense of the inevitable which calmed down his passion. Whenever he had been in his right senses, he had felt that this must be the end; and the thing for him now was to bear it with such courage and steadiness as he could muster to face the emergency. It was all over at least. There were no intermediary tortures to go through, and there was always some comfort in that.

His absence was not taken any notice of at the breakfast-table, though Sara gave many a wondering glance at the door, and had a puzzled, half-irritated look upon her face, which some of her friends perceived, though her father did not observe it. He, for his part, came down radiant. He looked weary, and explained that he had not slept very well; but he had never been in more genial spirits, never more affectionate or full of schemes for every body's pleasure. He called Jack apart, to tell him that, after looking over matters, he found he could let him have the hunter he wanted, a horse upon which his heart was set. When they were all talking at the table in the usual morning flutter of letters and mutual bits of news, Mr. Brownlow intimated that he had thoughts of taking Sara to Italy, where she had so long desired to go; "making up a party, and enjoying ourselves," he said. Sara looked up with a gleam of delight, but her eyes were immediately after diverted to the door, where somebody was coming in—somebody, but not the person she was looking for. As for Jack, he received the intimation of his father's liberality in perplexed silence; for if he was to marry, and sink into the position of a clerk in Masterton, hunters would be little in his way. But their father was too much absorbed in his own satisfaction to remark particularly how they both took his proposed kindness. He was overflowing to every body. Though he was always kind, that morning he was kinder than ever; and the whole party brightened up under his influence, notwithstanding Jack's perplexity, and Sara's wondering impatient glances at the door. Nobody asked what had become of the stranger. Mr. Brownlow's guests were free to come to breakfast when they liked, and no notice was taken of the defaulters. The meal, however, was so merry and friendly, that every body sat longer over it than usual. Several of the visitors were going away, and the sportsmen had laid aside their guns for the day to join the ladies in an excursion. There was plenty of time for every thing; pleasant bustle, pleasant idleness, no "wretched business," as Sara said, to quicken their steps; and she was, perhaps, the only one in the party who was ill at ease. She could not make out how it was that Powys did not come. She sat and joined with forced gayety in the general conversation, and she had not courage to ask frankly what had become of him. When they all began at last to disperse from the table, she made one feeble effort to satisfy herself. "Mr. Powys has never come down to breakfast," she said to Jack, avoiding his eye; "had not you better see if there is any reason?"

"If he is ill, perhaps, poor dear?" said Jack, with scorn. "Don't be afraid—probably he went out early; he is not the sort of fellow to fall ill."

"Probably some of you have insulted him!" said Sara, hotly, under her breath; but either Jack did not or would not hear. And she could not trust herself to look up in the face of the assembled company and ask. So she had to get up with all the rest, and go reluctantly away from the table, with a certain sense of impending misfortune upon her. A few minutes after, when she was sent for to go to her father in the library, Sara's courage failed her altogether. She felt he must have something important to say to her, something that could not be postponed. And her heart beat loudly as she went to him. When she entered the room Mr. Brownlow came forward to meet her. It struck her for the first time as he advanced that his face had changed; something that had been weighing upon him had passed away. The lines of his mouth had relaxed and softened; he was like what he used to be. It was almost the first time she fully realized that for some time past he had not been like himself. He came forward, and before she had fully mastered her first impression, took her into his arms.

"My dear child," he said, "I have sent for you to tell you that a great burden that has been upon my mind for some time has just been taken off. You have been very good to me, Sara, very patient and obedient and sweet; and though I never told you about it in so many words, I want you to be the first to know that it has passed away."

"Thank you, papa," said Sara, looking wistfully in his face. "I am sure I am very glad, though I don't know what you mean. Is it any thing about—? Am I to know what it was?" And she stopped, standing so close with his arm round her, and gave him an appealing look—a look that asked far more than her words—that seemed even to see into him, and divine; but that could not be.

"It is not worth while now," he said, smoothing her hair with his hand. "It is all over; and, my darling, I want you to know also that I set you free."

"Set me free?" said Sara, in a whisper; and in spite of herself she turned very pale.

"Yes, Sara, quite free. I ask no sacrifice of you now," said Mr. Brownlow, pressing her close with his arm. "Forgive me that I ever thought of it. Even at the worst, you know I told you to consult your own heart; and now you are free, quite free. All that is at an end."

"All what?" asked Sara, under her breath; and she turned her head away from him, resisting the effort he made to look at her. "What is it you set me free from?" she continued, in a petulant tone. "If you don't tell me in words, how am I to know?"

Mr. Brownlow was startled and checked in his effusiveness, but he could not be angry with her at such a moment. "Hush," he said, still smoothing her pretty hair, "we have never had many words about it. It is all at an end. I thought it would be a relief to you to hear."

"To hear what?" cried the girl, sharply, with her head averted; and then, to her father's utter consternation, she withdrew as far as she could from his arm, and suddenly burst into tears.

Mr. Brownlow was totally taken by surprise. He had not been able to read what was going on in his daughter's heart. He could not believe now that she understood him. He put his hand upon her arm and drew her back. "You mistake me, my darling," he said; "I mean that you are quite free, Sara—quite free. It was wrong of me to ask any promise from you, and it was foolish of you to give it. But Providence, thank God, has settled that. It is all over. There is no more necessity. Can't you forgive me? You have not suffered so much from it as I have done. Before I could have come to the point of sacrificing you—"

"Sacrificing me!" cried Sara, suddenly, flashing back upon him in a storm of passion and indignation, her cheeks scorching yet wet with tears, her big eyes swimming. "Is that all you think of? You had a right to sacrifice me if you liked—nobody would have said a word. They did it in the Bible. You might have cut me into little pieces if you liked. But oh, what right had you, how dared you to make a sacrifice of him?"

"Him!" cried Mr. Brownlow, and he took a step back in consternation and gazed at his child, who was transfigured, and a different creature. Her cheeks blazed under her tears, but she did not shrink. Weeping, blushing, wounded, ashamed, she still confronted him in the strength of some new feeling of which he had never dreamed.

"You never say a word about him!" cried Sara. "You speak of me, and you had a right to do whatever you like with me; but it is him whom you have sacrificed. He never would have thought of it but for you. He never would have come back after that time but for you. And then you expect me to think only of myself, and to be glad when you say I am free! How can I be free? I led him on and made him speak when he knew better. Oh, papa, you are cruel, cruel! He was doing you no harm, and you have made him wretched; and now you think it doesn't matter; but that is not the way with me!"

"Sara, are you mad?" cried Mr. Brownlow in his dismay; but Sara made him no answer. She sat down on the nearest chair, and turning round away from him, leaned her arms on the back of it, and put down her head on her arms. He could see that she was crying, but that was all; and nothing he could say, neither consolations, nor excuses, nor reproofs, would induce her to raise her head. It was the first quarrel she had ever had with the father who had been father and mother both to her; and the acuteness of her first disappointment, the first cross in her pleasant life, the unexpected humiliating end of her first dreams, roused a wild rebellion in her heart. She was wroth, and her heart was sore, and outraged. When he was called away by Willis about some business, he left her there, still twisted round upon her chair, with her face upon her folded arms, spending her very soul in tears. But the moment he was gone she sprang up and fled to the shelter of her own room. "They shall find that it is not the way with me!" she said to herself, and gave herself up willfully to thoughts of the banished lover who had been treated so cruelly. On that day at least, Sara avenged poor Powys's wrongs upon the company in general. She had a headache, and could not join in their excursion. And her eyes were still red with crying when next she was seen down stairs. Mr. Brownlow tried to persuade himself it was too violent to last, and thought it prudent to take no more notice, but was very obsequious and conciliatory all the evening to his naughty child. Even when it was thus brought before him, he did not make much account of the sacrifice of Powys. And he thought Sara would come round and see things by and by in their true light. But all the same the shock had a great effect upon him, and damped him strangely in the first effusion of his joy.

But he was kind, kinder to every body in his gratitude to Providence. Except that he had no pity for Powys, who seemed to him to have been all this time a kind of impostor, his good fortune softened his heart to every other creature. When he met Pamela on the road, though Pamela was the one other individual in the world with whom Jack's father was not in perfect charity, he yet stopped kindly to speak to her. "I hope your mother has not gone upon a long journey. I hope she is coming back," he said in a fatherly way. "She should not have left you by yourself alone."

"It was on business," said Pamela, not daring to lift her eyes. "She said she would be soon back."

"Then you must take great care of yourself while she is away," Mr. Brownlow said, and took off his hat as he left her, with the courtesy which was natural to him. He was so kind to every body, and that day in particular he looked after the pretty creature with a pang of compunction. He did not care much for Powys, but he was sorry for Pamela. "Poor little thing!" he said to himself—for while he said it he thought of launching Jack, as it was Jack's ambition to be launched, upon public life, getting him into the House of Commons, sending him out to the world, where he would soon forget his humble little love. Mr. Brownlow felt that this was what would happen, and his heart for the moment ached over poor Pamela. She was so pretty, and soft, and young, and then she reminded him—though of whom he could not quite say.

Thus the day went on; and the next day Mr. Brownlow went to the office, where every thing was as usual. He saw by his first glance that Powys was at his desk, and he was pleased, though he took no notice. Perhaps a certain unacknowledged compunction, after all, was in his mind. He even sent for Mr. Wrinkell and consulted him as to the fitness of the junior clerk for a more responsible post. Mr. Wrinkell was a cautious man, but he could not conceal a certain favoritism. "Ever since that first little cloud that passed over him, he has been worth any two in the office," he said—"any two, sir; but I don't think he is happy in his mind."

"Not happy?" said Mr. Brownlow; "but you know, Wrinkell, we can not be expected to remedy that."

"No, of course not," said Mr. Wrinkell; "it may be only seriousness, and then it will be all the better for him; but if it is not that, it is something that has gone wrong. At his age a cross in some fancy is enough sometimes—not that I have any ground for saying so; but still I think sometimes when I look at him that some little affair of that description may have gone wrong."

"It is possible enough," said Mr. Brownlow, with a smile, which was somewhat grim; "fortunately that sort of thing don't kill."

"N-no," said Mr. Wrinkell, gravely; but he did not say anymore, and his employer did not feel more comfortable after he was gone; and Powys was promoted accordingly, and did his business with a certain sternness, never moving, never looking round when Mr. Brownlow came into the office, taking no notice of him; till the lawyer, who had come to have a certain fondness for the young man, felt hurt and vexed, he could not have told why. He was glad to see him there—glad he was too manful and stouthearted to have disappeared and abandoned his work; but he would have felt grateful and indebted to him had he once raised his head and seemed conscious of his presence. Powys, however, was no more than human, and there was a limit to his powers. He was busy with his work, but yet the sense of his grievance was full in his mind. He was saying to himself, with less vehemence but more steadiness, what Sara had said. He never would have thought of it but for Mr. Brownlow—never would have gone back after that time but for him; and his heart was sore, and he could not forgive him like a Christian—not the first day.

However they had a cheerful evening at Brownlows that night. There were more reasons than one why it should be a night of triumph for the master of the house. His terrors had all died out of his mind. The cloud that had so long overshadowed him had vanished, and it was the last day! Nobody knew it but himself; doubtless nobody was thinking of any special crisis. Mr. Brownlow went, he scarcely knew from what feeling, in a kind of half-conscious bravado, to see old Mrs. Fennell, and found her still raving of something which seemed to him no longer alarming, but the merest idiocy. He was so genial and charitable that he even thought of Nancy and her troubles, and told her she must get a nurse to help her, and then she could be free to go and see her friends. "For I think you told me you had some friends," Mr. Brownlow said, with an amiability that cowed Nancy, and made her tremble. Nancy Christian! When he heard her mistress call her, he suddenly recollected the other name which he had seen so lately, and came back to ask her about a Mary Christian of the Isle of Man, and got certain particulars which were startling to him. Nancy could tell him who she was. She was a farmer's daughter related to the Fennells, and had married "a gentleman's son." The information gave Mr. Brownlow a curious shock, but he was a good deal exhausted with various emotions, and did not feel that much. So he went home, carrying a present for Sara—a pretty locket—though she had too many of such trinkets already. He meant to tell her it was an anniversary, though not what anniversary it was. And he took his check-book and wrote a check for a large amount for the chief charities in Masterton, but did not tear it out, leaving it there locked up with the book till to-morrow, for it was late, and the banks were shut. If any poor supplicant had come to him that day with a petition, right or wrong its prayer would have been granted. Mr. Brownlow had received a great deliverance from God—so he phrased it—and it was but his simple duty to deliver others if possible in sign of his gratitude. All but young Powys, whom he had deluded, and who had deluded him; all but Phœbe Thomson, who was just about to be consigned to oblivion, and about whom and whose fortunes henceforward no soul would have any inducement to care.

Sara, too, had softened a little out of that first rebellion which Mr. Brownlow knew could not last. She was not particularly cordial to her father, but still she wore the locket he had given her in sign of amity, and exerted herself at dinner to amuse the guests. Fresh people had arrived that day, and the house was very full—so full, that Mr. Brownlow had no chance of a moment's conversation with his children, except by positively detaining them after every body was gone, as Jack had done on the night of Powys's arrival. He took this step, though it was a very decided one, for he felt it necessary that some clear understanding should be come to. And he had such bribes to offer them. After every body else had retired, Jack and Sara came to him in the library. This room, which a little while ago had been the least interesting in the house, was gradually collecting associations round it, and becoming the scene of all the most important incidents in this eventful period of the family life. Jack came in half careless, half anxious, thinking something might be about to be said about his personal affairs, yet feeling that his father had no particular right to interfere, and no power to decide. And Sara was sulky. It is an ugly word, but it was the actual state of the case. She was injured, and sore in her heart, and yet she was too young and too much accustomed to her own way to consider the matter desperate, or to have reached the dignity of despair. So she was only sullen, offended, disposed to make herself disagreeable. It was not a promising audience whom Mr. Brownlow thus received with smiles in his own room. It was only about eleven o'clock, his impatience having hastened the hour of general separation; and the young people were not perfectly pleased with that, any more than with his other arrangements. Both the lamps in the library were lighted, and there was a fire burning. The room, too, seemed to have brightened up. Mr. Brownlow put Sara into one of the big chairs, with a tenderness which almost overcame her, and himself took up an Englishman's favorite position on the hearth.

"I want to speak to you both," he said. He was eager, and yet there was a certain embarrassment in his tone. "This is an important night in my life. I can't enter into particulars—indeed there is no room for them—but I have been waiting for this night to speak seriously to you both. Jack, I doubt whether you will ever do much at the business. I should have liked, had you given your mind to it, to keep it up; for a business like mine is a capital backing to a fortune, and without it you can't hope to be rich—not rich beyond competence, you know. However, it does not seem to me, I confess, that business, of our kind at least, is your turn."

"I was not aware I had been unsatisfactory, sir," said Jack. "I don't think I have been doing worse than usual—"

"That is not what I mean," said Mr. Brownlow. "I mean you are better adapted for something else. I wrote to my old friend Lord Dewsbury about you to-day. If any thing should turn up in the way he once proposed, I should not mind releasing you altogether from the office—and increasing your allowance. It could not be a great deal, recollect; but still if that is what you would really give your mind to—I should see that you had enough to keep your place."

Jack's eyes had gradually brightened as his father proceeded. Now he made a step forward, and a gleam of delight came to his face. "Do you really mean it?" he cried; "it is awfully good of you. Of course I should give my mind to it. It is what I most care for in the world—except—the business—" Jack paused, and other things besides the business came into his mind. "If you are making a sacrifice to please me—" he began slowly.

"We have all to make sacrifices," said Mr. Brownlow. "A few days ago I thought I should have had to make a sacrifice of a very different kind. Providence has been good to me, and now I should like to do the best for my children. There are only two of you," said Mr. Brownlow, softening. "It would be hard if I did not do all I could to make the best of your lives."

And then there was a pause. He meant what he said, and he had always been a good father, and they loved him dearly. But at this moment, though he was offering to his son the realization of his dreams, they both distrusted him, and he felt it. They looked at him askance, these two young creatures who owed every thing to him. They were doubtful of his great offers. They thought he was attempting to bribe them, beguile them out of the desire of their hearts. And he stood looking at them, feeling in his own heart that he was not natural but plausible and conciliatory, thinking of their good, no doubt, but also of his own will. He felt this, but still he was angry that they should feel it. And it was with still more conscious embarrassment that he began again.

"The time has come in my own life when I am ready to make a change," he said. "I want a little rest. I want to go away and see you enjoy yourselves, and take a holiday before I die. I can afford it after working so long. I want to take you to Italy, my darling, where you have so long wanted to go; but I should like to establish things on a new footing first. I should make some arrangement about the business; unless, indeed, Jack has changed his ideas. Public life is very uncertain. If you think," said Mr. Brownlow, not without a certain tinge of derision in his tone, "that you would rather be Brownlow of Masterton, with a safe, long-established hereditary connection to fall back upon, it is not for me to precipitate your decision. You can take time and think over what I say."

"There is no occasion for taking time to think," said Jack, with a little irritation. But there he stopped. It was getting toward midnight; the house was quiet; everything was still, except the wind sighing outside among the falling leaves. Sara, who was the least occupied of the three, had thought she heard the sound of wheels in the avenue, but it was so unlikely at that time of the night that she concluded it must be only the wind. As they all stood there, however, silent, the quiet was suddenly broken. All at once, into the midst of their conversation, came the sound of the great house-bell, rung violently. It made them all start, so unexpected was the sound, and so perfect was the stillness. At that hour who could be coming to disturb them? The bell was unusually large and loud, and the sound of it echoing down into the bowels, as it were, of the silent house, was startling enough. And then there was the sound of a voice outside. The library was at the back of the house; but still, when their attention was thus violently aroused, they could hear that there was a voice. And the bell rang again loudly—imperiously—wildly. Jack was the first to move. "Willis must be asleep," he said. "But who on earth can it be?" and he hastened toward the door, to give the untimely visitor entrance. But his father called him back.

"I hear Willis moving," he said; "never mind. It must be somebody by the last train from town. Did you ask any one? There is just time to have driven over from the last train."

"It must be some telegram," said Jack. "I expect nobody this week," and they all stood and waited; Sara, too, having risen from her chair. The young people were a little disturbed, though they feared nothing; and Mr. Brownlow looked at them tenderly, like a man who had nothing to fear.

"Happily we are all here," he said. "If it is a telegram, it can only be about business." He stood leaning against the mantle-piece, with his eyes fixed on the door. There was a flutter at his heart somehow, but he did not feel that he was afraid. And they could hear Willis fumbling over the door, and an impatient voice outside. Whatever it was, it was very urgent, and Jack, growing anxious in spite of himself, would have gone to see. But again his father called him back. Something chill and terrible was stealing over Mr. Brownlow; he was growing pale—he was hoarse when he spoke. But he neither moved, nor would he let his son move, and stood propping himself up, with a livid countenance, and gazing at the door.

When it opened they all started, and Mr. Brownlow himself gave a hoarse cry. It was not a telegram, nor was it a stranger. It was a figure they were well used to see, and with which they had no tragic associations. She came in like a ghost, black, pale, and swift, in a passion of eagerness, with a large old silver watch in her hand. "I am not too late," she said, with a gasp, and held it up close to Mr. Brownlow's face. And then she stood still and looked at him, and he knew it all if she had not said, another word. It was Pamela's mother, the woman whom, two days before, he had helped into the carrier's cart at his own gate.

CHAPTER XXXVI

MOMENTARY MADNESS

It would be difficult to describe the looks of the assembled party in the library at Brownlows at this moment. Jack, to whom every thing was doubly complicated by the fact that the intruder was Pamela's mother, and by the feeling that his own affairs must be somehow in question, made a step forward, thinking that her business must be with him, and fell back in double consternation when she passed him, looking only at his father. Sara stood aghast, knowing nothing—not even aware that there could be any thing to be anxious about—an impersonation of mere wonder and surprise. The two elder people were not surprised. Both of them knew what it meant. Mr. Brownlow in a moment passed from the shock of horror and dismay which had prostrated him at first, into that perfect calm which is never consistent with ignorance or innocence. The wonder of his children would have convinced any observer of their perfect unacquaintance with the matter. But he knew all about it—he was perfectly composed and master of himself in a second. Life goes fast at such a crisis. He felt at once as if he had always known it was to end like this—always foreseen it—and had been gradually prepared and wound up by degrees to meet the blow. All his uncertainty and doubt and self-delusions vanished from him on the spot. He knew who his visitor was without any explanation, and that she had come just in time—and that it was all over. Somehow he seemed to cease on the moment to be the principal in the matter. By the time Mrs. Preston had come up to him, he had become a calm professional spectator, watching the case on behalf of a client. The change was curious to himself, though he had no time just then to consider how it came about.

But the intruder was not calm. On the contrary, she was struggling with intense excitement, panting, trembling, compelled to stop on her way across the room to put her hand to her side, and gasp for the half-stifled breath. She took no notice of the young people who stood by. It is doubtful even whether she was aware of their presence. She went up gasping to the man she thought her enemy. "I am in time," she said. "I have come to claim my mother's money—the money you have robbed us of. I am in time—I know I am just in time! I have been at Doctors' Commons; it's no use telling me lies. I know every thing. I've come for my mother's money—the money you've robbed from me and mine!"

Jack came forward bewildered by these extraordinary words. "This is frenzy," he said. "The Rector is right. She must be mad. Mrs. Preston, come and I'll take you home. Don't let us make any row about it. She is Pamela's mother. Let me take her quietly away."

"I might be mad," said the strange apparition, "if wrong could make a woman mad. Don't talk to me of Pamela. Sir, you understand it's you I come to—it's you! Give me my mother's money! I'll not go away from here till I have justice. I'll have you taken up for a robber! I'll have you put in prison! It's justice I want—and my rights."

"Be quiet, Jack," said Mr. Brownlow; "let her alone. Go away—that is the best service you can do me. Mrs. Preston, you must explain yourself. Who was your mother, and what do you want with me?"

Then she made a rush forward to him and clutched his arm. He was standing in his former position leaning against the mantle-piece, firm, upright, pale, a strong man still, and with his energies unbroken. She rushed at him, a tottering, agitated woman, old and weak and half-frantic with excitement. "Give me my mother's money!" she cried, and gasped and choked, her passion being too much for her. At this instant the clock struck: it was a silvery, soft-tongued clock, and made the slow beats of time thrill into the silence. Mr. Brownlow laughed when he heard it—laughed not with triumph, but with that sense of the utter futility of all calculations which sometimes comes upon the mind with a strange sense of the humor of it, at the most terrible crisis. Let it strike—what did it matter?—nothing now could deliver him from his fate.

"I take you to witness I was here and claimed my money before it struck," cried the woman. "I was here. You can't change that. You villain give me my mother's money! Give me my money: you've had it for five-and-twenty years!"

"Compose yourself," said Mr. Brownlow, speaking to her as he might have done had he been the professional adviser of the man who was involved; "sit down and take your time; you were here before twelve, you shall have all the benefit of that; now tell me what your name is, and what is your claim."

Mrs. Preston sat down as he told her, and glared at him with her wild bright eyes; but notwithstanding the overwrought condition in which she was, she could not but recognize the calm of the voice which addressed her: a certain shade of uncertainty flickered over her countenance—she grew confused in the midst of her assurance—it seemed impossible that he could take it so quietly if he knew what she meant. And then her bodily fatigue, sleeplessness, and exhaustion were beginning to tell.

"You are trying to cheat me," she said, with difficulty restraining the impulse of her weakness to cry. "You are trying to cheat me! you know it better than I do, and I read it with my own eyes: you have had it for five-and-twenty years: and you try to face it out and cheat me now!"

Then the outburst came which had been kept back so long; she had eaten nothing all day; she had not slept the previous night; she had been traveling and rushing about till the solid earth seemed to be going round and round with her; she burst into sobbing and crying as she spoke; not tears—she was not capable of tears. When Mr. Brownlow, in his extraordinary self-possession, went to a side-table to bring a decanter of sherry which had been placed there, she made an effort to rise to stop him, but even that she was unable to do. He walked across the room while his astonished children still stood and looked on. He alone had all his wits about him, and sense enough to be compassionate. He filled out a glass of wine with a steady hand and brought it to her. "Take this," he said, "and then you will be more able to tell me what you mean."

Mrs. Preston looked up at him, struck dumb with wonder in the midst of her agitation. She was capable of thinking he meant to poison her—probably that was the first idea in her mind; but when she looked up and saw the expression in his face, it calmed her in spite of herself. She took the glass from him as if she could not help it, and swallowed the wine in an unwilling yet eager way—for her bodily exhaustion craved the needful support, though her mind was against it. She began to shake and tremble all over as Mr. Brownlow took the glass from her hand: his quietness overwhelmed her. If he had turned her out of the room, out of the house, it would have seemed more natural than this.

"Father," said Jack, interposing, "I have seen her like this before—I don't know what she has in her head, but of course I can't stand by and see her get into trouble: if you will go away I will take her home."

Mr. Brownlow smiled again, a curious smile of despair, once more seeing the humor, as it were, of the situation. "It will be better for you to take Sara away," he said; "go both of you—it does not matter." Then, having fallen into this momentary incoherence, he recovered himself and turned round to his visitor. "Now tell me," he said gently, "who you are and what you mean?"

But by this time it did not seem as if she were able to speak—she sat and stared at him, her dark eyes shining wildly out of her old pallid face. "I have seen the will—I have been at Doctors' Commons," she gulped out by degrees; "I know it must be true."

"Who are you?" said Mr. Brownlow.

The poor trembling creature got up and made a rush toward him again. "You know who I am," she said, "but that don't matter, as you say: I was Phœbe Thomson; give me my mother's money—ah! give me the money that belongs to my child! give me my fortune! there's witnesses that I came in time; I came in time—I came in time!" screamed forth the exhausted woman. She had lost all command of herself by this time, and shrieked out the words, growing louder and louder; then all at once, without any warning, she fell down at the feet of the man she was defying—fell in a dead bundle on the floor, in a faint—almost, as it seemed for the moment, dead.

Mr. Brownlow, for one dreadful second, thought she was dead. The moment was terrible beyond all description, worse than any thing that had yet befallen him; a thrill of hope, an awful sickening of suspense came over him; for the first time he, too, lost his senses: he did not stoop to raise her, nor take any means for her restoration, but stood looking down upon her, watching, as a man might watch the wild beast which had been about to kill him, writhing under some sudden shot. A man would not interpose in such a case with surgical aid for the wounded lion or tiger. Neither did Mr. Brownlow feel himself moved to interfere. He only stood and looked on. But his children were not wound up to the same state of feeling. Jack rushed forward and lifted his Pamela's mother from the floor, and Sara flew to her aid with feminine succors. They laid her on the sofa, and put water on her face, and did every thing they knew to restore her. Mr. Brownlow did not interfere; he could not bid them stop; it never even occurred to him to attempt to restrain their charitable offices. He left them to themselves, and walked heavily up and down the room on the other side, waiting till she should come to herself. For of course she would come to herself—he had no doubt of that. After the first instant it was clearly enough apparent to him that such a woman at such a moment would not die.

When Mrs. Preston came to herself, she tried to get up from the sofa, and looked at them all with a piteous look of terror and helplessness. She was a simply uneducated woman, making little distinction between different kinds of crime—and it seemed to her as if a man who had defrauded her (as she thought) all these years, might very well mean to murder her when he was found out. She did not see the difference. She shuddered as she fell back on the cushions unable to rise. "Would you like to kill me?" she said faintly, looking in their faces. She was afraid of them, and she was helpless and alone. She did not feel even as if she had the strength to cry out. And there were three of them—they could put out her feeble flickering flame of life if they pleased. As for the two young people whom she addressed in the first place, they supposed simply that she was raving. But Mr. Brownlow, who was, in his way, as highly strained as she was, caught the words. And the thought flashed through his mind as if some one had held up a picture to him. What would it matter if she were to die? She was old—she had lived long enough—she was not so happy that she should wish to live longer; and her child—others might do better for her child than she could. It was not his fault. It was her words that called up the picture before him, and he made a few steps forward and put his children away, and came up to the sofa and looked at her. An old, faint, feeble, worn-out woman. A touch would do it;—her life was like the last sere leaves fluttering on the end of the branches; a touch would do it. He came and looked at her, not knowing what he did, and put his children away. And there was something in his eyes which made her shrink into the corner of her couch and tremble, and be silent. He was looking to see how it could be done—by some awful unconscious impulse, altogether apart from any will or thought of his. And a touch would do it. This was what was in his eyes when he told his children to go away.

"Go—go to bed," he said, "I will take care of Mrs. Preston." There was a horrible appearance of meaning in his voice, but yet he did not know what he meant. He stood and looked down upon her gloomily. Yes, that was all that stood between him and peace; a woman whom any chance touch—any blast bitterer than usual—any accidental fall, might kill. "Go to bed, children," he repeated harshly. It seemed to him somehow as if it would be better, as if he would be more at liberty, when they were away.

"Oh, no—no," said Mrs. Preston, moaning. "Don't leave me—don't leave me. You wouldn't see any harm come to me, for my Pamela's sake!"

And then both his children looked into Mr. Brownlow's face. I can not tell what they saw there. I doubt whether they could have told themselves; but it was something that thrilled them through and through, which came back to them from time to time all their lives, and which they could never forget. Jack turned away from his father with a kind of horror, and went and placed himself beside Mrs. Preston at the head of the sofa. But Sara, though her dismay was still greater, went up to him and clasped his arm with both her hands. "Papa," she said, "come away. Come with me. I don't know what it means, but it is too much for you. Come, papa."

Mr. Brownlow once more put her away with his hand. "Go to bed, Sara," he said; and then freeing himself, he went across the room to the curtained windows, and stared out as if they were open, and came back again. The presence of his children was an oppression to him. He wanted them away. And then he stood again by the side of the sofa and looked at his visitor. "We can talk this over best alone," he said; and at the sound of his voice, and a movement which she thought Jack made to leave her, she gave a sudden cry.

"He will kill me if you go away!" she said. "Oh, don't leave me to him! I—don't mean to injure you—I—But you're in league with him," she exclaimed rising suddenly with the strength of excitement, and rushing to the other end of the room; "you are all against me. I shall be killed—I shall be killed! Murder! murder!—though I don't want to hurt you. I want nothing but my rights."

She got behind the writing-table in her insane terror, and threw herself down there on her knees, propping herself up against it, and watching them as from behind a barricade, with her pallid thin face supported on the table. With her hands she drew a chair to each side of her. She was like a wild creature painfully barricading herself—sheltering her feeble strength within intrenchments, and turning her face to the foe. Mr. Brownlow stood still and looked at her, but this time with a stupefied look which meant nothing; and as for Jack he stood aghast, half frightened, half angry, not knowing if she were mad, or what it was. When either of them moved, she crouched together and cried out, thinking they were about to rush upon her. For the moment she was all but mad—mad with excitement, fright, evil-thinking, and ignorance—ignorance most of all—seeing no reason why, if they had done one wrong, they should not do another. Kill or defraud, which did it matter?—and for the moment she was out of her senses, and knew not what she did or said.

Sara was the only one who retained her wits at this emergency. She stepped behind the screen made by the table without pausing to think about it. "Mrs. Preston," she said, "I don't know what is the matter with you. You look as if you had gone mad; but I am not frightened. What do you mean by calling murder here? Come with me to my room and go to bed. It is time every body was in bed. I will take care of you. You are tired to death, and not fit to be up. Come with me."

"You!" cried Mrs. Preston—"you! You that have had every thing my Pamela ought to have had! You that have been kept like a princess on my money! You!—but don't let them kill me," she cried out the next moment, shuddering and turning toward the other woman for protection. "You're but a girl. Come here and stand by me, and save me, and I'll stand by you. You shall always have a home. I'll be as good to you—but save me! don't let them kill me!" she cried, frantically throwing her arms round Sara's waist. It was a curious sight. The girl stood erect, her slight figure swaying with the unusual strain upon it, her face lit up with such powerful emotions as she had never known before, looking wistful, alarmed, wondering, proud, upon her father and her brother at the other side, while the old woman clung to her, crouching at her feet, hiding her face in her dress, clasping her waist as for life and death. Sara had accepted the office thrust upon her, whatever it was. She had become responsible for the terrified, exhausted claimant of all Mr. Brownlow's fortune—and turned round upon the two astonished men with something new to them, something that was almost defiance, in her eyes.

"I don't know what it means," she said, laying her long, soft, shapely hand upon Mrs. Preston's shoulder like the picture of a guardian angel; "but it has gone past your managing, and I must take charge of her. Jack, open the door, and keep out of the way. She must come with me."

And then, indeed, Mr. Brownlow within himself in the depths of his heart, uttered a groan, which made some outward echo. He was in the last crisis of his fate, and his cherished child forsook him and took his adversary's part. He withdrew himself and sank down into a chair, clearing the way, as she had bidden.

Sara had taken charge of her. Sara had covered the intruder for ever and ever with the shield of her protection; and yet it was for Sara alone that he could have found in his heart to murder this woman, as she said. When Sara stood forth and faced him in her young strength and pride, a sudden Lady of Succor, it cast him to the earth. And he gave that groan, and sank down and put himself aside, as it were. He could not carry on the struggle. When Sara heard it her heart smote her; she turned to him eagerly, not to comfort him but to defend herself.

"Well!" she said, "if it was nothing, you would not have minded. It must be something, or you would not have looked—" And then she stopped and shuddered. "I am going to take charge of her to-night," she added, low and hurriedly. "I will take her to my room, and stay with her all night. To-morrow, perhaps, we may know what it means. Jack, she can walk, if you will clear the way."

Then Mr. Brownlow looked up, with an indescribable pang at his heart, and saw his daughter lead, half carrying, his enemy away. "I will take her to my room, and stay with her all night." He had felt the emphasis and meaning that was in the words, and he had seen Sara's shudder. Good heavens! what was it for? Was he a man to do murder? What was it his child had read in his eye? In this horrible confusion of thought he sat and watched the stranger out. She had made good her lodgment, not only in the house, but in the innermost chamber, in Sara's room—in Sara's protecting presence, where nothing could get near her. And it was against him that his child had taken up this wretched woman's defense! He neither moved nor spoke for some minutes after they had left the room. The bitterness had all to be tasted and swallowed before his thoughts could go forward to other things, and to the real final question. By degrees, however, as he came to himself, he became aware that he was not yet left free to think about the final question. Jack was still beside him. He did not say any thing, but he was moving and fidgeting about the room with his hands in his pockets in a way which proved that he had something to say. As Mr. Brownlow came to himself he gradually woke to a perception of his son's restless figure beside him, and knew that he had another explanation to make.

"I don't want to trouble you," said Jack at last, abruptly, "but I should very much like to know, sir, what all this means. If Mrs. Preston is mad—as—God knows I don't want to think it," cried the young man, "but one must believe one's eyes—if she is mad, why did you give in to her, and humor her? Why did not you let me take her away?"

"I don't think she is mad," said Mr. Brownlow, slowly.

Upon which Jack came to a dead stop, and stared at his father—"Good heavens, sir," he said, "what can you mean?"

"I don't know," said Mr. Brownlow, getting up in his turn. "My head is not quite clear to-night. Leave me now. I'll tell you after. I'll tell you—sometime;—I mean in the morning." Then he walked once more across the room, and threw himself into the big easy-chair by the dying fire. One of the lamps had run down, and was flickering out, throwing strange quivers of light and shade about the room. An indescribable change had come over it; it had been bright, and now it looked desolate; it had been the home of peace, and now the very air was heavy with uncertainty and a kind of hovering horror. Mr. Brownlow threw himself wearily into the big chair, and covered his face with his hands. A moment after he seemed to recollect himself, and looked up and called Jack back. "My boy," he said, "something has happened to-night which I did not look for. You must consider every thing I said to you before as cancelled. It appears I was premature. I am sorry—for you, Jack."

"Don't be sorry for me," cried Jack, with a generous impulse. "It could not have made much matter anyhow—my life is decided, come what may."

Then his father looked up at him sharply, but with a quiver in his lip. "Ah!" he said; and Jack perceived somehow, he did not know how, that he had unwittingly inflicted a new wound. "It could not have made much matter—true," he said, and rose up and bowed to his son as if he had been a stranger. "That being the case, perhaps the less we say to each other the better now—"

"What have I said, sir?" cried Jack in amaze.

"Enough, enough," said Mr. Brownlow, "enough"—whether it was in answer to his question, or by way of putting an end to the conversation, Jack could not tell; and then his father waved him away, and sat down again, once more burying his face in his hands. Again the iron had entered his soul. Both of them!—all he had in the world—his fortune, his position, his son, his daughter, must all go? It seemed to him now as if the external things were nothing in comparison of these last. Sara, for whose sake alone he feared it—Jack, whom he had not petted—whom perhaps he had crossed a little as fathers will, but whom at bottom—never mind, never mind! he said to himself. It was the way of the world. Sons did not take up their father's cause nowadays as a matter of course. They had themselves to think of—in fact, it was right they should think of themselves. The world was of much more importance to Jack than it could be to himself, for of course a young man had twice the length of time to provide for that his father could possibly have. Never mind! He said it to himself with his head bowed down in his hands. But he did mind. "It would not make much matter anyhow"—no, not much matter. Jack would have it instead of Sara and Powys. It was the same kind of compromise that he had intended—only that the persons and the motive were changed.

Poor Jack in the mean time went about the room in a very disconsolate state. He was so startled in every way that he did not know what to think, and yet vague shadows of the truth were flickering about his mind. He knew something vaguely of the origin of his father's fortune, and nothing but that could explain it; and now he was offended at something. What could it be that he was offended at? It never occurred to Jack that his own words might bear the meaning that was set upon them; he was disconcerted and vexed, and did not know what to do. He went wandering about the room, lifting and replacing the books on the tables, and finally, after a long pause, he went up to his father again.

"I wish you'd have some confidence in me," he said. "I don't pretend to be wise, but still—And then if there is any thing hanging over us, it is best that a fellow should know—"

"There is nothing hanging over you," said Mr. Brownlow, raising his head, almost with bitterness. "It will not matter much anyhow, you know. Don't think of waiting for me. I have a good deal to think over. In short, I should be very glad if you would leave me to myself and go—"

"As you please," said Jack, who was at last offended in his turn; and after he had made a discontented promenade all round the room, he lounged toward the door, still hoping he might be called back again. But he was not called back. On the contrary, his father's head had sunk again into his hands, and he had evidently retired into himself, beyond the reach of all fellowship or sympathy. Jack veered gradually toward the door and went out of the room, with his hands in his pockets and great trouble and perplexity in his mind. It seemed to him that he saw what the trouble must be, and that of itself was not pleasant. But bad as it might be, it was not so bad as the way his father was taking it. Good heavens, if he should hurt the old woman!—but surely he was not capable of that. And then Jack returned upon his own case and felt wounded and sore. He was not a baby that his father should decline to take him into his confidence. He was not a fool that he should be supposed unequal to the emergency. Sleep was out of the question under the circumstances; and besides he did not want to meet any of the fellows who might have been disturbed by Mrs. Preston's cry, and might have come to his room for information. "Hang it all!" said Jack, as he threw himself on a sofa in the smoking-room, and lighted a dreary cigar. It was not a very serious malediction, but yet his mind was serious enough. Some terrible crisis in the history of his family was coming on, and he could only guess what it was. Something that involved not only his own prospects, but the prospects of his future wife. And yet nobody would tell him what was the meaning of it. It was hard lines for Jack.

When his son left the room, Mr. Brownlow lifted his head out of his hands. He looked eagerly round the room and made sure he was alone. And then his countenance relaxed a little. He could venture to look as he felt, to throw off every mask when he was alone. Then he got up and walked heavily about. Was it all true? Had she come at the last moment and made her claim? Had she lighted down upon him, tracked him out, just as he was saying, and at last permitting himself to think, that all was over? A strange confusion swept over him as he sat and looked around the empty room. Was it possible that all this had happened since he was last alone in it? It was only a few hours since; and he had been scarcely able to believe that so blessed a state of things could be true. He had sat there and planned every kind of kindness and bounty to every body by way of expressing his gratitude to God. Was it possible? Could every thing since then be so entirely changed? Or had he only dreamt the arrival of the sudden claimant, the striking of the clock too late, all the miseries of the night? As he asked himself these questions, a sudden shuddering came over him. There was one thing which he knew could be no dream. It was the suggestion which had come into his mind as he stood by the sofa. He seemed to see her before him, worn, old, feeble, and involuntarily his thoughts strayed away again to that horrible thought. What was the use of such a woman in the world? She had nothing before her but old age, infirmities, a lingering illness most likely, many sufferings and death—only death at the end; that was the best, the only event awaiting her. To the young, life may blossom out afresh at any moment, but the old can only die—that is all that remains for them. And a touch would do it. It might save her from a great deal of suffering—it would certainly save her from the trial of a new position, the difficult transition from poverty to wealth. If he was himself as old, Mr. Brownlow thought vaguely (all this was very vague—it was not breathed in articulate thought, much less in words) that he would be glad to be put quietly out of the way. Heaven knows he would be grateful enough to any one even at that moment who would put him out of the way.

And it would be so easy to do it; a touch would do it. The life was fluttering already in her pulses; very likely the first severe cold would bring her down like the leaves off the trees; and in the mean time what a difference her life would make. Mr. Brownlow got up and began to walk about, not able to keep still any longer. The second lamp was now beginning to flicker for want of oil, and the room was darkening, though he did not perceive it. It would be the kindest office that could be done to an old woman; he had often thought so. Suddenly there occurred to him a recollection of certain unhappy creatures in the work-house at Masterton, who were so old that nothing was any pleasure to them. He thought of the life-in-death he had seen among them, the tedious blank, the animal half-existence, the dead, dull doze, out of which only a bad fit of coughing or some other suffering roused them; and of his own passing reflection how kind it would be to mix them a sleeping potion only a little stronger, and let them be gone. It would be the best thing any one could do for them. It would be the best thing any one could do for her; and then all the trouble, all the vexation, all the misery and change that it would save!

As for the child, Mr. Brownlow said to himself that all should go well with the child. He would not interfere. Jack should marry her if he pleased—all should go well with her; and she would not have the difficult task of reconciling the world to her mother. In every way it seemed the desirable arrangement. If Providence would but interpose!—but then Providence never did interpose in such emergencies. Mr. Brownlow went slowly up and down the darkening room, and his thoughts, too, went into the darkness. They went on as it were in a whisper and hid themselves, and silence came—hideous silence, in which the heart stood still, the genial breath was interrupted. He did not know what he was doing. He went to the medicine-chest which was in one corner, and opened it and looked at it. He did not even make a pretense of looking for any thing; neither would the light have enabled him to look for any thing. He looked at it and he knew that death was there, but he did not put forth his hand to touch it. At that moment all at once the flickering flame went out—went out just as a life might do, after fluttering and quivering and making wild rallies, again and again. Mr. Brownlow, for his part, was almost glad there was no light. It made him easier—even the lamp had seemed to look at him and see something in his eye!

Five minutes after, he found himself, he could not have told how, at the door of Sara's room. It was not in his way—he could not make that excuse to himself—to tell the truth he did not make any excuse to himself. His mind was utterly confused, and had stopped thinking. He was there, having come there he did not know how; and being there he opened the door softly and went in. Perhaps, for any thing he could tell, the burden might have been too much for Sara. He went in softly, stealing so as not to disturb any sleeper. The room was dark, but not quite dark. There was a night-light burning, shaded, on the table, and the curtains were drawn at the head of the white bed: nothing stirred in the silence: only the sound of breathing, the irregular disturbed breathing of some one in a troubled sleep. Mr. Brownlow stole farther in, and softly put back one of the curtains of the bed. There she lay, old, pallid, wrinkled, worn out, breathing hard in her sleep, even then unable to forget the struggle she was engaged in, holding the coverlet fast with one old meagre hand, upon which all the veins stood out. What comfort was her life to her? And a touch would do it. He went a step nearer and stooped over her, not knowing what he did, not putting out a finger, incapable of any exertion, yet with an awful curiosity. Then all at once out of the darkness, swift as an angel on noiseless pinions, a white figure rose and rushed at him, carrying him away from the bed out to the door, unwitting, aghast, by the mere impetus of its own sudden motion. When they had got outside it was Sara's face that was turned upon him, pale as the face of the dead, with her hair hanging about it wildly, and the moisture standing in big beads on her forehead. "What were you going to do?" she seemed to shriek in his ear, though the shriek was only a whisper. He had left his candle outside, and it was by that faint light he could see the whiteness of her face.

"Do?" said Mr. Brownlow, with a strange sense of wonder. "Do?—nothing. What could I do?"

Then Sara threw herself upon him and wept aloud, wept so that the sound ran through the house, sobbing along the long listening passages. "Oh, papa, papa!" she cried, clinging to him. A look as of idiocy had come into his face. He had become totally confused—he did not know what she meant. What could he do? Why was she crying? And it was wrong to make a noise like this, when all the house was hushed and asleep.

"You must be quiet," he said. "There is no need to be so agitated; and you should have been in bed. It is very late. I am going to my room now."

"I will go with you," said Sara, trembling. Already she began to be ashamed of her terror, but her nerves would not calm down all at once. She put her hand on his arm and half led, half followed him through the corridor. "Papa, you did not mean—any thing?" she said, lifting up a face so white and tremulous and shaken with many emotions that it was scarcely possible to recognize it as hers. "You did not mean—any thing?" Her very lips quivered so that she could scarcely speak.

"Mean—what?" he said. "I am a little confused to-night. It was all so sudden. I don't seem to understand you. And I'm very tired. Things will be clearer to-morrow. Sara, I hope you are going to bed."

"Yes, papa," she said, like a child, though her lips quivered. He looked like a man who had fallen into sudden imbecility, comprehending nothing. And Sara's mind too was beginning to get confused. She could not understand any longer what his looks meant.

"And so am I," said Mr. Brownlow, with a sigh. Then he stooped and kissed her. "My darling, good-night. Things will be clearer to-morrow," he said. They had come to his door by this time. And it was there he stooped to kiss her, dismissing her as it seemed. But after she had turned to go back, he came out again and called her. He looked almost as old and as shaken as Mrs. Preston as he called her back: "Don't forsake me—don't you forsake me," he said hurriedly; "that was all—that was all: good-night."

And then he went in and shut his door. Sara, left to herself, went back along the corridor, not knowing what to think. Were they all mad, or going mad? What could the shock be which had made Pamela's humble mother frantic, and confused Mr. Brownlow's clear intellect? She lay down on her sofa to watch her patient, feeling as if she too was becoming idiotic. She could not sleep, young as she was: the awful shadow that had come across her mind had murdered sleep. She lay and listened to Mrs. Preston's irregular, interrupted breathing, far into the night. But sleep was not for Sara's eyes.

CHAPTER XXXVII

THE MORNING LIGHT

Of all painful things in this world there are few more painful than the feeling of rising up in the morning to a difficulty unsolved, a mystery unexplained. So long as the darkness is over with the night something can always be done. Calamity can be faced, misfortune met; but to get up in the morning light, and encounter afresh the darkness, and find no clue any more than you had at night, is hard work. This was what Jack felt when he had to face the sunshine, and remembered all that had happened, and the merry party that awaited him down stairs, and that he must amuse his visitors as if this day had been like any other. If he but knew what had really happened! But the utmost he could do was to guess at it, and that in the vaguest way. The young man went down stairs with a load on his mind, not so much of care as of uncertainty. Loss of fortune was a thing that could be met; but if there was loss of honor involved—if his father's brain was giving way with the pressure—if—Jack would not allow his thoughts to go any farther. He drew himself up with a sudden pull, and stopped short, and went down stairs. At the breakfast-table every thing looked horribly unchanged. The guests, the servants, the routine of the cheerful meal, were just as usual. Mr. Brownlow, too, was at the table, holding his usual place. There was an ashy look about his face, which produced inquiries concerning his health from every new arrival; but his answers were so brief and unencouraging that these questions soon died off into silence. And he ate nothing, and his hand shook as he put his cup of coffee to his pallid lips. All these were symptoms that might be accounted for in the simplest way by a little bodily derangement. But Jack, for his part, was afraid to meet his father's eye. "Where is Sara?" he asked, as he took his seat. And then he was met—for he was late, and most of the party were down before him—by a flutter of regrets and wonder. Poor Sara had a headache—so bad a headache that she would not even have any one go into her room. "Angelique was keeping the door like a little tiger," one of the young ladies said, "and would let nobody in." "And oh, tell me who it was that came so late last night," cried another. "You must know. We are all at such a pitch of curiosity. It must be a foreign prince, or the prime minister, or some great beauty, we can't make up our minds which; and, of course, it is breakfasting in its own room this morning. Nobody will tell us who it was. Do tell us!—we are all dying to know."

"As you will all be dreadfully disappointed," said Jack. "It was neither a prince nor a beauty. As for prime minister I don't know. Such things have been heard of as that a prime minister should be an old woman—"

"An old woman!" said his innocent interlocutor. "Then it must be Lady Motherwell. Oh, I don't wonder poor Sara has a headache. But you know you are only joking. Her dear Charley would never let her come storming to any body's door like that."

"It was not Lady Motherwell," said Jack. Heaven knows he was in no mood for jesting; but when it is a matter which is past talking of, what can a man do?

"Oh, then, I know who it must have been!" cried the spokeswoman of the party. She was, however, suddenly interrupted. Mr. Brownlow, who had scarcely said a word as yet to any one, interposed. There was something in his tone which somehow put them all to silence.

"I am sorry to put a stop to your speculations," he said. "It was only one of my clients on urgent business—that was all; business," he added, with a curious kind of apology, "which has kept me up half the night."

"Oh, Mr. Brownlow, I am so sorry. You are tired, and we have been teasing you," said the lively questioner, with quick compunction.

"No, not teasing me," he said, gravely. And then a dead silence ensued. It was not any thing in his words. His words were simple enough; and yet every one of his guests instantly began to think that his or her stay had been long enough, and that it was time to go away.

As Mr. Brownlow spoke he met Jack's eye, and returned his look steadily. So far he was himself again. He was impenetrable, antagonistic, almost defiant. But there was no hovering horror in his look. He was terribly grave, and ashy pale, and bore traces that what had happened was no light master. His look gave his son a sensation of relief, and perhaps encouraged him in levity of expression, though, Heaven knows, there was little levity in his mind.

"I told you," he said, "it might have been the prime minister, but it certainly was an old woman; and there I stop. I can't give any farther information; I am not one of the Privy Council." Then he laughed, but it was an uncomfortable laugh. It deepened the silence all around, and looked like a family quarrel, and made every body feel ill at ease.

"I don't think any one here can be much interested in details," said Mr. Brownlow, coldly; and then he rose to leave the table. It was his habit to leave the table early, and on ordinary occasions his departure made little commotion; but to-day it was different. They all clustered up to their feet as he went out of the room. Nobody knew what should be done that day. The men looked awkwardly at each other; the women tried hard to be the same as before, and failed, having Jack before them, who was far from looking the same. "I suppose, Jack, you will not go out to-day," one of his companions said, though they had not an idea why.

"I don't see why I shouldn't," said Jack, and then he made a pause; and every body looked at him. "After all," he continued, "you all know your way about; as Sara has a headache I had better stay;" and he hurried their departure that he might get rid of them. His father had not gone out; the dog-cart had come to the door, but it had been sent off again. He was in the library, Willis said in a whisper; and though he had been so many years with Mr. Brownlow and knew all his ways, Willis was obviously startled too. For one moment Jack thought of cross-questioning the butler to see what light he could throw upon the matter—if he had heard any thing on the previous night, or suspected any thing—but on second thoughts he dismissed the idea. Whatever it was, it was from his father himself that he ought to have the explanation. But though Mr. Brownlow was in the library Jack did not go to him there. He loitered about till his friends were gone, and till the ladies of the party, finding him very impracticable and with no amusement in him, had gone off upon their various ways. He did his best to be civil even playful, poor fellow, being for the moment every body's representative, both master and mistress of the house. But though there was no absolute deficiency in any thing he said or did, they were all too sharp-witted to be taken in. "He has something on his mind," one matron of the party said to the other. "They have something on all their minds, my dear," said the other, solemnly; and they talked very significantly and mysteriously of the Brownlows as they filled Sara's morning-room with their work and various devices, for it was a foggy, wretched day, and no one cared to venture out. Jack meanwhile drew a long breath of relief when all his guests were thus off his mind. He stood in the hall and hesitated, and saw Willis watching him from a corner with undisguised anxiety. Perhaps but for that he would have gone to his father; but with every body watching him, looking on and speculating what it might be, he could not go. And yet something must be done. At last, after he had watched the last man out and the last lady go away, he turned, and went slowly up stairs to Sara's door.

When his voice was heard there was a little rush within, and Sara came to him. She was very pale, and had the air of a watcher to whom the past night had brought no sleep. It even seemed to Jack that she was in the same dress that she had worn the previous night, though that was a delusion. As soon as she saw that it was her brother, and that he was alone, she sent the maid away, and taking him by the arm, drew him into the little outer room. There had not been any sentimental fraternity between them in a general way. They were very good friends, and fond of each other, but not given to manifestations of sympathy and devotion. But this time as soon as he was within the door and she had him to herself, Sara threw her arms round Jack, and leaned against him, and went off without any warning into a sudden burst of emotion—not tears exactly. It was rather a struggle against tears. She sobbed and her breast heaved, and she clasped him convulsively. Jack was terribly surprised and shocked, feeling that so unusual an outburst must have a serious cause, and he was very tender with his sister. It did not last more than a minute, but it did more to convince him of the gravity of the crisis than any thing else had done. Sara regained command of herself almost immediately and ceased sobbing, and raised her head from his shoulder. "She is there," she whispered, pointing to the inner room, and then she turned and went before him leading the way. The white curtains of Sara's bed were drawn at one side, so as to screen the interior of the chamber. Within that enclosure a fire was burning brightly, and seated by it in an easy-chair, wrapped in one of Sara's pretty dressing-gowns, with unaccustomed embroideries and soft frills and ribbons enclosing her brown worn hands and meagre throat, Mrs. Preston half sat, half reclined. The fire-light was flickering about her, and she lay back and looked at it and at every thing around her with a certain dreadful satisfaction. She looked round about upon the room and its comforts as people look on a new purchase. Enjoyment—a certain pleasure of possession—was written on her face.

When she saw Jack she moved a little, and drew the muslin wrapper more closely around her throat with a curious instinct of prudish propriety. It was the same woman to whose society he had accustomed himself as Pamela's mother, and whom he had tutored himself to look upon as a necessary part of his future household, but yet she was a different creature. He did not know her in this new development. He followed Sara into her presence with a new sense of repulsion, a reluctance and dislike which he had never felt before. And Mrs. Preston for her part received him with an air which was utterly inexplicable—an air of patronage which made his blood boil.

"I hope you are better," he said, not knowing how to begin; and then, after a pause, "Should not I go and tell Pamela that you are here? or would you like me to take you home?"

"I consider myself at home," said Mrs. Preston, sitting up suddenly and bursting into speech. "I will send for Pamela, when it is all settled, I am very thankful to your sister for taking care of me last night. She shall find that it will be to her advantage. Sit down—I am sorry, Mr. John, that I can not say the same for you."

"What is it you can not say for me?" said Jack: "I don't know in the least what you would be at, Mrs. Preston; I suppose there must be some explanation of this strange conduct. What does it mean?"

"You will find that it means a great deal," said the changed woman. "When you came to me to my poor little place, I did not want to have any thing to say to you; but I never thought of putting any meaning to what you, were doing. I was as innocent as a baby—I thought it was all love to my poor child. That was what I thought. And now you've stolen her heart away from me, and I know what it was for—I know what it was for."

"Then what was it for?" said Jack, abruptly. He was by turns red and pale with anger. He found it very hard to keep his temper now that he was personally assailed.

"It was for this," cried Pamela's mother, with a shrill ring in her voice, pointing, as it seemed, to the pretty furniture and pictures round her—"for all this, and the fine house, and the park, and the money—that was what it was for. You thought you'd marry her and keep it all, and that I should never know what was my rights. But now I do know;—and you would have killed me last night!" she cried wildly, drawing back, with renewed passion—"you and your father; you would have killed me; I should have been a dead woman by this time if it had not been for her!"

Jack made a hoarse exclamation in his throat as she spoke. The room seemed to be turning round with him. He seemed to be catching glimpses of her meaning through some wild chaos of misunderstanding and darkness. He himself had never wished her ill, not even when she promised to be a burden on him. "Is she mad?" he said, turning to Sara; but he felt that she was not mad; it was something more serious than that.

"I know my rights," she said, calming down instantaneously. "It's my house you've been living in, and my money that has made you all so fine. You need not start or pretend as if you didn't know. It was for that you came and beguiled my Pamela. You might have left me my Pamela; house, and money, and every thing, even down to my poor mother's blessing," said Mrs. Preston, breaking down pitifully, and falling into a passion of tears. "You have taken them all, you and yours; but you might have left me my child."

Jack stood aghast while all this was being poured forth upon him; but Sara for her part fell a-crying too. "She has been saying the same all night," said Sara; "what have we to do with her money or her mother's blessing? Oh, Jack, what have we to do with them? What does it mean? I don't understand any thing but about Pamela and you."

"Nor I," said Jack, in despair, and he made a little raid through the room in his consternation, that the sight of the two women crying might not make a fool of him; then he came back with the energy of desperation. "Look here, Mrs. Preston," he said, "there may be some money question between my father and you—I can't tell; but we have nothing to do with it. I know nothing about it. I think most likely you have been deceived somehow. But, right or wrong, this is not the way to clear it up. Money can not be claimed in this wild way. Get a lawyer who knows what he is doing to see after it for you; and in the mean time go home like a rational creature. You can not be permitted to make a disturbance here."

"You shall never have a penny of it," cried Mrs. Preston—"not a penny, if you should be starving—nor Pamela either; I will tell her all—that you wanted her for her money; and she will scorn you as I do—you shall have nothing from her or me."

"Answer for yourself," cried Jack, furious, "or be silent. She shall not be brought in. What do I care for your money? Sara, be quiet, and don't cry. She ought never to have been brought here."

"No," cried the old woman, in her passion, "I ought to have been cast out on the roadside, don't you think, to die if I liked? or I ought to have been killed, as you tried last night. That's what you would do to me, while you slept soft and lived high. But my time has come. It's you who must go to the door—the door!—and you need expect no pity from me."

She sat in her feebleness and poverty as on a throne, and defied them, and they stood together bewildered by their ignorance, and did not know what answer to make her. Though it sounded like madness, it might be true. For any thing they could tell, what she was saying might have some foundation unknown to them. Sara by this time had dried her tears, and indignation had begun to take the place of distress in her mind. She gave her brother an appealing look, and clasped her hands. "Jack, answer her—do you know what to say to her?" she cried, stamping her little foot on the ground with impatience; "somebody must know; are we to stand by and hear it all, and do nothing? Jack, answer her!—unless she is mad—"

"I think she must be partly mad," said Jack. "But it must be put a stop to somehow. Go and fetch my father. He is in the library. Whatever it may be, let us know at least what it means. I will stay with her here."

When she heard these words, the strange inmate of Sara's room came down from her height and relapsed into a feeble old woman. She called Sara not to go, to stay and protect her. She shrank back into her chair, drawing it away into a corner at the farthest distance possible, and sat there watchful and frightened, eying Jack as a hunted creature might eye the tiger which might at any moment spring upon it. Jack, for his part, with an exclamation of impatience, turned on his heel and went away from her, as far as space would permit. Impatience began to swallow up every other sentiment in his mind. He could not put up with it any longer. Whatever the truth might be, it was evident that it must be faced and acknowledged at once. While he kept walking about impatient and exasperated, all his respect for Pamela's mother died out of his mind; even, it must be owned, in his excitement, the image of Pamela herself went back into the mists. A certain disgust took possession of him. If it was true that his father had schemed and struggled for the possession of this woman's miserable money—if the threat of claiming it had moved him with some vague but awful temptation, such as Jack shuddered to think of; and if the idea of having rights and possessing something had changed the mild and humble woman who was Pamela's mother into this frantic and insulting fury, then what was there worth caring for, what was there left to believe in, in this world? Perhaps even Pamela herself had been changed by this terrible test. Jack did not wish for the wings of a dove, being too matter-of-fact for that. But he felt as if he would like to set out for New Zealand without saying a word to any body, without breathing a syllable to a single soul on the way. It seemed as if that would be the only thing to do—he himself might get frantic or desperate too like the others about a little money. The backwoods, sheep-shearing, any thing would be preferable to that.

This pause lasted for some minutes, for Sara did not immediately return. When she came back, however, a heavier footstep accompanied her up the stair. Mr. Brownlow came into the room, and went at once toward the farther corner. He had made up his mind; once more he had become perfectly composed, calm as an attorney watching his client's case. He called Jack to him, and went and stood by the table, facing Mrs. Preston. "I hear you have sent for me to know the meaning of all this," he said; "I will tell you, for you have a right to know. Twenty-five years ago, before either of you was born, I had some money left me, which was to be transferred to a woman called Phœbe Thomson, if she could be found out or appeared within twenty-five years. I searched for her everywhere, but I could not find her. Latterly I forgot her existence to a great extent. The five-and-twenty years were out last night, and just before the period ended this—lady—as you both know, appeared. She says she is Phœbe Thomson, the legatee I have told you of. She may be so—I have nothing to say against her; but the proof lies with her, not me. This is all the explanation there is to make."

When he had said it he drew a long breath of relief. It was the truth. It was not perhaps all the truth; but he had told the secret, which had weighed him down for months, and the burden was off his heart. He felt a little sick and giddy as he stood there before his children. He did not look them in the face. In his heart he knew there were many more particulars to tell. But it was not for them to judge of his heart. "I have told you the secret, so far as there is a secret," he said, with a faint smile at them, and then sat down suddenly, exhausted with the effort. It was not so difficult after all. Now that it was done, a faint wonder crossed his mind that he had not done it long ago, and saved himself all this trouble. But still he was glad to sit down. Somehow, it took the strength out of him as few things had done before.

"A legatee!" burst forth Sara in amazement, not understanding the word. "Is that all? Papa, she says the house is hers, and every thing is hers. She says we have no right here. Is it true?"

As for Jack, he looked his father steadily in the face, asking, Was it true? more imperiously than Sara's words did. If this were all, what was the meaning of the almost tragedy last night? They forgot the very existence of the woman who was the cause of it all as they turned upon him. Poverty and wealth were small matters in comparison. He was on his trial at an awful tribunal, before judges too much alarmed, too deeply interested, to be lenient. They turned their backs upon Mrs. Preston, who, notwithstanding her fear and her anxiety, could not bear the neglect. Their disregard of her roused her out of her own self-confidence and certainty, to listen with a certain forlorn eagerness. She had not paid much attention to what Mr. Brownlow said the first time. What did it matter what he said? Did not she know better? But when Jack and Sara turned their backs on her, and fixed their eyes on their father, she woke up with an intense mortification and disappointment at finding herself overlooked, and began to listen too.

Mr. Brownlow rose up as a man naturally does who has to plead guilty or not guilty for his life. He stood before them, putting his hand on the table to support himself. "It is not true," he said, "I do not deny that I have been thinking a great deal about this. If I had but known, I should have told you; but these are the real facts. If she is Phœbe Thomson, as she says—though of that we have no proof—she is entitled to fifty thousand pounds which her mother left her. That is the whole. To pay her her legacy may force me to leave this house, and change our mode of living; but she has nothing to do with the house—nothing here is hers, absolutely nothing. She has no more to do with Brownlows than your baker has, or your dress-maker. If she is Phœbe Thomson, I shall owe her money—nothing more. I might have told you, if I had but known."

What Mr. Brownlow meant was, that he would have told them had he known, after all, how little it would cost to tell it. After all, there was nothing disgraceful in the tale, notwithstanding the terrible shifts to which he had put himself to conceal it. He had spoken it out, and now his mind was free. If he had but known what a relief it would be! But he sat down as soon as he had finished speaking; and he did not feel as if he could pay much attention to any thing else. His mind was in a state of confusion about what had happened the previous night. It seemed to him that he had said or done something he ought not to have done or said. But now he had made his supreme disclosure, and given up the struggle. It did not much matter what occurred besides.

Mrs. Preston, however, who had been listening eagerly, and whom nobody regarded for the moment, rose up and made a step forward among them. "He may deny it," she said, trembling; "but I know he's known it all this time, and kept us out of our rights. Fifty pound—fifty thousand pound—what does he say? I know better. It is all mine, every penny, and he's been keeping us out of our rights. You've been all fed and nourished on what was mine—your horses and your carriages, and all your grandeur; and he says it's but fifty pounds! Don't you remember that there's One that protects the fatherless?" she cried out, almost screaming. The very sight of his composure made her wild and desperate. "You make no account of me," she cried—"no more than if I was the dust under your feet, and I'm the mistress of all—of all; and if it had not been for her you would have killed me last night."

These words penetrated even Mr. Brownlow's stupor; he gave a shudder as if with the cold.

"I was very hard driven last night," he said, as if to himself—"very hard put to it. I don't know what I may have said." Then he made a pause, and rose and went to his enemy, who fell back into the chair, and took fright as he approached her, putting out her two feeble hands to defend herself. "If you are Phœbe Thomson," he said, "you shall have your rights. I know nothing about you—I never thought of you. This house is mine, and you have nothing to do here. All you have any right to is your money, and you shall have your money when you prove your identity. But I can not leave you here to distress my child. If you are able to think at all, you must see that you ought to go home. Send for the carriage to take her home," Mr. Brownlow added, turning to his children. "If she is the person she calls herself, she is a relation of your mother's; and anyhow, she is weak and old. Take care of her. Sara, my darling, you are not to stay here with her, nor let her vex you; but I leave her in your hands."

"I will do what you tell me, papa," said Sara; and then he stood for a moment and looked at them wistfully. They had forsaken him last night; both of them—or at least so he fancied—had gone over to the enemy; and that had cut him to the heart. Now he turned to them wistfully, looking for a little support and comfort. It would not be so hard after all if his children went with him into captivity. They had both been so startled and excited that but for this look, and the lingering, expectant pause he made, neither would have thought of their father's feelings. But it was impossible to misunderstand him now. Sara, in her impulsive way, went up to him and put her arms round his neck. "Papa, it is we who have been hard upon you," she said; and as for Jack, who could not show his feelings by an embrace, he also made a kind of amende in an ungracious masculine way. He said, "I'm coming with you, sir. I'll see after the carriage," and marched off behind his father to the door. Neither of them took any farther notice of Mrs. Preston. It seemed to her as if they did not care. They were not afraid of her; they did not come obsequiously to her feet, as she had thought they would. On the contrary, they were banding together among themselves against her, making a league among themselves, taking no notice of her. And her own child was not there to comfort her heart. It was a great shock and downfall to the unhappy woman. She had been a good woman so long as she was untempted. But it had seemed to her, in the wonderful prospect of a great fortune, that every body would fall at her feet; that she would be able to do what she pleased—to deal with all her surroundings as she pleased. When she saw she could not do so, her mind grew confused—fifty pound, fifty thousand pound, which was it? And she was alone, and they were all banding themselves against her. Money seemed nothing in comparison to the elevation, the supremacy she had dreamed of. And they did not even take the trouble to look at her as they went away!

CHAPTER XXXVIII

MOTHER AND LOVER

Jack followed his father down stairs, and did not say a word. It had been an exciting morning; and now that he knew all, though the excitement had not as yet begun to flag, care came along with it. Suspense and mystery were hard, and yet at the same time easier to bear than reality. The calamity might have loomed larger while it was unknown, but at least it was unaccompanied by those real details from which there is no escape. When Mr. Brownlow and his son reached the bottom of the stair, they stopped, and turned and looked at each other. A certain shade of apology was in Mr. Brownlow's tone. "I thought it was all over last night," he said; "I thought you were all safe. You know my meaning now."

"Safe, sir, safe!" said Jack, "with this always hanging over our heads? I don't understand why we were not allowed to know; but never mind. I am glad it has come, and there is nothing more to look for. It bears interest, I suppose."

"That may be a matter of arrangement. I suppose it does," said Mr. Brownlow, with a sigh.

Jack gave vent to his feelings in a low, faint, prolonged whistle. "I'll go and tell them about the carriage," he said. This was all the communication that passed between the father and the son; but it was enough to show Mr. Brownlow that Jack was not thinking, as he might very naturally have thought, of his new position as the future son-in-law of the woman who had wrought so much harm. Jack's demeanor, though he did not say a word of sympathy to his father, was quite the contrary of this. He did not make any professions, but he took up the common family burden upon his shoulders. The fifty thousand pounds was comparatively little. It was a sum which could be measured and come to an end of; but the interest, that was the dreadful thought. Jack was practical, and his mind jumped at it on the moment. It was as a dark shadow which had come over him, and which he could not shake off. Brownlows was none of hers, and yet she might not be wrong after all in thinking that all was hers. The actual claim was heavy enough, but the possible claim was overwhelming. It seemed to Jack to go into the future and overshadow that as it overshadowed the present. No wonder Mr. Brownlow had been in despair—no wonder almost—The young man gave a very heavy sigh as he went into the stable-yard and gave his instructions. He stood and brooded over it with his brow knitted and his hands buried in his pockets, while the horses were put into the carriage. As for such luxuries, they counted for nothing, or at least so he thought for the moment—nothing to him; but a burden that would lie upon them for years—a shadow of debt and difficulty projected into the future—that seemed more than any man could bear. It will be seen from this that the idea of his own relations with Pamela making any difference in the matter had not crossed Jack's mind. He would have been angry had any one suggested it. Not that he thought of giving up Pamela; but in the mean time the idea of having any thing to do with Mrs. Preston was horrible to him, and he was not a young man who was always reasonable and sensible, and took every thing into consideration, any more than the rest of us. To tell the truth, he had no room in his thoughts for the idea of marriage or of Pamela at that moment. He strode round to the hall door as the coachman got on the box, and went up to Sara's room without stopping to think. "The carriage is here," he said, calling to Sara at the door. He would have taken the intruder down stairs, and put her into the carriage as courteously as if she had been a duchess; for, as we have already said, there was a certain fine natural politeness in the Brownlow blood. But when he heard the excited old woman still raving about her rights, and that they wanted to kill her, the young man became impatient. He was weary of her; and when she fell into threats of what she would do, disgust mingled with his impatience. Then all at once, while he waited, a sudden thought struck him of his little love. Poor little Pamela! what could she be thinking all this time? How would she feel when she heard that her mother had become their active enemy? In a moment there flitted before Jack, as he stood at the door, a sudden vision of the little uplifted face, pale as it had grown of late, with the wistful eyes wide open and the red lips apart, and the pretty rings of hair clustering about the forehead. What would Pamela think when she knew? What was to be done, now that this division, worse than any unkind sentence of a rich father, had come between them? It was no fault of hers, no fault of his; fate had come between them in the wildest unlooked-for way. And should they have to yield to it? The thought gave Jack such a sudden twinge in his own heart, that it roused him altogether out of his preoccupation. It roused him to that fine self-regard which is so natural, and which is reckoned a virtue nowadays. What did it matter about an old mother? Such people had had their day, and had no right to control the young whose day was still to come. Pamela's future and Jack's future were of more importance than any thing that could happen at the end, as it were, of Mrs. Preston's life, or even of Mr. Brownlow's life. This was the consideration that woke Jack up out of the strange maze he had fallen into on the subject of his own concerns. He turned on his heel all at once, and left Mrs. Preston arguing the matter with Sara, and went off down the avenue almost as rapidly as his own mare could have done it. No, by Jove! he was not going to give up. Mrs. Preston might eat her money if she liked—might ruin Brownlows if she liked; but she should not interfere between him and his love. And Jack felt that there was no time to lose, and that Pamela must know how matters stood, and what he expected of her, before her mother went back to poison her mind against him. He took no time to knock even at the door of Mrs. Swayne's cottage, but went in and took possession like an invading army. Probably, if he had been a young man of very delicate and susceptible mind, the very knowledge that Pamela might now be considered an heiress, and himself a poor man, would have closed up the way to him, and turned his steps forever from the door. But Jack was not of that fine order of humanity. He was a young man who liked his own way, and was determined not to be unhappy if he could help it, and held tenaciously by every thing that belonged to him. Such matter-of-fact natures are seldom moved by the sentimentalisms of self-sacrifice. He had not the smallest idea of sacrificing himself, if the truth must be told. He strode along, rushing like the wind, and went straight in at Mrs. Swayne's door. Nobody interrupted his passage or stood in his way; nobody even saw him but old Betty, who came out to her door to see who had passed so quickly, and shook her head over him. "He goes there a deal more than is good for him," Betty said, and then, as it was cold, shut the door.

Pamela had been sitting in the dingy parlor all alone; and, to tell the truth, she had been crying a little. She did not know where her mother was; she did not know when she was coming back. No message had reached her, nor letter, nor any sign of life, and she was frightened and very solitary. Jack, too, since he knew she was alone and could be seen at any hour, did not make so many anxious pilgrimages as he had done when Mrs. Preston was ill and the road was barred against him. She had no one to tell her fears to, no one to encourage and support her, and the poor child had broken down dreadfully. She was sitting at the window trying to read one of Mrs. Swayne's books, trying not to ask herself who it was that came so late to Brownlows last night? what was her mother doing? what was Jack doing? The book, as may be supposed, had small chance against all these anxieties. It had dropped upon the table before her, and her innocent tears had been dropping on it, when a sudden shadow flitted past the window, and a footstep rang on the steps, and Jack was in the room. The sight of him changed wonderfully the character of Pamela's tears, but yet it increased her agitation. Nobody in her small circle except herself had any faith in him; and she knew that, at this present moment, he ought not to come.

"No, I am not sorry to see you," she said, in answer to his accusation. "I am glad; but you should not come. Mamma is away. I am all alone."

"You have the more need of me," said Jack. "But listen, Pamela. Your mother is not away. She is here at Brownlows. She is coming directly. I rushed off to see you before she arrived. I must speak to you first. Remember you are mine—whatever happens, you are mine, and you can not forsake me."

"Forsake you?" cried Pamela, in pitiful accents. "Is it likely? If there is any forsaking, it will be you. You know—oh, you know you have not much to fear."

"I have every thing to fear," said Jack, speaking very fast; "your mother is breathing fire and flame against us all. She is coming back our enemy. She will tell you I have had a mercenary meaning from the beginning, and she will order you to give me up. But don't do it, Pamela. I am not the sort of man to be given up. We were going to be poor, and marry against my father's will; now we shall be poor, and marry against your mother's—that is all the difference. You have chosen me, and you must give up her and not me. That is all I have to say."

"Give up mamma?" cried Pamela, in amazement. "I don't know what you mean. You promised I was to have her with me, and take care of her always. She would die without me. Oh, Jack, why have you changed so soon?"

"It is not I that have changed," said Jack; "every thing has changed. This is what it will come to. It will be to give up her or me. I don't say I will die without you," said the young man—"no such luck; but—Look here, Pamela, this is what it will come to. You will have to choose between her and me."

"Oh no, no!" cried Pamela; "no! don't say so. I am not the one to choose. Don't turn away from me! don't look so pale and dreadful it is not me to choose."

"But it is you, by heavens!" cried Jack, in desperation. "Here she is coming! It is not your old mother who was to live with us—it is a different woman—here she is. Is it to be her or me?"

"Oh, Jack!" Pamela cried, thinking he was mad; and she submitted to his fierce embrace in utter bewilderment, not knowing what to imagine. To see the Brownlows carriage dash down the avenue and wheel round at the door and open to let Mrs. Preston forth was as great a wonder as if the earth had opened. She could not tell what was going to happen. It was a relief to her to be held fast and kept back—her consternation took her strength from her. She was actually unable to follow her first impulse and rush to the door.

Mrs. Preston came in by herself, quiet but tremulous. Her head shook a little, but there was no sign of weakness about her now. She had been defeated, but she had got over the bitterness of her defeat and was prepared for a struggle. Jack felt the difference when he looked at her. He had been contemptuous of her weak passion and repetition about her rights; but he saw the change in a moment, and he met her, standing up, holding Pamela fast, with his arm round her. Mrs. Preston had carried the war into her enemy's camp, and gone to his house to demand, as she thought, every thing he had in the world. These were Jack's reprisals—he came to her citadel and claimed every thing she had in the world. It was his, and, more than that, it was already given to him—his claim was allowed.

"You are here!" cried Mrs. Preston, passionately. "I thought you would be here! you have come before me to steal her from me. I knew how it would be!"

"I have come to claim what is mine," said Jack, "before you interfere. I know you will try to step between us; but you are not to step between us—do what you like, she is mine."

"Pamela," said Mrs. Preston, still, notwithstanding her late defeat, believing somehow strangely in the potency of the new fortune for which she felt every body should fall at her feet, "things have changed. Stand away from him, and listen to me. We're rich now—we shall have everything that heart ever desired; there is not a thing you can think of but what I can give it you. You've thought I was hard upon you, dear, but it was all for your sake. What do I care for money, but for your sake?—Every thing you can think of, Pamela—it will be like a fairy tale."

Pamela stood still for one moment, looking at her mother and her lover. She had disengaged herself from him, and stood, unrestrained, to make her election. "If it is so, mamma," she said, "I don't know what you mean—you know I don't understand; but if it is, there's no more difficulty. It does not matter so much whether Mr. Brownlow consents or not."

"Mr. Brownlow!" cried her mother; "Mr. Brownlow has been your enemy, child, since long before you were born. He has taken your money to bring up his own fine lady upon. He has sent his son here when he can't do any better, to marry you and keep the money. Sir, go away from my child. It's your money he wants; your money, not you."

Pamela turned round with surprise and terror in her face, and looked at Jack; then she smiled softly and shook her head. "Mamma, you are mistaken," she said in her soft little voice, and held out her hand to him. Mrs. Preston threw up her arms above her head wildly, and gave an exceeding bitter cry.

"I am her mother," she cried out, "her own mother, that have nursed her and watched over her, and given up every thing to her—and she chooses him rather than me—him that she has not known a year—that wants her for her money, or for her pretty face. She chooses him before me!"

She stood up alone, calling upon heaven and earth, as it were, to see; while the two clung together dismayed and pitiful, yet holding fast by each other still. It was the everlasting struggle so continually repeated; the past against the present and the future—the old love against the new—and not any question of worldly interest. It was the tragic figure of disappointment and desolation and age in face of hope and love and joy. What she had been doing was poor and mean enough. She had been intoxicated by the vision of sudden wealth, and had expected every body to be abject before her; but now a deeper element had come in. She forgot the fortune, the money, though it was still on her lips, and cried out, in the depth of her despair, over the loss of the only real wealth she had in the world. No tears came to her old eyes—her old meagre arms rose rigid, yet trembling. "She chooses him before me!" she said, with a cry of despair, which came from the bottom of her heart.

"Mamma," cried poor little Pamela, tearing her hand from that of her lover, and coming doubtfully into the midst between the two, "I don't choose! oh, mamma, how can I choose? I never was away from you in my life—he promised we never were to be parted. How am I to give him up? Oh, why, why should you ask me to give him up?" cried the poor child. Floods of tears came to her aid. She put her pretty hands together like a child at prayer—every line in her sweet face was in itself a supplication. Jack, behind her, stood and watched and said nothing. Perhaps he saw, notwithstanding, that it was against his interests—and in his heart had a certain mournful pity for the despair in the old woman's terrible face.

"But I expect you to choose," she said wildly; "things have come to that. It must be him or me—him or me; there's no midway between us. I am your old mother, your poor old mother, that would pluck my heart out of my breast to give it you. I've survived them all, and done without them all, and lived for your sake. And he is a young man that was taken with your pretty face—say it was your pretty face—say the best that can be said. If you were like death—if you lost all your beauty and your pretty ways—if you were ugly and ailing and miserable,—it would be all the same to me; I would love you all the more—all the more; and he—he would never look at you again. That's nature. I require you to choose. It must be him or me."

As she stood listening, a change came over Pamela's face. Her first appeal to her mother had been full of emotion, but of a gentle, hopeful, almost superficial kind. She had taken tears to her aid, and pleading looks, and believed in their success now as always. But as Mrs. Preston spoke, Pamela's little innocent soul was shaken as by an earthquake. She woke up and opened her eyes, and found that she was in a world new to her—a world no longer of prayers, and tears, and sweet yielding, and tender affection. It was not tender affection she had to do with now; it was fierce love, desperate and ruthless, ready to tear her asunder. Her tears dried up, her pretty cheeks grew pale as death, she looked from one to the other with a wild look of wonder, asking if it was true. When her mother's voice ceased, it seemed to Pamela that the world stood still for the moment, and every thing in heaven and earth held its breath. She looked at Jack; he stood motionless, with his face clouded over, and made no answer to her pitiful appeal. She looked at Mrs. Preston, and saw her mother's eager face hollow and excited, her eyes blazing, her cheeks burning with a strange hectic heat. For one moment she stood irresolute. Then she made one tottering step to her mother's side, and turned round and looked at her lover. Once more she clasped her hands, though she had no longer any hope in pleading. "I must stay here," she said, with a long-drawn sobbing sigh—"I must stay here, if I should die."

They stood thus and looked at each other for one of those moments which is as long as an age. The mother would have taken her child to her arms, but Pamela would not. "Not now, not now!" she said, putting back the embrace. Jack, for his part, stood and watched with an intensity of perception he had never exercised before—all power of speech seemed to have been taken from him. The struggle had ascended into a higher region of passion than he knew of. He turned and went to the door, with the intention, so far as he had any intention, of retiring for the moment from the contest. Then he came back again. Whatever the pressure on him might be, he could not leave Pamela so.

"Look here," he said abruptly; "I am going away. But if you think I accept this as a choice or decision, you are much mistaken. You force her to give in to you, and then you think I am to accept it! I'll do no such thing. She could not say any thing else, or do any thing else—but all the same, she is mine. You can't touch that, do what you like. Pamela, darling, don't lose heart; it's only for a little while."

He did not stop to listen to what her mother said; he turned at once and went out, unconsciously, in his excitement, thrusting Mrs. Swayne out of his way, who was in the passage. He went off up the avenue at a stretch without ever drawing breath. A hundred wild thoughts rose in his mind; her mother! what was her mother to him? He was ready to vow with Hamlet, that twenty thousand mothers could not have filled up his sum of love; and yet he was not blaming his Pamela. She could not have done otherwise. Why had he never been told? why had not he known that this downfall was hanging over him? Why had he been such a fool as to give in at all to the sweet temptation? Now, of course, when things had come this length, he would as soon have cut his own throat as given Pamela up. And what with love and rage, and the sudden calamity, and the gradual exasperation, he was beside himself, and did not well know what he was about. He was almost too much absorbed in his own affairs to be able to understand Sara, who came to him as he entered the house, and drew him aside into the dining-room to speak to him. Sara was pale enough to justify her pretext of headache, but otherwise she was full of energy and spirit, and met the emergency with a courageous heart.

"We must face it out as well as we can, Jack," she said, with her eyes shining out large and full from her white face. "We must keep up before all these people. They must not be able to go away and say that something went terribly wrong at Brownlows. We must keep it up to the last."

"Pshaw! what does it matter what they think or what they say?" said Jack, sitting down with a sigh of weariness. As for Sara, who was not tired, nor had any personal complication to bow her down, she blazed up at his indifference.

"It matters every thing!" she cried. "We may not be a county family any more, nor fine people, but we are always the Brownlows of Masterton. Nobody must have a word to say about it—for papa's sake."

"Every body will soon be at liberty to say what they please about it," said Jack. "Where is he? I had better go and talk to him, I suppose?"

"Papa is in the library," said Sara. "Jack, he wants our support. He wants us to stand by him—or, I mean, he wants you; as for me," she continued, with a flash of mingled softness and defiance, "he knows I would not forsake him; he wants you."

"Why shouldn't you forsake him?" said Jack, with a momentary growl; "and why should he be doubtful of me?"

But he did not wait for any answer. He took the decanter of sherry from the sideboard, and swallowed he did not know how much; and then he went off to the library to seek out his father. There was a certain stealthiness about the house—a feeling that the people belonging to it were having interviews in corners, that they were consulting each other, making solemn decisions, and that their guests were much in the way. Though Sara rushed away immediately to the room where her friends were, after waylaying her brother, her appearance did not alter the strong sense every body had of the state of affairs. The very servants slunk out of Jack's way, and stood aside in corners to watch him going into the library. He called the footman out of his hiding-place as he passed, and swore at him for an impertinent fool. The man had been doing nothing that was impertinent, and yet he did not feel that there was injustice in the accusation. Something very serious had happened, and the consciousness of it had gone all through the house.

Mr. Brownlow was sitting in the library doing nothing. That, at least, was his visible aspect. Within himself he had been calculating and reckoning up till his wearied brain whirled with the effort. He sat leaning his arms on the table and his head in his hands. By this time his powers of thought had failed him. He sat looking on, as it were, and saw the castle of his prosperity crumbling down into dust before him. Every thing he had ever aimed at seemed to drop from him. He had no longer any thing to conceal; but he knew that he had stood at the bar before his children, and had been pardoned but not justified. They would stand by him, but they did not approve him; and they had seen the veil of his heart lifted, and had looked in and found darker things there than he himself had ever been conscious of. He was so absorbed in this painful maze of thought that he did not even look up when Jack came in. Of course Jack would come; he knew that. Jack was ruined; they were all ruined. All for the advantage of a miserable woman who would get no comfort out of her inheritance, whose very life was hanging on a thread. It seemed hard to him that Providence, which had always been so kind to him, should permit it. When his son came in and drew a chair to the other side of the table he roused himself. "Is it you, Jack?" he said; "I am so tired that I fear I am stupid. I was very hard driven last night."

"Yes," said Jack, with a little shudder; and Mr. Brownlow looked at him, and their eyes met, and they knew what each had meant. It was a hard moment for the father who had been mad, and had come to his senses again, but yet did not know what horrible suspicion it was under which for a moment he had lain.

"I was hard driven," he repeated, pathetically—"very hard put to it. I had been standing out for a long time, and then in a moment I broke down—that is how it was. But I shall be able to talk it all over with you—by and by."

"That was what I came for, sir," said Jack. "We must know what we are to do."

And then Mr. Brownlow put down his supporting hands from his head, and steadied himself in a wearied wondering way. Jack for the moment had the authority on his side.

CHAPTER XXXIX

COMPOUND INTEREST

Mr. Brownlow and his son were a long time together. They talked until the autumn day darkened, and they had no more light for their calculations. Mr. Brownlow had been very weary, even stupefied. He had entered upon the conversation because he could not resist Jack's eagerness, and the decided claim he made to know fully a business which so much concerned him. He had a right to know, which his father could not dispute; but nevertheless all the events of the past twenty-four hours had worn Mr.

Brownlow out. He was stupefied; he did not know what had happened; he could not recollect the details. When his attention was fully arrested, a certain habit of business kept him on, and his mind was clear enough when they went into figures, and when he had to make his son aware of the magnitude of the misfortune which had almost thrown his own mind off its balance. The facts were beyond all comment. It was simple ruin; but such was the nature of the men, and their agreement in it, that they both worked out their reckoning unflinchingly, and when they saw what it was, did not so much as utter an exclamation. They laid down, the one his pen and the other his pencil, as the twilight darkened round them. There was no controversy between them. It was nobody's fault. Jack might have added a sting to every thing by reproaching his father for the ignorance in which he had been brought up, but he had no mind for any such useless exasperation. Things were as bad as bad could be; therefore they brought their calculations to an end very quietly, and came to the same conclusion as the darkness closed over them. They sat for a minute on opposite sides of the table, not looking at each other, with their papers before them, and their minds filled with one sombre thought. Whether it was that or the mere fall of day which was closing round them neither could have told—only that under this dull oppression there was in Jack's mind a certain wild suppressed impatience, an overwhelming sense of all that was included in the crisis; while his father in the midst of it could not repress a strange longing to throw himself down upon the sofa, to close his eyes, to be alone in the silence and darkness. Rest was his most imperative want. The young man's mind was thrilling with a desire to be up and at his troubles, to fight and make some head against them. But then things were new to Jack; whereas to Mr. Brownlow, who had already made a long and not guiltless struggle, the only thing apparent and desirable was rest—to lie down and be quiet for a little, to have no question asked him, nothing said to him, or, if it should please God, to sleep.

Jack, however, was not the man, under the circumstances, to let his father get either sleep or rest. After they had made all the calculations possible, and said every thing that was to be said, he did not go away, but sat silent, biting his nails and pondering much in his mind. They had been thus for about half an hour without exchanging a word, when he suddenly broke into speech.

"It must go into Chancery, I suppose?" he said. "She has got to prove her identity, and all that. You will have time at least to realize all your investments. Too much time perhaps."

"She is an old woman," said Mr. Brownlow. He was thinking of nothing beyond the mere matter of fact, and there was no meaning in his voice, but yet it startled his son. "And you were to marry her daughter. I had almost forgotten that. You were very decided on the subject last time you spoke to me. In that case every thing would be yours."

"I hope she may live forever!" said Jack, getting up from his chair; "and she has no intention of giving me her daughter now—not that her intention matters much," he said to himself, half muttering, as he stood with his hand on the table. The change was bewildering. He would have his Pamela still, whatever any body might say; but to run away with his pretty penniless darling, and work for her and defy the world for her, was very different from running away with the little heiress who had a right to every penny he had supposed his own. It was very hard upon him; but all the same he had no intention of giving in. No idea of self-sacrifice ever crossed his mind. It made the whole matter more confusing, more disagreeable—but any body's intention mattered very little, father or mother; he meant to have his love and his way all the same.

"It does matter," said Mr. Brownlow. "It had much better never go into Chancery at all. I never had any objections to the girl—you need not be impatient. I always liked the girl. She is like your mother. I never knew what it was—" Then Mr. Brownlow made a little pause. "Poor Bessie!" he said, though it was an exclamation that did not seem called for. It was this fortune that had first made him think of Bessie. It was for her sake—for the sake of making a very foolish marriage—that he had made use of the money which at first was nothing but a plague and burden to him. Somehow she seemed to come up before him now it was melting away, and he knew that the charm of Pamela's dewy eyes and fresh face had been their resemblance to Bessie. The thought softened his heart, and yet made it sting and ache. "This matter is too important for temper or pride," he went on, recovering himself. "If we are to treat as enemies, of course I must resist, and it will be a long suit, and perhaps outlive us all. But if you are to be her daughter's husband, the question is different. You are the natural negotiator between us."

"I can't be; it is impossible," cried Jack; and then he sat down again in his chair in a sort of sullen fury with himself. Of course he was the natural negotiator. It was weakness itself to think of flinching from so plain a duty; and yet he would rather have faced a battery or led a forlorn hope.

"You must be," said Mr. Brownlow. "We are all excited at this present moment; but there can be no doubt of what your position entails. You are my son, and you are, against my will, contrary to my advice, engaged to her daughter. Unless you mean to throw off the girl you love because she has suddenly become an heiress—"

"I mean nothing of the sort," cried Jack, angrily. "I shall never throw her off."

"Then you can't help having an interest in her fortune;—and doing the best you can for her," said his father, after a pause.

Then again silence fell upon the two. It was natural and reasonable, but it was utterly repugnant, even though one of them thus urged it, to both. A thing may be recommended by good sense, and by all the force of personal interest, and yet may be more detestable than if it was alike foolish and wicked. This was how it seemed to Jack; and for Mr. Brownlow, in the whirl of ruin which had sucked him in, it was as yet but a poor consolation that his son might get the benefit. Acting by the dictates of nature he would rather have kept his son at his side to share his fortune and stand by him. Yet it was his duty to advise Jack to go over to the other side and take every thing he had from him, and negotiate the transfer of his fortune—to "do the best he could," in short, for his father's adversary. It was not an expedient agreeable to either, and yet it was a thing which reason and common sense demanded should be done.

While they sat thus gloomily together, the household went on in a strangely uncomfortable way outside. The men came straggling in from their shooting, or whatever they had been doing; and, though Sara was with the ladies, every body knew by instinct, as it seemed, that her father and brother were consulting together over something very serious, shut up in the library, Mr. Brownlow neglecting his business and Jack his pleasure. If it had only been business that was neglected, nobody would have been surprised; but when things were thus pushed beyond that natural regard for appearances which is born with Englishmen, they must be serious indeed. Then, of course, to make matters worse, the gentlemen came in earlier than usual. It was their curiosity, the elder ladies said to each other, for every body knows that it is men who are the true gossips and ferret every thing out; but, however that might be, it threw additional embarrassment upon Sara, who stood bravely at her post—a little flushed, perhaps, and unnaturally gay, but holding out with dauntless courage. She had every thing to take on her own shoulders. That night, as it happened by unlucky chance, there was to be a dinner-party. Sir Charles Motherwell and his mother were coming, and were to stay all night; and the rector was coming, he who knew the house better than any body else, and would be most quick of all to discover the difference in it. The recollection of the gathering in the evening had gone out of Mr. Brownlow's mind and even Jack had forgotten all about it. "Like men!" Sara said to herself, indignantly. She had every thing to do, though she had not slept all night, and had not escaped her share of the excitement of the day. She had to give all the orders and make all the arrangements, and now sat dauntless pouring out the tea, keeping every body at bay, acknowledging the importance of the crisis only by unusual depth of color on her cheek, and an unusual translucent sheen in her big eyes. They did not flash or sparkle as other eyes might have done, but shone like globes full of some weird and visionary light. She had an answer ready for every body, and yet all the while she was racking her mind to think what could they be doing down stairs, what decision could they be coming to? She was doing her part stoutly in ignorance and patience, spreading her pretty draperies before them, as it were, and keeping the world at arm's length. "Oh, yes, the Motherwells are coming," she said, "but they will come dressed for dinner, which none of us are as yet. They are only at Ridley—they have not very far to come. Yes, I think we had better have a dance. Jack is not good for much in that way. He never was. He was always an out-of-doors sort of boy."

"He does not seem to care for out-of-doors either," said one of the young ladies; "and, Sara, I wonder what has happened to him. He always looks as if he were thinking of something else."

"Something else than—what?" said Sara. "He has something else than us to think of—if that is what you mean. He is not one of your idle people—" which speech was met by a burst of laughter.

"Oh no; he is very diligent; he loves business," said young Keppel. "We are all aware of that."

"He is not at the bar, you know," retorted the dauntless Sara. "He has not briefs pouring in upon him like—some people. But it is very good of you to take so much notice of us between the circuits—is that the right word? And to reward you, you shall manage the dance? Does Sir Charles dance? I suppose so—all common people do."

"Sara, my love, don't speak so," said one of the matrons. "The Motherwells are one of the best families in the country. I don't know what you mean by common people."

"I mean people who are just like other people," said Sara, "as we all are. If we did not wear different colored dresses and have different-colored hair and eyes, I don't see how we could be told from each other. As for gentlemen generally, you know one never knows which is which!" she cried, appealing to the candor of her friends. "We pretend to do it, to please them. Half of them have light beards and half of them have dark, and one never gets any farther; except with those whom one has the honor to know," said Sara, rising and making a courtesy to the young men who were round her. Then, amid laughter and remonstrances, they all went fluttering away—too early, as most of the young people thought—to their rooms to dress. And some of them thought Sara "really too bad;" and some were sure the gentlemen did not like it. The gentlemen, however, did not seem to mind. They said to each other, "By Jove! how pretty she was to-night;" and some of them wondered how much money she would have; and some supposed she would marry Charley Motherwell after all. And, for the moment, what with dinner approaching and the prospect of the dance after, both the ladies and the men forgot to wonder what could be the matter with the family, and what Mr. Brownlow was saying to Jack.

But as for Sara, she did not forget. Though she was first to move, she was still in the drawing-room when they all went away, and came pitifully up to the big fire which sent gleams of light about through all the dark room, and knelt down on the hearth and warmed her hands, and shivered, not with cold, but excitement. Her eyes were big and nervous and dilated; but though her tears came easily enough on ordinary occasions, to-night she did not cry. She knelt before the fire and held out her hands to it, and then wrung them hard together, wondering how she should ever be able to go through the evening, and what they were doing down stairs, and whether she should not go and remind them of the dinner. It seemed to her as if for the moment she had got rid of her enemies, and had time to think; but she was too restless to think, and every moment seemed an hour to her. As soon as the steps and voices of the guests became inaudible on the stairs, she got up, and went down to seek them out in the library. There were two or three servants in the hall, more than had any right to be there, and Willis, who was standing at the foot of the stairs, came up to her in a doubtful, hesitating way. A gentleman had come up from the office, he said; but he did not like to disturb Master, as was a-talking with Mr. John in the library. The gentleman was in the dining-room. Would Miss Sara see him, or was her papa to be told? Sara was so much excited already, that she saw in this visitor only some new trouble, and jumped at the idea of meeting it herself, and perhaps saving her father something. "I will see him," she said; and she called up all her resolution, and went rapidly, with the haste of desperation, into the dining-room. The door had closed behind her, and she had glided past the long, brilliant, flower-decked table to where somebody was standing by the fire-place ere she really thought what she was doing. When the stranger started and spoke, Sara woke up as from a dream; and when she found it was Powys who was looking at her—looking anxious, wistful, tender, not like the other people—the poor girl's composure failed her. She gave him one glance, and then all the tears that had been gathering in her eyes suddenly burst forth. "Oh, Mr. Powys, tell me what it is all about!" she cried, holding out her hands to him. And he, not knowing what he was doing, not thinking of himself or of his love, only penetrated to the heart by her tears, sprang forward and took her into his arms and comforted her. There was one moment in which neither of them knew. For that brief instant they clung to each other unwitting, and then they fell apart, and stood and looked at each other, and trembled, not knowing in their confusion and consciousness and trouble what to say.

"Don't be angry with me!" he cried; "I did not know what I was doing—I did not mean—forgive me!—you were crying, and I could not bear it; how could I stand still and see you cry?"

"I am not angry," said Sara, softly. Never in her life had she spoken so softly before. "I know you did not mean it; I am in such terrible trouble; and they never told me it was you."

Then Powys crept closer once more, poor young fellow, knowing he ought not, but too far gone for reason. "But it is I," he said, softly touching the hand with which she leaned on the mantle piece,—"to serve you—to do any thing—any thing! only tell me what there is that I can do?"

Then she looked up with her big lucid eyes, and two big tears in them, and smiled at him though her heart felt like to burst, and put out her hands again, knowing this time what she was doing; and he took them, half-crazed with the joy and the wickedness. "I came up with some papers," he said; "I came against my will; I never thought, I never hoped to see you; and your father will think I have done it dishonorably on purpose; tell me, oh, tell me, what I can do."

"I don't think you can do any thing," said Sara, "nor any body else. I should not speak to you, but I can't help it. We are in great trouble. And then you are the only one I could speak to," said the girl, with unconscious self-betrayal. "I think we have lost every thing we have in the world."

"Lost every thing!" said Powys; his eyes began to dance, and his cheek to burn—"lost every thing!" It was he now who trembled with eagerness, and surprise, and joy. "I don't want to be glad," he cried, "but I could work for you, slave for you—I shouldn't mind what I did—"

"Oh, hush!" cried Sara, interrupting him, "I think I hear papa: it might not matter for us, but it is him we ought to think of. We have got people coming, and I don't know what to do—I must go to papa."

Then the young man stood and looked at her wistfully. "I can't help you with that," he said, "I can't be any good to you—the only thing I can do is to go away; but, Sara! you have only to tell me; you know—"

"Yes," she said, lifting her eyes to him once more, and the two big tears fell, and her lips quivered as she tried to smile; she was not angry—"yes," she said, "I know;" and then there were sounds outside, and in a moment this strange, wild, sweet surprise was over. Sara rushed out to the library without another word, and Powys, tingling to the very points of his fingers, gave his bundle of papers to Willis to be given to Mr. Brownlow, and said he would come back, and rushed out into the glare of Lady Motherwell's lamps as her carriage came sweeping up the avenue. He did not know who the little old lady was, nor who the tall figure with the black mustache might be in the corner of the carriage; but they both remarked him as he came down the steps at a bound. It gave them their first impression of something unusual about the house. "It is seven now," Lady Motherwell said, "and dinner ought to be in half an hour—what an odd moment to go away." She was still more surprised to see no one but servants when she entered, and to be shown into the deserted drawing-room where there was not a sign of any one about. "I don't know what they mean by it, Charley," Lady Motherwell said; "Mr. Brownlow or somebody was always here to receive us before." Sir Charles did not say any thing, but he pulled his mustache, and he, too, thought it was rather queer.

When Sara rushed into the library not five minutes before Lady Motherwell's arrival, the consultation there had been broken up. Jack, notwithstanding his many preoccupations, had yet presence of mind enough to remember that it was time to dress, as well as to perceive that all had been said that could be said. Mr. Brownlow was alone. He had stolen to the sofa for which he had been longing all the afternoon, and had laid himself down on it. The room was very dimly lighted by a pair of candles on the mantle-piece. It was a large room, and the faint twinkle of those distant lights made it look ghostly, and it was a very strange sight to see Mr. Brownlow lying on a sofa. He roused himself when Sara came in, but it was with an effort, and he was very reluctant to be disturbed. "Seven o'clock!" he said—"is it seven o'clock? but leave me a little longer, my darling; ten minutes is enough for dress."

"Oh, papa," said Sara, "it is dreadful to think of dress at all, or any thing so trifling, on such a day; but we must do it—people will think—; I am sure even already they may be thinking—"

"Yes," said Mr. Brownlow, vaguely—"I don't think it matters—I would rather have five minutes' sleep."

"Papa," said Sara in desperation, "I have just seen Mr. Powys—he has come with some papers—that is, I think he has gone away. He came to—to—I mean he told me he was sent to—I did not understand what it was, but he has gone away—"

"Ah, he has gone away," said Mr. Brownlow, sitting up; "that is all right—all right. And there are the Motherwells coming. Sara, I think Charles Motherwell is a very honest sort of man."

"Yes, papa," said Sara. She was too much excited and disturbed to perceive clearly what he meant, and yet the contrast of the two names struck her dimly. At such a moment what was Charles Motherwell to her?

"I think he's a very good fellow," said Mr. Brownlow, rising; and he went and stirred the smoldering fire. Then he came up to where she stood, watching him. "We shall have to go and live in the house at Masterton," he said, with a sigh. "It will be a strange place for such a creature as you."

"I don't see why it should be strange for me," said Sara; and then her face blazed suddenly with a color her father did not understand. "Papa, I shall have you all to myself," she said, hurriedly, feeling in her heart more than half a hypocrite. "There will be no troublesome parties like this, and nobody we don't want to see."

Mr. Brownlow looked at her half suspiciously; but he did not know what had happened in those two minutes beside the fruit and flowers in the dining-room. He made a desperate effort to recover himself, and to take courage and play out his part steadily to the end.

"We must get through it to-night," he said. "We must keep up for to-night. Go and put on all your pretty things, my darling. You have had to bear the brunt of every thing to-day."

"No, papa; it does not matter," said Sara, smothering the longing she had to cry, and tell him—tell him?—she did not know what. And then she turned and put her one question. "Is it true?—have we nothing? Is it all as that terrible woman said?"

Mr. Brownlow put his hand on her arm and leaned upon her, slight prop as she was. "You were born in the old house in Masterton," he said, with a certain tone of appeal in his voice; "your mother lived in it. It was bright enough once." Then he stopped and led her gently toward the door. "But, Sara, don't forget," he said hurriedly, "I think a great deal of Charles Motherwell—I am sure he is kind and honest and true."

"He has nothing to do with us!" said Sara, with a thrill of fear.

"I don't know," said Mr. Brownlow, almost humbly. "I don't know—if it might be best for you—"

And then he kissed her and sent her away. Sara flew to her own room with her heart beating so loud that it almost choked her. So many excitements all pressing on her together—so many things to think of—was almost more than an ordinary brain could bear. And to dress in all her bravery and go down and look as if nothing had happened—to sit at the head of the table just there where she had been standing half an hour before—to smile and talk and look her best as if every thing was steady under her feet, and she knew of no volcano! And then, to crown all, Sir Charles Motherwell! In the height of her excitement it was perhaps a relief to her to think how at least she would crush that one pretendant. If it should be the last act of her reign at Brownlows, there would be a certain poetic justice in it. If he was so foolish, if he was so persistent, Sara savagely resolved that she would let him propose this time. And then! But then she cried, to Angelique's great discomfiture, without any apparent reason. What was to be done with a young lady who left herself but twenty minutes to dress in, and wept in an unprovoked and exasperating way in the middle of it? Sara was so shaken and driven about by emotion and by self-restraint that she was humble to Angelique in the midst of all her own tumults of soul.

CHAPTER XL

The dinner passed over without, so far as the guests were aware, any special feature in it. Jack might look out of sorts, perhaps, but then Jack had been out of sorts for some time past. As for Sara, the roses on her cheeks were so much brighter than usual, that some people went so far as to suppose she had stooped to the vulgar arts of the toilet. Sir Charles Motherwell was by her side, and she was talking to him with more than ordinary vivacity. Mr. Brownlow, for his part, looked just as usual. People do not trouble themselves to observe whether the head of the house, when it is a man of his age, looks pale or otherwise. He talked just as usual; and though, perhaps, it was he who had suffered most in this crisis, it did not cost him so much now as it did to his son and daughter. And the new people who came only for the evening, and knew nothing about it, amused the people who were living at Brownlows, and had felt in the air some indication of the storm. Every thing went on well, to the amazement of those who were principally concerned—that is to say, every thing went on like a dream; the hours and all the sayings and doings in them, even those which they themselves did and said, swept on, and carried with them the three who had anxieties so much deeper at heart. Sara's cheeks kept burning crimson all the night; and Mr. Brownlow stood apart and talked heavily with one or other of his guests; and Jack did the best he could—going so far as to dance, which was an exercise he did not much enjoy. And the guests called it "a very pleasant evening," with more than ordinary sincerity. When the greater part of those heavy hours had passed, and they began to see the end of their trial, a servant came into the room and addressed himself to Jack, who was just then standing with his partner in the pause of a waltz. Sara, though she was herself flying round the room at the moment, saw it, and lost breath. Mr. Brownlow saw it from the little inner drawing-room. It seemed to them that every eye was fixed upon that one point, but the fact was nobody even noticed it but themselves and Jack's partner, who was naturally indignant when he gave up her hand and took her back to her seat. Somebody wanted to see him, the servant said—somebody who would not take any answer, but insisted on seeing Mr. John—somebody from the cottages at the gate. It was Willis himself who came, and he detracted in no way from the importance of the communication. His looks were grave enough for a plenipotentiary. His master, looking at him, felt that Willis must know all; but Willis, to tell the truth, knew nothing. He felt that something was wrong, and, with the instinct of a British domestic, recognized that it was his duty to make the most of it—that was all. Jack went out following him, but the people who did not know there was any thing significant in his going, took very little notice of it. The only visible consequence was, that thenceforward Sara was too tired to dance, and Mr. Brownlow forgot what he was saying in the middle of a sentence. Simple as the cause might be, it was alarming to them.

Jack asked the man no questions as he went down stairs; he was himself wound-up and ready for any thing. Whatever additional hardship or burden might come, his position could scarcely be made worse. So he was in a manner indifferent. What could it matter? In the hall he found Mrs. Swayne standing wrapped up in a big shawl. She was excited, and fluttered, and breathless, and almost unable to speak, and the shawl which was thrown over her head showed that she had come in haste. She put her hand on Jack's arm, and drew him to a side out of hearing of the servants, and then her message burst forth.

"It's not what I ever thought I'd come to. It ain't what I'd do, if e'er a one of us were in our right senses," she cried. "But you must come down to her this very moment. Come along with me, Mr. John. It's that dark I've struck my foot again' every tree, and I've come that fast I ain't got a bit of breath left in my body. Come down to her this very moment. Come along with me."

"What is the matter?" said Jack.

"Matter! It's matter enough," gasped Mrs. Swayne, "or it never would have been me to come leaving my man in his rheumatics, and the street door open, and an old shawl over my head. And there ain't one minute to be lost. Get your hat and something to keep you warm, and I'll tell you by the way. It's bitter cold outside."

In spite of himself Jack hesitated. His pride rose up against the summons. Pamela had left him and gone over to her mother's side, and her mother was no longer a nameless poor woman, but the hard creditor who was about to ruin him and his. Though he had vowed that he would never give her up, yet somehow at that moment his pride got the better of his love. He hesitated, and stood looking at the breathless messenger, who herself, in her turn, began to look at him with a certain contempt.

"If you ain't a-coming, Mr. John," said Mrs. Swayne, "say so—that's all as I ask. Not as I would be any way surprised. It's like men. When you don't want 'em, they'll come fast enough; but when you're in need, and they might be of some use—Ugh! that ain't my way. I wouldn't be the wretch as would leave that poor young critter in her trouble, all alone."

"All alone—what do you mean?" said Jack, following her to the door, and snatching his hat as he passed. "How can she be alone? Did she send you? What trouble is she in? Woman, can't you tell me what you mean?"

"I won't be called woman by you, not if you was ten times as grand—not if you was a duke or a lord," said Mrs. Swayne, rushing out into the night. Beyond the circle of the household lights, the gleaming lamp at the door and lighted windows, the avenue was black as only a path in the heart of the country can be. The night was intensely dark, the rain drizzling, and now and then a shower of leaves falling with the rain. Two or three long strides brought Jack up with the indignant Mrs. Swayne, who ran and stumbled, but made indifferent progress. He took hold of her arm, and in his excitement unconsciously gave her a shake.

"Keep by me and I'll guide you," he said; "and tell me in a word what is the matter, and how she happens to be alone."

Then Mrs. Swayne's passion gave way to tears. "You'd think yourself alone," she cried, "If you was left with one as has had a shock, and don't know you no more than Adam, and ne'er a soul in the house, now I'm gone, but poor old Swayne with his rheumatics, as can't stir, not to save his life. You'd think it yourself if it was you. But catch a man a-forgetting of hisself like that; and the first thought in her mind was for you. Oh me! oh me! She thought you'd ha' come like an arrow out of a bow."

"A shock?" said Jack vaguely to himself; and then he let go his hold of Mrs. Swayne's arm. "I can't wait for you," he said; "I can be there quicker than you." And he rushed wildly into the darkness, forsaking her. He was at the gate before the bewildered woman, thus abandoned, could make two steps in advance. As he dashed past old Betty's cottage, he saw inside the lighted window a face he knew, and though he did not recognize who it was, a certain sense of help at hand came over him. Another moment and he was in Mrs. Swayne's cottage, so far recollecting himself as to tread more softly as he rushed up the dark and narrow stair. When he opened the door, Pamela gave but one glance round to greet him. She was alone, as Mrs. Swayne had said. On the bed by which she stood lay a marble figure, dead to all appearance except for its eyes. Those eyes moved in the strangest, most terrible way, looking wildly round and round, now at the ceiling, now at the window, now at Pamela, imperious and yet agonized. And poor little Pamela, soft girlish creature, stood desperate, trying to read what they said.

She had not a word to give to Jack—not even a look, except for one brief moment. "What does she want—what does she want?" she cried. "Oh, mamma! mamma! will you not try to speak?"

"Is there no one with you?" said Jack. "Have you sent for the doctor? How long has she been like this? My darling! my poor little darling! Has the doctor seen her yet?"

"I sent for you," said Pamela, piteously. "Oh, what does she want? I think she could speak if she would only try."

"It is the doctor she wants," cried Jack. "That is the first thing;" and he turned and rushed down stairs still more rapidly than he had come up. The first thing he did was to go across to old Betty's cottage, and send the old woman to Pamela's aid, or at least, if aid was impossible, to remain with her. There he found Powys, who was waiting till the guests went away from Brownlows. Him Jack placed in Mrs. Swayne's parlor, to be ready to lend any assistance that might be wanted, or to call succor from the great house if necessary; and then he himself buttoned his coat and set off on a wild race over hedge and field for the doctor. The nearest doctor was in Dewsbury, a mile and a half away. Jack knew every step of the country, and plunged into the unseen by-ways and across the ploughed fields; in so short a time that Mrs. Swayne had scarcely reached her own house before he dashed back again in the doctor's gig. Then he went into the dark little parlor to wait and take breath. He was in evening-dress, just as he had been dancing; his light varnished boots were heavy with ploughed soil and wet earth, his shirt wet with rain, his whole appearance wild and disheveled. Powys looked at him with the strange mixture of repugnance and liking that existed between the young men, and drew forward a chair for him before the dying fire.

"Why did not you let me go?" he said. "I was in better trim for it than you."

"You did not know the way," said Jack; "besides there are things that nobody can do for one." Then he added, after a pause, "Her daughter is going to be my wife."

"Ah!" said Powys, with a sigh, half of sympathy, half of envy. He did not think of Jack's circumstances in any speculative way, but only as comparing them with his own hard and humble fate, who should never have a wife, as he said to himself—to whom it was mere presumption, madness, to think of love at all.

"Yes," said Jack, putting his wet feet to the fire; and then he too gave forth a big sigh from his excited breast, and felt the liking grow stronger than the repugnance, and that he must speak to some one or die.

"It is a pretty mess," he said; "I thought they were very poor, and it turns out she has a right to almost all my father has—trust-money that was left to him if he could not find her; and he was never able to find her. And, at last, after all was settled between us, she turns up; and now, I suppose, she's going to die."

"I hope not," said Powys, not knowing what answer to make.

"It's easy to say you hope not," said Jack, "but she will—you'll see she will. I never saw such a woman. And then what am I to do?—forsake my poor Pamela, who does not know a word of it, because she is an heiress, or marry her and rob my father? You may think yours is a hard case, but I'd like to know what you would do if you were me?"

"I should not forsake her, anyhow," said Powys, kindling with the thought.

"And neither shall I, by Jove," said Jack, getting up in his vehemence. "What should I care for fathers and mothers, or any fellow in the world? It's all that cursed money—that's what it always is. It comes in your way and in my way wherever a man turns—not that one can get on without it either," said Jack, suddenly sitting down and leaning over the fire with his face propped up in his two hands.

"Some of us have got to do without it," said Powys, with a short laugh, though he did not see any thing amusing in it. Yet there was a certain bitter drollery in the contrast between his own little salary and the family he had already to support on it, and Jack's difficulties at finding that his Cinderella had turned into a fairy princess. Jack gave a hasty glance at him, as if fearing that he himself was being laughed at. But poor Powys had a sigh coming so close after his laugh that it was impossible to suspect him of mockery. Jack sighed too, for company. His heart was opened; and the chance of talking to any body was a godsend to him in that moment of suspense.

"Were you to have been with us this evening?" he said. "Why did not you come? My father always likes to see you."

"He does not care to see me now," said Powys, with a little bitterness; "I don't know why. I went up to carry him some papers, against my will. He took me to your house as first against my own judgment. It would have been better for me I had walked over a precipice or been struck down like the poor lady up stairs."

"No," said Jack, pitying, and yet there was a touch of condescension in his voice. "Don't say so—not so bad as that. A man may make a mistake, and yet it need not kill him. There's the doctor—I must hear what he has to say."

The doctor came in looking very grave. He said there were signs of some terrible mental tumult and shock she had received; that all the symptoms were of the worst kind, and that he had no hope whatever for her life. She might recover her faculties and be able to speak; but it was almost certain she must die. This was the verdict pronounced upon Mrs. Preston as the carriage lamps of the departing guests began to gleam down the avenue, and old Betty rushed across to open the gates, and the horses came prancing out into the road. Pamela caught a momentary glimpse of them as she moved about the room, and it suddenly occurred to her to remember her own childish delight at the sight when she first came. And oh, how many things had happened since then! And this last of all which she understood least. She was sick with terror and wonder, and her head ached and her heart throbbed. They were her mother's eyes which looked at her so, and yet she was afraid of them. How was she ever to live out the endless night?

It was a dreadful night for more people than Pamela. Powys went up to the great house very shortly after to carry the news to Mr. Brownlow, who was so much overcome by it that he shivered and trembled and looked for the moment like a feeble old man. He sank down into his chair, and could not speak at first. "God forgive me," he said when he had recovered himself. "I am afraid I had ill thoughts of her—very ill thoughts in my head. Sara, you heard all—was I harsh to her? It could not be any thing I said?"

"No, papa," said Sara, trembling, and she came to him and drew his head for a moment to her young, tremulous, courageous breast. And Powys stood looking on with a pang in his heart. He did not understand what all this meant, but he knew that she was his and yet could not be his. He dared not go and console her as he had done in his madness when they were alone.

Mr. Brownlow would not go to bed; he sat and watched, and sent for news through the whole long night. And Powys, who knew only by Jack's short and incoherent story what important issues were involved, served him faithfully as his messenger coming and going. The thoughts that arose in Mr. Brownlow's mind were not to be described. It was not possible that compunction such as that which moved him at first could be his only feeling. As the hours went on, a certain strange mixture of satisfaction and reproach against Providence came into his mind. He said Providence in his mind, being afraid and ashamed to say God. If Providence was about to remove this obstacle out of his way, it would seem but fitting and natural; but why, then why, when it was to be, not have done it a few days sooner? Two days sooner?—that would have made all the difference. Now the evil she had done would not die with her, though it might be lessened. In these unconscious inarticulate thoughts, which came by no will of his, which haunted him indeed against his will, there rose a certain upbraiding against the tardy fate. It was too late. The harm was done. As it was, it seemed natural that his enemy should be taken out of his way, for Providence had ever been very kind to him—but why should it be this one day too late?

Jack sat down stairs in Mrs. Swayne's parlor all the night. The fire went out, and he had not the heart to have it lighted: one miserable candle burned dully in the chill air. Now and then Powys came in from the darkness without, glowing from his rapid walk; sometimes Mrs. Swayne came creaking down stairs to tell him there was no change; once or twice he himself stole up to see the same awful sight. Poor Pamela, for her part, sat by the bedside half stupefied by her vigil. She had not spirit enough left to give one answering look to her lover. Her brain was racking with devices to make out what her mother meant. She kept talking to her, pleading with her, entreating—oh, if she would but try to speak! and ever in desperation making another and another effort to get at her meaning. Jack could not bear the sight. The misery, and darkness, and suspense down stairs were less dreadful at least than this. Even the doctor, though he knew nothing of what lay below, had been apparently excited by the external aspect of affairs, and came again before day-break to see if any change were perceptible. It was that hour of all others most chilling and miserable; that hour which every watcher knows, just before dawn, when the darkness seems more intense, the cold more keen, the night more lingering and wretched than at any other moment. Jack in his damp and thin dress walked shivering about the little black parlor, unable to keep still.

She might die and make no sign; and if she did so, was it possible still to ignore all that had happened, and to bestow her just heritage on Pamela only under cover as his wife? This was the question that racked him as he waited and listened; but when the doctor went up just before day-break a commotion was heard in the room above. Jack stood still for a moment holding his breath, and then he rushed up stairs. Before he got into the room there arose suddenly a hoarse voice, which was scarcely intelligible. It was Mrs. Preston who was speaking. "What was it? what was it?" she was crying wildly. "What did I tell you, child?" and then, as he opened the door, a great outcry filled the air. "Oh, my God, I've forgotten—I've forgotten!" cried the dying woman. She was sitting up in her bed in a last wild rally of all her powers. Motion and speech had come back to her. She was propping herself up on her two thin arms, thrusting herself forward with a strained and excessive muscular action, such as extreme weakness sometimes is equal to. As she looked round wildly with the same eager impotent look that had wrung the beholders' hearts while she was speechless, her eye fell on Jack, who was standing at the door. She gave a sudden shriek of mingled triumph and entreaty. "You can tell them," she said—"you can tell me—come and tell me—tell me! Pamela, there is one that knows."

"Oh, mamma, I don't want to hear," cried Pamela; "oh, lie down and take what the doctor says; oh, mamma, mamma, if you care for me! Don't sit up and wear out your strength, and break my heart."

"It's for you—it's all for you!" cried the sufferer; and she moved the hands on which she was supporting herself, and threw forward her ghastly head, upon which Death itself seemed to have set its mark. "I've no time to lose—I'm dying, and I've forgotten it all. Oh, my God, to think I should forget! Come here, if you are a man, and tell me what it was!"

Jack stepped forward like a man in a dream. He saw that she might fall and die the next moment; her worn bony arms began to tremble, her head fell forward, her eyes staring at him seemed to loosen in their sockets. Perhaps she had but half an hour longer to live. The strength of death was in her no less than its awful weakness. "Tell me," she repeated, in a kind of babble, as if she could not stop. Pamela, who never thought nor questioned what her mother's real meaning was, kept trying, with tears and all her soft force, to lay her down on the pillows; and the doctor, who thought her raving, stood by and looked on with a calm professional eye, attributing all her excitement to the delirium of death. In the midst of this preoccupied group Jack stood forward, held by her eye. An unspeakable struggle was going on in his mind. Nobody believed there was any meaning in her words. Was it he that must give them a meaning, and furnish forth the testimony that was needed against himself? It was but to be silent, that was all, and no one would be the wiser. Mrs. Swayne, too, was in the room, curious but unsuspicious. They all thought it was she who was "wandering," and not that he had any thing to tell.

Then once more she raised her voice, which grew harsher and weaker every moment. "I am dying," she cried; "if you will not tell me I will speak to God. I will speak to him—about it—he—will send word—somehow. Oh my God, tell me—tell me—what was it?—before I die."

Then they all looked at him, not with any real suspicion, but wondering. Jack was as pale almost as the dying creature who thus appealed to him. "I will tell you," he said, in a broken voice. "It was about money. I can't speak about legacies and interest here. I will speak of it—when—you are better. I will see—that she has her rights."

"Money!" cried Mrs. Preston, catching at the word—"money—my mother's money—that is what it was. A fortune, Pamela! and you'll have friends—plenty of friends when I'm gone. Pamela, Pamela, it's all for you."

Then she fell back rigid, not yielding, but conquered; for a moment it seemed as if some dreadful fit was coming on; but presently she relapsed into the state in which she had been before—dumb, rigid, motionless, with a frame of ice, and two eyes of fire. Jack staggered out of the room, broken and worn out; the very doctor, when he followed, begged for wine, and swallowed it eagerly. It was more than even his professional nerves could bear.

"She ought to have died then," he said; "by all sort of rules she ought to have died; but I don't see much difference in her state now; she might go on like that for days—no one can say."

Jack was not able to make any answer; he was worn out as if with hard work; his forehead was damp with exhaustion; he too gulped down some of the wine Mrs. Swayne brought them, but he had no strength to make any reply.

"Mr. Brownlow, let me advise you to go home," said the doctor; "no one can do any good here. You must make the young lady lie down, Mrs. Swayne. There will be no immediate change, and there is nothing to be done but to watch her. If she should recover consciousness again, don't cross her in any thing: give her the drops if possible, and watch—that's all that can be done. I shall come back in the course of the day."

And in the grey dawning Jack too went home. He was changed; conflict and doubt had gone out of him. In their place a sombre cloud seemed to have taken him up. It was justice, remorseless and uncompromising, that thus overshadowed him. Expediency was not to be his guide—not though it should be a thousand times better, wiser, more desirable, than any other course of action. It was not what was best that had now to be considered, but only what was right. It never occurred to him that any farther struggle could be made. He felt himself no longer Pamela's betrothed lover, whose natural place was to defend and protect her, but her legal guardian and adviser, bound to consider her interests and make the best of every thing; the champion, not of herself, but of her fortune—that fortune which seemed to step between and separate them forever. When he was half-way up the avenue it occurred to him that he had forgotten Powys, and then he went back again to look for him. He had grown as a brother to him during this long night. Powys, however, was gone. Before Jack left the house he had set off for Masterton with the instinct of a man who has his daily work to do, and can not indulge in late hours. Poor fellow! Jack thought in his heart. It was hard upon him to be sacrificed to Mr. Brownlow's freak and Sara's vanity. But though he was himself likely to be a fellow-sufferer, it did not occur to Jack to intercede for Powys, or even to imagine that now he need not be sacrificed. Such an idea never entered into his head. Every thing was quiet in Brownlows when he went home. Mr. Brownlow had been persuaded to go to his room, and except the weary and reproachful servant who admitted Jack, there was nobody to be seen. He went up to his own room in the cold early day-light, passing by the doors of his visitors with a certain bitterness, and at the same time contempt. He was scornful of them for their ignorance, for their indifference, for their faculty of being amused and seeing no deeper. A parcel of fools! he said to himself; and yet he knew very well they were not fools, and was more thankful than he could express that their thoughts were directed to other matters, and that they were as yet unsuspicious of the real state of affairs. Every body was quite unsuspicious, even the people who surrounded Pamela. They saw something was amiss, but they had no idea what it was. Only himself, in short, knew to its full extent the trouble which had overwhelmed him. Only he knew that it was his hard fate to be his father's adversary, and the legal adviser of his betrothed bride; separated from the one by his opposition, from the other by his guardianship. He would win the money away from his own flesh and blood, and he would lose them in doing so; he would win it for his love, and in the act he would lose Pamela. Neither son nor lover henceforward, neither happy and prosperous in taking his own will, nor beloved and cherished in standing by those who belonged to him. He would establish Pamela's rights, and secure her in her fortune, but never could he share that fortune. It was an inexorable fate which had overtaken him. Just as Brutus, but with no praise for being just; this was to be his destiny. Jack flung himself listlessly on his bed, and turned his face from the light. It was a cruel fate.

CHAPTER XLI

SIR CHARLES MOTHERWELL

The guests at Brownlows next morning got up with minds a little relieved. Notwithstanding the evident excitement of the family, things had passed over quietly enough, and nothing had happened, and indifferent spectators easily accustom themselves to any atmosphere, and forget the peculiarities in it. There might still be a smell of brimstone in the air, but their organs were habituated, and failed to perceive it. After breakfast Sir Charles Motherwell had a little talk with Mr. Brownlow, as his smoked his morning cigar in the avenue; but nobody, except perhaps his mother, who was alive to his movements, took any notice of what he was doing. Once more the men in the house were left to themselves; but it did not strike them so oddly as on the day before. And Sara, for her part, was easier in her mind. She could not help it. It might be wicked even, but she could not help it. She was sorry Mrs. Preston should die; but since Providence had so willed it, no doubt it was the best for every body. This instinctive argument came to Sara as to all the rest. Nobody was doing it. It was Providence, and it was for the best. And Jack would marry Pamela, and Sara would go with her father to Masterton, and, but for the shock of Mrs. Preston's death, which would wear off in the course of nature, all would go merry as a marriage bell. This was how she had planned it all out to herself; and she saw no difficulty in it. Accordingly, she had very much recovered her spirits. Of course, the house at Masterton would not be so pleasant as Brownlows; at least—in some things it might not be so pleasant—but—And so, though she might be a little impatient, and a little preoccupied, things were decidedly brighter with Sara that morning. She was in the dining-room as usual, giving the housekeeper the benefit of her views about dinner, when Sir Charles came in. He saw her, and he lingered in the hall waiting for her, and her vengeful project of the previous night occurred to Sara. If she was to be persecuted any more about him, she would let him propose; charitably, feelingly, she had staved off that last ceremony; but now, if she was to be threatened with him—if he was to be thrown in her face—And he looked very sheepish and awkward as he stood in the hall, pulling at the black mustache which was so like a respirator. She saw him, and she prolonged his suspense, poor fellow. She bethought herself of a great many things she had to say to the housekeeper. And he stood outside, like a faithful dog, and waited. When she saw that he would not go away, Sara gave in to necessity. "Lady Motherwell is in the morning-room, and all the rest," she said, as she joined him; and then turned to lead the way up stairs.

"I don't want to see my mother," he said, with a slight shudder, she thought; and then he made a very bold effort. "Fine morning," said Sir Charles; "aw—would you mind taking a little walk?"

"Taking a walk?" said Sara, in amaze.

"Aw—yes—or—I'd like to speak to you for ten minutes," said Sir Charles, with growing embarrassment; "fact is, Miss Brownlow, I don't want to see my mother."

"That is very odd," said Sara, tempted to laughter; "but still you might walk by yourself, without seeing Lady Motherwell. There would not be much protection in having me."

"It was not for—protection, nor—nor that sort of thing," stammered Sir Charles, growing very red—"fact is, Miss Brownlow, it was something I had to say—to you—"

"Oh!" said Sara: she saw it was coming now; and fortified by her resolution, she made no farther effort to smother it. This, at least, she could do, and nobody had any right to interfere with her. She might be in her very last days of sovereignty; a few hours might see her fallen—fallen from her high estate; but at least she could refuse Charley Motherwell. That was a right of which neither cruel father nor adverse fortune could deprive her. She made no farther resistance, or attempt to get away. "If it is only to speak to me, we can talk in the library," she said; "it is too early to go out." And so saying she led the way into Mr. Brownlow's room. Notwithstanding the strange scenes she had seen in it, it did not chill Sara in her present mood. But it evidently had a solemnizing effect on Sir Charles. She walked across to the fire, which was burning cheerfully, and placed herself in one of the big chairs which stood by, arranging her pretty skirts within its heavy arms, which was a troublesome operation; and then she pointed graciously to the other. "Sit down," she said, "and tell me what it is about."

It was not an encouraging opening for a bashful lover. It was not like this that she had received Powys's sudden wild declarations, his outbursts of passionate presumption. She had been timid enough then, and had faltered and failed to herself, somewhat as poor Sir Charles was doing. He did not accept her kind invitation to seat himself, but stood before her in front of the fire, and looked more awkward than ever. Poor fellow, he had a great deal on his mind.

"Miss Brownlow," he burst out, all at once, after he had fidgeted about for five minutes, pulling his mustache and looking at her, "I am a bad fellow to talk. I never know what to say. I've got into heaps of scrapes from people mistaking what I mean."

"Indeed, I am sure I am very sorry," said Sara; "but I think I always understand what you mean."

"Yes," he said, with relief, "aw—I've observed that. You're one that does, and my mother's one; but never mind my mother just now," he went on precipitately. "For instance, when a fellow wants to ask a girl to marry him, every thing has to be understood—a mistake about that would be awful—would be dreadful—I mean, you know, it wouldn't do."

"It wouldn't do at all," said Sara, looking at him with terrible composure, and without even the ghost of a smile.

"Yes," said Sir Charles, revolving on his own axis, "it might be a horrid mess. That's why I wanted to see you, to set out with, before I spoke to my mother. My mother's a little old-fashioned. I've just been talking to Mr. Brownlow. I can make my—aw—any girl very comfortable. It's not a bad old place; and as for settlements and that sort of thing—"

"I should be very glad to give you my advice, I am sure," said Sara, demurely; "but I should like first to know who the lady is."

"The lady!" cried Sir Charles—"aw—upon my word, it's too bad. That's why I said every thing must be very plain. Miss Brownlow, there's not a girl in the world but yourself—not one!—aw—you know what I mean. I'd go down on my knees, or any thing; only you'd laugh, I know, and I'd lose my—my head." All this he said with immense rapidity, moving up and down before her. Then he suddenly came to a stand-still and looked into her face. "I know I can't talk," he said; "but you know, of course, it's you. What would be the good of coming like this, and—and making a fool of myself, if it wasn't you?"

"But it can't be me, Sir Charles," said Sara, growing, in spite of herself, out of sympathy, a little agitated, and forgetting the humor of the situation. "It can't be me—don't say any more. If you only knew what has been happening to us—"

"I know," cried Sir Charles, coming a step closer; "that's why—though I don't mean that's why from the commencement, for I only heard this morning; and that's why I don't want to see my mother. You need not think it matters to me—I've got plenty, and we could have your father to live with us, if you like."

Sara stood up with the intention of making him a stately and serious answer, but as she looked at his eager face, bent forward and gazing down at her, a sudden change came over her feelings. She had been laughing at him a moment before; now all at once, without any apparent provocation, she burst into tears. Sir Charles was very much dismayed. It did not occur to him to take advantage of her weeping, as Powys had done. He stared, and he drew a step farther back, and fell into a state of consternation. "I've said something I ought not to have said," he exclaimed; "I know I'm a wretched fellow to talk; but then I thought you would understand."

"I do understand," cried Sara, in her impulsive way; "and papa was quite right, and I am a horrid wretch, and you are the best man in the world!"

"Not so much as that," said Sir Charles, with a smile of satisfaction, which showed all his teeth under his black mustache; "but as long as you are pleased—Don't cry. We'll settle it all between us, and make him comfortable; and as for you and me—"

He made a step forward, beaming with content as he spoke, and poor Sara, drying her eyes hastily, and waking up to the urgency of the situation, retreated as he advanced.

"But, Sir Charles," she cried, clasping her hands—"oh! what a wretch I am to take you in and vex you. Stop! I did not mean that. I meant—oh! I could kill myself—I think you are the best and kindest and truest man in the world, but it can never be me!"

Sir Charles stopped short. That air of flattered vanity and imbecile self-satisfaction with which most men receive the idea of being loved, suddenly yielded in his face to intense surprise. "Why? how? what? I don't understand," he stammered; and stood amazed, utterly at a loss to know what she could mean.

"It can never be me!" cried Sara. "I am not much good. I don't deserve to be cared for. You will find somebody else a great deal nicer. There are girls in the house even—there is Fanny. Don't be angry. I don't think there is any thing particular in me."

"But it is only you I fancy," cried Sir Charles, deluded, poor man, by this humility, and once more lighting up with complaisance and self-satisfaction. "Fact is, we could be very comfortable together. I don't know about any other girls. You're nice enough for me."

Then Sara sank once more into the chair where a few minutes before she had established herself with such state and dignity. "Don't say any more," she cried again, clasping her hands. "Don't! I shall like you and be grateful to you all my life; but it can never be me!"

If Sara had been so foolish as to imagine that her unimpassioned suitor would be easily got rid of, she now found out her error. He stared at her, and he took a little walk around the table, and then he came back again. The facts of the case had not penetrated his mind. Her delicate intimations had no effect upon him. "If you like me," he said, "that's enough—fact is, I don't see how any girl could be nicer. They say all girls talk like this at first. You and I might be very comfortable; and as for my mother—you know if you wanted to have the house to yourself—"

"Would you be so wicked as to go and turn out your mother?" cried Sara, suddenly flashing into indignation, "and for a girl you know next to nothing about? Sir Charles, I never should have expected this of you."

Poor Sir Charles fell back utterly disconcerted. "It was all to make you comfortable," he said. "Of course I'd like my mother to stay. It was all for you."

"And I told you it could never be me," cried Sara—"never! I am going to Masterton with papa to take care of him. It is he who wants me most. And then I must say good-bye to every body; I shall only be the attorney's daughter at Masterton; we shall be quite different; but, Sir Charles, I shall always like you and wish you well. You have been so very good and kind to me."

Then Sara waved her hand to him and went toward the door. As for Sir Charles, he was too much bewildered to speak for the first moment. He stood and stared and let her pass him. It had never entered into his mind that this interview was to come to so abrupt an end. But before she left the room he had made a long step after her. "We could take care of him at Motherwell," he said, "just as well. Miss Brownlow, look here. It don't make any difference to me. If you had not a penny, you are just the same as you always were. If you like me, that is enough for me."

"But I don't like you!" said Sara, in desperation, turning round upon him with her eyes flashing fiercely, her mouth quivering pathetically, her tears falling fast. "I mean I like somebody else better. Don't, please, say any more—thanks for being so good and kind to me; and good-bye—good-bye!"

Then she seized his hand like the vehement creature she was, and clasped it close in her soft hands, and turned and fled. That was the only word for it. She fled, never pausing to look back. And Sir Charles, utterly bewildered and disconcerted, stayed behind. The first thing he did was to walk back to the fire, the natural attraction of a man in trouble. Then he caught a glimpse of his own discomfited countenance in the glass. "By George!" he said to himself, and turned his back upon the rueful visage. It was the wildest oath he ever permitted himself, poor fellow, and he showed the most overwhelming perturbation. He stood there a long time, thinking it over. He was not a man of very fine feelings, and yet he felt very much cast down. Though his imagination was not brilliant, it served to recall her to him with all her charms. And his honest heart ached. "What do I care for other girls?" he said to himself. "What good is Fanny to me?" He stood half the morning on the hearth-rug, sometimes turning round to look at his own dejected countenance in the glass, and sometimes to poke the fire. He had no heart to put himself within reach of his mother, or to look at the other girls. When the bell rang for luncheon he rushed out into the damp woods. Such a thing had never happened in his respectable life before: and this was the end of Sir Charles Motherwell's little romance.

Sara, though she did not regret Sir Charles, was more agitated than she could have supposed possible when she left the library; there are young ladies, no doubt, who are hardened to it; but an ordinary mortal feels a little sympathetic trouble in most cases, when she has had to decide (so far) upon another creature's fate. And though he was not bright, he had behaved very well; and then her own affairs were in such utter confusion. She could not even look her future in the face, and say she had any prospects. If she were to live a hundred years, how could she ever marry her father's clerk? and how could he so much as dream of marrying her—he who had nothing, and a family to maintain? Poor Sara went to her own room, and had a good cry over Sir Charles in the first (but least) place, and herself in the second. What was to become of her? To be the attorney's daughter in Masterton was not the brightest of fates—and beyond that—She cried, and she did not get any satisfaction from the thought of having refused Sir Charles. It was very, very good and nice of him—and oh, if it had only been Fanny on whom he had set his fancy! Her eyes were still red when she went down stairs, and it surprised her much to see her father leaving the morning-room as she approached. Lady Motherwell was there with a very excited and pale face, and one or two other ladies with a look of consternation about them. One who was leaving the room stopped as she did so, took Sara in her arms, though it was quite uncalled for, and gave her a hasty kiss. "My poor dear!" said this kind woman. As for Lady Motherwell, she was in quite a different state of mind.

"Where is Charley?" she cried. "Miss Brownlow, I wish you would tell me where my son is. It is very strange. He is a young man who never cares to be long away from his mother; but since we have been in this house, he has forsaken me."

"I saw him in the library," said Sara. "I think he is there now. I will go and call him, if you like." This she said because she was angry; and without any intention of doing what she said.

"I am much obliged to you, I am sure," said the old lady, who, up to this moment, had been so sweet to Sara, and called her by every caressing name. "I will ring and send a servant, if you will permit me. We have just been hearing some news that my dear boy ought to know."

"If it is something papa has been telling you, I think Sir Charles knows already," said Sara. Lady Motherwell gave her head an angry toss, and rang the bell violently. She took no farther notice of the girl whom she had professed to be so fond of. "Inquire if Sir Charles Motherwell is below," she said. "Tell him I have ordered my carriage, and that his man is putting up his things. We are going in half an hour."

It was at this moment the luncheon bell rang, and Sir Charles plunged wildly out into the woods. Perhaps the sound of the bell mollified Lady Motherwell. She was an old lady who liked luncheon. Probably it occurred to her that to have some refreshment before she left would do nobody any harm. Her son could not make any proposals at table under her very eyes; or perhaps a touch of human feeling came over her. "I meant to say we are going directly after luncheon," she said, turning to Sara. "You will be very glad to get rid of us all, if Mr. Brownlow really means what he says."

"Oh, yes, he means it," said Sara, with a little smile of bitterness, "but it is always best to have luncheon first. I think you will find your son down stairs."

"You seem to know," said Lady Motherwell; "perhaps that is why we have had so little of your company this morning. The society of young men is pleasanter than that of old ladies like me."

"The society of some young men is pleasant enough," said Sara, unable to suppress the retort; and she stood aside and let her guest pass, sweeping in her long silken robes. Lady Motherwell headed the procession; and of the ladies who followed, two or three made little consoling speeches to Sara as they clustered after her. "It will not turn out half so bad as your papa supposes," said one. "I don't see that he had any need to tell. We have all had our losses—but we don't go and publish them to all the world."

"And if it should be as bad, never mind, Sara," said another. "We shall all be as fond of you as ever. You must not think it hard-hearted if we go away."

"Oh, Sara dear, I shall be so sorry to leave you; but he would not have told us," said a third, "if he had not wanted us to go away."

"I don't know what you all mean," said Sara. "I think you want to make me lose my senses. Is it papa that wants you to go away?"

"He told us he had lost a great deal of money, and perhaps he might be ruined," said the last of all, twining her arm in Sara's. "You must come to us, dear, if there is any breaking-up. But perhaps it may not be as bad as he says."

"Perhaps not," said Sara, holding up her head proudly. It was the only answer she made. She swept past them all to her place at the head of the table, with a grandeur that was quite unusual, and looked round upon her guests like a young queen. "Papa," she said, at the top of her sweet young voice, addressing him at the other end of the table, "when you have unpleasant news to tell, you should not tell it before luncheon. I hope it will not hurt any body's appetite." This was all the notice she took of the embarrassing information that had thrown such a cloud of confusion over the guests. Mr. Brownlow, too, had recovered his calm. He had meant only to tell Lady Motherwell, knowing at the moment that her son was pleading his suit with Sara down stairs. He had told Sir Charles, and the news had but made him more eager; and, with a certain subtle instinct that came of his profession, Mr. Brownlow, that nobody might be able to blame him, went and told the mother too. It was Lady Motherwell's amazed and indignant exclamations that spread the news. And now both he and the old lady were equally on tenter-hooks of expectation. They wanted to know what had come of it. Sara, for any thing they knew, might be Sir Charley's betrothed at this moment. Mr. Brownlow, with a kind of hope, tried to read what was in his child's face, and Lady Motherwell looked at her with a kind of despair. Sara, roused to her full strength, smiled and baffled them both.

"Sir Charles is in the library," she said. "Call him, Willis; he might be too much engaged—he might not hear the bell."

But at this moment another bell was heard, which struck strangely upon the excited nerves of the company. It was the bell at the door, which, as that door was always open, and there was continually some servant or other in the hall, was never rung. On this occasion it was pulled wildly, as by some one in overwhelming haste. The dining-room door was open at the moment, and the conversation at table was so hushed and uncomfortable, that the voice outside was clearly audible. It was something about "Miss Sara," and "to come directly." They all heard it, their attention being generally aroused. Then came a rush which made every one start and turn round. It was Mrs. Swayne, with her bonnet thrust over her eyes, red and breathless with running. "She's a-dying—she's a-dying," said the intruder. "And I'm ready to drop. And, Miss Sara, she's a-calling for you."

Sara rose up, feeling her self-command put to the utmost test. But before she could even ask a question, Jack, who had been sitting very silently at the middle of the table, started up and rushed to the door. Mrs. Swayne put him back with her hand. "It's Miss Sara," she said—"Miss Sara—Miss Sara—that's who she's a-calling of. Keep out of her sight, and don't aggravate her. Miss Sara, it's you."

And then the room seemed to reel round poor Sara, who had come to the end of her powers. She knew no more about it until she felt the fresh air blowing in her face, as she was half led, half carried, down the avenue. What she was to do, or what was expected from her, she knew not. The fate of the house and of all belonging to it had come into her innocent hands.

CHAPTER XLII

It was Jack who hurried his sister down the avenue in obedience to that peremptory summons. The effects of the fresh air and rapid movement roused her, as we have said, and nobody but herself had been aware that her strength had ever failed her. Jack was wound up to the last pitch of suspense and agitation; but he could not say a word to her—would not tell her what she was to do. "How can I tell till I see what is wanted of you?" he said, savagely. She did not know what might be laid upon her, or why she was sent for; but she was left to accept the office alone. He gave her no help except his arm to support her down the avenue—a support which was not of much use to Sara, for her brother walked at such a pace that she was scarcely able to keep up with him. He was walking a great deal more rapidly than he was at all aware. Things had come to a climax in Jack's mind. He was burning with feverish irritation, anxiety, eagerness, and panic. He had thought that his mind was made up, and that nothing farther would disturb him. But in a moment he had become more disturbed than ever. The end that must decide every thing had come.

There was a certain air of excitement about Swayne's cottages as they approached. Old Betty's lodge was closed and vacant for one thing, and the gates set wide open; and the blinds were down in Mrs. Swayne's windows, and her neighbor stood in the little garden outside watching, with her hand on the door. She was waiting for their coming; and Betty within, who was utterly useless so far as the patient was concerned, flitted up and down stairs looking for the arrival of the visitor who was so anxiously expected. They received Sara with a mixture of eager curiosity and deference. "She's been a-calling for you, Miss," said Mrs. Swayne's neighbor, "as if she would go out of her mind." "She's a-calling for you now," cried old Betty; "she don't seem to have another thought in her head—and the rector by the bedside all the same, and her so near her latter end!" Even Mr. Swayne himself, with his wife's shawl round him, had come to the kitchen door to join in the general sentiment. "The Lord be praised as you've come, Miss Sara," he said. "I thought as she'd have driven me wild." This preface was not of a kind to calm Sara's nerves. She went up stairs confused with all the salutations addressed to her, and full of awe, almost of fear. To be sent for by a woman on her death-bed was of itself something alarming and awful. And this woman above all.

As for Jack, all that he heard of this babble was the intimation that the rector was there. It added another spark, if that were possible, to the fire in his heart. The doctor knew all about it—now here was another, yet another, to be taken into the dying woman's confidence. Though nobody asked for him, and though his presence seemed little desirable, he went up after his sister without saying a word to any one. They could hear the voice of the patient as they approached—a voice almost unintelligible, thick and babbling, like the voice of an idiot, and incessant. Mrs. Preston's eyes still blazing with wild anxiety and suspicion met Sara's wondering, wistful gaze as she went timidly into the room. Pamela stood by like a ghost with utter weariness and a kind of dull despair in her pallid face. She could not understand what it all meant. To her the mot of the enigma, which had been wanting at the commencement, could now never be supplied, for she was too completely worn out in body and mind to be able to receive a new idea. She beckoned to Sara almost impatiently as she opened the door. "Yes, mamma, she has come—she has come," said Pamela. Mr. Hardcastle was standing behind her with his prayer-book in his hand, looking concerned and impatient. He was amazed at the neglect with which he was being treated in the first place, and, to do him justice, he also felt strongly that, as Betty said, she was near her latter end, and other interests should be foremost in her mind. Old Betty herself came pressing in after Jack, and Mrs. Swayne followed her a few minutes later, and the neighbor stood outside on the landing. Their curiosity was roused to such a pitch that it eclipsed every other feeling—not that the women were hard-hearted or indifferent to the solemn moment which was at hand, they all wanted to know what she could have to say to Sara, and they were all curious to witness the tragedy about to be enacted and to see whether she made a good end.

"Ah, she's come," said Mrs. Preston in her thick voice. "Bring her here to me. Not him—I don't want him. Sara! come here! It's you I can speak to—only you. Give me something. I have a dozen words to say, and I must say them strong."

"Here, mamma," said Pamela, who watched with a sort of mechanical accuracy every indication of her mother's will; and she put her soft arm under Mrs. Preston's head and raised her with a strain of her slight girlish form, which at another moment would have been impossible. Jack made a step forward involuntarily to help her, but stopped short, arrested by the dying woman's eyes, which she fixed upon him over Pamela's shoulder as the cordial which was to give her strength to speak was put to her lips. She stopped even at that moment to look at him. "Not you," she said, hoarsely—"not you." It was not that he cared what she said, or even understood it, in his own excitement; but Pamela had her back turned upon him as she supported her mother; and Jack felt with a pang of poignant humiliation that there was no place for him there. Even her interests, the charge of her, seemed to be passing out of his hands.

"If you are going to speak to me—about—any thing," cried Sara, "I don't know what it is—nor why you should send for me; but do you want all these people too?"

Mrs. Preston looked at them vaguely—but she took no notice of what Sara said. "I have sent for you," she cried, uttering two or three words at a time, as if making a last effort to be intelligible, "because you saved me. I leave her to you; you're only a girl; you will not kill her; for the sake of her money. My mother's money! And to think we might all have been—comfortable—and happy! and now, I'm going to die!"

"Oh, mamma!" cried Pamela, clasping her hands wildly, "if you would but put away every thing from your mind—if you would but stop, thinking, and do what the doctor says, you might get better yet."

The dying woman made an attempt as it were to shake her head—she made a dreadful attempt to smile. "Poor child!" she said, and something like a tear got into her dilated eyes, "she don't know. That's life; never to know—till the very last—when you might have been happy—and comfortable; and then to die—"

"Mrs. Preston," cried Sara, going up to the bed, "I don't know what you mean or what I can do; but, oh, if you will only listen to Pamela! You are strong—you can speak and remember every thing. Oh, can't you try to live for her sake? We will all pray," she cried with tears, "every one of us—if you will only try! Oh, Mr. Hardcastle, pray for her—why should she die, and she so strong? and to leave Pamela like this!"

"Hush," said Mr. Hardcastle, almost sternly, "Sara, you forget there are things more important than life."

"Not to Pamela!" cried Sara, carried away by the vehemence of her feelings. "Oh, Mrs. Preston, try! You are strong yet—you could live if you were to try."

A kind of spasm passed over the poor woman's face. Perhaps a momentary hope of being able to make that effort crossed her mind—perhaps it was only a terrible smile at the vanity of the proposal. But it passed and left her eyes more wild in their passionate entreaty than before, "You don't—answer," she said; "you forsake me—like the rest. Sara! Sara! you are killing me. She is killing me. Give me an answer. Oh, my God, she will not speak!"

Sara looked round upon them all in her dismay. "You should have the doctor," she said: her inexperienced mind had seized upon Pamela's incoherent remonstrance. "Where is the doctor? Oh, could not something be done for her if he was here?"

Then Pamela gave a low cry. Her mother, who had been motionless for hours, after a wild struggle turned her head round upon the pillow. Her palsied fingers fluttered on the coverlid as if with an attempt to stretch themselves out toward Sara. Her eyes were ready to start from their sockets. "She will not speak to me!" she cried—"although she saved me. I make her guardian of my child. Do you hear?—is there any one to hear me? She is to take care of my Pamela. She is killing me. Sara, Sara! do you hear? I am speaking to you. You are to take care of my Pamela. I leave her to you—"

"Do what she says," said a low voice at Sara's shoulder. "Promise any thing—every thing. She must not be thwarted now."

Sara did not know who it was that spoke. She made a step forward, recovering her native impetuosity. She laid her warm living hand upon the cold half-dead one of the dying woman and left it there, though the touch thrilled to her heart. "I will take care of her," she said, "I promise, as if she was my sister. Do you hear me now, Mrs. Preston? I promise with all my heart. Oh, Pamela, I don't think she hears me! I have said it too late—she is going to die."

The doctor, who had spoken to Sara, came forward and drew her softly from the bedside. "Take her away," he said to Jack, who all this while had been looking on. "Take them both away—they can do no good here—"

Sara, who was trembling in every limb, fell back upon her brother's supporting arm; but when Jack held out his other hand to Pamela she made him no reply. She was weaker than Sara, but she was a hundred times stronger. She gave him one pitiful look and returned to her mother. That was her place, come what might; and she was so young, that even now she could not recognize that there was no hope.

Then Jack took his sister down stairs. They went into the little parlor, which was full to his mind of so many associations. Sara had not, like Pamela, the support of intense and overwhelming emotion. She was shaken to the very depths by this extraordinary trial. As soon as it was over she fell into hysterical sobbing like a child. She could not restrain herself. She sunk upon the little black sofa in the parlor, where Mrs. Preston had so often rested, and hid her face in her hands to keep down as far as she could the irrepressible sobs. Jack had begun to walk about the room and seemed to take no notice; but he was thinking in his heart how small a matter it was to her in comparison with what it was to Pamela, though it was she and not Pamela who indulged in this show of sorrow. He was unkind to his sister; he was bitter against her, and against all the world. It was his natural charge that had been transferred to her hands; and who was Sara that she should have such a guardianship given to her? He vowed to himself that it was he and only he who should take care of Pamela. Sara? a girl who knew nothing about it—a child with no power to take care of herself—the woman must be mad. He went to the door with a little excitement as the sound became audible of other people coming down stairs. The spectators who had crowded into Mrs. Preston's sick room were being sent away, and old Betty, thus deprived of one source of interest, came in courtesying to make herself useful to Sara. "Poor soul, she's awful bad;" said Betty, "but, Miss Sara, don't you take on; you've been a comfort to her. She's a deal easier in her mind; she's found friends for her girl, as was always her great thought. Don't you take on—"

"Oh, Betty, is she dead?" cried Sara, to whom the sympathy even of this old woman was a consolation, excited as she was.

"No, Miss," said Betty, shaking her head. "It ain't so easy getting shut o' this life. She ain't dead, nor won't be not yet awhile—judging by all as I've seen in my day."

"Then she is getting better," cried Sara, clasping her hands. "Oh, Jack, thank God! she is going to live."

Old Betty again shook her head. "Miss Sara, you're young," she said; "you don't know no better. She ain't a-going to live. But them things take more nor a minute. This world had need to be a better place than it is to most on us; for it's hard work a-getting in and it's harder work a-getting out. She may lie like that for days and days. Most folks get to be glad at last when it's over. It's weary work, both for them as is nursin' and them as is dyin'; but it's what we all has to go through," said Betty, with a conventional sigh.

This time, however, Betty, with all her experience, was not a true prophet. The strength of the dying woman was fictitious. As soon as she had got beyond the point at which her mind could still work, her body went down like so much dead weight; consciousness and intelligence had failed her while Sara was in the act of making her promise, and in a few minutes the rector, excited and rather angry, joined the others down stairs. "You should have waited, Sara," he said, severely; "no worldly affairs could be so important as to justify—And then what can you do for the poor girl? I would humor the fancies of the dying as much as any one; but if the poor thing is left destitute, unless you take her into your service—"

"Mr. Hardcastle," exclaimed Jack, furious, "do you know whom you are speaking of? Miss Preston is my betrothed wife."

The rector fell back in dismay for a moment. Then he recovered himself with a certain dignity. "My dear Jack," he said, "this is not a moment to discuss any act of youthful folly. Your good father ought to know of this. Don't, I beg of you, don't say any thing more to me."

"And all that we have in the world belongs to Pamela," said Sara, with a sigh. Mr. Hardcastle looked at the brother and sister, and his usual discrimination forsook him. He thought they were both out of their senses. As there was nobody else to communicate with, he looked round at old Betty, who stood listening eagerly; and Betty, too, elevated her eyebrows, and shook her head. Were they going mad? Was there some idiocy in the air which affected every body? The rector went to the window, and turned his back upon them, and looked out in his bewilderment. He felt very sorry for poor Mr. Brownlow. Then he seemed to get a glimmering of the meaning of it all. It was for Sara's aid in securing this marriage that the poor creature up stairs had been so anxious. Her mind had been passionately occupied about merely worldly interests to the last; and for this he and his higher consolation had been thrust away. Poor Brownlow! Mr. Hardcastle thought of his own dutiful Fanny, who never gave way to any vagaries. And he buttoned his coat with a friendly instinct. "I am going to see your father, as I can be of no farther use here," he said; and there was a world of disapproval in his tone.

But just then there were some hurried movements above, and a cry. It was Pamela, who was calling on her mother, appealing to an ear which no longer heard. They all knew instinctively what it meant. Sara started up, trembling and clasping her hands. She had never been in the same house with death before—never that she knew of; and a dreadful sense that Mrs. Preston had suddenly become a spiritual presence, and was everywhere about her, seized upon the girl. "I promise," she said, wildly, with lips that gave forth very little sound. As for Jack, he too started as if something had struck him. He went up to his sister, though he had been angry with her, and took her into his arms for a moment. "Sara, go to her," he said. He forgot all about secondary things—his heart bled for his Pamela. "Go to her!" he cried; and something like a sob came from his breast. Not for the poor soul that was gone—not for her to whom at last the trouble and toil were over; for the young creature who remained behind to profit by all the mother's unrewarded pains—for the living, not for the dead.

The doctor came down stairs shortly after; and though he was grave, there was a professional tone about him which dispelled the awe of the group below. "It is all over," he said, "and a very good thing too for that poor girl. She could not have stood it much longer. I am very glad Miss Brownlow has gone to her. It's excessively good of your sister. I was obliged to interfere, you know. Nobody need hold themselves bound, unless they please, by a promise extorted like that; but in such a case one never can tell what might have happened. The patient must be humored. I feared—"

"No more," said Jack—"don't say any more; you did what was quite right. It is Miss Preston who must be considered now. Could she be removed at once? Would it be safe to take her away at once? for my sister, of course, I mean."

"Miss Preston?" said the doctor, a little puzzled. "Oh, the daughter, you mean, poor thing! It would be the very best plan to take her away; but she is a good little thing, and she wouldn't go."

"Never mind your opinion of her," cried Jack, keeping his temper with difficulty. "Tell me if we can take her away?"

"She will not go," said the doctor, offended in his turn. "As for opinions, I have a right to my opinion if she was the queen. She's not the sort of girl to be taken away. After the funeral it may be done, perhaps. Good-morning. I shall see her to-morrow. Mr. Hardcastle, if you like I can set you down at the rectory—I am going that way."

"Thanks, I have to go somewhere else first," said the rector; and the other parish functionary departed accordingly, going softly for the first dozen steps out of respect for the dead. Then Mr. Hardcastle put on his hat, and looked at Jack.

"I am going to Brownlows," he said. "I am very sorry to have such an office to fulfill; but your father must know, Jack, what has been going on here to-day."

Jack was in no merry mood, but he was unable to retain a short hard laugh which relieved him as well as any other expression of feeling. "Yes, you are free to tell him," he said, and he felt disposed to laugh again loudly when he looked at the rector's severe and disapproving face. It gave him a certain cynical and grim amusement to see it. How blind and stupid every body was! What immovable, shallow dolts, to look on at all those mysteries of death and ruin, and never to be a whit the wiser! He could have laughed, but his laughter, such as it was, was internal—that too might be misunderstood. He waved old Betty impatiently away, and he turned his back on Mr. Hardcastle who was going. When he turned round again both were gone. He even paused to think they were not so unlike each other; Betty perhaps on the whole had most understanding of the two. He went to the window and watched the old woman cross reluctantly to the lodge, and the rector enter the avenue. Betty, however, could not stay away. She came stealing back again, not perceiving Jack, looking cautiously round to make sure that both the rector and the doctor were out of sight. She stopped to speak to the neighbor who was at her door, and they shook their heads over the sad story, and then Betty crept into Mrs. Swayne's cottage and stole up stairs. Jack took the pains to watch all this, but it was not because he was interested in old Betty. He was reluctant to go back to his own thoughts—to face the situation in which he found himself. When he could delay no longer, he sat down at the table as if he had work to do, and buried his head in his hands. Yes, she was dead, poor woman! The fortune which had excited her almost to madness, which had changed her from an humble, tender creature anxious to serve every body, into an elated tyrant eager to tramp the world under foot, had never reached her grasp. Poor soul! At the very last moment of her life to undergo this awful temptation and to fall under it, and give the lie to all her dutiful and pious existence! Instead of pondering over his own difficulty, these were the reflections in which Jack's mind plunged itself. She had gone where money could do her no good, and yet at the very end she had agitated and even stained her spotless life for it, leaving painful recollections behind her, though she had been a good woman, perhaps even shortening her own days. What a hard fate it was! how cruel to have had the irresistible temptation so late, and to have no time left her to efface the recollection of her momentary frenzy. Jack's heart grew soft toward her as it all came before him. Poor soul! Poor woman! no time even to say her prayers and ask God's pardon before she died; perhaps, however, on the whole, though Mr. Hardcastle might be of a different opinion, God, who knew all, was less likely to be deceived by that ebullition than man. When he tried to think of his own course of action at this difficult moment, his mind went off at a tangent. It was in vain that he attempted to consider what he was to do. The quiet of death had fallen over the agitated house in which he sat, and his own agitation died out in that chilly calm. Then he got up with a kind of dull composure in his mind to go home. Every thing must be postponed now until the few first days of darkness were over. It was the only tribute that could be paid to the dead.

Before he went away Sara came to him for a moment. Her eyes were red with crying, but she had recovered herself. "Tell papa I must stay with her," said Sara. "I can not leave her. I don't think she could have borne it much longer; and there is only me to take care of her now."

"You? to take care of her?" cried Jack. "How long is this folly to last? Am not I to see her?" and then his flash of resentment died away. "Sara, if you are not good to her, tender to her!" he said with tears coming into his eyes in spite of him. "And she so young! not much more than a child. Why can't I bring down the carriage for her, and take her home?"

"And leave her mother here!" said Sara, turning away with the impatience of excitement. As for Jack, he was walking about in the passage while she spoke to him from the stair. He could have cried like one of the girls—he could have taken his sister in his arms, or have stormed at her. A hundred contradictory contending feelings were in his heart.

"Her mother is dead," he said. "What good can she do here now? why can't you show her the reason of it? she would be much better at Brownlows. The doctor said so. She will come with you."

"Never while her mother lies there," cried Sara—"her poor mother who loved her so! I know what is in her heart; and she shall do as she pleases. Tell papa, unless he wants me, that I must stay here."

And she stayed, and Jack went up the avenue alone. He met two carriages coming down, and had to stop and tell why he had not been present to say good-bye, and what had detained Sara. The ladies in the carriages stared very strangely at his few brief words of apology. And they gazed at each other in consternation as they passed on. It might be very good of Sara to go and watch by a sick-bed, but to leave her guests for it, to let them all depart without a word as if it had been a hotel—altogether it was a strange family. Mr. Brownlow had told them he expected to be ruined, though there was no visible appearance of it. And Sara had rushed away from them, from the head of the table without a word, on the very last day, to attend a poor woman's death-bed. Not very much like Sara, they said; and they began to give each other significant looks and to ask if the Brownlows had "any thing wrong" in their blood. They were so new as a county family. People had no information about their grandfathers and grandmothers; but they looked as if they were all mad—that was the fact. It was the strangest way to treat their guests.

And there were some of the guests, as Jack found on returning to the house, who were not going to leave till the next day. They were sulky and offended, as was natural. To make arrangements for a pleasant visit, and to be all but turned out before the time you had yourself fixed—and then to have your mind confused by vague stories about ruin and loss, and somebody who was dying! It was not to be supposed that any one could be pleased. Mr. Hardcastle had been there, and he had not mended matters. He had told one or two men how sorry he was for poor Brownlow—how he feared Jack had got entangled somehow, and had been so foolish as to involve his sister—and how things were in a bad way. All sorts of vague rumors were floating about the house—the servants were prepared for any thing, from the reduction of their wages to the arrest of their master. They watched the door anxiously, and cast furtive looks down the avenue, that they might not be taken unprepared; and Mr. Willis secretly removed a good deal of the plate into a dark corner of the wine cellar. "Master might want it," he said to himself—judging it not off the cards that master might be obliged to run away, and might be glad of a silver tea-pot or so to pay his expenses.

How they could have got through the evening it is impossible to tell, had not Sara appeared before dinner, very pale, with red eyes, and a melancholy face. Every body rushed at her when she appeared—in a kind of consternation. And for a moment it seemed to both her father and brother that their adversary had come alive, and that the struggle was to begin again. Sara's explanation, however, was the simple one that Pamela had fallen asleep, and that she had thought they would want her at home for dinner. So she went and dressed herself, like a martyr, and carried them through the embarrassed meal. It was she upon whom the chief burden fell, and she took up the weight and carried it without flinching. So the long confused eventful day came to an end. When it was late and all the bewildered people had retired to their rooms, Mr. Brownlow and Jack took her down the avenue, guarding her tenderly, one on either side. There was little said between them, but their hearts were full—a kind of gratitude, a kind of sorrow, a certain pervading sense of union and sympathy had come into their minds; and the two men regarded with a half wondering, half pitying enthusiasm, a waking up of all the springs of natural love, the soft creature between them, the indulged, petted, faulty girl who now had every thing to do. They both kissed her when they left her, with an overflowing of their hearts, and stood and looked at the dark cottage with the faint lights in its windows, saying nothing. In the upper window was the dim glow of the light in the chamber of the dead—the needless pathetic glimmer which shone faintly over the covered face and closed eyes; below, in the little parlor, where a bed had been hastily prepared for her, Pamela was sleeping in her profound exhaustion, almost as pale as her mother, shaded from the dim candlelight. The father and son did not speak, but they grasped each other's hands closely as they looked at the house, and turned away and walked home in silence. A certain confusion, consolation, and calm, all mingled with wonder and suspense, had come over them—words were of no use at that moment. And Sara went in and took up her guardianship—and slept and waked and watched all night long in the weakness and strength of her youth.

CHAPTER XLIII

THE LIGHT OF COMMON DAY

Next morning Mr. Brownlow resumed his regular habits, and went down to the office, reassuring the household a little by this step, which seemed a return to ordinary life. He looked wistfully and with a certain solemnity at the closed windows of Mrs. Swayne's cottage as he passed. The chief point of interest to him was that Sara was there; and yet it was impossible not to think at the same time of the woman who had crossed his path so fatally, and now had been taken out of his way. In one sense she was taken out of his way. It was not to be supposed that the lawyer could look at the situation in which he found himself with any sentimental or superlative resolutions. His mind was quieted out of all the terrors which had at first overwhelmed him. It was no longer ruin that stared him in the face. The mother could have exacted interest and compound interest; the daughter, who was Jack's betrothed bride, could, of course, be dealt with in a different way. Jack's sense that he was no longer her lover, but the guardian of her interests—that his business was to win every penny of her fortune for her, and then leave her to its enjoyment—did not, of course, affect Mr. Brownlow. He was thinking of nothing fantastical, nothing exaggerated. Pamela was Jack's betrothed. She was in Sara's guardianship. From this day he considered her as a member of his family; and after all the troubles he had undergone, this solution on the whole seemed to Mr. Brownlow a very easy, a very seemly and becoming one. She should have, as Jack's wife, her mother's fifty thousand pounds; and when he himself died, every thing except a moderate portion for Sara should go into his son's hands. It was an arrangement which made his heart ache; for Sara would have to come down from all her grandeur, to become only what her father's daughter had a right to be in the Masterton house, to have but an humble provision made for her, and to relinquish all her luxurious habits and ambitions. If it had been Jack upon whom such a necessity had fallen, Mr. Brownlow could have borne it; but Sara! Nevertheless it was just and right and necessary. There was nothing else to be done, nothing else to be thought of. And both Sara and her father would have to submit, unless, indeed, Sir Charles Motherwell—Mr. Brownlow's eye kindled a little as he thought of his late visitor, and then he shook his head sadly in a kind of self-communing. If any thing had come of that, could Sara have been silent on the subject? Would Sir Charles himself have gone away without a sign? Yet every moment since then had been so full of excitement and occupation, that he still retained a hope. In the midst of the awe and agitation attending Mrs. Preston's death his child could scarcely have paused to tell him of a love-tale. When he entered the familiar office and saw every thing going on just as it had done, Mr. Brownlow felt like a man fallen from the skies. It seemed to him years since he had been there, and he could not but feel a thrill of wonder to find all his papers in their places, and to listen to Mr. Wrinkell's questions about business matters which seemed to have stood still while his own destiny was getting decided. "Are you still at that point?" he said, almost peevishly. "I should have thought that would have been decided long ago."

"It is only three days, if you recollect, since I consulted you about it," Mr. Wrinkell replied, with offended dignity, "and you gave me no distinct answer." Only three days! It might have been three centuries, for any thing Mr. Brownlow knew.

Then he sat down at his desk and addressed himself very heartily to his business. A mass of work had accumulated of course, and he took it up with an energy he had not felt for ages. He had been working in the dark all this time, working languidly, not knowing who might be the better for it. Now his whole soul was in his occupation; every additional shilling he could make would be so much for his child. More and more as he became accustomed to the thought his mind cleared and courage and steadiness returned to him. It was true that he was at the age when men think of retiring from work, but he was a strong and vigorous man still, in possession of all his powers. Jack would withdraw, would marry, would enter on his independent career, and carry out probably the very programme his father had drawn out for him before that midnight visitor arrived whose appearance had changed every thing. Poor creature, after all she had not changed every thing. She had changed but little. Sara only had lost by her appearance. That was the sting of the whole matter; and Mr. Brownlow applied himself with double energy, with the eager impulse and vigor of a young man, to the work before him. Every thing he could add to his store would be the better for Sara, and he felt that this was motive sufficient for any man worthy of the name.

When it came to be time for luncheon he went out—not to refresh himself with food, for which he had little appetite, but to make a visit which perhaps was a kind of ill-natured relief to him amid the pressure of his many thoughts. He went to Mrs. Fennell's lodgings to pay one of his generally unwilling but dutiful visits. This time he was not unwilling. He went with an unaffected quietness which was very different from the forced calm of his last appearance there. Mrs. Fennell was seated as usual in her great chair, but she had not on her best cap, and was accordingly cowed and discouraged to begin with; and Nancy, who was with her, made a pretense of leaving the room. "Stay," said Mr. Brownlow, "I want you. It is best that you too should hear what I am going to say."

"At your service, sir," said Nancy, dropping him a defiant courtesy. As for Mrs. Fennell, she had begun to tremble immediately with excitement and curiosity.

"What is it, John Brownlow?" she said. "What's happened? It's a sight to see you so soon again. It isn't for nothing, we may be sure. What do you want of me and Nancy now?"

"I want nothing of you," said Mr. Brownlow. "I came to tell you something you ought to know. Phœbe Thomson is found, Mrs. Fennell. She came to me the other night."

"Good Lord!" cried the old woman; and then a wild light got up in her eyes and she looked at him fiercely. "Came to you?—and you let her come, and let her go, and owned her, you coward! Tell me next you have given her up the children's money—my Bessie's children? That's what you call a man! Oh, good Lord—good Lord! You owned her, and you tell it to my very face!"

Then there was a little pause. The two old women looked at him, one with impotent fury, the other with suppressed exultation. "I always said so!" said Nancy. His simple words had produced effect enough, if that was what he wanted. He looked at them both, and a faint smile came over his face, a smile in which there was no mirth and which lasted but a moment. He felt ashamed of himself next minute that he could have been tempted to smile.

"John Brownlow," said Mrs. Fennell, rising in her exasperation, "I'm an old poor failing woman, and you're a fine strong man, but I'd have fought different for my Bessie's children. Didn't I tell you she came to me, that you might be on your guard. And you a lawyer? Oh, good Lord—good Lord! I'd have kept it safer for them if it had been me. I'd have turned her out of my door for an impostor and a vagabond! I'd have hunted her to death first if it had been me. And you to tell me her name clean out as quiet as a judge and look me in the face! Oh you coward! you poor creature! Never, if she had torn me with wild horses, would she have got it out of me."

"He could not have acted different," said Nancy, with suppressed excitement. "Sit down, mistress, or you'll do yourself a harm. The best lawyer in the world couldn't turn a woman away as knowed her rights."

Mr. Brownlow held up his hand to prevent the angry exclamation that was on Mrs. Fennell's lips. "Hush," he said, "my story is not done. It is a very sad story. Poor soul, she will never get much good of the money. Phœbe Thomson is dead."

They both turned on him with a look which all his life he never forgot. Would they themselves have been capable of such a deed? Was it the natural suggestion of the crisis? The look made him sick and faint. He turned so as to confront both the old women. "I don't know who her counselor was," he said, with unconscious solemnity, "but it must have been some one who believed me a knave and a liar. Had she come to me and proved to me who she was, she might have been living now. Poor soul, she did not do that. She was sent to London instead to find out for herself about her mother's will, and she came down in haste, finding there was not a moment to lose. And she was driven mad with fright and suspicion and fatigue; an old woman too—she could not bear it. And now, instead of enjoying what was hers, she is dead. This is what comes of evil counsel. She might have lived and had some comfort of her life had she been honest and straightforward and come to me."

Mr. Brownlow said this with the conviction and fervor of an upright man. All the evil thoughts he had himself entertained, all his schemes to baffle his unknown adversary, had faded from his mind. It was not a fictitious but a real forgetfulness. He spoke in the superiority of high principle and of a character above reproach. He did not remember that he had tacitly conspired with Mrs. Fennell, or that he had willfully rejected the opportunity of finding Phœbe Thomson out after her visit to his mother-in-law. Perhaps his excuse to himself was that, at the moment, his suspicions were all directed to a wrong point. But I don't think he felt any occasion to excuse himself—he simply forgot. If she had lived she should have had all, every penny, though it cost him his ruin; and now she was dead by the visitation of God, and every thing was changed. It is strange and yet it was true. He looked at them both with a superiority which was not assumed, and he believed what he said.

As for his hearers, they were both stunned by this solemn address. Mrs. Fennell dropped into her chair, and in her surprise and relief and consternation began to cry. As for Nancy, she was completely cowed and broken down for some minutes. It was she who had done all this, and every word told upon her. She was overwhelmed by Mr. Brownlow's rectitude, by his honor and truth, which owing to her had been thus fatally distrusted. And she was struck at the same time by a cruel disappointment which gave force to every word. She stood and looked at Mr. Brownlow, quailing before him. Then a faint gleam of returning courage came over her. She drew a deep breath to give herself the power of speech. "There is her child still," she said, with a gasp, and faced him with a certain bravado again.

"Ah, I see you know!" he said; "that is the strangest part of all. For a long time past, before we knew who they were, and much against my will, her child had taken Jack's fancy; he was determined to marry her, though I told him he should have nothing from me; now in the strange arrangements of Providence—" said Mr. Brownlow. But there he stopped; something seemed to stifle him; he could not go on speaking about the dispensations of Providence; he got up when he had reached this point, with a sudden sense that after all he had no right to speak as if God and himself—or Providence, as he preferred to say—were in partnership; his hands were not clean enough for that. He stopped, and asked after Mrs. Fennell, if she had all the comforts she wanted, and then he made what haste he could away.

He even felt half ashamed of himself as he went down stairs. His mother-in-law, excited as she had been by the first piece of news he told her, had but half understood the second. He left her sobbing weakly over her Bessie's children who were being robbed and ruined. Nancy went to the door with him in a servile despair. She understood it all well enough. There was no more hope for her, no more dazzling expectations of such a retirement as Betty's lodge and its ease and independence. To serve old Mrs. Fennell's whims all the rest of her days; to be pensioned on some pittance, or turned out upon the world for her misdeeds in her old age when Mrs. Fennell should die—this was all that she had before her now.

When Mr. Brownlow went back after having fulfilled this duty, he went up stairs into the house instead of going to the office, and with a caprice which he himself scarcely understood, called Powys, who was standing at the door, to follow him. It seemed to him as if, it was so long ago, Powys too must have recovered from his heart-break. He took the young man with him over the silent, empty, echoing house. "This is where I began my married life," he said, stopping on the cold hearth in the drawing-room, and looking round him. It was a pretty old-fashioned room, running all the breadth of the house, with windows at each end, and a perpetual cross-light, pale at one side, rosy and full of sunshine at the other. It was not a lofty room, like the drawing-room at Brownlows, nor was it rich with gold and dainty colors; but yet there was something in the subdued tone of the old curtains, the old Turkey carpet, the japanned screens and little tables, the old-world look of every thing, which was neither ungraceful nor unrefined. "I am coming back to live here," he said after an interval, with a sigh. He could not tell why he made this confidential communication to the young man, who grew pale, and gazed at him eagerly, and could not find a word to say in reply. Mr. Brownlow was not thinking of Powys's looks, nor of his feelings; he was occupied with himself, as was natural enough; he took the young fellow into his confidence, if that could be called confidence, because he liked him, and had seen more of him than any body else near. What the intelligence might be to Powys Mr. Brownlow did not stop to think; but he went over the house in his company, consulting him about the alterations to be made. Somehow he had returned to his first feeling toward Powys—and he wanted to be kind to him, to make up to him for not being Phœbe Thomson's son; they were fellow-sufferers so far as that was concerned—at least such was the feeling in Mr. Brownlow's mind, though he could not well have explained how.

Later in the afternoon he had some visitors. Altogether it was an exciting day. The first who came to him was Sir Charles Motherwell, who had ridden in from Ridley, where he was staying, to see him, and whose appearance awoke a certain surprise and expectation in Mr. Brownlow's mind; he thought Sara must have accepted him after all. But the baronet's looks did not justify his hope; Sir Charles was very glum, very rueful, and pulled at his mustache more than ever. He came in, and held out his hand, and put down his hat, and then pulled off his gloves and threw them into it, as if he were about to perform some delicate operation; when he had got through all these ceremonies, he sank into the chair which stood ready for Mr. Brownlow's clients, and heaved a profound sigh.

"I thought I'd come and tell you," he said, "though it ain't pleasant news; I tried my luck, as I said I would—not that I've got any luck. She—she—wouldn't hear of it, Brownlow. I'd have done any thing in the world she liked to say—you know I would; she might have sold the old place, or done what she pleased; but she wouldn't, you know, not if I'd gone down on my knees—it was all of no use." He had never uttered so many sentences all on end in his life before, poor fellow. He got up now, and walked as far as the office wall would let him, and whistled dolefully, and then he returned to his chair, and breathed another deep sigh. "It was all of no use."

"I am very sorry," said Mr. Brownlow—"very sorry; she would have chosen a good man if she had chosen you; but you know I can't interfere."

"Do you think I want any one to interfere?" said Sir Charles, with momentary resentment. "Look here, Brownlow, I'll tell you how it is; she said she liked some one else better than me—I'd like to wring the fellow's neck!" said the disappointed lover, with a little outburst; "but if there's money, or any thing in the way, I thought I might lend him a hand—not in my own name, you know. I suppose a girl ain't the master to like whom she ought to like, no more than I am," said Sir Charles, disconsolately, "but she's got to be given in to, Brownlow. I'd lend him a hand, if that was what was wanting. As long as she's happy and has her way, a man can always pull through."

Mr. Brownlow started a little at this strange speech, but in the end the confused generosity of the speaker carried him out of himself. "You are a good fellow, Motherwell," he said heartily, holding out his hand—"you are the best fellow I know."

"Ah, so she said," said poor Sir Charles, with a hoarse little laugh—he was not bright, poor fellow, but he felt the sarcasm; "I'd a deal rather she had praised me less and liked me more—"

And he ended with another big sigh. Mr. Brownlow had to make himself very uncomfortable by way of discouraging Sir Charles's generosities. He had to protest that he knew no one whom Sara could prefer. He had to say at last peremptorily that it was a matter which he could not discuss, before his anxious and melancholy visitor could be got rid of. It was not a pleasant thought to Mr. Brownlow. He did not like to hear of Sara preferring any man. He could have given her to Charley Motherwell, who would have been her slave, and could have assured her position, and endowed her with a title such as it was; but Sara in love was not an idea pleasant to her father, besides the uneasy wonder who could be the object of her preference. He tried to go back and recollect, but his memory failed him. Then there came a dim vision to his mind of a moment when his child had turned from him—when she had wept and rejected his embrace and his sympathy. How long was that ago? But he did not seem able to tell. It was before—that was all he knew. Every thing had happened since. He had told her she was free, and she had turned upon him and upbraided him—for what? Years seemed to lie between him and that half-forgotten scene. He tried in vain to resume the thread of his plans and arrangements. In spite of himself his reluctant yet eager thoughts kept going back and back to that day. How long was it since he had thought Powys the heir? How long since the moment of unlooked-for blessedness when he believed himself free? It was on that day that Sara had turned from him and cried—that day when he was so full of comfort, so anxious to show his gratitude to God—when he had drawn that check for the Masterton charities, which—by, the way, how had he distributed the money? Catching at this point of circumstance, Mr. Brownlow made an effort to escape from his recollections. He did not want to recall that foolish premature delight. It might have been years ago, to judge by his feelings; but he knew that could not be the case. It had become late in the afternoon by this time, and the clerks were mostly gone. There was nobody whom he could ask what had been done about the check for the charities; and he had just drawn toward him the dispatch-box with his papers which had been brought from Brownlows with him, to ascertain for himself, when the office-boy came pulling his forelock to ask if he would see a lady who was waiting. Mr. Brownlow said No, at first, for it was past office hours, and then he said Yes, no longer feeling any tremor at the prospect of a strange visitor. He could believe it was a simple client now, not a messenger of fate coming to ruin and betray, as for a long time he had been in the way of feeling. Such ease of mind would be cheaply purchased even with fifty thousand pounds. The lady came in, accordingly, and Mr. Brownlow received her with his usual courtesy, which was, however, a little disturbed when he looked at her. Not that he had any real occasion to be disturbed. A far-off flutter of his past anxieties, a kind of echo, came over him at the sight of her pleasant homely face. He had thought she was Phœbe Thomson the last time he had seen her. He had shrunk from her, and lost his self-possession altogether. Even now a minute had elapsed before he could quite command himself, and remember the real condition of affairs.

"Good day, Mrs. Powys," he said; "I am sorry to have' kept you waiting. Why did not you send me word who it was?"

"I thought you might have been engaged, sir," said Mrs. Powys; "I wasn't sure if you would remember me, Mr. Brownlow. I came to you once before, when I was in trouble, and you were very kind—too kind," she added, with a sigh. "No, no, it is not the same thing. If my poor boy has troubles still, he does not hide his heart from me now."

"That is well," said Mr. Brownlow, coldly. He thought some appeal was going to be made to him on behalf of Powys and his folly. Though he was in reality fond of Powys, he stiffened instinctively at the thought. "It is growing late," he went on; "I was just going. Is there any thing in which I can be of use to you?" He laid his hand on his dispatch-box as he spoke. His manner had been very different when he was afraid of her; and yet he was not unkind or unreasonable. She was his clerk's mother; he would have exerted himself, and done much to secure the family any real benefit; but he did not mean that they should thrust themselves into his affairs.

"It is something my poor boy didn't like to ask," said Mrs. Powys, with a little timidity. "He had offended you that day, or he thought he had offended you; and he would not do any thing to bring it back to your mind. I am sure if he went wrong, Mr. Brownlow, he didn't mean to—There's nothing in this world he would not do for you."

"Went wrong—offended me?" said Mr. Brownlow; "I don't think he ever offended me. What is it he wants? There are certain subjects which I can not enter upon either with him or you—"

"Oh, not that—not that," said Mrs. Powys, with tears. "If he's been foolish he's punished for it, my poor boy! And he would not ask you for his papers, not to bring it back to your mind." 'Mother,' he said, 'he's worried, and I can't vex him.' He would lose all his own hopes for that. But I'm his mother, Mr. Brownlow. I have a feeling for my son's interests as you have for yours. His papers, poor boy, are no good to you."

"His papers?" said Mr. Brownlow, with amaze, looking at her. For the moment his old confusion of mind came back to him; he could not quite feel yet that Powys's papers could be innocent of all reference to himself.

"My poor husband's letters, sir," said Mrs. Powys, drying her eyes; "the papers he took to you when he thought—; but that is neither here nor there. I've found my poor Charley's mother, Mr. Brownlow; she's living, though she's an old woman. I have been tracing it out to the best of my ability, and I've found her. Likely enough she'll have nothing to say to me. I am but a poor woman, never brought up to be a lady; but it's different with my boy."

"Ah, his papers!" said Mr. Brownlow. This, too, belonged to his previous stage of existence. It was clear that he had to be driven back to that day of vain terror and equally vain relief. It came back to him now in every particular—the packet he had found on his writing-table; his long confused poring over it; his summons to Powys in the middle of the night, and discovery of the mistake he had been making; even the blue dawn of the morning through the great window in the staircase as he went up to bed, a man delivered. All this rushed back on his memory. He took his keys and opened the dispatch-box, which he had been about to open when Mrs. Powys came in. Probably the papers would be there. He began even to recollect what these papers were as he opened the box. "So you have found your husband's family?" he said; "I hope they are in a position to help you. I should be very glad to hear that, for your son's sake."

"You are very kind, Mr. Brownlow," said Mrs. Powys. "I have found my poor Charley's mother. She's old now, poor lady, and she's lost all her children: and at long and last she's bethought herself of us, and wrote a letter to Canada to inquire. I got it sent on this morning—only this morning. I don't know what she can do for my boy; but she's Lady Powys, and that counts for something here."

"Lady Powys?" cried Mr. Brownlow, looking up with a handful of papers in his hand, and struck with consternation. "She used to live near Masterton; if you knew she was your husband's mother, why did not you apply to her before? Are you sure you are making no mistake? Lady Powys! I had no idea your relations were—"

"My husband was a gentleman, sir," said Mrs. Powys proudly. "He gave up his friends and his family, poor fellow, for me. I don't pretend I was his equal—and it might have been better for him if he'd thought more of himself; but he was always known for a gentleman wherever he went; and my boy is his father's son," said the proud mother. She would have been glad to humble the rich lawyer who had sent her boy away from his house, and forbidden him, tacitly at least, his daughter's presence. "We did not know that his grandmamma was a lady of title," she added, with candor. "My poor Charley used to say it was in the family; but his folks have come to it, poor fellow, since his time."

"Lady Powys!" Mr. Brownlow said to himself, with a curious confusion of thoughts. He knew Lady Powys well enough, poor old woman. She had accumulated a ghostly fortune by surviving every body that belonged to her. He remembered all about her, and the look of scared dismay and despair that came into her eyes as death after death among her own children made her richer, and left her more desolate. And what if this was an heir for her—this young fellow whom he had always liked even in spite of himself? He had always liked him. He was glad to remember that. He sought out his papers with his heart softening more and more. Lady Powys's grandson was a very different person from his nameless Canadian clerk.

"Here they are," he said. "I have been much occupied, and I have never had time to look at them; but I am very glad to hear you have friends who can be of use to you. I know Lady Powys. You should send your boy to her, that would be the best way. And, by the bye, he told me your name was Christian. If you are the same as I suppose, we are a kind of connections too."

Mrs. Powys was so utterly amazed by this statement, that Mr. Brownlow had to enter deeply into details to satisfy her. Possibly he would not have mentioned it at all but for Lady Powys. Such inducements work without a man being aware of them. He said afterward, and he believed, that his reference to the family connection between them was drawn out "in the course of conversation." When she went away, he felt as if there could never cease to be something extraordinary raining down upon him out of heaven. Lady Powys! that was different. And before he closed his dispatch-box, he looked at his check-book which was there, to see if there were any particulars about the charities on the counter-foil. The first thing that met his eyes was the check itself, left there, never so much as torn out of the book; and, could it be possible, good heavens? it was dated only four days before. When he had mastered this astonishing fact, Mr. Brownlow paused over it a minute, and then tore it into little pieces with a sigh. He could not afford such benefactions now.

CHAPTER XLIV

PAMELA'S MIND

The Brownlow family scarcely met again until after Mrs. Preston's funeral. Sara did not even attempt to leave her forlorn charge, or to bring her away from Mrs. Swayne's on the funeral day. On the first dreary night after all was over the two girls sat alone in the darkened rooms, and clung to each other. Poor little Pamela had no more tears to shed. She looked like the shadow of herself, a white transparent creature, fragile as a vision. She had no questions to ask, no curiosity about any thing. She was willing that Sara should arrange and decide, and take every thing upon herself. She did not care to know, or even seem to remember, the mysteries her mother had talked of on her death-bed. When Sara began to explain to her, Pamela had stopped the explanation. She had grown pale and faint, and begged that she might hear no more. "I don't want to know," she cried hoarsely, with a kind of sick horror; "if you knew how it changed her, Sara. Oh, if you knew what she used to be!" And then she would burst into fits of sobbing, which shook her delicate frame. It had changed her tender mother into a frantic woman. It had clouded and obscured her at the end, and made her outset on that last lonely journey such a one as Pamela could not dwell upon. And there was nobody but Pamela who would ever know how different she had once been—how different all her life had been to these few days or weeks. Accordingly the poor child allowed herself to be guided as Sara pleased, and obeyed her, to spare herself an explanation. She went into the carriage next morning without a word, and was driven up the avenue to the great house which she had once entered as an humble visitor, and from which she had been so long absent. Now she entered it in very different guise, no longer stealing up the stairs to Sara's room, to wait for her young patroness there. It was she now who was every body's chief object. Mr. Brownlow himself came to meet her, and lifted her out of the carriage, and kissed her on the forehead like a father. He said, "My poor child!" as he looked at her white little face. And Jack stood behind watching. She saw him and every thing round her as in a dream. She did not seem to herself to have any power of independent speech or movement. When she tried to make a step forward, she staggered and trembled. And then all at once for one moment every thing grew clear to Pamela, and her heart once more began to beat. As she made that faltering uncertain step forward, and swayed as if she would have fallen, Jack rushed to her side. He did not say a word, poor fellow; he too had lost his voice—but he drew her arm through his and pressed it trembling to his side, and led her into the place that was to be her home. It was all clear for a moment, and then it was all dark, and Pamela knew no more about it until she woke up sometime later and found herself lying on a sofa in a large, lofty, quiet room. She woke up to remember her troubles anew, and to feel all afresh as at the first moment, but yet her life was changed. Her heart was wounded and bleeding with more than mere natural grief—she was alone in the world. Yet there was a certain sweetness—a balm in the air—a soothing she knew not what or how. He had carried her there and laid her down out of his arms, and kissed her in her swoon, with an outburst of love and despair. It seemed to him as if he ought to leave her and go away and be seen no more—but yet he was not going to leave her. His principles and his pride gave way in one instant before her wan little face. How could any man with a heart in his breast desert such a tender fragile creature in the moment of her necessity? Jack went out and wandered about the woods after that, and spoke to nobody. He began to see, after all, that a man can not arbitrarily decide on his own conduct; that, in fact, a hundred little softenings or hardenings—a multitude of unforeseen circumstances are always coming in. And he ventured to make no new resolutions; only time could decide what he was to do.

When Pamela had rested for a few days, and regained her self-command, and become capable of looking at the people who surrounded her, Mr. Brownlow, who considered an explanation necessary, called together a solemn meeting of every body concerned. It was Sara's desire too, for Sara felt the responsibilities of her guardianship great, and was rather pleased that they should be recognized. They met round the fire in the drawing-room, as Pamela was not able yet to go down stairs. Mr. Brownlow's dispatch-box in which he had kept his papers lately was brought up and put on the table; and Jack was there, not sitting with the rest, but straying about the other end of the room in an agitated way, looking at the pictures, which he knew by heart. He had scarcely exchanged a word with Pamela since she came to Brownlows. They had never seen each other alone. It was what he had himself thought proper and necessary under the circumstances, but still it chafed him notwithstanding. Pamela sat by the fire in her deep mourning, looking a little more like herself. Her chair was close to the bright fire, and she held out her hands to it with a nervous shiver. Sara too was in a black dress, and stood on the other side, looking down with a certain affectionate importance upon her ward. She was very sorry for Pamela, and deeply aware of the change which had taken place in the circumstances of all the party. But Sara was Sara still. She was very tender, but she was important. She felt the dignity of her position; and she did not mean that any one should forget how dignified and authoritative that position was.

"Papa, I have brought Pamela as you told me," said Sara; "but there must not be too much said to her. She is not strong enough yet. Only what is indispensable must be said."

"I will try not to weary her," said Mr. Brownlow, and then he went to Pamela's side in his fatherly way, and took one of her chilly little hands. "My dear," he said, "I have some things to speak of that must be explained to you. You must know clearly why you have been brought here, and what are your prospects, and the connection between us. You have been very brave, and have trusted us, and I thank you; but you must hear how it is. Tell me if I tire you; for I have a great deal to say."

"Indeed I am quite content, quite content!" cried Pamela; "why should you take all this trouble? You brought me here because you are very kind. It is I who have to thank you."

"That is what she wants to think," said Sara. "I told her we were not kind, but she will not believe me. She prefers her own way."

"Oh, please!" said poor little Pamela; "it is not for my own way. If you liked me, that would be the best. Yes, that was what I wanted to think—"

She broke off faltering, and Jack, who had been at the other end of the room, and whom her faint little voice could not have reached, found himself, he did not know how, at the back of her chair. But he did not speak—he could not speak, his lips were sealed.

"You must not be foolish, Pamela," said her guardian, solemnly; "of course we love you, but that has nothing to do with it. Listen to papa, and he will tell you every thing. Only let me know when you are tired."

Then Mr. Brownlow tried again. "You are quite right," he said, soothing the trembling girl; "in every case this house would have been your proper shelter. Do you know you are Sara's cousin, one of her relations? Perhaps that will be a comfort to you. Long ago, before you were born, your grandmother, whom you never saw, made a will, and left her money to me in trust for your mother. My poor child! She is not able to be spoken to yet."

"Oh, no, I am not able, I will never be able," cried Pamela, before any one else could interfere. "I don't want ever to hear of it. Oh, Mr. Brownlow, if I am Sara's cousin, let me stay with her, and never mind any more. I don't want any more."

"But there must be more, my dear child," said Mr. Brownlow, again taking her cold little hand into his. "I will wait, if you prefer it, till you are stronger. But we must go through this explanation, Pamela, for every body's sake. Would you rather it should be on another day?"

She paused before she answered, and Sara, who was watching her, saw, without quite understanding, a pathetic appealing glance which Pamela cast behind her. Jack would have understood, but he did not see. And though he was still near her, he was not, as he had been for a moment, at the back of her chair. Pamela paused as if she were waiting for help. "If there was any one you could say it to for me—" she said, hesitating; and then the sudden tears came dropping over her white cheeks. "I forgot I was alone and had nobody," she continued in a voice which wrung her lover's heart. "I will try to listen now."

Then Mr. Brownlow resumed. He told her the story of the money truly enough, and with hearty belief in his story, yet setting every thing, as was natural, in its best light. He was not excusing himself, but he was unconsciously using all his power to show how naturally every thing had happened, how impossible it was that he could have foreseen, and how anxious he had always been for news of the heir. It was skillfully told, and yet Mr. Brownlow did not mean it to be skillful. Now that it was all over, he had forgotten many things that told against himself, and his narrative was not for Pamela only, but for his own children. His children listened with so great an interest, that they did not for the moment observe Pamela. She sat with her hands clasped on her knees, bending forward toward the fire. She gave no sign of interest, but listened passively without a change on her face. She was going through an inevitable and necessary trial. That was all. Her thoughts strayed away from it. They strayed back into the beaten paths of grief; they strayed into wistful wonderings why Jack did not answer her; why he did not assume his proper place, and act for her as he ought to do. Could he have changed? Pamela felt faint and sick as that thought mingled with all the rest. But still she could bear it, whatever might be required of her. It was simply a matter of time. She would listen, but she had never promised to understand. Mr. Brownlow's voice went on like the sound of an instrument in her ears. He was speaking of things she knew nothing about, cared nothing about. Jack would have understood, but Jack had not undertaken this duty for her. Even Sara, no doubt, would understand. And Pamela sat quiet, and looked as if she were listening. That was all that could be expected of her. At last there came certain words that roused her attention in spite of herself.

"My poor child, I don't want to vex you," Mr. Brownlow said; "if your mother had lived we should probably have gone to law, for she would have accepted no compromise, and I should have been obliged to defend myself. You inherit all her rights, but not her prejudices, Pamela. You must try to understand what I am saying. You must believe that I mean you well, that I will deal honorably with you. If she had done so, she might have been—"

Pamela started up to her feet, taking them all utterly by surprise. "I don't want to know any thing about it," she cried. "Oh, you don't know, you don't know! It changed her so. She was never like that before. She was as kind, and as tender, and as soft! There never was any one like her. You don't know what she was! It changed her. Oh, Jack," cried the poor girl, turning round to him and holding out her hands in appeal, "you can tell! She never was like that before. You know she never was like that before!"

Sara had rushed to Pamela's aid before Jack. She supported her in her arms, and did all she could to soothe her. "We know that," she said, with the ready unquestioning partisanship of a woman. "I can tell. I have seen her. Dear Pamela, don't tremble so. We were all fond of her; sit down and listen to papa."

Then poor Pamela sat down again to undergo the rest of her trial. She dried her eyes and grew dull and stupid in her mind, and felt the words flowing on without any meaning in them. She could bear it. They could not insist upon her understanding what they meant. When Mr. Brownlow came to an end there followed a long pause. They expected she would say something, but she had nothing to say; her head was dizzy with the sound that had been in her ears so long. She sat in the midst of them, all waiting and looking at her, and was silent. Then Mr. Brownlow touched her arm softly, and bent over her with a look of alarm in his eyes.

"Pamela," he said, "you have heard all? You know what I mean? My dear, have you nothing to say?"

Pamela sat upright and looked round the room, and shook off his hand from her arm. "I have nothing to say," she cried, with a petulant outburst of grief and wretchedness, "if he has nothing. He was to have done every thing for me. He has said so hundreds and hundreds of times. But now—And how can I understand? Why does not he speak and say he has given me up, if he has given me up? And what does it all matter to me? Let me go away."

"I give you up!" cried Jack. He made but one step to her from the other end of the room, and caught her as she turned blindly to the door. It was with a flush of passion and confusion that he spoke, "I give you up? Not for my life."

"Then why don't you speak for me, and tell them?" cried Pamela, with the heat of momentary desperation. Then she sank back upon his supporting arm. She had no need now to pretend to listen any longer. She closed her eyes when they laid her on the sofa, and laid down her head with a certain pleasant helplessness. "Jack knows," she said softly. It was to herself rather than to others she spoke. But the words touched them all in the strangest way. As for Jack, he stood and looked at her with an indescribable face. Man as he was, he could have wept. The petulance, the little outburst of anger, the blind trust and helplessness broke up all the restraints in which he had bound himself. In a moment he had forgotten all his confused reasonings. Natural right was stronger than any thing conventional. Of course it was he who ought to speak for her—ought to act for her. Sara's guardianship, somewhat to Sara's surprise, came to an instant and summary end.

Mr. Brownlow was as much relieved as Pamela, and as glad as she was when the conference thus came to an end. He would have done his duty to her now in any circumstances, however difficult it might have been, but Jack's agency of course made every thing easier. They talked it all over afterward apart, without the confusing presence of the two girls; and Jack had his own opinions, his own ideas on that subject as on most others. It was all settled about the fifty thousand pounds, and the changed life that would be possible to the heiress and her husband. Jack's idea was, that he would take his little bride abroad, and show her every thing, and accustom her to her altered existence, which was by no means a novel thought. And on his return he would be free to enter upon public life, or any thing else he pleased. But he was generous in his prosperity. His sister had been preferred to him all his life—was she to be sacrificed to him now? He interfered, with that natural sense of knowing best, which comes so easily to a young man, and especially to one who has just had a great and unlooked-for success in the world—on Sara's behalf.

"I don't like to think of Sara being the sufferer," he said. "I feel as if Pamela was exacting every thing, or I at least on her behalf. It would not be pleasant either for her or me to feel so. I don't think we are considering Sara as much as we ought."

Mr. Brownlow smiled. He might have been offended had he not been amused. That any one should think of defending his darling from his thoughtlessness! "Sara is going with me," he said.

"But she can not carry on the business," insisted Jack. "Pamela's claims are mine now. I am not going to stand by and see Sara suffer."

"She shall not suffer," said Mr. Brownlow, with impatience; and he rose and ended the consultation. By degrees a new and yet an old device had stolen into his mind. He had repulsed and shut it out, but it had come back like a pertinacious fairy shedding a curious light over his path. He could not have told whether he most liked or disliked this old-new thought. But he cherished it secretly, and never permitted himself to breathe a word about it to any one. And under its influence it began to seem possible to him that all might be for the best, as people say—that Brownlows might melt away like a vision and yet nobody suffer. Sara was going to Masterton with her father to the old house in which she was born. She had refused Sir Charles and his title, and all the honors and delights he could have given her. Perhaps another kind of reward which she could prize more might be awaiting her. Perhaps, indeed—it was just possible—she might like better to be happy and make every body happy round her, than to have a fine house and a pair of greys. Mr. Brownlow felt that such an idea was almost wicked on his part, but yet it would come, thrilling him with anticipations which were brighter than any visions he had ventured to entertain for many a long year. "Sara is going with me," he said to every body who spoke to him on the subject. And grew a little irritated when he perceived the blank looks with which every body received the information. He forgot that he had thought it the most dreadful downfall that could overwhelm him once. That was not his opinion now.

Brownlows lost its agitated aspect from the moment when Mr. Brownlow and Jack came out of the library, having finished their consultation. Jack went off, whistling softly, taking three steps at a time, to the drawing-room, where Pamela still lay on the sofa under Sara's care. Mr. Brownlow remained down stairs, but when he rung for lights the first glance at him satisfied Willis that all was right. Nothing was said, but every body knew that the crisis was over; and in a moment every thing fell, as if by magic, into its usual current. Willis went down to his cellar very quietly and brought the plate out of it, feeling a little ashamed of himself. And though the guests were dismissed, the house regained its composure, its comfort, and almost its gayety. The only thing was that the family had lost a relation, whose daughter had come to live at Brownlows—and were in mourning accordingly—a fact which prevented parties, or any special merry-making, when Christmas came.

Though indeed before Christmas came the little invalid of the party—she whom they all petted, and took care of—began to come out from behind the clouds with the natural elasticity of her youth. Pamela would shut herself up for a whole day now and then, full of remorse and compunction, thinking she had not enough wept. But she was only eighteen—her health was coming back to her—she was surrounded by love and tenderness, and saw before her, daily growing brighter and brighter, all the promises and hopes of a new life. It was not in nature that sorrow should overcome all these sweet influences. She brightened like a star over which the clouds come and go, and at every break shone sweeter, and got back the roses to her cheeks, and the light to her eyes. It was a pretty sight to watch her coming out of the shadows, and so Jack thought, who was waiting for her and counting the weeks. When the ice was bearing on Dewsbury Mere—which was rather late that year, for it was in the early spring that the frosts were hardest—he took her by the crisp frozen paths across the park to see the skaters. The world was all white, and Pamela stood in her mourning, distinct against the snow, leaning on Jack's arm. As they stood and looked on, the carrier's cart came lumbering along toward the Mere. Hobson walked before cracking his whip, with his red comforter, which was very effective in the frosty landscape; and the breath of the horses rose like steam into the chill air. Pamela and Jack looked at each other. They said both together, "You remember?" Little more than a year before they had looked at each other there for the first time. The carrier's cart had been coming and going daily, and was no wonder to behold; and Hobson could not have been more surprised had the coin spun down upon his head out of the open sky, than he was when Jack tossed a sovereign at him as he passed. "For bringing me my little wife," he said; but this was not in Hobson's, but in Pamela's ear.

CHAPTER XLV

CONCLUSION

Within six months all these changes had actually taken place, occasioning a greater amount of gossip and animadversion in the county than any other modern event has been known to do. Even that adventure of young Keppel's of Ridley, when he ran away with the heiress, was nothing to it. Running away with heiresses, if you only can manage it, is a natural enough proceeding. But when a family melts somehow out of the position it has held for many years, and I glides uncomplainingly into a different one, and gives no distinct explanation, the neighborhood has naturally reason to feel aggrieved. There was nothing sudden or painful about the change. For half a year or so they all continued very quietly at Brownlows, seeing few people by reason of Pamela's mourning, yet not rejecting the civilities of their friends; and then Pamela and Jack were married. Nobody knew very distinctly who she was. It was a pretty name, people said, and not a common name—not like the name of a girl he had picked up in the village, as some others suggested; and if that had been the case, was it natural that his father and sister should have taken up his bride so warmly, and received her into their house? Yet why should they have received her into their house? Surely she must have some friends. When the astounding events which followed became known, the county held its breath, and not without reason. As soon as the stir of the wedding was over, and the young people departed, it became known suddenly one morning that Mr. Brownlow and his daughter had driven down quietly in the carriage with the greys for the last time, and had settled themselves—heaven knew why!—in the house at Masterton for good. Brownlows was not to be sold: it was to be Jack's habitation when he came home, or in the mean time, while he was away, it might be let if a satisfactory tenant should turn up. There was no house in the county more luxuriously fitted up or more comfortable; and many people invented friends who were in want of a house simply in order to have an excuse for going over it, and investigating all its details, unsubdued by the presence of any of the owners. And Sara Brownlow had gone to Masterton!—she, the young princess, for whom nothing was too good—who had taken all the dignities of her position as mistress of her father's house so naturally—and who was as little like a Masterton girl, shut up in an old-fashioned town house, as can be conceived. How was she to bear it? Why should Jack have a residence which was so manifestly beyond his means and beyond his wants? Why should Mr. Brownlow deprive himself, at his age—a man still in the vigor and strength of life—of the handsome house and style of living he had been used to? It was a subject very mysterious to the neighborhood. For a long time no little assemblage of people could get together anywhere near without a discussion of these circumstances; and yet there was no fuss made about the change, and none of the parties concerned had a word of complaint or lamentation to say.

But when the two, who thus exiled themselves out of their paradise, were in the carriage together driving away after all the excitements of the period—after having seen Jack and his bride go forth into the world from their doors only two days before—Mr. Brownlow's heart suddenly misgave him. They were rolling out of the familiar gates at the moment, leaving old Betty dropping her courtesy at the roadside. It was difficult to keep from an involuntary glance across the road to Mrs. Swayne's cottage. Was it possible to believe that all this was over forever, and a new world begun? He looked at Sara in all her spring bravery—as bright, as fearless, as full of sweet presumption and confidence as ever—nestled into the corner of the carriage, which seemed her natural position, and casting glances of involuntary supervision and patronage around her, as became the queen of the place. He looked at her, and thought of the house in the High Street, and his heart misgave him. How could she bear it? Had she not miscalculated her strength?

"Sara," he said, taking her hand in his, as he sat by her side, "this will be a hard trial for you—you don't know how hard it will be."

Sara looked round at him, having been busy with very different thoughts. "What will be a hard trial?" she said. "Leaving Brownlows? oh, yes! especially if it is let; but that can only be temporary, you know, papa. Jack and Pamela don't mean to stay away forever."

"But your reign is over forever, my poor child," said Mr. Brownlow; and he clasped her hand between his, and patted and caressed it. "When Pamela comes back it will be a very different matter. You are saying farewell, my darling, to all your past life."

When he said this, Sara stood up in the carriage suddenly, and looked back at Brownlows, and across the field to where the spire of Dewsbury church rose up among the scanty foliage of the trees. She waved her hand to them with a pretty gesture of leave-taking. "Then farewell to all my past life!" said Sara, gayly. She had a tear in her eye, but that she managed to hide. "I like the present best of all. Papa, you must be satisfied that I am most happy with you."

With him! was that indeed the explanation of all? Mr. Brownlow looked at her anxiously, but he could not penetrate into the mysteries that lay under Sara's smile. If she thought of some one else besides her father, his thoughts too were traveling in the same direction. Thus they took possession of the house in the High Street. Whether Sara suffered from the change nobody could tell. She was full of delight in the novelty and all the quaint half-remembered details of the old family house. She was never done making discoveries—old portraits, antique bits of furniture—things that had been considered old-fashioned lumber, but which, under her touch, became gracious heir-looms and relics of the past. Old Lady Motherwell, having recovered her temper, took the lead in visiting the fallen princess. The old lady felt that a sign of her approval was due to the girl who had been so considerate and Christian-minded as to refuse Sir Charles when she lost her fortune. She went full of condolences, and found to her consternation nothing but gayety. Sara was so full of the excellence and beauty of her new surroundings that she was incapable of any other thought. Even Lady Motherwell allowed that her satisfaction was either real or so very cleverly feigned as to be as good as real; and the county finally grew bewildered, and asked itself whether the removal was really a downfall at all, or simply a new caprice on the part of a capricious girl, whose indulgent father could never say her nay?

All the time Powys kept steadily at work. Six months had passed, and he had seen her only in the company of others. They had never met alone since that moment in the dining-room at Brownlows, when Sara's fortitude had given way, and he had comforted her. In the mean time his position too had changed. Old Lady Powys, who once had lived near Masterton, had put the whole matter into Mr. Brownlow's hands. She had written volumes of letters to him, and required from him not only investigation into the circumstances, but full details, moral and physical, about her son's family—their looks, their manners, their character, every thing about them. It is too late to introduce Lady Powys here; perhaps an occasion may arise for presenting her ladyship to the notice of persons interested in her grandson's fortunes. She was as much a miser as was consistent with the character and habits of a great lady; if, indeed, she was not, as she asserted herself to be, a poor woman. But anyhow she was prepared to do her duty toward her grandchildren. She had little to leave them, she declared. All the family possessions were in the hands of Sir Alberic Powys, her other grandson, who was like his mother's family, and no favorite with the old lady; but her poor Charley's son should have something if she had any interest left; and as for the girls and their mother, she had a cottage vacant in her own immediate neighborhood, where they could live and be educated. Mr. Brownlow, for the moment, kept the greater part of this information to himself. He said nothing about it to his daughter. He did not even profess to notice the wistful looks which Sara, sometimes in spite of herself, cast at the office. He never invited Powys, though he was so near at hand; and the young man himself, still more tantalized and doubtful than Sara, did not yet venture to storm the castle in which his princess was confined. She saw him from her window sometimes, and knew what the look meant which he directed wistfully at the house, scanning it all over, as if every red brick in its wall, and every shining twinkling pane, had become precious to him. Perhaps such a moment of suspense has a certain secret sweetness in it, if not to the man involved, at least to the woman, who is in no doubt about the devotion she inspires, and knows that she can reward it when she so pleases. Perhaps Sara had come to be tacitly aware that no opposition was to be expected from her father. Perhaps it was a sudden impulse of mingled compassion and impatience which moved her at last.

For there came a day on which the two met face to face, without the presence of witnesses. Sara was coming in from a walk. She was arrayed in bright muslin, clouds of white, with tinges of rosy color, and the sunshine outside caught the ripple of gold in her hair under her hat, just as it had done the day Powys saw her first and followed her up the great staircase at Brownlows to see the Claude. She had time to see him approaching, and to make up her mind what she should do; and found an excuse for lingering ten minutes at least on the broad step at the front door, talking with some passer-by. And old Willis, who had more to do in the High Street than he had at Brownlows, had grown tired of waiting, and had left the door open behind her—

Sara was standing all alone on the threshold when Powys came up. His heart too was beating loud. The sun was in the west, and she was standing in the full blaze of the light, with one hand on the open door. Powys was too much excited to think of the fine images that might have been appropriate to the occasion. He stopped short when he came to the steps which alone parted her from him. He had his hat off, and his face was flushed and anxious. There was a moment's pause—a pause during which the world and their hearts stood still, and the very breath failed upon their lips. And even then she did nothing that she might not have done to a common acquaintance, as people say. She made a step back into the house, and then she held out her hand to him. "It is so long since I have seen you—come in!" said Sara. And Powys made but one stride, and was within beside her. He closed the door, thrusting it to with his disengaged arm; and I suppose it was time.

When Sara stood in the sunshine, blinded with the light, blushing like a rose, and said "Come in!" to her lover, she knew very well, of course, that she had decided her fate. The picture was so pretty that it was disconcerting to have it shut out all at once by the impetuous young fellow who went in like a bomb, blazing and ardent, and thrust to the door upon that act of taking possession. The sunshine went in with them in a momentary flood. The clouds and the storms and the difficulties were over. I think that here the historian's office ends:—there is no more to say.

Margaret Oliphant – A Short Biography

Margaret Oliphant Wilson was born on April 4th, 1828 to Francis W. Wilson, a clerk, and Margaret Oliphant, at Wallyford, near Musselburgh, East Lothian.

She spent her childhood at Lasswade, near Dalkeith, Glasgow before moving to Liverpool.

Her youth was spent in establishing a writing style so much so that, in 1849, she had her first novel published: Passages in the Life of Mrs. Margaret Maitland based on the Scottish Free Church movement. It met with some success and was a good start to her career.

Two years later, in 1851, her third book Caleb Field was published. It was also now that she met the publisher William Blackwood in Edinburgh and was asked to contribute to his well-received Blackwood's Magazine. It was to be a lifetimes endeavor. Over the course of the relationship she would have well over 100 articles published.

In May 1852, Margaret married her cousin, Frank Wilson Oliphant, at Birkenhead, and they settled at Harrington Square, Camden, London. He was an artist working primarily in stained glass. With the marriage she became Margaret Oliphant Wilson Oliphant.

Their marriage produced six children but three tragically died in infancy.

When her husband developed signs of the dreaded consumption (tuberculosis) they moved, on the advice of doctors, to warmer climes. In January 1859 it was to Florence, and then to Rome where, sadly, he died.

Margaret was naturally devastated but was also now left without support and only her income from her writing. She returned to England and took up the task of supporting her three remaining children by her literary activity.

By now she was being published both as an established novelist and regularly in Blackwood's Magazine, amongst others. Her incredible and prolific work rate increased both her commercial reputation and the size of her reading audience.

Against this her domestic life continued to be tragic, full of sorrow and disappointment.

In January 1864 her only remaining daughter Maggie died and was buried in her father's grave in Rome. Her brother, who had emigrated to Canada, was shortly afterwards involved in financial ruin. Margaret generously offered a home to him and his children, adding another demand to her already heavy responsibilities.

In 1866 she settled at Windsor to be closer to her sons, who were being educated at near-by Eton School. That year, her second cousin, Annie Louisa Walker, came to live with her as a companion-housekeeper. Windsor was now to be her home for the rest of her life.

Her literary career for three decades was one of constant delivery and success. Whether she wrote historical works or across several genres in fiction: domestic realism, historical, romance or supernatural she was successful.

For more than thirty years she pursued a varied literary career but family life continued to bring problems.

The literary ambitions she wished for her sons were unfulfilled. Cyril Francis, the eldest, died in 1890, leaving a Life of Alfred de Musset, incorporated in his mother's Foreign Classics for English Readers. The younger, Francis, who she nicknamed 'Cecco', collaborated with her in the Victorian Age of English Literature and won a position at the British Museum, but was rejected by Sir Andrew Clark, a famous physician. Cecco died in 1894.

With the last of her children now lost to her, she had but little further interest in life. Her health steadily and inexorably declined.

Margaret Oliphant Wilson Oliphant died at the age of 69 in Wimbledon on 20th June 1897. She is buried in Eton beside her sons.

At her death, Margaret was still working on Annals of a Publishing House, a record of Blackwood's Magazine with which she had enjoyed such a successful relationship.

Her Autobiography and Letters, which present a thoughtful picture of her domestic anxieties, was published in 1899. Only parts were written with a wider audience in mind: she had originally intended the Autobiography for her son, but he died before she could finish it.

Opinions on Oliphant's work are split, with some critics seeing her as a 'domestic novelist', while others recognize her work as influential and important to the Victorian literature canon. Critical reception from her contemporaries is also divided. John Skelton took the view that Oliphant wrote too much and too quickly. Writing a Blackwood's article called 'A Little Chat About Mrs. Oliphant', he asked, "Had Mrs. Oliphant concentrated her powers, what might she not have done? We might have had another Charlotte Brontë or another George Eliot." However not all of the contemporary reception was negative. The esteemed M. R. James admired Oliphant's supernatural fiction, concluding that "the religious ghost story, as it may be called, was never done better than by Mrs. Oliphant in 'The Open Door' and 'A Beleaguered City'. Mary Butts lavished praise on Oliphant's ghost story 'The Library Window', describing it as "one masterpiece of sober loveliness".

More modern critics of Oliphant's work include Virginia Woolf, who asked in Three Guineas whether Oliphant's autobiography does not lead the reader "to deplore the fact that Mrs. Oliphant sold her brain, her very admirable brain, prostituted her culture and enslaved her intellectual liberty in order that she might earn her living and educate her children."

Whatever the merits of their cases Margaret Oliphant has been shamefully neglected in modern years. She is now becoming more widely recognised as a leading writer of her day.

Margaret Oliphant – A Concise Bibliography

A canon of more than 120 works, including novels, travel books, histories, and volumes of literary criticism.

Novels

Margaret Maitland (1849)
Merkland (1850)
Caleb Field (1851)
John Drayton (1851)
Adam Graeme (1852)
The Melvilles (1852)
Katie Stewart (1852)
Harry Muir (1853)
Ailieford (1853)
The Quiet Heart (1854)
Magdalen Hepburn (1854)
Zaidee (1855)
Lilliesleaf (1855)
Christian Melville (1855)
The Athelings (1857)
The Days of My Life (1857)
Orphans (1858)
The Laird of Norlaw (1858)
Agnes Hopetoun's Schools and Holidays (1859)
Lucy Crofton (1860)
The House on the Moor (1861)
The Last of the Mortimers (1862)
Heart and Cross (1863)
Salem Chapel (1863)
The Rector (1863)
Doctor's Family (1863)
The Perpetual Curate (1864)
Miss Marjoribanks (1866)
Phoebe Junior (1876)
A Son of the Soil (1865)
Agnes (1866)
Madonna Mary (1867)
Brownlows (1868)
The Minister's Wife (1869)
The Three Brothers (1870)

John: A Love Story (1870)
Squire Arden (1871)
At his Gates (1872)
Ombra (1872
May (1873)
Innocent (1873)
The Story of Valentine and his Brother (1875)
A Rose in June (1874)
For Love and Life (1874)
Whiteladies (1875)
An Odd Couple (1875)
The Curate in Charge (1876)
Carità (1877)
Young Musgrave (1877)
Mrs. Arthur (1877)
The Primrose Path (1878)
Within the Precincts (1879)
The Fugitives (1879)
A Beleaguered City (1879)
The Greatest Heiress in England (1880)
He That Will Not When He May (1880)
In Trust (1881)
Harry Joscelyn (1881)
Lady Jane (1882)
A Little Pilgrim in the Unseen (1882)
The Lady Lindores (1883)
Sir Tom (1883)
Hester (1883)
It Was a Lover and his Lass (1883)
The Lady's Walk (1883)
The Wizard's Son (1884)
Madam (1884)
The Prodigals and their Inheritance (1885)
Oliver's Bride (1885)
A Country Gentleman and his Family (1886)
A House Divided Against Itself (1886)
Effie Ogilvie (1886)
A Poor Gentleman (1886)
The Son of his Father (1886)
Joyce (1888)
Cousin Mary (1888)
The Land of Darkness (1888)
Lady Car (1889)
Kirsteen (1890)
The Mystery of Mrs. Biencarrow (1890)
Sons and Daughters (1890)
The Railway Man and his Children (1891)
The Heir Presumptive and the Heir Apparent (1891)

The Marriage of Elinor (1891)
Janet (1891)
The Cuckoo in the Nest (1892)
Diana Trelawny (1892)
The Sorceress (1893)
A House in Bloomsbury (1894)
Sir Robert's Fortune (1894)
Who Was Lost and is Found (1894)
Lady William (1894)
Two Strangers (1895)
Old Mr. Tredgold (1895)
The Unjust Steward (1896)
The Ways of Life (1897)

Short stories

Neighbours on the Green (1889)
A Widow's Tale and Other Stories (1898)
That Little Cutty (1898)
The Open Door (1918)

Selected Articles

Mary Russel Mitford (Blackwood's Magazine, Vol. 75, 1854)
Evelin and Pepys (Blackwood's Magazine, Vol. 76, 1854)
The Holy Land (Blackwood's Magazine, Vol. 76, 1854)
Mr. Thackeray and his Novels (Blackwood's Magazine, Vol. 77, 1855)
Bulwer (Blackwood's Magazine, Vol. 77, 1855)
Charles Dickens (Blackwood's Magazine, Vol. 77, 1855)
Modern Novelists—Great and Small (Blackwood's Magazine, Vol. 77, 1855)
Modern Light Literature: Poetry (Blackwood's Magazine, Vol. 79, 1856)
Religion in Common Life (Blackwood's Magazine, Vol. 79, 1856)
Sydney Smith (Blackwood's Magazine, Vol. 79, 1856)
The Laws Concerning Women (Blackwood's Magazine, Vol. 79, 1856)
The Art of Caviling (Blackwood's Magazine, Vol. 80, 1856)
Béranger (Blackwood's Magazine, Vol. 83, 1858)
The Condition of Women (Blackwood's Magazine, Vol. 83, 1858)
The Missionary Explorer (Blackwood's Magazine, Vol. 83, 1858)
Religious Memoirs (Blackwood's Magazine, Vol. 83, 1858)
Social Science (Blackwood's Magazine, Vol. 88, 1860)
Scotland and her Accusers (Blackwood's Magazine, Vol. 90, 1861)
The Chronicles of Carlingford (Blackwood's Magazine 1862–1865)
Girolamo Savonarola (Blackwood's Magazine, Vol. 93, 1863)
The Life of Jesus (Blackwood's Magazine, Vol. 96, 1864)
Giacomo Leopardi (Blackwood's Magazine, Vol. 98, 1865)
The Great Unrepresented (Blackwood's Magazine, Vol. 100, 1866)
Mill on the Subjection of Women (The Edinburgh Review, Vol. 130, 1869)

The Opium-Eater (Blackwood's Magazine, Vol. 122, 1877)
Russian and Nihilism in the Novels of I. Tourgeniéf (Blackwood's Magazine, Vol. 127, 1880)
School and College (Blackwood's Magazine, Vol. 128, 1880)
The Grievances of Women (Fraser's Magazine, New Series, Vol. 21, 1880)
Mrs. Carlyle (The Contemporary Review, Vol. 43, May 1883)
The Ethics of Biography (The Contemporary Review, July 1883)
Victor Hugo (The Contemporary Review, Vol. 48, July/December 1885)
A Venetian Dynasty (The Contemporary Review, Vol. 50, August 1886)
Laurence Oliphant (Blackwood's Magazine, Vol. 145, 1889)
Tennyson (Blackwood's Magazine, Vol. 152, 1892)
Addison, the Humorist (Century Magazine, Vol. 48, 1894)
The Anti-Marriage League (Blackwood's Magazine, Vol. 159, 1896)

Biographies

Edward Irving (1862)
Francis of Assisi (1871)
Count de Montalembert (1872)
Dante (1877)
Cervantes (1880)
Life of Sheridan in the English Men of Letters series (1883)
John Tulloch (1888)
Laurence Oliphant (1892)

Historical & Critical Works

Historical Sketches of the Reign of George II (1869)
The Makers of Florence (1876)
A Literary History of England from 1760 to 1825 (1882)
The Makers of Venice (1887)
Royal Edinburgh (1890)
Jerusalem (1891)
The Makers of Modern Rome (1895)
William Blackwood and his Sons (1897)
The Sisters Brontë. In: Women Novelists of Queen Victoria's Reign (1897)